Lyre O' Theldar

Song of Light

C. R. Adkins

ISBN: 979-8-9896032-1-3

Thanks to GetCovers for the gorgeous cover art.

Cover art designed by GetCovers

Map of Threa

Ss'al Akum
(the Great Wastes)
Aegân Mtns.
Bassar
Home of the Urz
Cajnaeg Cronan
THE
Capitol
of the
Aelys
THE
AE
Grynwood
Richmont
Capitol
of the
Dworves
The Wild Lands
Doraegonoran
ATSAR
Plainskeep
Bythatsar
Lotheliel
Nitenmile
Dunn Mtns.
Muthport
Bestford
Farmersrest
Uenairu's
Home
Aronoran
Isle of the
Master Order
N
W
E
S
~ 160 Km
Ragnor

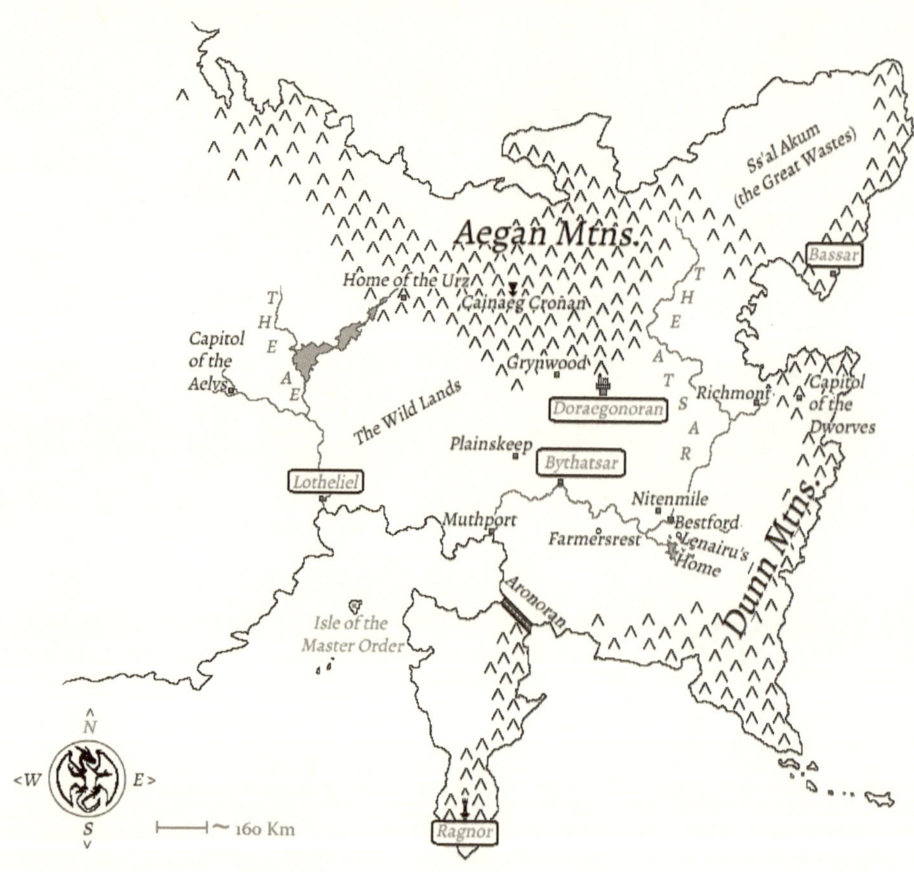

Chapter 1

The soft, warm light of a morning's sun broke gently through the cracks of the wooden shutter boards, streaming brightly into the darkened room of the red-brick dormitory, and lighted kindly upon the face of the room's soundly slumbering occupant. With a snort the human boy, Zurthaud, arose.

However, he did not stay long within his cozy, thickly quilted coverlet and soft warm bed, for this was a day above other days. Quickly he donned his finest breeches, tunic, and rough leathery jacket. Hastily he shod his feet with newly shined black leather boots, the standard uniform for his station, and pausing only slightly to wash his face and comb his thick, dark hair, he bolted out the door of his room and down the main hall of the sleeping quarters.

The sprightly young Human was a cadet, the lowest ranking of member, of the Order of Paladins. The Order of Paladins was once was a group of many thousands of volunteers, an army, of all those on the world of Threa who sought to do good, to uphold justice and truth; they were once peacekeepers and lawmakers. Once they were, for now the once busy halls were empty, even as was the spirit of the Order. Not many cared overmuch about truth seeking or peace upholding these days.

It was through the halls of the Citadel, their castle, his father's castle, that he now bolted, stirring the usually still air with his abrupt passing. His father, Orthard, sat in the utmost seat of the ruling High Council- the Lord Consul, and acted as though he were a king, holding sway over nearly all aspects of Paladin life. Even though Zurthaud was the son of such a man, he had been raised lowly, among the other cadets in the barracks of The Order, like a true soldier boy, given no privilege due to his father's rank.

He had to study and train hard for his bread, to be quick of mind and feet, sure of skill to avoid the chastening of his instructors, and Zurthaud had come to expect the callousness of this rough militaristic life as natural to him. Yet, he still desired above all other things the love and approval of his father. For whatever reason, be it pride, disregard, even hate, Orthard had given little to no attention, let alone any affection or love, to his son, perhaps, on the best of occasions giving Zurthaud some mild praise, like one would throw a bone to a dog.

Through his father's plain disregard, the demeaning martial life had been made nigh intolerable. It was more like being an orphan, or a ghost, for the boy, but made worse by the fact that he actually had a live father who did not want him, and he both abhorred Orthard, and aspired to his favor all the more for it. Though, indeed, unbeknownst to a boy this age, or even those full grown and long living under such wretched shadows, the poor treatment and neglect spoke more of what kind of man and father was Orthard, rather than what manner of son was Zurthaud.

But, Zurthaud had no time to dwell on such thoughts; they had not even crossed his mind as he hurriedly passed through the halls of the Human barrack's dormitories, one of many such stone and brick buildings that composed the massive Citadel. His thoughts were on this day, this morning. Only recently he had ceased to dwell so fixedly upon his inward desires for his father's praise, for one person had brought love and warmth into his life when this cold, harsh, loveless existence was all that he had ever known.

She was a beautiful female, full of grace and power, a warrior and a scholar, quite unlike any other person the boy had ever known.

As Zurthaud's own mother had died when he was very young and his father was purposefully ever detached from the boy, this female had been the first person ever to offer affection to him, had given him his first hug and kiss, had taught him how to be a better soldier, student, and even a better man. As he raced through the castle, in such haste that he didn't even bother to sniff of the delicious smells wafting from the hearty breakfast being prepared in the mess hall, as he hurriedly passed by its welcoming and open double doors, his thoughts remained solely upon her.

He was rushing off to meet her, as he did many times every day; she was the reason he was up so early and running through these dimly lit hallways, nearly bowling over the chef's assistants as they hauled in food-stuffs for the kitchen he had just passed. He was so excited for her and for today that Zurthaud barely muttered an apology as he raced on, dashing down the hallway past the cursing cooks.

Today was a day above others, for on this day, one of the last two female Dragons of the Order would select her mate before the attending High Council. This was she, upon whom Zurthaud's thoughts were centered- a Dragoness.

When Humankind had utterly failed to give any sympathy or worth to the life of a simple and common boy, a benevolent soul, a Dragon, had sustained him with compassion and kindness. She was the only one who had kept him going through his darkest days, when the ear boxing and whippings, piled onto the shouted curses and mocking teases, along with the absence of any parental love, and the incorporated isolation of a Paladin-in-training's life had all caused him to run, with teary eyes and a heart heavy with depressive self-loathing, straight into her loving, motherly arms. He was truly grateful for her, and they had grown into the best and closest of friends.

This whole affair, the Dragons' mating selection, having been made by the Humans an exciting event through all the gossip, announcements, and other hullabaloo, was, at least for Zurthaud, somewhat odd. The two Dragons were most certainly not going to mate in public, let alone in the presence of Humans, let alone in front of the members of the reviled High Council.

The Dragons, of all the peoples of Threa, were the most noble, moral, and private.

Normally, no one but the Dragons themselves would know who was mated with whom, or who was related, or even what each individual's names were. It was just a ridiculous ceremony, only just lately concocted by the High Council for to make the regal Dragons bow and scrape to their whims. Only with their unwanted approval could the pair begin to legally raise a family within the Order's walls, hopefully restoring some female Dragons to their ranks.

The High Council, and Zurthaud's father, Orthard, in particular, seemed to take delight in making such demands upon the other members, especially the non-Humans of the Order, and to the point of apparent debasement, yet had the Aelvs, Dworvs, and Dragons of the Order done nothing to deserve such hateful oppression and ridicule. Orthard even openly admitted that he thought all other sentient beings to be beneath Humans, unworthy to share the same soil, and did not waste any opportunity to impose such precepts upon the other councilors, and the whole of the Order.

This degrading ritual was but one of their many new regulations that only segregated and "dehumanized" the other sentient people. Zurthaud did not like any of it, did not like being called a "rider" and his Dragoness friend being called a "steed" or "beast" by the other Human Paladins.

The only reason he was excited for today, for his friend having to abase herself and humiliate her people before the High Council, was that now she and her mate, with whom she had fallen desperately in love and had already been together for many months now, could have the blessing of these powerful men; rather than hide their love from the Humans, they could now openly regard each other without fear of punishment or other retaliation.

As he rounded the last darkened corner and sped out of the barracks into the open grassy lawn of the main courtyard, Zurthaud thought about how his father had changed so drastically the Order, even in his own short and discriminatorily iron-fisted rule.

Just recently, the last Aelven and Dworvish members of the lower ruling councils were removed from office. They were no longer allowed to serve as soldiers and could only be scholars or mages, engineers or smiths; they were even denied companionship with the Dragons, being deemed too untrustworthy to become a "rider". Hardly any Aelvs or Dworvs could tolerate this treatment; many had willfully departed from the ranks of the Order, retreating back to their own realms and leaving only a few members behind, mostly to report the goings on to their respective royalty and governments.

The Dragons had fared worse, and only because they had stayed dutifully loyal to the Order, not forsaking their membership. Seemingly for this and for their persistent refusal to be fully subjugated in complete, though peaceful, defiance, Orthard had hated them the most of all non-Humans.

There had not been a Dragon in the ruling councils since Zurthaud had been born, and every day they were viewed and treated more and more like animals, rather than as people.

The other Humans of the Order had begun embracing Orthard's harmful philosophy, seeking less and less to communicate with, much less befriend, any other people, and while the Humans had retained the role as "riders" and warriors, contact with Dragons was discouraged. The Human Paladins of this new school of thought who did choose to retain the title of "rider", hardly spoke to their Dragons, and certainly did not have any kind of friendship with them.

"Rider"

He hated that word. He and his dragoness friend, and presumably the other Dragons, preferred the old term for the unique relationship that was the focal point of the Order, the true nature of the Paladins of old, "Companions", and Zurthaud was, indeed, companions with his Dragoness.

She had been the only person who had ever desired to be his friend. He even knew her name, "Lethira", when no Human had even heard the name of a Dragon in decades.

But, all this was a mystery to the simple Human boy.

"Why?" Zurthaud wondered, as he jogged across the cool dewy grasses of the courtyard, breathing in the sweet scents of the luscious young fruit and spice trees that grew along the paths in neat rows.

Why would anyone want to subdue the free spirit of another person, even to the point of renouncing their sentience; how could anyone harbor that much hate for another creature, just for being different than oneself? He did not have much time to ponder upon so deep a question, for Zurthaud quickly reached the other end of the courtyard and bolted through an archway that led to the Dragons' quarters.

While the architecture of the compound was mostly brown and gray stone, cut square and basic uniformly throughout, aside from the Aelvs' need for the excessive presence of plant life and the Dworvs' mountainside mine delving, the Dragons' section of the compound was very different. Their size alone warranted either bigger buildings or fewer rooms, as they averaged at triple the height of a tall man, and they preferred very open and high living quarters.

Their section of the castle was, in fact, a single tall and wide tower, circular in shape, with the lower floors used only for storage and custodial access for the other races. The upper rooms each had a large balcony, by which the Dragons entered and exited their dormitories. The very top floor was used as a communal area and had a dome covering it; the only entrances to this top floor, arched openings at the base of the dome, allowed Dragons exclusive access.

As Zurthaud gazed skyward at the awe-inspiring structure, he remembered that he had been told of the dome's purpose, a place of meeting, but mainly the Dragons' place of worship, their temple. Although he had never been taken up to their temple, while others wondered at the strange noises that came from there on certain nights, Zurthaud knew that it was only the Dragons singing praise to The Creator, Whom they called The Eloigal; they were a very reverent and spiritual race.

The rest of the Dragons' quarter was a large courtyard, wherein they ate their meals together and had their other more mundane daily activities; it was here that Zurthaud had first met his companion, had trained in the martial arts of the Order with her, had learned how to ride and move atop a Dragon in flight.

As he climbed a staircase to the outer wall where the High Council would watch and judge the pairing, the memory of their first flight together- Lethira taking off into the open sky without so much as a warning, him screaming and clinging for dear life to her longer neck spines- brought a smile to his face.

When he at last reached his destination atop the high stone wall, some of the High Council members waved a greeting, but his father only came over to him, a disapproving frown smeared all over his grim, barely shaven face.

"Where have you been, boy? They could start at any minute and you would miss the whole point of your presence." Huffed Orthard as he gruffly grabbed Zurthaud by the arm and hoisted him to the edge of the wall against the parapets and under the hastily prepared awning where the rest of the Councilors reclined in carved wooden chairs.

"Good morning to you as well, father." Bluntly replied Zurthaud, embarrassed by his rough handling in front of the other men.

Orthard curled his lip in disapproval of his son's sarcasm before replying, "The only reason you were allowed to become a 'Rider', much less view your Dragon's pairing, is so that we can know for certain who her mate is, so we can make sure they are reproducing properly. You shall find out for us if they are hiding their eggs away, smuggling them out to the wilds, or simply not mating at all to spite us. This is one of the last two Dragonesses in the Order, and you are our spy against them. I will not have you squandering such a precious opportunity with your childish petulance."

Paying his father absolutely no heed while he ranted, with glance askance, Zurthaud watched the male Dragons assembling in the courtyard below.

They were such magnificent creatures, beautiful and terrible all at the same time. Their tall graceful necks extended from heads ornamented with long, elegant muzzles, crested brows, and horned scalps down to chests that could rival a lower millstone with their hugeness and hard thick muscles. They had six limbs in all, two fore-legs that extended to surprisingly human-like four-fingered, clawed hands, two powerful, curved aft-legs, and between-behind the shoulders-two glorious wing arms.

While a Dragon was upon the ground their wings could remain neatly tucked into tight folds upon their backs, but if they were stretched out as if in flight, the strong arms and silken, fleshy folds of these appendages were amazingly large, more than fully capable of powering their flying. Their tails were thick and long, yet slightly flattened vertically to give stability while in the air, but were flexible and always curved or curled in some way, betraying to the learned the emotions of their bearers.

Their scaly exterior was harder than any natural substance, completely impenetrable, and yet still softly skin-like to the touch; the colors and shades of their skins were unique to every Dragon and more variable than displayed in even the most vivid rainbow. They were the epitome of strength and power, the paragon of nature's wrath and beauty.

In all, Zurthaud wondered how men like his father could not but reverence such resplendent beings. Instead, Orthard imposed such crude and perverse mandates upon them as this mating selection, and for such a debased reason as to control their population.

However, Zurthaud too had often wondered about this strange mystery of their populace. Indeed, where had all the female Dragons gone? It must have happened slowly, over much time, and before he had been old enough to walk, yet surely the Dragonesses' numbers had dwindled until now there were only these two left.

And, it was not as if there were Dragon populations living apart from the Order in the wild. The city where the Order had established its stronghold was originally a Dragon city, their only one. Doraegonoran was the name they had given it, and it was still called by that name to the present day, even though most of the people who lived there no longer knew what the name meant. All the Dragons that lived on Threa had been here, initial members of the Order, for it was their race who had founded the Order of Paladins. Lethira had even once mentioned to him that in such golden days of yesteryear, though the sun were obscured, the sky would brighten, shimmering with the myriad iridescence of the multitude of colorful Dragons flying overhead, and yet, over the centuries, the number of Dragon members had dwindled from those many, many thousands to just the nigh three hundred that remained.

"Where is that blasted Dragoness? She made known to us that she would choose a mate today, and yet here we are waiting!" Impatiently stated one of the Councilmen, startling Zurthaud from his reverie.

"You expected a Dragon to keep time? They have no brains; they wear no clothes, thus no pockets, thus no time-pieces, nor the ability to read one." Orthard replied, his more usual expression, a wickedly curved smile, creeping across his mug, as he released his grip on Zurthaud's shoulder and returned to his seat, while the other councilmen obligatorily cracked up over the poor joke.

Zurthaud knew that the Dragons below had heard them, but they did nothing other than wince slightly, or flick their tails in annoyance, or dig their claws into the sandy earth. He knew that any one of the young males could suddenly rise up and easily slay all the men on the wall, but surprisingly, the Dragons always seemed to restrain themselves around such abuse, even worse.

Lethira's actual mate was among those young Dragon males in the courtyard below, and whose anger at the Human's disparaging remarks was more obviously displayed.

Theros was his name, a handsome specimen, with lush earthy red on his back and striking silver of his belly. He had wrath and fire in his eyes upon hearing the Humans' cruel jesting, and he thrashed his tail violently from side to side to show it. He did not like any Humans, even Zurthaud, always claiming that he was a spy for his wicked father, and Theros had only put up with his presence in their quarter because Zurthaud was Lethira's companion. He was only complying with the High Council's mandate now because she had made him do so.

Though Theros had simply wanted to bite Orthard in half and spit out his remains on the rest of the High Council, the plan they had actually concocted, placating the Council and pulling them through the whole embarrassing ordeal, to keep their now illegal love hidden from the High Council and Orthard, was for her to simply choose him after a moment of pretending to evaluate the other males. It was a clever scheme, easy, no worry of failure, even compliant with the High Council's wishes, and Zurthaud truly was no spy, leastways not for his base father. He could keep a secret, especially if Lethira was the one who had entrusted him with it.

After a while of waiting, eyes on the sky and the lofty reaches of the Dragons' tower, Zurthaud began to worry that, perhaps, Lethira had changed the plan without him knowing; still, she surely would have told Theros about any deviations and he yet stood, albeit impatiently, among the other males.

Finally, Lethira did suddenly dart out of her chambers, and all the councilmen clapped and joked rudely about her lateness. However, something was amiss, and Zurthaud could almost feel an awful presence in the very air. The only other Dragoness of the Order, Ilara, tore out of the chamber after her, tailing Lethira much too closely to be an escort.

"Father, something is not right about them, the way they are flying." He announced, eyes still on the two Dragonesses in the sky.

They were screaming down toward the courtyard too fast to land properly, the other female following too close for Lethira to accomplish even the most abrupt stopping technique without being rammed into.

"Why should we care how they fly; it is how they bed that matters." Jocularly sneered Orthard, coaxing more bawdy jokes and laughter from the other councilmen, completely oblivious to the imminent disaster.

But, Zurthaud was not listening to them; he was running again, running back down the winding steps to the courtyard below, he and the Dragons in the yard had their total concentration focused on the two females flying, no, falling closer and closer to the earth.

Lethira's mate, Theros, roared an alarm, just as Zurthaud reached the very bottom stone step, and the two females crashed into the sandy earth of the courtyard, at the very base of the wall, right under were the councilmen still sat. It was no accident.

The two Dragonesses were fighting!

Dragons would play fight often, even jocularly wrestle to settle mild disputes, but they never tore at each other with tooth and claw, shedding each other's blood, as now Lethira and the other Dragoness did. Their blood now heavily shed in thick, oily crimson sprays and splatters as the two females twined about each other in a vicious battle to the death.

The youngest males stood back, stiffened with fright and shock at the sheer horror of the scene before them. They had never seen such atrocity as Dragon shedding Dragon's blood. It was unheard of among their kind; it was evil, an abomination. But, Zurthaud raced across the courtyard toward his battling friend. He joined Lethira's mate and some of the other Dragons, trying to pull the females apart, yet, in the end, he was too small to do much good. He was violently flung back out of the fray by a stray tail and his head smacked soundly against the outer stone wall.

The last thing he remembered was someone firing a blast of magic at the writhing mass of warring Dragonesses; he fell unconscious and saw no more.

<><><><><>

Orthard grimaced at the disgusting mess below him. Where two Dragonesses had been fighting a moment before, there now was only one, and it lay in a pile, dying in a pool of its own blood.

"Someone, explain to me what just happened." Orthard demanded, as he leaned over the parapets for to get a better view of the courtyard below, truly confused by what had just occurred, yet still without any empathy.

The sky overhead was slowly beginning to darken with the heavy clouds of rain as the other Dragons called out, summoning their physicians to tend to the lone dying female.

"You killed her! You blasted her with magic!" Roared one of the young males, a muscular red, but so thickly covered with sand and dark Dragon's blood that one could not truly tell what color he was. He had been one of the first to jump in attempting to separate the two females, and was now charging straight for Orthard.

However, several of the other Dragons grabbed hold of him before he could take but a few enraged paces. They had to tackle him, as he struggled against his brethren, attempting to violently mangle, if not utterly destroy, the head of the Order. It took a total of five others to haul him away across the courtyard and up into the air, to the domed roof of their tower.

"The Human bastard killed my Lethira!" The young male shouted and much more, as his fellow Dragons, flying, carried him up the height of the tower to the top chamber, where still his muffled cries could be heard.

"Well, that was all so...entertaining." Leered Orthard, showing his contempt for the whole fiasco, paying no heed that his life had almost been taken by that angry red male. Though his fellow councilmen had noticed and had sheltered themselves behind the coarse stone parapets a few good paces away from where Orthard was standing. "But, it was still not I who had fired the magic blast." Orthard truthfully, if not disdainfully stated, as the other Councilmen also denied the charge.

For now, the Dragons believed them, and although a few still glowered and growled at the onlooking council, the majority returned their attentions to the remaining female. Despite the care of a couple of Dragon physicians, who had come hastily upon being summoned and worked quickly and tirelessly, the last Dragoness of the Order heaved a weary last breath and died.

The Dragons all bowed their heads in silent prayers; having done everything they could to help the poor female, they now went into mourning. Eventually, the flammable gasses that reside within the bodies of Dragons, being the means by which they breathe fire, leaked out through the sphincters that in life would have held them back, and the body began to spontaneously combust. Although completely inflammable in life, after a Dragon has died, their bodies immediately lose their unnatural immunity to fire.

One by one, as the rain started to drip down from the darkened heavens, the onlookers took wing, up to the top of their domed tower, for to begin their funeral services. Only a single aged white male Dragon was left behind, the leader of the physicians, the best of their healers.

Orthard cared nothing for the Dragons pretending to have enough sense to mourn for their dead, but he nevertheless had stayed to watch the whole ordeal.

He too now descended the stairs of the outer wall of the courtyard, long after the other Councilors had either summoned Human aid for Zurthaud's unconscious state or simply left the scene. He casually sauntered over to this last remaining Dragon doctor, actually planning on performing some duty related to his job, now leading investigations into unlawful activity, but of course, not out of concern for the Dragons or their dead but of selfish interest and necessity.

"So, tell me, doctor, who did kill your last two females." Orthard demandingly questioned of this Dragon elder, the only one who had stayed behind to watch the body slowly burn to ash.

This Dragon was, indeed, a much older one than the rest; one whom Orthard recognized as being the last Dragon to sit on the High Council. The rain spattered and fell in rivulets off his ancient wrinkled hide, streaming to the ground, mixing the rain and his tears with the dead female's blood.

"You are speaking to me?" Asked the elder Dragon, as if in disbelief, but he continued, nevertheless. "I believe, someone saw that it was your son who fired the magic bolt, but I cannot be entirely certain. I am far more concerned as to why Dragon's blood was spilled by fellow Dragon this dark day. An abomination has just occurred before our very eyes, in this most sacred of places, and we could neither do anything to foresee or avert it." Slowly, sadly replied the elderly Dragon, and he spoke no more, only staring into the inferno that was once his kin.

But, even the Dragon doctor eventually left, only as soon as he was satisfied with the proper self-cremation of the body, and he too soared up to the domed temple atop the solitary tower.

"Of course, a Dragon would blame MY son." Fumingly muttered Orthard, as he turned to see about his boy.

Zurthaud had already been attended by some Human doctors that the other councilmen had called for and was, at last, being carried away on a stretcher. Despite his harsh treatment of the boy, deep down Orthard did care somewhat for his son, as much as such a base and gruff man as himself could care for anything, and did only want good for him, but Orthard never did fully grasp the concept of love, did not have any idea how to show it, or even how to properly raise a child. Still, He was, indeed, grateful that his son was yet alive, the last surviving piece of his beloved mother, and Orthard jealously wondered how his son had become so powerful as to slay, that is, to completely disappear a whole Dragoness. Some strange measure of pride came over him, as he watched the councilmen and the doctors hasten his boy away to the infirmary.

However, his vile attentions were not held long on so insignificant a person as his son. Strangely enough, he was far more morbidly interested in the smoldering remains of the dead Dragoness' body, and he returned to it for further investigation. He hated the Dragons with all his being, and he regarded them as no more than animals, beasts of burden at that. But, the more he pondered the words of that old Dragon doctor, the more curious he also became as to the "why" of the Dragonesses' battle.

"Perhaps, they were both interested in the same male, and it was a lovers' quarrel. Then again, what can animals know of love?" He thought to himself, as he gazed into the blazing, disintegrating corpse.

Orthard's attention was abruptly caught by a strange object amongst the flames. It was smooth and round, about the size of a bushel-basket or a large pot, and it was the only thing about the natural funeral pyre that was not being destroyed by the all-consuming fire.

He examined it, captivated, uncaring that he had been left alone in this field to be soaked through by the steady rain, until at last he recognized what it was.

An egg! A Dragon's egg!

"So indeed, they had been hiding their eggs from us. I shall get them for this, for going against the Council's wishes that all mating pairs be recognized. Oh, but what fun I shall have deciding upon their punishment; which of their rights or freedoms shall I do away with next?" Gleefully mused Orthard, but his mouth dropped from its usual wicked smile to a gasp of wonder, as a far more vile plot formed within his brain.

He would take the egg, raise the hatchling under his authority, his ideology, and use it to force subservience out of the Dragons. If it was female, it would be the very last female Dragon in the world, and he could make the Dragons bow to his whim in order to mate with it. To save their species from extinction, they would have to do every little thing he said, believe every thought he desired to be true for them. He would force breed them into the animals that they truly were, and in only a few generations' time.

Orthard's crooked smile returned as he dreamed of the squalid future he had planned for them, but he eventually came to himself, realizing that he would first need to acquire the egg from the depths of the firestorm which now surrounded it and without anyone knowing of what he was doing.

Glancing once again around the empty wet courtyard for to make certain that he was surely alone, Orthard set about the daunting task, for although the rain was very heavy, it did little to impede the constancy or temperature of the powerful flames.

In life, a Dragon's fire-breath could melt both stone and steel. It was no different in death, and Orthard had been standing well away from it, because of the intense heat emanating from it. He knew that no earthly thing could shield him from the blaze, and to wait until the flame died out would either mean being found out or risking the egg dying from exposure. So it was that Orthard turned his conniving to the supernatural force of magic.

Humans could not naturally utilize the strange powers that Dragons called magic, but riders who formed a pact with their Dragons were given the ability to channel the magic of their partners. It was never their own power that fueled the magic but their Dragon's, and the Human riders could not do anything with their magic that their Dragon objected to. Now that the Dragons no longer made these pacts with the Humans, even with those who had in the latter decades been trained to ride them, only the elder Humans of the Order had the ability.

Luckily, Orthard was one of the last few who had made this pact, and though he had long left from communing with his Dragon partner, he now tapped into that flow of power again. To his great surprise and amusement, he found that he could still summon enough of the peculiar ability to shield himself from the, otherwise, deadly scorching flames, but Orthard's magic was not very strong, a Human's channeling of a Dragon's magic never was, despite the fact that it took practice and much focus for a Human to effectively utilize magic at all, a fact that Orthard had really quite neglected for some time now.

He quickly rushed in, grabbed up the hot Dragon's egg, and jumped out from the inferno, just in time to avoid being consumed by the blazing pyre; even still, his tunic and robes had been singed and his boots had been blackened by the ash.

However, Orthard cared not for that, nor for his hands burnt sorely by the hot egg, for in them he held the destruction of all Dragon-kind and the rise of the supremacy of man. His wicked smile burst forth to new repugnancy as he held the heavy, smoking egg up to eye-level, reveling in his victory, soaking in the pouring rain. As he was about to leave, to sneak the egg back to his personal chambers under the folds of his soggy robes, he spotted something else among the ashes of the corpse.

It lay about the neck area of the smoking, black smudge in the sandy earth, that which was once a Dragoness; it lay out of the reach of the pyre that was still burning hotly about the body region of the corpse. So intrigued by the item's unusual nature, he stooped to gather it into his arms also. Pulling the unnaturally cooled metal out from its shallow burial in the blood stained and ash ridden earth, Orthard held it up to his eyes also. It appeared to be some kind of jewelry, a necklace, perhaps; it was a single dark, blood-red gem affixed to a chain wrought of a devious black metal.

But, now some noise coming from the Dragon's tower startled Orthard, and he hastened on his sneaking way, at last leaving in peace and the rain, the ashen remnants of the burning, smoldering corpse.

Chapter 2

Far to the South and West, across plains of golden grass waving cheerily in the dancing breeze, stand dark forests of grim pines, still and stark, densely packed like an army at attention with their spiny green spears held high against the moody gray skies. And beyond, loom the high, cloud capped mountains, sage and majestic, watching the world turn, and without word or sound stoically proffer wisdom and tranquility. Past all these lies the bay of a dark sea, so named Crydan, for it cuts a cold and raging way fiercely deep into the heart of the land, crashing so mightily and constant that it had long ago separated a certain lone island from its mother mainland.

For an island this far South, the weather was surprisingly nasty; icy winds blew in gales across the surface of the water, chopping the waves and biting the trees. Trees once used to the warmth of the sun, palms and exotic fruit bearers, now grew pale and deathly ill, for this island had once been used to the merry temperature that so commonly graced others, far distant sisters from separate seas, yet of the same latitude.

Perhaps, as a memory of the sorrow that this island saw, the wind frigidly whispers dirges to the ocean, or perhaps, in reenactment of the sanguine struggle that took place here so long ago, it too desires to coldly kill, not men and Dragon now, but only shrubs and plants and small creatures unused to its bitter touch.

But, the cold wind was not the only ancient onlooker that spoke in hushed murmurs of war and murder; nestled against two low, gently sloping peaks, the various ruined stone structures that lay within the island's middle did also silently testify to horrors long passed. These buildings, by their battle won decay, gave light to the suddenness of that long forgotten desolating violation, of which they were the only survivors. They and the lone man-like figure who tread upon the barren shore were the only ones left to tell tale of that horrific night.

He was tall for a Human, almost too tall, yet slim, excessively pale in color and robed with a dark tunic; A vizored steel helm, black as the shadows that twisted in his broken mind, covered his head and hid his eyes from both the light and any who might wish to see his countenance, not that this forgotten place received any guests to look upon him, not since the original inhabitants.

He remembered how they had taken him in, those noble and sage warriors; when he had nothing to offer, they taught him how to live: farming, hunting, how to fight: with sword, with magic, on Dragon's back. They were no ordinary people; they were The Order of Masters, or rather, they had been.

They were all dead now, all but him.

Many years ago, too many to keep count, when he had been but a child, barely of age, the Dark Horde came and slaughtered them, his friends, his family, too terrible night for a child to behold, yet had he witnessed it. Yet, had his life had been spared, and by none other than the one to oversee the murderous, bloody conflict. For what purpose, he knew not, perhaps, only to bear witness to the utter destruction that had come upon the poor souls who had once inhabited this place, they who had long and bravely defied the evil of the Shadow Lord.

As the last surviving member, or perhaps because of the fracture in his soul, this unbearable loss, he had stayed upon the desolate island, tending what had been left of their fields, repairing and maintaining the structures as best he could.

Perhaps, he felt that this was the best monument to their memory that he could accomplish; he had no chance of ever taking revenge for them. The Dark One was unattainable, and those who had betrayed him and his family, those who had stood by and done nothing while they were slaughtered like animals, those of the Order of Paladins, they, he had long forgotten about. His resentful anger for them no longer boiled hot; he was now only waiting, waiting until the end, his end.

As he finished hoeing a row of potatoes, about the only crop left that would grow upon the frigid island, it began to rain down upon his head, or rather, his helm. The merry "plinks" of the falling shower tapping upon his metal covering were a signal for him to move from the once lush, now near barren, garden to the indoors, lest he freeze to death. He had managed to very finely restore the nesting houses, the low domed buildings once used in lodging Dragon mothers when they were brooding a clutch of eggs. He now used them as his living quarters, proving very sturdy and being designed to retain warmth especially well, for the main barracks and most of the other prominent structures had been irreparably demolished.

Down the cracked cobblestone paths he heavily trod, making his way slowly toward his favorite of these nesting house, the one he had chosen to sleep within. Hoe over his shoulder, eyes ahead, daydreaming of long ago happiness, he nearly slipped in the pools and trails of viscous liquid that covered the path. Regaining his usually sure footing and wondering what this fluid could be, so dark and slick, he dipped his hand down into the fetid gel and lifted it to his helm to sniff of it.

It was Dragon blood!

He could not mistake that all too familiar, acrid smell. Had a foul tormentor returned to now haunt even his waking moments with nightmares of that awful night when Dragons had roared and bled and died alongside screaming men and Aelvs and Dworvs? He dropped his gardening tool, and even as he had stooped to investigate the blood, he fell to his knees with the weighty memory of such things, things that no child should have experienced.

But, no, he should not be so ruled by his fears, controlled by emotion; he remembered the lessons he had been taught. If there was Dragon blood here, there was a wounded or dead Dragon nearby. Perhaps, he would succumb to whatever had thus injured such an impenetrable creature as a Dragon, but perhaps, he may also have an opportunity to heal someone who had been hurt.

He slowly rose to his feet and began to follow the trail of blood spatters and smears; it turned a corner in the stony path and went right into an open nesting house, the one just across from his own modified dwelling. He stepped inside the arched doorway, and was soundly startled by the threatening hiss of an enraged and injured Dragoness, but he had not jumped, though startled, had not moved, his training had been too exceptional. His reflex was to stand perfectly still, and a good thing he had. He suspected that the Dragoness might have just killed him had he made much more sudden movement.

"Who are you? Where am I?" She spat, almost roaring, had she the energy to roar.

He could tell that she had been very sorely hurt, noticing a broken leg, exposed ribs, several nasty gashes, all of which were still bleeding fiercely upon the sandy floor of the round chamber. But, he was not used to talking; he had not spoken in decades, so that he was very slow to respond, replying in an almost slow-motion speech.

"My name is Anur..." He tardily, unnaturally calmly stated. "You are in the nesting houses of the Order of Masters. You are severely injured. I do not know if I can help, but if you let me, I will try to heal you, as best I can."

He saw the look of surprise on her face when he mentioned the name of his people, his family, but he did not wait for her to respond with questions or even thanks. He slowly backed out the door he had entered from, then ran across the cracked cobblestone path, to his home, to hastily fetch all the medical supplies he could find within; shortly he returned with arms full of needles and poultices, bandages and blankets.

The Dragoness still seemed distrusting of him, but he did not hold it against her. His heart was kind, though his appearance dark and his voice callous. Because he could not possibly fathom how she had gotten here, he supposed that she was just as stupefied as he as to how she had so suddenly come to so isolated a place. However, thanks to his patience and gentleness, the Dragoness eventually lowered her head, ceased her snarl, allowing him to come closer and begin the work of bandaging and stitching, a seemingly impossible task with all the wounds she bore.

To break the silence and to better understand where she was, who was caring for her, the Dragoness sought conversation with the strange, apparently, last surviving Master.

"My name is Lethira, and I thank you for your kindness." She spake unto him, through her tired ragged breathing. "I had heard tales of the Master Order when I was but a child, the elite of the elite, paragons of combat, smithy, lore, and magic, graduates from the Order of Paladins, but I had thought that they had all been destroyed long ago, when I was but a hatchling." Spake the Dragoness, loosing from the tensions of battle and yet feeling no better, recovering no strength at all.

"They were." Anur haltingly responded, memories of the past painfully dredging up to the surface of his mind. "I am the only one left."

"What happened to them? Was it the Dark One, or did the Order just diminish and finally dissolve, as was told to us, as is written in the books of history?" She prodded, needing any distraction from the pain that wracked her body.

"We were besieged by innumerable forces from the Shadow Lands, for the Order of Paladins ignored our cry for aid. Our pleas for help fell on deaf ears, and eventually we were overcome and utterly annihilated. I alone was spared, a harmless boy, to tell the tale of our demise." He responded, slowing then stopping his work as he relived those dread hours, but he came to himself as Lethira's blood still trickled out upon his hands, wetting them. He realized that the task at hand was far too important to fall prey to his hopeless reminiscing, and he returned to his work of healing with fervor. "Now I have told the tale of our sorrows, and I can move on to something else." Said he, with some new resolve, not just on mending these wounds but, perhaps, upon all of his life as well. "Tell me, how did you come to be here? Who did this to you?" He asked, appalled at the viciously effective handiwork of her attacker, trying with all his might to find some way to save her from the unearthly clutches of cold, pallid death.

"It does not matter; she could not help herself." The Dragoness reflected, but she returned her gaze to him, looking him straight in the eye as sternly as she could manage, and firmly grabbed his arm with her hand. "My life does not even matter now, for I know death is upon me. What is important now is the life of my child. Though she is still soon for her birthing, I want for only one last thing, that I could see her live before I pass on. Can you induce my labor?" She pleaded.

It was as if she could see right through his visor, right into his own eyes. He would have shunned the gaze of another being before, but this Dragoness he allowed into his heart. He truly, sincerely pitied her and any compassion that had so long been suppressed inside himself finally burst forth into tears and a promise.

"I am learned in such medical knowledge. I pledge to you Lethira, that you shall deliver your child alive, but please, allow me to attempt saving your life also." He swore to her, slightly hoping that the tears that fell out through the bottom of his helm would go unnoticed.

"Anur, may your unwarranted kindness, that of a complete stranger, be blessed profoundly by Eloigal, for I have no life left and nothing else or better with which thank you." She said, pressing her lips to kiss his helmeted forehead, thus blessing him.

For hours he stitched and sewed, bandaged and sopped blood till every thread he had was used up, every scrap of cloth he owned worthy of dressing was soaked by Lethira's injuries. Still the Dragoness' life flowed fast from her, and there was nothing more he could do for her, as he had never been trained in any healing magics, only the usual corporal medicine. He silently cursed himself for not having been taught in these, for he wondered with such knowledge if he could, indeed, save this Dragoness.

"It is too late for me." Lethira finally said to him, after silently watching him, as he sat back on his haunches, exhausted and not knowing what else to do. "I am ready to die. Do nothing else for me, but let all your concern be as mine, for my daughter."

Though he had desperately fought for her life, Anur had to admit the futility of his work; he doubted whether an army of the Master Order's healers would have been able to save this Dragoness by now. For every stitch and bandage he had put on, there were more than twenty gaping wounds in her flesh, each one clean through the scale and hide straight to the muscle and bone.

In their mutual silence, Anur now turned his sole attention to her egg. Frantically, trying to induce labor upon the Dragoness, he gave her many of the herbs and several poultices that he had learned to mix for such uses. Through the late hours of the day they struggled together, until the dark of night began creeping in, forcing Anur to light several lanterns and a fire for warmth. Finally, she began to contract, and not long after, heaving and groaning, with her last measure of strength, she pushed forth the egg from within herself.

As, Anur hastened to swaddle it properly and gently lay it before Lethira, the mother Dragon's tears mingled with the shiny dew of birth upon the eggs milky, Turquoise colored surface, for she knew that her life was now very short. She could spend no time with her child, could love it for only so little a while. With her muzzle pressed gently against the hard, warm shell of the little, premature egg in the passion of a mother's loving kiss, Lethira sang unto her child.

Although, Anur could not understand a word of the song, he knew that it was in the old Dragon language, the language her people had spoken long before they ever had met Humans. It was a beautiful sorrowful melody, the like of which he had never before heard, simple in tune yet deep in meaning.

"What did you sing to your child?" Anur kindly asked, as Lethira finished the mournful tune.

He gently patted and caressed her as she lay her head down upon the sand, her strength rapidly leaving from her body.

"I said that I love her, that I wish that I could be with her. I told her goodbye from this first moment that I held her, and I regret, by horrible fate, our time together was so short. I did not wish to leave her at all, let alone without anything given her by her own mother, so I blessed her. Her song shall have power; her voice shall have magic. She will bring light to the darkest of hearts and places; everywhere she goes, she will bring warmth and joy, peace and love." Lethira replied, every breath becoming more and more ragged, every word becoming more and more arduous. "Though you have done so much kindness unto me already, I must ask one more thing from you, friend Anur. Please, take care of my little one."

Before answering, Anur had to swallow a tightness in his throat. Never before had he cared for another person; he barely cared for himself. He doubted his ability to raise a Dragoness, but there was nothing for it. He could not refuse a mother's dying request. "I promise unto you; I shall raise her as best I can." Anur swore to her. "This child is female, then, as you have called her daughter; what do you name her?" Anur asked, fighting back the tears in his eyes, the sorrow in his heart.

"Her name is... Feldara- Daughter of Light." Lethira replied, a last smile spreading across her face as she closed her eyes.

Anur kept gently stroking the Dragoness' head until, in one long final, tired breath, Lethira's spirit left her exhausted body. He could have sworn that he had seen it hasten out from her, but that he knew souls were invisible. He quietly lay down her head in the blood stained sand and, knowing that Dragons burn when they die, crawled a short, safe, distance away; he could barely believe what had just happened, all too quickly, before his very eyes.

The first person, a Dragon even, that should happen upon his lonesome isolation, had just died in his arms, and the weight of sorrow for her fate and for his own helplessness to save her clung heavily about him, like the dark storm that now raged without. He sat there, fists clenching tightly the warm red sand on the floor, with the pain of a thousand such nightmarish memories flooding quickly from their recesses in the hidden, forgotten parts of his mind and back into the fore of his thoughts.

Suddenly, he was there again, truly there on that black night, seeing all of his comrades, his family falling slain about him as he, the helpless boy, looked on in horror. As her body's self-imposed funeral pyre engulfed Lethira in hottest flame, Anur screamed, the hoarse bellowing scream of a man deprived of all sanity or hope. He screamed until all his air was gone from his lungs, pulling his head down between his knees and sobbing uncontrollably.

He kept on until one would think that he would never recover, that indeed he would perish in his own insanity, but something caught his eye, distracted his thoughts. Pale, Turquoise blue in color, round and smooth, slowly Anur realized it to be the egg of the departed Lethira, and slowly he began to remember something other than terror, deep loss, and sorrow.

He remembered his promise to Lethira, his charge, the innocent child who was Feldara; slowly, calmly he rose to his feet, silent and sober. He tenderly grabbed up the egg in the only piece of cloth he had not bandaged her mother with, his own cloak, and he wrapped her snugly. He took Lethira's egg, warm with life and still slightly damp from birth, out from the nesting house, across the cobblestone path, protectively shielding it from the pouring rain, and he set Feldara's egg in his own abode, right in the warmest most comfortable spot he could manage, in his own bed.

Anur sat there beside that Dragon's egg for a good long while staring into the serene opaque colors of the shell, wondering how it was that he of all people could raise a Dragon, how had he recovered from his rabid stupor only moments before, for at the time, he was sure that he would be lost forever in that living nightmare of his own memories.

She had saved him, the egg, Feldara, and now he would return the favor.

Chapter 3

Only a day after the death of the Order's last Dragoness, Orthard had finally found a flaw in his plan; to salvage the Order's Dragons, he would need a female Dragon. As he paced back and forth within his lavish private chambers, over and over again upon the thick, black haired bison rug that covered the greater part of the cool stone floor, all while drinking a little and twirling a lot of his favorite Aelven wine in a crystal goblet, he concentrated on how to turn this utter loss about.

When he had taken the dead female's egg out from her ashes, he had little time to check it, but after he had safely gotten back to his chambers without anyone noticing the Dragon blood sopping his clothes, or the giant Dragon egg in his arms, or the unusual burnt odor about him, especially his actually burnt hands, which indeed, had been no easy feat, he had finally bothered to inspect the egg for possible imperfections or medically unsafe deformities, besides which to satisfy his own unhealthy curiosities. What he had discovered was, by far, worse than any possible retardation of growth or malformation; this had utterly ruined his conspiring, had completely nullified all of his hopes to finally subdue the animals who wished they were men.

His schemes had been abruptly thwarted, for the last Dragon egg was, indeed, a male!

While Dragons could tell right away which sex their children were, other species, such as Humans like Orthard, could only inspect the inside contents of the egg by holding it in front of a light source. Once illuminated, male and female Dragonets could easily be distinguished by the position and quantity of the spines that protruded from their necks. Females had spines along the back and sides of their necks; males had more spines altogether but none on the sides of the neck, only the back.

Upon finding this, he had somehow restrained himself from merely smashing the unborn Dragonet upon the floor in enraged disappointment, and it was truly fortunate he had not, as nothing and no one could have saved him from the consequential Draconic wrath due such wickedness. Orthard now had to find some way of salvaging his egg theft, for if they found him out, the other Dragons would not take kindly to this lack of respect for either their dead or their young.

He cared little what they said or thought, but he knew that they must have a breaking point to their bestially simplistic patience. To think of how easily they could rip Orthard in twain or quarters made him shudder with fear, and disgust, and hate. He had known from long ago, when first he had begun his oppressive rule, to slowly, tediously apply his boot to their heads, his subjugation of their freedom, lest they rise together against him; he knew to boil them slowly, as a cook could so do with live frogs. Not even considering leaving the pot, they would heat slowly until poached in their own juices.

Yet, Orthard still feared being drawn and quartered by the angry Dragons far less than he did the other Councilmen, for if they found out what he had done, his enemies could use this incident as an opportunity to depose him from the comfortably lofty position of head of the Order, shaming him by taking his power, and replacing him with some weaker, marionette imbecile of their own.

In any case, his plans to dominate the last Dragons through breeding rights had been demolished. A sad thing too, he thought, for he had so wished to see the animalistic depravity that certainly those semi-sentient beasts could have been dragged down into.

Just the thought of finally disposing with the last vestiges of civility borne by those creatures that pretended at intelligence, brought a contented smile to Orthard's face. Only Humans deserved the spot at the top of the food chain, the social hierarchy, the evolutionary tree; all other creatures must be made subservient, especially those who bore some defiant remnant of sentient thought.

Orthard had dreams of a Human ruled society, where even the highly sophisticated Aelvs and Dworvs were brought low into the role of inhuman servants. If such creatures could eventually evolve into the semi-sentients that they now were, certainly after a few millennia of Human suppression, the chief of animals, these other lesser species could be pushed back into the primordial forms from which their ancestors had sprung.

Orthard stopped his pacing and grimaced as he recalled the Dragons' belief in a Creator, that which they had always proliferated amongst the Humans. Ever since the two species had met, the Dragons had always traveled about from one Human settlement to another preaching their "religion". They had even visited Orthard's home town once when he was a lad, but even then he had been too smart to be captivated by their fanciful stories of a loving God that lived everywhere, that longed to commune with His creation.

He had known the truth. Through pain and sorrow, toil and tears, he had learned that there was only the here and now, no afterlife, no spiritual realm. All things had come about from time and some accident of the stars, and there was certainly no God, no Creator, no balance or order. Never mind that the Order of Paladins had sprung up from these few traveling Dragons who had also protected the Humans from diverse catastrophe and the Dark Horde.

A knock on the door interrupted Orthard's trail of thought, and he hastened to cover the male Dragon egg with something. Scrambling about, he finally decided to throw the coverlet from his bed over it, even as he turned and hopped toward the entrance of his opulent apartment.

"What is it?" Nearly screamed Orthard, flinging aside the heavy oak door along with his glass of wine.

A lone paige boy, startled by the abruptness of Orthard's loud inquiry, stumbled backward, falling over a chair that had sat along the wall in the hallway, and with a painfully loud thud, landed soundly on the stone floor upon his backside.

"Well, boy, speak. Why do you interrupt my privacy?" Demanded a slightly bemused and greatly annoyed Orthard.

"Lord Orthard," Stuttered the paige in response, as he scrambled back to his feet, "The Serpen ambassador is here. He has requested an audience with your excellency."

His message complete, the paige boy picked himself off the floor, bowed quickly, and hurriedly limped back down the corridor from whence he came, leaving Orthard to seethe over this unexpected and unpleasant turn of events.

The Serpen were lanky, scaly, darkly colored, yellow eyed, bipedal creatures, little more than walking snakes in the eyes of Orthard. Living in the desert just to the North of the Order's territory, they were the unpleasant and untrustworthy neighbor of the civilized nations, for the Serpen had sided with the Dark Horde in the last great war. Their treacherous actions along with their strategic position had almost caused the collapse of the Order and its allies. Only with a great deal of luck and the powerful alliance of Dragons, Men, Aelvs, and Dworvs had the civilized peoples prevailed.

Since their evil, old, traitorous king had died, they now sought to renew the bonds of peace that they had broken, but as of yet had not gained any ground. Orthard had made sure of that; he had been playing with their hopes of regaining the Order's friendship, imposing hefty tributes and even once threatening war against them. He had enjoyed leading the Serpen around like dogs, or rather snakes, on a leash, having them do all sorts of purposeless, menial, or even dicey tasks that he considered beneath the Order's attentions. The unexpected visit, which at another time would have been a welcome diversion, a chance to impose upon and manipulate these peoples, was now very bothersome, for Orthard knew now that he was embroiled in this whole ruined, control-the-Dragons debacle, he must rid himself of the useless, incriminating egg at once.

However, with only a little more consideration, the crafty Orthard was able to find a solution. The Serpen people that he had toyed with for so long might actually now prove very useful, and with one of his customary wicked grins, Orthard grabbed the male Dragon egg, still concealed under one of his lighter silken bed sheets, and merrily strode down toward the main hall to meet his guests.

<><><><><>

Ulam had been waiting for some time now. He, the ambassador of the Serpen people to the Order of Paladins, the Vizier and second only to the Serpen king, was usually not a person to be kept waiting. With his fine crimson robes and golden jewelry, far more refined, and warm, than the simple embroidered linen waist-cloth that was the usual garb of Serpen, Ulam fully displayed the last remnants their nobility's wealth and power, but all Serpen, even one so esteemed as he, now waited on the call and beck of Lord Orthard.

As the Serpen had for ages past lived alone in the Northern wastes eking out a meager living amongst the sandy desert and barren steppes, they required no help from the outside world, no aid from the other civilized peoples. To bow so low before a foreign power was a great shame upon their people, and the Serpen people did bow very low before Orthard.

Ulam completely disagreed with the young prince's, Shar Koman's, wish that the relationship his father had spoiled be renewed. Indeed, he thought truly awful the act of betrayal that their past king had committed against the other nations, a political move Ulam had never supported, for he understood the grievous consequences of allying with the Dark Horde and its evil master. Still, to trade their freedom for the leash of the Order, their prideful solidarity for table scraps, would have been too much to bear were Ulam any less loyal.

None of his opinions on these issues mattered, Ulam was loyal, even to death, to the young prince, still but a child at eight years of age, who only last year had become king. Ulam would never go against his sovereign, and the young prince needed his most faithful of servants especially now.

Political intrigue never ceased, foreign and local powers threatened to undermine their feeble government, and to top the whole pint off, a boy who had once been a squalling babe that a younger Ulam had cared for and guarded with his own life, now had the royal responsibility of running a whole nation soundly thrust upon his youthfully incapable shoulders.

For this reason and it alone- loyalty- Ulam sat in the cold, stone hall of the Dragon riders, slightly shivering in the chillier climate, waiting to meet with such an obscenely honorless person as Lord Orthard. Ulam licked his eyes with his long forked tongue and, with his clawed fingers, scratched the particularly rough crest-like scales atop his head. He hated waiting; somehow, it always made him feel itchy. The cold, shaded hall did not help either, for though the Order's territory was further South than the even the closest desert of the Serpen Kingdom, the reflective white sands kept the ground and the air warmer all year round. Ulam also hated the cold; somehow, it always made him feel irritable.

They were alone in the vast hall, discourteously, inhospitably ignored; the Human courtiers, nobles and representatives of nobles, all non-members of the Order, who hung about seeking favors from Orthard or other members of the High Council, who had only moments before filled this chamber with music and some dancing, had hastened out in disgust upon spying the Serpen. Ulam could fully not blame them for their hatred of his people, but still, the harsh remarks and cold treatment were very hard to bear. Surely, Ulam was loyal to a fault, for to endure such bad handling and weather for his king.

Eventually, after untold hours of waiting, eye licking, scratching, shivering, and some grumbling, Lord Orthard, bowled into the room like a hurricane, and Ulam's guards and entourage hastened to make way for him. Out of respect for his own king's wishes, and not at all for the base personage of Orthard, Ulam himself rose from the carved wood chair that he had been occupying.

He had particularly liked this chair, as such wooden objects were not common in his homeland. To own a single fruit or nut tree was considered wealth to the Serpen; it meant that, in a desert, one owned enough water to sustain the tree. He paused slightly, reminiscing upon the days when many families owned entire oases, but the war and the heavy taxes and tributes that followed were taking their toll on his nation. If their standing with the other civilized folk of the realms did not improve in the next few generations, Ulam expected that his people would cease to own any trees, and the society that they had worked so long and hard to build up and sustain might itself crumble, leaving the Serpen to wander the desert as their nomadic ancestors had done many, many generations ago.

However, Ulam could not afford to think long upon the delightful wooden chair, the future, or days since gone. Thinly veiling his disdainful frown, he quickly bowed in greeting of the hated Lord Orthard, for he saw that the tyrant was expectantly awaiting such obeisance.

"My Lord Orthard," Welcomed Ulam in his best attempt at Human language, which still sounded more like one continuous hiss than the delicately intricate words that Humans used to speak with. "We have finished gathering and counting the Dworvs' security tax along with our own. We not only bring you the bounty of our and their halls, but also humbly ask if there is anything else that we might undertake for your grace's pleasure and the restoration of our nations' fellowship."

Without acknowledgment or greeting, Orthard waved his hand casually, if not abruptly, rudely signaling for Ulam to cease talking.

"These taxes were to be expected at the first of the month; it is now the second week thereof." Orthard stated as he pushed past the ambassador and, after looking about to check whether or not anyone other than Serpen were occupying the main hall, revealed the male Dragon egg from under his cloak and placed it in the chair that Ulam had formerly occupied. "However, I will overlook punishment of your slothful collection. In light of new events, the High Council has decided to reward your lowly nation's efforts toward goodwill by giving you an opportunity to prove your trustworthiness. I present you with this male Dragon's egg; you shall care for it and raise it to maturity." Lied Orthard so nonchalantly, so seamlessly, that his own mother could have believed him.

Orthard left the egg on the chair and turned his attentions to absentmindedly sifting his hands through the large chests full of gold coin that the Serpen had retrieved and laid before him, while he thought over this new and fortuitous twist of circumstances. The snakes would take home the Dragon egg and raise the chick, and it would never again be seen in the halls of the Order, thus clearing Orthard's name from the whole messy plot. Although, the Serpen were just as likely to eat or mishandle the egg than raise it to adulthood properly; if it ever did show up again, no one would believe the word of the Serpen over the Head of the Order. He smiled his usual wicked smile as he picked up a particularly large handful of coin.

"Beautiful." Orthard actually spoke aloud.

Absolutely speechless, Ulam carefully removed the silk drape from the Dragon's egg, as he ignored Orthard's admiration of the atrociously sumptuous piles of gold. He gently ran his scaly hand over the egg's warm, smooth, black and green surface.

The Dragons were very much feared by the Serpen, but not hated. In all their encounters with the Serpen the Dragons had been just and noble, if not fierce and extremely dangerous, and his people had learned what destruction that the Dragons could bring in the last war; still, to be given a Dragon's egg...

After a moment of grasping at the reality of what he had just been told and recovering from the following stupefaction, Ulam had to doubt the authenticity of Orthard's offer. He contemplated whether or not Lord Orthard had the authority to take a Dragon's egg from its mother, sincerely doubting that one would so casually lend her child to a foreign land, especially the Serpen, even to be raised by them.

Yet again, Ulam wondered if he could truly dismiss so gracious and auspiciously glorious a gift to his people, for never before had a Serpen been the companion of a Dragon, never before had there been a Serpen "rider".

"You are much too kind, my Lord." Ulam thanked, after coming back to his senses, this time, bowing very low to the uncaring Orthard. Thinking quickly, he added, "How can we accept such a gift? Indeed, how could a Dragon mother part thus with her own offspring?" Ulam sneakily inquired, hoping not to be fooled into a trap, especially not one that ended with him and his caravan being chased and burned to death by angry Dragons.

Orthard only paused for but a second, yet promptly decided that the truth would serve him better than a lie in this particular instance. "The mother is dead, and none of the other Dragons offered to raise this egg. It is an orphan." Replied Orthard, taking great pride in his own wit, and he ceased to lustfully admire the chests of gold to turn his full, disdainful attention back toward the Serpen ambassador.

Ulam had no reason to inquire further, but he had a suspicion that Orthard was hiding something; perhaps, he even needed to be rid of this egg. Ulam seriously considered refusing the gift and walking right out of the hall, but he knew that an alliance with the Order meant far too much to his people. Not taking the egg might even do worse than break the feeble ties of peace; Orthard would probably twist this around to where the Serpen had actually stolen the Dragon child and use that as an excuse to raise taxes, declare war, or worse. Besides, having a Dragon around who was loyal to the king would pretty much destroy any local political rivals' hopes of usurping authority by force of arms.

"Well, be off with you, and see to it that you do not flaunt the ugly thing all over the place. I will not have you break it." Orthard demanded, after observing the Serpen thinking about the offer far too much for his liking.

The last thing he needed was for the crafty beasts to snoop about trying to find answers, but the Serpen ambassador relented, offering more thanks and flattering praise of Orthard's generosity. At length, satisfied with the disposal of the male Dragon's egg, Orthard strode back out of the main hall calling for some servants to fetch the gold and bring it to the Order's treasury, as the Serpen again bowed lowly at his departure.

"We had best leave at once." Ulam ordered his guards, as soon as Orthard had exited the room. "Who knows what manner of trickery the Head of the Order has bestowed upon us with his so called 'gift'."

But, as his attendants hastily scrambled about gathering their supplies and belongings, Ulam again sat in the charming wooden chair, carefully lifting into his arms and stroking the large Dragon egg. He was very much reminded of his own children, by this Dragon child, and he knew that it was not the egg's fault that he had become part of Orthard's scheming. He determined within himself that this Dragonet would, indeed, be raised as best his people could hope to raise one of his kind, loved and cherished, and perhaps, would one day rejoin his kindred here.

However, he would first have to return with Ulam to his new home, and an arduous trek over the great expanse of desert sand would be no small challenge.

Chapter 4

Zurthaud awoke with a start, bolting upright in the linen sheeted bed. Icy sweat poured from his skin, as his heart thudded in his chest and his breath came rapidly and shallow, yet as he sat there, slowly beginning to recognize his calm surroundings, his terror did subside. By the noonday sun streaming through the large windows into the spacious brightly lit room and the various medical devices laying nearby his bedside on trays and tables, he guessed that he was in the infirmary of the Order's Citadel, in one of the quieter suites along the outer wall of the Keep, thankfully well distanced from the oftentimes gruesome operating theaters, busy staff quarters, and storage rooms located in the more central halls. Once his heart quit racing and he had oriented himself, with much difficulty, Zurthaud wearily arose from his bed and staggered across the sun-warmed stone floor out onto the balcony, not at all recalling why he had been placed in the hospital, still wondering at the soreness that ached throughout his head and back.

He tiredly leaned upon the low stone parapet and looked out across the Order's stronghold; from this vantage point he could see nearly the entirety of the fortress, the bailey courtyard, the outer keep walls, and all seven of the terraced city walls and the giant Human metropolis that sprawled in between and beyond those.

"So, you are awake now." Spoke a large, booming voice to his left.

It was a voice only a Dragon could have, so powerful and resonant, deep but still unwarped, clear as the midday air that warmly kissed Zurthaud's cheeks.

He turned about and found that it was so. A Dragon was, indeed, lying upon the edge of the small balcony, and slowly, as his mind was still quite foggy, Zurthaud recognized him as Lethira's mate, Theros. Though usually uncaring of Zurthaud, the large, muscular, red male had obviously been waiting outside his hospital room for him. At first, Zurthaud could not comprehend why this was so, but eventually the gears of his dazed mind began to turn.

He abruptly remembered much of what had happened.

"Lethira!" He screamed, salivating from a recently set dislocated jaw, panicking with the awful, bloody fight he had recalled. "Where is she? Is Lethira all right?" He fearfully, shoutingly asked of the Dragon.

"You mean to tell me you have no recollection of what happened to her! I have been waiting at your bedside almost two days to find that out myself." The Dragon shot back at Zurthaud with just as much surprise as anger. "Was it you who had blasted her with magic, as they have been saying? Did you kill her who called you 'friend', and I 'my beloved'?" He viciously interrogated.

Theros was livid, more than furious, and the sight of a Dragon in such rage severely terrified the poor Human boy, but Zurthaud was still too groggy from the concussion he had apparently suffered to offer any answer to this questioning. He could barely even stand, and suddenly staggering, he almost fell to the stone floor. Thankfully, he was able to catch himself against the lintel of the balcony's entrance, but there he stayed, leaning heavily against the doorway, unable to move without much involuntary shaking.

Theros only snarled at this showing of weakness, concentrating his seething fury on Zurthaud, growing dangerously closer to hostility, and Zurthaud, still not recalling his part in the struggle between the two Dragonesses, could only marvel at why.

"Tell me!" The Dragon roared. "Was it you who killed her!" And, he came toward Zurthaud lifting his massive taloned hand as if to strike down the Human.

"Stop this!" Loudly shouted another large, gravelly voice from above.

Zurthaud lifted his gaze to see that it was another Dragon, white as new fallen snow and much older than Theros, as displayed by his wrinkled brow and hide, though his silver eyes still did sparkle with the fieriness of intelligence and fierce determination. Though he spoke forcefully and with great volume, he was calm, even as much as Theros was angry; even as he swiftly winged a landing upon the balcony before them both, he offered no aggression.

"Stay out of this, old one! I shall take vengeance for my beloved!" Theros returned, though his raised paw had begun to tremble with the emotional deliberation of such violence.

But, the elder Dragon only stepped in between the two, protecting Zurthaud from any possible attack by Theros. The old one gave such an admonishing glower to the younger, slightly smaller Dragon, that he had to lower his hand and turn away his enraged face.

"You shame yourself, and our people, even pretending to strike a Human, for they are the weaker race, completely unable to defend themselves from a Dragon's wrath, and much less this injured child." Spake the old Dragon, and seeing that Theros was fully chastised, he turned his attentions to Zurthaud. "Do not fear me, child, nor my people; we shall not harm you." He gently spoke. "Come, you are pale with exertion and fright; let me help you to a seat."

He then stretched out his hand so that Zurthaud could hold himself steady with one of the Dragon's fingers, each as long and thick as the Human boy's legs, and he carefully led him over to one of the low stone benches that sat out upon the balcony against the hospital's wall. Only once he was again off his feet did Zurthaud realize how much effort he had put into just standing, for his body had truly been drained by his injured state. He had to breathe very heavily, as if he had been out jogging, for a good while before he felt well again.

"My name is Serc." Said the old white Dragon, resuming their conversation once he observed that Zurthaud could again breathe easier. "I am the oldest living Dragon in the Order and one of their healers. Though you do not know me, I do know who you are, Zurthaud, the son of Orthard, the only young Human trained to ride upon a Dragon's back in decades, for we have all been watching you. I must ask you some questions now, and I expect you to answer them honestly."

Zurthaud nodded in understanding; he had nothing to hide, though he could barely remember the occurrences of the other day. He knew he had not killed Lethira; it was impossible to contemplate such a thing. He simply could not have done it. However, Theros certainly thought he had, and that ate at Zurthaud like a ravenous wolf. He had to clear his name before the Dragons; surely they knew how much he had loved Lethira.

"We know that your father sent you to us to spy upon our doings, but did Orthard order you to kill Lethira?" Serc began.

Zurthaud did not even need to think to answer. "No, and if he had, I would not have done it. I never did spy for him, for I loved Lethira. I only ever told him things that did not matter, or made up things, and only when he forced me to report to him."

"Very well, then." Continued the elder Dragon, seeming somewhat surprised that Zurthaud had not been faithful to his father in any espionage. "Do you remember casting magic at Lethira?" He asked.

A dark cloud came over Zurthaud's thoughts, for he did now recall firing a blast of magic at his friend, the very same magic he had been taught to wield by her. Suddenly, it seemed very possible that he had slain his only friend, and Zurthaud's soul sank, lower in his own mind than the depths of the earth.

Yet, the magic Lethira had taught him had only ever been of a gentle nature: some defensive shields of various kinds of energy, a source of light when there was no other to be found, and a spell for teleporting objects.

"Zurthaud, please answer the question." Serc appealed, becoming more concerned with each passing second of silence.

Even Theros had quit his shamed sulking at the other end of the balcony and pricked his ears in anticipation of Zurthaud's answer.

At last, like an opened floodgate, memory of the past event rushed into Zurthaud's mind, and he could clearly recall what had happened in every detail.

"I did!" He excitedly shouted, seemingly admitting his guilt to the surprise of both Dragons. "I had cast the teleportation spell at her, wishing her to safety." He declared, relieved within his own self that he had not been the cause of his beloved friend's death, alleviated in remembering and knowing the truth.

"To where?" Shouted Theros, as he excitedly covered the distance of the balcony in two strides, planting his own face directly before Zurthaud's. "To where did you teleport her?" He shouted again, as dumbstruck Zurthaud could not answer him.

In his haste to rescue Lethira, Zurthaud had never envisioned a destination for her, as he was supposed to, for when teleporting is used, one must send an object to its destination with their thoughtful well-wishes. Otherwise, who could know where the object would go: to nowhere, to the stars and the cold blackness that surrounds them, to annihilation. Zurthaud stuttered and choked, for he may well have doomed his friend to a fate worse than the sudden death of a magical attack.

"Back away from the boy." Serc commanded, again coming to the Human's rescue, moving Theros apart from Zurthaud with his great forearm. "He does not know where. It was an ill-formed spell, with no destination in mind, and it changes nothing that Lethira was transported away. If Ilara's wounds were any clue to go upon, then by now, your mate has also passed on, regardless of where she went." He said, becoming more gentle in tone as he spoke, for Serc knew the hurt of losing Lethira still burned painfully in Theros' heart.

Even so, the young Dragon began to weep, for his hope had risen beyond all hope only the moment before, to now, once he realized the impossibility of his expectation, crashing down again unto despondency. Serc did pity the poor Theros, seeing him in such bereavement, and held him in comforting embrace, but the young male did only sob the more for his beloved.

For him, there was no sun, no air, no joy, nor life without Lethira, such was their bond, and now that Theros had allowed his rage to subside long enough for that small glimmer of hope to shine into his heart, his front of wrathful vengeance had been broken down and shattered, revealing what he truly was, only an utterly destroyed young lover.

Zurthaud did pity him also, for he too shared the pain of a lost best of friends. His own loss weighed heavily again within him, seeing the grown Dragons shed so many tears, and he could not bear his grief alone. He rose slowly from the bench and staggeringly strode over to the Dragons, and did put his small arm around Theros, as best as he could manage.

"Theros, I am sorry. I am so sorry." Zurthaud blubbered, tears streaming from his own eyes, even as he rested his head upon the Dragon's side.

The shared moment of mourning did break the bonds of hate that had chained the young Dragon's heart, for Theros did take notice of the Human boy. His anger now softened and faded toward Humans and Zurthaud in particular, for he remembered how his mate had cared for him, had practically raised the boy as her own child. Deep within himself he had truly believed that Zurthaud was not responsible for her demise, but he just could not let the blame pass so easily from those living. He had so desperately desired the closure of justice or vengeance, not for blood or even righting of wrongs, but just so he could do something, anything to fix this.

Now, he could not. He must now only accept his beloved mate's passing, having been unable to do anything to prevent or divert it. It caused Theros to feel weak, powerless, and yet free, free now of such grave responsibility.

"I know that you loved her also Zurthaud." Theros quietly responded, as they eased their grip on each other, coming to the end of their bout of grieving. "I am sorry for blaming you for her death, for listening to untruth. I should never have allowed myself to hold you accountable, for surely it was not your claws that had cut her."

As Zurthaud returned to his seat on the bench and the two Dragons also reclined upon the large open balcony, Serc shook his head in befuddled doubt.

"I am not so sure we can either blame Ilara, for indeed, her actions were not those of a Dragon's, not a sane one. We all know, from being taught as children, that to shed another Dragon's blood is such an appalling wickedness, and it has happened so rarely throughout the past. I know not how her heart could have become so black, or her mind so crazed, as to even consider such violent action." Gravely pondered the wizened elder.

"Was it a lover's quarrel?" Zurthaud asked of Theros. "Did she also desire to be your mate?"

"No, certainly not. She was my friend only and like a sister to Lethira." Theros sincerely denied. He then looked about carefully, as if to catch someone watching them, and brought his head near to Zurthaud, with voice low in response. "She was already mated with Sicaron, the black, our greatest scout, but he is still on one of his tours of espionage in the Shadow Lands. She was eagerly awaiting his return."

"I fear that no natural disease or emotional state could have caused such madness in a Dragon." Serc explained. "I fear that a shadow has come North, that somehow, the dark powers were able to possess her, twist her mind, or control her body against her will and cause this great evil to befall us."

"What do you mean by this?" Zurthaud confusedly asked, for he had never heard of such a shadow or any kind of evil darkness. These notions were as foreign to him as the Serpen.

Serc realized this. He had expected it. "I will tell you now of things that have left the knowledge of Humans and the Order, and frighteningly so, for it was within my own lifetime that I have seen them forget the evils in this world, wasting their days on frivolities and neglecting their duties, as if disillusioned by the same darkness that we fear and battle"

"One hundred years ago to this day, a great darkness rose in the South. An evil Lord of Shadow, a terrible giant and warlord, the Kragon, built his tower in that wasteland and raised an army, the Dark Horde, from the savage races: the Goblins, Trolls, Ogres, and a new vile creature, the Nokre. By some magic or deception, he turned one of our own against us, Dragas, a Dragon extraordinarily skilled in magic, and they two with their army made war against the civilized world."

"My own father fought in that great struggle, while I, just a hatchling, hid with my mother and siblings in our temple. He did not ever return from that day, and many others would have neither, were it but for our great champion, Rathnyalgr, the Dragon who was Lord Consul in that time. He defeated Dragas and the Kragon and banished their hordes to the Southern wasteland, the Shadow Lands, and we built a great wall, the Aronoran, to border and protect our lands, from the eastern Blue Sea to the mouth of the great Atsar River at the Crydan."

"The wall has kept the Order safe from the Dark Horde for generations of men, leading them to believe that there is, indeed, no great evil beyond them, lulling them into dullness and doldrum, until now, for Orthard no longer posts a full guard upon it. The darkness seems to be growing again, the shadow spreading, for the savages grow in number and more restless, as storm clouds gather in the skies above the Shadow Lands, and the dark tower, the Ragnor, still stands untouched, foreboding. More so, now the same power of the Kragon, to turn the hearts of Dragons to evil, has again revealed its awful presence."

"We Dragons have smelled it in the air, heard it in the wind, and have now felt it shed our own blood, but the High Council is far from listening to us. The pride of Orthard shall be his undoing. He hearkens not to our warnings, denying us even the ability to speak before them, denying us even the dignity of civility, and he shall drag us all down with him to share in his doom. It seems the Kragon will soon return, and we Dragons, mighty though we are, fear the coming darkness He shall find us weak and ill-prepared to face him; if the Order continues as we are now, he shall easily overcome us and plunge the world into chaos."

Zurthaud was taken aback, for the only stories he had ever heard of the Shadow Lord were fairy-tales used to scare children off to bed. Never had he imagined such things could be real, never before had he been given reason to doubt the words of a Dragon, for they rarely, if ever, lied. Now he found himself doing both, and he did not know how to respond.

"Why have you told me these things? What can I do to affect any of this?" He exclaimed.

"That is why I had come here," Chuckled the elder Dragon, "I have been watching you, Zurthaud: how you have dutifully grown in knowledge, strength, and skill, at the head of all your classes, how you have the respect and friendship of all your peers, and especially how you took to Lethira. Even though we thought you a spy at the time, you learned well from her the basics of partnering with a Dragon, and you are the only Human in years to have ridden Dragon-back. You shall be the first of a new generation of Paladins, along with your fellow young cadets; not even in secret, for your father thinks still to control you and use you as a weapon against us and has given you all freedom to go about among us, we will teach you the old ways: the sword, magic, and how to live and fight alongside a Dragon partner. You may even be able to convince him to let you recruit among your comrades, for now, anyone who can keep this secret, then more later as our movement gains strength in numbers and influence. In time, the Order can be strong again, and you could be the catalyst."

"What?" Zurthaud and Theros simultaneously gasped.

"How can I do this? Why me? I am just a boy." Zurthaud asked very much frightened by this enormous responsibility, while Theros pretended not to be so shocked by Serc's improbable scheme, though his tail did flick agitatedly.

"You may doubt yourself, Zurthaud, but you are the ledge upon which the Order's future hangs. As his son, no other Paladin but for you could escape Orthard's admonishing; only you can lead him along, letting him think you are still his inside agent, all the while helping us to raise up an army to stand against the coming darkness. You may see yourself as only a boy set to an impossible task, but I see the beginnings of a man who can stand for righteousness, the foundations of a great leader." Serc spake encouragingly. "The choice is yours, of course. No one can force you to accept this task, for it shall be a great work, a life's work. However, I strongly urge you to consider it, for the reward is also great- a life free from the fear of evil and separation from the tyranny of men like your father. And of course, I and many others whom you can depend upon shall be at your side the whole journey through."

Zurthaud pondered deeply upon this crucial decision, and he might have rejected Serc's offer but for Theros. The Dragon came up beside Zurthaud and comfortingly placed his large clawed hand upon the boy's shoulder.

"I shall be with you also, as your companion." Softly spoke Theros. "It is what Lethira would have wished."

Only then did Zurthaud find the strength to do what he knew was right, the only way to save the Order and fight off the coming storm. He slowly nodded his head, accepting his new role, taking on his destiny. What at first had seemed hopeless now felt conquerable, if he had such friends as Theros and Serc with him to help bear the task each day.

"I will do as you have asked." Zurthaud agreed.

"It is settled then." Said Serc, smiling with a big, toothy Dragon's grin. "We will start your training tomorrow."

Chapter 5

As hours often go, they turn into days, and days into weeks, then months, but Anur was patient. His solitary life had taught him the value of patience, the ability to wait.

Ever since the Dragoness Lethira had lain her egg and passed from the world, Anur had strictly kept his heartfelt promise, to raise the Dragonet that would eventually hatch from the beautiful Turquoise colored egg, that which even now lay sedentary by the small clay hearth of Anur's home, amongst a makeshift nest of old blankets and quilts. Almost an entire year had passed, and still he waited patiently upon this egg.

At first, he had only paid it little heed, making sure it was warm, keeping it safe, for long had it been since he last offered any affection to another creature. He was unused to such feelings, yet after a while, he began stroking the Dragon's egg, touching it, caring for it. Eventually, he found himself talking to "it", or rather "her", for he had now come so far as to know that which lived inside the protective shell was an actual person.

After so long a time lovingly tending his precious charge, Anur began to regard Lethira's egg as his, his child, his adoptive daughter, and his heart grew warm again with the love he gave for her. He called her by name, Feldara, while he lay beside her, keeping her snug in the chill autumn nights. He told her everything he knew about the world, his life, his hopes for her future, about the goings on of each and every day, anything and everything, and the more Anur spoke to her, regarded her as a person, as his own child, the more he loved her, and the more he healed from his past wounds. He began to find that he had actually become a whole, stable person once again.

These days passed all too quickly for him, as he soon realized, for when he returned to his abode one wintry evening, carrying a basketful of fresh potatoes for his dinner, all the while wistfully speculating when spring would again come, or if it would even make a difference in the climate of this particularly cold island, he noticed a crack in the smooth surface of the egg's shell.

He dropped everything he had in his arms, at first very worried that somehow the egg had been damaged, and ran quickly over to inspect his little Dragon, but he breathed a sigh of relief, as he realized not harm but a greater wonder was taking place.

Feldara was hatching from her egg!

The day, the hour, the moment for which he had long been waiting was finally here, and he could barely contain his excitement. At first, the crack remained for hours only a single fissure in the glassy surface of the Dragon's egg, but soon much splintering began to appear around its surface, as the whole began to bulge at times, and to rock fairly violently in intervals, outward signs of the struggling infant within. At last, after nearly the whole night had gone, the entire shell of the egg seemed to give way all at once, and the baby Dragon plopped out from within it.

Quickly, Anur grabbed some of the warm wet towels that he had been preparing and began to clean the remains of the albuminous fluid off the newly hatched Dragonet. All his practice with talking, as he had made with the egg all these long months, now came into full use, for he spoke calmingly to the little Dragoness, while she blindly protested his efforts. He soon finished with the task and sat down on the floor a little way from her, for to get a good look at her.

She was, on her back, face, and neck, the same Turquoise blue as her shell, while her belly and eyes were a warm, mellow gold hue.

Anur thought these colors strikingly contrasting and yet still quite complementary, altogether the most vivid and bright colors of any Dragon, even the Dragonesses, he had ever seen. The little Dragonet was truly beautiful, and Anur simply sat in awe of her for a moment, until she began to whimper for what should have been her parents.

She opened her eyes for the first time then, for to see where her mother and father should be, and Anur, in compassion, was moved to speak.

"Feldara, I know that I am not your parent, but I promised your mother that I would raise you as my own. I now promise you that I will do my very best at this, even though I am not a Dragon." He said softly, sadly wishing that he was, indeed, a Dragon, so as to better take care of her, or better yet, that her mother was still alive.

However, the baby Dragon would have none of his speech making; at last finding his location, she gurgled playfully and smiled at him while she did her very best to crawl toward him with her untried infant legs. She did not know or care about the differences between them, for she had become familiar with Anur's voice through her egg, had already learned to recognize his scent and to associate these things with the constant loving care that he had already been providing her.

She finally reached him where he sat and climbed up in his lap, and after a few short, affectionate nips at his dark cloak, fell soundly asleep, exhausted with the tremendous exploits of hatching and crawling towards her beloved guardian.

Now for the first time in many years, he too donned a smile under his black vizored helm, as he gently stroked the snoring Dragonet.

"Well met, Feldara." He chuckled, as his heart swelled with joy.

As days go, they turn into weeks, and the weeks into months, then years. The strange chill that had once blasted across the sea and turned the island unnaturally cold, had ceased in the Spring following Feldara's birth. It was as if the sun itself was welcoming the baby Dragon into the world, and Anur did, indeed, wonder at how quickly the warmth returned and beckoned forth the plants and animals that had once long ago enjoyed its tropical impinging. The once desolate ruin again became alive with the verdant greens of palms and ferns, and Anur was made to work exceedingly hard to keep the lush growth from reclaiming the abandoned compound that he called home.

Little Feldara also shared that home with him, playing in his small house at first, then in the grounds nearby, and finally she became bold enough to explore the whole of the ruined fortress. He had to watch her closely in order to match pace with her energy, keeping her from getting into things and situations that could hurt her. She grew so fast that Anur hardly knew what to do about it, but he doggedly pursued his role as parent, with much love for the Dragonet.

When the animals, the birds, reptiles, and even, surprisingly, many goats and deer had returned in sufficient number, and Anur had become weary of nearly constantly fetching food of all sorts for to feed his ever growing Dragoness, he took Feldara out into the wilds of the two low hills that towered over the rest of their island and taught her how to hunt and track prey. She became very proficient at startling and scaring away many things, but eventually she mastered the task and soon was able to provide enough meat even for the both of them. But, her hunting was like that of a Human, from the ground and not from the air, not as the way of Dragons, and Anur despised himself for it.

He wished that he could teach her how to fly and how to breathe fire, but he could not. He was physically incapable of these things, and thus thought himself inadequate to teach them to her. Nevertheless, she loved him dearly and eagerly learned anything that he would teach her: how to fight, how to use magic, how to garden, how to fish.

And, Anur did teach her everything he knew, everything he had learned from the Order of Masters, and when that seemed not enough to him, he began to teach her from the burnt out library's vast number of books and scrolls that remained intact after the Order had been destroyed. She read all of Threa's history, a few of the great works of literature, the sciences, and much more. She was very smart and drank up each word like they were the very air and water that did sustain her life.

Together they lived and grew peacefully, until Feldara was sixteen years of age, a stunningly beautiful young Dragoness. She now became restless and bored of all the tired books, the seemingly small ruins, even the wild jungles about the two small hills, and she began to wander alone about the island, searching for anything to intrigue or amuse herself with. She often walked up to the highest spot on the larger of the two low slopes and would gaze out over the sea to the shore of the mainland beyond, wondering within herself what strange and wonderful things lay beyond the horizon.

But, Anur would have none of this; he only desired for her the safety of his little island. He, like all parents, could not too quickly accept that she was growing up, desiring anything other than their simple happy life together.

Thus, they began to be in conflict much of the time, for each day she would ask him if they could build a boat or a raft or somehow go off to the far shore for an adventure, and each day he would respond the same...

"No." Again said Anur, as he, bare chested, loins girded, cast the net out once more into the tide pool. He was aiming for a group of bright blue fish that he knew tasted particularly sweet, but they were small and fast, and he was currently being distracted.

"You say the same thing every day, no, no, no. Is that all you ever say?" Angrily replied Feldara, as the fair, young, Turquoise blue and gold Dragoness leaped about him slapping and splashing the water with frustration.

She was now about twelve feet tall, stunted in growth for a Dragoness of her age, probably due to her premature birth from her mother's womb, yet still she could easily overpower Anur. However, she was very good, and would never even dream of doing such a thing, for she still loved and respected him, even when he was being difficult, like on this day.

____

"I say the same thing, because my answer is the same, no. Should I not say what I mean; otherwise I would be lying." Anur coyly responded, poised to strike, patiently waiting until Feldara quit moving and scaring the fish to cast his net again.

"Must you be so smart with me? Why then do you always have the same answer?" She asked, purposefully jumping into the deeper tide pool just in front of him and huffily sitting down right where the fish had been a moment before, so that she and Anur were both now eye to eye.

"Because, I always have the same reason for my answer. The outside world is dangerous, full of horrid, violent people and creatures. Now, do you want to eat fish tonight, or am I wasting my time with this net?" He answered, sportively casting the net on her head.

She splashed him furiously, in reply, and pouted, but after he shook his head to get the saltwater out of his helmet, he only gently took the net off from about her horns.

"When will you realize, the most wonderful place in the whole earth is this, your own home. Going about the wide world is only lonely and wearisome, especially if you have nothing to return to each night, and our island is an unusually pleasant spot to call home." He chided, as he stroked the boney crest at the top of her head.

"I only want to go off for a day, an hour at least, please?" She begged, letting him hold her head.

However, Anur only glared at her through his dark visor, through which Feldara had never seen his eyes. As long as she had known him, Anur had never taken his helmet from off his head, and she often found herself wondering what he looked like under there, what color his eyes were, if he had any hair like a Human. Today, she guessed that she would actually not want to see his grumpy face glowering at her, and she gave up on asking for him to take her to the far shore. She would have anything, or in this case nothing, rather than for him to be upset with her.

"Alright, I have changed my mind. I do not want to go to the far shore, because I suppose you are right, as usual." Sarcastically conceded Feldara, as she hopped out of the tide pool and sauntered off.

However, she still begrudged him his lack of adventure, his satisfaction with the peacefully mundane life that they shared on the island. She thought, if she did not change her scenery or see something new quite soon, she would become so bored as to die, yet she still would not have Anur mad at her for anything. Feldara scribbled some lines in the white sand with her claws, as the tide gently splashed around her ankles, all the while thinking about how to get what she wanted without upsetting Anur. She would have to leave the island in secret, without him ever knowing, what he did not know could not cause him grief, and on this line of thinking, she justified and arranged a plan to escape and go exploring without him.

So, that same night, when she was sure that Anur had fallen asleep beside her on the large solitary futon that they shared as a bed, she arose quickly and quietly, and silently sneaked out the door. She did her best to muffle her footsteps while along the cobblestone paths of the abandoned compound, hoping not to make too much noise with the crunching and scuffling of something her size and weight and, of course, the clacking of her claws.

Anur had never really explained why the place had been abandoned, why they were living here. She knew that it was once the secret stronghold of the Master Order, but other than that, and the plain fact that she had been born here, she could find very little about this place in the books she had read.

She had recently come to think that Anur was keeping plenteous secrets from her, like his helmeted face, as if he assumed that she would never need to know about certain things that were unsafe or unimportant to him, and Feldara presumed that if she asked, he would certainly never answer truthfully, if at all. In trying to quiet her insatiable curiosity about the world, about life, she had asked him often enough what lay across the sea upon the mainland, but as she thought likely, he had never really answered her.

"Nothing more than a world full of darkness and woe." He would say and nothing more.

She wondered if there were different flowers out there that smelled lovely or strange, different animals, ones which tasted good and which ones were unpleasant to eat. She knew that there were other people, other places; she had read about Doraegonoran the great city; the Citadel, the fortress of the Paladins; about the forest havens of the Aelvs; the underground cities of the Dworvs. She had always dreamed of visiting those fabulous elsewheres, but tonight she would see for herself, what the rest of the world looked like. She would explore to her heart's content, until dawn, at least; then she would have to race back home, climb back into bed, pretend that nothing had happened, all so that Anur would never find out.

She, at last, with the night still young, climbed to her favorite spot atop the island's highest peak and looked out over the waves. A calm, but steady wind was blowing her way; it was just what she needed, not a boat or a raft.

She had already been keeping a few secrets from Anur to get back at him; in the quiet hours of the morning or the late night, whenever she could be alone, she had been practicing.

As she slowly opened her wings to greet and be filled with the night air, Feldara giggled with the sensuous caress of the wind against the tender folds of skin that were her young wings. She had, indeed, been practicing her flying, and she thought she was quite good at it now.

Although her first attempts in the months past had been utter flops at best, last week she had been able to get up into the strong wind and soar for as long as she had liked, and though her landings had been a little rough, she thought she had managed herself quite well. Like the sails of a great graceful ship, her wings quickly became full of the joyful breeze, and she jumped and flapped all at once and was thus rapidly lifted into the sky.

Soaring upon the wind is, to a Dragon, like taking a breath; they could not imagine life without the exultant feat, and no less Feldara. She delighted in the soft, chill touch of the night air; the briny spray and smell upon the wind coming up from the ocean below, thrilled her senses. She reveled in the swiftness at which she passed over the sparkling waters as, in the pale moon's light, they shimmered magnificently as any diamond.

With the ability to fly whither she wanted, the cramped ground of the lonely island was boredom and a cage to her. She only wished that Anur could have come with her, but surely he would have disliked the whole ordeal, never-mind ever having approved of the outing as a whole.

But, she would worry about Anur later, as now the great ominous shadow of the lands beyond sprang boldly from the gloomy sea fog about it. Dark, ancient, rocky cliffs, enshrouded by the night, spread out before the sea, like a wall of shielded warriors, forcing back its ferocious thrashings as they stoically defended the land beyond. Feldara hastened above this sight, for she had viewed it a thousand times afar off upon her island home.

Up over the cliffs to the plains and forests beyond she soared, and she marveled at each difference between this new land and her home.

Gone were the semi-tropical jungles that overran the island; they had been substituted in this new place by the tall black pine forests and the occasional towering oak or maple. The ferns were replaced by the many tall plains of grasses which, by droves, merrily waved at her in the wind.

She decided to land now, so as to better explore this strange new world, for though she could see all below her clearly enough in the pale moon's light, she desired to touch and to smell all these new and wonderful things. Upon a grassy bluff, right before the forest of black pines and right above the sea, she disembarked from the lofty currents, and she ran about gleefully enjoying the new sensations of the touch of grass and the smell of pine. She took off into the coniferous forests, sniffing of each tree and jumping about as the pine needles pricked the undersides of her hands and feet, and she soon became hopelessly lost among them.

After some time of blissfully purposeless wandering, a few lights off in the distance caught her eye. They were like little lanterns, the kind which a Human might carry to help them see better in the dark, but these lights were all sorts of colors and floated about in dizzying undulating patterns. Feldara had never needed a lantern, for a Dragon's eyes could see well in the dark. To her, the bright light of the full moon was clear as midday, and under these thickly woven boughs of the tall evergreens, which did blot out almost entirely the moonlight, she could see about half as well as an owl.

Overjoyed with the new discovery of the lights, Feldara hastened towards them to investigate their source, but as she neared the strange illuminations, they scattered about the happy little forest glade that had, opening the thick evergreen canopy, let in a small sliver of radiance from the full moon's glow.

"Do not be frightened little lights." She cheerily called out to them, not really expecting a response.

However, the curious orbs of light did resume their frolicking, taking particular care to come as close as they dared to the young Dragoness. Mystified by their unexpected and uncannily sentient response, Feldara warranted these strange objects closer inspection, and peering intently at them she found that there were tiny creatures inside the light orbs, little faerie-like pixies, as nimble and quaint as any she had ever read about.

Through the deep hours of the night, she romped and played among them, dancing and prancing about the small forest clearing, until, surely just before the sun's first smiling rays of morning, a chilling noise echoed through the prickly boughs of the forest.

It was a haunting sound that scattered the fey; they took off into their burrows in the hollow trees and under the caps of large mushrooms. Feldara had heard this noise only once before, and that from off in the distance while she stayed safe upon her and Anur's island. She recognized it as the howling of wolves, but these howls were deeper, larger than that of any wolf she could think of and were full of dark malice and wicked intent. They were coming ever nearer.

Even though Feldara was a Dragon and had little reason to fear much of anything in the natural world, she was frightened to her very core by this howling, and she took off running in the opposite direction from them. Through, the scraping boughs of pine that uncaringly, almost malevolently, reached for her face to gouge out her eyes, she sped, full pace for a Dragon on the ground, but by the nearing of the cries, she could tell that the wolf pack was gaining on her.

"If only I can make it to the open ground, then I can just fly away," Thought Feldara, "If only I had just stayed in bed."

Not once in her flight from the abnormally frightening wolves did she consider turning about to fight. The thought may have occurred to an older Dragon, but it was well enough that she had not. Some instinct of hers had warned truthfully, for these were no normal wolves.

Suddenly, she broke through the dark forest, once again free from the ensnaring clutches of the evergreens, even returning to the very same shore where she had before landed. She opened her wings to the helpful wind, for to whisk her fast away from her trouble.

However, the pack was too close upon her, and right behind her, they also broke through into the open. Before she could even fully spread her wings to the still darkened sky, much before she could have leaped into the safety of the wind's comforting, billowing grasp, several of the great wolves pounced upon her, dragging her to the ground.

She had feared, but now as she fought with them in the dirt: biting, clawing, flailing, she saw that her assailants were no ordinary wolves; these were much bigger than was natural, every bit as large as she, much bulkier, and uglier, and nailed upon their claws and fangs were talons fashioned from a black metal. Worgs they were called, the hounds of the Dark One.

The biting and clawing of normal wolves would have done nothing to a Dragon's naturally impenetrable hide, but the ghastly, dark metal upon the fangs and paws of these beasts of shadow easily ripped into her scales and deeper. Despite her struggling, her ferocious defense, there were far too many werewolves for her to emerge victorious. Though she killed the two that had pounced upon her at the first, she could feel her blood flowing from her, her strength fading from her limbs. She tired, as the pack backed away, regrouping in the confidence that she could no longer escape into the sky above.

From deep within her, she roared at them in utter defiance. Though she may fall here today, Feldara knew, as did all Dragons, that she would rise again, in spirit at once, and her body later onward, at the end of all things. She knew at the very moment of her death, she would be in the arms of the Eloigal, apart from all these horrid things, no more to worry about the world's troubles, but even so, the love of life, the pride of Dragons, would not let her just lie down and succumb to these monsters. She only wished that she could have talked with Anur one more time, made sure he knew that she loved him, told him that she was sorry for running away from home.

A few tears fell from her eyes at the thought of not seeing Anur again, at least, for a very long while, of causing him grief by just disappearing one night. She doubted he would ever find out what had happened to her.

Upon noticing her tears, the monsters across from her uttered awful gurgling noises. Feldara could have sworn that they were laughing at her, mocking her crying, but she had no time to wonder at this, for the pack again, ever so slowly now, closed in on her, salivating profusely with the thought of her becoming their next meal. She tensed, preparing herself, summoning all the last bits of her strength to fight off these monsters one last time, but she never got the chance.

A bright flash of pale green light tore through the darkness, peeling apart and ripping through the fabric of night and reality. It blazed past Feldara and struck the nearest werewolf, which upon contact, immediately and violently disintegrated in a glowing ball of green fire. Anur quickly followed after the luminous bolt of magic, coming to stand between Feldara and the now enraged wolf pack and drew from his belt one of the ancient swords from their island's once useless armory.

Feldara was so overjoyed by Anur's sudden unexpected appearance that the tears of regret she had shed earlier now turned into abundant tears of grateful relief. She smiled, glad beyond words for his rescuing, but could not remain standing. She stumbled to the ground and lay there, the sheer exhaustion of her battling and the loss of blood finally mixing with the utterly emotional expectation of death and the sudden, unanticipated removal thereof, by none less than the one person in the world that she knew and loved. It all finally drove her tired body to unconsciousness.

Slowly, uncontrollably her legs gave way and her eyes began to close, as the world darkened further, even as the first rays of the morning sun triumphantly rose above the horizon and Anur danced about in the frenzy of bladed battling, methodically, almost easily disposing of the rest of the wolf pack.

Chapter 6

The young jet-black Dragon, Malok, soared over the shimmering wriggling, tenebrous expanse below him. He knew that he was dreaming, for the earth and trees never had undulated so fluidly in reality, never had the moon seemed so purple or the faeries darted about so thickly and briskly.

He was far from the sandy wastes of his home, the land of the Serpen, they who had raised him.

He had been cared for, since the time he had hatched, by the King's own personal aide, Ulam, a greatly venerated personage among his people. The King himself, Shar, was his best of friends, and the two had grown up together, played together in the labyrinthine tunnels of the Serpen palace, studied together under Ulam's careful and strict tutelage, and had caused all manner of mischief together.

But, he was alone in this dream world now, and he realized no matter how hard he tried, he could not change the dream or even wake. He desperately attempted to turn around and fly away, for he knew now that he was about to be caught in one of his numerous nightmares that had plagued him his whole life through. Try as he might, he continued to soar above the dark, wobbling pine trees below, headed toward some, as yet unknown, destination.

Soon a bright figure caught his eye below, and unable to otherwise alter his course, he hastened toward the glowing shape. As he descended from on high, drawing nearer and nearer to the lightened one, he recognized it as a uniquely Turquoise colored Dragoness. He landed right beside her, and enamored by her radiant beauty attempted to say hello. Even if she could have heard Malok, she could not have understood what he said, for as he spoke, he realized that she could not possibly interpret his adopted Serpen tongue, but would rather speak the language of Men and Aelvs, the common tongue.

However, his confusedly awkward attempts at greeting the enchanting, mysteriously glowing, Dragoness were suddenly violently interrupted, as from out of nowhere, vicious monsters leaped upon her and began to eat her alive, even as she fought with them.

Malok threw himself into the fray as well, for to defend this beautiful female, but he had no power over his dream. His claws struck upon nothing; his teeth bit at the air.

Suddenly, the trees melted and fell backward all at once, and both the Dragoness and the vile creatures dissipated into the darkness. Malok was lifted into the air by an unknown power, not his own wings, and a bright red glow began to fill the sky. Before his eyes, there slowly appeared an armored giant fearsome and full of malevolence, wreathed in dark fire, his face, or rather lack thereof, hidden by nothing but shadow in his visor-less horned helm.

"Who are you!" Screamed Malok in utter terror, at the wine-red armored giant.

The faceless giant did not answer; it only coldly stared at Malok and his racing heart for what seemed an eternity. Salvation only came when the dream abruptly ended, and just as the Dark One finally moved, at last reaching out with a single clawed, metal gauntlet for to grab Malok's throat, surely killing him, the young Dragon found himself roaring uncontrollably, tangled in a mess of bedding upon the floor of his own room.

Both Ulam and Shar were already by his side, and the King's personal guard looked on from the safety of the room beyond, where were the King's chambers.

Malok could not yet explain himself properly, so soon after violently waking from this nightmare, and stuttered and muttered over words of embarrassed apology, as he noticed the commotion he had caused. His bed was a shredded pile of strewn stuffing and plush fabric, and he had rolled over and smashed into the low table and his bookshelf. Books and scrolls lay scattered across the floor, some more worse for wear than others.

"There is no need for apology, for there is no harm done." Comforted Ulam, who was as much a father to Malok as anyone had ever been. "You had another of your visions. Many people have suffered violent ones like this, and never in all of history has a single person learned to truly control their dreams."

"Speak for yourself, Ulam." Shar joked, as he helped Malok out of the tangled mass of bed sheets. "These silk coverings, the books, the extra large, Dragon-sized bed- have all been harmed and will all need to be replaced, along with the hours of sleep I have missed."

Although Malok knew Shar spoke in jest, he did feel clumsily guilty about destroying all these precious objects. Furniture was a luxury that only a very few Serpen could afford, and even though the country had begun to prosper under Shar's wise rule, most Serpen still slept on the sandy floor of their subterranean homes and had no books or scrolls to read, let alone fine wooden tables and shelves.

"These material things can be done without. Your friend has suffered a terrible dream tonight; what if he had never awakened?" Chided Ulam, as he began straightening the room, forcing the reluctant royal guards to help, for the regular servants were always allowed to their own homes for the night.

"Besides, such a gift, or curse, that of unfathomable foresight, of itself alone, is worth more than finely crafted wood, as Malok has proven time and again. I still remember how you had found the long lost Sovereign's Stone among the possessions of house Uzil." Recollected Ulam, a contented smile beginning to creep across his face. "That pompous toad Uzil and his family have long been enemies of the crown, yet in one night you had deflated all their scheming, brought them so low in the eyes of the people and the other houses that they shall never rise again. How elatedly I recall watching you unassumingly dig out the spot in the wall of his great room, right in the midst of that jubilee that he had organized to gain favor with the other houses. Oh, the look on his face when you produced that unmistakable ruby, while all the other lords looked on stupefied. I would have been pleased enough were you simply destroying his rat tunnel of a manor, but no, you held out your hand for all to see the still damp and sandy gem. I almost died laughing when you innocently said, 'Look, I found it.'"

"I was not even attempting to incriminate house Uzil. While I was at the party, I just simply remembered seeing in my dreams the exact location of the Sovereign's Stone." Malok abashedly protested, as Ulam ceased his reminiscing and resumed a less smug expression; though the young Dragon did have to admit to being proud of solving an ages old mystery and discrediting the enemies of his best friend.

"But, never has he been so frightened before, to thrash about in panic." Shar had to point out, truly being worried for his friend's health. "I am concerned, Malok; what did you see in your dream that caused you such fear?" He inquired.

Malok then recounted to them his recent nightmare, making careful detail of everything. By the time he had finished, the guards and Ulam had cleaned up what they could without a proper maid's knowledgeable help, and they were all sitting on the floor, fixedly listening to him as if he were telling an audience of children some important legend of old. Then noticing their lingering presence, Ulam flicked his forked tongue and shot a disapproving glare to dismiss the guards, who probably should not have stayed to be distracted from their duty by the tale, and they quietly arose and left with haste.

"What do you think it all meant?" Malok asked of his two friends, as he also tried to make some sense of how he could again sleep upon his thoroughly carved bed.

"It must have been something that had actually happened, for you to have been so enraptured by the Dragoness and her attack. Perhaps, it was your mother, how she had died." Gently ventured Shar, hoping not to upset his friend with his guess.

"No, I would have recognized my own mother; would I not?" Malok pressed.

He was nearly positive that the Dragoness he had seen was not his mother; she felt too young, even the same age as he.

"Then another Dragoness that you are tied to, a twin or sibling, perhaps; nevertheless, a real person, who had been slain by the workings of the Shadow Lord." Ulam proposed, and they all became sorely saddened by this idea.

But, Malok did not feel this to be quite right either, for he withheld from them how he had seen before this particular apparition, this Bright Dragoness. Yet, never before had she been endangered; only had Malok looked upon her, enamored by her shining beauty. For some time, they all sat in thoughtful silence, each with their own theories as to the identity of the Dragoness and what the dream could have meant, until Ulam stifled a yawn with the sleeve of his night robes.

"Perhaps, more answers shall be revealed to us in the morning." He suggested, rising and bidding them both goodnight.

The older Serpen determinedly slithered back to his own chambers, which were down the hall from the King's, for he was, indeed, getting too old for such late night excitement and craved more and more his soft bed.

Shar also wished his friend a more restful sleep, cordially kissing the Dragon upon his large crested forehead before leaving to his own bed.

Malok lay awake for some time thereafter, still fearfully dwelling upon the horrible Shadow Lord's armored form and disturbing lack of visage under the demonically horned helm, but he soon drifted off to a more peaceful slumber than before, thankfully devoid of any dreaming.

<><><><><>

Malok arose with the dawning of the sun, refreshed and fully rested despite the awful vision he had encountered the night before. With a morning lave of his face and hands, the fear that had been caused by the dark dream was washed away.

He raced out his own private, specially built exit, from his room to the very top of the small frontage of a stone castle that crowned the sandy mound, under which lay the main palace complex. The small mound, and the diminutive castle atop, slightly overlooked the grand center of the Serpen Kingdom, Bassar, the chief city of their nation. To the eyes of foreigners, it seemed little more than a large mass of mounds that stretched from the lone castle tower to the docks of the nearby bay and seaport, but underneath each mound lay a Serpen home or business. Some of the wealthier ones could be distinguished by the oasis that sat at the front of the entrance of the mound; even a single fruit or nut palm tree signified the prominence of the house or enterprise that lay, in tunnels, under the surface of the desert soil.

Over these Malok stretched his wings, at least, daily, for he loved the freedom and quiet peacefulness of the wide open sky above the empty desert. As he soared overhead, many of the Serpen would come out of their holes just to see him, and often the children would playfully race after his winged paths in the sky, dreaming above hope that they could make pace with him. He brought joy to the hearts of all who saw him, so that when he landed here or there, they would call him by name, singing his praise, or offer him wares or food. The people treasured him as they did their own sovereign, a national symbol in which they all could take pride, but also an individual whom many of them knew personally and all loved. He was the Dragon of the Serpen, and he was ever proud to be called so, for he loved his adoptive people every bit as much in return.

Today was no different. Malok leaped off the small stone castle's roof and let the warm currents carry him high into the air, but instead of heading into town, he took off in the opposite direction, toward the mountains, for to find some breakfast. He hunted for most of his food, rather than eat from the table of the King, for he knew that was a table the people themselves spread from the sweat of their labor. The various game from the nearby mountains, goat and antelope, and the fish from the nearby sea were his main source of sustenance.

Finding a couple of delicious young rams upon the tall craggy slopes, he took his breakfast to the crystal shore of the dazzlingly sunlit morning sea, and watched the Serpen wives make clean their laundry in the surf, while he ate his meal. As it splashed up against his black, clawed hands and blood red meal, the colors of his meat and of the surf once again brought to Malok's mind the image of that dazzling Bright Dragoness of his latest night terror and the consequent and horrifying visage of the grim Shadow Lord.

Perhaps, it was better he not worry about such things as dreams and visions. After all, who was he to care, a nobody, an orphan, abandoned and unwanted by his own kind, yet still clawing at the back of his mind, the images, almost too distinct and lucid to be real, vividly lingered. Could it be that, in his own dreaming, he had seen the actual death of so fair a Dragoness, but why, he wondered, should such phantasms appear unto him at all, unless he were destined, almost required, to do something about them.

Suddenly, revelation came upon him, striking swiftly like a lightning bolt. The vision of the Turquoise Dragoness could have been of the future, or the near present, rather than the past; If so, she could still be alive and in severe peril, in dire need of rescue! Such urgency of plight caused Malok to forget his breakfast where it lay and swiftly wing back to the palace.

The guards quickly scrambled to get out of his way, as he abruptly descended and, hardly without stopping to land, sped back into his room. Through his own chambers he bolted on and slammed open the iron doorway that led directly to the King's adjacent bedchamber.

"Shar!" Malok shouted, nearly roaring in enthusiasm, surprising his friend.

This morning was, possibly, not the best time to drop in on the juvenile king, as he and a beautiful young Serpen girl, one whom the yet unwed sovereign had been eying passionately now for several months, had only just begun sharing a secretly intimate moment.

Thankfully, they were both quite virtuous, even in their ardent lover's pursuit, and were merely conversing, fully clothed, only sitting upon the edge of the King's bed. Even so, they could now only stare open mouthed at the Dragon, embarrassed at the effortless exposal of their clandestine dalliance.

"What is the matter, my friend?" Shar finally stuttered in response, after a short moment of dumbstruck silence.

Malok smiled sympathetically and bowed to the Serpen princess-to-be, as she quickly and quietly left the chamber with as much dignity as she could muster through her humiliated astonishment. With much agony, Shar watched her go, desperately hoping that their relationship had not been tarnished by this episode of glorious chagrin.

Malok waited until she had closed the doors behind her before continuing. "We must set out at once for the city of Doraegonoran, for the Order of Paladins. The Dragoness that I saw last night in my dream may still be alive, and we must go to her rescue!" He frantically exclaimed.

"Slow your slithering." Demanded Shar, rather excessively emphasizing the colloquial expression with a gesture of his hands.

The Serpen King, after recovering from his earlier stupefaction, was, understandably, aggravated by his Dragon friend, for the ruining of this private morning with his, possibly, future queen. Nevertheless, Shar was a good friend and valued greatly Malok's happiness; he continued to inquire about the dream.

"I thought you saw this Dragoness being killed by some dark beasts under the control of the Shadow Lord. How can we save her if she is already dead?" Asked the king, but quickly the realization dawned on him as it had Malok.

If this dream of Malok's was, indeed, a vision of what could happen, then they, good and noble beings, were honor-bound to do everything possible to deliver this Dragoness from such a fate.

"Are you certain that this is even a vision and not just a regular nightmare?" Shar asked, not so much in disbelief of his friend, but out of having no desire to travel to the Order's realm.

____

"I am certain, that if I do nothing, the darkness will consume this Dragoness. I know that Ulam has cautioned me against returning to the place of my birth, to the Citadel of the Order, but if I have been given so great a gift as to see the future, and I now do nothing to save a life, that which I know shall certainly perish without my intervention, then I am no better than a dog and would shame my kin if I were to still call myself Dragon." Malok stated, assuming a rare noble posture that was so uncommon for the blithely youthful male.

"You are in the right, my friend," Conceded Shar, with but a little deliberation. "But I cannot let you go alone. I must accompany you. Yet, let me first say farewell to some people about the palace, and we must make sure to let Ulam know that we are leaving this time. He did not quite enjoy the last instance we up and left the kingdom in his stewardship, however capable." Shar replied, embracing his friend.

The King summoned the guards at the entrance to the royal chambers, for to take word of his departure unto Ulam, and he himself left in another direction, after the way in which his consort had earlier left.

Afterward, they met again upon the roof of the palace, to gather together all their supplies, which became quite an ordeal, as Shar had started off wanting to take most every comfort he enjoyed here with him upon the road, but as his sumptuous bed was obviously too bulky for Malok to carry Dragon-back, they eventually pared his list down to: a simple, hooded traveler's cloak over plain Serpen waist-cloth to wear, a map, a compass, a water-skin and another satchel for food and other small stuffs, and a short, unadorned sickle-sword for his weapon.

With a few hours having gone by, somehow, nearly the whole city had heard of what was happening and had turned out to what was supposed to have been a rather inconspicuous departure, and the throngs of loyal and loving subjects cheered, blew horns, and waved farewell with hands and banners to the two, Serpen Dragon and Serpen King. As they prepared to take off from the modest castle above the city, before they could yet leave, Ulam took them aside and, having to shout over the gathered crowds, gave them special advice for their journey.

"My lord Shar, reveal your identity to no one, for the Humans of the Order have no love for our people; do not test what they might do should they know who you are. Above all, beware lord Orthard, the both of you. His conspiring was to keep you here, Malok, apart from your people, for whatever reason; who would know what he should do, if he finds you back among the Paladins." At this Ulam discretely handed an item to Shar, a gemstone which Malok thought he recognized. "Be safe." He finally wished of them.

With a nod and a smile, and Shar fastened well upon his back, Malok leaped into the air, and they swiftly headed South, toward the Order's realm.

It was only one of a few times Shar had ridden Dragon-back, and he was as yet to be comfortable so high above the warm consoling touch of the sandy desert. Once they were well away from Bassar, Malok decided to start a conversation with the trembling Serpen upon his shoulders, so as to pass the time and help ease his friend.

"So, I will forgive your rudeness earlier, in the lack of introductions, but you must acquaint me with your new female friend, the next time we meet." Malok glibly jested, but as the wind muffled completely any rebuttal, Shar could only smack the Dragon soundly with his long tail.

Chapter 7

Sixteen years ago Zurthaud had undertaken the daring mission of rebuilding the Order of Paladins, training a new generation of Humans and other sentient beings to accept each other as people, to work together, especially on Dragon-back, to prepare, in the old ways, for the imminent struggle with the Shadow Lord and his armies, all the while, right under the nose of his own bigoted father.

Had Orthard known the full reason why his son spent every waking hour among the Dragons and his select peers, he would have surely disciplined or even expelled him for thus challenging his rule, but the Lord Consul could not have known, as Zurthaud reported only tales at the required briefings of the Dragons doings, which became ever more sporadic- less than yearly- due to the choice dullness of their contents.

Sixteen years ago he had been but a boy when the Shadow Lord had revealed his hand through the deaths of the last two Dragonesses of the Order, thus dooming the race of Dragons, for no more females of their kind existed. Now Zurthaud was a young man, full of strength and knowledge. He had, with himself, raised up his childhood friends, Human boys, cadets of the Order, alongside many others, to become these Paladins who were the companions of Dragons, who knew how to ride and fight Dragon-back, who had mastered the unnatural ability to wield magic, who now regarded each other as friends and brothers.

Now Zurthaud, as he soared through the air upon his Dragon companion, almost got his head taken off by a well aimed ballistae bolt;

thankfully, Theros was looking out for him and, with a flick of his wings, swerved quickly to the side, causing the bolt to miss by mere inches.

"You are so welcome." He snidely shouted back at Zurthaud, over the rush of the wind.

He and his fellow Paladins were currently embroiled in a fierce battle against a regiment of the Dark Horde that had dared to wander deep into the Order's territory. With great numbers, ballistae, and trebuchet, they had been besieging the large walled town of Bythatsar that lay about sixty miles South of Doraegonoran, along the North bank of the Atsar river. Though the multitude of Goblins, Trolls, and Ogres had taken the gatehouse on the southern shore and the bridge across the river, they had as yet to take any ground on the North side, and Zurthaud intended to keep it that way.

Historically, the Atsar River had served as an excellent barrier to the Dark Horde, in ages past preventing them from ever making it all the way to Doraegonoran, that is, until the more easily defended Great Wall, the Aronoran, had been built at the true border of the Shadow Lands. However, recently, not even the supreme blockade of the unassailable Aronoran was stopping the Dark Horde, for with its guard reduced to a skeleton crew, a the Lord Consul's order no less, and for some time now, the wicked creatures had found it no longer well manned and had begun crossing in ever greater numbers over into Order lands, sacking farms and attacking smaller villages to the South. Still, never before had the enemy made such a bold move, as to deploy so large and organized a force against so prominent a target as this well defended and affluent city.

Bythatsar was, indeed, like many towns of the Order's territory, the Human's realm, walled and fortified, modern and bustling with trade, ruled by a duly elected mayor who paid tribute to the Order in exchange for their protection, but in the days before the Aronoran, it had been a symbol of freedom to the people, the last obstacle, never captured nor desolated, between Doraegonoran and the Shadow Lands. Just the thought of such boldness from the enemy as to desecrate so illustrious an icon of enduring and triumphant spirit infuriated Zurthaud.

Even more enraging still, his father had refused to increase the guard at the Aronoran and had even refused to send any reinforcement to this town, filled with many more merchants and farmers than soldiers. For sure, Bythatsar had a town guard comprised of trained and volunteer militia, but Zurthaud saw, from the moment he and his Paladins had arrived, that they would have certainly been overrun by the well armed and organized Dark Horde, if they had not come any sooner.

And, the Paladins had come, four hundred strong: two hundred Dragons with their two hundred riders, nearly the full might of their true army, Zurthaud's faithful. They had fought fiercely all day, burning and smiting with blade, claw, and magic, but the enemy was still determined to end the siege and swarm into the city. The Dark Horde had already crossed the river by way of the bridge, which, along with the fortified gatehouse on the South shore, served as the town's first line of defense; they now brought forth a heavily roofed and iron-wheeled battering ram to knock down the town's gate on the North shore, the last line of defense for all the helpless people inside.

"Let us make another pass for the ram." Zurthaud yelled at his companion, for the wind of Theros' battle speed necessitated such volume.

"It is too well guarded by the ballistae they mounted in the gatehouse towers." Theros shouted back, circling high in the air above the raging warfare below. "I cannot get close enough for a clean shot with my fire-breath, without slowing down a little, and you have seen how well they have been aiming all day. They already snagged Galrag in the arm with a Black-iron bolt."

Zurthaud nodded in response, for he knew how deadly the savage metal, Black-iron, could be. It was the only thing in the world that could pierce a Dragon's hide and by no natural means at that. Found only in the Shadow Lands, it was truly infected with some dark power, reflecting no light at all and able to cut so easily, as by some corrosive magic, into the Dragons' scales.

Fortunately, they had suffered no casualties as of yet, for Galrag, the elder, dark green Dragon who had been covering their left wing and, as a renowned general, been helping to strategize their army's attacks, had only suffered a flesh wound in his arm. Still, Zurthaud had ordered him off the field of battle, to take up a defensive position inside the town.

Of a sudden, an idea, seeming crazed at first, but becoming all the more sensible as time passed, came to Zurthaud.

"What if I were to do the scorching?"Asked the young Human, a smile, all too wickedly curved, too much like his father's, yet infinitely less malicious, spreading across his ruggedly handsome face.

"Oh, no. I know what you think. I will not permit it." Theros shouted back at Zurthaud, but his friend was nowhere to be found.

Zurthaud had leaped off the back of his Dragon and was rapidly falling to sure doom upon either the stone bridge below or the velocity hardened water.

"Catch me!" He shouted back up at his Dragon friend, even as Theros hastened after him.

Zurthaud then began to charge a great ball of magic between the palms of his two hands, but the question now was what the magic should do. A blast of force too strong could destroy the battering ram, the bridge, and even both of the town's gates, maybe even rebounding back upon Zurthaud, thus killing himself, thereby making this maneuver, the magic, and helping save this town all an utter waste of time. On the other hand, a blast of force too weak would accomplish nothing other than to alert the enemy below to his presence, which could also get him and Theros killed and, otherwise, accomplish nothing.

Thinking quickly, and the more so as his altitude rapidly decreased, Zurthaud charged the magic to mostly create heat and fire where it should land, with just enough punch to cut through the ram's armor, and just as quickly, he released it upon the battering ram. The red orb of light shot from his hands like a rocket and easily burst through the roof of the ram, immediately exploding the insides of it into a ball of flames as hot as any Dragon's breath; the surviving Goblin and Troll operators promptly scrambled out from the innards of the ram, which began to be consumed, rather quickly, by the magic fire ball.

Zurthaud would then have celebrated but that he still plummeted straight toward the inferno which had once been a proudly terrifying siege engine, and just as he was beginning to reconsider this choice in tactic, Theros suddenly caught him by the arms and, being mindful of terminal velocity's force, so as not to rip the man's appendages clean off, began to gently, yet urgently slow their descent.

"That was so stupid! Curse you, Zurthaud! How many times do I have to tell you to stay on my back while we are flying? You could have died." Theros scoldingly shouted as they narrowly avoided landing in the fire on the bridge.

As it was, they almost crashed into the Atsar River, but for Theros slowing their descent enough to at last defy gravity without causing his Human any harm. Even so, Zurthaud's boot heels licked the surface of the water like skipping stones.

"Calm down. You caught me; I knew you would." Zurthaud responded, nearly chuckling with the humor of the situation and an acute adrenaline rush.

"Well, I am so glad you have such faith in me." Theros sarcastically remarked, as he dodged the horde's retaliatory ballistae fire.

Upon seeing their ram destroyed and the boldness of the Paladins, the Dark Horde then silently gave up their hope of winning the town. Slowly at first, but ever quickening, their army began to flee the battle in unorganized retreat, leaving behind both dead and wounded, whole and shattered weaponry, heading straight for the border and their various camps.

"Shall we pursue them?" Theros asked, as he and Zurthaud regrouped with the rest of the Paladins in the skies above the town.

"No, but we should send a scout after them, to make sure they cross back over the border into their own country." Zurthaud replied, as he climbed back atop Theros and into his usual spot between two large neck spines at the Dragon's broad shoulders.

Some companions would use a saddle, for their own sake, to ride upon their Dragons' backs, as they aided in comfort and security, but Zurthaud had never found them to be particularly useful, other than for holding the rider in place with a special full-body harness. He thought them too restrictive of his movements atop and across a Dragon's back; besides which, Theros would probably never have approved of one.

While he and Zurthaud had become the best of friends over these sixteen years, Theros still had the remains of his juvenile temper, and a greater portion of pride than most Dragons. Yet, had he softened in his heart toward Humans in general, not just toward Zurthaud. His condemnation and hatred toward the weaker race had ceased, and he had even come to show respect and care for the younger Humans whom he and Zurthaud had trained. It was these students who now fought beside them, along with scant few of the older Humans and Aelvs who had never cared for Orthard's discriminating mandates. These were the true Paladins, and Theros considered them worthy of regard.

With the Dark Horde gone, they now turned to helping the citizens of the town recover from the assault, healing the injured and repairing the broken and demolished structures. It was hours still after the battle had ended before they could stop working, before they could say the day had been won, and though no members of the Order had fallen, casualties among the people of Bythatsar were very great. As Zurthaud and Theros walked the streets seeing to the finishing of their aid toward the people, they could not help but let their eyes wet at the sight of such sorrows as had befallen the townsfolk. Children cried out for their mothers and fathers to no answer, parents tearfully cradled the lifeless in their arms; despite all their heroic actions, their help in restoring the town, and all their sympathy and compassion for them, the Paladins could not diminish the suffering of those whose loved ones had perished.

"I wish we had pursued those monsters." Zurthaud uttered in regret.

"Perhaps, we should have cut them all down, but things might not have worked in our favor in the Shadow Lands. Besides, the people of Bythatsar needed our help repairing their walls and towers; it would have taken them days or weeks to do so without our magic, leaving them open to another attack." Theros replied, for once unusually cool headed.

Having walked the streets of the town and seen that all the Paladins could accomplish toward the peoples' relief had been done, they two found the Mayor of Bythatsar, debriefed him of the battle's result and the casualties suffered, and with many condolences for the city's losses, gave notice of their departure.

Lastly, before they could leave, they made sure to check up on their only injured from that day, the elder Dragon who was once the highest commanding officer in all the Order. Before Zurthaud had been born, the old, green one had been removed from his official position by order of Orthard, but all the Dragons, and even Zurthaud's fellow companions still called him by title more than name. He was the one who had overseen most of their soldierly training, in both drill and tactics, and was revered by all who knew him for his martial prowess.

He was clearly not thrilled to have been taken out, and rather early, from, in his earlier stated opinion, so light a skirmish, and as Zurthaud and Theros found him, already attended by the town's doctors, he could clearly be heard grumbling about it. His son, Galrath, only a shade lighter of green than his father and just slightly younger than Theros, was already with him, and he welcomed their arrival, for he was good friends with both Theros and Zurthaud.

"How is the General?" Zurthaud slyly asked of Galrath, seeing that the elder Dragon was too busy fussing with the doctor over his healthcare to have yet noticed them.

"Oh, he is quite wroth to have at all been wounded, much less ordered from the field." Galrath relayed with a wry smile. "He will probably want an apology from you for that, but otherwise he will be fine," Then turning to his father, he yelled. "As long as he lets the good Human doctor waste his several yards of gauze on him, rather than stitching the wound closed."

This finally caught the General's attention long enough for him to realize Zurthaud and Theros had come to see about him and to make reply.

"Any proper physician knows that it is much better to suture a Dragon for a wound like this; I even learned that in the teachings on field dressings."

"The poor doctor has probably never seen a Dragon, much less tended to one; besides, you know he has neither a needle large enough nor wrought of

Black-iron, as this is the only time that foul metal is good for anything."
Galrath, all in defense of the appreciative Human physician, shouted in return,
as he invited Theros and Zurthaud to sit with them while the doctor finished
his work.

"It is good to see that you are well enough to argue." Theros greeted, as
he sat down near the grumbling Galrag.

"Well enough? I was shot and missed the whole battle and ordered
from the field by this, this hatchling." Aggravatedly complained the towering
Dragon, but he had a sly smile for Zurthaud, not anger or jealousy.
"Congratulations on surviving your first battle, a victory even." He proudly
chuckled to the Human. "If you were not already, officially, a higher rank than
I, I truly would think about promoting you, Zurthaud, yet after witnessing that
last maneuver, I begin to question your sanity, much less your fitness for
leadership."

Zurthaud, scratched his head in embarrassment and mumblingly
stammered some kind of explanation for his reckless tactic, but as Galrag was
being rather jocular and not entirely serious, Theros was game to banter.

"Come now, how could you not?" He jokingly replied. "Besides you and
me and Galrath, he is the most senior member present. Would you really risk
the chain of command being broken?"

"No, and I jest." The elder Dragon confirmed, but then turning more
serious. "Yet, speaking of command, I doubt your father, Lord Consul Orthard,
can be further misled regarding your purpose and intentions among us. It was
against his direct orders that we came to this city's aide, and you were not only
with us, but also, since I fell to a blow, leading us. He will surely catch wind of
your deeds today, and he may very well try to punish you, and us, for it."

"I am not afraid of my father." Zurthaud stated bravely.

"But, you must be wary of him." Galrag sternly advised. "You
remember what happened to my Aelven companion, Reythanuil, for disobeying
the Lord Consul's direct orders. He was tried, 'legally', almost found guilty of

treason, 'legally', and exiled, 'legally'; I could not put that man past doing the same to you, though you were his own flesh and blood."

With that somber thought lingering among them like a bad taste in the mouth, the doctor finally finished with his wrapping of the large Dragon's truly enormous arm, and though the General heartily thanked him, they all knew the poor Human physician had only wasted time and resources. For, as soon as they would return home, the stubborn general would have Serc redo the dressing.

With the Dragon's roaring bugle call, the Paladins assembled to leave. Though still in the throes of bereavement for their dead, the brave townsfolk let out a loud and grateful cheer for the Paladins, as the Dragons together, a massive flock of iridescence, in a rush of hot wind and lucent color, all took off from the ground at once. As a group, they spiraled in the skies above the town for a moment, a magnificent display of power and beauty, until they had all caught up with one another, and finally, waving farewell to the people of Bythatsar, they all winged off toward Doraegonoran and the Citadel.

Looking back over his shoulder at the black smoke that still rose like somber pillars from the ashes about the town. Zurthaud could not take his mind off the misery of those unfortunates, especially the children. "What shall we do about this, Theros?" He asked of his companion. "Children should not have to grow up as órphans because of the evils in the world."

"I know not, only that we must prepare for the coming storm." Theros answered, unsure of what the future held as their fate.

"But, we have prepared, and we are strong now, great in number." Zurthaud argued. "I think it is time we took this fight to the enemy. I think it high time we cause the Shadow Lord to tremble in his boots, and not for our own selves, for our own glory or victory, but for those people, their children, and those like them."

Theros thought long and hard about his friends words. Ever since the dark tower of Ragnor had appeared on the barren black plains of the South , the lands forever enshrouded by the most ominous of storm clouds, thunderheads which brought neither rain nor storm only darkness, never had any army dared assail that vile fortress. It was thought nigh impenetrable with its ring of mountains fortified with myriad minor battlements and towers, and its sheer height, being the tallest structure in all of Threa.

"I care far more for your safety than to let you go off alone to battle the whole army of darkness and its master. At least, let us bring this matter before the other Paladins, those that follow the old ways, and let them decide. If they would go to war, then I will go to war with you; if not, then I will find some rope or chain to tie you down with." Theros finally stated, chuckling at his last little quip.

Although Zurthaud had to admit the wisdom of his friend's response, going through with Theros' plan meant that Zurthaud would have to face his worst and most persistent enemy- public speaking.

<><><><><>

That night, Zurthaud and Theros' had prepared for the occasion in their shared apartment, in the sole tower of the Dragon's quarters, for after Lethira had passed on that sad day sixteen years ago, and he and Theros had started to become good friends, Zurthaud had moved in there with the Dragon.

"You have practiced this speech on me ten times already, and I thought it fine every time." Encouraged the Dragon, as Zurthaud paced anxiously about the large main living room. "Just tell them what you had told me earlier today, what you feel in your heart to be true, and you shall do fine."

"I wish I had not said anything to Serc; if only I had kept my mouth shut. You know how bad I am at speech making. I speak so boringly that you were always the one to lecture the cadets." Griped Zurthaud as he let loose his worries upon his friend. "I doubt I shall convince a single person."

"I said you shall do fine." Theros insisted more aggressively, as he helped Zurthaud get upon his shoulders. "Besides which, it is far too late to back out now, for tonight, all the Dragons and their companions have gathered for their say in the direction our Order will take, whether to fight or to stand fast."

Before Zurthaud could argue any further, the Dragon had strode out the arched doorway of their apartment and off the edge of the balcony without, and after falling only a few feet, stretching his wings out fully, Theros lifted them up to the domed top of the Dragon's tower.

As the roaring wind rushed by his ears, causing words to be silenced and thoughts to sound, Zurthaud let his mind drift back to earlier that day, for after the battle at the town of Bythatsar, he had confronted Serc with his plans to move offensively against the machinations of the Shadow Lord, hoping that the eldest Dragon of the Order would see the wisdom in his words. Actually, quite the opposite had occurred. Serc had vehemently opposed any aggression toward the Dark Horde, and was especially against Zurthaud's plans of attacking the Ragnor itself.

Instead of gaining an ally who would publicly support his strategy of attack when Zurthaud would argue his cause and explain his plan before the

Paladins gathered here tonight at the Dragon's temple, Serc was now going to oppose Zurthaud and openly denounce his strategy before the same audience.

Not that Zurthaud was already nervous enough, having to make speech before all these friends and comrades, but now he would have to be especially eloquent and convincing to the point of out-speaking the venerable Dragon doctor. Zurthaud had never been very apt in the art of speech-making, had never been particularly pronounced with his words, and he doubted if he could persuade the Paladins to follow him in the path that he thought best for defeating the evils that slowly encroached about them.

But, all these worries would have to wait a moment, for as the two reached the balcony of the dome, the only entrance, designed exclusively for Dragons and their companions, Zurthaud remembered the first time he had entered this holy place.

The Dragons had brought him here, after he had officially become a companion to Theros. They had inducted him truly into the Order of Paladins with the long ignored sacred observances and had even introduced him to their faith.

At first he had not really cared, neither believing nor disbelieving, yet each day since, the solitary God that had created the universe and longed to commune with his creation, The Eloigal, seemed to prove Himself more and more real to Zurthaud. The young Human could almost palpably feel His presence when he and the Dragons worshiped here; when he had begun praying to Eloigal, Zurthaud really did feel as if there was someone listening. Circumstance itself, an inanimate, dispassionately unconcerned force, even seemed to prove Eloigal's presence, as Zurthaud's life could have been ended many times by now, but for the benevolent providence of some slight adjustment to how the world should have kept on turning. The Dragons had said that these, those unannounced little miracles, were the foundation of magic, the bending of reality.

Following tradition and out of respect for the Dragons within and for The Eloigal, to Whom the whole world belonged, let alone this holy temple, Zurthaud took off his boots and laid them at the doorway when he dismounted from Theros' back, and they both entered barefoot into the large atrium of the dome.

He looked into the eyes of his friend of sixteen years, with whom he had only grown closer in bond with the passing of these years, and Theros returned Zurthaud's gaze with a supportive nod and a smile. He had made clear, after Serc's disagreement them, that they were comrades together until the end, that he would support Zurthaud even if his own kind did not. Whatever Zurthaud chose to do, if anything was in this meeting allowed, Theros would guard his backside.

Together they ceremoniously laved with purest water, which sat in large, ornate wash basins placed about the large atrium at the various entrances to the large inner chamber, for to cleanse their hands and their faces before they would enter the sanctuary of the domed temple, and finishing, Zurthaud heaved a large sigh, as the water rolled in rivulets down his face and back into the vessel.

It was not his first time speaking to many people, but to all the Dragons and their companions at once, truly a large crowd, that caused him such anxiety; not only that, but he was also trying to persuade them to follow his leadership over that of the honorable Serc. Zurthaud had only just commanded troops in battle against the forces of darkness. Never had he to stand in front of the entirety of his soldiers and, with much articulate communication, convince them to follow his leading and inspire them to victory.

"You will do fine." Again encouraged Theros, sensing his friend's anxiety; he lightly, comfortingly placed his enormous hand over Zurthaud's shoulder. "If we cannot convince them to take action, it will not be because you did not speak well enough. Just tell us what you believe in your heart; we all are your friends here."

The words soothed the pounding in Zurthaud's chest only a little, as he was, indeed, very uneasy, more so than he had been all his life long. He desperately hoped to convince the Dragons to take action, for he knew, without a doubt, that the time was right. The Dark One's forces were weak, weak in the battle for Bythatsar, and now certainly weaker. Surely, with the amount of foes slain in that conflict, The Shadow Lord had as yet to rebuild his full strength, and in such stark contrast, the Paladins had proven very strong and were growing even stronger by the day. Zurthaud was certain that now was the time for attack, to push back against the oncoming darkness.

"Let us go in together." He asked of his companion. "Your presence gives me much strength." And his fiend's large Dragon hand upon his shoulder he clasped with his own.

They two entered then, ascending the small flight of stairs that separated the atrium from the large interior sanctuary.

Within, the number of Dragons and their two-legged companions were already heatedly debating the subject. Their raucous conversation nauseatingly reverberated again and again off of the round, smooth, Dragon-fire carved white stone walls of the sanctum, swelling into an almost intolerable roar.

Zurthaud looked around at all the faces he knew so well, Dragons, Men, Aelvs, and Dworvs, but he could not take comfort in a single one. They all were turned in bitter argument against their neighbor, uncommonly strained in frustration with their brethren, and it so sickened Zurthaud that, instead, he lifted his eyes to the domed ceiling.

Even though he had gazed upon the Dragon-painted frescoes at least a thousand times, he took consolation in each of the scenes, which he recognized as being from the history scrolls and books he had studied, the greatest heroes and deeds of the Order. Each one had the Dragon's symbol of the Eloigal's presence painted above them, a raised hand, Human or Dragon, with the first two fingers extended above a loosely closed fist. The repetition of the sign's appearing was to stand for the Eloigal's constant workings in the lives of mortals, and while some times may seem harsh, would always be guiding safely the souls of Men and Dragons.

With his gaze, Zurthaud also lifted up a silent prayer, asking for special guidance in this time of needful decisiveness, and he knew that he was heard, even though the great dome still reverberated the clamorous disputing of the assembly.

Serc now entered the sanctuary from its opposite side. Seemingly also disturbed by the earnest divisions among his brethren, he let his gaze fall commandingly around the room, easily silencing all the Dragons with but a purposeful stare; even the Humans, Aelvs, and Dworvs quickly followed suit. Zurthaud had expected a look of contention or even disappointment when Serc turned his eyes upon him, but the old Dragon held no ill will. His eyes only spoke of understanding; even if he did oppose Zurthaud's perspective, Serc had only friendship in his heart toward the young man.

They had known each other for the same sixteen years Zurthaud had been befriended by Theros, and Serc had been no less a companion than he. Most everything that Zurthaud had taught his recruits bout being a Paladin and companion to Dragons had at first been taught to him by Serc, and even now that he stood in opposition to his ideas, Zurthaud knew the kind elder Dragon as a more sincerely caring, parental, mentor than his own father had ever been.

"Good evening to all of you." Greeted the old Dragon doctor, as he continued to look about the ever quieting room. "This night we shall convene as an orderly council, what can only be regarded as the true Order of Paladins. As such, we must conduct ourselves in an honorable manner and not like the foolish squabbling of Orthard's lower councils. We have come together to discuss and then to cast lots toward either of two plans of action, for a terrible dark tide is swelling against us, sixteen years ago having reared its awful cresting in the deaths of the Order's last two Dragonesses. Most recently we have seen the armies of the Dark One attempt to annihilate the populous of a peaceful Human settlement within our lands. Though we have defended many souls this day and, indeed, reclaimed the town from those evil forces, we cannot afford to name it a victory when so many had perished."

"In question tonight is whether we follow either of two strategies: Shall we continue to gather our strength and bolster our defenses, preparing for the next attack from Ragnor, or shall we take to the offensive and launch a surprise attack against the very seat of The Dark One's power? Zurthaud, please elaborate upon your bold plan."

With that, as a respectful signal for Zurthaud to begin speaking, Serc bowed to him in the old Draconic style, right hand hovering over his horns, the left arm crossing in front of his chest, and lowering his head and neck.

Zurthaud took a deep breath, hopefully exhaling all his fears, and waited until Serc had found a seat to begin speaking.

Trembling, he lifted his voice, falteringly at the first. "All of you here know me. I have grown up in the Order, wholly a student of its teachings. Hopefully unlike my father, I have by now proven to you my trustworthiness, the soundness of my knowledge, the excellence of my training."

Someone off to his right lauded him for his bravery earlier today, how he had leaped from the sky to destroy the enemy's ram. Zurthaud had led them well there, no one had fallen that day, but he wondered to himself if he could continue to lead them so well, if he was capable. He had always strongly doubted himself, and he knew not whether that was a good or ill trait, to judge himself so strictly.

However, he still continued once the cheering had subsided, gaining in confidence with the emboldening rallying of his friends.

"But, the Order is more than one Human. We risk many lives with this bold move, for I plan to strike at, as it were, the very head of the snake. I propose that under the cover of night, we sneak into the Dark Tower by way of an opening in the roof."

Some older Human now interrupted him, asking how he had known that there was such an opening, for it was not common knowledge.

"I have studied well the ancient scrolls that detail the layout of The Ragnor. By my guess they were written several years after the first battle with the Shadow Lord, but there has been little change over the years in the Tower's structure, as the reports from last decade's scouting missions against the Ragnor inform. The opening was believed to have been built for a long dead Dragon companion of the Shadow Lord, as an entrance for him into the Tower, and has been consistently reported until the very last scouting mission, during which one of our spies was killed with a ballistae bolt wrought of Black-iron. All these scrolls are still available for anyone to read in the vast Order library." Said he, bravely defending his facts before the audience, silencing the scoffing of those who did not fully support him.

"As I was saying, we shall enter by way of this rooftop opening and seek out The Shadow Lord himself, who should be located in the top floors of his own tower. As he would only be expecting an attack from the ground below, he may even be upon this very top floor itself, and certainly shall be taken unaware. When we have found him, we shall kill him and thus swiftly end this ongoing war once and for all."

Zurthaud then bowed to his audience, most of which cheered or applauded, and again to Serc, respectfully signifying the end of his speech, and he retired to a seat among the small wooden chairs that had been placed out in rows for the humanoid members.

Theros followed after him and congratulated his simple, yet sincerely communication while taking a seat beside Zurthaud, as nearly all of the younger members applauded his risky, yet ingenious plan. Though Zurthaud had not spoken with any great oratory, they knew to take the fight to the enemy so early would surely catch the dark forces off guard; they agreed with Zurthaud.

But, the older Dragons did not approve, even though some of them still applauded; they knew how dangerous it would be to assume that they could catch off guard the powerful Shadow Lord. They did not wish to take that chance.

Serc arose once more from where he had been seated and waited patiently for the applause and acclamations to subside. It was his turn to speak, and he would, no doubt, provide the more eloquent counterargument.

"Well spoken, my friend." He stated, for though he did not approve of Zurthaud's plan of action, he knew that it was, indeed, very likely the best possible strategy for attacking their enemy.

Serc did also want this war to be over with as quickly as possible, but he knew that the cost of lives could be very great. His longing for victory were tempered by ages of wisdom, and his desire for war was cooled by his experiences of loss.

"If ever an attack upon the Ragnor were to succeed, this would surely be the strategy with which it was accomplished. However, I believe that such an attack would not prevail against the formidable adversary of the Dark One. Many Humans and Aelvs and Dworvs and Dragons would surely die in the attempt, and thus the Order would be weakened, crushed, by the loss of so many brave souls. Even if we were so to succeed, at what cost would come our victory? Have we so quickly forgotten who it is that we fight against, or have we forgotten that we are not warriors, only peacekeepers. Shall we risk everything we have, all that we have worked so hard to preserve and restore, in one battle against so mighty, so terrible a foe? I believe that we must prepare ourselves: shore up our walls, stock our armory, recruit and train many more new fighting members, and could we even then possibly hope to stand against the coming darkness? The storm clouds gather over Ragnor, and we say that we are strong? I tell you, we have not yet even tasted the bite of the wind."

"I saw it in the days of my youth, how the darkness would overtake us, for our ancestors, far mightier in magic and number than we, faced without fear of death, the full front of the thunderheads, stared down the lightning, and the Dark Horde still would have overtaken them, the great and dreadful Dark One would have overwhelmed them were it not for only The Eloigal's providence. Rathnyalgr, the hero whom He had raised up for us, took his special Dragon-fire forged blade and plunged it deep into the heart of the Dark One, thus vanquishing him, or at least driving deep into the void his terrible presence. And, the peace that came from that victory has lasted from thence until that rueful day sixteen years ago."

"Only with the aid of Eloigal can we again hope to stand against so great a foe. We must prepare here while we can, growing in strength, all praying for and waiting upon His providence."

With that, Serc bowed to Zurthaud and his audience, signaling the end of his speech, and returned to his seat at the far end of the sanctuary. Silence followed him to his chair, until the humbled Paladins came to and slowly began applauding his great rhetoric.

Zurthaud had to admit the soundness of Serc's plan; there was no risk, not yet, only preparation. But, to wait upon The Eloigal, while each new day could bring news of another conquered town or city, until the Shadow Lord would finally choose to show his full strength, Zurthaud knew not if he could do such a thing with any manner of patience or faith.

In either case, it was up to the decision of the other members now, and they started to quietly converse amongst themselves. However, the din soon reached the same nauseating volume that Zurthaud had walked in on.

When the bickering did not cease, as Human, Aelv, Dworv, and Dragon continued expressing their individual opinions, trying to convince one another to join either side, the large older green Dragon, Galrag, the great general, slowly got up to speak. As his arms till was wounded, though, indeed, now sewn rather than bandaged, he limped his way to the center of the room. All silenced their conversing, for Galrag was equally well respected as Serc. His opinion would most likely sway the undecided members.

"It is with all due respect to Zurthaud that I say this." The older Dragon huffed, as he struggled not to put weight on his injured leg. "An all out attack upon the Ragnor is complete foolishness. With its multitude black iron ballistae, it is too well defended against any aerial assault, and an attack from the ground would mean blindly charging through the hordes of darkness and, if we miraculously passed through that, a doomed ascent of the Tower's insides, where surely a deathtrap waits about every corner, all just to reach the Dark One, whose dreadful powers have never been measured."

"We are too few in number to even consider that plan as a possible course of action, and not even your stealthy surprise attack would be without risk, even in the approach. One lantern, a flash of moonlight reflecting off steel or scale would be enough to alert their rigorous vigilance and ruin us all. I would barely be in favor of reconnaissance of the Tower, as that often proves to be the death of some brave young scout. Even Serc's plan is only a hope, only a prayer against the insurmountable odds, for we just do not have the strength that our Order has had in bygone years."

With that, Galrag returned to his seat, and even though a few still rose to speak in favor of Zurthaud's plan, the decision of the many had been swayed by the few simple words of the wizened commander.

Aelanur, a gold Dragon that had served his whole life as the ministering priest of the temple, who had beforehand been chosen to delegate the voting, arose to call for and count the raised hands of the lots, the "ayes" and "nays" and, it quickly became clear that Galrag's doubts and Serc's better oratory had won the votes of the majority.

The decision was made to prepare for the coming storm, rather than to fly out into it.

"I know that none of these Dragons are cowards, not even Serc, whose plan it is to hide behind our walls, but I still believe that they are wrong. We must act now, before the Shadow Lord can regroup his forces." Argued Zurthaud.

After the disappointing conclusion to the meeting, he and Theros had taken off to a peaceful spot just outside the Order's fortress; it was a series of low rocky cliffs just beyond the plateau upon which the city of Doraegonoran had been built. Beyond all the lights of homes and shops and the bustle of the unceasing commerce, the magnificent gray stone walls of the impressive outer defenses, past the whole city, and more or less under it, by way of the edge of the great cliffs, Zurthaud and Theros had found such a concealed private spot.

Here they had talked often, upon their favorite rocky ledge, under a spaciously cavernous overhang, when their topics warranted such privacy as to not be had even within their own apartment in the Dragons' Quarter tower, as they did tonight.

"I do not agree with you, but if I know you, Zurthaud, you would go off alone to the Ragnor, to face the Dark One. And, I cannot allow that." Theros nervously chuckled, slightly bemused by his friends troubled self-talk and pacing, yet deathly afraid of the thought of entering that bastion of evil.

Zurthaud's mind was set like a lock, to come free only once he had accomplished what he thought, what he truly hoped would be the sure end of this age-old struggle against the dark forces. As he paced, his boots scuffed against the smooth floor, and the noise echoed about the overhang and off into the night sky beyond. Silence followed, as although the two already knew what was to be done next, they deeply contemplated the action that they were about to take, for it was considered treason to go against the will of the Order.

The wing-beats of multiple Dragons arriving outside broke the quiet, as several of Zurthaud's and Theros' closest friends arrived. These few young men and Dragons had been with them the longest of any of his recruits; they had been his first enlistees, his closest friends. Now they had all joined together under his vision of a preemptive strike; they all stood behind Zurthaud, truly loyal to him, despite the decision of the other Paladins.

Their names and race were thus: Silecs a brown and gray Dragon, with Arthaud, his Human companion; Caelon a blue Dragon, and his Human Companion, Losal; Teror a green and gold Dragon, and his Aelven Companion, Anfanuil; Thol, a dark red Dragon, and his Human companion, Baltor; and lastly, but by no means least, Galrath, the son of Galrag, every bit as stubbornly for Zurthaud as his father was against, with his Human companion, Dyreft.

"Thank you all for coming, but before we go any further, if any of you wish to turn back now, while there is still the opportunity, I would hold no ill will against you. What we are about to do is not only daring, it is also in direct contradiction to the will of the Order. It is high treason, and we could be expelled from the Paladins, or worse, were we to be found out." Zurthaud asked, staring each of his friends in the eye.

They knew the risk, yet not a single man or Dragon left from the group. They had stood behind Zurthaud when all others had been swayed by the words of their elders, and they would again stand behind him now, even at the cost of their lives, such was the loyalty of each and every one of them.

"Very well, I shall count you all in. We will leave for the Ragnor in two days; make preparation in secret, and meet again here at the setting of the sun on the second day. Many of us will not live to see the sun rise on the third day, but hopefully, our comrades and descendants shall never again face what we go to do. In two days time, we shall slay the Shadow Lord."

Chapter 8

Feldara awoke to an overwhelming pounding that sorely resounded throughout her brain, and when she reached with her hand to touch her pulsating forehead, arcs of fiery torment flashed through the entirety of her body. She roared with the unspeakable pain.

"Try not to move." Anur's voice called out to her from behind her field of vision, for he was at her back, stitching a gash in her body with a newly acquired Black-iron needle and some strong thin thread. "It is the Worg's venom that brings you such pain; moving only pumps it through your blood, making its effects that much worse."

"Anur!" She cried out to him, so relieved by the comforting sound of his voice.

But, then she remembered what she had done, how she had run away from home, deceiving him and ruining their bond of trust, and putting them both in danger; she was crushed under the weight of her guilt.

"I am so sorry for what I have done." She sobbed, fighting the jolts of pain as she tried to crane her neck about so as to see, at least, his helmeted head.

"Do not move." He said again, raising his voice, truly angry that she had before so foolishly disobeyed him, but his heart softened toward her. He could not help but love his precious charge. "You need not ever again speak of what happened last night. You disobeyed me, to your own detriment, but I am just glad that you are still alive. I cannot, I will not mourn another Dragoness on this island." He spake more kindly, emotions of fear and relief mixing in his words.

From what she could see of herself and her surroundings, Feldara was back home on the island in the circular domed building opposite her and Anur's shared home, the doors of which he had mysteriously kept locked. Inside upon the sandy floor lay a multitude of items, mostly those of common usage: medicinal supplies, vials full of myriad poultices and tonics, various tools for gardening, masonry, and carpentry, but scattered among these were racks upon which hung many weapons: swords, spears, maces, bows and arrows. Feldara wondered at these instruments of war, for until last night, she had never seen such weapons being used, had only read about their battle techniques in books and scrolls. Though he had hunted with a bow and fished with a spear at times, Anur had never carried a sword about, and she never would have believed him capable of wielding one so effectively.

She saw next that she lay upon a wooden cart, large yet low to the ground. This she recognized, having used it herself to help haul loads of brick and stone from the loose piles that had lain in and by the more decayed structures of the compound, for so she had helped Anur, in maintaining their home. It had been a beloved tool and plaything of her childhood, and on one instance, before she could yet fly, she had tried to use it as a raft. However, the heavy cart would not float, and she had ended up having to help Anur dig it out of the dense wet sand of the surf.

As low to the ground the cart was, it still rose, upon its four stubby wheels, at least a foot from the floor and she began to wonder how it was that Anur had managed to haul her large unconscious form atop it, for that matter, how she had gotten from the dangers of the far shore all the way back home, all without drowning. Yet, another question plagued her thoughts more so, for how Anur had even found out she had left the island at all, she could not fathom.

"How were you able to come across the sea and rescue me?" She asked, having nothing better to distract herself from the dreadful pain that pulsed through her body than to satisfy her curiosity. "How did you even know that I had left?"

Anur paused a while before answering her, for although he was, indeed, overjoyed to have her back safe and alive, he was still so disappointed that she had tried to deceive him, to go off on her own, that he did not truly feel like talking plainly with her, as if nothing had happened between them. But, his anger was not against her person, only how she had so poorly treated his trust, and he slowly answered her. His love for her was that of a good father's, without conditions.

"I had built a boat some time ago; I had kept it hidden from you for a few years, but I figured that it would eventually be useful, that perhaps, some day we should go off and see, at least, the far shore, albeit not toward the coast you happened upon. That was the Western border of the Shadow Lands that you stumbled upon; it was why the wolves were there so large and bold as to attack a Dragoness." He pensively mused.

Upon hearing of this long hidden means of easy escape from their island prison, feelings of betrayal and resentment swirled among Feldara's thoughts; that Anur should, in hypocrisy, pretend at having no desire to leave their isolated home and yet have made in secret this boat, this palpable expression of adventure and freedom, and still, time and again, refuse and suppress her own want for such liberation, burned sore her conscience, worse than if salt were rubbed into her wounds. Even so, because of her own guilt at disobeying him and getting into much danger, Feldara kept silent and hid these poisonous thoughts of enmity in her heart.

"We shall, indeed, leave from this place, for now we must." He continued. "At least one beast escaped my blade, and now their masters shall hear of a Dragoness and her companion in the North and West of their domain. They shall come for us in force. We shall flee to the Aelven Lands, the farther Northern shore, and shall seek refuge among one of their great fortified cities. It is the closest place we can run to, and also where we can find treatment for the venom which those Worgs bore in their Black-iron fangs. I have not the medical knowledge for how to treat such an ailment, as these kinds of monsters and their ilk were long thought extinct."

"It does hurt awfully." Feldara complained, for she could not tell the difference in pain between the sutures Anur had made to mend the deeper wounds from any of the rest of her whole body.

"It is very potent, having caused you to black out last night, for your wounds are not so severe that you had fainted from blood loss. I only pray that you do not pass out again, or that the debilitating effects worsen or become permanent." Anur morosely commented. "I have even heard that, left untreated, it can turn Men and Aelvs into Worgs."

"How long shall we be gone?" Feldara asked, thinking for a moment that, should her throbbing body become well again, this might have been her wish granted, to leave from their reclusive little home.

"We shall never again return here!" Anur nearly shouted, as he ceased his stitching to address her most forcefully. "Or, there shall never again be a day when we are at peace. We must flee from the Darkness that pursues us, for they shall come. They shall hunt us until we find safer refuge among the fortified cities of the Aelvs or Humans, and even then we might not yet be safe."

Feldara shed not a few more tears upon hearing this news that they should forever leave their home, running for their lives, to treat her for a disease that might not be curable, and she sobbed a great deal longer than either of them really cared for. Almost until Anur was done with her mending did she continue her crying, in spite of several attempts to quit. All the frustrated adventuring, eminent death, unexpected salvation, and now pain and hindsight had taken its emotional toll on her, and she, even being a Dragoness, just found it insurmountable to remain dry eyed.

About noon, Anur brought her some fish for midday meal. The warm grilled meat calmed her much more than words alone, even those spoken in compassion and sincerity by her mentor, and she ate with vigor, suddenly realizing the hunger that pain and trial had caused her to forget.

As soon as they were done with their simple meal, Anur again explained that they should make haste, for the Dark One's minions would soon be on their trail, eventually tracking them to their little island.

So, they left, slowly at first and truly emotional, and though well he hid it, the thought that he should, possibly forever, abandon out of necessity the only home he had ever known, wore heavily upon Anur. Steps falteringly tardy with reminiscence, he rolled her out of the old nesting house, upon the cart, along with as many food stocks and supplies as he thought they would need, including a couple of swords, a knife, and a good sturdy spear. He carted the whole mound of stuff and Dragoness, himself, down unto the white sands of the beach where waited a pontoon raft of grand size and fine make, even for its untried shipwright.

He easily rolled the cart upon it, balanced it in the center of the raft, and tied it down tightly to the pontoons, so as to not roll about or even slip over the side into the water. "Thus, ending the trip rather quickly." Anur then somberly jested, attempting to lighten the mood.

With the shaft of the long sturdy spear, he slowly pushed them away from the shore, and they were off. They remained at the mercy of the tides' courses until they got a distance away from the surf of the shoreline, whereupon Anur was able to paddle with an oar or steer effectively with the rudder; besides which, he also raised the single masted vessel's lone sail, a great triangular sheet that Feldara thought she had remembered him making only a year ago.

The journey across the waves had taken her only a few minutes of soaring upon her silken wings, but by boat, even wind powered, the trip took almost the rest of the day. Evening was fast approaching by the time they had come within sight of the far Northern shore, and by the time they had landed and Anur had disembarked everything he had brought, night was looming on the far side of the sunset. However dark it was becoming, Anur still had no desire to stop and pitch camp.

They were only so many miles North and West of where Feldara had been attacked, and she could see, across the other side of the bay, the hazy outline of that same dark pine forest. Shadowy clouds full of storm and thunder began to accumulate ominously over the black evergreens, but no wind or rain did they bring.

"We must clear this area quickly, and make haste for the border of the Aelven lands." Anur said, as he doggedly pulled the cart forward, simply abandoning his lovely little boat in the surf.

He knew the nature of those thunderheads. They were not the friendly rainstorms that often graced the island with life-giving fresh water, but were, rather, the manifestation of evil darkness that overspread the skies of the Shadow Lands. They were emissaries of Ragnor, signals of the nearness of the Dark One's presence, and Anur feared them greatly.

However, Feldara's gaze lingered upon their quaint raft, even as it slowly faded into the distance; she had dearly enjoyed the boat ride, almost as much as she had loved flying over the waters. It seemed such a shame to let so neat and well made a craft just drift away on the tide, but Anur knew the direness of their situation. If by dark they had not, at least, reached the border of the Aelven realm, they may as well consider themselves dead.

As twilight began to end and the shadows grew ever tall and powerful, overwhelming the sinking golden sun, they two cleared the grassy plains that had stretched from the beach unto the deciduous forests that they now entered. After stumbling in the darkened bush for some time, Anur and Feldara happened upon a narrow and well hidden dirt road that wound off to the Northern and Western horizons.

"We can stay here for the night." Anur said letting go of the cart, and beginning to unpack some comforts. "We have reached the Aelven lands at last. This is their highway, and it stretches from their outposts at the edge of the Western wilds all the way to their capitol, Verdeliel, which lies far to the Northwest of here."

Feldara struggled to ease herself off of the cart, and every motion she made sent the same scorching pain through her limbs.

However, she found the struggle worthwhile, as laying on the wooden surface of the cart for so long, even shifting positions from time to time, had worn sore some spots on her body. The cool grass, upon which she now lay, soothed a little her burning flesh and did not chafe the bruises that the cart had caused her.

"We should look rather funny to the passer-by, a man pulling a rickety potato cart loaded with stuff and a Dragoness." She joked, as Anur gathered wood for a fire.

She had not contemplated how abnormally strong Anur would have to be, impossibly strong for a Human, to be able to haul her ton and the half of supplies all the way up from the coast. The thought had never even crossed her mind, even after he had so easily slain those Worgs; she was used to Anur's exceptionally strange abilities, took them for granted as being those of any ordinary Human, never mind his odd pale gray skin. As he lay half a tree in a pile, inside a small ring of gathered stones, She saw him only as a person, her teacher, beloved caregiver, and best friend.

"Can you yet breathe fire?" He asked of Feldara, as he returned to the cart, rummaging through its contents attempting to locate a flint in the encroaching dark.

She, at least, attempted to do so, but only ended up showering the bundle of twigs with spittle and hot air. She sighed in derision of her own futile attempt to set the kindling aflame, but as he triumphantly returned with the flint-stone, Anur only encouragingly patted her head, assuring her that she would soon be up to the task.

Dragons could not breathe fire until after they had reached puberty; it was their mark of adulthood. And, though she was comforted by Anur's words, that she would soon be breathing flame to her heart's content, Feldara reviled despondently her own immaturity. Despite this, Anur had soon enough a roaring fire blazing before them, warming against the chill air and cooking their simple meal made from Anur's supplies. To the both of them, dried, salted fish and roasted potatoes had never tasted so good.

After their dinner, as the creatures of the night sang and chirped in harmonious chorus for their uncustomary audience, they sat in the contentment of each other's company, a pleasurable respite at the end of such a long day's travels. Anur was careful not to lean against her tonight, as he was accustomed to, for Feldara was still so very sore from the nasty Worg venom, her stitches, and the bumpy cart ride. Yet, he did gently stroke her, as he often did, upon her back, the back of her neck, the boney crest atop her head, all her usual favorite spots.

"Anur," She spoke suddenly, abruptly breaking the calmness of their quiet evening, "Why is it that you always wear that helm upon your head?"

It was true. He had not ever taken off the helm but in private, even sleeping and eating with it upon his head. Feldara had always wondered why Anur wore the masked helm, but she never had the nerve to ask about it before. Now everything was different. Her whole world had changed, let alone their relationship, and she could not stand for there to be such secrets between the two of them.

Anur fingered the cold metallic surface with his rough hands, clearly very emotionally attached to his facial covering, but he eventually relented and began to slowly lift the black metal helm.

"It is an old habit, a relic of my past. Even before I was taken in by the Masters, I always had some sort of head covering; this one is just the latest I had picked up, from about the compound, after the... incident. Through the years, I can never remember a time when I felt comfortable without one, and I suppose; in my darkest time, I lost the desire to remove this one from my head." He mutteringly explained.

"Well, I should like to see your face; would you show it to me, please?" She pleaded, and not out of just blindly childish curiosity. Feldara only desired to look upon the visage of the one person she loved most in the world, that person whose eyes she had not yet looked into.

For a moment, it seemed that Anur would not consent to this silly inquiry, but his Dragoness was far more dear to him than any feelings of comfort, no matter how deeply ingrained in his psyche. After a moment of deliberation, he finally relented

"You must promise to not be alarmed by what you see." He demanded, pausing the removal of his cap. "For, I am very different from...other men. You must swear to love me still, even upon seeing what I truly look like."

"Surely not, I mean, surely not that you are so different. Are you deformed? I promise I won't laugh or make fun; I am your best friend and I always will be." She swore confusedly, not imagining what could possibly be so unnerving about his appearance.

"Swear to me." He insisted.

"I swear, that I shall always love you for who you are, not what you look like; you will always be Anur, my friend, not matter your countenance." She vowed.

Satisfied, he took the vizored helm from off his head revealing a face not Human at all, for his scalp was bald of any hair and strangely, yet symmetrically, shaped. His ears were longer than should be and pointed; his chin, thicker and more muscular than would be a man's, jutted out, with pointed teeth peeking out here and there from the lower lip. He had no nose, but only slits for nostrils, and even so, his eyes were the most unusual of all his features. With deep violet irises and blackness where the whites would have been, they matched well with his oddly gray skin.

In all, Anur appeared to be no Human, and feeling quite uneasy without his covering, all while a curious Dragoness intently stared him down, he quickly replaced the helm upon his head.

"Are you a Troll?" Feldara jokingly asked, for, indeed, the baldness, pointy ears, and thick chin did combine to give Anur a very Troll-like appearance, to the point where, if any casual observer had seen him helmet-less, they would have also assumed that he was a Troll, if a fairly small one at that.

"I do not think so, but truth be told, I have no idea what I am." Anur replied, "I only know that others have always been frightened by my appearance, and hiding my face from them, helped allow me to feel accepted."

Rising from his seat, obviously displeased with the whole ordeal, he began to stalk away, muttering about fetching more firewood.

"I know what you are." Feldara called after him, stopping him cold in his tracks. "You are my friend."

Anur paused long enough to whisper an emotional thank you, but still proceeded to wander off into the night, to actually gather more firewood.

It had been one of the hardest things he had ever done, letting his charge, his only companion, his best friend, see his true face, a face he had been told his whole life was ugly or strange and to be kept hidden. He had known that he could not keep his visage secret from her forever, yet Anur was gratefully surprised by her kind, innocently naïve, and accepting response. She had helped, as only good friends can, to lift such a heavy burden from his shoulders.

From his position in the shadows, bent over gathering the dead dry branches to fuel their fire, he watched her slowly, yawning, sink into slumber, but he denied himself this pleasure, as he unloaded his armful of wood onto the flames. He stood guard the whole night through, all too knowledgeable, even fearful, of the enemy they were running from.

The night passed without any worrisome incidence; Feldara had slept very soundly, much to Anur's annoyance, snoring the whole way through. She awoke with the sunrise, and sleepily drank in the morning light. However, Anur did not wish to stay at their campsite much longer, not even for a hot breakfast, and he soon had the whole camp packed up and was helping Feldara to clamber back aboard the cart. With every movement of her muscles, a new jolt of pain arced through her body, just as strong and piercing as it had been the day before.

The venom was truly awful; impervious to her body's defenses, it just coursed over and over again through her blood and tissue.

"How is it that this venom does not dissipate?" Feldara snarled in frustration, as she finally eased herself onto the low cart and lay down amidst the stacks of supplies.

"I think it must feed off of the body, just enough to keep itself present, just enough to continue your misery, for such are the vile fancies of the Dark One." Anur explained, as he took up the cart once more and began to slowly pull the load down the dirt highway.

The bright and chill morning wore slowly onward, as the two steadily trundled down the path, and as Anur had become too short of breath to pull the heavy cart and keep a conversation going at the same time, Feldara ended up observing her surroundings for entertainment.

The grasses seemed to her eyes more green and lush here than anywhere else she had seen before; the trees also looked much healthier, as did every other green thing. The birds were more numerous and seemingly chirped louder and more boldly than even on her happy island home; even the insects, who were present everywhere, appeared to be in greater number, scampering, crawling, and flitting about ever more spiritedly. It was the joyous vivacity of the Aelvs that so infected this place, transferred to all living things in their realm, enriching the flourishing of all life, for their power and place in the world was among the green and the growing.

In the distance, just past the tree line to Feldara's right, a brook babbled merrily, assuredly joining up with its brethren on its lengthy flowing journey to the Crydan Sea, and several deer, lazy, carefree, and apparently unafraid of even a Dragoness, crossed the path in front of them, heading toward the fresh water of the stream.

Anur chuckled at the sight of the fair sized herd, as they caused him to stop at their crossing, lest he run into them.

"Surely, we are in the Aelven lands now, for even the deer have no fear of being hunted." He said, pausing to set the cart down, as he waited for the whole of the herd to cross the road.

However, Feldara was a little peeved by the audacity of these hinds; she had hunted their kind and the wild goats to near extinction on her little island. They had always cowered before her, had always run from her; she had liked that feeling of power, of dominance over her prey. Now these Aelven deer even came up to the cart to sniff of her and the supplies.

She decided to take a swipe at one, a little fawn, and she caught it. It bleated and scrambled to free itself from her claws, as the others of the herd now bolted away in surprise, but Feldara could not bring herself to do anything more to the fearless and innocently inquisitive hart, she being not at all hungry. Besides for food, she had no use for a deer, so Feldara reluctantly decided to set the poor thing free, still annoyed by its presumptuous disregard of her predatory nature. The fawn then quickly bounded away to rejoin its kin, who just out of sight in the cover of the brush, had been waiting to see about its fate.

Anur had not thought much of the whole debacle; he could care less about the fate of a single deer, especially if it were to be sustenance for a sentient being. But, for a Dragon to kill, when not for food or in defense, would have been a waste, an offense in the eyes of all Dragons, and something that they two in particular really had no time for to stop their traveling.

"Are you done playing with your food?" Anur asked, belying his bemusement with her antics, as he resumed pulling them down the road.

"Why were those deer so fearless? Have they no respect for the mighty Dragon?" She asked, her pride still ruffled.

____

"They have no reason to fear Dragon, or Man. Most likely, they had never seen or smelled anything like me, other than Aelvs, and Aelvs would never have reason to harm a deer, as they are all nearly completely vegetarian in their diet. Dragons they may have never seen or smelled before, ever at all, as these lands are so sparsely populated by your people." Anur explained, and this somewhat quieted Feldara's indignation.

Until noontide, the morning passed with the quiet and tedium of afore the encounter with the herd of deer. But, as the shadows declined with the sun's inevitable rise, the pair came upon a great wooden-beam gate blocking the road, at the side of which stood a lone wood tower. To the left and right of the gate, for as far as their eyes could see, a high, plank boarded wall stretched, straight and unbroken, even through the thickness of the denser forest.

As they approached the closed gate, no one hailed them, and from what Feldara could see, there was also no one present within the tower.

"Is it abandoned?" She asked, really having hoped to finally meet some Aelvs here and dismaying that now she would not.

"No, it is not. They are watching us, for these lands border the Shadow Lands. They wish to fully see who we are, before they will open their defenses to strangers, such as us." Anur calmly replied.

Eventually, as they two stood there waiting to pass through the closed gate, a voice called out to them. "Who are those that seek to enter the Aelven realm, friend or foe?"

"Friend, a Dragoness and her companion in need of medicine for the Worg's bite." Anur called up to the tower.

Silence followed for a minute, as apparently the Aelvs considered their new guests, but at last, the voice called out to them again.

"You are welcome to pass on into our lands." Replied the voice, albeit drastically more cheerfully than before.

The gates then flung open, revealing a guard of Aelven rangers, ten or so strong, with more leaning out to wave and shout greetings from the windows and galleries of the tower above.

"Welcome Dragoness and your companion, to the realm of the Aelvs." Greeted one of their number, as he bowed in salutation. "I am Finiriel, keeper of the gates and commander of this border wall defending the Aelven homeland. May I ask the names of our visiting guests?"

"Well met, Finiriel." Feldara replied, speaking over Anur who was not quite so quick to respond. "I am Feldara and this is Anur."

Feldara then discovered that all the fantastic descriptions of Aelvs from her book reading back home could not compare with seeing them in reality, for these people were the image of grace, having all the fine qualities of the nimblest legendary nymph or dryad. They were smaller and leaner than an average man in stature, smaller still than Anur who was very tall for a man, but what they lacked in size they made up for in personality.

Each of them were exponentially more mirthful and fair than any of the old scrolls had mentioned, as if never they could long be held down by any woe, nor have such unrestrained happiness recorded by words. Child-like they seemed, and yet with many immortal years, their slanted, bright eyes were darkened with unrevealed wisdom.

However, it was their hair that caught Feldara's eye, partly because such long flowing locks were a foreign concept to her, for Dragons, and Anur, are all hairless, yet mostly because their gorgeous flaxen strands caught the light so well, even as a Dragon's scales, and reflected the blond and silver of their natural colors in glorious, shimmering halos about their heads.

"Surely beautiful names both, although I know not the meaning of Anur; is it Dworvish? But, never-mind. About those Worg bites, did you encounter the foul beasts within our lands, or perchance you were only nearby, for we have not seen such beasts in an age, since the Great War, and had hoped never again to catch sight of the foul monsters?" Finiriel blatheringly inquired, interrupting her thoughts, even as he motioned for two of his rangers to take the cart from off Anur's shoulders, and finding that three could barely budge it, asked for another four more to help wheel it down the road.

Feldara only blushed at this question, for she was still too embarrassedly remorseful of her juvenile actions. Anur noticed and quickly answered in her stead.

"We were attacked two nights ago, on the Eastern shore of the bay reaching from the Crydan Sea into the Shadow Lands, just to the South."Anur spake, cunningly sparing Feldara any further loss of dignity by the simple change of subject. "We dispatched the beasts, and other than that, there is not much more to tell, but is it true that the children of Rathnyalgr, the famed Dragon healer, make their home in Lotheliel? If so, then we seek their expert aid in curing these venomous wounds."

"Why yes, they do still reside within the walls, indeed, within the rocky walls of the gray cliffs on the far side of that fair city, that which some would call the true capitol of the Aelven land, for therein is our center of art and music making, and therein is our greatest trade done with the foreign peoples of the world. Yes, Rathnyaling, the very son of Rathnyalgr himself, does there practice medicine, and some say that he is even better a doctor than his father ever was. If anyone can cure my fair lady Dragoness of the awful Worg poison, it is surely Rathnyaling." Blithely chatted Finiriel, and, though already having answered the question at the first, on he continued until Anur's ears hurt.

But, Feldara thought his personable, talkative habit rather endearing, herself, and listened very intently, as now the ten of them traveled down the road together.

It was some time later, as they had trundled merrily down the highway, that conversation grew tiresome even to the Aelvs, and Finiriel with the help of the majority of his cohorts, eagerly suggested that they pass the time in song. Much to the displeasure of Anur, yet the delight of Feldara, the eight Aelvs broke into tune after tune. Playfully bawdy drinking songs, mournful dirges of days long past, the usual romantic ballads, even worshipful songs of praise to Eloigal- these and more, melody after melody, continued the Aelvs, until, rather forcefully, Anur insisted that they enjoy the peacefully quiet nature of the countryside.

However, it was not long thereafter, rounding the crest of a tall ridge, the seven Aelv rangers, huffing and puffing to push and pull the Dragoness laden cart uphill, their commander, Anur, and Feldara completely oblivious to their struggling, that they espied the marvelous Aelven metropolis below them.

Aelven cities were in no way like unto their Human counterparts, as Feldara could see and Finiriel described. All the buildings were made out of magically hollowed giant trees, and the roads were of boardwalks spread between the gaps in the boughs. The lights were made all of luminescent fungus and, utilizing wind and watermills, the factories and utilities ran by the power of the wind and the nearby Ae River.

"I am sorry, my dear Dragoness; there is no fire making allowed throughout the city, but for in designated kitchen and trade working areas." Explained Finiriel, yet Feldara only lowered her head, slightly ashamed that she would have no choice in containing her fire.

They all ventured down the other side of the large hill toward the magnificent city, the seven Aelven rangers, descending the rise, having a horrible time preventing the heavy cartload from careening out of control, as their commander recalled the wonders of Aelven design to both Anur, and Feldara; they three again perfectly oblivious to the others' struggling.

Finally, as the sun began to set below the high hills and rocky cliffs that lay at the far end of the city, the company reached the magnificent wall and gates, which like the border wall and gate were made all of wood, yet on a much grander scale. This gate, unlike the one at the border, opened quickly to them with many joyous shouts of welcome from the Aelvs within, for they did recognize Finiriel and his men.

"As the Rathnyalgrs will not be expecting company this late, you may lodge at the gatehouse inn tonight, if you wish, for it has fine accommodations. Upon the morrow, you can ask anyone in town about the doctor's residence, and they shall provide good directions to you. Oh, and expect excellent hospitality, for it is not very often anymore that we receive Dragons and Riders from the Order, let alone any travelers, these days." With that, Finiriel bade them a lengthy farewell, as he and his exhausted underlings headed back to their post at the border.

Feldara and Anur were, indeed, showered with the generous cordiality of the Aelven host that had come out to greet them, and they soon were well fed and asleep in a warm, comfortable Aelven bed.

Chapter 9

Two nights ago, they had all sworn to meet here again. Now they had all returned, not a Man or Dragon among them unwilling to give their very lives for this mission. There were twelve of them in all, five Dragons and their five Human riders, led by Zurthaud and Theros.

"If any one of you wishes to back out now, this will be your last chance; otherwise, I must be able to completely rely upon you until the very end." Gravely spoke Zurthaud to them, his voice echoing throughout the small rocky overhang, the same place they had gathered two nights earlier.

Not a one of the brave company said a word, nor did they turn back toward the entrance, for they all trusted Zurthaud and believed in his cause. Zurthaud himself heaved a huge sigh, for he was not so sure of his own leadership as were these true friends. Thankfully, Theros was at his side, and the large Dragon gave him a gentle and encouraging nuzzle.

They checked all the supplies to be brought with them: rope for climbing, perhaps even to scale the great tower; their many weapons, the long pole-swords which the 'riders' would use in airborne combat upon their Dragon's backs, bow and arrows for at least three of them, and of course, their short-swords as primary weapons.

However, they took no food, not even water did they bring for refreshment, for they neither planned to tarry long nor have any need of it. If their plan went awry, sustenance would be the last of their trouble in the Shadow Lands.

"Very well, we have all that we need, let us go and do what we have set out to accomplish." Zurthaud commanded, and with a little help from Theros sizeable foreleg, Zurthaud clambered aboard his friend's massive shoulders. "Let us rid Threa of the Darkness!"

With a shout and a cheer, they flew off into the crisp night, the wind biting at their faces, as they sped as fast as the Dragons could soar, and as the Dragon flies, what was a lengthy journey of days on foot took only a few hours. Soon after passing over the Aronoran wall, the healthy green of the Human kingdoms' soft, rolling plains was replaced by the stark grays and blacks of the drear wastes of the Shadow Lands. Not long thereafter, they could espy from afar the Tower itself, at first only a thin black needle stretching up into the ominously clouded sky. It was as a shadow of shadows, for even in the pitch-black moonless night, they could trace its shape, starkly profiled against all the black night about. As closer they came, the ring of low mountains that surrounded the Tower of Ragnor began to jut from the horizon, and they could clearly see the lights from the lesser, guardian battlements and towers atop their peaks and plateaus.

Strangely enough, tales of the tower's halo of umbrous thunderheads seemed unfounded, for as shortly they closed in on their destination, the night sky was so clear that Zurthaud had to signal for their group to ascend to a height where the enemies in the fortresses on the mountains below could neither hear their wing-beats nor see their silhouettes against the stars. So, they remained hidden by darkness alone, and no clouds, and began circling about the very top of the tower for to spot their opening and to land.

"There it is!" Zurthaud shouted to Theros over the roar of the wind, pointing at the obviously gaping hole amongst the eminent spines and spires of the otherwise flat roof of the Ragnor, and at his command they all began to slowly, as silently as possible, descend toward the opening.

The group landed there upon the outside of the roof, muffling the thump of their landings in the periodic gusts of billowing air currents that swept ragged the Black-iron surface of the Tower. Not a one of them felt welcome here, for although they had encountered no resistance so far, it was in the soul of every sentient being, and especially the Dragons, to hate this dark place. Zurthaud had to summon all of his courage as their leader to descend first, down the ropes they had dropped into the gaping maw of the roof-hole, down into the depths of the Ragnor.

Even before he hit the floor, Zurthaud began scanning the inside of the first, highest floor of the tower. It was a massive single room with two levels, one of which was above the spot where his rope had landed, yet what immediately caught his eye was a large cave or fireplace-like gap carved into the wall. The enormity of the structure frightened Zurthaud, for he thought he recognized it as being some sort of Dragon's den. Surely a very large Dragon, indeed, a giant among giants, perhaps, the long dead companion of the Shadow Lord, had called home the enormous crack, the makeshift cave.

Two sets of bannistered stairs, unusually elegant for so gloomy a castle, ran, spiraling, up the sides of the ominous cave-like gap, leading to the smaller second level above, more or less only a balcony, a roof for the large cavernous crag. Upon this second level sat a curious instrument, that Zurthaud recognized some sort of virginal, with several sets of keyboard, attached, by various mechanics, to a bellows and gigantic flute-like pipes lining the wall behind. However conspicuous or gilded, there were no signs of life within this first spacious room, no enemies, no dark lord. Even the cave was empty, without any gargantuan evil Dragon lying coiled within, and quiet was the whole of this first floor.

The opulence of every detail took Zurthaud by surprise, for he had expected the Dark One to have lived in a rather pallid, disheveled estate. Instead, the Black-iron walls were smothered with intricate carvings, and statues, although of gruesome subject, neatly ornamented the whole of the room.

At last his attentions came upon the very epicenter of this great round chamber, a lone black iron stand, simple yet elegant in design, and upon it an seemingly ordinary book. Zurthaud did walk over to it, as the others made their way in through the hole in the roof, and he opened it, quickly thumbing through the pages. Though he had immediately recognized the imposed value of this book, which had been placed so prominently within the room, the tome was unreadable to Zurthaud, as all the writing was in the ancient Dragon language. Still, he decided to hold onto it for future study, as, perhaps, it contained some valuable knowledge about their enemy, and he tucked it away in one of his jacket's pockets.

"Spread out, find an access to the second lowest level." Zurthaud whispered, trying to stay focused on the task at hand, rather than become distracted by the appalling sights.

Eventually, as they were all searching, Theros did find a door that led to a twisting staircase, presumably winding around the entire outer edge of the Tower, very conveniently leading to all floors, and after drawing lots, Thol and Baltor were chosen to stand guard of their only escape route. The rest of the company exited through Theros' door.

They had to walk single-file to descend the staircase, with the Dragons barely fitting through the narrow, dimly candle-lit corridor, which after one long, winding flight, led to the next floor. Again, Zurthaud took point, entering first this new floor, but the second level was not a singular room as had been the topmost floor; within, a large central hall led to five rooms, two on each side of the hall and one at the very end thereof. There were no doors on the giant square lintels; so as the group slowly went down the hall, they paused to look into each one.

The first room on the left was a treasury, filled to overflowing with innumerable mounds of gold, gems, and other items of wealth. They paused for a moment there, to look at all the marvelous things, the whole of which was greater than even the entire treasury of the Order, but there were no enemies within, no Shadow Lord.

"Keep moving, and take nothing. This wealth is all ill-gotten." Zurthaud whispered, knowing full well that none of them would have lifted a single coin from the enormous piles of gold, for they all knew how the Shadow Lord had violently amassed his treasure.

The first room on the right was a map room, wherein the Shadow Lord had drawn up all his plans of conquest, but none of the pieces for strategizing were laid thereupon the large center table-map, except for a tiny model of the Ragnor and a large, painted, red 'x' where would have stood Doraegonoran. Again not a single living thing was within this room.

The next room on the left must have been some sort of trophy room. Zurthaud took one look within and retched, and no one else braved a look, save Theros who espied the severed, embalmed heads of several Dragons among the other unsavory items. He too became sickened and, though turning away quickly, gagged at the room's sight and smell, yet no living thing was among the items of this room.

The final room on the right of the hall was a bedchamber of sorts, but it was also disappointingly empty, save for the unusable, mangled and broken furniture.

They, at last, came to the end of the hall, where lay the final room of this second level, and they slowly peered within, expecting at any moment to see the Dark One within, busy about some foul work. Instead, this large circular chamber had only a mysterious single legged water basin standing in the very center and was otherwise completely empty. Zurthaud, frustrated by not finding their target so soon, and fearful of their time running short, whispered a curse and turned about to exit the bare room.

However, as he did just so, the odd basin and the smoking, foggy water within, caught his attention, causing him to take a second look. What he had at first assumed was an ordinary reflection of himself appeared to be an image of the group as a whole, as seen from the top down, that is, from the ceiling.

With this viewpoint one could have easily watched them searching about this level of the Ragnor, and Zurthaud began to fear that the Shadow Lord was aware of their presence within his tower. Instead of being taken by surprise, their foe could even now be watching them.

"We need to get back to the roof!" Zurthaud shouted to everyone's astonishment, but they did not waste breath questioning why he had broken the profound silence.

The company raced after him, for he had taken off, sprinting to the doorway at the end of the hall. Even as they did so, a booming, trumpet-like blast sounded from the floor above them, and the noise of it shook the whole of the Ragnor with its thundering reverberations.

Anfanuil, as an Aelv more sensitive to sound than the rest, nearly toppled over with the deafening blare, but Zurthaud noticed and caught him in time to prevent his stumbling, and they continued to run toward the door at the end of the hall. Zurthaud, Theros, Galrath, Dyreft, Caelon and Anfanuil all managed to cleanly exit the floor and begin ascending the staircase without, when the Nokre then came upon them.

Up from the levels below, almost as a liquid they seemed to seep, a teeming living mass of teeth and evil. Alone, a Nokre was a Human sized, hunched back, ape-like, reptilian, that wore only simple chain mail scraps and a large horned face-mask that had not even tiny eye-holes, but only bore, where their faces should be, the inscribed emblem of the Shadow Lord, a repugnantly twisted 'x'-like shape. They carried no weapons, but their very sharp pointed teeth and long nails were formed entirely of Black-iron. It was written of them, that they were not ever a living people or created animals, but were only the physical manifestations of the Dark One's evil will. Alone they were weaker than an average man, but the Nokre never fought alone. They always came in great number, and no Nokre horde Zurthaud had ever seen could match the number of this raving, aggregating swarm that now came, eerily, wickedly silent, bounding up the stair toward them.

With the Dragons having to ascend single-file and backwards up the staircase, it was inevitable that at least one would be cut off from the group, even with them breathing their explosive fire against the Nokre, even with their heads reaching over each other's shoulders, providing a nearly continuous stream of flame. Even with this ceaseless fiery death and the spending of every last one of their companions arrows, two of the Dragons were, indeed, trapped on that second floor, Teror and Silecs, doomed to be overwhelmed and slaughtered by the Nokre swarm, ripped apart piece by piece, as had fallen already their two Human comrades, Losal and Arthaud.

Zurthaud could not bear to watch the hopeless scene, as the two Dragons were forced back into the hall that would become their tomb, Nokre upon Nokre sickeningly crawling within after them, but there was nothing to be done for them without losing all the rest of the group. Soon the flashes of warm red light from their blasts of fire ceased to illumine the further part of the bend in the staircase, yet did Anfanuil scream after his Dragon Companion and had to be restrained by both Dragons and men to keep him from going to his, now surely dead, friend.

The Dragons' fire would nearly disintegrate the Nokre on contact, and even the Black-iron walls and floor were beginning to glow red and soften with the heat. This did help scorch the Nokre, even if they were not caught in the direct blasting inferno, but they cared not for pain and clambered on despite their flesh burning and reeking, melting and sticking to the floor. However, a Dragon cannot breath flame indefinitely; they do come to a point where they need to rest in order to replenish the combustible gasses within their second lungs. If they kept spurting fire, eventually nothing would come out but for hot air, and already a few of the Dragon's streams of flame were starting to sputter and lose continuity. Still came the seething Nokre, seemingly unending in number.

Finally, Dyreft and Zurthaud had reached the door of the top floor, all the while dragging after them the sobbing Anfanuil, and held it fast open for their companions. They shouted encouragement, as the Dragons, whose flaming breath had each now utterly failed, raced for the way out.

Theros exited, then Galrath, but Caelon was gotten by the tail and thus slowed. Screaming and roaring in pain and indignation, he was overcome by the horde within claw's reach of the door, as the rest of the group slammed it fast shut, knowing full well that there was nothing to be done for him. The Dragon's final cries echoed hurtfully in the hearts of the company's remainder, but were brief and muffled by the thick Black-iron door, hopefully signifying a swift death.

While Anfanuil, the tender Aelv, sat and wept and the rest of the company took a dreadfully earned breather, Zurthaud did a head-count in the relative safety of the topmost floor, as the ferocious banging of the Nokre throng upon the door had done little to open it. Three Humans remained, counting himself and Baltor guarding the exit, one Aelv, and three Dragons, counting Theros and Thol, but as Zurthaud turned about to look upon the two he had left guarding the entrance, he found out what had become of them.

They hung, bleeding, stapled by huge nails wrought of Black-iron to the balcony, over the entrance to the empty abysmal crevice. Baltor was already dead, but Thol who, because of a wicked gash down his throat removing his vocal chords, had been unable to cry out in warning, still panted with the last remnants of life and raspingly wheezed as loud as he could in attempt to warn the others.

Zurthaud, utterly shocked by the grisly sight, gasped and fell over upon his backside, causing the rest of the party to look on as well. A few of them gagged; all were appalled by the horrid display. None of them expected the tremendous noise that blared out thereafter; it was of the same blast that had resounded at the first, before the Nokre assault. It now sounded again, but was this time followed by a haunting and complex melody in high, shrill registers. The tune did continually crescendo with louder and deeper voices swirling in ugly, contrapuntal non-harmonies, but there was nothing jovial about this music. Its tone was despairing, its mood, depressing. At length, it ended just as violently as it began, an anti-climactic cluster of rapid and continuously fading nonsense.

Zurthaud looked up to where he had spotted the odd instrument's keyboards, and surely, there was a player there where had not been one before. He was tall, enormously so, for a Human, as a two-legged creature, even challenging the Ogres in sheer height. The giant figure, he who had relished in song while Dragons and Humans had died below, now turned to face his horrified audience. It was the Shadow Lord himself, clothed in his faceless horned helm, evilly spiked wine-red armor, and heavy, shrouding, black cape

"Welcome to Ragnor." Boomed an otherworldly, demonically deep voice, resounding from the empty void where should have been the face of the Dark One, as he held arms high and open wide to them. "It has been a long time since I have entertained guests; so please, forgive the overdramatic welcoming. I could not help myself for to greet your expected, no, anticipated, arrival with a tune of my own composition." Spoke he without any hint of humor, as he ploddingly descended the staircase that led to the lower level of the room.

However, the Dark One paused, upon seeing that the Dragon which he had nailed to the edge of the balcony was still alive and gasping for life. The armored figure raised a hand ever so slightly, and viciously zapped a few bolts of bright, yet terrible and black, lightning into the body of the bleeding Thol. A smell of burning flesh enveloped the room and much smoke, for the Dragon had been eradicated, burned to ash ever so quickly, leaving only the memory of a scream and some scorched blood upon the floor.

He casually resumed descending the rest of the stair, turning his non-gaze toward Zurthaud as he finished the last step.

"You have led these men and Dragons here to only their doom, Zurthaud, for you cannot hope to kill me. I shall not, I cannot, die."

"I have watched you all these years, from the very same seeing bowl that just now I let you also look into, how you grew in wisdom, power, and pride. Oh, the utter terror upon your visage when you then realized the trap into which I had lured you, that now despite all your best effort and skill, the blood of your fallen comrades shall be upon your own head. Indeed, it was well earned, for I have listened long enough to your hypocrisy, your arrogant self-righteousness."

"I now know, thanks to this futile attempt, among other matters, that you are not the One, the Child of Light, the one who was promised to destroy my darkness, but I have found 'Her'. You cannot save her from me. Even now, my hunters close in on her, and you do not even know her name." Mockingly spake the Shadow Lord. "Once I slay 'Her', no flesh shall be left to withstand my darkness, and I shall be free to annihilate all life from the face of this world."

However, Zurthaud was still proudly standing before the ghastly fiend. He had taken not a word to heart, though indeed there was much truth mixed in with their enemy's lies and boasts. He would remain proud, and hopeful, and fight this evil to his own bitter end; neither would he let his friends give up their own hope.

"You have yet to slay us here, and there are still many more Dragons in the Order." He challenged, now overcoming his stupefaction at the undue knowledge and power that this evil being bore, now setting aside his own questions about the riddles that the Shadow Lord had spoken, now only angry at the nonchalance of this foe, especially over the deaths of such good people. "For, every thousand Nokre is only worth one half of a Dragon."

"Oh child, I send not only Nokre to fight Dragons. This time, I shall not waste even one of my miserable thralls in war against the Order, for I have bested the work of Dragons with the folly of Men. My armies shall march in through the gates of Doraegonoran unchallenged, long after the last Dragon has left from therein," Returned the Dark One, "Longer still, after all of you here before me are cut down."

They all questioned these sayings of the Dark One, for they knew not that he spoke the truth to them but in riddles, about the "child of light" and "the folly of men". However, the giant, armored menace did not give them long to ponder his cryptic ridiculing; without a single stride, he crossed the vast distance between himself and Zurthaud's group and cut down both Anfanuil and Dyreft with one swift stroke of a fell two-handed sword that he had brought forth from nowhere. Although, Aelvs were usually more lithe and quicker than Humans, this only served to get the poor dead Aelv's head only half chopped from his shoulders, as the Shadow Lord moved with such impossible speed.

Theros then aimed to pounce upon the monster and roaring leaped through the air toward him, but even the speed of a Dragon could not match the Dark One's quickness. He had sidestepped the attack, dodging Theros' deadly claws by only a little, and let him, rather, fall upon the outstretched blade of the bastard-sword.

Sorely wounded, Theros limped away, as yelling with fury, thinking Theros had been slain, Zurthaud raced over for a counter-attack. Only a few parries later, and the Dark one was pressing hard his own attack upon Zurthaud, his foul attentions focused seemingly exclusively on the only Human whose swordsmanship could barely match his terrible speed and power.

Galrath saw his opportunity and attempted to bite and claw at the surprisingly agile and powerfully deadly warlord, but his strikes fell on air, as the Shadow Lord continued to press his attack against Zurthaud.

Finally, the wine-red armored demon caught Zurthaud with a movement he could not avoid or block, and he ran the Human straight and cleanly through the middle with a great lunging stab of the awful blade. Even though Galrath landed a good blow thereafter, as the Shadow Lord had paused to impale Zurthaud, the Dark One merely shrugged off a strike that would have sent any mortal foe plummeting through space in two halves. As Zurthaud fell to the floor, his lifeblood quickly seeping from what was not an outright fatal wound, the Shadow Lord turned about and cleanly decapitated the unsuspecting Galrath with a single backhanded swipe of his fearsome blade.

"What did I tell you? That you were not 'the One', that you would fall before me like grass before the cutter's scythe, and yet still you stood, rather than attempting to escape through my nice hole in the roof. Fool! Now all your comrades lie dead about you, the full weight of their corpses drowning you in a sea of guilt and blood. I shall give you a deserving fate; slowly, tortuously shall I take even your very last breath from you." The Dark One taunted, as he strode triumphantly around the vast room, his blood stained, yet empty, visage gloating over each of his kills.

Suddenly, he came back around to Zurthaud. "Now, return my book." Said he becoming quite wroth.

Zurthaud did not answer the fell enemy, for he was in so much pain, yet did he now realize the full importance of this item, as being so precious to their foe. He clutched it, holding it closer to his chest inside his coat. This only served to further infuriate the Shadow Lord, and full of violent rage, he trod swiftly over toward Zurthaud.

However, Theros was not slain, and as the Shadow Lord came upon Zurthaud, for to end his life, the Dragon cast a dreadful spell of red magic upon the fiend. The magic blast would have surely killed any other mortal, but it only took the Shadow Lord off guard. As the menacing warlord was flung across the room and into the depths of the empty Dragon's lair by the magic's forceful eruption, Theros took wing and, grabbing Zurthaud in his arms, hastened with all his might for the exit in the roof.

With an unearthly roar of pure rage, uncannily like to that of a Dragon's, the Shadow Lord, from where he lay upon his side, unleashed more of his black lightning after them, and, indeed, clipped Theros' hind parts, scorching him so awfully, that the Dragon screamed in pain and nearly dropped his cargo. But, Theros clung only the tighter to Zurthaud and did not let go, and they cleared the hole in the roof just as more of the Dark One's lightning seared hotly after them, failing by inches to destroy them and exploding harmlessly on the inner part of the ceiling.

Slowly, sorely was their winged flight homeward, and Zurthaud was conscious for hardly a moment of it, as his life was flowing fast from him. Yet, they were immediately safe from the awful grasp of the all-too-powerful Lord of Darkness and each felt that relief, even as soon as they had crossed back into the borders of the Order's realm.

"Theros, I have failed. I have failed the Order, and I have failed our friends who died tonight. Their sacrifice was in vain; I have ruined everything." Zurthaud muttered, losing consciousness.

"Be still my friend; hold onto life. We are almost home. All of us knew the risk of entering the Ragnor; we knew we would not all come out alive. We Dragons know more than anyone, that none who have entered there have lived. Yet, did we trust your leadership, yet did we believe in your cause. We hoped beyond all good sense, beyond all hope, for the best of outcomes, and that is all for which we had tried. Now, just hold onto your life; do not leave me just yet." Theros begged, though with his own grievous wounds, death lingered not far away.

However, the wing-beats of Theros' hastened flight, his pleading cries for to hold on a little longer, only grew ever fainter in Zurthaud's ears, and the world around him faded into numb blackness.

Chapter 10

Feldara awoke early in the sunny, open-aired Aelven apartment, and blinking one eye open then the next, she noticed, first of all, Anur, still soundly asleep in the bed beside her, snoring softly, his heavy breaths pinging metallically against the inside of his helm. While it was not unusual for the two to share a single bed, as they had done so out of necessity for sixteen years, it was very odd for Anur to still be asleep when she arose, and Feldara thought that he must, indeed, feel much safer within the Aelven lands, to be so comfortable as to rise late. However, she soon ceased her admiration at this small wonder, as she wanted for a drink of water, a giant whiff of crisp morning air, and for other morning duties.

Her wounds quickly healing, in spite of the vile Worg venom, Feldara had begun, by last night's dinner, to feel quite a bit better, even well enough to walk, rather than be pushed about on the clumsy potato cart. So, gently, with every motion still fighting the constant, but slightly lessened, pain of the Worg venom, she clambered out of the plush, downy bed, and after checking to make sure she had not accidentally stirred her friend into rising, and to her great delight, finding herself successful, made her way quietly toward the door. Not really looking where she was going, her first steps creaked soundly upon the wooden porch of the apartment, but her succeeding footfalls landed upon nothing.

The next thing Feldara knew, she was suddenly about to fall down the length of a very tall tree, for she had forgotten their ascent the night before of the great oak, many times the size of any regular tree.

It was within the trees that the Aelvs dwelt, in fine wooden apartments that entwined with the numerous boughs, and normally there would have been a railing at the edges of the balconies. But, Anur and Feldara had been placed in quarters designed for the comfort of Dragons and their companions, meaning no safeguarding balustrade, for the ease of a Dragon's winged landings and departures.

As she plummeted downward with a startled yelp, her weakened back-legs giving way, she reached out with her front talons, and with them, dug deeply into the tree's dense bark, stopping her fall almost as soon as it had begun. And, Feldara stuck right there, clinging to the bark of the tree for dear life. Her wings too weak to fly back up to the apartment's porch, she attempted to swing her hind-legs back up to the ledge above, and after a couple of failed attempts that ended with her facing her own rear-end, with her clawed feet, she finally managed to grab firmly hold of the balcony that formerly she had been standing safely upon.

However, what to do next, Feldara wondered, as she had no momentum or strength left with which to swing her front end back up to the balcony, and she certainly could not climb down the immensely tall tree head first. Falling was out of the question; so, there she stayed for, at least, a few minutes, utterly stranded in that awkward position, until the Aelvs on the ground below began to point and take notice of her predicament.

Many of them looked on and laughed lightheartedly, not really at the possibility of her falling, but rather at the comically awkward position that she had managed to get into, and then only because they thought she was fully capable of using her wings to get safely out of the ridiculous spot. They could not possibly have known that the Worg venom had so sapped her strength that she could not even hope to spread her wings at all.

Thankfully, other more informed Aelvs, the staff of the inn and particularly the innkeeper, who had inquired himself why she had come to his establishment on a potato cart, of all the available manner of transportation, had heard of her predicament and were already rushing to help.

Soon some ropes were lowered about her waist, and once securely harnessed, she was hoisted back up to the refuge of the balcony. Once returned to the safety of the boardwalk and after regaining her composure, Feldara heartily thanked each of the Aelvs who had rescued her, and after being given an explanation for her amusing circumstances, those who had asked why she could not have just flown away or even glided gently to the earth below, the crowd wished her well and dispersed to their usual business, leaving Feldara alone again upon the wood platform.

"I must be cured of this awful venom." She mused to herself, thinking about the source of her unusually irksome trouble, as she checked to see if Anur had yet awoken.

But, Anur was yet asleep, still snoring softly, as he had been throughout the whole dilemma. Feldara was slightly annoyed that he could remain so restfully oblivious of her undignified situation, not being able to have lifted a finger to help her, and she loudly huffed at him, as only a Dragoness could. Even then Anur did not awake, causing Feldara even more frustration, but also a little worry, as Anur had always been a light sleeper and would usually wake at the slightest noise or provocation.

"He must be very tired, as he had stayed up all of the night before to keep watch." She reasoned to herself.

She too was tired, tired of being wheeled about in carts, of longing for the joyful, lofty freedom that only being a Dragon and the boundless sky could supply, and after only a little deliberation she determined not to wait on the pleasantly slumbering Anur, to set out on her own again, to find this famed Dragon doctor and be rid of her plaguing disease once and for all.

And, this time she determined to not be so unaware of her surroundings, as she, after resting a good while to recover from the terrible strain and venomous hurt she had suffered throughout her little accident, stepped foot out the door of the apartment again. She swore to herself that she would not get into trouble by ignoring those wiser than she and going where it was not safe, as she had done in the dark pine forest two nights ago. This time she resolved to be wise and not foolish and not get into any mischief, and the very first thing she did was to wisely ask for directions to the doctor's house.

____

"Ho, innkeeper, I thank you again for your aid." Said she, upon entering the common room within the base of the massive tree's hollowed trunk.

"Oh, think nothing of it, Lady Dragoness. Knowing of your ailment, I could not just stand idly by." Returned the ruddy cheeked, rather round- and such was uncommon for the light-footed folk- Aelv, even as he tended other guests and matters from behind a large, well stocked bar counter.

"Do you happen to know where is the residence of the Rathnyalgrs? I will be seeing them so as to ensure your Dragon roping skills will no longer be needed." She inquired.

After a good round of laughter from all the Aelven customers and staff, even the kind innkeeper, much to Feldara's dismay, for she had not intended her dry humor to evoke such an exaggerated response, the good master of the inn did give her the address and some general directions.

After being informed of the location and the general direction of Rathnyalgrs' house, Feldara set off at more a brisk pace, being slightly indignant of the earlier volume of humor at her expense and wanting to not appear so helpless, but she soon found herself in constant misery, with the Worg venom coursing through her veins. She eventually had to stop to rest and catch her breath, and then again quite soon after. It was not until she began to walk at a much slower pace, like that of the elderly- toddling along so carefully- or a snail, that she could keep strolling for quite some time without the need to rest.

So, she kept strolling and toddling, beginning to finally look about and exploring the wondrous city, until she accidentally walked right into an open aired cafe upon the side of the street and knocked over some empty tables and chairs, and even a couple of occupied ones.

Fortunately for her, the Aelvs were, generally, quite carefree folk and, after cleaning up the trouble she had gotten into, the owners cheerfully accepted Feldara's apology, and even kindly offered her a gratuitous breakfast. As they had not received Dragon visitors from the Order in many decades, the other Aelvs of the city likewise cordially welcomed her, whither she wandered.

All the bright-faced, brighter-eyed, jovial Aelven people would greet her and the morning with song and a quaint salutation, every bit as happy and luminous as their spectacular metropolis.

So many sights did Feldara marvel at. The tall trees, she had grown accustomed to seeing being used as buildings, yet toward the industrial section of the city, into which she had now wandered, the Aelvs had begun mixing with magic this use of the trees along with much more conventional stone masonry. Much of the heart of the city was built this way, the structures being half of stone and brick and the other half of tree, each part bent and melded together in harmoniously magical quality. Arches were half of bough and brick, windows of glass and flowers, tower-topping weather vanes and spires of pines and steel.

Feldara soon came upon the great river that ran right through the center of Lotheliel, the Ae, but even this forceful obstacle of nature was compatible with the development of the Aelven city, serving in so many uses: a main causeway, with many small boats ferrying people about, powering mills and enterprises of all sorts with wheels and cogs that turned and spiraled in the constant flow of the water. Feldara was not so compatible with the vast expanse of water; she was stopped in her tracks by the Ae. She took one look at the size of the boats at the crossing, as several Aelvs attempted to coax her onto one of them, and found that she became unable bring herself to trust the tiny canoes to carry her weight. Shuddering to think of what would happen should she, beleaguered as she was, fall into the water, she opted for the alternative, traveling across the canal by means of the many tree-bough, stone, and iron bridges that spanned it.

As she crossed over the Ae, through the center of Lotheliel, past the grand City Hall adorned with magnificent statues of heroes and days long past and large bubbling fountains tossing spray high into the air, she entered the artisan quarter, where she encountered many skillful works, finely crafted wares, and such sweet jubilant music. A young Aelv even excitedly offered to paint her portrait, a rare chance for him to capture the form and beauty of a Dragoness, but she could not afford to stand still for as long as he deemed would be necessary and regretfully passed onward, leaving the pouting, disappointed artist to sulkingly return to his quiet shop.

Everywhere she looked there was a sight to behold, a smell to discover, a person to meet; truly, if she were not so enjoying the experience, Feldara might have become overwhelmed by it all. However, she kept her ultimate direction in mind, her goal constant; slowly and casually, resting often her sore, aching body, she finally meandered her way to the extreme opposite side of the great city, where dwelt the renowned Dragon doctors.

By means of again asking for more specific direction, she eventually made it there, for every Aelv she passed by, smiling and courteous, was always so helpful as to point her in the right way. Feldara doubted that there were any dangerous, bad, or even grumpy Aelvs, as they always seemed so jovial, and even though she had read tales of the Dark Aelvs of the far North, among other Aelven unpleasantness, she was certain that none of those creatures resided in such a fantastically idyllic place as this.

She finally made it to the complete opposite side of the city a few hours after noontide, and hastening her steps as much as she could, Feldara happily traversed into the Dragon's quarter. It was bare of any Aelven buildings and separated from the rest of the city, for the Dragon's desire for greater privacy, by a large public park, full of walking trails, flower gardens, and thick evergreen and deciduous groves.

As she quickly cleared this serene commons and neared the tall, white granite cliffs that made up the entire North wall of the city, she gazed up in awe at the height of the majestic rock face, the whole of which was dotted with the balconies and round entrances of a multitude of Dragon apartments, and each of these decorated round about with carved and chiseled artwork of various nature.

But, these grand sights did not long hold Feldara's attention, as she was so very excited to finally meet some other Dragons. She only wondered if any such multitude of her kind lived within these august dwellings, yet after asking a few passersby, she learned that, sadly, most of the marvelous apartments had, long ago, been abandoned. The cliff-face housing was only occupied by Rathnyalgr's immediate kin, with many of the vacancies being reserved for the Paladins, especially the High Councilmen of the Order and their Dragons, but unfortunately, the latter party had not visited the city for untold many years.

"Not in about an hundred years." Informed one of the Aelvs whom she had asked, and it would be so great a number to Humans, even Dragons, that Aelvs would simply call "not recently", for the merry folk do not age, wither, or die by natural causes. They continue on and on, immortal- in the crudest sense of that word- until either war or unnatural plague take them or the end of all things.

As she came under the very shadow of this monolithic natural dwelling, Feldara's troubles only seemed to multiply, as she had quickly run into a big problem. In order to gain entrance to the Dragon apartments, one had to be able to fly, for there were no stairs that reached them. As of yet, Feldara was not exactly capable of becoming airborne. Just the simple walk through the city had too often tired her out, and even now her veins pounded and ached with the ferocious Worg venom from her quickened pace through the park.

So, she sat at the feet of the smooth faced precipice for a good long while, gathering her breath and wondering if the doctor was even home, and if he was, how she was to get up the height of the cliff. Yet, just as she was about to give up hope of ever being healed and turn about to go back the long, weary way to her room at the inn, dark shadows began to alight upon her from the sky above.

Thinking these shadows no more than clouds, and hopefully not rain clouds, she paid them little heed, until a familiar sound wafted to her ears. The beating of silken Dragon wings, caused her to turn her head up to the air, and her eyes were greeted by the sight of many Dragons and Dragonesses flying in and out of the apartments above her head. They quickly took notice of her, and greeted her as they all swooped down to land beside her.

The younger Dragons eagerly welcomed Feldara, as they were all about her age and very happy to have received a guest, let alone a youth such as they, while the three present elder Dragons practiced a measure more of polite restraint in their warm salutations. As they introduced themselves as the extended family of Rathnyalgr, Feldara learned not only all of their names: Crasra, whose mate was Rathnyaling, the son of Rathnyalgr, and their children: Sengis, Calidon, Vol, Chassia, and Sachru; and Rathnyala, Rathnyaling's sister, and her mate, Yuronon, and their children: Aris, Rath, Thinru, Ruderon, and Nyalanya, but also a little about each one of them.

She found, through a good hour of introduction and friendly conversation, that despite the predominance of red colorings for Rathnyala and her brother and all their children- while Yuronon was slate gray and Crasra so light a blue as to be almost white- and their shared knowledge and passion for the medicinal arts, though each quite disparate in personality, very wonderful people.

"So, can any of you treat me for this awful Worg venom?" Feldara asked, as the subject of her visit's purpose came about while they had all stretched their wings, reclining and sunning themselves upon the cool dewy grass before the cliff-face.

"I have no knowledge of Worg bites." Offered Sengis, the smallest male yet, among his siblings, the most adept of his father's medical apprentices. "Do you remember how to cure a Dragon's blood of this disease, Auntie?" He asked of his aunt Rathnyala.

But, the Dragoness only shook her head 'no'. Yuronon her mate, who was the only one of their family who actually had absolutely no knowledge, training, or inclination toward anything medical, also jocularly answered a negative, causing giggles to erupt from his younger family members. The rest of the siblings and cousins answered the same, not a one of the Dragons and Dragonesses gathered there had ever encountered the Worg's bite or its cure.

"Truly it is a rare condition, for a Worg's teeth usually cannot penetrate a Dragon's hide. The Humans and other two-legs that are thus infected usually never can be treated, for they become Worgs themselves after only a few hours of being bitten." Explained Rathnyala, who was the most medicinally learned Dragon in their company, in the city, and perhaps, the world, alongside her nephew and her brother.

However, she motioned with a finger and began digging within a great leather satchel that hung about her neck. After a long moment of gracelessly rummaging through the cluttered pouch, while Yuronon mockingly mimicked his mate's searching, again much to everyone's amusement, she withdrew a small tome, though thick for its diminutive size. Inscribed upon the worn cover of the volume was the title: "A Dragon's Guide to a Dragon's Ailments".

"Let me see if there is anything herein." She suggested, as she began thumbing through the pertinent sections. "This might take a moment; the print is so small it may as well be the Dworvish edition."

The Dragons all waited in silence thereafter as Rathnyala scoured the book for anything on Worg's bite, but many moments passed and still she read on, leaving the less medicinally inclined family members to grow bored and restless. At length, Yuronon rose with much stretching from his place on the ground beside his mate.

"Very well then, the day grows long, and we shall all be famished soon. Let us invite our guest to wait inside our home as we prepare a feast in honor of her visit." He wisely advised, much to the delight of the other younger Dragons.

It was then that Feldara tragically remembered that she had left Anur still soundly asleep in their cozy apartment on the other side of the city, and she sorely wished that she had woken him, so to, at least, have explained where she would be going. He was certainly now searching diligently, and angrily, throughout the whole of the city looking for her.

As the male Dragons started to take off into the air, for to either hunt or buy the meat for their feast, Feldara asked them send word to Anur of her safety and to also bring him with them upon their return. The Dragons graciously obliged themselves to her request, and Feldara gladly thought to dwell no more upon it, as she was hoisted up by several of the younger females to their lovely apartments on the cliff above.

Although, her body was still weak, Feldara had nearly become tolerant of the constant scorching of the painful venom, and after arriving within the Dragon-fire carved halls, offered to do anything she could in aiding the other Dragonesses, who rushed about, busily preparing for the bounteous meal that was soon to be served. She first aided in laying out a large red linen upon a long, low table in the great common room, that which connected the other various apartments that were owned by the Rathnyalgrs, for to house so many adult and juvenile Dragons required much space, indeed. She also set upon the red linen large pewter plates, of which Feldara was very curious, never before having seen their like, let alone eaten off such finery; to go with these plates were big pewter goblets, which, as Feldara was told, would hold their drink while they ate.

Never before had Feldara considered being able to drink while she ate, for on their island, she and Anur's only source of fresh-water was the deep well at its center, and their only drinking vessel, the bucket with which they drew it up . She was now worried that she should look a fool in front of all her refined hosts, but Crasra must have seen her distress. The older Dragoness, took her aside and kindly showed her the use of the new utensils, and even some Dragon etiquette.

"But, do remember, dear, here we are all your friends, and growing up in the wilds, apart from more refined society, is nothing to be ashamed of. I myself was raised in the northern Aegan Mountains, far above the Aelven capitol, and there the Dragons have absolutely no manners, nor the use thereof." Jestingly consoled the lovely wife of Rathnyaling.

Nevertheless, Feldara made a mental note to neither take a drink from her chalice with her mouth full, nor to talk while chewing, nor to dig her whole face into a carcass for a bite.

As the sun began to droop ever so slightly from the peak of its noontide height, and all the male Dragons had as yet to return, and Rathnyala still sat on the ground below the cliffs, fixedly reading through her book, Feldara and the other young Dragonesses began to grow rather concerned.

Although she had spent her time diligently, preparing to go with their meat a wonderful cold salad of potatoes, boiled eggs, onions, and spiced dressing, the like of which Feldara had also never before seen nor tasted, Crasra too became worried, for she knew that a hunt among seven large Dragon males should not take so long. She was also fairly distressed that her mate had as yet to return home from his doctor's visits of the day; as disease and injury were a rarity in the Aelven lands, a Dragon doctor should not have worked for such long hours at a time.

She was just about to go off after their males to look for them, when, suddenly, a sound of many bodies entering the apartment fluttered noisily at the doorway. The Dragonesses all hastened to the entryway in the joyous anticipation of a happy reunion with their kin and the start of a gladsome evening of mirthful feasting, but the visitors they received were unexpected, to say the least.

They were tall Human-like creatures, for what was to be seen of their skin was too pale and coarse to be Human; the majority of their appearance was cloaked in thick black robes, under which they wore chain mail wrought of Black-iron and thick leather belts full of pockets, knives, and all manner of sharp utensil. Upon their heads were helms with dark vizors, seeming to Feldara quite similar to, if not exactly the same make as, Anur's. To reach the Rathnyalgrs' lofty Dragon apartment, they had apparently rappelled down from above the rocky cliff face, and now they entered into it, twenty strong, with Black-iron swords drawn and ready.

"Who are you? What are you doing in my home?" Viciously snarled Crasra, startled and angry to see such menacing and uninvited guests.

The darkly robed men laughed a little before their leader responded. "We are the Dark Hunters, the strongest of the Kragon's servants; we have come for the Dragoness that seeks healing from you, the bright one. If you let us have her, we will leave in peace, for we have no quarrel with you." He offered in a deep gravelly voice that sounded more dead than quick.

But, the Dragonesses of Rathnyaling's family did not consider, even for a moment, giving ear to such a demand, for Dragons regard all of their own kind as kin, no matter how distantly related. They would never have betrayed another Dragon to such seemingly dark and evil strangers. Nevertheless, Feldara, who had to walk at a slower pace than the other females, was in the back of the group, behind all the other Dragonesses, quite out of sight from the odd villains who had come looking for her.

"There are no Dragonesses here that are not of my blood." Somewhat lied Crasra, for she did not yet wish to engage in combat with an enemy of which she knew nothing, lest she endanger her nearby daughters. "You will leave this place right now, for what you seek is not here."

However, the dark men did not heed her words; they did neither leave nor turn to go. "We know you are lying to us; we saw her enter this house. Now, step aside or die." Harshly spat the leader, as his pack of ruffians readied for battle.

Crasra attacked first, breathing an explosion of hot Dragon fire into the entryway, and the fiery blast covered the corridor from wall to wall. Some of the foul warriors, screaming with the pain of swift disintegration, withered in the heat, but the rest were quicker and shielded themselves with magic, for there was no room within the entrance hallway to avoid the fire-breath. Eventually, Crasra's breath of flame began to grow thin, and she began to back into the depths of the apartment, forcing her daughters and Feldara to retreat along with her.

As the last of her blazing defense dissipated into the air, the leader of the black-armored men cried out. "Kill them all. Leave none alive, but for the bright one." And, they did hasten further into the home, after the Dragonesses.

There were no doors to bar the way within the Dragon apartment, so that the only barrier between the females and these Dark Hunters was the scorching hot stone walls and floor, which had even begun to melt slightly from the heat of Crasra's fire. However, this was no defense against their thrown weapons, and the men began to thicken the air with Black-iron throwing knives and other darts.

"What will we do, mother?" Frightenedly asked Sachru, as Crasra was forced to shield herself and her charges with magic.

Just as the floor began to cool enough for the Dark Hunters to come across and engage the females, and it seemed as though they might not live through a battle with such powerful foes, more noise echoed into the apartment from the entrance. This time, it was definitely the sound of Dragon's wings, and with it a loud roar of rage and savagery, that which comes from a father and husband earnestly desiring the safety of his household.

The males had returned home, and they rushed into the apartment full ready for battle. Yet, the first of their company to enter the fray was no Dragon. It was none other than Anur, for he, having been brought with them, had been sorely searching the whole day long for Feldara. Having found her whereabouts, and now seeing the danger that she was in, he charged into battle, as protective and fierce as any of the Dragon males.

Feldara's heart soared to see him, there again at just the right time to save her, effectively swinging his favorite short sword in skillful parries and offensives against the evil intruders. The Dragons then entered closely after Anur, and with much rage they fought with tooth and claw and magic against the invaders. Rathnyaling, who had also come back with the others, joined the scrap, as well. He and Yuronon also used their fiery breath to scorch the foes, whereas their sons, but for Calidon the tallest, strongest, and most developed of the young males, yet could not.

Though they fought tirelessly and heatedly, the Dark Hunters could not hope to battle so many Dragons, for the males tore into them with almost reckless abandon, seeking to protect their family, and the females did also opportunistically attack from their end, finishing off any who survived the initial onslaught, except Feldara for, because of her condition, she was pushed to the very back of the entrance hallway and kept out of the fight,.

At last, Anur and the leader of these Dark Hunters faced off with lightning flashes of sword-play, but they were equals in combat and could get no advantage over each other, until the captain spake unto him.

"Why do you fight against us, brother? Do you not fear our master? Or, have you been deceived by these weak-minded folk?" He maliciously interrogated.

And hearing this, Anur did pause his attack and slightly lower his sword, for he had begun to notice their appearance, that it was striking in resemblance to his own. With his free hand he felt of his helm, which seemed to him identical to his foes'.

But, it was a ploy, a ruse, by the cunning hunter, for to make an opening in Anur's defense, to distract him for even a moment. The Dark Hunter stabbed quickly at Anur, making full use of his advantage, and landed a cut on Anur's arm, drawing blood and hurting him greatly.

However, Yuronon had also his eye on the hunters' captain, and just as the fell warrior was about to finish off Anur, much to Feldara's dismay, the large Dragon made his own ploy. Reaching across the hallway, Yuronon took the hunter by surprise, as he was distracted by Anur's vulnerability, and he cleanly clawed the man in twain.

The few surviving Dark Hunters, seeing all hope lost with the life of their leader, their most powerful member, attempted an escape, but they were hard pressed to flee from such tight quarters packed with so many thrashing, slashing, battling Dragons. At last, one of them did break free from the slaughter and hastily escaped. He used one of their ropes to rappel down the remainder of the cliff face and took off running toward the city gates, completely unnoticed by any of the Dragons or Anur.

Finally, the last of the black robed men was slain, and with the battle won and wistful silence returning to the hallways of the apartment, the Dragons rested a moment, breathing heavily with their exertion and adrenaline fueled battle rage.

"Who were those awful men? I mean, what were they doing here? How did they get into the city, past the guards?" Finally, asked Nyalanya, after they had all rested a good while and began cleaning up the mess of blood and carcasses.

"They were part of the attack upon the city; I assume." Offered Rathnyaling, and he told them of what had occurred that had made them so late to dinner.

"I had just finished tending the poor magistrate, for as you know he has been ill with a rare fever, the cure of which is not known to any other doctor in the city beside myself, when I received word that there was an attack at the South gate of the city. Many were there wounded and they desired my aid in tending them, so I gladly obliged. When I arrived, Yuronon and the boys were already there, helping to destroy the enemy force from above. It was a giant pack of Worgs, some with Goblin riders, and a battalion or so of Trolls, hardly enough to conquer the whole of the city, especially with our presence here, but they had caught the wall guards by surprise and were about to open the outer gates and become a scourge to the civilians, slaying many within. Surely they would have, if not for this brave man and I. At first, I mistook Anur for one of the enemy, for there were certainly more of those dark robed hooligans leading the enemy forces. But, we found each other comrades, thanks to Finiriel's presence, and together with Yuronon and our sons, and the Aelven rangers and regulars, we won the day, and drove back to the border those foul beasts." Proudly explained the Doctor, as some of his family applauded. He continued, motioning to Feldara. "It was only after the battle that I found out Anur was your companion, Feldara, for he had been concerned of your whereabouts, and made mention of you when he noticed my medical skill being employed after the battle."

Mention of his own prowess as a physician only caused Rathnyaling to assess the families' injuries, and extensively examining them all, he found only small cuts or bruises among the lot of them, aside from Anur's thoroughly lacerated arm.

"I shall stitch that up quickly." Said the Dragon doctor to Anur, or rather to Anur's wound, for Rathnyaling was looking at it rather closely when he spoke. "And, with my special poultice, it should heal just fine and sooner than would normally be the case."

Feldara too did come closer to Anur, for to see how badly he had been hurt. Yet, he had not such good intentions toward her.

"I had been worried to sickness for you, Feldara." He crossly chided her. "You should not have gone off on your own, even to here. You should have waited for me to rise and come with you, for I have all day been searching for you throughout the city. For shame, that you caused me such grief."

The words stung her, for Feldara was now going through the pain of moving her ill and tired body over to him, simply out of concern for his well-being, and he had so scolded her, as if she were a hatchling, and in front of all these Dragons, her peers and betters. She was sorely embarrassed, and if Dragons could bashfully flush, she would have. In truth, she had not meant to worry Anur so; she simply had not thought it through, how he should earnestly desire to know where she was going, if she was safe or not.

Yet, Anur was not intending to be so unkind. He had been truly worried for her, unto much bitter, gut-wrenching sorrow, and was so relieved beyond words that she had been safe within the Rathnyalgrs' home and not endangered by the Dark Horde's attack at the city gate. The only words he found after such emotional stress of a lost child, and then a battle for their life, were harsher than intended, but he had not a second to apologize for his tone or explain his agony. Rathnyaling broke the awkwardness of the silence that had followed Anur's stern rebuke, replacing any response from either the worried unto sickness Anur or the abashed Feldara by remembering that he had one more patient whom he had not yet checked.

"Where is Rathnyala?" He asked, as he went about his home gathering bandages, needle, and thread, much to the utter consternation of Yuronon, her mate, who had also not thought to look for her.

They all then began to worry for her sake, for they had not seen her since before the females had started preparing for their meal. As the sun began to set, Yuronon hastened to venture without, for to see what had become of her, but there ended being no need for that.

For, Rathnyala suddenly burst into the apartment, a gigantic smile spread across her face. "I have found it!" She elatedly cried. "I have found a cure for the Worg's bite." And, it seemed that she had been completely undisturbed by the whole battle with the hunters, instead being completely engrossed within her medical tome, unaware of the outside world, for she wrinkled her nose at smelling the burnt flesh and seeing some remnants of the battle, and frowning, asked a simple question.

"What happened in here?"

Chapter 11

As dawn broke over the horizon, its light reflecting a warm red from the burning hot sands of the desert, Malok and Shar passed over the very last of the tall, gently sloping dunes. The crossing of the Akum, the Great Wastes, the Serpen name for the vast, barren desert that separated their kingdom from the Order's realm, had been particularly dangerous this time. As there was absolutely no cover out in the empty heart of the wastes, they had been forced to outrun several dangerously thick dust storms, learning firsthand the old saying, "Never trust the sand."

Many trade caravans of the Serpen would cross the desert on foot, and a few of the inexperienced, unprepared, or unlucky ones would never be seen or heard from again, victims of the sun and the heat or even such a sandy, impromptu burial amidst the howling winds of the frequent sandstorms. To travel by night and conserve water was common knowledge and practice, but even the wizened traveler could still meet an untimely demise by neglecting the smallest of details and warning signs.

However, the desert was behind them, and now a completely strange new world stretched suddenly beneath their winged traveling and before their eyes unto the distant panorama beyond. The tall, ice-capped, northern Aegan Mountains rose majestically before them, reaching high into the atmosphere, until their very tops were shrouded by the mist of slowly melting glaciers and low lying clouds.

As they stopped among the heights of these rocky giants, by a small brook on one of the grassy, sloping steppes, for to refresh themselves with the first source of crisp, clear fresh water they had seen in the whole two day journey by Dragon's wing, they decided to make camp and rest for a while, for not only were they wearied from their travels but were also fully mesmerized by the beauty of the immeasurably abundant plant life and greenery that had seemingly sprung up from what was once barren ground. They had to marvel at such lush vegetation, for neither of them had felt the tingling of a grass carpet underneath their feet before, nor ever seen so much green at one time, for though they had heard tales of distant verdant lands, never before had they seen with their own eyes, nor had imagined, such abundant flora.

"I wonder how much it must rain here, for this grass to grow so green and the trees so tall and plentiful. Surely a more blessed place never existed." Shar wondered aloud, as he stretched himself out upon the cool sedges, freshly wet with the morning dew.

"I agree." Confirmed Malok, as he took a large drink from the chill mountain stream.

They both attempted together to relax for a bit, but their excitement over the new sights and wonders of the magnificently emerald land and their complete rejuvenation from the long, hot desert journey by the frigid clear water and the bed of soft wet grass, let them not linger idly for very long. They slept but a little and were ready to further explore this enchanting domain.

Soon they were again soaring loftily in the sublime currents of the mountain breezes, and their shadow darted quickly after them across the faces of hills that were low enough to not necessitate a bypass round about.

Many of the tall foreboding peaks were just too high, possibly, for even a Dragon to surmount, as there would be little enough air to breath at the utmost of their extraordinary limits, but quickly did they pass by these magnificent kings of edifices, as they descended to the lower altitudes.

"Surely, the city, Doraegonoran, should be somewhere about these lower foot hills; we could spot it at any moment." Malok called up to his friend who sat upon the back of his shoulders.

Such a notable location would not be hard to find, even among the mountains, and, as surely as he had spoken it, so it was that they sighted the great city of cities afar off in the distance. What at first had seemed but a dark strip of unusually placed shadow atop the very last of the steppes of the Northern Mountains, upon the very edge of the wide open, rolling grassy plains of the Human Realm, turned out to be just the outline of the city, and its great walls, towers, and the castle of the Paladins, only grew larger and more defined as they drew ever closer, until at last, the city was spread out below them, a thousand, thousand homes and many hundreds of shops, mills, and metalworks. The grand park, filled to abundance with more variety and number of trees than in the whole Serpen Kingdom, sprawled near the center of the city, and the vast grain and crop fields that lay beyond the eleven tiered city walls stretched out unto the Southern horizon.

The two foreigners' eyes drank in the fabulous wonders of the world-renowned metropolis as they had only moments ago, desert travelers, thirstily filled themselves with sweetest water, but indeed, the glorious sight to truly steal away their breath was the august Citadel that was the headquarters of the Order of Paladins, which stood at the North end of the great city, that nearest the shadow of the mountains.

The great castle was ringed about with a double set of walls, each of these thicker and taller than the small frontage of a fortress that was the Serpen king's home.

Behind these impressive walls were the quarters, dividing the castle grounds for the four represented civilized races, each, aside from the Dragon's quarter, comprised of several towers and buildings and joined fast to one another by an inner courtyard and strong inner walls. They all were connected, by means of the inner walls, to the main tower, the Keep of the Citadel, where was the stored treasury, the medical ward, library, and the high and lower councils' judicial chambers.

"How shall we go about this?" Malok then wondered aloud, for, as Serpen were not exactly beloved by the rest of the civilized world, he had been pondering the manner of his companion's welcome. "Should we announce ourselves and our intentions to the head of the Order, at the first, or should we introduce ourselves to the lower members before seeking audience with the High Council?"

"You should know by now that I never think so far ahead when I have no throne to sit upon." Joked Shar in response, but he too dreaded a meeting with the awful Orthard, who had subjugated his people so tyrannically. "I think it would be best if as few people knew that we are here as possible, for none in this city should think half so highly of me, though I be the king of my people, as they would of the horse dung in the common stables. Let us warn, maybe, only this Dragoness, and then quickly return to our home, before we incite riot or worse."

"I never thought you would be so cowardly before the enraged voice of the people, for it seemed that the angry mobs were common enough, back home." Malok returned, also in jest, for both he and Shar knew the fairness and goodness of his rule.

Shar faked laughter in sarcastic response, as they approached the Dragon's quarter, both silently agreeing with this aforementioned plan of action, both hoping to be well received, but very much doubting that possibility.

However, the jovial smirk faded quickly from the young Dragon's lips, as Malok had always secretly longed to be among his kin, to be taught by Dragons about their own ways, for he had not ever been able to learn such knowledge from the Serpen. Ulam, try as he might, could not read the old Draconic language, and as wise and learned as the old Serpen was, he still was not capable of using magic, nor of revealing the knowledge of Dragons unto Malok. Although he deeply loved his adoptive people, Malok had always yearned to be what he had not ever been, to be what he seemed on the outside but thought not of himself, fully Dragon, what he was created to be.

But, there was no warm welcome from the Order's Dragons, as the two descended in lazy spirals to the castle below. There remained but a few Human guards upon the outer walls, and they seemed more interested in gambling and drinking than in keeping watch. Over all, as they observed the barren courtyards, the empty living quarters, the silent towers, they both began to feel that something was amiss; the whole fortress was much too still and stark for to live up to its own reputation as the gathering place of all the Paladins and lawmakers of the land.

"Where is everyone?" Shar whispered in Malok's ear, spread out flat upon his friend's back, hoping to stay unnoticed for the remainder of their hopefully short visit.

"They saw us coming and are waiting in hiding for us to pass by, after which they shall jump out and yell, 'surprise!'" Nervously teased Malok, as he himself could not imagine why the skies above were not impossibly filled with Dragons, or the gardens with plant tending Aelvs, or the forges with crafting Dworvs, as all the books of history told thereof.

As they circled about the fortress, Shar voiced his disbelief of Malok's statement, apparently, still unaware that his friend was being silly, while Malok craned his neck about to see whether there might be some Dragons within the lone tower that surely was their living space. No other building, save for the Keep, that holding the chambers of the High Council on its topmost floor, rivaled the height and enormity of this tower, but the entryways were the real differentiating mark, as they were all at least three times the size of those used by the other sentient races, clearly meant to accommodate Dragons.

They decided together to land within the spacious courtyard of this area, which surely was the Dragon's quarters, and the dust scattered before them in pulses, echoing the soft wing-beats that slowly let them down to the ground. However, as soon as Malok landed upon a bare spot of soil, an unusual sensation came upon him. His hard scales seemed to tingle, and he felt as if something had grabbed hold of him. For a while longer than he would have liked, he stood there unmoving, breathing heavily with the surreal presence of death and despair clinging close to his heart, but, out of surprise and reflex more than will, he took a step back onto the grassier spots of the field and the unusual and terrible sensation quickly passed from him.

Little could the young Dragon know what did instinctively his spirit, that not seventeen years ago his own mother had bled and died upon this very same patch of earth. Malok dug his talons into the dry sandy ground, as the tremendous grip of emotion slowly left from his body.

"What is wrong with you?" Shar hissed, and though truly concerned for his friend's sudden fit, he anxiously began scanning the skies for Dragons.

A chill wind struck Malok in the back, accompanied by more scattering of the dust, abruptly startling him out of his stupor. Malok whirled about, nearly flinging Shar off his shoulders, but he was relieved to see that only an elderly white Dragon had silently landed upon the wall behind them.

His face was roughened from the experiences of a long productive life, and his skin was wrinkled and sagging in places. But, the sternness which Malok perceived in the old Dragon's countenance was only matched by the comically odd package which he carried about his neck, a satchel full of local wild herbs and flowers. The old one spoke first, for Malok was speechlessly in awe at his first encounter with his own kind.

"I take it, you are not from around here, for I have never seen your faces before. I am Serc, the chief Dragon physician of the Order. May I ask your names?" Said he.

Although Malok fluently spoke the common tongue, his Serpen accent was laid bare, particularly in the drawn out "s" sounds, as he recovered from the impact of seeing another Dragon for the first time and responded. "I am Malok, an orphan, raised by the great Serpen ambassador Ulam, alongside here my good friend Shar." Malok politely replied, bowing slightly, but in the unusual Serpen manner.

However well he hid his surprise, Serc was taken aback by both the dialect and mannerisms of this new Dragon acquaintance. Never had he expected in all his life to hear of such a thing as a Dragon raised by the Serpen, yet here was this youngster speaking with the peculiarities of their tongue, following their customs, and with a Serpen companion, no less.

"Are you surprised by this news?" Asked Shar, quickly and somewhat contemptuously upon noticing the astonishment that had quickly hidden behind Serc's blank expression, for he knew that they who lived within the realm of the Order were often prone to discriminate against his people. "Surely one as long lived as yourself can remember the gift of my friend's egg to the Serpen people by your lord Orthard."

"I neither recall nor can I believe any such thing, and yet, here you both stand." Serc replied, his tail confoundedly twitching to and fro as he stared at them, completely stunned by Shar's words.

The old doctor marveled at how or why an orphaned Dragon had come into Orthard's possession, only to be given to the Serpen, as if his people were such livestock, to be traded about like coin or wares. He could not fathom such an atrocity, and in perplexity, he dug deeply into his vast store of memories trying to recall any instance of how this could have happened. However, the young Dragon's smell was as foreign as his accent, and his countenance, being not of Serc's direct kindred, was unrecognizable to him. Besides which, no solid proofs materialized in wracking his brain for some such tale or the whisper thereof, at least none that could warrant as anything more than speculation, and Serc, at last catching himself amidst the awkward moment of stupefaction, resumed their conversation.

"Whatever your story, as a Dragon, you and your companion are both welcome here. I have no condescension towards your upbringing, however unusual, nor do I bear any hatred toward the Serpen. In the time of their betrayal, they were only deceived by the Dark One, as any people could have been. Even so, you have unwittingly chosen an evil hour to come here, amongst unfortunate occurrences, only to witness sorrowful days. I would explain further, but I must now hasten to the tower. Please, do accompany me." With that the old doctor motioned an invitation to the domed temple at the top of the Dragon's tower, out of the wind and cold morning air.

They three then lifted into the sky again and soared up to the heights of the tower. In but a few wing-beats, they were within the atrium of the large chapel, but Serc did not pause to converse here. He quickly laved his hands and face with water from the standing basins within this grand parlor and instructed the two foreigners to do the same, for to show reverence due this holy place and He for Whom it was built. The aged Dragon then led them up the small flight of stairs, up to the sanctuary, only halting to tell his guests a bit of the essential history of this august place, the importance of reverence within these walls, for the top floor of their tower was, indeed, a temple, made for the worshipers of Eloigal to gather within. Though the Dragons' name for The One True God was unfamiliar to the two outsiders, they gladly heeded Serc's instructions, for they too, as all Serpen, did worship the Eloigal.

They then continued on into the sanctuary, and as he entered therein, Malok, along with every other new visitor, was captivated by the many intricacies of the temple's architecture. The murals of famous actions of the Order upon the ceiling above particularly held his attention, to the point that he almost did not notice the other occupants of the room.

A large crowd of Dragons had gathered with their companions, strangely enough in this holiest of places, about a younger Human, who lay unconscious upon a small cot in the middle of the floor. Apparently, the man had been severely injured in his abdominal region, for this area was heavily bandaged. Even now, Serc replaced the older wrappings with fresh ones soaked in a healing poultice made from the flora that had been in his satchel.

There was also a red Dragon beside the Human, who at first seemed better off, but as Malok neared the scene he could see that terrible burns had been scorched all along his legs and backside. The whole room Malok could have mistaken for a hospital were it not for the elderly golden Dragon in the background, garbed with priestly vestments about his neck, lighting candles and incense while whispering prayers.

"My brothers, these two are visitors from the Serpen lands, Malok and Shar." Spake Serc to the multitude of other Paladins gathered thereabout, as they began to notice the strangers that had entered with him. "Treat them well. Honor them as our guests, for so they are."

Slowly, as Serc resumed busying himself with tending the still grievous wounds of the Human, members of the crowd came, one by one, to make acquaintance with Malok and Shar; all were friendly toward them, in spite of the two traveler's less than propitious Serpen origin, in spite of their own downcast countenance, in spite of the sad presence of the injured man and Dragon among them. All the while, Malok wondered why the man lay here in so holy a place, wounded to the point of fatality, all while the red, burnt legged Dragon sat in bereavement alongside him, with so large a crowd of Paladins gathered around them. Remembering the sore words of Serc, he thought they had surely interrupted the proceedings of a funeral, and finally could no longer help himself but to ask.

"What has happened here, to the Human upon the cot and to the Dragon who lies beside him." Malok inquired of an especially important looking elderly green Dragon, who had introduced himself as Galrag.

The aged general sighed, lowering his head with the pitch of his voice, as he gravely replied. "Last night, those two, Theros, the Dragon, and his companion Zurthaud, with a small group of comrades, brave warriors all, attempted to destroy our longstanding enemy the Dark One. They all fell to his foul blade. My son, my only son was among the slain, and only they returned alive. Though he has returned home, Zurthaud may not live through another night, for some dark power has taken hold of him and keeps his body from healing of a grievous wound. Serc is doing all he knows how, for to keep his flesh from simply rotting away, but all his medicines have proven useless. We may well be gathered here for a funeral, indeed."

Galrag did pause here for a moment; then remembering through his own spoken words that his son had been slain, he wept tears anew. Bitterness would have welled in his heart for Zurthaud's foolish company, but that it was now so broken that he could not bring himself to hate or speak any ill word toward them. "Oh, my dear son, if only you had listened to my words," Grieved the old Dragon, and others of the Order had then to comfort him and lead him away to rest, so great was his sorrow over the loss of his son, Galrath.

Malok and Shar became sorely disconcerted at this sight, but worse news was yet to cut the newcomer's ears and hearts, for as the Paladins did address them, and they two did inquire further into the depressive misery that permeated the heart of everyone here gathered, they heard full well the doom that had befallen these few true members of the Order.

"When Orthard heard wind of this failed attempt to destroy the Evil One, though he neither cares for the life of his son nor even believes that the Dark Lord still lives, he, in his thirst for power and hatred for all those who are not Human, used the incident as an excuse to further enthrall our people." Informed one Dragon.

"He brought false witness to the High Council: that we were responsible for the death of his son, completely neglecting the attempt to destroy the Dark One, that we had unnecessarily stirred up the folk of the

Shadow Lands, whom Orthard had the audacity to call 'peaceful', and, worst of all, that we had neither found any evidence of the Dark One's existence. We could offer no proof to the contrary, not even the survivors' testimony, as Zurthaud has not awoken since that dark night, and though his word would not be taken into consideration anyway, Theros' injuries are still too painful for him to be moved from where he lies." Spake another Human Paladin.

Many others told them the rumors of how Orthard planned to use the incident to enslave the Dragons, forcing them into harsh labor within the toxic depths of the sulfur mines, never again to see the light of the sun, all as punishment for their crimes of disobeying the will of the High Council and causing the death of Zurthaud.

It was then that Malok fully understood the words of Serc, from before, for not only had brave young Paladins died horrible deaths just last night, but also the faithful few of the Order here gathered were in danger of losing their freedom. Surely, the Dark One was plotting havoc for the world, even now working to end all good things. Through greeting the rest of those gathered he held back his tears, until he had been acquainted with everyone in the room, but as the last to welcome him finished their salutations, he could restrain his sorrow no longer and had to excuse himself, exiting back out into the vestibule.

Shar had noticed and did also accompany him without, and as Malok sat down upon the lowest of the stairs leading up to the sanctuary, he sat beside him, while the Dragon let forth his sobbing.

"What evil has befallen my kin?" Malok cried out through his tears.

"Malok, I do not know what to say." Shar began, trying to comfort his friend, even as he recalled that he had never been good at such things. "I wish I could say that your dream of finally reuniting with your people could have been realized, every bit as wonderful and happy as you had imagined, but there is sorrow here, as much as anywhere else in the world."

"I knew that there was conflict within the Order, but never had I imagined that such sadness and turmoil could exist where my people dwell. I would that I had never come here, to face such despair, but that is not true. I have always been wanting to come back here, to learn and know what I truly am. I just wish that I could do something to help, to ease their suffering." The young Dragon ranted through his tears.

"Who knows, but that you can?" Shar encouraged. "Perhaps, there is some purpose here for you, that it was by no coincidence your vision had brought you here just at this time; perhaps, you can help them."

"Surely, I am not that special." Malok argued, lifting his face to stare back at his friend.

Shar held his gaze, looking his friend directly in the eye. "Surely, you are! So says the Serpen King." He forcefully, if not teasingly, contended, even as he embraced his friend.

"The Serpen King?" Interrupted someone behind them.

Surprised, they two spun around from their spot on the steps, and saw that it was Serc who had eavesdropped upon them. The elder Dragon had apparently finished with his tending of Zurthaud's wound, and had come without for some fresh air and to check on the whereabouts of his two new acquaintances.

"I had no idea that we were so honored by the presence of such a venerable guest." Spake the Dragon doctor, as a sly smirk crept across his face. "But, then again, that was your intention."

"Yes, it was." Shar boldly replied. "I had hoped not to attract any undue attention during our stay here, especially that of the High Council or its dread lord, and I, as your guest, would that you honor my wish."

"The view of the Paladins toward your people has changed much during your own rule, lord Shar." Humbly replied Serc, though his uncanny smile did not dissipate. "Nevertheless, I completely understand the want for your identity to remain hidden from certain others, for seemingly, none can fathom the wickedness conspired in the minds of men. Who knows what scheme they would concoct to gain politically or monetarily, from kidnappings, or otherwise abusing your presence. Your secret is safely entrusted with me."

He then turned to address Malok, placing his large clawed hand upon the young Dragon's shoulder, for he could see that tears had flowed from his reddened eyes. "I hope the tragedies that have befallen us have not so severely upset you. Take heart, for we are not alone in this battle against the dark forces of our world. This temple was built as a testament to that fact, a monument to Eloigal's proven faithfulness toward us, and when times become so dark and drear as these, it is then that His power shines brighter, when goodness and righteousness blaze like the sun, to burn and scatter the shadows."

These words did comfort Malok most of all, for he had known them to be true, only in the moment of sorrow having forgotten them. Perhaps, he could be part of this bright shining of goodness to combat the evils his people now faced; perhaps, he truly was here in this place, at this time for a purpose. His usual calm, composed, and happier demeanor returned to Malok, as he thanked Serc for the timely well-spoken words.

"I must inquire, what has brought you to the Order's realm? Was it that you wished to return to the place of your birth and rejoin your kin?" Serc asked, as he too sat upon the steps beside them.

"We have come seeking a Bright Dragoness, which my companion had seen attacked by the dark powers in a vision." Explained Shar, being the quicker to answer.

"Well, I am sorry to say that there are no Dragonesses here, for the last two were destroyed by unspeakable evil almost sixteen years ago." Serc solemnly replied, and Malok hung his head low, weary from hearing such poor news.

He had been hoping that his quest could have ended, even today, having arrived at the best possible spot to find other Dragons, and his heart grew heavy again over the calamity that had befallen so once great a place.

Serc continued, attempting to lessen the blow of the ill news just mentioned.

"Nevertheless, the gift of visions is quite a remarkable trait; I am surprised that you have received it, seeing you were raised outside the Order with no formal training in magic." He commented regarding Malok. "Perhaps, it was one of these Dragonesses in the past hour of their demise which you saw; if you were to be properly educated, you may well be able to clarify that which you had seen."

But, Malok was certain of what he had seen. He needed no clarification, and with new resolve he arose and replied. "No, the Dragoness I saw was young, my own age, and she is yet alive, somewhere out in this world. If she is not here, then we cannot so tarry."

"But, you have only just arrived here from a long trek across the Great Wastes. Surely, you could spend a day's rest recuperating in our hospitality. I would be honored to have you as guests in my own apartment." Offered Serc.

Though sincere in his statement, another motive in this invitation was withheld from the two foreigners, for the elder Dragon could not help but to wonder at the peculiar origins of this extraordinary young Dragon. Too many questions remained, especially the matter of parentage, for Serc to simply allow them to leave so soon, and he was sure with but a day or two, further investigation would successfully disclose such inquiries.

However, Malok shook his head "no". Though the young male now had made peace with the plight of his kind and had calmed his heart, he could not forget his true mission, his reason for traveling so far in the first place. He could not abandon the Bright Dragoness, for the thought haunted him, that even now she could be in grave peril.

"We really must be going, before it grows too dark to travel." He explained motioning for Shar to join him as he strode toward the great, arched doors of the temple.

"Wait. The hour, indeed, grows late. Please, be my guests for tonight, and if tomorrow you shall leave, we could then, possibly, spare a Paladin or two to accompany and aid in your search." Offered the elder Dragon.

This second offer caused the pair to pause their leaving, for in Serpen culture, to then refuse a host's third invitation would have been a severe insult. They did wish not to be so bad of guests, and though Shar, through their constant adventuring, had become accustomed to periods of living naturally off the land, he then did give Malok such a garish look, so as to belie his want for the comforts of civilization, that the Dragon truly had to reconsider their host's offer.

Chapter 12

Though the incident with the Dark Hunters and the ensuing battle had frightened and upset Feldara, Anur, and the Rathnyalgr family, they had afterward managed to recover quite a lovely evening together. After they had laughed long and fully over Rathnyala's befuddlement, who apparently, had sat reading the large medical tome, completely obliviousness to the savage fighting that had gone on above her, unbothered by any of the Dark Hunters or the cacophony of her family's struggle with them, they finally could rejoice in their relative freedom from injury and overall safety. Aside from the ugly gash in Anur's arm, not a one of them had been hurt, save, thanks to Anur's indurate parentage, Feldara's pride, for though their attackers had been fierce enough and armed with Black-iron, all of the Dragons had, thankfully, managed to remain unscathed.

After Rathnyaling had bandaged up Anur's wound they, at last, all gathered around the low wooden table within the spacious dining hall, making sure to retrieve any goblets or platters that had been scattered about by the fighting, and enjoyed the meal that beforehand they had prepared. As the males had hunted a little before they had noticed and joined the battle at the gates of the city, the meat was scarce, but they managed well enough to thoroughly savor the remnants of their feast and the glad wholesomeness of each others' company.

It was then, after they had finished their jovial meal, that Rathnyala was able to reveal the formula for the cure that would dissolve the Worg venom within Feldara's body.

It was a relatively simple cure, however odd and distasteful, and all the ingredients that they needed were already within the doctor's medical supplies: a sprig of pine from the dark forests of the Shadow Lands, a cluster of berries from the Northerly Wolfsbane plant, a single Worg's hair, and a good driblet of Dragon spittle.

With Rathnyaling eagerly watching the process and taking notes, his sister added a measure of fresh, clear water to the blend while compounding it together with a mortar and pestle, and then heated it all in a copper pot over a fire. By the time the substance had been melded together, cooked, and then cooled, it smelled so awful that none of the Dragons could bear to be near it, save for the two fascinated physicians and Feldara, who could not hope to escape out the door of the apartment as had everyone else. Anur did also stay, saying he did not mind the smell and would remain by Feldara's side until she had drunk it and was well again, yet he did gag and cough often.

At last, the foul concoction was ready for consumption, and Rathnyala filled a measured goblet to the brim for Feldara's dose. Wrinkling her nose, nearly retching from the odoriferous solution, Feldara hoisted the cup to her lips and, for to get it over with, quickly slurped down the disgusting, slimy liquid. The taste was so bad that she nearly vomited back up the foul concoction, but she calmed herself and, for her own good health, forced her stomach to retain its contents.

Almost immediately, she began to feel better. Her muscles began to relax and loosen, no longer aching with the foul venom's effect, and her blood quickly pumped away the awful burning sensation that had plagued her veins. A new glow flooded her cheeks, like the golden reflection of sunlight, and her heart was lightened.

That night was Feldara's best sleep ever, though she had hardly been coaxed to bed at all, staying up to terribly late hours with the rejuvenating properties of the cure, and her hosts graciously accommodated her heightened vitality by talking and playing quiet games until, at last, they were too tired to stay awake any longer.

When she arose with the dawn the next morning, there was no more pain in the slightest of her movements; not a trace of the evil poison remained in her. So, she decided to go hunting, even though the sun had just crested the horizon, and the Rathnyaling's still slumbered, tired from last night's antics and their unusually late bedtime. Off of the enormous, comfortable cushion of a Dragon-sized bed she clambered, careful not to wake the daughters of Rathnyaling, whose room she had shared, and out into the halls she trotted. Though she tried to be very sneaky, so as not to wake her kind hosts, in her excitement and haste, she could not keep her claws from clacking against the cool, smooth stone floor, but in the end, clumsily boisterous as she had been, she did make it to the entrance hallway without disturbing any of the other Dragons.

She had long relished this moment, to finally be free again from the shackles of the dirt, to soar on high, as she used to, as she longed, as any Dragon lived to be. Not that she loathed the earth, for Feldara did enjoy walking about upon the ground, and there must always be a place to land and rest when one's desiring of flight has worn them weary through constant wind-fighting and wing-flapping. Still, nothing else could compare to the purest freedom of flight.

"Free again" She thought to herself, beaming a smile that none but a Dragon could bear, toothy, though kind and joyful, and enormously wide.

Yet, a belligerently unwanted voice casually graced her hearing. "Where do you think you are going?" Anur questioned from where he had been lurking, unseen, in the doorway.

"I am going hunting." Feldara defiantly whipped back at him, surprised at his unexpected appearance and displeased with his seeming condescension.

But, Anur's intentions had not been to ruthlessly corral the young Dragoness with chains of tyrannical parentage, and he could not help his voice seeming so cold, it being his personality, so cracked by his injured past.

"Not without me." He stated, as blithely as he could, for he too was happy for Feldara's wellness.

As bad as the Worg venom had been for Feldara, Anur also had felt the pain, like a knife, deep in his own heart, for in his paternal love, he had groaned within as she had without. He would have done anything to take that pain from her, but now that she was well again, he too could rejoice.

As surprised as she had been about Anur's inferred derision, Feldara was even more astonished by his willingness to join in her wild outing, and she just stared at him for a moment, mouth agape.

"So, are we going hunting, or not?" He questioned again, rubbing his arm that had been injured the night before.

Though he had been cut deeply, Anur had healed quickly, abnormally so for most creatures, and now only the stitching, that which itched terribly, still marked the spot where he had been cut and held his skin tightly together.

The smile quickly returned to Feldara's face, as she happily replied, for she had forgotten that Anur could, indeed, enjoy himself and be mirthful, even a fun person, at times. As an adolescent, she had forgotten how he involved himself in whatever she loved, forcing himself on occasion, to take sincere interest in her passions and pastimes.

Elatedly, she helped him mount upon her shoulders, almost throwing him over like a sack of potatoes, as she dashed out the doorway of the Rathnyalgrs' apartment.

She misjudged the length of the balcony, and fell over the edge thereof, quickly plummeting down the cliff face. But, she did not care at all, for the fall only gave her flight some excellent starting momentum. Laughing with pure joy, she snapped her wings open just before they both hit the ground. The wind caught them, and filling her silken appendages with lifting air, they careened back up into the sky.

At length, she, still giggling uncontrollably, came to a more peaceful glide, at an altitude about double the height of the very tall Aelven tree-houses, and as the wind was no longer rushing past her ears and the pure joy of speed and the freedom of the sky no longer pounded so severely in her heart, she finally realized that Anur was clutching tightly, white-fistedly, to her neck spines.

She apologized to him, seeing his distress, but he was silent for a good moment longer before replying.

"Let us not do that again today." He suggested, his voice audibly near trembling, his hands just barely shaking.

"All right, 'grandfather'" She teased, "I should want to keep my back dry, anyway."

He crossed his arms over his chest, pouting, and grumpily replied. "I was on Yuronon's back yesterday, and we were in a battle. Never, through all the thick fighting, did he do any maneuver like that ridiculous stunt."

Before, Feldara would have obeyed his suggestion, had Anur not called her fabulous dive 'ridiculous'. Now she was determined to have a little more fun with her mentor, since he was, for the very first time ever, completely at her mercy.

"Hold onto your dinky hat, old man, because my flying is not ridiculous!" She shouted at him, and even as he started to protest, she shifted her weight to the left and tilted her wings ever so slightly.

Plummeting, turning, she fell into a truly fearsome barrel roll, through which she had to curl her wings tighter to her body, for to keep them from twining together and breaking. Still diving, she did a little loop, curling over her own body so fast it nearly gave her a headache, but she cut her descent just short of the tops of the trees this time, so that she could jet along, just above their crests, like the waves of the sea. With a flap of her wings and another little roll, she was flying upside down, with Anur's head just above the same treetops.

Anur had been screaming for quite some time now, nearly non-stop since the bottom of her dive, and had been clinging onto her for dear life itself, so she decided to show a little mercy. She ended the thrill ride just as soon as it had begun, with another quick flap of her powerful wings, and now they were soaring along, right side up, quite peacefully again.

"How was that for 'ridiculous'." She playfully mocked, as she calmly lofted back up to her previous altitude.

But, Anur did not answer immediately, and Feldara worried that she had taken her jesting a little too far. She had only meant to have some fun with him, to show him how well she could fly. He had never been endangered by the whole ordeal, for Feldara had kept close watch for his presence upon her back. Never would she have let him fall. Yet, she began to fret that he might never again wish to ride upon her back and revel in the fresh air and the wind's freedom with her, and that would have been far worse to her than any scolding.

He allayed her dread, and his own, with some laughter, which slowly and softly, at first, pierced the silence between them, but then grew, as his adrenaline rush faded with the anxiety from such rapid sky-diving, to a full, loud chuckle. The sound caught Feldara by surprise at the first, for though Anur was mostly peaceful and even happy at times, hardly had she ever heard him laugh, even such as he did now. Laughter was just not a great part of his character, but soon, hearing his jollity, she could not keep her own smile hidden. They shared loudly their joy together for a while, a rare experience for them both, and a great relief from their current standoffish position toward each other.

Anur had, indeed, not despised her crazy antics, as he had let on with his words, but had only been scared by them. He could not ever hate flying, for that was one of Feldara's loves. Though he could not fully enjoy these delirious feats as could a Dragon, he would always love his charge enough to endure, and truly enjoy, their shared activities.

They continued their outing in peace, at last, finding their actual goal, a large herd of deer, perfect for a Dragon's breakfast.

Unlike the ones Feldara and Anur had met on their way to Lotheliel, these deer, being in close proximity to an entire clan of carnivorous Dragons, did fear them and bolted as soon as they detected a change in the wind's pressure or perchance heard the beat of Feldara's wings. However, the deer, skittish as they were, could not outrun Feldara, and could only hide in the thickest of forest cover. Luckily for the deer, such thickets were plentiful in the woodlands of the Aelven realm, and Feldara had to make a few attempts before she could even get close to them.

Eventually, she did manage to outsmart the excitable beasts, figuring out that she could approach the herd from the direction that the densest brush was located and scatter them in the opposite direction thereof, toward clearer meadows, and at length she caught one. Having gathered her meal, they landed in a grassy, little glade upon a small, rounded hill, and once upon the ground again, Anur hopped off and walking to the base of the small hill, where a brook crookedly ran through the forest.

While Feldara sated her hunger with the warm, delicious flesh of the deer, he refreshed himself with the cool water of the stream, fully ridding himself of his earlier terror born of winged frolicking; only after she had finished all that she wanted of the deer, did Anur return to sit with her and partake of some leftover bits of meat, which he roasted over a small, hastily constructed, fire.

"I did enjoy flying with you today, however much you did scare me at the first." He said, at length, breaking the silence that they had shared with their meal. "Yet, I do have another reason for coming along with you this morning."

"You mean to say that you did not just wish to enjoy my company?" Feldara playfully questioned, yet did she sigh within herself, thinking that Anur must always have some alternate motive in spending time with her.

However, Anur's motives were double and he truly had wished to spend this morning with Feldara. He only also had something truly urgent to discuss with her, and in contrast to Feldara's inner musings, it had neither detracted nor added to his desire to be with her.

"Those dark men that we fought off yesterday, did they say who they were?" He questioned. "Were they after you?"

"They called themselves the Dark Hunters, the chief servants of the Kragon, whoever that is. They were looking for a 'Bright One'." She replied, not really dwelling on the matter, not considering how important that information was. Slowly, she began to realize that her incident in the Shadow Lands must be connected to these men, to the battle at the gates of Lotheliel. "Were they speaking of me? Am I this 'Bright One'?" She asked, already knowing the answer.

Anur silently mused over the recent happenings, plotting possible courses of action, before he responded, for if anyone knew the direness of the situation they found themselves in, it was him.

"The Kragon is the true name of the Dark One, as you might recall from your studies of the ancient Dragon language. We are never to speak that name aloud, at least, not in polite company. It is a curse and a foul word, not worthy of a good Dragon's tongue. If these Dark Hunters are his servants, and they do want you, then we are truly worse off than I had thought before. I reasoned, for certain, a Worg pack or a Troll or Goblin hunting party would follow our trail to our island home, and we would be safe there no longer, but when we arrived in this fair land, I thought that, possibly, we could now be beyond the reach of whatever monsters had been pursuing us. I thought that the dark folk would not dare enter the Aelven kingdom, but I now know that we cannot stay here, not a day longer."

"But, Anur!" Feldara loudly protested, for she had just gotten to know the only other Dragons she had ever met, the kind Rathnyalgrs. She could not bear to think of leaving such sincerely good folk, having only spent such a short time with them.

However, Anur sternly interrupted her contentions before she had even fully said those two words. "Be silent! If the Dark One really has found interest in you, then nothing will stop him. He will not cease his attempts to reach you, even if he has to annihilate everything that stands in between. He will slaughter every Aelv, burn their forests to ash; not even the Rathnyalgrs could stand against his full might. He would kill them all just to get to you, and I would not see that happen. We cannot endanger these kind people by our presence; even though, as we saw yesterday, in their goodness they would willingly die on your behalf, I could never ask them do so. We must flee to the stronghold of the Order, to Doraegonoran, and maybe, even beyond there. We might never cease our running, all our lives long."

Feldara pouted, but truly she was despondent. She could not imagine her entire day, let alone her entire life on the run. "What kind of life is that?" Dejectedly, she thought aloud.

Anur stroked her large hand, as they sat on the grass together. "I know not, but I will do everything in my power to keep that abomination away from you. I will protect your life with my own."

She affectionately laid her head on his shoulder, for she knew that Anur was more than trustworthy. He did truly love her, and if need be, he would die for her. He was as close to a father as he could be, being without scales. They just sat there holding each other, silently dreading the future together, until Anur let go her hand and rose to leave.

"Let us go. We should be polite to our hosts and say our farewells before we leave the Aelven lands." He said.

She arose also, with a great heavy sigh, for the morning that had started out so well had turned dark and gray. Anur then leaped upon her shoulders and they took off again into the sky, but not before he had a good, long look at the same terrible, dark thunderheads, that which had followed them from their home, out of the Shadow Lands, rising ominously in the South.

<><><><><>

"You are leaving, so soon?" Rathnyaling asked of Anur and Feldara.

He had been wondering where the two of them had gone so early in the morning, but once they had returned from hunting their own breakfast, he and his family had been expecting them to stay in their company, at least until noontide, and afterward not really leaving the city. Most visitors would stay a month or two in Lotheliel, exploring all the finer points of the luminous metropolis, such as the crafters' and artisan's quarter, the plethora of eateries, the multitude of theaters, shows, and circuses, not to mention the nearing yearly visit of the Aelven Queen, which was to be accompanied by a great feasting holiday. In truth, his own feelings were rather hurt that such beloved guests would depart from his own house, and after spending so little time there.

However, Anur did offer his reasoning behind it, while Feldara tried to go along with her mentor without disrespectfully retaliating or tearing up. The Rathnyalgrs were the only other Dragons she had ever met, and she had so wished to learn more from them, to know them better. They had already taught her so much about who Dragons were, how they acted, especially how they accepted complete strangers into their own home simply because there was need; they had not even thought of turning her over to those Dark Hunters, even when it meant their own personal safety was at stake.

It was this honor, this pride and righteousness of character that caused Rathnyaling to now reject Anur's plans for a quick departure.

"If she is, indeed, in so much danger, would it not be best for Feldara to stay within my home, under my protection?" Rathnyaling proposed, hopeful that Anur would reconsider.

"Your home would not be safe enough. As we have seen, the enemy is fully capable of sneaking past all the Aelven defenses. Even with their forces on high alert, as they now are, it would only be a matter of time before the Dark Hunters, or worse, entered your house again, and I dread to think what should happen if they caught us unaware or, more simply, outnumbered and overpowered us, all of us. You put your own family in danger by giving us refuge. It is out of gratitude, not discontent, for your great, unwarranted friendship that we must bid you so quick a farewell." Anur replied, unshakeable in his conviction, sincere in his reasoning.

Rathnyaling did have to consider Anur's counsel then, for his words were well spoken and, as much as the doctor hated to admit, were surely true.

"Very well, I know that you are right in your deductions, though I wish that such evils had not to be feared by Man and Dragon. I shall accompany you back to your apartment, for to retrieve anything you had left there, and, from there, shall bless your journey." Said he, sadly relenting to the unavoidable course of action.

Then, the whole family of the Rathnyalgrs, who had gathered about to hear what should happen, did one by one wish them safe travels. All the females' eyes were wet and some of the young males' too, but not one of them bawled so much as Yuronon, for though he was a massive Dragon, when not in the heat of battle, he was a very gentle soul. They embraced both Anur and Feldara and kissed them on the foreheads and spoke silent and open prayers for their health and well-being, until, having said goodbye to all of them, at least thrice, Anur mounted Feldara's shoulders and they slowly exited the Rathnyalgrs' apartment, taking off into the sky with Rathnyaling and, surprisingly, one of his sons, Calidon, following.

It was but a short trip across the city on Dragon's wings, for what had taken the better part of yesterday for Feldara to travel on foot with her body tainted by the painful Worg venom, was only a couple minutes' flight. Anur then had to direct her course, for to land at the balcony of the little inn at the city gates that had accommodated them the night before, as she, having only seen the city from the ground, could not recognize many of the locations from above. They quickly landed upon the small balcony, with hardly room to spare for three Dragons, and Anur, hastening within their lodging, began rummaging through their belongings, seeking only what they would need.

Feldara, thinking herself only obstructive to Anur's rapid packing, sought to inquire why Calidon was also accompanying them.

"My son has had for many years now a great passion to join the Order, to become a Paladin. I had not thought of it at the first, but he was quick to remind me that, since you are also going that way and I have not yet found the time to make the journey, he would be an excellent addition to your party. He is an expert hunter and bears a little of what medical knowledge I have taught him and his siblings, though he surely has no love for medicine, nor is in any way inclined toward doctoring. I would that you take him with you, if for nothing else, than to repay the kindness that I have shown you." Rathnyaling explained, all while the young Calidon did his best to make himself seem more worthy of the adventure and their company.

Though Feldara was not so inclined, as yet, to think on such things, for she had only just met any Dragons, let alone youths like her, she did consider Calidon to be quite handsome, strong, and large for his age, and did express that he would make a great candidate for to join their expedition.

Anur, after returning from selling the rough potato cart and some other unnecessary items to the innkeeper, to pay for their night's stay, had much more to be convinced of that prospect.

"I am very concerned for his safety, as I shall have enough of a time seeing to Feldara's wellness, much less having to keep an eye on another Dragon. Not that he is a poor son, or that I suspect he will be trouble, but I do not wish any harm to come upon him because of us." Anur reasonably objected.

"I can take care of myself." Simultaneously protested both Calidon and Feldara, bringing Rathnyaling much amusement.

"He is wanting to be a Paladin; so, let this be his first assignment, to escort you through the wilderness. I have great faith in my son, for he is a Dragon, made of stronger flesh than Humans. He shall surely be a great aid to your quest, and as he so bluntly stated, he will be well capable of fending for himself in the wilds. Though as a father, I can only worry for my son's well-being, if you three were to watch each others' backs, I doubt that there should be much danger that you could not overcome." Rathnyaling gently contended, trying to subdue his own lingering reservations, so that his child's hopes of joining the Paladins could, at last, be fulfilled.

At last, Anur did reluctantly yield, much to the open delight of Calidon, who gave a shout of joy, and the inner happiness of Feldara, who did want the companionship of other Dragons, much more specifically the company of this comely young male. They then did bid their farewells to Rathnyaling, and Anur did try to pay him for the kindness that had been shown him and Feldara, even offering coin from the sale of their excess gear. But, the kind doctor would have none of that.

"My hospitality I freely extended, and it was my sister who produced your medical treatment. I will accept no payment for such things, for you two are my friends. You are always welcome in my home and in Lotheliel." Rathnyaling gently refused, a generous smile beaming across his face.

They, now three, then did lift off again from the small balcony of that gate-side inn, and waving goodbye to the gracious and compassionate Rathnyaling and letting their eyes drink in, one last time, the beauty of the wondrous city of Lotheliel, they departed to the East and headed straight for the Citadel of the Order, the realm of the Humans and the Paladins, and the city of Doraegonoran.

Chapter 13

After he had fed them a good meal of tasty, local game: deer and a few mountain goats, Serc had entertained his two guests, Malok and Shar, with tales of the great deeds of the heroes of old, those mighty Paladins whose legends had far outlived them. From the renowned Rathnyalgr, who had slain the Dark One nearly a century ago, to the fabled first Paladins, a Human whose name had long been forgotten and his companion Aldaru, a pure white Dragoness whose blindingly magnificent beauty was rumored to be the only weapon she ever wielded, Serc regaled the two foreigners until the very late hours of the night. Only when it began to near midnight's hour did he finally end his story telling.

"I must now bid you good night, before I become too tired to rise at a decent hour tomorrow." The old Dragon had yawned.

And at that, he had proceeded to show Malok and Shar a spare room within the surprisingly spacious apartment, which had easily accommodated all three of them in its main hall. Serc had laid out a couple of Dragon-sized bedrolls for them there, with even a few pillows, and then had shuffled off to his own sleeping quarters.

It was upon these Malok now lay, incapable of sleep, and it was not necessarily due to the elder Dragon's profusely deafening snore, which seemed to plow through the solid stone walls as if they were thin paper. Nor was it due to anything else without his own body, for Shar was now dozing peacefully, having managed to muffle Serc's clamorous breathing enough by burying his head under the enormous Dragon-sized pillows.

What now drove rest far from his mind was, rather, all those legends of greatness to which he had listened; how every time when the hero had a choice between good and evil, they chose good to unfathomably fortunate consequence. One, maybe two, well-timed or righteous decisions had changed the course of their lives and benefited future generations long after their souls had left from Threa. There Malok lay wondering if he too could aspire to such honor, such valor, for he wanted to do what was right, to help his fellow beings along their way through this world. So then, he pondered if he should stay here within these walls, where surely there was work to be done, needs that required meeting, wounds to heal, and wrongs to right.

Every time he thought he had decided to stay with the Paladins, the image of that Bright Dragoness filled his mind's eye, and he could not help but to yearn within his soul for her. He had for the longest time dreamed of her, as far back into his youth as he could remember, had almost bonded with her on some level, as if he knew her like a close friend. Could he truly abandon her now that she was in danger, or was she even of reality, rather than a figment of his imagination?

However, even the quickest mind in the constant strain of worry must needs fall prey to the unstoppable predator sleep, and so Malok eventually drifted into an anxiously uneasy state of being, that which lies between the realms of consciousness and deep dreaming. Once there, the world around him began to shimmer and writhe, as it had done before in his recurring nightmares, and Malok grew ever more restless and disturbed, fearful that he should once again enter into one of his customary visions.

Yet, as he lay there quietly, still very aware of Shar sleeping beside him and Serc, with his incessant nasal drone ringing throughout the background, he began to realize that the horrors which usually plagued him were not appearing, and might even pass him by on this night.

He almost shouted in hesitantly restrained joy, but that he wished not to disturb the others' rest. Instead Malok decided to rise from his sleep and walk about a little, for to soothe his excited state. When he did so, he felt a strange sensation course throughout his body, as if he were a twine or rope being unbraided, and the memory of a noise, that of a muffled tearing sound, seemed to echo at the corner of imagination and reality. As he turned about to see what he had broken, Malok could find nothing, except that out of the corner of his eye he caught a glimpse of another Dragon's black, clawed hand and arm.

The sight surprised Malok for he did not remember going to bed with another Dragon beside him, and he sprang backward from the spot he was standing. He promptly spun about to face the unexpected guest, but as he slipped quite easily through the normally solid stone wall of the apartment, which while spacious, could hardly accommodate young Dragons leaping about within, he seemed to think that he recognized the other Dragon from somewhere. Hardly noticing the break in reality he had accomplished by seamlessly passing through the wall's structure, as if he were a ghost, Malok stepped out of the wall as easily as he had phased into it, and he attempted to identify the form of the young intruder.

The poor young Dragon was a little lean for a male his age, midnight black from head to toe for coloration, and was sleeping rather fitfully, gritting his jaw and furrowing his crested brow with much restless dreaming. Malok slowly reached for the other Dragon's hand, for to gently wake him from this disturbed rest, but he then recognized at whom he was staring.

His hand slowly fell back to the floor and his mouth hung agape in shock, for he now realized that it was himself upon which he gazed.

The perplexity of this insane disruption of reality caused Malok's head to spin, a nauseating dizziness, for it was quite unlike staring at his own reflection, which would be mirrored in reverse of all his features. This out of body experience was unnatural and sickening in every way, and he had to step back and avert his gaze to keep from becoming ill.

As he did so, Malok stepped a little too far and again passed through the wall of Serc's apartment, yet this time did he take notice of this feat and did marvel that he could do something so apparitional. Slowly, he began to come to the conclusion that he was not half-asleep, as he had previously assumed, but instead, truly had been caught up within another of his night terrors. However, he also realized that, on this occasion, he was able to exercise some control over the ongoings of this dream, being his freedom of movement and thinking remained intact. Normally, he could not restrain himself, usually being forced along through some foretelling specter, and would arrive at a destination or sight not of his own choosing. Marveling at this propitious change in power, he wondered if, perhaps, he could use this new ability to his advantage.

Immediately, Malok thought of Zurthaud and his strange illness; perhaps, while in this dream-like state, he could examine the Human and find some missed clue, only now revealed in the apparitional world, to healing Zurthaud's grievous wound. Now that he had his courage gathered and fearful anxiousness allayed, Malok walked, or rather floated, over to the entrance of Serc's apartment and, spreading wide his wings, though doubting the need to do so, flew back up to the domed top of the Dragon's tower.

As he neared the large arched doorways of the temple, Malok began to notice an obvious difference in how the structure now appeared as compared to when he had viewed it while awake. The inner walls seemed to glow with a warm golden light, like that of a glorious summer's evening, and as he landed upon one of the attached balconies, a great calm flooded into all of his senses. The cheerful light and peaceful sensation only grew in strength as he passed on through the outer court and up the small flight of steps into the sanctuary, so that he soon was penetrated and enraptured by delightful serenity.

But, the light did not emanate from the room's center and the feelings of comfort slowly, reluctantly dissipated, as Malok looked upon the prone form of Zurthaud lying beside his companion Theros. The place where they lay in the middle of the room was eerily devoid of the golden aura that covered all other places within the temple, and instead a thick misty shroud of darkness spewed forth from the wound in Zurthaud's chest, spilling out onto the floor and rising like morning fog, densely covering them both in its blackness.

It seemed to Malok as the very manifestation, metaphysical though it was, of Zurthaud's malady, that which was the source of the pestilence which slowly drained away the Human's life.

Mystified, the young Dragon could not tear his eyes from the disgusting seep of the liquid darkness, and his drifting steps only brought him closer to it, until the wound from which it frothed was right before his nose. Closer still was Malok drawn unto it by some will other than his own, pulled into it, below the surface of Zurthaud's skin, deep into the oozing black of the world beyond the wound. He had to shut his eyes for the twisted horror of it, dropping through the corpse-like body of the Human, and he did not open them again until, instead of the sickly wet limpness of the wound portal, the cold flat expanse of a stone floor was felt beneath his feet.

To what he then opened his eyes was no better than that foul, otherworldly experience from which he had come, for as he looked about, Malok found this whole new place stark and drear, stinking of death and decay, and filled with an empty, groaning spirit, seeming exactly opposite in every way from the joyful temple wherein he was only moments before.

Defying logic and physics, from a comparatively smaller basin of smoking water, so known by the sloshing about of the fluid and vapor, Malok had spewed forth and out therefrom to flop upon the cold stone floor of a large round room, bare of all else other than the standing basin of dark liquid from which he still flowed, his tail being the last of what slurped out from the nether orifice, and a singular arched open doorway. His heart pounding in his chest, a horribly loud drumbeat for so dark and dreary a place, Malok slowly arose from the floor and, scanning about every way for enemies, cautiously proceeded without the room.

Before him without the basin's room, was a dimly lit hallway with four other such rooms as that from which he just exited, two on either side, and as quick glimpses within these offered no kind viewing, he entered not within them and only passed on down the hallway to its end, at which was another open doorway leading to some stairs.

Here, Malok knew not whether to ascend or descend other than that, to a Dragon, the higher ground is always more desirable, and so he did ascend, even a small flight unto another entryway, which did have a door, but it was rather swung open and not shut before him.

Timidly peeking out from the stairwell, Malok sought to survey this room without being spotted by anyone yet within. From where the Dragon stood, eyes barely poking above the last of the stairs and the floor, as a crocodile breaching only its head above water, he could see that he was on the lower of two levels in a great round chamber, levels which were connected by a set of great rounded staircases. Betwixt these stairs, in the expanse from the floor of one level to the floor of the next, was the maw of a great stygian hollow, as black within its deep recess as a moonless night.

As Malok took in the bleak sight, a lone figure on the upper level eventually caught his attention; it was some sort of grand statue, an armored giant seated upon a black throne. Bewildered by this strange ornament's presence, Malok flitted up one of the balustraded stairs to get a closer look, and only once he reached the top and was nigh upon it did he really recognize its form. It was the dreaded Shadow Lord himself, sitting stoically upon his vile ruler's seat.

If Malok were not so weightless in this dream-world, he surely would now have tumbled all the way down the same stairs he had ascended, for he jumped backward in shock and terror of seeing his nightmares' culminations before him again. As weight and mass and gravity were not so powerful in this phantom dream-state, he only came to a gentle landing, though on his backside, upon the top few steps.

Gasping for breath, he lay there upon the stair, all the while anticipating the ominous tyrant to rise and strike him dead with a single blow, yet by and by, as his heart rate slowly decreased from panic, Malok began to realize, by hearing of the heavy metallic pinging of labored breathing from behind the Dark One's savage helm, that the enemy of life itself was unashamedly sleeping.

Not wishing to waste such a grand opportunity, Malok quickly arose, casting aside the instinctual fear that all living creatures had toward this wicked foe, and hurriedly, he began looking about the large chamber for any sign of a connection or cause of Zurthaud's illness. Eventually, as he frantically searched, he found another ghastly seepage of the same umbrous cloud as that which flowed from Zurthaud's mortal injury. This time it poured forth from the tip of an enormous bastard sword, which Malok surmised to be the very same weapon used to inflict the devastating wound, that which now sapped Zurthaud's life from him.

He would now have hastily grabbed for this instrument of evil, but for that it sat quite comfortably on the Shadow Lord's lap, as if he were daring anyone to take it from him. He would have left it there, but that Malok knew this evil sword was somehow the key to the Human's healing. Only then did he resolve to take it, if only without waking its fiendish owner, for if the Dark One were to be roused, he might, indeed, espy Malok, even through the curtain separating dreams from reality. For, if Malok could now see the world about him, though augmented from what was normal, and if the dread lord could sense Malok in the same manner, what horrors then would he inflict upon the unfortunate intruder?

With caution, much fear, and uneasy trembling, the young Dragon sought to retrieve the blade, and moving ever so slowly, he began to subtly slide the great sword from its owner's grasp.

With a snort, the Shadow Lord suddenly moved, and Malok froze in his place, unable to do anything else for fright and the unexpectedness of this spurt of wakefulness.

Though, it soon became clear, as the Dark One's helmeted head lolled unconsciously to an awkward angle, that he was still soundly asleep, Malok found it even more difficult now to concentrate on this meticulous removal of the large blade, for the horned helmeted head of the Dark Lord had, indeed, drooped to where the blackness of the faceless visor now stared directly at the poor Dragon, as though the evil Shadow Lord were even now watching him steal his precious hero slayer.

After what seemed a year and a half of carefully sliding the great sword from the Shadow Lord's lap, Malok finally had removed the fell blade from its wielder's grasp and straightaway set about studying the source of the oozing darkness which so tied this sword to Zurthaud's affliction. However, try as he might, with all manner of spells that the young Dragon knew- and these were few, with all measure of physical force that he inflicted- even beating the blade against the hard stone floor, Malok could neither break the sword nor destroy the vile life-leeching mist, and he spent ever more time in his growing number of attempts to do so.

"You should know, that the sword only responds to its master." Eventually breathed a deep, grating voice, from behind Malok.

The young Dragon whirled about, tentatively seeking the source of the voice, and found that somehow, being lost in his efforts to unmake the wicked blade and its vile magics, he had managed to turn his back upon the dozing warlord. Malok shuddered to think that he had been unknowingly observed by the Shadow Lord, and even more did he fear that it was the Dark One's voice which had just now spoken to him.

Yet, as Malok nervously looked on, the Shadow Lord did not move, nor offered any sort of evidence that he was anything other than soundly sleeping, for still did heavy, restful breathing emanate from the black void where should have been the face of the Dark One.

However, was it just his imagining or had the cruelly horned helmet of the Shadow Lord been facing another direction than it was now, for Malok had thought that the Dark One's head had been lolled to the side facing where he had before stood when trying pluck the sword from his grip. Now after Malok had moved about, in his wrestling with the wickedly enchanted blade, it was again staring straight into Malok's soul.

"Oh, I am not awake, if that is what you are wondering." Rang the deep voice again, and this time Malok felt even more certain that it had come forth from the direction the Shadow Lord was seated. *"Yes, I am speaking to you."* Continued the voice, and now Malok was positive that it was the evil one hailing him, and all the more he frantically continued his attempts to break the dark magic of the bastard sword, knowing that his time would now be short upon the earth.

"Why do you waste your breath taunting me, when so easily you could strike me down?" Asked Malok, even as he began hurriedly backing down the staircase, dragging the sword along with him.

The dark lord laughed before responding. *"I am asleep, young Dragon, dreaming even, and like most other beings, yet unlike your most peculiar ability, while I am sleeping I do not have full control of my body. I can only now see you through my dreaming, traipsing about as if you were the master of the dream-world. I should like to have such a useful skill. I could give the word 'nightmare' a novel definition, but instead, I can only watch you, watch you taking what is not yours, seeking to break what is not yours. You ought to be* _ashamed of yourself, little thief."_ Mocked the Shadow Lord, though his form did not move, and his restful breathing continued on, unhindered by the words he spoke, as they were unnaturally proceeding forth, not from his mouth.

Having found himself to be in no immediate danger from the Dark One, Malok continued his struggling with the enchantments about the fell blade when he had reached the bottom of the stairs, but there seemed to be no breaking the dreadful spell, either with force of mind or body. The Dragon was about to give up hope of ever succeeding with destroying the sword and the curse it had placed upon Zurthaud, when the dream-world around him began to quake and buckle.

"Ah, it seems you are losing control of your dream powers. Perhaps, you are waking, with the sun rising above the horizon where you are resting, shining its golden rays into your little eyes and ending all hope of ever healing poor Zurthaud. Oh, yes, I know what you have been about, and I swear to you that when I wake, and that not being long now, for I rouse even as we speak, I shall hide my sword from you. I shall conceal it so well that you shall never again find it, at least, not before Zurthaud has died. Maybe, after that I shall then also use it to kill you." Ridiculed the Shadow Lord, even as a Black-iron clawed finger of his gauntleted hands began to twitch.

Panicking with this dire news, Malok paced about upon the bottom level of the great room, trying with all his might and mind to think of a way he could break the grim spell, but even as he felt his true body waking from dreaming, he could find no solution.

At last, the Dark One arose from his slumber, and he leaped down from the second level. Quickly, he crossed the expanse of the room and was almost upon the trembling Malok, who still clung protectively onto the sword with both hands. Suddenly, a flash of bright light flooded into the Dragon's eyes, and he reflexively closed them, gasping in surprise and terror. Before Malok knew what was happening, he felt himself lying upon the cold stone floor.

A large hand grabbed him by the shoulder and began shaking him, and Malok hissed and roared his defiance.

"You shall not take it from me!" He shouted, eyes still closed for fear of his terrible attacker.

"Wake up, you fool of a Dragon!" Shouted back another voice, but it was not the deathly chill, deep voice of the Dark One. It was lighter, warmer, almost jovial by comparison.

Malok opened his eyes, at last, bewildered by the sudden change in speakers, and he saw the face of another Dragon staring concernedly down at him. Slowly, Malok began to recognize it as the visage of the injured Theros.

"Where am I? What am I doing here?" Malok asked, still shouting at the top of his lungs.

Theros winced with the volume at which he was addressed, and as the echoes of the shouting reverberated upon the walls about them, he annoyedly replied. "You are in the temple atop the tower in the Dragon's Quarter of the Order's Citadel, in Doraegonoran, most specifically. What you are doing here at such an hour, with that... thing in your arms, I know not, but I do know this, if you keep shouting and screaming like you have been, I will decidedly throw you out and hope you open your wings before you arrive at the bottom floor."

At first Malok was confused, not so much by Theros' thinly disguised threat, but as to what, indeed, was he holding in his arms. He could feel it now, when before he had been distracted by the ongoings of his dream and his subsequent, abrupt awakening. It was long, cold, hard, and sharp, made of metal, to which he held fast, cradling it tightly in both arms and against his chest. Astounded, he looked down to see that which he held was a sword identical to the one that, in his dream, he had taken from the Shadow Lord.

Almost every detail of the thick, rough blade and the strong, finely crafted hilt seemed alike, but surely it was not the very same weapon. Malok wondered, truly, could he now thieve in the real world while he was yet soundly asleep and in the world of dreams? Though no oozing, darkling mist emanated from the edge of the blade, and its appearance seemed now not half so ghastly as the dread life-ender which he had grabbed onto with his surreal form; though he doubted and questioned the possibility, the young Dragon had to admit that the sword which he now held in his actual hands could be no other.

"I think this is the weapon of the Shadow Lord, the very same sword which did strike down your friend, Zurthaud" Spake Malok, slowly, and far more quietly than before. "I think I stole it; maybe it is the key to his healing."

Theros' brow furrowed and his tail whipped back and forth, as astounded by the young Dragon's claim, he intently stared at the sword first, then at Malok, then back at the sword again; his expression clearly belied his own doubts of the sword's origin, yet as he gazed upon the fell blade, Theros slowly, surely recognized its reviled shape.

"Where,... How did you get this?" Asked the completely astonished Theros.

Malok then proceeded to recount his night's adventure, recalling every single part in full clarity, leaving no detail out, and Theros could but sit in silent amazement. The older Dragon had never heard of such a thing, as to walk about in a world of dreams, nor for those who did so to have such an effect on the actual physical world, as to pilfer treasured objects from their terrible, mighty owners. He had not a clue how to respond to Malok's tale, nor what to do with the Shadow Lord's blade, but he knew of one who might.

"I can hardly believe what you are telling me, but that I recognize the sword. We must send for Serc, at once! Surely, he shall know what to make of this, what to do with the blade."

Chapter 14

They had made good time, Anur, Feldara, and Calidon, swiftly journeying across the vast and mostly uninhabited rolling, grassy plains and scattered forests that separated the Order's Realm from the Aelven Kingdom. In the late hours of the night before, they had only just arrived in this no-man's-land of wilderness, only just barely departing from the heavily wooded Aelven land, and having pitched a hasty camp, with a diminutive fire for to help keep Anur warm through the chill night, all three of them had promptly fallen fast asleep, little knowing the awesome beauty of the land all about them. But, now that they had all risen early to the sun's cresting of the horizon, instantly dispelling the misty morning's fog, they truly witnessed the great wide-openness, the grandeur, of this land.

It was nothing like the realms Feldara had ever before seen, though she had only been in the three now. It was, by far, more aerated and spacious than the grim, dark pine forests on the coast of the Shadow Lands, and the sedges and tall grasses flourished here like they never did on either her beloved island home, or even within the borders of the verdant Aelven realm. From their camp's vantage point on the crest of a low hill, she could see these grassy plains stretch out to the distant horizon, unbroken in their dales and mounds but for clusters of wild flowers or a small strand of trees dotted here or there and a river, windingly flowing way too far in the distance to be heard or even glimpsed but by a Dragon's excellent eyes.

To the far North, the jagged, violet hued line signifying the lofty heights of distant mountains barely peeked over the horizon's edge, promising an ultimate boundary to the, otherwise, seemingly unending flat prairie lands, but so distant were these majestic border guards that even Feldara had trouble spying them. Not so with the dreary thunderheads that loomed ever closer from the Southwest, for they were well within sight, appearing to have followed Anur and Feldara from their own island, the very start of their travels. By now even Calidon had noticed their unnatural presence, but they did only discuss with each other what possibly this storm could be doing so far out of any usual weather pattern, as mere clouds surely could not harm anyone, only perhaps, providing an unpleasant, unwarranted soaking.

But, as Anur finished packing his satchel with the bedroll and the other few items he had brought along, a large low noise pervaded their camp. It was like a very large dog's growling, yet the tone lasted longer and ended with a gurgle. At first, the two Dragons looked about searching for the source of this strange utterance, fearing it to be some sort of unknown predator lurking just beyond their sight in the tall grass, or perhaps a far distant thundering of the approaching storm, but Anur allayed their fears.

"Sorry, it was my stomach. May I suggest we find some breakfast." He apprehensively confessed.

After a good laugh, much to Anur's demur, Feldara let him up on her shoulder, and they all took off into the sky, hunting for their breakfast over the glistening, windswept plains.

They had not to search for long at all, as Calidon had spotted a large herd of some strange herbivores from their earlier vantage point, and they now only winged their way over toward the odd beasts.

From high up in the atmosphere, Feldara could see that these creatures were some kind of bovine, with the characteristically thick muscular bodies, short wide muzzles, and small, slightly curved horns, but the like of which she had never seen before, even in the many tomes she had read on the matter, those from which, back on their island home, Anur had taught her of the world. But, as curious as Feldara was, greater still was her hunger for meat; as long as these animals were not poisonous, she was going to eat of them.

As the Dragons had come from far away and were now so far above the herd, the cow-like prey were completely unaware and only milled about- eating, play-fighting, sleeping, and otherwise- oblivious to their present danger, but even as the two Dragons flew closer and the hot gusts of air from their wing beats at last descended onto the ground below, billowing the grass in gentle, yet constant, bursts, the dumb beasts still took no notice of their airborne stalkers, even when the skittish deer of the Aelven lands, that which lived within range of the Rathnyalings, would have long turned tail and fled for brushy cover.

Feldara wondered at this too, that these creatures could either be so stupid or unaware; perhaps, they were simply unused to being hunted from above, their only danger coming from the earthbound carnivores. But, not for too long did she ponder on this either, for Calidon had already started his killing dive, and Feldara had to keep pace, staying in sync with her hunting partner, lest he scatter the herd and she end up with nothing.

The kill was so easy as to be tragic, for the creatures were taken by surprise even unto the very end of two of their herd's number. Even as the two Dragons landed violently upon the backs of their prey, tackling them and snapping their spines all at once, the rest of the herd stood in shock at the whole ferocious scene, until one of the smarter ones finally fled a distance away. Only when the Dragons had started to skin their kills for eating did the rest of the buffalo, as after their landing Anur and Calidon had identified them, finally realize what had happened and scatter abroad, regrouping at what they thought to be a safe location only a little farther away.

"I almost feel ashamed to eat of such pitiful creatures as these buffalo." Said Feldara, once Anur had jumped from off her back. "They barely noticed us, even when we came right in among them."

Calidon had to agree, wishing to have given the bison more fair a chance at escape, for though Dragons must eat of flesh, for the wholeness of their health and the strength of their bodies, never are they ungrateful for, or unaware of, the sacrifice of life that is given so they may live. Such responsibility and reverence was taught to Dragonets at a young age, to be thankful for their meat, both to the Eloigal Who ultimately provided the sustenance and to the prey itself for the giving of its life.

Anur, though not so concerned as his Draconic companions, was also disturbed by the ease with which such beasts were taken, but he knew the value of a cow compared to people.

"We should not feel so ashamed, for, though all life is precious, the lives of people are worth more than the animals. We needed this meat for our nourishment, and we take it gratefully, neither wasting nor wanting. Besides which, the buffalo will learn from this. Before, this herd had never known of Dragons, and now they never again will forget them. We shall not hunt of them so easily again." Anur said.

And, being relieved by his wise words, they hungrily devoured the buffalo, for Anur and Feldara had not eaten since breakfast yesterday, as they had been traveling so hard, while Calidon divulged that he had not even eaten that much, skipping yesterday's breakfast, having awoken late, only having time to rise and leave with them. As starved as they were, Anur and the two Dragons made short work of their meal, quickly devouring the carcasses.

While the meat was warm, Feldara found buffalo to taste quite excellent, yet did its tenderness fade quickly if it was allowed to sit, as Anur had to do with his portion. For, he would not eat strange creatures raw, wanting to avoid parasites, of which Dragons had no need to worry because of their strong stomach juices, and he had to take the time to build a fire with which to cook. Luckily, all that he must do today, as the night before, was to gather some fuel for the flames and, kicking away the plants with his hard leather boots, make a wide ring of bare earth about, for Calidon was of the maturity that he could breathe flame and did happily oblige.

No longer did Anur have to tediously light a fire from flint and steel, thanks to the helpful male. In mere seconds, he was cooking his own little buffalo roast on the growing blaze, yet Feldara, though she knew and welcomed the time saving benefit of a fire-breathing comrade, looked on in slight jealousy. She had now been trying to breathe flame for a few years, desperately attempting to prove her usefulness in this way to Anur.

Even though she knew that male Dragons matured more quickly than females, she resented herself for being so underdeveloped and unable to aid her mentor in such a distinctively Draconic way, and simply hated the fact that her fire had not been the one he cooked on.

However, early morning began to wear on, as the sun climbed higher into the sky, and they hastened to depart and make good time across these open, beautiful, yet isolated plains. All too soon, Anur again mounted Feldara's shoulder and they moved on, leaping into the darkening sky, heading Northwest, even as the threatening storm clouds ever neared their location, blotting out the sun with their heavy, umbrous wings.

For a while, they flew on in peace, with nothing but the rushing of breezes and the cyclic rhythm of flapping Dragon's wings to separate noise from thought, but the wind began to pick up, a strong headwind, slowing them greatly. Still the thunderheads above encroached upon them, fighting far better than they, supernaturally even, the gusting currents; until at last, the three travelers were completely overtaken by the rushing squall.

Then came the rain.

At the first, little droplets began to drizzle down, gently wetting the group, but soon these grew in size and speed until they began to pelt and sting, as if becoming hailstones. Finally, the heavens let loose the downpour, and a deluge broke out upon them, soaking them to the bone and causing them need to land, for so poor was their visibility now.

Anur had to signal Calidon to stop, through much shouting and pointing, for though he had been soaring as close to Feldara as possible, he could barely see, or be seen by, them.

When at last they did get his attention and Anur had explained their course of action, they three did then slow their beating wings and make quick descent to the safety of the earth below, for as they now saw, flashes of lightning sizzled hotly and frequently through these dark clouds, followed by deafening cracks of pealing thunder.

Feldara remembered Anur having told her that Dragons of old did not fear the electric storms, for they could summon strong magic to protect themselves from the treacherous lightning or even harness it in their teeth and horns to be wielded as a tool or weapon. Not so these two youngsters, Feldara especially trembled at the thought of being scorched, instantly zapped, flash-fried by a sudden unavoidable jolt of electric death, and hurriedly sought the refuge of solid ground.

By the time they did touch down to earth, hasty as their landing was, the whole wide prairie had turned into a sloppy, muddy swamp, and they now squelched onward, on foot, through the thick, gloppy marsh, trying to find some manner of shelter. Still the rain poured down, turning the air bitter cold and freezing their drenched hides, impeding their vision, and slowing their progress to a crawl. Many times Anur, who was leading them now, had to look back to make sure that his charges were, indeed, following him, not having lost themselves in the enveloping deluge and tall sedge curtains, and once Feldara fell a little behind, causing him to stop and wait for her, all the while hoping she had not gone too far astray. Once was enough for Anur, he then decided to tie them together by the wrist with a lengthy cord he had brought along, and this did help to keep them together.

On and on they slogged through the boggy mire and the torrential rainstorm, for hours and hours they trod, until at last they met with some higher ground, a small mound upon which sat a clump of broad-leafed trees.

So relieved by this sight, by the much firmer ground beneath their tired feet, by the relatively drier spot of grass beneath the trees' boughs, that Anur decided that they should stop and rest here for a bit, perhaps, even wait out the rain.

But, the rain did not cease, though they sat and rested, hoping for the sky to clear, about an hour's time, and they all began to wonder how it was that the clouds could contain so much water, as to drench the whole of these plains so unceasingly. At length, Anur got up again, and not because he wished to.

"We cannot stay here much longer, for though we are a little drier now, if the rain continues as it is, these fields will be immensely flooded. We must move on to higher ground, unless you both wish to sleep underwater tonight." Anur wisely proposed.

However, the poor young Dragons were so weary of plodding through the miry bog, which once was beautiful, dry grassland, that the only response they could offer was an unhappy, whining groan, yet they did all get up reluctantly.

"I saw some mountains far to the North, this morning." Offered Feldara, at length. "We could try for them. Even if we cannot make the whole distance, surely the land will rise to meet them, offering some refuge from the wash of this storm."

They all thought this very sound counsel, and after Anur took a bearing from his surroundings, the direction of the wind, and anything else he could use to point himself Northward, they all loathingly followed him, back out into the downpour, heading North, hopefully to higher ground and shelter from the rain and flood.

For the whole rest of the day, until the world began to fade into the sunset absent dark of a clouded evening, the group slogged on through the mucky fen, but never did they seem to achieve any higher an elevation. The stands of trees were so sparse, so thin of cover and thoroughly soaked, that even they now offered no shelter, no dry spot beneath them, no relief to the worn trio, and they despondently trod onward.

The dark began to deepen along with Feldara's despair, and she began to wonder if the deluge would ever cease, if she could finally rest her tired sore feet in a dry place, by a warm fire, at the end of this horrible day. But, as she tediously plodded through the slough, she rather painfully knocked her hand against something hard within the mud, breaking her free from these more hopeful reveries and bringing a curse to her lips. Upon inspection, she did find it to be, as expected, a rock, and she angrily threw the good sized stone away from her path.

Still, more and more rocks did she encounter, causing her to watch her step considerably more closely, until it seemed that the whole of the ground below her was loose stone, wettened by only a slight covering of mud. The simple act of walking, which had before been made so difficult by the dense, viscous quagmire, now became easier again upon this rocky ground, and the trio began to comprehend that they had, at last, made it to the higher land they had been heading toward. Though still completely drenched, bared to the watery elements, at the realization of their hard won goal, they all felt like rejoicing, yet not a one had the energy for anything more than to keep on treading.

"Let us find some place to make camp." Yelled Anur, over the howling wind and pouring rain, as he loosed them from the cord so that they could spread out their search.

They then did gladly peel their eyes for any sort of shelter, for even the most slightly drier of places in which to rest. As they walked on, looking for such a spot, Feldara eventually came upon a couple of giant boulders jammed against one another so as to provide an angular roof and slanting walls, and upon closer examination, she found there to be plenty enough room underneath this monolithic rocky crag for all three of them.

"Over here!" She called out to Anur and Calidon, shouting over the deluge. "Under these rocks!"

Faster than expected, they two did also hasten, from where they had been seeking about, toward the homely structure, which seemed to them as fine as any roadside tavern, and they joined Feldara under the pleasantly dry stone lean-to.

For a good long while, they only sat huddled together, shivering from the wet and cold of the rain, utterly worn out by their day's march, but Anur had a mind to be warmed of a fire, as was his usual wont.

"I shall go out and fetch some tinder for a fire." He said, after they had dried a little from each others' warmth.

"Nothing will burn after being soaked by this downpour." Feldara harshly derided, with a snort. "All you will do is get wet again, return drenched with an armful of soaked twigs, thereby bringing the wet into our shelter, and spread your wetness around until we are all wet again."

"Well, a Dragon's fire could, possibly, should, light logs even so soppy as whatever Anur brings back." Calidon meekly offered, abashedly trying to soften the disrespectful tone with which Feldara had addressed her mentor.

"Be silent, you foot-licker." Feldara viciously spat back at Calidon, causing the bigger, stronger Dragon to cower.

She did not know why her tone was now so harsh, her words so nasty, for "foot-licker" was not a nice name to call anyone who tried to make peace between friends.

Such a title would have been more earned by Orthard's cronies, the High Council members, who would pretentiously serve and flatter the vile lord for some small reward or another. Perhaps, it was the lingering feelings of jealousy, which had been aroused by Calidon's ability to breathe flame while she still could not; certainly, it was the long day's travel, which had tried her mind and body to the breaking point. Whatever the case, she had uttered the remarks, knowing little why, and had earned something not seen very often, by her or anyone.

Anur was mad, and not just mad, quite livid. He had not slogged through mud all day, patiently leading these two young Dragons through a storm in which they well would have been lost without his aid, that at his quicker walking pace, he could have left them in, just to be mocked and have crass, unearned insults thrown about every which way. He quickly stomped right up to Feldara's face, which now bore an expression of trepid surprise, and jutted a bony pointed finger right at her bright golden eyes.

"I shall not have this kind of behavior from you, Feldara. We have all been plodding through this slough, every bit as much as you, and I will not now put up with your foul attitude. Calidon does not deserve your insult, and I have no need for your smart mouth." He stated, with a loud, firm, and angry voice.

For a fraction of a second, Feldara considered simply taking this well earned correction, but after so long a day, she had not so much control of her tongue as she would have liked. Her temper welled up inside her like the hot fire Anur had wished to make, and all the rotten thoughts that she had kept hidden, had buried all these years, thoughts that she hoped to have dismissed as being too loathsome and unkind, like the storm about them, burst forth in violent rage.

"This kind of behavior from me? You are the one who always treats me like a child, embarrasses me in public, talks down to me, as if I do not understand. You impose stupid rules upon me that make no sense. You never let me have any fun, and when I actually do manage to find some, you arrive and ruin the whole thing. When I laugh, you sigh, and when I am melancholy, you do not care. Everything that I like, you despise, and I hate your dismal outlook on all of life. A sunny day would be as this one to you. I hated all the times you spent lecturing me on boring topics from musty old books, and when I asked you to spend time having fun with me, you always found something else to do. I hated your boring little life, your stupid little island, and I hate your stupid little hat that hides your face. I just hate everything about you, you stupid old man. You are not even my father, so quit pretending like it!" She screamed right into Anur's face, eyes burning with anger and tears.

However, Anur did not react as Feldara thought he should. He did not yell back at her. He did not strike her, and he had never, ever in all her life, even made as if he would. His pointed finger had wilted the whole tantrum through, until now his arm lay at his side, fist tightly closed. His head had lowered until now the chin of his "stupid little hat" sullenly rested on his chest. For a while, he stood there, silent as the rocks all about them, trembling from emotion and weariness, but at last, Anur offered a reply.

"You are right." He tremulously whispered, voice cracking from the knife wound in his heart. "I am not your father."

With that, he slowly turned and walked out of the small rock shelter, back out into the pouring rain. With every fiber of her being, Feldara wished to call out to him, to run out there after him and hug him tightly, begging his forgiveness, but she did not. She somehow kept her lips pursed and feet firmly planted, but her tears she could not hold back. They streamed regret all down her face, long after her mentor's silhouette had faded into the downpour.

She had not meant a word of what she said, aside from hating Anur's vizored helm, that which hid his beloved face from her. Truly, she disliked being corrected and scolded, being led about or unnecessarily guided, but she knew that this counsel only meant Anur cared enough for her to do so, to help her become a decent person. While she knew that Anur was seldom excited, she had never felt that he despised her joys, and he had never expressed as such. She did not even know why she had said those things.

She had been bored to death by some of the old scrolls they had read together back home, but she had also loved some of them and had cherished his tutelage, knowing all that he had taught her was beneficial. Feldara knew that Anur had shared his whole life with her, and could not fathom why she had said otherwise. Through this whole time she had spent away from it, she actually had found herself longing for the peaceful mundanity of their simple island life, and found that the farther she had gone from their home, the more she had wished to be back there again.

Most of all, Feldara absolutely hated herself for her last words to Anur, that final sting of venomous nail driven piercingly right through his heart, into the soft flesh of his own perceived vulnerabilities, for though Anur was no Dragon, nor even came close to knowing all of a Dragon's knowledge, or doing any of a Dragon's deeds, or even the ability to teach these to her, Feldara knew that no one in the whole world was more qualified for that kingly title of father as he. No one in all of Threa had poured out as much love for her as Anur; indeed, compared to the water that poured all about them, it would be ten-hundred-thousand-million-billion-trillion fold. His whole life he had given away to her, her care and well-being.

A long while Feldara stood there silent, watching the entrance to their little cave-like shelter hoping and dreading Anur's return. Her tears dripped profusely in loud plinks upon the stony floor of the small cavern, though sound washed into inaudibility by the roaring storm without, as she thought of all the ways she should apologize to him, but by and by, he did not return.

She grew restless and worried, but also more and more tired. Eventually, Feldara had to lie down, as had Calidon. The poor young male, having witnessed such a thing and already intimidated by the much more spirited and outgoing Feldara, had silently sat in the far corner, uttering not a peep lest he also incur her wrath. But, he now did summon up a little courage, and spoke his mind.

"I know what it is like to be chided by parents, and often I had thought somewhat as you. But, never did I speak out on it, for I first had to remember all that they had given up for me." He softly said, and not condescendingly.

Calidon spoke as a friend seeking a friend, with much compassion, earnestly attempting to make peace, for though he was large, strong of body, and big of mouth, his heart was warm and humble.

Yet, Feldara did not reply. Her words had so disturbed her own heart, for she wondered how could she possibly harbor such ill-willed resentment toward one who had given up everything for her. They lay there, her facing the doorway, he crouched in the corner facing her, both of their eyes growing heavier by the moment, and still Anur had not returned.

Feldara, like often times before, prayed a few words to Eloigal before sleep took her into its welcoming embrace. She asked for His forgiveness first, for having at all uttered such hurtful, untrue things, and that Anur would forgive her also, that he would not leave her all alone, gone forever, never to be seen again, but that he would come back, so she could tell him how sorry she was. But, the long tiresome day quickened and deepened the comforting arms of slumber, so that before Anur had yet returned, unable to resist any longer, Feldara fastly fell into them.

Chapter 15

Morning broke again, but not into the usual golden splendor of a radiant dawn. A murky, pallid sky blearily smeared the light into a cold, depressing after-storm, for the sunrise only added visibility, rather than happy, luminous beams, to the dismal, gray world. Feldara only awoke because of the cold, for shivering and coiling about herself, she had slowly resumed awareness. Immediately, she wished a return to her dreaming state, for while the rain was long gone, her hateful words to Anur and his wounded reply had not left from her remembrance. They replayed over and over again in her mind, like a perpetually turning wheel of regret, another cog in the unstoppable, incorrigible mill of time.

But, Feldara also recalled that Anur had not come back to their little stone crag shelter while she was yet awake last night, and this frightening thought jolted her into wakefulness. Feldara lifted her head up from where she lay, looking over her curled body, all about the small space under the rocky overhang, but there was no sign of her beloved mentor. She arose, hoping for him to be about somewhere without the small cave, noticing that, strangely, Anur had not built any kind of fire within their shelter as he said he would, but whither she looked, there was neither any trace of him outside the two great rocks.

Feldara began to despair at the thought that Anur could have really left her, perhaps, going all the way back to his island, never to see her again, yet she still subconsciously knew that it was not in his character to do such a thing. Even the absence of the fire, which he had set in his mind to make, was unnatural for him. They had argued before, though never quite so maliciously, and he never had left her then. Why then would he now go, when she needed him most?

It was then that Feldara recalled a moment, now seeming so long ago, that one dark, foul winter Anur had needed to go off alone to their island's two wooded hills and hunt for food, for their supplies had run very low. As the weather had become so cold and bad, almost as it had been in the days before Feldara had hatched, Anur had determined that Feldara was too small, too young to go with him and be anything more than in danger of freezing to death in the snow and blizzard that was plaguing the island. Still, Feldara was so distraught that he was leaving her that she had clung to his boots sobbing and begging him to stay, but he set her down and comforted her with a warm embrace.

He had already prepared all that she would have needed in the meanwhile, and she would mostly be sleeping in hibernation during his short week's absence, as very young Dragons so do in winter time. Yet, did he patiently explain the necessity of his trip, that he would certainly come back, but that had not been good enough for little Feldara, she only pouted plaintively. He then did swear to her, as he had sworn before to her mother, that he would never forsake her, that he would always be there for her. Only then did she finally relent and let him go off hunting, and he did certainly come home again, and with much game.

Feldara knew, without question, that Anur would never break a promise or neglect to do what he said he would, even something so trivial as building a fire, and especially not something so cherished as his youthful charge. Even being so hatefully, so groaningly ruefully, disowned, Anur would keep his word, and yet still he was nowhere to be found.

Something was amiss.

By now, Feldara's frantic searching had caused Calidon to stir from his slumber. Blinking his eyes open, and sleepily yawning, he slowly lifted his head from the corner where he had lain.

"Help me find him!" Feldara blatantly shouted at the sleepy male.

She was so distraught now, nearly in tears again with worry and guilt, that she forgot to mention for whom they should be searching, and only caused the still groggy Calidon to cluelessly stare back at her. Slowly he pursed his lips, to begin asking the name of this individual for whom she sought, but Feldara could not wait long enough for him to get a word out.

"Anur is gone!" She yelled at him.

Calidon sprung to life, craning his neck to look all about the small cavern, and rising to his feet, searching without, as Feldara had done. Still to no avail, He returned, with a surprising amount of initiative, to question Feldara.

"Anur did not return at all last night?" He asked of her, truly concerned for her mentor's sake.

Feldara could only shake her head "no", for her legs were trembling with the gravity of this crisis, as she fast became weary of regret's dread weight. In her heart she knew that Anur would not forsake her, but in her head, all manner of doubts, like demons, danced maniacally with last night's foolish, hurtful words.

"Perhaps, you truly did hurt him so, last night, that he is going back to your home." Calidon somberly, if not callously, carelessly, mumbled.

Fire crept back into Feldara's heart with her reply. "Anur is of greater character than to let a few harsh, foolish words so affect him. He would never just up and abandon us. I know something is wrong."

Left to her inward self, she may have kept on doubting, assuming that her misspoken words could ever stop the beating heart of her parent, but by speaking the truth, she had forced herself to believe it, had dispelled the falseness of guilt-borne self-loathing from her heart. Anur never would ever leave her, for he loved her unconditionally, just as a father should. Even if Feldara had spat in his face, beaten him to the ground, even killed him, Anur would have still loved her, still been there for her with the gloomy gray dawn, and if death could not part Feldara from Anur's love and care, certainly no adolescent's tirade, wrought of a long tiring day, could do so. Feldara now not only knew, but believed in her heart that this was true.

If Anur had not come back by now, something terrible had befallen him, and Feldara made this fact just as plain to Calidon.

"Then, let us take to the air. We can search more effectively from such a better vantage point." He recommended, becoming more careful in his speech, more gentle in his tone.

They did so, running from out their shelter and leaping into the sky.

The night before had been too dark and shrouded with pouring rain for them to fully take in their surroundings, but as soon as they had risen but a little from the earth, Feldara and Calidon could now see where yesterday's travel had ended. Feldara had thought last evening that they had only made it to the higher ground that must accompany the foot hills that lie about a mountain range; however, she now saw that they had passed all such raised earth, passing even the low hills before them, and had indeed, come all the way to the very same mountains which she had espied so far in the distance yesterday morning. So much ground had they covered the day before that the mere thought of it caused Feldara's feet to ache again, but it was well that they had gone this far.

The plains which had been drenched so thoroughly last night now appeared in the distance as a great shimmering lake or river, completely filled with water. Even up to the foothills the water came, having risen enough to submerge many trees of the plain and sufficiently cover the trunks of those at the base of the foothills, and Feldara could not help to wonder how the buffalo, being such stupid creatures, had managed to survive such disastrous storm and flood.

"Look, there!" Calidon shouted to her, for observing the wonder of the world about her and searching desperately for Anur, she had fallen behind him.

"What is it?" She asked, craning her neck to look at the ground where he was pointing, for to her eyes, there was nothing.

"It is a trail, a mark of disturbed leaves and soil, cutting through the underbrush of the forest, leading straight into the heart of the mountains."

He said, slightly baffled that she could not see plainly such obvious trace of movement through the wood, not considering that she did not have the training in hunting and tracking that he had received.

Though she still had trouble spotting the "trail" which Calidon had tried to point out to her, Feldara did see that it truly was a forest directly below them, the grasses of the plains having mingled with more and more trees and brush, until there was no more room between them for the sun to shine down through the enveloping boughs to feed them. These trees, though not quite as lush and lively as those in the Aelven land, here did grow just as old and tall and numerous, despite the inhospitable rocky ground, which, for lack of finer nourishment, caused them to gnarl and twist into rough, ragged shapes.

Taller and older still were the snow-capped peaks, which rose above all other things, far above even the loftiness of the two Dragons' winged paths. Their somber majesty, ascending above all other earthly things for to touch the heavens themselves, and their stark, cold, beauty- ominous stony guardians of the world's deep fissures- caused Feldara to pause and marvel at their height and breadth, for never before had she seen in such close proximity the grandeur of a mountain.

However, she did pause only for a moment. Finding Anur, making sure he was alright, was her first priority, and apologizing to him for her foul, misspoken words was second.

"Here, the trail starts. Let us descend and look about for clues." Calidon suggested, and Feldara nodded a reply.

The closer the two came to ground, to that patch of scuffled, upturned loam and leaf-litter, which Feldara could finally now see, the more it seemed that something horrible, indeed, had befallen Anur, for signs of struggle showed themselves all about the little glade where was the trail's head.

Many boot prints did Feldara find in the muddier spots of soil, too many for one Anur to have left behind without having run about like an imbecile, and broken branches hung all around the small clearing. Eventually Calidon found a substantial piece of evidence, one that surely signified a tussle between Anur and some unknown assailants. He excitedly called Feldara over to the far side of the meadow, where about he had been intensively searching.

"Look! I have found a sword." He exclaimed, showing Feldara the short blade. "It has not been here long, for the blade still shines nicely. It was under a pile of leaves, as if someone hastily wished it not be found."

Immediately Feldara recognized it as one of Anur's, for he did keep a short blade on him at all times. He could even magically summon to his hand a few of the enchanted weapons that lay in the remnants of the Master Order's armory, from back home on their island, but this one, this particular short, straight, double-edged blade was, by far, his favorite. Anur had brought it along especially with his few other things, and it had rarely left his side.

Feldara audibly groaned, worrying what could have transpired to cause Anur to leave so treasured an object. She held it close to her, wishing for all the world that it would trade places with her beloved guardian.

"Do not worry." Calidon awkwardly attempted at comforting her. "I am sure he is alright. Anur seems very tough, for a Human. Let us follow the trail, see where it leads. We shall find more answers at its end, rather than here."

Feldara was worried to sickness for Anur's sake, to the point that she felt her heart melting with anxiety. All she wanted was to find Anur, for this whole rotten experience to be done with, for him to be safe, but she doubted that she could walk even another ten steps, and this not of her weariness left over from the long walk the day before, but of her fearful, tiresomely draining concern for Anur's well-being.

She barely knew what she was doing, but Feldara did then lean into Calidon, resting her neck and head on his large warm chest. A simple hug was all that she desperately needed, and he gallantly complied, letting her tears and trembling fall upon his strong, broad shoulders, as he gently wrapped his large forearm about her. For a moment, at least, Feldara did rest her frantic thoughts in the kind embrace of this grand young male, but they both knew that time was now very earnestly crucial. Anur's life could well be in jeopardy.

Having received the strength she need to keep going through this awful trial, she reluctantly let herself go of Calidon's sturdy and compassionate, though discomfited, consolation, and they both strode off in the direction that went the trail, the evidential track of whatever had confronted and overcome Anur.

"Whoever did this to Anur must have been a formidable foe." Feldara mused aloud, having noticed the wide path of slicked mud, upturned leaves, and scattered stones, signifying how he had been unwillingly, or unconsciously, dragged along the way.

"Perhaps not, there seem to be multiple tracks along the trail. It could have been a large mob, maybe ten or more assailants from the look of it." Calidon postulated, pointing out the many boot-prints along the path, some more distinguished than others, pressed deep with the weight of their bearers into the soppy ground.

"I meant that we have as yet seen no dead bodies. Either they returned to their hideout carrying their slain, for to keep us from more easily tracking them, or less likely, they took Anur by complete surprise." Feldara snorted. "I had already noticed there were more than one set of foot-prints, even back in the glade." She continued, slightly hoping to have impressed Calidon with her keen observations.

"I guess the latter, because we found no trace of blood, or anything to indicate Anur had put up any kind of fight." Calidon unthinkingly replied, but he quickly changed his answer seeing the annoyed look Feldara shot back at him. "Of course, they could also have really cleaned up after themselves." He backpedalled.

"Shut up." Bluntly spat Feldara, not really wanting to discuss the issue any longer and definitely not wishing to hear of her mentor's ability in combat being defamed by anyone other than herself.

So, on and on they followed on foot, and in silence, this trace of Anur's capture as it wound its way deep into the highlands, for miles they walked following the trail, as Feldara thought it would be too hard to spot again from easier traveling in the air above. All the while, as they went upward and upward upon the same slopes which earlier they had spied from below, the terrain grew ever more rocky and steep and more difficult to cover quickly.

At last, they broke through the enshrouding tree line of piney forests, and continued on, up and across the bare stony heights of the true mountainous landscape.

Here the trees broke from solid forest to scattered strands, mostly of pine and other conifers, and the grasses, though longer here, were just as scattered as the trees. Bare rock, gray and bleak was mostly what covered the ground, even as gray and bleak clouds covered the sky.

Morning had drawn on to mid-day when they were still in the forest; now noontide was fading to evening as they scaled these rocky heights. Though scrabbling up the embankments, the lofty ramparts of natural stone, was easy enough for the clawed hands and feet of a Dragon, the whole day had gone by and night was approaching fast by the time they had reached level ground again, and eventually following their trail upon these barren rocks became ever more difficult due to the oncoming dark and the lack of muddy slides and other clear traces more easily left behind in the grasses and wet soils of lower altitudes. They had to halt, though Feldara wished to press onward, but there would likely be no better place to stop further on than this cleft they had come upon.

It was not large, but it was roomy enough for both of them to move about upon freely. There was even a gaping overhang near the back of it, against the wall of the next mountain's ridge-line, under which they could take shelter against the chill night air of this altitude.

"Let us stop here for the night." Suggested Calidon. "I know you do not wish to, but stumbling about the mountains in the dark is only a good way to get killed. We cannot do any more for Anur until morning."

Feldara said nothing, for she knew he was right. She simply trudged to the back of the small overhang and slumped to the ground. They were both tired, having neither eaten nor slept since the morning of the day before, but there was no energy left in them now to hunt for a dinner of mountain goat or even to light a fire. Calidon plopped on the ground a short distance from her and quickly was snoring, but Feldara could hardly sleep at all tired though she was. She was too anxious for Anur's sake, and tears began to creep into her eyes again. Slowly she curled up close to Calidon's side, for his warmth had brought her much comfort earlier in the morning. Half-asleep he lay one of his arms over her, but Feldara was too tired to care. She let her strong escort embrace her again, and before she knew it, she was asleep in his arms.

- 195 -

<><><><>

Calidon's struggling woke Feldara the next morning, for apparently he was now, in his fully conscious mind, not so comfortable letting her rest right against him, snuggled twixt his forearms against his chest.

"Um,.. excuse me." He mumbled, realizing he had woken Feldara, but to her great annoyance he still continued to, as kindly as possible, shove her off of his other arm.

Feldara groaned, hating the waking light, along with her ill-spoken words, her life, and everything else. Had she only but kept her mouth shut, none of his would have happened. She thought to herself, and still more, had she only but stayed content upon her island home, definitely would she not be in this horrid mess. Being hunted, running for her life, losing her best friend- all these incidents were beginning to take their toll on the poor Dragoness.

Calidon finally freeing himself from her unmoving lump of a body broke her inner turmoil, and she too rose up, at last.

"Let us go." She stated, already striding out from the overhang.

"Do you not want me to find you something to eat first?" Calidon asked, every bit as much wanting some food for himself, yet having the brilliance and presence of mind to pose his inquiry so delicately.

Feldara did not answer. She merely rounded about the overhang and proceeded on up and over it along to the top of the mountain's ridge. Calidon apparently wanted more of a conversation, for he sped out after her and even overtook her.

"Feldara stop!" He cried, suddenly becoming a little bold, even fierce.

She could not meet his gaze, partly because she was so weary, mostly because she was so depressed. She hated herself so much right now that if she had any more energy she probably would have used it to fling herself down from off theses heights and neglect to open her wings or even try to slow her fall. All the woes she had inflicted upon herself, upon Anur, and upon everyone she had ever met crowded into her thoughts and beat her down with lashes of guilt and remorse, but Calidon grabbed her firmly by both shoulders, shaking her a little.

"Stop punishing yourself for what happened to Anur!" He shouted into her face, and he set her down rather hard upon the ground. "You are not to move from this spot until I return, and you will eat whatever I bring back. Because, you are not to blame for the evil that hunts you; you are not to blame for the woes that have befallen us. Even if you had never come here, even if you had never been born, the Dark One would still be trying to ruin everyone's lives and his servants would still be about seeking to accomplish that by any means. Yes, you said some hurtful words, but that was all those were, words. You have shown your love for Anur many times before, and you prove it still by even coming this far, seeking him when he is lost. So, continue in this quest of love, this rescue, but cease this bout of self-loathing and sadness!"

And after only a slight pause, just to make sure she was not going to argue with him, Calidon jumped up into the air and took off, but Feldara probably could not have resisted his reasoning anyway. Fatigue had so overcome her that she felt not even strong enough to respond. So, she lay back against whatever tree that she found to be there and rested.

A little while later, Feldara found out that she had slept more while Calidon had gone, for he had woken her again with his bumbling. However, he had brought back two wild goats and a full one of the canteens Anur had brought. Seemingly, he had flown all the way back to their camp under the two leaning rocks and back to retrieve this treasured water bearer and had caught their meal along the way. It had not even taken him very long, for it was now only about noon, as Feldara guessed by the height of the sun.

He laid one of the goats at Feldara's feet and proceeded to eat the other in silence. Finally, after a good while of staring at her meal, hunger overcame the resentment she held toward herself. She allowed herself to eat, and with the meat came strength and vigor, clearing the mind from the clouds of tiredness and depression. It helped her to forgive herself, for though Feldara could not yet fully relinquish this darkness of thought, she now had some strength to grow resolve and confidence. She could find Anur, defeat his captors, and apologize to him. They could get back on their road, reach the Citadel of the Order, and finally be free from the clutches of the Dark One. It was possible.

Soon they had both finished their goats, and they then split the water. Though, it was not much of a drink for a Dragon-sized thirst, coming from one of Anur's Human sized canteens, it was enough. Calidon, of course let her drink her portion first, and as she handed the bottle over to him, their eyes met again.

"Thank you." Feldara said, simply and kindly.

"I am only sorry it was not much of a meal, but I figured goat would be better than nothing." Said Calidon shrugging it off.

"No, I mean, Thank you for everything." She insisted, for he had been very patient with her harshness, attentive to her needs, and very kind.

It was Calidon's turn to say nothing, partly because he was drinking water from a canteen, mostly because he was too modest and bashful for his own good.

At last, after a good rest and this simple meal, the two Dragons got moving again. Rolling atop the ridge of this next mountain, they made better time, but soon they came to the end of this crest. Immediately before them rose a high, straight cliff, reaching up to a higher sister peak, thus connecting the mountain they had afore scaled with this new, loftier one. Climbing up this, as the track of their enemies surely went, they at last came to the entrance of a craggy canyon-like pass, which cut right through this mountain and between several more, into the very heart of the range and beyond.

"The trail leads through here, but it seems too good a spot for an ambush. We might be heading into a trap, or something." Hesitantly spoke Calidon, breaking the silence by noting the high, steep sides of the ravine they would be following the tracks through.

"What other choice do we have? We must rescue Anur, for he has, and would do again the same for us." Feldara boldly replied, somewhat hoping that the idiots who had dared attack her beloved Anur would show themselves, so that she could tear them to pieces.

So, they carefully, quietly entered the crack in the mountain, stealthily stepping so as not to even clack their claws against the rocky ground, and against both of their better judgments, on they pursued after Anur's captors. After only a little way in, the rock walls about them began to narrow the passage, and from then on they had to walk single file for the tightness of it. Feldara, of course, had taken the lead, while Calidon, though having gallantly objected, was forced to bring up the rear.

"I do not like this, if we encounter danger, we are too cramped in here to even spread our wings to fly out. We should go back and soar over this ravine, just to make sure we are not being so deceived, for we cannot help Anur if we are in the same predicament." Suggested Calidon, just as they had walked about a quarter mile in the same fashion, he behind and she in front with only barely enough room for them to turn about in the confining space of the crag.

However, just as Feldara was about to heed this wise counsel and turn back around with him, exactly as Calidon had predicted, a trap was, indeed, sprung for them. A great boulder crashed into place just behind Calidon, blocking their way out, as another huge rock fell into the pathway before Feldara, blocking their way forward.

"Good, let them come. I shall kill them for taking Anur!" Growled Feldara, but she did not get a chance to act upon her words.

A large brutish form fell from the heights of the cliff walls above them, and with a sound smack, bashed poor Calidon upon the head with a crude wooden club. The unfortunate young male fell unconscious to the ground, as their attacker spun to face the thoroughly stunned Feldara.

As much as she was taken unaware by the ferocity of the assault, now that the element of surprise had gone from the assailant, Feldara was even more taken aback by the form of the attacking warrior.

It was not a Human, nor even one of the mysterious, black robed Dark Hunters, as Feldara had supposed had captured Anur. It was rather, a bear, or what appeared to be a bear, though it did walk easily upon its hind two feet, carried the, now broken, club with well formed, if not fat, clawed hands. Its shaggy, dark brown fur covered body was civilly clothed with a finely knitted wool tunic, cloak, and coarse pantaloons and, fastened over these, bits of leather and metal lamellar armor. Albeit for its unshod, clawed feet and the viciously snarling expression on its muzzle, the bear-person seemed quite sentient and full of enough wits to have easily designed this trap. Besides the clothes and its ferocious visage, Feldara could only take in the bear-person's immense height and brawn, almost as tall and wide as herself, before another bear-warrior apparently did the same to her as the other had done to Calidon.

Chapter 16

After leaving the Shadow Lord's sword in Theros' hands, Malok had sped as fast as his wings could carry him, nearly falling from the tower's top, back down to Serc's apartment, and woke the elder Dragon from his rest. This had been no easy task, for Serc was quite grumpy being roused so soon from his slumber. But, after explaining what had occurred last night in its surreal entirety, Malok had grabbed the still groggy Shar and hurried the skeptical, yet willing, Dragon doctor out his door and back up to the temple's sanctuary. They now stood therein, as shocked as any of the other Paladins gathered, who having heard themselves of what had occurred, had slowly begun congregating, all gawking over the supernaturally acquired blade.

"Truly, this could be no other weapon than the very sword of the Dark One." Serc exclaimed, after having spent a good long while examining it. "Again, how did you come by this blade?" He asked, still questioning the young Dragon's tale of pilfering the living world while asleep.

Of course, while Serc had been busy with analyzing the sword, Malok had told Shar of what had happened at the first opportunity; he above all others could Malok trust with this knowledge, while Theros and Serc knew, albeit only out of circumstance and necessity. Yet, Malok had became uneasy of the growing crowd about them and did not wish to divulge his dream-thieving capabilities to any more than must know of them, for power such as this was abnormal, even for Dragon magic. The many would consider it dangerous and unwieldy and attempt to limit or restrain its usage, and if any devious fiends, such as Orthard, were to hear of this ability, they would no doubt attempt to manipulate it, and its wielder, to their own ends.

Indeed, it was a dangerous quality, and Malok had already reasoned that anything could now be possible with this strange new ability. He could become an unstoppable assassin, or as last night, an untouchable thief. Literally, any door was open to him, and that notion of limitless power within his own clawed hands scared him, as it would any honest person. Malok, as young and inexperienced with Dragon magic as he was, realized that he had opened a door that should have been kept locked, the private and sacred door of the subconscious mind. Therefore, he remained silent, only shaking his head 'no', in answering Serc.

Fortunately, the elder Dragon seemed to understand Malok's position, and he did not press him for a reply.

"The trick now will be knowing how to use it, for to dispel the enchantment on Zurthaud." Serc pondered aloud, causing speculative murmurings to arise from those gathered.

"Maybe the answer hides within the little black book that Zurthaud brought back with him, for it did seem rather importantly placed in the Dark One's chambers." Suggested Theros, after a moment remembering how especially angered the Shadow Lord had been when Zurthaud had kept hold of it.

"I had already given the tome a cursory examination, to ascertain even such a possibility, but as much as I had wished not, by necessity I must now dig further into the undoubtedly reviled contents of that book of horrors and hope that, perchance, the spell we need is written therein." Serc offered.

He nodded toward Aelanur, the Dragon's priest, who then sauntered off to fetch the vile book from where they had stored it away amongst the other tomes and scrolls within the temple's sizeable library. He was an unusual Dragon, and not just because of his uncommon and resplendent, golden coloring, for having been voluntarily consecrated to this sacred service, he had rarely, if ever left the temple's hallowed halls and served night and day therein maintaining the library and relics, burning sweet smelling incense, and offering up constant prayers. As such, his muscle structure and wings were not as well-developed as other Dragons, and he relied upon them to provide his portion of meat. They did so gladly, though, not begrudgingly, for they understood his service, his work, was just as important to their survival even as that of any hunter.

Shortly, Aelanur returned with the small, black leather bound book, all the while gritting his teeth with such a tortured expression on his face, as if merely holding it caused him immense pain, and nearly tossing it at Serc's feet, he quickly rid his hands of the wretched article.

"It is written in ancient Draconic. That much I know by the letters of the title, for it says, 'The Book of Shadow' upon it." Relayed the elderly priest.

"Yes, and that means either you, Galrag, or I are the only ones here able to read the text." Serc replied, for the ancient speech had not been taught to the younger Dragons.

The elder Dragons had, indeed, ceased to commonly teach Old Draconic among the Order not only due to the rise of Basic Elvish as the common tongue of the various peoples of Threa, but also because the ancient language truly was hard to master.

The written text was primordial, based off of the shapes of actual contorted positions of the Draconic body, which had early on been used to communicate over longer distances than the voice could carry, while the spoken word was highly contextual, included more guttural, natural sounds that other races found hard to produce- like growling and snorting, and of peculiar etymology when compared to the other Threan tongues. Therefore, had it regrettably fallen out of use, while the Shadow Lord's book only showed its extraordinary age, for Serc had himself been of the last class of Paladins to be taught, as proper education, this mysterious language.

"I have not the strength of heart, or stomach, to bring my eyes down upon whatever heinous writings are within that book. Besides which, I would serve Zurthaud better with prayer." Sincerely returned the gentle priest, as he resumed his duties.

"Though I too fear what lies further within these dark pages, only I am left to do it, for Galrag is still in mourning for his son, and should not be expected so soon to delve his already tortured mind into so tortuous a volume.

Anyway, it shall take some time for me to decipher the text, as my Old Draconic is quite out of practice." Serc explained, as he wincingly opened the evil book.

He then did plow into the depths of it, though every part of his being told him just to cease from reading and close it up again, for the words therein were truly vile, full of malice and darkness. The very pages themselves seemed to drain his strength from him, for Serc began to tremble quite vividly. Constantly, it seemed he had to rub his eyes, stretch his neck, or look away to refresh himself even the slightest from the abominable narrative within. Many times he had to slow the pace of his reading, this being determined by the rate at which he moved his lips, silently mouthing out the more difficult, more foreign Draconic words. Even so, the aged doctor kept on for hours reading, tirelessly sacrificing his health and innocence for the good of the others, for Zurthaud.

At length, Serc had to take a break from deciphering the deplorable text, and he rose, trembling so forcefully now that the other Dragons sought to help him.

"I am fine." Serc insisted; though he did not stop them from aiding him as he took another seat nearby his patient. "Just let me change Zurthaud's bandages and I will continue."

At this point they were all loudly interrupted from the usual serenity of the temple, as another Dragon with his Human companion suddenly bolted within, and they, panting with the exertion of haste, skidded to a halt before Serc. They did not wait for inquiries before giving out their crucial news, for they were well known as spies in the High Council's chambers, the Dragon being capable of invisibility with magic and the Human being a certain paige boy to Lord Orthard himself.

"Tomorrow afternoon Orthard has planned to bring before the High Council the matter of our punishment for Zurthaud's death."

"He will propose we serve out our days within the sulfur mines." They frantically shouted.

Immediately, the room began to fill with the clamorous whisperings of outrage and fear, as the Paladins all began conversing with each other about the horrible news, for they knew as well as anyone, that such a sentence was unto death. These sulfur mines, with their foul mineral namesake, were filled with the noxious fumes produced by mining the substance. Any lengthy amount of time spent within the shafts would bring slow, painful death to the miners, as gradually their lungs would decompose from the poisonous atmosphere. As it was so certain a demise, there were very few mines for sulfur in existence and only the criminally condemned worked them, for Orthard to demand this as their unjust punishment was unspeakably hateful, unaccountably evil.

"No one is going to be condemned to the sulfur mines!" Shouted Serc, surprising and silencing all those gathered. "We will deal with this threat to our lives as we have done all the others. First, we must concentrate on Zurthaud's healing, and I will need quiet for that. Either leave or become so."

Having finished with the redressing of Zurthaud's grave wound, Serc again tottered over to where he had laid the book and resumed reading. The tension within the sanctuary, which before had been one of excitement and hope, had now changed to a soundless, anxious despair, as they all breathlessly awaited the announcement to come forth from Serc's lips, that of triumph and rejoicing, having finally found the enchantment for which he had been so earnestly searching, but many more hours still passed and there was nothing proceeding from the poor doctor other than pained groaning. The book was, indeed taking its dark toll on Serc's soul, for his trembling became so profound that he had asked others to turn the pages, lest he rend or tear them, and he grew ever colder, as if exposed to an icy wind. More often now did he mouth the words, for though the text had stayed constantly difficult in reading, it now became ever harder for Serc to focus upon.

At long last, sound did come forth from the elder Dragon's lips, but it was not of cheer, nor of insight. Instead of merely silently forming the shapes of the words in his mouth, by accident, fortune, or fate he now sounded out the hateful text. The whole building seemed to shake with the power that resonated from Serc's voicing, and candles were snuffed out by the blackness that, as a ghastly spirit, seemed to fill the whole of the room.

The words which he spoke were thus:

Tse djonts <u>this</u> kror.

Aownyou kood

Necs tse krag <u>this</u>.

Reg,

Ownyou soon sic <u>thal</u>,

Adj res kror,

Djoon ownyou hay no.

Serc, though at first not realizing what he had done, seemed just as terrified as everyone else gathered when he finally understood that he had spoken the terrible passage aloud, for there had truly been dark power in these words, the effects of which still reverberated throughout the temple. Thankfully, a force greater than the umbrous qualities of the black book's words also resided within the sanctuary, perhaps, also within the walls or the burning incense and candles, but most assuredly within those gathered therein. The black void which had filled the room with its terrible presence was quickly dissipated, beaten out, by the sweeter, warmer, more powerful spirit that dwelt within the Dragon's temple.

"I am sorry. I do not know what came over me, but the words just fell off my tongue." Serc apologized, as he forcibly closed his eyes and tore his head away from the horrid book.

"What did it all mean?" Enthusiastically asked Theros, completely disregarding the awful, dark apparition, only hoping that they had finally found the key to curing Zurthaud.

However, Serc shook his head "no" in response.

"All it said was that the sword's power is a leeching death, and that it could be controlled by the command of its wielder, the same that Malok already surmised." Explained the elder Dragon, as he cast the vile book from his hands. "It is the right spell, the only one, for this horrible magic, but completely useless to us." He exclaimed in exasperation.

They all became very downcast at this, for they had thought themselves so near the end of this battle for the life of so dear a friend and captain. Tears sprang to many eyes, as the malevolent darkness that had entered the room through speaking the powerful words in the black book, even that kind, warm spirit which had so completely dispelled it, was replaced by a new spirit, one within each heart, borne of despondent sorrow.

Malok felt this not the least of all, yet he could not help but to hope. Surely there was more they could do to save the life of this beloved Human, but already most of the congregated Paladins had given up expectation of such. Some had even started to leave, having lost all anticipation of anything good happening today within their own holy temple, and fearing that they would soon be witnesses at yet another funeral.

Yet, did the young black Dragon hope. He had known from the night before that the cure for this wound was not of medicine or anything natural, that it was of the spirit and directly tied to the wicked blade, which he now held again in his hands. Almost unwittingly had he strode back over to where it had been laid, forgotten at the moment when Serc had begun reading from the black book. He wondered now if, perhaps, there was a way that he could control this blade, become its wielder, command its power, and if so, could he possibly terminate its life-sapping spell?

"What are you doing with that?" Shar hissed at him, interrupting his thoughts, for as he did most everywhere else, he had followed his friend over to the sword.

"I was thinking, if the wielder of the blade controls its life-draining spell and could thus stop it with but a whim, perhaps I could become the owner of this weapon and end its curse with my will." Malok hesitantly theorized.

"Do you not know how evil that blade is, how many of your kind and my kind it has slain over the years? There is innocent blood on the hands of the Shadow Lord, on this blade, and I would not have you share in any part of that." Shar insistently pursued. "Besides, no one would dare ask this of you." Said he, moving to take the weapon from Malok's hand.

"I would choose this, if it means saving a life, let alone one so beloved by his friends. How could I live with myself otherwise, knowing that I had the power, or even the possibility, to do good and only stood idle to watch as others suffered?" Spake Malok, and before anyone else could notice or attempt to stop him, as best he knew how, he channeled his will into the terrible sword.

Instead of trying to destroy or attempting to break its power, as he had at the first sought to do when in the dreaming-realm, Malok used his magic endeavoring to control the awful blade, to seek its name and to own it, and at the first, the darkling sword truly did fight with him. Black lightning crackled off from the pommel and the blade itself, scorching his hands, and Malok screamed with pain. Wondering what had occurred, the Paladins turned about just in time to see the young Dragon struggle with the monstrous sword. Completely astounded, they could but watch the grievous weapon, glowing red hot from its thundering, as it tormented the poor Dragon, but it did not fight Malok for so long, at least not with force.

The more it seemed to submit to Malok's will, the more the cunning sword tried to drag him down into its own deep, old murderous intent, that which was purposely imbedded by the Shadow Lord at its making. These abominable apparitions of death and gore swirled into the young Dragon's mind, attempting to either sway him to accommodate their atrocious violence or drown him within the guilt of its past gruesome, depraved actions. Just when it seemed that he would finally give in to this dark will, a hand was laid upon his, lessening the sword's dreadful grasp on Malok's mind.

It was Shar who had touched him, and though the Serpen king knew no magic, Malok could palpably sense the warmth of his companion's friendship flood into his spirit, fighting back against the sword's swelling tides of maddening, chaotic force of will. Soon many others laid their hands upon him as well, first Serc and Theros, then all the other Paladins, all lending him their strength to his own. With a brilliant flash of light, Malok, at last, overcame the dark will imbued within the blade, thanks in part to the spiritual aid of so many others, and the foul weapon hurt him no more, neither in body or mind.

"What have you done?" Serc asked, surprised at what had transpired, for though he had unquestioningly aided Malok, this sort of struggling between an owner's and a sword's will was not yet recollected from his many years of wisdom.

"This blade's power is no longer of death, for it is now mine. No longer shall it be wielded against the good people of this world. No longer shall it drain life, not Zurthaud's nor any others'." Spake Malok, meaning to reply to Serc's inquiry.

However, he had unbeknownst concluded transferring the sword's ownership with his spoken word, and the power of death left the sword. Immediately, being now unable to do that which its dark maker had intended for it, the blade rusted, the leather wrapping on the handle cracked and unraveled, and the pommel fell straight off. The whole sword suddenly broke apart in Malok's hands, as if from great age, for its raw materials could not physically bear the strain of the evil weapon becoming essentially purposeless, devoid of all dark power. By the time the Paladins had taken their hands from Malok's arms, shoulders, and head, it had disintegrated into no more than a pile of rusty brown dust upon the temple floor.

"Not since the days of my youth have Paladins laid hands upon their brethren for such effect as the accumulation of our strength," Serc happily reminisced. "But, this kind of transference of ownership, a truly difficult technique, was a skill only commonly practiced by the Order of Masters. How is it that you have succeeded in it?" He asked, still bewildered by the whole experienced.

"I know not how, only that I had reasoned undoing the spell would require me to become the owner of that fell blade, either that or convince the Shadow Lord to cease from being evil." Malok smiled, happy and honestly proud that his efforts to solve this riddle had succeeded so well.

"What of Zurthaud?" Theros asked, as they all became aware of the repercussions of Malok's actions.

They rushed over to his bedside, and indeed his condition had improved.

No longer was the rotten stench of death about him. His breathing had become full and restful, and his fever had disappeared. Altogether, the young Human seemed as if he could wake from his slumber at any moment, but for the nasty gash still cutting through his chest. For, though the life-draining effect of the now destroyed sword had ceased, Zurthaud had still to mend naturally from his wound, as Serc confirmed by peeking under his bandages.

"He is in the clear now, and should be whole again quite soon, maybe only a day or two with healing magics." Serc confirmed.

However, it was sooner than they thought that Zurthaud was well enough to rise from his death-like state, for he stirred, at last, from his long slumber. He coughed thrice, emitting some blood, but sat upright, nonetheless. This was greeted by none other than a loud chorus of joy from the Paladins, for they shouted jubilantly and praised the Eloigal, as surely it was He who had ordained this miraculous intervention in Zurthaud's healing, and his good servant Malok through whose clever actions had the healing come.

"Theros, where is Theros?" Zurthaud feebly inquired after he had finished with his coughing fit.

"I am right here." Loudly spoke his friend, as he had nearly to shout over the raucous merriment going on about them. "It is good to see you among the living." Said he more softly, as he neared Zurthaud with a warm embrace.

"I had a nightmare, that all of Threa was enshrouded in darkness, that Doraegonoran had fallen, and most horribly that I watched as you died by the Shadow Lord's own hand. I myself could have died of sorrow and fear for the dreams that I had, and all so real." Zurthaud whispered frightenedly. "What has happened? How did I come to be here in the temple?" He asked becoming more and more anxious.

"Calm yourself. All is well, for no one, no army, no dark lord, has even approached the city. I carried you here from the Ragnor, but your father refused your admission to the medical ward, pronounced you dead and commanded we bury your body. I had nowhere else to bring you, rather, no better place to bring you, for Serc has made this temple your sacred hospital, where he has cared for you the past few days. You know, your foolish father plans to punish us for your death." Consoled Theros.

"He shall now have a hard time of that." Zurthaud chuckled, slowly quieting from the rampant fear of his dreams.

"As for what happened, you did almost die, almost, but this young Dragon here, to whom I owe a great debt of gratitude, saved your life." Theros explained, as Serc pushed Malok forward through the crowd to Zurthaud's bedside.

Though he had done these great deeds, Malok did not wish to assume vanity in them, and was uneager to accept the praise and cheers of the gathered Paladins as they applauded his, now, two fantastical accomplishments. He did, however, wish to finally meet this Human who had earned the respect and devotion of all these good folk.

"I do not recall your name, good Dragon, but surely it must be the dreams playing with my memory. Anyway, I thank you, from the depths of my heart. I owe you my life." Conveyed Zurthaud, as after firmly clasping Malok's great hand with his own, he again lay back to rest.

Little did he realize, but Zurthaud could not have possibly remembered Malok, as the Dragon had arrived only after their fatal attempt to storm the Ragnor and slay the Shadow Lord. Serc and Theros remedied this by introducing him and retelling his origin, while Zurthaud listened intently.

"A Dragon raised by the Serpen is not so outrageous, for I see that they have dealt kindly and wisely with their charge. How my father could get his hands on a Dragon's egg without being torn to pieces is the true mystery, and I can only wonder how it was possible?" Zurthaud questioned aloud, after the gathered crowd had, at length, lulled in their joyful accolades. "Do you know the name of your mother?" He asked after some inner debate, questioning whether Malok could have been the son of Lethira, for though Zurthaud had not known of her and Theros having conceived children in their all too brief time as lovers, he now suspected it.

But, Malok only shook his head, "no". "I had hoped to find such answers in coming here." He stated, his voice falling with that crushed hope.

"He is not mine, if that is what you are implying, though I would have been proud to call him my son." Firmly, yet kindly, denied Theros, for as a Dragon, he could clearly determine this, most assuredly, by scent.

Theros' train of thought was interrupted by Serc's insensitive prodding, for the doctor had not been allowed a chance to examine his injuries while Zurthaud had been in so dire need of medical aid.

"Perhaps, now you shall let me tend your wounds, stubborn young Dragon. You shall be fortunate to ever run again, with these burns." Serc chided, as aside, he took the longest look he had since been allowed of Theros' burnt hind legs.

"Nevertheless, my father has committed many crimes, this egg thievery not the least of which. Perhaps, I have not fully considered the consequences or the price, but I think we can no longer ignore his oppressive regime." Gravely spoke Zurthaud.

"It was revealed to us this morning while you were still unconscious that Orthard wishes to condemn every Dragon within the Order to work in the sulfur mines. As much as we have striven to avoid such action, as much as I hate to say, I fear we have no other option than to forcibly overthrow his ridiculous, tyrannical rule." Replied Serc, only briefly allowing an interruption of his coarse medical attentions.

For, as much as every Paladin here hated the vile reign of Lord Orthard, they still wished not to openly oppose the law of their realm. They had struggled to remain obedient and considerate of even the most incredulous of stipulations, for they, unlike Lord Orthard, the other members of the corrupt High Council, or the uncaring, common soldiers of the Order who bore the name of Paladin but did nothing to earn it, were honest in their belief of right and wrong, good and evil, justice and mercy, and wholly pursued these. Rebellion, even such a peaceful one as they intended, would undoubtedly be met with opposition, which would incur violence, perhaps, even the deaths of many.

So it was, that they, first the Dragons, then those who had followed Zurthaud's leading and sided with them, had been long-suffering under the villainous Orthard's cruel boot and had only now, when it meant their certain doom should they continue on in peaceful acceptance of the law, even contemplated revolt.

"Very well, let every Paladin here who agrees with Serc and I give a vote, yea or nay." Zurthaud proposed.

Not a single one gave forth a "nay", not a single voice among the Paladins gathered, for they had all suffered long under Orthard's rule. All shouted forth together a resounding "yea".

"Then, I am not alone in this. Let us go and unseat this despot, my father, from where he sits comfortably lording over us, even as we sorrow." Spoke Zurthaud.

And, the Paladins together then gave a loud shout, of frustrated outrage, of patriotic want for freedom. So loud it was that Malok thought surely Orthard could hear them, even from his lofty, gilded chambers, and he wondered if the fool were quaking in his boots at this fearsome racket they were making. The young Dragon so overcome by the emotion of the throng in their rallying cry could not help but to also lift up his voice to roar with them, and Shar, glancing about, did also join, more so that he did not seem foolish when everyone else was shouting except for him.

"First, you must rest and mend. This will give us time to plan our next move, for the 'what' is decided to do, now is the 'how' to be considered, strategized." Wisely suggested Serc, after much of the shouting had quieted, and all those who heard agreed.

All except for Theros, for with Serc's distracted care, he had only been able to painfully grunt during all this excitement.

Chapter 17

Feldara slowly came to, mostly from the cold dampness of the environment around her, but she soon became aware of the other factor that had driven her into pained wakefulness, a throbbing in her skull, a reminder of what had become of her. Her eyes flashed open, as she instantly recalled the sound blow that Calidon had received to his head and the one she had also obtained. Whirling, she promptly scanned the area about for her attacker.

She saw no one but herself in the small, round, gray stone cave in which she had been placed, and it was a short look, as there was barely enough room within this rocky prison for her own self, let alone another, and that lying down, not sitting or standing. This brought her little comfort, and not just because of the pounding in her head, which was now so forceful that she found herself uselessly rubbing with her fingers the tender point of impact in the absent minded hope of lessening the blaring soreness. Feldara was deeply concerned for Calidon's fate, for Anur whom she had yet to cease worrying about.

She called out for them, but there was no answer. Having nothing better to do, she fought back against the pain, and searched about the room again, hoping to find some manner of escape. At last she found the door, or what seemed to be the door to her little prison, for it was a crack in the otherwise seamless rock wall about her. This crack went around in a rough circular shape on one side of the room, likely meaning that it was evidential of a large rock rolled into place to serve as a shut door.

Upon further inspection of this door, Feldara saw where it was that the light poured into this cavern, thus allowing her to see, for there was a small slit near the top of the door, not nearly wide enough for her to put her clawed fingers through, for to search without for some lever or hold allowing her freedom. However, it was surely wide enough for her to get a glimpse of the world without, and she crawled over to this thin slit in the round stone door, as she could only crawl in the limited space, lest she hit her already sore head on the ceiling, and peeked through to observe the outside world.

Feldara could see very little through this tiny vantage point, but what she saw was quite unusual. Just outside her door were a couple of the bear-people who had attacked her, apparently they were her prison guards. Beyond them, she found that her particular cell was inside a short tunnel, most likely dug into the side of one of the mountains, and beyond this, she could only catch glimpses, glimpses of what seemed like a small town or village. Feldara assumed this, because she could see one and an half log structures, possibly houses or communal buildings, in and out of which stomped more bear-people, some of them big and mean-looking, others smaller and seemingly more friendly, some perhaps even children, for these were very small and ran about rather rambunctiously, likely in play, making all sorts of noise, some of which was assuredly laughter.

The whole sight would have not seemed so bad to Feldara, but that she was a captive of these strange creatures and knew not what they wanted with her. That was about to change, for at length, another bear-person made his way around the corner of the short tunnel, from whence Feldara could not see, and proceeded to walk down the length of it toward her.

The other two bear guards stood aside as he looked within the small rocky prison at Feldara. He backed away quickly when he noticed she was looking straight back at him, and surprisingly, he shouted in at her.

"No breath fire at me! Other one do this; I no like it. No breath fire!" Screamed the bear-person at her, to Feldara's astonishment, speaking a broken, heavily accented, simplistic version of the common tongue.

Feldara had expected them to have their own bear-ish grunting, snorting, roaring speech, but to hear one of them speaking the mutual language of the civilized races made them appear now much more than the animalistic barbarians that she had previously thought them to be. Still Feldara did not know how to respond to this bear-person, whether in anger or in assurance that, indeed, she would not treat them poorly, so she remained silent, mostly out of astonishment.

"You no breath fire, I give you meat." Spoke the bear-person again, but upon not receiving a response from Feldara he resumed his shouting. "No speaking bad, rude, when others speak at you. Speak!"

"Why should I talk to you when you attacked my friend, hit me on the head, and stuck me in this little hole?" Feldara retorted, becoming angered that she should be criticized for rudeness by the very people who had assaulted her.

"I sorry for that. It not our choice. Tiny, black people make us do it." Spoke the bear-person, apparently somewhat apologetic for what had happened to Feldara. "You still want meat? No breath fire at me?"

As much as she would have liked to breathe fire at this consternating bear for her past woes and her current incarceration, whether or not he was responsible, Feldara knew that she physically could not. Besides which, she truly was hungry; even the thought of meat had caused her to salivate, as she had not eaten since yesterday, and that only the little mountain goat Calidon had brought her.

"I will not burn you with my fiery breath, and yes, I would like something to eat." She relented, craftily hiding her physical limitations

The bear-warrior, with the help of his two compatriots, then tardily rolled away the heavy stone door from the entrance to the cell. Only once the large round rock was secured within its precisely carved niche in the side of the tunnel wall, did the one bear who had addressed Feldara step into the small room, and though he was so large that he had to bend his knees in order to fit within, he still managed to hold one of their crude wooden clubs above his head with one hand, while still offering a large leg, seemingly of deer, with the other.

"Are you going to hit me again while I am trying to eat?" Feldara snarled, almost hoping the bear would give her a reason to attack it.

The bear-person, then seemed to consider how horribly he was behaving, treating Feldara as if she were an uncouth animal, easily inclined to violence at any provocation and devoid of reasoning, and surprisingly, he lowered his club.

"I sorry. We forget our way, to welcome strangers. My name Gorod." Spoke the bear, as he tossed the ham and a flagon of, hopefully for her great thirst, water at Feldara's feet. "We, my people, Urz, once live simple, in peace, but tiny-black-people come. They bring giant-warrior and many other small-bad-people. They challenge our chief, his honor; so he must agree, but their champion, giant-warrior, best our chief. Now, we must do what they say. They rule over us, make us do bad things."

She could not listen intently to his drawled speech, as Feldara hungrily tucked into the deer ham which had been smoked and salted to much savor, and thirstily guzzled the flagon's entire contents, indeed, sweet, cold mountain spring water, but she did understand enough of what Gorod was saying. The "tiny-black-people" that he had mentioned must be the Dark Hunters. She could think of no other foe that could easily match this description, other than, perhaps, the Nokre, that which she had read about yet, thankfully, never seen, but the Dark One's puppets had not life or will enough to act so independently, to plot or plan or control an entire race of people, much less communicate effectively. Apparently the Dark Hunters had known of these Urz or had been spying upon them and had observed their government to be no more complicated than rule by the strongest, fittest warrior. The giant-warrior to oppose the Urz chief, Feldara concluded must be an Ogre, as not many other creatures would seem giant to these Urz, nor could defeat these bear-people in battle, but the Ogre, seemingly, had won over their chief in single combat, and the Urz were forced by their own laws to submit to the Dark Hunters' commands.

Feldara then started to empathize more with their plight, seeing that they were as much prisoners as she, for though they might risk breaking their word of honor and try to fight off the Dark Hunters themselves, even strong warriors would have a hard time of it and would suffer many casualties if these many other small, bad-people were a good number of the Dark Horde.

Still, to be so honor bound that an evil tyrant, who did not even belong to your people, could overthrow your own leader and command your people to do what they knew to be wrong, seemed awfully stupid to Feldara. Yet, dwelling upon this information caused the beginning of a plan to formulate in Feldara's mind, of how she could attain freedom and by using this simple honor system to her advantage, just as her enemies had.

"My name is Feldara," She bluntly introduced herself in between a mouthful of venison, for she could not exactly say that it was nice to be acquainted, given the current circumstances. Immediately after finishing her bite, Feldara made her proposition, a bold one and yet all that she could think of to free herself and her companions. "What if I were to challenge the giant warrior, defeat him, and give back rule of your people to your chief?" She asked. "Would you then let my friends and I go free?"

Gorod laughed heartily, or at least seemed to, for the Urz laugh was very much like a heavy breathing mixed with a snore and a growl, nearly indistinct from harsher growls and breaths.

"You!" He chortled. "You no defeat even Barzul, and he dumbest hunter in village. He one who bash your head, make you angry. No, no you not win. Giant warrior defeat you too. No point trying."

With that Gorod turned to leave, still laughing in the gruff Urz manner, but Feldara could not let this chance slip by so easily.

"Wait, wait. Barzul only won because he took me by surprise. I could beat him easily in a fair fight, especially with my fire-breath, and I would do the same to the Ogre, er the giant-warrior. Besides, if I lose, even if I die, what would it matter to you? Another of your strong warriors could challenge them after I weaken the giant-warrior." Feldara pleaded, trying her best not to sound desperate and only confident in her fighting skill, even though she was outright lying about her ability to breathe fire.

Gorod, not knowing of Feldara's late blooming, turned about and seemed to thoroughly consider her foolhardy plan, as he slowly stroked his extended lower lip with his fingers, like a Human or a Dworv with their beard.

"Yes, maybe, this is good plan." He finally replied, using his head's bobbing to emphasize. "My people know your kind, good warriors. I take you to Bjarz. See what they say. If yes, then yes. If no, you stay prisoner like tiny-black-men say so."

With that Gorod motioned for Feldara to exit her confinement, as he also stepped without the round doorway, but he stopped mid-stride, as though he had forgotten something.

"I warn you. No trick me." Said he, brandishing his rough wooden club.

Feldara only snorted in reply, for she had not yet even considered that course of action as a possibility; though now that Gorod had mentioned deception, she was truly sorry to not have been cunning enough to think of that first, seeing as how trusting the Urz were, or at least this specific one.

Apparently satisfied with her half answer, Gorod turned and spoke in the rough, growling Urz language to the two door guards and again motioned for Feldara to follow. These two then accompanied Feldara and Gorod out through the opening of the tunnel, though with much grunting chuckles, apparently having also been told of Feldara's absurd plot.

As the sun blindingly shone into Feldara's eyes, now sensitive to the light after having been accustomed to the relative dark of the tunnel and its prison cell, the world without slowly became visible to her. What had once seemed to be only a primitive village was revealed to be a large town or city of the Urz, for the communal building Feldara had seen was only one of hundreds, and the Urz running about only a handful of the populous. The many structures were all alike in their make, having large stones for the foundation with log sides and heavily thatched roofs, being square or rectangular in shape and altogether symmetrical, seemingly very civilized and comfortable. The streets were of cobblestone, all pressed into the rocky earth so as to become a flat road and very smooth, and though there were many Urz carrying on about them, it was not crowded. Trees and grasses grew thick upon the hillocks and bare spots between the outspread dwellings and shops, and the whole of the city, as it wound its way along the side of a sloping ridge right up to the very top of the mountain, seemed aerated and open to the blue sky above. Feldara could not help but to stare at the unsophisticated, austere masonry of the quaint structures among these other beauteous sights of the city, even as the natives could not help but to gawk at her. Every eye that she passed by was upon her, from the smallest cub to the greatest hunter, as Gorod escorted her up and through the city toward the Bjarz' lodge.

"Look. We are simple people." Spoke Gorod, motioning to the craftsmen at work, the mongers selling, the shoppers haggling, and the children playing, as they strode past what must be their marketplace.

Shops of all sorts lined the open aired square, with types of smithies, tanners, clothiers, bakers, and butchers all present, albeit in the Urz' utilization. No money traded hands, only goods, barter, for the sellers and tradesmen were compelled not only to benefit themselves but to ensure the welfare and survival of their people. They were more communal than most societies, for as Feldara witnessed, the Urz lived and worked together more as an extended family, a tribe, than the other peoples she had seen or read about.

"We no warriors. We hunters, makers, but tiny-black-men no like this. They say 'you must fight for us!' So, you see, it is truth when I say we sorry for what we do to you. They want us make war with other people, your people. We no do this, but they try make us. You defeat giant-warrior; then we be free, live simple again." Gorod said, as he stopped to rest, watching the market's business.

But after only a short while, they continued on again, slowly making their way up the ridge and through the town. Eventually, nearly all the Urz residents had taken notice of the strange creature that was Feldara passing through their town, and they started to crowd around her, trying to get a good look. By their unashamed staring, Feldara could tell that they had not seen many Dragons before. She could also tell that they had arrived at their destination when they came upon the Bjarz' residence, for it was at least twice as large as the other buildings, had a higher double-roof, and had a profound coat of red paint upon the stones of its base.

However, there was no pause to marvel at the exterior of the grand lodge; into the building, through the round, rolling stone doorway, Gorod pushed her, even as the other two Urz accompanying them shouted gruffly at the assembly, causing the crowd to disperse.

Barely inside, just past the lintel, Feldara finally had to stop. It was her turn again to gaze in awe, for the whole of the lodge was gloriously furnished. Solid oak was the floor, amber and shiny with care and polishing, and large scarlet colored tapestries draped the timbered walls. The long main hall was pillared with great redwood trunks, sanded and shined until the piney wood seemed every bit as richly crimson as blood, and a great carpet of hides, fur side up, lay upon the center of the floor, covering its main causeway from the entrance to the very end of the hall.

Upon long log benches, at massive oak tables that stretched down the length of the hall, sat many Urz, each of them seeming as tall and strong as Gorod. They all turned to see who had interrupted their feasting, for indeed, they were in the middle of a banquet, with a large fire roaring and roasting meats near the center of the tables. At the very end of the hall, was an elevated pinewood platform, upon which sat a special seat, decorated with lustrous metal, rich carvings, and fine wool and furs, and every inch of it declared that it must be the chief's throne. As Feldara wistfully noticed that the throne of their people was empty, whispered conversation, or as quiet as the Urz could manage, spread throughout the hall, for all music had ceased, all eating had stopped, as the Urz lords stared in astonishment at their unexpected guest.

"These are Bjarz." Gorod explained, gesticulating to the gathered Urz. "They all great hunters, protectors of our people."

"So, if these are your leaders, where is your chief?" Feldara asked, scanning about the room for an Urz even bigger and stronger than these.

"I was chief." Gorod confessed, his voice tinged with somber regret.

Nevertheless, he strode right up to the edge of the table, and seeing that all were hushed and looking at both him and Feldara, he began speaking. Though Feldara could not understand a word of what Gorod was saying in the grumbling Urz speech, she could tell that it was full of spirit and patriotism. She had not fully realized it at the time, until moments before when she had seen their market, with all the plain happy folk living in harmony, and now this great hall with the gathered nobles, how much her offer, to defeat the giant-warrior and save their people, had meant to them.

She had only been focused on her own problems, her own worries for the small circle that included only Anur and Calidon. Her plan now, when so hastily and foolishly concocted, mostly as an excuse to find her friend's whereabouts, seemed ever so untruthful, and Feldara felt ashamed to think that she might have wished to use or deceive these honest folk. However, new fervor came to her, filled her heart like the fire that should fill her lungs, to live up to her bold words and remain true to her word.

When Gorod had finished, after only a few moments of deliberation, all the bear lords raised their right paw, nearly in unison, and gave a great shout, for they, being too good-natured to even consider war and violence against other peaceful beings and hating the oppression of their new masters, were quite finished with the reign, however short, of the wicked Dark Hunters.

Despite the positive consensus of all the other Urz nobles, there was one in the room who did seem to detract. To Feldara, he seemed not a lord like the other gathered Urz, for he had not sat at the table with the others, but rather upon the small set of steps that led from the floor to the top of the dais, upon which was Gorod's throne, and was dressed in a robe of cloth and animal furs rather than the piecemeal armor of his brethren. He was also much older than the other Urz, with white shaggy fur, and saggy, wrinkly skin, and he had to lean heavily on a gnarled staff, as he rose to address the others. He spoke slowly and hushed, and by the time he had finished and returned to his seat the room had become deathly quiet.

"What is going on?" Feldara impatiently asked of Gorod, curious as to what was being said and frustrated that she could understand none of it.

"I chief, but chief no more. Tiny-black-man chief now. So, I tell your words to Bjarz, these Urz. They say together, we go with your words." Gorod explained, quite well to his own liking, but far from satisfying Feldara's curiosity.

"So, you had a vote. Good. Who was the old one? What did he say?" Feldara determinedly inquired.

"He our spirit-man, Znakar. He say, 'Be careful. We fail, more tiny-black-men come for us. They servants of great shadow, far to South. We must be sure of you.' Tomorrow he test you, see what you made of, before we let you fight, if we let you fight." Gorod replied.

"What happens to me if I do not pass the test?" Feldara wondered aloud, becoming less and less sure of this rash course of action by the minute.

"We must keep you prisoner, like tiny-black-men want. Maybe, they kill you at the end. We be sorry for that, but we can do nothing. They threaten my people, the children. Giant-warrior wants to see what we taste like." Returned Gorod. "Come now; I take you back."

However, Feldara resisted being forced to leave, as Gorod had begun nudging her. She had as yet to see Calidon or even hear of Anur.

"Wait. I want to see my friends. Please, take me to them." She pleaded, now caring not at all if she seemed plaintive.

Gorod seemed to think about this for a moment, as he again stroked his protruding lip, but at last he consented with a grunt.

"I take you to other-black-man, your friend, but other Fire-breather you no see. Tiny-black-men have him where we not go without them see us. They not see us with you out of cave; would be very bad." Said he, stating his conditions.

Feldara could do nothing but agree, for she was still a prisoner, indeed, by her word even more than of the Urz' or the Dark Hunters' power. She followed Gorod out of the chief's hall and back down the sloping main, and only, road that cut through the Urz city, back to where her cell was. Just as Feldara thought they were not going to take her to Anur and were only uncaringly taking her back to the prison where she had before been held, they turned a corner about the tunnel and proceeded into another adjacent cavern, which besides being longer and with a few other side passages that led to other cells, was exactly identical to the one where she had been incarcerated.

At the end of this cavern was the last round, rolling, cell door. With a nod from Gorod, the two accompanying Urz guards shoved it open, and Feldara slowly stepped inside.

As Feldara's eyes again adjusted to the change in lighting from the bright outside to the deep, inner darkness of the prison, she could already see the form of her beloved mentor sitting huddled against the far wall. Without hesitation, and regretfully without any word of greeting, Feldara rushed over to him for a good, long, reuniting embrace, but Anur did not recognize her immediately, as his back had been turned to them. At first, he struggled against whom he thought was an attacker.

"Anur it is I, Feldara." She groaningly shouted, wishing only to hold and be held by him.

It was then that Anur turned toward her, realizing who she was, and it was then that Feldara's eyes finally adjusted to the blackness about them. She could see that his helmet had been taken from him, along with his good clothes. He was left with nothing but a plain ragged tunic and he bore bruises and nasty welts where he had been beaten and otherwise abused.

However, Anur cared not for anything else in the world than the sight of his beautiful Dragoness before him, and he wept profusely and resisted her no longer, embracing her and kissing her again and again upon her cheek and neck.

"Oh, Feldara, why did you have to come here? Though I am glad to see you, I would wish you a thousand miles from here." He whispered, for his voice was cracked and dry from the agonies inflicted upon him.

"Oh, Anur, I am sorry, so sorry, for what I had said to you. I would give anything to take it all back. I would give anything just to be back on our little island with you. I do not hate you. I love you, and I am so sorry." She blubbered through her tears, even as he cradled her large head in his arms and stroked the crest above her eyes just as she liked best.

"Hush child, hush. It was but the road and the rain talking that night. Speak not ever of it again." He comforted, and for the longest moment ever, they just sat together in that dark, little cave.

Sniffling from the entrance caught their attention, and Feldara turned to see that Gorod and his men were tearing up and trying to hide it by shuffling their feet, looking away to wipe their eyes, and blowing their noses profusely. She could tell that they had not been the ones to harm Anur, for the Urz were truly gentle folk. It was the Dark Hunters who had caused all their misery, all of her recent wretchedness, and she longed to make them pay in blood for every misdeed. She was fully committed now to her rashly spoken words, they were now her honest intentions, to defeat the Ogre and cast down its cruel masters, to bring about justice for herself, for Anur and Calidon, and for the Urz.

"Please, let me stay here tonight." She asked of Gorod, for she could not bear to be another night apart from Anur now that she had found him, and in such poor condition.

Gorod could only nod in reply, and he and the other Urz turned and strode out the door, closing it only after promising to bring more meat later. They had accomplished their goal of not shedding a single tear publicly, and after seeing such a heart-wrenching scene, it had surely been a hard won battle.

Anur and Feldara cared not for such things, for their hearts and minds could now rest easier knowing, at least, that they were together again, and that, together, they could rely upon each other and withstand most any difficulty to come their way. In that rest, in that strong peace, they remained, and not even waiting for the evening meal, they could not help but to drift away to sleep, still held fast in each other's arms.

Chapter 18

The sunrise could not wake Feldara this morning, for she and Anur were too far back within the cave-prison to clearly see the light of daybreak, even through the common slit carved into each cell's stone door. Unfortunately, that which did wake her was far less gentle than the splashing of golden rays across one's face, for Gorod had arrived, quite early, to bring her to the test he and his people had prepared the night before. Clearly having no desire to wait for Feldara to arise naturally, he had begun pushing her with his clawed foot. Of course, upon becoming conscious, her response was to growl viciously at him, but the Urz took it only as a good sign that she would do well that day.

"Rise! Rise!" He sportively shouted. "Today we see what Fire-bringers can do."

"Only after I have eaten." Feldara sleepily grumbled. "I think I shall have some bear for breakfast."

At this Gorod took a little offense, as expressed by some loud snuffling, but he did leave off from kicking her, saying that he would return with some meat.

"What does he mean by that?" Asked Anur, as he too arose, though having been awake earlier and closely watching Gorod's every movement

It was then that Feldara realized that there was another difficulty in her plan, lying hidden, unforeseen until now, for she still had to convince Anur to go along with it. Sheepishly, she turned to face him and slowly explained her hastily construed plot to overthrow the Dark Hunters and rescue them all.

She could read his every facial expression now that his helmet had been removed, but instead of the anger or sternness of face she had expected and had always imagined upon him whenever she had done foolish things like this, there was only an anguished grimace, as if he could see and feel all the horrible ways this could go wrong all at once and could not bear the thought of her harm or failure a second longer. It shocked and surprised Feldara at first, for she was unused to seeing anything there and felt awkward now that she could look directly into his eyes through a whole conversation. She almost wished to look away, but at the same time, it was one of those longings for which her heart had always pined, to see his face, his response when she spoke.

When she finished he was slow to reply, but it was still the expected Anur answer.

"No. I cannot let you do this. It is much too risky of a plan. If that Ogre gets hold of you, it will tear you limb from limb, and unless these Dark Hunters are fools, they will never agree to this. Whether you win or lose, they surely will not honor their end and just imprison you again, or kill you. Besides that, judging from my forced, though thankfully brief, visits to their camp, where the rack was my bed and the scourge my meat, they surely have a full battalion of Trolls here at their command, along with twice as many Goblins; if the Urz cause too much trouble for them, they will just conquer the town by force." He firmly objected.

"What other choice do we have?" She asked, not rebelliously, only speaking the truth. "You are yet in no condition to fight, and I have not as yet seen Calidon. Besides which, even if we could escape, how could we leave these people to such a fate as being oppressed by the Dark Horde?"

Neither was she simply using the Urz as leverage to force Anur to concede, for through her tour of the town and her time spent with Gorod, Feldara had genuinely become compassionate for their plight. She truly could not, would not, leave without even trying to rescue them. Anur too had to admit he could not just abandon the Urz to such a dark fate as unwillingly becoming part of the Dark Horde, even his loving parental desire to protect his charge could not ultimately undermine his righteous character and the good which he knew was greater of need.

———————

"You are right." Anur relented, though not happily, and he pensively held his jaw. "I only wish there were another way, in which you were not endangered. If only we could somehow meet with Calidon, he surely would be more than a match for a single Ogre." Anur suddenly remembered that he had yet to see hide or wing of his other young charge, and a grieved expression came upon his face. "Where is he? I forgot to ask yesterday why he was not with you."

"The Dark Hunters are holding him elsewhere." Feldara answered, trying not to be surprised at seeing any emotion on Anur's face, which she had been so used to seeing helmeted. "Gorod spoke of it yesterday. I can only hope that he is well, for I have not been allowed to see him since we came here."

"Yet, I did not catch glimpse of him in their camp, unless, and I hope not, that grate near the middle covered a pit, into which they had thrown him." Anur anxiously mused.

With that they became sorely worried for the young male's sake. They could only guess as to why he had been separated from them, but Gorod then returned, cutting off any further conversation. He had brought more of the same venison hams and flagons of water as from yesterday, and both Anur and Feldara were more hungry than they had realized, too famished to even converse between bites and drinks.

"Good, eat; get stronger." Encouraged Gorod. "The test is strength."

After they had finished with their breakfast, Gorod and the two jail guards led them out of the prison and across the spacious lawn before it. He led them all the way across this open grassy area to the edge of a cliff, that which was the end of the plateau, spreading about and before the prison at the bottom of the ridge that upon which their city was built. All the Bjarz and the ancient Urz holy man, the Znakar, were already gathered before them, standing about or sitting on stones and stumps, and they watched Feldara intently as she passed among them, sizing her up with but a gaze.

She puffed out her chest as well as she could, trying her best to look noble and strong, even though her heart was racing with excitement and anticipation, for she knew not at all what had been planned as her test of strength.

At last, when they had gotten to the opposite end of the crowd and stood before the very edge of the cliff so that Feldara could look down its length to see that, though it was a steep drop off and quite far, it was sloped kindly enough that one could possibly make it all the way down, or up, through walking or easy climbing.

"Here your test." Said Gorod, as he pointed to a nearby rock.

It was not an ordinary boulder like the others in that field, not in that it was quite large, easily being two-thirds as tall as Anur, but that it seemed to have been chiseled and even polished so as to become nearly perfectly round. There was even a slight sheen on its surface, as if it had been waxed or wettened in some way, for to make its surface quite smooth.

"Push off edge." Gorod commanded, emphasizing vehemently with his own arms.

Feldara walked over to the great rock, which sat only about ten feet back from the cliff, and felt of it with her clawed hands. It was not particularly heavy for its size, though, indeed, being a rock, and a rather large one at that, it was weighty for any object that had to be moved by sheer force of body. She positioned herself and pushed on it and found the great boulder to roll quite well, even on the rough grassy earth, mostly due to its finely smoothed surface. Without much more effort than could be expected, she pushed the rock right off the plateau and it rolled merrily down the length of the slope, about a hundred feet, and crashed somewhere among the trees at the base thereof, remaining perfectly intact the whole journey through, even to its end.

"Was that your test of strength?" Feldara snorted, thinking it much too easily accomplished.

"No." Replied Gorod, and a large Urz smirk spread across his muzzle as he pointed to the ground under his feet. "Now bring back up."

Immediately upon hearing this, the enormity of the challenge hit Feldara, and all her pride and confidence immediately deflated, as this task, with the weight of the rounded stone and the enormity of the sloping drop, seemed impossible to accomplish even for a large, strong Dragon male like Yuronon. She only barely kept her jaw from dropping open, as Anur gave her a look of grave concern, but this was a task that must be done, if ever she, Anur, or Calidon were to be freed. So, she only asked a few questions of Gorod.

"How long do I have to roll that rock back up here?" Was her first inquiry, as she stifled the need to swallow conspicuously.

"Until sun-down." Gorod replied, still bearing an awful smirk on his face.

"What happens if I cannot push it all the way back up in the time allotted?" She delicately posed, trying to save some dignity.

"Nothing. You go back to hole. Tiny-black-men come, take you away." Gorod replied, his smirk disappearing. "Bjarz lose respect for you, but that no matter. Do this, and you are stronger than all Urz. No Urz rolls big rock like this up hill, ever; only smaller rock. Many try rock this big; all fail. Do this, and you fight giant-warrior." Explained he, and he patted her heartily, once upon the forearm. "Udash! Means, 'Good luck.'"

It really was not luck that she needed, at all, but rather a miracle, Feldara thought to herself as she spread her wings and glided down to the bottom of the cliff. Straightaway, she began looking for the boulder among the dense pine strand that she had last seen it roll into; though, it was not hard to trace such a heavy object's course. It had forced a deep muddy track through the loamy, pine needle blanketed turf and had even felled some smaller conifers when it had broken through the thickly woven boughs.

Feldara finally found it at the base of a larger spruce, one that in its grand age had not yielded to the great stone orb's ever lessened kinetic powers. Even so, the tree had received an ugly knock and had been shaken to the dropping of many fresh cones from the impact. The rock itself had received no such damage, not even small chips or gouges, and was only worse for wear by the clumping of mud and debris upon the majority of its once shiny surface.

But, Feldara did not waste any time with observations. As soon as she had spotted the stone, she put herself on its side facing opposite the steep hill and began rolling it back along the track whence it had come.

It was not easy going, for the great boulder was so cumbersome, and there was an incline, however slight, all the way from this piney knoll sitting near the base of the mountain to the very base of the cliff. Still, on and on Feldara worked, slowly pushing the boulder forward and upward.

She was not a stranger to hard labor, for even when she was little, Anur had her helping him with whatever task he had done in maintaining their livelihood upon their small island. She had fished with him and hunted, which were her favorite tasks, but also she had helped him garden their meager crop, which had seemed such a bore to her, for as a Dragon, she would not eat most of their harvest, save potatoes and a few other heartier, "meatier" vegetables. They had also repaired many of the devastated buildings together, with her doing more and more of the heavy lifting of stones and beams as she had grown bigger and stronger.

However, this great rock was the heaviest thing she had ever set her hand to moving, and the sun crept up the sky unto noontide before she had even reached the base of the great cliff from whence she had rolled this accursed boulder. Feldara had to rest a moment here, for to catch her breath.

If Dragons could sweat, she would have then, but they do not. Instead, her wings had opened ever more slightly to let out her excess heat, and her tongue did loll from her mouth, though not quite in the obscene panting of a dog. She sat upon the grass there, beside the irksome stone, which by now had become horribly filthy from rolling back up the same miry track of its descent, and looking above to the top of the cliff she saw many of the Urz lords looking down at her. Among them was Gorod, and seeing her look his way, he did smile and wave at her.

Feldara was too tired now to even wave back, so she tried to smile instead, but it must have seemed the most weary, defeated grin ever. She knew not how this rock could ever get back up that steep slope, for it had taken the better part of her strength only to roll it back up to the foot of the large hill. She could not contemplate giving up. She knew that all their freedom: of the Urz, Anur, Calidon, and herself, rested upon her aching shoulders.

Her tired legs having eventually ceased their trembling, she got up, but just as she was about to resume rolling the stone, she spotted Anur coming down the far side of the cliff toward her. He had taken the easy route, which Feldara had assumed would be off limits for her rolling exercise, a well tended path up the hillside, skirting around the crescent-shaped overarching of the cliff.

"How are you faring?" He asked when he had reached her.

"Not well." She simply responded, still breathing heavily. "This rock is very heavy."

"I was allowed to bring you water and some food, but I was instructed not to help you move the rock." Anur said holding out some dried bit of meat and a large water-skin.

Feldara took the meat and chewed upon it, again sitting with her back to the great boulder, and with several big gulps of water, she downed its spice and dryness after only a few chews. She would have preferred fresh meat, over the chewy dried jerky, but it was much better than eating nothing. Having finished her lunch, she sat sipping the water for a while, as silence engulfed her, but at length, she could not hold back her inner turmoil.

"Anur, what am I going to do? I shall never roll this giant stone back up this hill. It is too steep, and the rock is much too heavy. I am afraid that this time I have gotten too big of a mouthful for me to swallow." She whined, wishing that she could just give up and knowing that she could never do so.

"What do you mean, 'this time'?" Anur asked blithely, trying to lighten her mood, but seeing that effort go to naught, he took his more usual serious tone. "Have you tried viewing this test as a puzzle, trying to see any way other than the obvious to more easily accomplish this task?" He asked, though himself knowing not of any simpler solution, nor expecting the unsophisticated Urz to have imbedded one within this brutish challenge.

Still, this question did cause Feldara to ponder over any other means by which she could get such a heavy load up so high a slope. If she tried simply rolling it, the ball-shaped rock would be against her the whole way, fighting alongside gravity, eventually winning and rolling away down the hill again. She had no rope with which to make a pulley or even a harness, but that along with tools of any kind, such as a larger felled tree utilized as a lever or stop, was probably against the yet unspoken rules that the Urz had in place for this contest. She could try rolling the rounded boulder about the escarpment and up the gentler slope of the path which Anur had walked down for to greet her, but Feldara did neither think that would be allowed, nor would it be much less difficult than simply rolling the great ball straightaway up the course whence it had come.

She sat there almost a good hour, sipping the last of the water and thinking, but no credible plan jumped into her head, no moment of inspiration was conjured from her many plots. So, at last, Feldara rose again, thinking only of the enormous struggle ahead, planning only to do what was the obvious, for that seemed all there was to be done about it, to roll the big rock straight back up the steep hill. However, as she got up, she had need to stretch her wings, as they had gotten a little stiff from being unused and leaned against for so long.

She flapped them a little, pumping some life back into the tingling, inactive appendages, and suddenly the flash of insight for which long had she sought leaped into her mind like lightning from an angry black cloud. She suddenly knew the answer, how she would prevail when all the Urz who had tried before had failed, and it was not because she was simply stronger than they. Feldara would use what was special about her, what made her different from them, to conquer what they never had before, and with vigor, she returned to rolling the rock.

Neither was it upward the hill as everyone had expected.

She had turned her back to the gathered crowd of Bjarz, and was now pushing the great stone back down the mountain from whence she had come. Many hushed conversations exploded all at once from the cliff above, as the Urz lords, bewildered by this change of direction, confusedly pondered what could she mean to be doing by rolling the rock back down the hill, and they began to wonder if this was a sign of her quitting. Even Anur questioned her drastic change of tactic.

"You do know that you are rolling that rock the wrong way?" He asked, only half-assured that his Dragoness had concocted some kind of plan.

"Just trust me." She grunted, giving him a little smile from an askance glance, as she could not afford more distraction while struggling against the weight of the boulder.

Feldara found it much easier going with gravity down through the sloping, pine forested steppe than it had been coming up against it, and she made great headway returning within an hour's time to the very same spot where the ball had ceased its rolling against the side of that sturdy conifer. Here Feldara struggled a little, having to push the large stone up and out of the trench it had made, but once she had succeeded with that task and had the big round rock on unmarred ground, without any deep muddy track to restrain its motion, the going became fairly quick, indeed. As the great boulder began to roll more and more freely, it gathered speed, enough so that Feldara had hardly to push it at all, but rather, she trotted along behind it and pushed it sideways in either direction to avoid clumps of brambles and tree stumps in her immediate path.

She had gotten out of sight of the cliff, but Anur and the Urz accompanying him had followed along and were now a little way off to her side and were running to match pace with her. At last, Feldara found what she had been looking for, the end of the pine strand and therefore the end of this steppe. She broke suddenly through the shade of the boughs into a clear afternoon and proceeded to the sudden drop from this plateau, another cliff, not half so kindly sloping as the one she had rolled her stone down. It was, rather, a sheer drop-off, falling thousands of feet to its bottom; it was the very ultimate end of the great, high mountain range, with only open sky beyond it, and the distant grasslands far below.

Yet, Feldara did not slow her pace as she sped her rolling stone toward the fast approaching cliff; she only quickened, having now to run after the great rock, forcing her witnesses to race after her. Anur's face was tightened into miserable grimacing, for he knew not what his precious charge was about to do, but still he kept silence, choosing to trust her decision, whatever it was.

At the very last second, before the large round rock rolled straight off the vast expanse and into the empty air, Feldara clutched onto its smooth surface and with her talons dug into the stone as best she could. As Anur, now unable to hold his peace, shouted something inaudible over the rush of wind biting the bare escarpment, she held on as if for life itself to the careening boulder, or rather death itself, for it plunged fiercely downward and over the edge.

The force of weight and gravity tore at Feldara, as she and the great stone both descended the better part of an hundred feet in mere seconds, but she knew that this moment was most crucial, she had to act quickly, or the two conflicting forces soon to be unleashed would wrench her apart. The Dragoness flicked her wing arms, and the glorious silken folds opened to the wind. Bulging with the lifting power, they fought as allies with her, even against the supreme force of magnetism, gravity itself, against the weight of the hefty rock, too massive for her to have so conquered alone on flat ground.

Still, though she had spread her splendid, mighty wings as quick as she could, prevention or even lessening of these two powers' fight was not fully achieved, and the consequences upon her flesh were terribly painful. Lift and gravity battled within her own body, and rent her insides, pulled her muscles, stretched and beat at her wings, and threatened to lose her grip on the, suddenly tenfold burden of the heavy stone. Feldara cried out from the hurt it caused her, abrupt and acutely horrendous, but with a tremendous flap of her powerful limbs, as quickly as it started, the battle ended.

She had won.

Soaring now over rock and field, she turned and easily ascended above the edge of the cliff she had fallen from only moments before. Anur was standing there, his face beaming with pride as he smiled up at her, for his Dragoness had overcome, and not with force or wit alone, but with both together had she bested all the strength and smartness of the Bear-people.

She did not pause above them, but rather let the momentum she had gained from her bone shattering dive continue to propel her toward the stone's final rest. In less than a minute, she was hovering over the very spot from where she had rolled the smoothed rock down the slope, and all the Bjarz were agape gazing up at her. Not even the sly Gorod could contain his amazement, though he had, indeed, desired her success.

Feldara dropped the great stone orb from the last few feet of her descent and it thudded heavily to the ground at the feet of the nearest Bjarz, and yet no one cheered for her as she landed, not even a smile was passed among them. Feldara's smug grin of triumph was replaced by a disdainful frown, for she began to realize that, even past their amazement of its accomplishment, they were, and only out of pride for their own strength, considering her victory a cheat.

Indeed, she had not "rolled" the stone back up the hill, but that was not what Gorod had asked her to do. All that he said was to "bring" the stone back up the steep hill, and he had given her no specification as how that was to be accomplished. From his poor description of the rules of contest, using tools, taking the easier path, or even utilizing magic, had Feldara the knowledge, should have been acceptable, but the Urz lords began shouting angrily, pointing their fat clawed fingers at her and Gorod and each other.

"They think you cheat." Said Gorod, as he approached her. "They say, 'No flying is allowed.' I too think you cheat a little, but it clear you brought stone back up here with strength, strength of wings."

"Then, why are they so upset?" Feldara bitingly asked, making clear in her voice how unhappy she was with their response.

"You just do what no Urz ever dream of, bringing a rock this big up hill. You disgrace us and our sons with your strength." Gorod replied, becoming a little defensive himself. "Now they decide whether to count your rock or no. Some talk beating you with clubs just for besting champion's rocks."

With that last comment, Feldara had to restrain her anger, for she knew it would only hurt her cause if she lost her temper and began retaliating. It certainly would not help their situation either, for they would hate her and her people and might even consider joining with the Dark Horde. However, she still could not comprehend how these stupid bears could prattle and argue about something so small when their entire way of life was so direly threatened; she could not understand the useless squabbling of nobles and their politics.

However, not all the Bjarz gathered were against her. Gorod was much experienced in their politic and was already going about calming and gathering his close allies, even while attempting to sway the opposition, but it was the Znakar that raised his voice and quieted the Urz lords.

With a shout, he silenced the bickering mob and then proceeded to reminded them that the rules of the contest did not define what kind of strength was to be used in returning the rock to the top of the hill, and that they must accept with honor that her Dragon's strength was greater than any that the Urz could muster. Or, at least, that is what Gorod translated to Feldara.

He was the voice of reason, nearly quoting Feldara's own thoughts, that it was ridiculous to quarrel over so little a discrepancy when their very freedom was now at stake. Only thanks should be offered to the Dragoness who had willingly and selflessly provided an opportunity to redeem their lives from such cruel masters.

Gorod then utilized this moment of silence and reason to ignite the crowd with optimism, for their champion was this Dragon who had proven her strength greater than all the Urz and surely could free them from the terrible Ogre. And, though Feldara could not understand a word of that which was spoken, by the time that they two had finished, the whole crowd of Bjarz had verily begun cheering.

"What did you say to them?" She asked, as Gorod returned to her from his swift campaigning.

"I say only, 'Trust you for champion.' It was Znakar who shame them like little children for bickering when bigger are worries. He say, 'You victory fair, you have different strength, so we not dishonored.'" He explained, and he then gave her such a hearty pat on her tired shoulder that Feldara nearly fell over. "Udzem, good job! You, now champion!"Gorod heartily exclaimed, as his smile returned and the Bjarz intensified in shouting her praise.

<><><><><>

That night, after Feldara had been given the remainder of the day to recuperate from her ordeal, the Urz brought her and Anur up to the chief's lodge to feast and toast her achievement, for somewhat to show that they had no more enmity with her for outdoing their strongest warriors and nobles, but mostly because, as Gorod had explained while escorting them back up through the town, the Urz used any and every excuse that they could to party and drink.

Feldara cared not for their foul, smelly, potato derived liquor, though every Urz had a large flagon, which they refilled several times during the night, but she did appreciate the roasted boar and goat, freshly grilled over the hearth right in the middle of the great hall. What captured her attention most of all was the decorations they had prepared for the feast, for myriad colored paper lanterns had been strung in long lines from house to house, crisscrossing the street at many points and intersecting each other in a luminous web of festivity.

The speed at which the celebration had been prepared only reminded Feldara of the simplicity and happiness, the gentleness and love of life, and the sprightly making of fun that these people had within them, ready to spring out at any instant from their coarser exterior gruffness, like the first lilies of spring from winter's lingering snow. It brought joy to her heart and forgetfulness to her mind, seeing all this merrymaking, the young Urz dancing, the women- who were the only ones trusted with preparing a good dinner- old and young, running about with cooking and serving food and drink, even a little music played blithely on crude plucked strings, flute, and a few drums and cymbals. In all the joyous merriment, as they jubilantly shouted their version of her name, "Feltra", she almost forgot why they were even celebrating, why she was even here.

Suddenly, the hall's door opened harshly with a loud bang, and the jolting noise and what followed it brought her back to the present.

The musicians stopped their playing, and all eyes turned to the great hall's entrance, as in strode the most deplorable of party crashers, the most unwanted of fiends. It was none other than the Dark Hunters, only four in number now, but with them they brought a rabble of stunted grunting, pig-like

Goblins, tall, stony, lizard-like Trolls, and one giant, Black-iron mail clad Ogre, who had to stoop quite a bit to even enter the hall, though with its enormous, wickedly spiked, Black-iron mace it could just as easily have made its own door.

"Well, well, it seems our friends and subjects have decided to throw a party, and apparently thought it imprudent to invite us." Sneered the raspy voice of one Dark Hunter, apparently their captain, as he casually strode up through the great hall, to the chief's dais, and sat down in the throne thereon. "Please, let me not interrupt your merrymaking."

The Urz did not answer, though the bear-women did rush all the children quickly from the hall, and the Bjarz silently grabbed for their weapons.

"Come now, stay your hands, for why would I have need to quarrel with my loyal subjects?" Continued the leering Dark Hunter Captain, having noticed the sudden, yet subtle, rush for armament. "Unless of course, you have forgotten to keep imprisoned our special guest." Said he gesturing toward Feldara. "Or, you had forgotten whom it is that I serve, he who shall cast down your mountains, should I return empty-handed to his land, he whom your nightmares cannot display more terribly than is in actuality, the magnificent and deathly Lord of Shadow, the Kragon."

At this point he snatched the drink from Gorod's own hand, who had been sitting nearby on the steps before the throne, yet not upon it, and he paused to take a sip from the vessel, lifting the visor of his helm only slightly so that his face could still not be seen

"And yet," He continued. "I do see that you have quite disregarded your instructions, for our prisoner sits in a place of honor in my hall. Have you also forgotten about my, no... our, master?"

Gorod did not flinch when his cup was taken, nor now did he let his anger pour forth unchecked at the belligerence of the Dark Hunter captain. He stood and replied in a calm, restrained voice. "Since you defeat me with your champion, I be sore. I no like your rule, and now I challenge with my champion. I choose my prisoner, Fire-bringer, fight for me against your giant-warrior, win back right as chief." He explained pointing back at Feldara, for she sat near the very middle of the long table with Anur at her side. "She best your champion, I be chief again, and she go free. She lose, she stay prisoner, and we fight in your war."

The Dark Hunter captain then did thoughtfully consider this, for he had been desirous of forcing the Urz to obey without necessarily conquering or killing them all. His master greatly coveted their strength, size, and strategic location, in the northern mountains, above and between the Human and Aelv realms, as an invaluable asset in whatever schemes were planned for the coming war.

"I suppose I can afford to humor your customs, seeing as I also did use them to subjugate you." He venomously relented. "Yet, even if our champion loses and you think yourselves free of the dark hand that stretches forth in iron, crushing grip over these lands, we will have rule over you. We shall take the Dragoness, and my master's will shall be done."

With that he rose and proceeded to leave, confident that he would prevail, and having nothing more to say, he tossed his drink, goblet and all back at Gorod, who stoically received the wet, rude gesture, though a wrathful tremor spread through his tightening limbs. The rabble followed their leader out through the door, with the large Ogre leaving last, and Feldara used this opportunity to measure her opponent. True, the Ogre was huge and intimidating with its spiked weapon, armor, and horned helm, but it was very slow and seemingly very dull in thought, possibly even to the point of being incapable of speech. It would be a terrible challenge, but Feldara knew within herself that she could defeat this foe. She was far smarter than any such creature, and much quicker. She would use these two advantages to her benefit and its demise, but something about the Dark Hunter captain's surety of her capture and their horrid victory unsettled her.

Anur noticed this and patted her arm gently.

"I saw you overcome so massive an obstacle today; I have no doubt now that this one shall topple tomorrow." He said encouragingly, as he looked into her golden eyes with his own. "But, if something goes awry, know that I will jump into the fray, rules or no rules. I will have your back, and if need be, I will die defending you."

She had nothing to say in reply to that, no argument, nothing to add; so, instead she laid her head in his arms. It was all she had ever needed or wanted from him, for him to be there for her, as her father and friend.

The party was over now. Even though the vile darklings had gone, no one felt like celebrating anymore.

Gorod, still stinking from the spill of his own beverage tossed back upon him, led them to their sleeping quarters, but it was not back down the hill to the prison caves. Instead, he took them to a room within the chief's lodge, down a side corridor apart from the main hall, and there they slept, albeit restlessly, eagerly awaiting the coming dawn.

Chapter 19

It was one hour before noon according to the small sundial that Zurthaud had placed out on the balcony of the temple atop the Dragon's tower. An important hour noon was, for then it would be decided if the true Paladins of the Order would revolt, or bear for yet another day, month, or year the oppressive tyranny of his father, the despicable Orthard.

However, it was other men who would determine their course, not themselves, for they only longed to continue in the true duty of the Order, to fight against the oncoming tide of darkness. It was the High Council that would cast the vote: whether or not to commit a crime against life and morality itself, inhumane and barbaric, befitting more the savages of the Dark Horde rather than the lofty governing bodies of a civilized society. At the behest of lord Orthard, they would make their decision by the stroke of noon, whether to send the last few Dragons of the Order to work as slaves within the terrible sulfur mines, a doom of certain death, a slow, yet sure execution by means of the foul sulfur fumes, or to not do so and continue on in the tense cold-war that had been silently, politically raging since a Dragon had last sat at the High Council with them.

Zurthaud was not alone as he waited for this important mid-day hour, for Theros his companion was by his side, as always. The large male Dragon stretched his massive red wings in the bright sunlight, catching in them the heat and energy of the noontide sun. He was recovering well and quickly from the horrible burns which the Shadow Lord had inflicted on him, and though he, probably, never again could bound and leap and race with them as a young Dragon, he had nearly regained all other use of his scorched back legs.

____

This was thanks to the incredible healing skill of Serc, the aged Dragon physician who also sat with him upon the great porch of the temple, but unlike the pensive Human, the doctor's own attentions were still focused upon the little black book Zurthaud had stolen from the very stronghold of the Dark Lord,

That tome had cost the lives of ten Paladins, and nearly Zurthaud's own, to bring it back, and though nothing could be considered worth the lives of his friends, he had found it to be somewhat a token for their sacrifice, so that now they could not be called vainly spent. Once the spell on the sword had been broken, the entire book seemed to have lost much of the dreadful energy which had before so sapped the reader of strength and will; so that when Zurthaud had been cured of his deathly malady, Serc had been able to fully concentrate upon scouring the dark text for other useful bits of information. Though the aged Dragon still trembled slightly as he scanned through the tome and had to rest from it often, it held no greater power than to unsettle his stomach with the more unsavory passages.

After Zurthaud's healing, many had wanted to discard the dreaded tome, but the Human had insisted on saving it. It was not out of any desire to see the piece of excessively morbid literature kept from flames, for the book had no value apart from the possibility of revealing a weakness of the Dark Lord. More than any other reason, the cause of the young black Dragon, Malok, and his friend, Shar, was why Serc still continued his research in the evil lore of the black book, rather than burning it, for they were pursuing a Bright Dragoness from Malok's supernatural dreams.

A fabulous connection had Zurthaud drawn from the "Bright One", which the Shadow Lord had mentioned with fear and trembling, to this Dragoness from Malok's visions. Though the Human did not understand the full meaning of the allusion, for he still thought that all Dragonesses had died and their noble race had come to its end.

The young black Dragon and his Serpen companion had already left in the early hours of the morning, and though they had wished to stay and help the Paladins retake their stronghold and right the wrongs of Orthard, Zurthaud had insisted that they get a head start in the crucial search. They could not afford to wait any longer, lest the Shadow Lord find "her" first. If their quest to find her could bring about a person, a weapon, that not only caused the darkness to fear, but actually had the power to defeat it, there might be some hope of ending the war against the dark powers, slaying the Shadow Lord, and bringing peace back to Threa

And so, the Paladins had made plans to meet up with them at a predetermined place along their border with the wilds and the Aelven lands beyond, only after this business had been completed.

"Have you seen the wicked barbs on those accursed Black-iron bolts?" Asked Theros, though not truly concerned with the ammunition for the new ballistae lord Orthard had ordered to be mounted upon the walls of the Keep, meaning only to break the silence that had grown broodingly in the few minutes of their inward reflections.

Apparently, word or wind of their knowledge and disapproval of this new ruling had reached Orthard's ears, and the vile despot had made preparations in anticipation of any disorganized, outbreaks of defiance.

Surely, he had mounted these new ballistae and had given his men new armaments- all of accursed Black-iron, but he had not gone to any further, more excessive measures, keeping only the same watches of guards, and these not observing the Dragons any more closely than usual. The arrogant lord seemed to think that any reaction to his plans would be feeble or ill contrived. It was this oversight and underestimation that would cost him, for the true Paladins were far more ordered and ready than the despot could know.

"I am looking at them right now and the soldiers manning them. The fools are playing dice, gambling rather than attending their post. We shall catch them quite off guard." Zurthaud replied, giving his companion an askance smirk.

"Phonies," Snuffed the Dragon , "They should have left off pretending to be Paladins years ago. They are ill-trained, unprepared for any kind of assault, let alone ours, which your father even had the foresight to anticipate."

"This is true. While we have grown strong, learning, training, and flourishing together, thanks in no small part to Zurthaud's leadership, they have fattened and become slothful, weak even. They could not withstand the storm to come." Serc chimed in, greatly encouraging Zurthaud.

It appeared to the eyes of Zurthaud, as he looked upon the elder Dragon, that the aged doctor had seemingly grown even older in the short time that he had spent reading from the black tome.

He rued the fact that neither Galrag nor Aelanur could be called upon to read the contents of the dark book, for when it still had its defense of dark magic, it had very much injured the cherished Serc, who was more like a grandfather to his people and a beloved friend to Zurthaud than a mere medical officer.

"How goes your journey into the dark mind?" Zurthaud asked, regretful having not earlier voiced more concern for his friend's health.

"It is fraught with much useless bragging, and self-worship, ludicrously self-centered, but there is so much information, seemingly every single one of his schematics, plans, devices, and spells. In truth you spoke, for it is every bit as close to the Dark One's very thoughts anyone would ever wish to go." Serc replied, glad to take his attentions from the evil text. "Even the impractical, down to the childishly unrealistic, designs are written herein, such as for that darkling instrument which he had played upon while slaughtering Dragons. It functions on compressed air within several giant bellows that blow wind through massive pipes, some of which span nearly the whole length of the tower. One activates the bellows, and selects which pipe receives the air by fingering the keys upon a manual. Truly ridiculous, one could just blow into a flute and be done with it, rather than fool with all these extravagant mechanisms." Serc explained, as if in fascination, though he were not; the knowledge of the black book was too evil to be inspiring. "In my spare time, I shall make translations of as many of these writings as I can, although excluding the most horrid parts, but out of all the listed spells, there is one that stands out to me as most disturbing. I have already begun interpreting it, for it is a very terrible and dangerous incantation, a method for using magic and Dragon-stones to subdue another's will and control their body. I have not gotten quite to the end of this spell's description, but I believe the name for it is something like, stone of blood, or Bloodstones."

Theros mused long over this, for he now suspected that this was the method by which his mate had been killed, the reason why the other Dragoness Ilara had gone mad and attacked her. "Do you think…" Theros began to speak, yet he could not finish his words. Remembrance of that dark day only troubled him, and he became woefully silent.

"I do." Serc replied, knowing Theros' train of thought, and he comfortingly patted the poor Dragon on the shoulder. "I just do not know how it happened, for the both of them were watched so closely. They always had someone with them. Even greater a mystery, I was the one who witnessed her pyre, and I cannot recall seeing any Dragon-stones among Ilara's ashes. Nevertheless, I am sure it was by this dark power that Dragon shed Dragon's blood on that day."

They became somber and did not talk much thereafter, even though they could feel their adrenaline rise in anticipation of what was to come.

Suddenly, the noontide bells chiming in the great clock-towers of the city broke them from their reveries, and they now awaited only one thing- their messengers. Their couriers now came bolting out of the Keep and flew up toward the Dragon's tower like an arrow, speedily bringing the news, good or ill. It was the slender young Dragon and his Human companion, the former paige boy of Lord Orthard, the same spies from the day before, and in less than a minute's time, they had raced unto the very balcony upon which Zurthaud stood. Hastily, they spat out their report.

"It is decided. Lord Orthard has gotten his way. The High Council has voted eight to four that the Dragons be sentenced to life's labor within the sulfur mines." They shouted hurriedly, all in one breath.

Unexpectedly, Zurthaud laughed, a full resounding guffaw.

He was no longer intimidated by his father. He no longer feared anything, for he had faced the Shadow Lord, a living nightmare, and had courted with death itself. Besides which, he knew that no power of men could stand against what was to be unleashed upon them today.

____

"All right, let us begin." He said, and he motioned for the spies to sound the signal.

The young Human put to his lips a long, slightly curved horn, a Dragon's horn, salvaged from the ashes of a long forgotten victim of a long forgotten battle, salvaged more recently, in need, from the Dragon temple's dusty library shelves, and forth from the horn came a loud note, clean yet deep, full bodied, speaking of spring and autumn, and feasting and the hunt all at once. Though it was unbeknownst to any of that age, there was magic in the sounding of that ancient horn whose name had been long forgotten, so that all Dragons who heard it were awakened, awakened in fire and power from their self-imposed restraints of civility. They were aroused unto battle, and unto battle they did go.

Up from the ground right below the walls where they had been lying in wait, hidden from the eyes of the guards above them, all together, they promptly leaped into the sky, every last one of the Order's Dragons, each with their Human, Dworv, or Aelv companion. They were barely two hundred strong, but they whirled about in the air so thickly in intertwining patterns and with myriad colors, and the high-noon sun so beat its shining brightness down luminously upon them, that it seemed the sky had suddenly burst forth into an explosion of iridescence.

"For the Order and the true Paladins!" Zurthaud cried aloud, even as he climbed upon Theros' back and they also took off into the air.

A thunder, as from great black clouds of storm, rolled from the trumpeting roars of the replying Dragons and companions, so as to shake the very stone of the Citadel, and they descended upon the terrible ballistae of the pitifully shaken followers of Orthard.

They did not fire but one shot from any of the four new ballistae mounted on the inner wall of the Keep, and this shot was so poorly and frantically aimed that it hit nothing but the ground in front of the turret. No more bolts came from the ballistae, but neither was any blood of the hapless lackeys shed.

The Dragons in their terrible wrath so frightened the Humans that many, completely overwhelmed with dismay, fell down upon their faces before them, and the rest ran about senselessly, as if for their very lives, though the Dragons restrained themselves and did not even attempt to strike them. Only the weapons were broken, and the ballistae foremost were violently dismantled.

Any Humans that fled or seemed to desire resistance or escape were set upon with a heavy clawed hand and gently, but inescapably, pressed to the ground, while those who had showed fear and respect and remained upon their faces were not bothered much at all.

For a good while it seemed as if there was not any organized opposition, so that the companions of the Dragons had naught to do but dismount and gather up all their captives into chain gangs and herd them into holding within the Order's barracks, but eventually they came to a more prepared regiment of men, whose ears had heard the rumor of battle and whose hearts had not quite melted.

These were the loyalists of lord Orthard- mostly mercenary soldiers, unafraid of battle and hired with much gold from the ranks of soldiery associated with the lords of the Human Realm's provinces; some, the older men who had agreed with his harsh rulings, even some of which had been true Paladins of old, yet all battle hardened and unwavering. These loyalists had sealed off the inner wall's gates, with a heavy portcullis before the ancient entrance, and had completely enclosed the Keep from aerial attack, barring off the windows and balconies with specially made Black-iron shutters and bolted doors. Even now they had formed a resistance in the bailey before the Keep's main entrance; having issued forth from postern portals on either side of the courtyard, they blocked access to the great door in tightly formed phalanxes with thick, heavy Black-iron shields and long Black-iron pikes turned toward their foes.

Seeing that blood might be shed there, Zurthaud motioned for Theros to land before the shield wall, so that he might reason with their captain. Even as they touched ground and Zurthaud dismounted, he spoke earnestly with them.

"My good men, and faithful servants of the Order, has my father so deceived you that even now you stand ready to die and to kill your own brethren before the very gates of our hallowed halls? Turn aside your weapons and let us in, for we wish only to right the grievous wrongs that my father, and he alone, has committed against us. Not a drop of Paladin's blood needs to be shed this day, not even my father's; do not defend his lawlessness and self-serving with your honest swords." Spoke Zurthaud as sincerely and poignantly as he could, for he truly wished no harm to befall these men, nor even the High Councilmen, nor even his father.

Their ambition here was not violence; their objective was neither war nor conquest. Rather, they merely wished to unseat unfair rulers from their positions of power, to remove them from the place where they could hold sway over others' lives, and none of these men, the simple foot soldiers that had blindly followed command, did the true Paladins hold responsible for what had slowly, imperceptibly grown, as a poison, between them.

Indeed, some of these loyalists seemed to lower their weapons and shields, ready to give up rather than face off in battle against such powerful foes, but the captain of these men was a crude, stupid, old soldier, which Zurthaud had remembered as being a particularly nasty drill sergeant to the young cadets, cruel and swift in unearned punishment and curses. He opened his mouth loudly and unwisely.

"Well, if it is not the same son of a donkey whom we had since thought dead. Are you come back to the land of the living by the power of these dumb animals, or were you deceiving us the whole while, like a little priss, just to get some attention from your daddy?" He jeered, trying to make mockery of Zurthaud's sincerely spoken words.

"I only seek to bring justice to the man who has so cruelly mistreated the other races. None of you will be harmed so long as you surrender your arms and let us pass." Calmly spoke Zurthaud, giving no credence to the captain's impetuousness.

The stubborn, grim soldier only chortled upon hearing this. "Do you hear this boy? The phantom prince wants our weapons, the only thing keeping him and the stupid, giant lizard at bay. Well, you can very well have my spear, right through your slimy, yellow gut." Spake he with less mirth than before.

But, Zurthaud stood his ground, and again spoke calmly to the soldiers. "I would not advise such action; it would make my friend very angry. Besides, as I said, there is no need for conflict or bloodshed; we are only here for the vile Orthard. The rest of you will be let go free."

Upon seeing his men waver, having heard three times now from the honorable Zurthaud, that their lives would be spared and that they could go free if they only surrendered, the captain became wroth, as he had always been quick to do.

"Do not let this cur's fancy tongue fool you, men." He brazenly screamed. "It is filled with lies and poison like theirs." And, he pointed at the increasingly more irate Theros to emphasize. "The bastard son of Orthard is no longer a Human like us; he must be possessed, or sick in the mind, or a wraith they conjured with their magic. Either way, the scum was better off dead!" And with the last insult, the stupid man let fly his spear, well-aimed and with great force, straight for Zurthaud.

However, the bolt never reached its target, for even as the javelin left the fingers of its idiotic owner, Theros wrathfully charged the unit, scattering the men asunder with either their own legs or his, and the well-thrown shaft, never even got close to its target, merely scathing the Dragon's armored skin with its Black-iron tip, and sticking not, fell clattering to the ground.

In that same second's time, Theros had singled out the unfortunate captain and bitten him cleanly in half even before the fool had time to scream, and the rest of the men fled wildly, as Theros roared furiously and poured hot flame onto the mess that was once their bold leader, thus wiping clean the ground from his dirtiness. Back into the walls of the Keep, through the same postern gates ran the terrified soldiers, with not a one turning back to pay any respect or even glance at the captain's ash pile, smoldering away in the otherwise happy, sunny afternoon.

"Theros!" Zurthaud gasped, for neither had he any time to restrain his companion from committing such a terrible act of violence.

"What? That bastard tried to kill you, and yet you would defend his fate. Let one fool die so that the rest of the pitiful lambs might not be slaughtered." The Dragon hotly retorted, as gray trails of smoke slowly fumed from his nostrils.

"I would have had no one die this day, no matter how stupid or deserving. I knew that you would step in to block that javelin from hitting me, and I was willing to bear his insults, if it meant that we could easily enter these gates, but now that we have shed the blood of one of my father's men, they will draw together in fear. We might have a prolonged siege now, rather than a quick coup." Zurthaud chided, returning to his usual seat atop his friend's shoulders.

"I would rather tear this stone fortress apart brick by brick, alone, with my bare hands, over the course of decades rather than suffer that vulgar imbecile's scoffing a second longer." Theros growled as he lifted off into the air again.

But, he was regretful for his actions later, if only slightly, for it happened as Zurthaud had feared, that by the time they had rounded up the soldiers they had captured and secured the gatehouse of the Keep's outer wall from assaults by reinforcements from the other garrisons on the walls of the city, the Keep had been shut up tightly and locked in for a long besieging. The thought of having to demolish so well built and impregnable a structure seemed a daunting task even for the Dragons, especially Theros who really hoped no one else had heard him offer to tear the massive stone fortress apart with his bare hands.

"Blast! With the speed of our assault, though it was not a surprise by any means, I had hoped we should procure, at least, one of the balcony entrances." Serc unhappily remarked. "Now we shall be in for a greatly protracted engagement, for they have plenty of food stuffs to hold out for several months, at the very least, and the stones of the walls and towers were laid with magic so that we cannot easily dismantle them in that manner. We shall have to make siege engines of our own, a ram to tear down the gates, perhaps, for those will be the weakest parts."

The whistle of arrows ripping through the air caught their attention, for the archers of the Keep had regained their courage and begun firing Black-iron tipped bolts at the Paladins who had stayed within the bailey yard. Most clattered harmlessly against the cobblestone paved courtyard, but a few found their mark in the hides of unlucky Dragons.

They hissed with annoyance, for the bodkin tips, though darkly imbued to pass easily through their scales, could not penetrate very deeply into their thick hides. Still, it did cause them enough pain and trouble for the Paladins to relocate beyond the range of the marksmen in the Keep's galleries.

As they rested and licked their wounds, easily pulling the arrows from their shallow moorings, the Paladins regrouped, gathering up their foray scattered members and establishing a base camp upon the ramparts of the Human quarter's barracks, wherein they had stowed their prisoners.

"I was hoping to talk some sense into the underlings, but now it seems that their commanders will be able to spur them on to fight past the initial panic." Zurthaud observed, as he gazed over the battlements at the well defended keep. "We really do not have the time for a siege, for we must soon join with Malok and Shar in the search for the Bright Dragoness, lest we come too late and our efforts here become worthless."

"I know of a way we can enter the Keep with need for neither engine nor siege." Interrupted a familiar gruff voice.

It was the Dragon general, Galrag. Though the time of mourning his beloved son had hardly begun, he had resumed his position as the wisest of military officers; having forgiven Zurthaud for the reckless, yet hopeful espionage which had led to the death of his own flesh, and knowing how desperately his comrades needed his counsel and strength for this day, he overcame his own need for time of grieving to once again commune with his comrades of old, offering freely his expert advice.

His comrades, not yet expecting his return to duty, already happily surprised at his appearing, would have then heartily welcomed him, but that the elder general, as completely in his element- here in battle- as a fish in water, thoroughly engrossed in his strategizing, continued to expound upon his plan.

"There is an underground entrance which the Dworvs had dug in the days when they were still given passage into the Keep, for their chiefs would venture long into the mines within the mountains behind the city and had still wanted quick access returning to the Citadel. There is one shaft that goes from the Dworvs' quarter to the mines and from the mines to the Keep and another directly from the Dworvish quarter to the Keep. Now, Orthard in his shrewdness, saw fit to destroy the tunnel that leads directly to the Dworvish quarter, but according to my knowledge, the other passage that leads into the basement of the Keep from the mines was never found. We should be able to sneak in from there, but even if both ways are blocked, the rock under the Keep is not enchanted and will be much easier to remove than the walls above."

"How is it, though we are nearly the same age and were graduates of the same class, that you always can remember these curious bits of information that seemed to have slipped free from my mind?" Serc questioned, in mock annoyance, though he did hurry to lightly embrace his friend, before the big green general could continue his discussion of tactics, or resist.

"It is not that you are senile, my friend." Deeply chuckled Galrag, bemused by the affection, for which he understood the reasoning, though still, in his gruff martial nature, slightly embarrassed by it. "You only forget that I was always a soldier, and you a doctor. While your head was filled with the lore of herbs and potions, I was taught the ways of battle, including memorizing every detail of the Citadel's schematics."

"This is a sound plan, and seeing as it is the best way to quickly gain entrance to the castle, I vote we commit to it immediately." Zurthaud emphatically suggested, for he wished this conflict well over with by day's end.

"Do not be so hasty." Galrag interjected. "Those tunnels were only built to accommodate a Dworv-sized person, and a Dragon is no such creature. This venture will be very risky, for you shall have only Humans, Dworves, or Aelvs to go with you through those mines. If you do elect this strategy, I advise you to take with you a good company of our smaller comrades, for if you manage to access the Keep undetected through there, you will then have to make your way through the under parts of the fortress to the main gate, or any such entrance that is Dragon-sized, before we will be able to give you aid. There is also a chance that your father might remember these tunnels and set a trap for you, and then once captured, in the worst instance, use you as hostages to negotiate our surrender. Of course, he might just kill you instead, which would be better for our cause than your imprisonment, but I digress."

"Always one for kind words are you, Galrag." Theros muttered, as he plucked an arrow from one of his wing arms.

"No, he is right Theros. At this point, I would be better a martyr for truth than a prisoner for leverage." Zurthaud solemnly agreed, and he vowed to himself not to let the latter be an option if it came to such decisions. "Still, this is our best and quickest route into the Keep. I vote 'yea'."

And, so did vote any other Humans and Aelvs nearby who had overheard the plan.

"Very well." Zurthaud declared, seeing that the yea's had prevailed. "Help me to gather some volunteers. I would say a quarter of our non-Dragon Paladins would be the right number for such an attack, not too many to be noticed, missing from our siege or present within the Keep, and not so few that we could be easily overwhelmed once inside."

Chapter 20

It was chill in the spacious wooden hall when Feldara awoke early that morning, and immediately the dread of the challenge to come hit her like lightening striking a tree. For all the anxiety bubbling up within her, she could lie at rest no longer, though she had futilely tried and ended up only fidgeting about so much that she woke Anur also. So, she got up from their shared bed of a simple futon, more or less only a blanket between them and the hard wood floor, and went out from the cramped back area of the great chief's lodge.

As she wandered into the main hall, she found, that someone had already stoked the fire in the central hearth, and that meat and some kind of soup or warm beverage were being heated upon it. Gorod was already sitting there before the hearth, apparently also unable to continue sleeping, and Feldara sat down next to him, for a long while only in silence, watching the embers glow and the flames dance.

"Today is the day." She mumbled, trying to start a conversation to break the uncomfortable quiet of the empty hall, but Gorod did not respond further than grunting an affirmative.

He took a piece of meat from the skewers upon which it had been roasting and shared it with her, chewing his half and more or less casually tossing the other in her direction, but he did now speak.

"I was fool. When giant, black warrior came, I thought I win easy, no trouble. I thought I strongest warrior on all mountains everywhere, but at end, my people lose freedom, because of me, because of my pride. Now, everything we love on this mountain, maybe we lose, because of me." Spoke he staring remorsefully into the fire, but then he turned to her. "You are gift from heavens, Fire-bringer Feltra. I praying you win. We see your strength yesterday; now, we see again. Help free us from bad people."

Feldara sat in stunned silence, still amazed that, on her shoulders, these people placed the hopes of their entire race. If she faltered now, it would mean far more than her capture or death, and she found no words, either of comfort or confidence, with which to reply. Instead, she tried to change the subject.

"Will you sit on your throne again when you become chief once more?" She asked, having noticed that not once, since she had met him, had Gorod even touched the carved ivory and wood chair.

Gorod at first seemed a little surprised by this question, but he lowered his gaze again, back to the fire, as he replied despondently. "<u>If</u> I chief again, I still be one who fails, one who almost lose everything for people. Maybe, I never sit in seat again; maybe, I no worth anymore."

Feldara became a little irked by this response, for in the short time that she had come to know Gorod, she had found him only to be respectable, sensible, dependable, well liked by all his people, and even having a witty sense of humor. She could not stand to let someone so honorable loath themselves so openly.

"Maybe, I worded the question wrongly." She began emphatically. "I shall rephrase it. Since you are the chief, why are you not sitting in your chair? Because no matter what the tiny, smart-mouthed man might say, to your people and everyone who meets you, you still are the chief of the Urz. Though I am no Urz historian, I would still venture to say that, even now, you are one of their best chiefs ever. Just you wait until this battle is over today, then there will not be an enemy left to lay claim to your throne, and you shall have to sit on it. I shall make you sit on it."

"You make me do nothing." He replied tartly, though a slight smile had returned to his once grim face and confidence into his doubting heart. "It still, <u>if</u> I chief again. You no know you win or lose. Be careful. Giant warrior look slow, stupid, then he fight. He quicker than think, maybe no smarter."

It was then that the most earnest question that had been lingering at the back of her mind all the time she had spent among the Urz leaped into the front, for, in the chaos of these last two days- first, having found Anur, and then becoming engaged with the test of the smooth stone, then the half-party of the night before, she had forgotten to ask about the fate of her other friend. Where Calidon was being held, what had happened to him, how he was faring- all these questions had somehow slipped from mentioning with the more present distractions of her own troubles.

"Do you remember saying to me that you had seen our other friend, the other Dragon?" She asked of Gorod, who nodded an affirmative. "Do you know what has become of him?" She earnestly inquired, for she had not meant to disregard poor Calidon's fate.

However, Gorod wagged his head sadly. "I give him food two days ago, when he wake up, but he breath fire at me. Not nice. I no see him again, but tell other Urz, feed him. They come back to me with his meat, say, 'Tiny-black-men-chief no let us feed Fire-bringer.' I try, see, maybe I feed him, but tiny-black-men no let me see him. I say, 'Is mean no feed someone, even enemies.' But, they laugh; they say, 'We no care, go away or we kill him. Then, who will you give meat?' I know he is your friend, so I leave then. No more Urz go up there, where tiny-black-men make house. I sorry, Feltra. He no eat, three days, but I can do nothing."

Tears welled in Feldara's eyes as she thought about the miserable Dragon sitting all alone in a horrible little hole without any food or comfort for three whole days, all the while being mocked or beaten or worse by the Dark Hunters, but these were soon replaced by fiery anger and a desire to end the terrible cruelties of the vile oppressors.

"When does the challenge start?" Feldara furiously asked, fully ready, even eager, to face her foes and destroy them.

"Challenge is when you want, but eat first; food make you strong. Wait for Bjarz get ready. We help if evil people break words; I think they will. They bad when win, be more bad when lose." Gorod wisely advised.

So it was, that by the time Feldara had eaten and Anur got up and ate, and the Bjarz had all awoken, eaten and gotten ready, it was late morning, drawing unto noontide, and her adrenaline was pumping excitement through her so that she could not at all sit still but had to pace about or twitch her tail uncontrollably.

Eventually, Gorod was able to gather everyone together and lead them on out of the chief's lodge to where the battle would be, but Anur drew Feldara aside.

"Do not be discouraged if you are unable to see me watching in the crowd." Said he, with more than a little deviousness in his low whispering voice. "I shall be there, but in a more advantageous position for counterattack than the other spectators, and if there is even a shadow of treachery, I shall not let my chance for vengeance pass by."

Feldara was a little surprised by this sort of talk from her usually mild guardian, but she had nearly forgotten how he had so effortlessly dispatched the Worgs who had attacked her in the Shadow Lands or how furiously he had fought the Dark Hunters in the home of Rathnyaling. She now recalled how proud and skilled a warrior he was, his whole life being spent learning, practicing, and teaching the ways of the Order of Masters, and also surmised now why he was hungering retribution for his foes.

"It really did upset you, how they sneaked upon you in the middle of the night, overpowering and capturing you." Feldara guessed, a fiendish grin spreading across her muzzle, more in joy of discovering that Anur took pride in his martial abilities and showed any emotion at all.

"More than you guess." He grimly replied, as he took a small short sword, more like a knife for the Urz, from the ones laid upon the great hall's table, those that were prepared for the Bjarz' mustering. "But, know this, even if you cannot see me, I will be there, and I will lay everything aside to protect you."

"I know you would, but I venture you shall not get the chance." She confidently responded. "You are looking at the strongest Dragoness the Urz have ever seen; never you mind that I am, for most of them, also the only one."

Anur affectionately pressed his hand to her shoulder and patted her heartily. "Leave off your smart mouthing; you shall have no need of it on the battleground." He kindly, soberly chided and he turned and disappeared quickly into the throng of Urz warriors.

Feldara sighed, more than a little relieved of her tension and anxiousness, for she had genuinely needed and wanted Anur's encouragement this day. With his mere few words and brief touch, her looming struggle already seemed lessened in dread and difficulty, and without anything more to do, no further preparations, Feldara followed the mob of Urz as they slowly began to march out from the chief's lodge and up the mountain.

Where the Urz city had been built on the upward slope of the highest ridge upon the mountain and the chief's lodge had been built the furthest up that ridge, assuming a loftier place above the roofs of the common buildings and the marketplace, there was still a good bit more ridge-line that rose above the chief's dwelling. The single road that had gone through the Urz' city continued on, climbing ever higher up the mountain. At last, after narrowing down to a mere path and much twisting and turning, for to make the steepness of the hike easier with switchbacks, upon the highest peak of the mountain, where the ridge ultimately crested, did the trail end.

Before them, in a vast hollowing centered in the mountain's coned extremity, stood a circle of bare earth lined with monolithic gray stones. These stones were laid long side flat upon the ground and joined end to end and ran up the sides of the hollowing like a flight of stairs, so that the bare circle was enclosed about with these stones but for two gaps at either end, one right before Feldara and the other on the direct far side of the circle.

It was cold upon the bleak mountain top, but Feldara did not shiver from the temperature, only from the excitement of anticipation. Upon the far side of the stone circle her enemies were already gathered, for here was their encampment, upon the very heights of the mountain. Unbeknownst to Feldara, here was also once the Urz' most sacred site, for out of all their settled locations, this one was highest upon Threa and therefore closest to the heavenly home of Eloigal, whom they called Boag, and here had the foul Dark Hunters desecrated their holy place with their loathsome presence- shoddy, hasty, Goblin constructed towers and walls, and ragged, filthy black tents.

It was insult upon insult for the Urz to bear the sight of this hideous effigy of a fortification upon their own holy ground, and as they gathered on their side of the rocky arena, they roared their battle-cries in defiance and anger. The enemy: the Goblin horde, the Troll legion, and the lone Ogre brute, responded with their own howls of war.

Feldara thought it strange that her Ogre opponent also be among the audience before the start of their fight, but she paid no more heed to that slight portent as she entered the ring of stones. Truly, she could barely have heard her own thoughts through the ruckus that the Bjarz unleashed upon seeing their champion come forward to do battle, for they stomped their feet and pounded their clubs and swords upon their wooden bucklers and redoubled the volume of their roaring and shouting; after which the response of the enemy seemed rather lacking.

At length, a lone black-robed figure rose above the enemy horde upon the far side of the arena, for the Dark Hunter captain stood upon a litter borne by the shoulders of four Trolls. He raised his arms to quiet the crowd, and more out of a desire to see the challenge begin than paying any heed to the authority of the vile figure, did the Urz settle down their war chanting.

"My loyal subjects." Began the Dark Hunter captain, with his usual disdainful false-friendship. "Today I am challenged for the right of chief by Gorod your former ruler. He who already proved too weak to defeat my champion, wishes for a rematch with a new contender of his own. Out of graciousness and respect for your customs do I now concede to this."

At this statement, much booing and other rude, yet warranted, gestures were offered in raucous cacophony by the Urz lords, who had not ever tasted of this viper-tongued fool's "graciousness", but the Dark Hunter's leader held up his arms again and waited for the crowd to quiet.

"However, since my opponent has offered up a new warrior to represent him, I could only do the same, for what is the fun in seeing the same fighters do battle over and over again? Besides, who ever heard of an Ogre defeating a Dragon? Even Og, the legendary Ogre king, 'the killer of two', has only succeeded twice." He wickedly eluded.

Everyone's heart began to sink hearing these words, especially Feldara's, for by now they all were certain that she could have slain the Ogre warrior. They could now only guess as to who would be her adversary.

"Without further delay," Shouted the Dark Hunter captain, his grating voice full of wicked glee for his surprise. "For our champion, I present to you, Calidon 'the bloodthirsty!'"

From beyond the shadows of the gap between the stones, the entrance on the far side of the arena, came the poor Dragon male. Though Feldara had inwardly laughed at his title of "bloodthirsty" and mentally denied even the possibility that Calidon would dare to strike her, let alone battle to the death against her for an enemy that all hated, instantly, she could see that something was amiss about him.

He was being dragged along by the other three Dark Hunters on a chain and collar of Black-iron as he driveled and staggered all over the place, and his eyes were clouded by some oozing blackness. All in all, he seemed either as though he were drunk with far too much of something many times stronger than wine or had been driven to madness. Feldara, all at once, pitied and loathed him, as if by some otherworldly power he had been made an instinctual foe, but if she now detested Calidon for what was done to him, she all the more hated they who had worked this evil.

"What have you done to him!?!" She roared at the terrible Dark Hunters.

Their captain only laughed, a horrible, diabolical cackle, as the other three drew Calidon's head down to their mouths and inaudibly whispered dreadful commands into his ears. They pointed at Feldara with their crooked gloved fingers, and at last unhooked the chain from his Black-iron collar.

As if drawn by a power far surpassing his own, Calidon ran, staggering and tottering, down the length of the bare circle, mouth agape and tongue dementedly wagging. Straight for Feldara he came, much to her dismay, for her heart ached with sickening thought that he would attempt to cause her harm, and even more nauseating, that she may have to hurt him, perhaps even kill him, just to stay alive.

Not a one of the Urz cheered or encouraged her to fight, though the enemy grew ever more noisy, for they knew that this was an unfair battle, to make friend fight with friend, to inspire the abomination of Dragon shedding Dragon's blood. They became deathly silent, sure that their champion would die by the hand of her friend and foe, either from being unwilling to bring harm to him and selflessly giving up or becoming overpowered by the raw animalistic ferocity which her enemy now displayed.

In truth, Feldara thought about fighting back for an instant, as Calidon closed in upon her, blind in his deranged fury, for he seemed now more beast than person. However, she could find neither strength nor hatred to raise her claws to strike at him, and ashamedly she lowered her head in defeat. She could not bring herself to wound, much less slay, Calidon, but as he drew nigh unto her and lunged the final few feet, with his jaws open and reaching for her neck, she did find enough will to resist death, even if for only a little while.

She sidestepped his clumsy, swooning attack and leaped away to the left, as Calidon, having put his whole body into that lunging strike, flopped soundly upon the ground, and Feldara took the brief opportunity to scan about the arena, knowing that Anur was watching, as he said he would, and wondering if he too could not bring himself to kill Calidon. Surely, he too was struggling with this unexpected revelation, for no interruption or distraction now occurred that Feldara could notice. Seeing that she was alone in this conflict, with neither her desired miracle from heaven nor the aide of any mortal coming directly to her assistance, Feldara began thinking of ways she could contend with Calidon without causing him any more pain than already seemed to beleaguer him, yet this was only her mind working in her usual intelligence and not of any want for victory. Against so dismal and dire a situation, facing an opponent so beloved and pitiful, Feldara now felt drained of all her optimism and readiness from before, and the thought of triumph now seemed only distant and vain.

As Calidon rose from the ground and turned again upon her, Feldara had to spread her wings and flap them quickly to back-step out of his attack range, for now he came more calculatingly, as if the power that was controlling him had adjusted to the craftiness of its foe. He took a big breath and poured forth flame from his mouth, the brightness of which Feldara had to shield her eyes, though the fire could not hurt her, and seeing her so dazed, he quickly followed with another lunging strike.

This time, Feldara was caught by his outstretched claws, and they tore into her arm. She was thrown to the ground by his superior might, for he was a large male for his age, far larger than her, being small for her age. Calidon was upon her, even as her breath was knocked from her lungs, but Feldara stretched forth her bleeding forearm and pushed aside a fatal bite from his jaws. She held his head away from her, even as she tried, mostly unsuccessfully, to avoid his flailing claws.

"Calidon it is I, Feldara. Do you not know me?" She pleadingly yelled at him, even as another of his claws nicked her side.

Somehow, Feldara managed to throw him off or squirm away from him, and he did not straightaway press his attack. For, in his eagerness to attack her and her earnest defense, she had unintentionally scored his belly with kicks from her taloned feet, and he was sore and bleeding even as she.

A laugh from the balcony interrupted her thoughts, for she pondered still how to contend with such a possessed victim of an enemy. It was the Dark Hunter captain whose chortling had risen over the droning jeers of his minions, and he now addressed his seemingly soon to be defeated foe.

"It is no use to reason with the controlled mind, for no power on all of Threa can undo the enchantment of my master's Bloodstones. The Dragon is fully enthralled by his magic, as you will soon be." He wildly gloated. "Do not fear, I shall not allow him to kill you, as I have very specific instructions, but I am sure the Kragon will not mind a little spoiling. You might as well give up and save yourself some pain now, for I am sure much more awaits in the future my master has planned for you."

The rest of the mocking words fell deaf on Feldara's ears, for upon hearing "Bloodstone" she had suddenly become fascinated by the chain that Calidon bore about his neck. It was not the searing of his scales and the underlying rottenness of wound that the Black-iron had burnt into him, nor the darkling metal itself, which was the bane of Dragons, but rather the sole jewel that decorated the otherwise plain collar that her attentions became fixed upon. It was a deep red, as blood or wine, and light did not pass through, but was rather sucked into its depths, so that it emanated only a darkness of evil and malice.

Now that Feldara thought on it, this wicked aura seemed every bit the same as the oozing darkness that clouded Calidon's eyes and connected by the same terrible spell, but how to get at this gem when her enemy was so intent on her demise, was beyond her reckoning. She could not breath fire for a distraction or even to directly harm the stone, and Feldara had no knowledge of magic, for the magic that Anur had learned was that of a Human's, drawn from the power of their Dragon companion. As such, he had not been able to teach her the source of her people's special power, and all the scrolls on their island had been for advanced techniques and spells, not any beginners' training.

With nothing else coming to mind, she tried talking to him again.

"Calidon, it is I, Feldara. Do you not remember me?" She asked again, taking slow strides toward him.

He did not respond, as he turned to face her, but neither did he rush to attack her. So, she continued to move forward slowly, even as she spoke soothingly to him.

"Surely you remember me, how we met? I was limping through the Aelven city, your home, and I came all the way to the lawn before your house, where your family lives. You and your brothers and sisters, your mother, and your aunt and uncle, all came down to greet me. You took me into your home, and showed me kindness, and we fought off an attack on your city and your family and I. Then, you came along with me and Anur on this journey, because you wanted to be a Paladin." She calmly explained, even as she drew near to him.

Still, Calidon did not respond, though he yet did not move, only standing still as a stone, wheezing and slobbering. The gathered crowd, even the monsters of the Dark Horde hushed, waiting to see what would happen.

"Surely, you remember Anur? He led us through that terrible storm, and then, um, we got separated, because I acted and spoke foolishly. He was captured by those villains." She said gesturing toward the Dark Hunters, and to her surprise Calidon turned to glare at them with his unseeing eyes. "And, of course, you must remember how brave you were, how gallantly you helped me to look for him. You must remember how you comforted me in my darkest hour of woe. You are so dear a friend to me, as my own brother, more than a brother even." She tenderly spoke, tears gathering in her eyes as she remembered his overflowing of compassion for her, his kind and giving nature that was not this sickly apparition of Calidon that stood before her.

Suddenly, on his face came such an expression of pain and woe, that tears of pity did stream from her eyes, even as she came right up against him. She embraced him again, as she had done before, seeming now a lifetime ago, in the forest below the mountains when she had thought Anur and all hope were forever gone, and his own hot tears fell in large drops upon her back, as his arms, trembling in desperate struggle against the force that conspired to consume him with darkness, reached for her and embraced her also. He made a sound as if choking, as if he were trying to say something but could not, but still he clung to her as if she were his lifeline, his only hope in the encroaching darkness.

"Hurt her, you mindless puppet! Subdue her! Kill her, even!" Screamed the Dark Hunter captain from the top of the walls, but his voice went unheeded.

As they embraced, Feldara's nose touched upon the singular jewel of Calidon's collar, and her tears flowed down her muzzle onto it. A light began to shine between them, emanating from the gemstone, which before had been dead to all light. It now burned hot from its contact with Feldara and her tears, and suddenly, being able to no longer withstand the opposing forces of light and goodness, it burst asunder. The Black-iron collar disintegrated from about Calidon's neck and he gasped, as if finally able to get a breath after long being submerged underwater. He looked down into her eyes, with the oozing black magic gone, seeing for his own self again, the first time since he had been enslaved by the darkness, and he whispered into her ears with a faint weak voice.

"You saved me." Said he, as if he were amazed that it was possible and yet so thankful that it was, but he said no more. Nor, did he move from her arms, for he had not the strength of body or mind to yet do either.

<><><><><>

"Kill them! Kill them all!" Shouted the captain of the Dark Hunters, seeing that his plot to destroy Feldara had failed, and his Troll guards sounded an attack on a drear horn.

However, Gorod was already prepared for this, for while they had all been watching the Dragons in the arena, he had moved his forces into strategic positions. They now had the high ground all around the stone circle, and they shouted one final Urz battle cry, even as they descended upon their foes.

The Goblins were outmatched in every way by the Urz, so that they could either be club fodder or attempt to stay as archers and attack from range, but even though the Urz were superior in might, the Trolls did put up a fight with the advantageous reach of their long spears and polearms. The Ogre, however, was a terrible adversary, for it waded among the ranks of the Bjarz and flailed its huge Black-iron mace about wildly, scattering and slaying them easily with deadly powerful strokes.

This menace did Gorod soon find himself alone with, for now none of the other Bjarz could, nor would, get close enough to attack or be attacked by the horrible creature. The brute laughed seeing its earlier foe, which it had already defeated, again standing before it, and it abandoned all caution in frantic assault. Yet, this time, Gorod was prepared for his foe; he used the Ogre's slower movements and clumsiness against it, for every time the beast missed wide with a heavy swing of its dreadful mace, the Urz lord would leap inside its defense and strike a quick blow.

Before the Ogre could recover or strike back at him, Gorod would leap away, and in this method did he attack the Ogre over and over again. About the fifth round of this feinting assault, the Ogre had become infuriated, for though its Black-iron mail had saved it from a fatal blow, many of these feigning strikes had hit well, and in its wrath it abandoned what little sense it had and all caution. Wildly, it swung the giant mace round and round, smashing the ground, smashing rocks, smashing unfortunate Goblins and Trolls, but each time Gorod was too quick to be caught by the bludgeoning.

At last, with one final attempt, the Ogre, now tiring from all its wrathful exertion, swung its mighty mace, and plunged it, not into Gorod, for he had slyly dodged away, but into the branches of a stubbornly gnarly old tree.

So deeply and forcefully did the Ogre bash his mace into the poor bramble, that the flanges thereon scored and stuck within the wood, and almost in vengeance of its smashing, did the obstinate bush not again relinquish its steady grip on the Ogre's offending weapon.

Seeing his foe so disarmed, as though trying mightily, the Ogre could neither dislodge his weapon nor uproot the stroppy tree, Gorod pressed his advantage, and with one ferocious stroke of his club, he broke the hands of his foe, so that they hung limp and unusable from the Ogre's wrists. With two more furious swipes, Gorod broke both kneecaps of the, now wailing, beast, and unable to do anything else, the Ogre fell and lay, rolling in pain, upon the ground; until Gorod removed its horned helmet and smashed his club repeatedly against its skull.

With the few final strokes, Gorod had slain the foe who had before bested him, and all the Bjarz took notice. They raised another riotous shout, which when translated was, "Long live the chief," as Gorod sat upon his defeated foe, smiling a big Urz smile by jutting his lower lip out and down while also grinning in the normal manner, as he rested from the thickest of the battle.

Once the Ogre had been defeated, the tide turned against the Dark Horde, and the Bjarz renewed their assault, now pressing in on them from three sides. Their commander attempted an organized retreat to the only viable escape route, their ramshackle fort, so that they might hide out therein and await reinforcement, but as they backed toward the crooked gates with the rearguard of the Troll legion forming a pike wall to stave off the Urz, the Dark Hunter captain realized he had himself been deceived.

Anur had been busy while everyone's attention had been held fast by the two scuffling Dragons, for he had sneaked around behind all their forces, silently killed every Goblin watchman in their camp, and securely shut the gates thereof, so that their only path for withdrawal was now completely blocked off. In an effort to provide Feldara a distraction and buy her time to act, all the tents and stores he had set ablaze, and as Anur leaped down from the high ramparts to land directly before his nemesis, only now did they see the putrid, black smoke billowing up from behind the scrappy walls.

The Dark Hunter captain was truly astounded by Anur's unexpected espionage, but he regained his composure, realizing his fate was now sealed as fast as the gates of his intended haven. "I should have expected no less from one of our own, but you must tell me, before either of us fall here today, why have you turned from our master, from our people? What has caused to you to follow the light?" Hissing, he asked.

"I am not one of 'your own'. You are not 'my people', and the darkness was never my master. As for why I still follow the light, look no further than yon Dragoness." Anur coldly replied, though he could not help his curiosity being piqued by these encounters with the Dark Hunters.

Anur had always wondered about his past, for the Masters had never told him much about it. In truth, they probably knew little more than he, as they had found him but a young starving boy, too weak to move or speak, on the coasts of the Shadow Lands. Meeting now these people who wore similar garb as he, with nearly identical helms, who called him "brother" and "one of us", only brought more questions to his mind.

The Dark Hunter captain did only stare back at the glaring visage of the angered Anur, but eventually he responded. "I see that the truth has been withheld from you, for you to doubt so heartily our estrangement. However, I shall show you why we name you our brother." Said he, as he removed his own helm.

To Anur's shock and horror, the face that was revealed seemed none other than his own, for it was pale, gray skinned, with the same violet irises set in deep black eyes, bald, and with strong jutting chin. It was as if Anur now gazed in a mirror, but for that the face before him belied a darker soul. In the eyes was malicious intent, and in the demeanor was only suffering and the desire to bring it upon others.

"It is not too late to change sides, for then you shall be with your own people, with the victors. And, we shall tell you everything you ever wanted to know about yourself and your past." Wickedly tempted the Dark Hunter, sensing Anur's internal queries.

For but a moment it seemed as if Anur really could accept this invitation, for in the offer, perhaps by villainous design, was every answer that he had all his life longed to know. However, the boy who was once of the race of the Dark Hunters was not anymore.

He had been raised in the tutelage of the wisest and fairest, and had been taught goodness, kindness, honesty, and loyalty by his adoptive family.

"As I afore told you, I am already with my people." Anur sternly replied, meaning the Master Order before their demise and now his Dragoness ward, and with that he unhesitatingly charged in.

His assault did not catch off-guard the Dark Hunter's captain, and he produced a blade of his own, a jagged, cruelly curved scimitar. They matched blow after blow with parry and block, but they two seemed equal in skill and strength. More and more furiously did they fence at each other, having to drag out seldom used tricks and maneuvers from deep within their martial repertoire in attempt to gain an advantage, but in the end, it was the Dark Hunter captain that first pulled off an uncheckable, unavoidable move. It was the same tactic that the last Dark Hunter to go against Anur had used, landing upon him the only blow he had suffered in many long years, but this time, though even quicker and more fluid was the strike of their leader, Anur was able to avoid a cut from the saw-edged blade.

He dropped his sword from his hand, even as his foe had pinned it against the ground, and as the Dark Hunter captain made the very same upward slice, for to wound head or shoulder, Anur ducked so quickly, as if he had gone limp. Before the Dark Hunter could realize his miss and bring his curved sword back down again, Anur grabbed up again his weapon and rose with a stab of his own, neatly impaling his enemy.

There was still life in the Dark Hunter's leader, as he had been determined to bring down his foe with him, and did follow through with his attempted return slash, but Anur lifted his free arm and caught his enemy by the wrist of the sword hand, so that the stroke never fell. Though, his eyes did meet those of the Dark Hunter, and he could not help but to wonder, as they glared back at him, hatefully indignant in defeat, if he had, perhaps, slain his own father or other blood kin. But, life flowed with blood fast from the cruel leader of the Dark Hunters, and he slumped against Anur, and finally vanquished, fell to the ground, still clutching tightly his weapon.

The soldiers of the Dark Horde, who had been so busy defending themselves from the Urz onslaught that they had not noticed Anur's battle with their leader, did now see their captain's demise and began to fight the more viciously, in panicked, though futile, effort to survive, or else broke rank and attempt to flee. There was still no way for them to escape, as Anur had cut off their only route, and they could not hope, no matter how savage a cornered animal they were, to outfight the overwhelming force of mighty Bjarz. In the end, not a one of the Dark Horde was left alive; none escaped; none surrendered. They were all slain, and their corpses piled high where they had stood ground.

A loud, deep shout of victory was roared from the dry battle-worn throats of the triumphant Urz, and they began to sing old songs of conflicts won. Today they had overthrown the oppressive rule of the un-chief and destroyed his army, and they opened the doors of the enemy fort and looted every salvageable item from therein, that which had been stolen as tribute from their own homes and hands.

Still singing victoriously, they then piled all of their fallen foes within, for by now, thanks to Anur's kindling, nearly the whole of the camp ablaze, a hot consuming pyre to obliterate their vile presence and cleanse the defiled land, and only after finishing with that foul task, did they, at last, return to the great stone arena, to regroup and count their own losses.

Feldara was still there, still holding poor Calidon in her arms, for he had been too weak to move, let alone join the fray about them, and she had not wanted to leave him alone while a battle raged not a stone's throw from where they had sat. Anur, at length, came up to them, while the Bjarz counted their dead and wounded, for he had been unable to do so while the battle raged. Being caught behind the enemies' line of defense, he had endured the fiercest fighting of any warrior there, and he had only now been able to return to his Dragons after being dug up out of the mound of dead foes he had made about himself.

"Are you both alright?" He asked.

"I am; Calidon caused me no great harm." Feldara replied as she turned to face her mentor.

Anur looked like a nightmare come to life, with green and black Goblin and Troll blood caked all over his body, soaking his plain, ragged prison clothes, and he smelled every bit as horrid.

"Are you injured?" She asked of him, seeing that Anur appeared so wretched.

"There is naught but a scratch or two upon me." He replied, lying not, for he was, indeed, so proficient a combatant. "And, you, Calidon, are you well?" Asked he of the poor Dragon.

For, he knew that the young male had suffered far more than either he or Feldara. He had been kept long in their enemy's possession, being tortured and otherwise abused, and all alone.

"I think so." Calidon slowly replied, for thought and word had only recently been allowed to flow freely through his mind, where before they had been restricted and confined. "I was lost in the dark for so long. From the time that they subdued me and put that chain around my neck until now, I could see nothing but shadows in the murk all about me, and I knew that my will was not my own anymore. I could not control my body or even my own thoughts, but you." He turned to look Feldara in the eyes. "You were the only one I could see, like a lamp, clear and bright in a darkened room, or a star in an otherwise empty sky. Please, believe me when I say that I tried to stop myself from hurting you, the only other person that I could see amidst the shadow, but I just could not do anything. I was powerless within that all-consuming darkness, but you saved me. Somehow, you had power over the darkness, as the sun has power over the night. You cleared my mind and burned away the shadows. I am free because of you."

At this the young male bowed low to Feldara in the old style of Dragons, with the right hand placed over the horns and the left crossed under the body. "Thank You." He gratefully spoke, and tears welled in his eyes.

To be freed from such inescapable enthrallment when never was there hope or expectation to ever be liberated from so strong an evil force was, only yesterday, so unimaginable an impossibility to the young male, that now, being, indeed, free from the chains of darkness, he could not contain his emotion, and it flowed unrestrained from him in big happy tears, much joyful trembling, and something between a sob and an jubilant giggle.

They all then began to laugh, a little at first, and then more, as they realized the depth of despair Calidon had been plucked from and, of course, the glorious victory over the Dark Horde, but they soon quieted down, for still death loomed heavily all about them. The few Urz who had fallen were now being carried down the ridge on the shields of their brethren, to be buried in a sacred cave at the very foot of the mountain, thus to become part of the roots of the great peak, the strong foundation of their people, ever memorialized in the rock and stone of their descendants' livelihood and home.

When the last body had been gathered and all others, injured and whole, were accounted for and began to make their way down the path whence they had come, Gorod came over to join Feldara, Anur, and Calidon as they still sat, silently resting in peace and the warming afternoon sunlight.

"Good, fire-bringers and tiny-black-man-friend all live. I happy for you, but you scare me little bit, Feltra. For moment, I think you lose to save friend, but I glad I wrong." Happily stated the Urz. "Come down with us now, to bottom of mountain. All my people go, to honor warriors who fall this day. We make big feast again."

As weary as they all were, Anur somehow managed to find the strength to attempt a refusal, trying to get across that they had to get going, but Gorod did not quite understand.

"What you mean, having leave?" He gruffly snarled.

"If we do not go as soon as possible, more of these monsters, the Dark Horde, will come, perhaps more than your warriors can fight. The Shadow Lord is looking for her, the crux of some dark design, and we cannot risk endangering your people or ourselves by staying in one place too long." Anur tried to explain, but no one, not even he was ready for the road ahead.

They were all weary from the battle and their unpleasant stay in the captivity of their defeated tormentors. Even Calidon, who knew how wise it was of Anur to desire movement when the Shadow Lord might have yet heard about this little instance: his slaves being freed, his armies being crushed by those very same would-be slaves, his new Dragon puppet being freed by Feldara, did not lift his voice to protest a little more rest, more time to recover.

"Let come." Gorod boastfully grunted. "We kill, no matter how many."

Anur now seemed to have no more energy to argue with the insistent Urz chief, for he relented by tiredly lowering his head.

"I do not think it will hurt so much to have, maybe, one or two day's rest here, for surely there were no messengers to escape from this battle. If no one reports this defeat, how will the dark forces learn of it until, perhaps, they begin to miss a report from this camp." Feldara optimistically suggested, being not the least worn among them and truly desiring a little longer with a roof over her head and a pillow under it.

"Good, good, you stay for ceremony of new chiefs. You see me seat again, Feltra." Gorod happily answered, before anyone had time to object.

With that, they four arose, with Feldara and Gorod helping Calidon to walk, and also began their trek down the mountainside. However, Anur did lag behind and gave a last look about the field of battle, for he did recall there being three other Dark Hunters present at its start and did wonder if the others whom he did not go against were also with their leader among the slain. Still, his delay was not to locate their corpses, but if it were, perhaps, it would have alarmed him not to have found their bodies.

Since the day he had been without his helmet, Anur had felt slightly naked, a little lost, and constantly woozy in the glaring sunlight, so that he had been wishing for it, for it had been taken from him by the Dark Hunters when he had been captured.

He had lived in it, having had it upon him when he was found by the Masters, having had it refitted and reforged by the Master's armorers as he had grown, with it nearly constantly upon his head. Though having taken for himself a black robe, boots, and gloves, and a coat of Black-iron chainmail from the battle's spoils, he had been distraught to not find his own helm during that brief pillaging of the enemy camp, and sadly, he figured that now it was gone forever, that it had been cast aside somewhere in that camp or melted down to recycle the Black-iron from which it had been fashioned.

Yet, to Anur it was not some piece of scrap metal that he had lost; it was a part of him, his identity. So, even as the rest of the party began to move on out of sight, and the wind picked up and gray clouds began to cover the open sky above the mountain, with purpose in his stride regarding this, he trod back over to where he had slain his doppelganger, remembering there could be one last possibility of regaining his persona.

Indeed, the body of his foe had been moved, but there on the ground where it had been cast before their battle, in a pool of its former bearer's blood, there still lay the helm previously worn by the captain of the Dark Hunters. Without thinking twice, Anur took it up in his arms. The dark vizored helm then had a new owner.

Chapter 21

Malok and Shar had been traveling quite quickly over the wide rolling leas and scattered farmlands of the Human's realm. With only half the day gone by, the two had nearly made it to the Atsar River at its closest crossing, but they were nowhere near surveying the whole of such an expansive land. From the far eastern mountains of Dunn and the coast, where was the Dworvish Kingdom, to the Aronoran border wall which blocked off the Shadow Lands, to the great wilderness that spanned the gap between the more settled area in the Southeastern portion and the Aelven Lands, spread all the vastness of the Order's realm, and they had the whole of it to search, and even beyond.

Seeming a whole other age ago, were their lives spent in the royal home of the Serpen Kingdom, for so many leagues had passed beneath them. All the comforts and pleasures, sorrows and battles of the past had they abandoned for the sake of one Dragoness, and it now seemed to Malok, as the miles raced by under the slow, steady beat of his wing's flapping, that perhaps, he had been foolish to think such a quest at all achievable in his one lifetime.

Even with the promised help of the Order, such a great land, much more the remainder of all Threa, seemed far too immense a space to investigate, and he began to wonder if his whole life would be spent in a fruitless pursuit of his dreams, if ever he would find the object of his hunt, if such a Bright Dragoness was anything more than the contrivances of his own imagination.

Nevertheless, he could not back down now, not when he had come so far, not when he had already accomplished so much, not when proofs, even those questionable evidences of the Dark One's wily words, had been presented and seemed to collude with what he believed to be true. Even so, the more he thought upon the road ahead, the less enthusiastic Malok became, and the more hopeless of ever succeeding in this impossible undertaking.

Indeed, even their starting direction to begin their quest, to head South unto the Atsar and then follow it West until its mouth at the sea, had been at random, for only the night before had they divided up their search with the other Paladins that should assist them after the coup's end.

Shar, wishing to break the silence of their prolonged flight, spoke out. "I should like a bite of meat soon, for it is about noontide, and we had left without eating even a morsel of breakfast. Perhaps, we can stop here in this little village and buy something."

Which little village he had meant, Malok found hard to guess, for all along their flight, the ground below had been dotted with well spaced Human settlements. Some were larger towns, enclosed with sturdy palisade, and others were little more than a few farmers' huts banding together against the wilds. The great majority of these were more as Shar had described, a little village circling about a highway road, with a few homes, businesses, a temple for the residents, and a tavern for any weary travelers passing through.

Signaling that he would do so, Malok just selected the nearest one of the these and began a lazy, spiraling descent toward the earth, more as a notice to the inhabitants below that they should soon be visited upon than any need for a slow landing.

As they approached, they could already see the locals shielding with their hands their straining eyes to get a good look at the Dragon coming toward them. Little did the two foreigners know, but that these villages and their people had been nearly completely forsaken by the Order under the rule of Orthard. As such, the common folk held no great respect or love for Paladins, whose seemingly only duty was to collect as tribute their hard earned money, while out of necessity, these peasants, and their landlords, had formed their own militias to compensate for the neglectfully owed protection. Even Zurthaud's sincere, though limited, efforts to mend the relationships with the people of this realm had brought only so much success in winning back their hearts and trust.

Nevertheless, the sight of a Dragon, gloriously magnificent, seeking to land in their own small hamlet was still worth beholding to these people, they who had seen so little of their protectors of late, and that lateness, in most cases, of many decades. All the young children, who could not understand the old graybeards' disdain for such amazing creatures and the lucky men and women who had chance to fly among the clouds upon their backs, did gather joyously in the streets, shouting, running about, and jumping up and down with excitement.

Malok could only think of home and all the beloved Serpen children who used to do the same whenever he had come within sight of them, the only difference in these youngsters was the shape of their outer flesh and their lack of knowing his name, which the little Serpen would merrily shout. He did now smile and wave at them, even as his feet touched ground and the billowing dust of his wings' fluttering had dissipated.

Then, Shar dismounted.

All the adults gasped and the children backed away a few paces, and even though the Serpen king saved his and their own grace by pretending not to notice, his feelings had been wounded, especially through the fear of the little ones, by this unearned apprehension.

Through the kind acceptance of the true Paladins, he had nearly forgotten the rest of the world's apprehension and prejudice toward his people, but a wizened old man then came up to greet them, breaking the aghast silence of the small crowd gathered about. He proceeded to introduce himself and somewhat begrudgingly welcome their guests, only thinly disguising his distrust of Dragon and Serpen alike with a practiced courtesy.

"Hello. Welcome to our village, master Dragon and... other guest." Began the old man, not too unkindly. "This is the Hamlet of Nitenmile, the last village on the road between here and the town of Bestford, at the river crossing. By election, I am this hamlet's head man, Sutton being my name, and you are free to purchase any food, drink, or other common traveling supplies that you wish, if that is, indeed, your purpose for stopping here. You are with Zurthaud's men, yes? Seeing that you are a Dragon and your companion is a um,.. We just assumed you were passing through and not here to collect more tax. We did just make our monthly payment of tribute, and I do still have the receipt from the last Paladins who took our hard earned money. Though might I say, gladly do we buy the esteemed protection of the Order."

The nervousness and presumption in this elderly man's patronizing blathering fast made clear to Malok what had occurred out in these isolated fiefdoms. While Zurthaud had spent much time making good the duty and honesty of the Order, Orthard, for to fill his own greedy coffers, had longer still been bleeding dry the purses of these poor farmers, and they had become bitter toward the levy collecting thieves who so called themselves Paladin.

"Please, slow your speech and be at ease. Truly, we are friends of Zurthaud and have no interest in taking anything more from you than the meat we shall pay for, but do not call the fools who have treated you so poorly 'Paladin', as it would only insult those who actually are." Malok tactfully replied.

Sutton did then offer a slight smile, causing the care-earned wrinkles of his face to deepen, and he spoke plainly, without the mask of false-friendship. "I thought as much, for never in all my years has a Dragon ever asked a tribute from us, nor any of their companions, but we never can be too careful these days. Our stockpiles of wheat and corn are getting dangerously low, so that we fear any further tax before the coming winter, and speak not of coin, as most folk here barely have two to rub together. But, I am now forgetting my manners, for I admit, knowing that you follow the honorable Zurthaud has put us all at such ease. May I ask your names and offer you refreshment at our inn?"

Malok did then introduce Shar and himself to the gathered townsfolk as they made their way down the street to the local common-house, and by the time they had made it to the door thereof, they had all become quite friendly, so that the past wrongs of Orthard's men were somewhat lessened by the kindness and gentleness of the two strangers. Even Shar began to receive more civility, being addressed by name and spoken to, rather than be ignored or asked questions through Malok, as if the Serpen king were a dumb beast who could not understand, and eventually the children did acclimate to him, coming close enough to stare and inquisitively poke at his scaly skin, which was still rather rude but much more likeable to him than their previous fearing.

Once Malok managed to squeeze through the door of the tavern, which while a large building for the Humans, was barely roomy enough for him to turn about within, they ordered a simple meal, for simple was the only available fare. It was only salted beef with a little mead to drink, but out of generosity and Shar's hefty wallet, they paid well for it, with extra for the serving maid and a round of drink for those who had lingered about the table to hear tale of the travelers' news. The children then had to be shooed away by the responsible adults, for they were not allowed to partake of strong drink, free or otherwise. Though, they had a hard time of it, for the young ones had become fascinated by Shar's custom of swallowing whole, not chewing, large morsels of food, as was the Serpen way.

"What news can you bring us from The City, my friends?" Asked Sutton, only after his thirst had been slaked and his guests had been filled. "We heard rumor that there were to be some big changes, but the details, as always, are harder to come by than the general gossip."

"It is truly so, but I fear to say any more about it. I do not know yet if we can rejoice in what was to transpire, but know this, Lord Orthard has threatened good people like yourselves long enough, and there was something to be done about it. His latest offense, daring to sentence my people to death in the sulfur mines, was at the very end of our tolerance." Malok replied, wishing not to tell more than he should, lest any of Orthard's spies catch wind of their plot.

The young Dragon did not yet know that by now the battle to retake the Order's stronghold and overthrow Orthard's tyrannical oppression had already commenced and was well along. Even so, the inn erupted with a chorus of approval and shouts of affirmation, upon hearing word that the Dragons might finally be fed up with their hated despot; clearly, there were no snitches among these folk.

"We, however, are on another quest, for though we count them our friends, we are not officially Paladins ourselves." Continued Malok, after the crowd had again quieted down. "We are searching for a Bright Dragoness, for we think that she may be in danger from the dark powers."

Upon hearing mention of their hunt for the Bright Dragoness, Sutton and the other villagers became silent, and all smiles faded from the room. Yet, it was not from new-found hatred or fear; it was of veneration and deepest respect that the townsfolk abandoned all careless jollity.

"Surely you mean 'her'." Sutton suddenly exclaimed. "Why, I mean 'The Dragoness'. We do not know her name, but if anyone deserves to be called 'bright', it is her. She is a saint to us, defending our town from all attack or even the very presence of the enemy. She alone must be the reason, unless there are others helping her, that the Dark Horde has yet here to cross the river, for she watches over us, and all the other hamlets about, even feeding the poor in winter tide with meat from her own hunting. Though we had lost faith in the Order, still we reverence her and all the free Dragons, for your people have not forsaken the old oaths. Truly, it was they who brought us the word of God and helped to build our temples. Why, I can remember my great-grandfather telling me the story of the first time a Dragon came to this village..."

Even much more did Sutton intend to say in the extolment of the free Dragons, but Malok, upon hearing of a Dragoness nearby, heard naught else and, nearly bursting with excitement, suddenly interrupted.

"Where? Where is this Dragoness?" He little less than shouted.

More timidly did Sutton answer. "She lived in a cave by a small lake, not fifty miles due South on the far side of the Atsar, but it has been some time since we have seen her, so that where she resides now, I do not know. The other side of the river, from the forests before its water to the great border wall, has become a rather unfriendly place. Stories come of whole fiefs emptying, either through fear of the Dark Horde or an actual attack from it. Why, old Farmersrest, a nice fortified town, stood on the open grasslands for ages, but one night passes and, come morning, nothing remains there but ashes, no graves, nor even any sign of the dead or their desecration, just gone, without any trace."

But, Malok neither heard nor cared for the danger before him, for news had come to him of, perhaps, the very person for whom he had been searching. Hastily, he downed the rest of his mead and motioned for Shar to also finish his meal.

"We must now be going, for if this is the same Bright Dragoness I have been seeking, I might, much more quickly than expected, be nearing the very end of my quest. I thank you, Sutton, and all your people, for your hospitality. May you be blessed all your days." Spake the young Dragon even as he darted out the door.

"We always have to leave so soon, and I was just getting to like the locals." Shar jocularly complained, as he trotted along close behind his friend.

But, Malok's mind was already turned to the culmination of his search, so that he did not answer only quickly hoisting his friend onto his shoulders, he bolted off into the blue sky, even as the townsfolk began to disperse out into the street for to wave and call farewell and then to go on about their day.

It was almost an hour past noon when Malok touched ground again. He and Shar had raced across the last stretch of open plains that had spread before the looming Atsar, and as they had so quickly passed over the mighty river, the gushing torrent of the rain-gorged watercourse had for only a moment caught their attention. The Order's realm on the far side of the Atsar seemed a completely different world from the farmland and plains on the other, with its vast sedges, creeping thickly from the overreaching waters, turning into patches of woods and eventually dense forest, but Malok paid little heed to the wondrous landscape. He was focused entirely on one thing, finding the Bright Dragoness.

Quickly soaring over many miles of the lush semi-tropical woodland, they now came within sight of what Malok surmised to be the lake whereabout the aforementioned Dragoness was said to have lived, for in contrast to all the other wetlands they had passed over, this small lake had little to no vegetation growing on its banks or in its depths, such as long marsh grass, cattails, or even algae, and the North shore, that which was closest to the nearby forest, had been smoothed with a lining of fine sand and pebbles. So clean and clear was the pool that it seemed more of glass than water, and it reflected near flawlessly the trees about, and the skies above, and even the young Dragon's descent therefrom.

As Malok neared the smooth North shore, there appeared under the trees, and right before the lake, large hillocks, great earthen mounds, that surely were the cave dwelling of said Dragoness, for there was a quaint little pathway, obviously crafted, of flat stones carefully laid in the conjoining sand, leading only a short distance from the very shore of the lake to a shadowy cleft in the side of the closest hill.

Before the doorway of this Dragon lair upon the lake's shore, which he now saw clearly to have been carved out all by Dragon-fire, Malok landed as quickly as he could, and pausing only long enough for Shar to speedily dismount, he called out a greeting.

At first Malok supposed that Sutton had been correct in surmising the Dragoness had abandoned these lands, for no voice quickly answered his call. For the short while they waited, it seemed that all was silent about the small lake, as not even the water made a sound of splashing, though the wind rippled it in soft waves against the sandy shore.

However, his uncertainty was soon allayed and replaced by excited glee, for out from the darkness of the tunnel-like cave of a home stepped forth the most stunningly beautiful sight that Malok had yet seen. Though the young Dragon had gazed upon many natural wonders of earth and water, sunsets and sunrises, never before had his eyes beheld a Dragoness, and he began to tremble with the overpowering emotion that coursed through his mind and body.

She was radiantly silver, like the moon's glow on a cold, lucid winter's night, and graceful were her legs and long arms, tail and neck. Her eyes seemed almost luminously gleaming, for they shone of a supernaturally brilliant fire. Yet, her greeting was kind, even humble, a surprise from a being seemingly so far beyond mortality and the familiarities of daily life.

"Welcome to my home, young Dragon and his friend." Spoke she, with a low voice, soft as silk and warmly sweet like amber honey, as if soothing music poured from her lips with each word. "What do you seek here?"

For a good while, Malok could do naught but stare back at her, mouth agape, in wonderment, but after a moment, and a knock in the side from Shar, he overcame his stupefaction.

"I have come from my homeland seeking a Bright Dragoness that I had seen in my dreams, and when I was told that there was a Dragoness living here, I came as quickly as I was able to see if you were she." He stuttered.

Still, as soon as these first mesmerized seconds had passed, even though this Dragoness was truly beautiful beyond words, Malok realized that she was not the one for whom he had been searching. This comely female was at least twice the age of the Dragoness of whom he had dreamed, old enough to be his own mother, and though they both seemed aglow of supernal brilliance, the light was not the same, as they were, indeed, of two different souls. Whereas the Dragoness from his dreams shone with a golden fire like the sun, this one here was of a sliver glow like the moon, similar because of a shared luminescence but of completely opposite quality.

Either the Dragoness before him had read his facial expression most adeptly or, seemingly, sensed his thoughts even before he had put them to words, for she now did answer openly his inward doubting.

"It is surely not I whom you seek, but perhaps, I can help in your quest." Said she, letting a gentle smile grow upon her lips. "Yet, I am forgetting myself. My name is Lenairu." She said, slowly bowing in the old style of Dragons, and she fell silent waiting for Malok to reciprocate.

The young Dragon was still so captivated by the beautiful Lenairu's grace and poise, that he almost forgot to return the mannerly gesture and succeeded only in a clumsily hastened Serpen style obeisance.

"I am Malok." He abashedly replied, wishing that he had half the courteousness of his host.

"It is an odd name to accompany your foreign mannerisms, though not at all reviled or displeasing, for Dragons do not despise any honest creature or people. I only mean that I am truly curious about your origin, and how you came to be in the company and culture of the Serpen." She asked, the sincerity and warmth of her smile never fading from her lips.

"It is a long story, and I do not have many of the important details, as I am still trying to figure out most of it." Malok replied a little sheepishly, for though he did not resent having his peculiarities noted, it still bothered him that they were so blatantly obvious to strangers, especially other Dragons.

Though Malok truly loved his adopted people, and never would disown them, he deeply desired to be accepted and respected by his kindred. He wanted, as he had sought his whole life, and indeed, tasted of among the Paladins, to be fully Dragon, who he was, and to be seen as such, not as a Serpen, or even a Dragon who lived among the Serpen, and even the love and acceptance of his adopted people, though gratefully received, could not abate or replace this most profound need to be acknowledged as one of their own by his kind.

However, this too did the Dragoness seem to most insightfully perceive, for her facial expression and tone of voice changed again becoming even more compassionate, almost motherly.

"I meant not to demean your earned habits, for I suppose that you have lived long among the Serpen people. Their ways have become yours, and there is no wrong in that. It is part of who you are and of what constitutes your uniqueness, and you should neither be ashamed nor embarrassed of your adopted manners and people." She softly voiced, speaking peace into Malok's yearnings and shame. "In fact, I should wish to learn more about you, and your friend, whom you have neglected to yet introduce. Please, let us enter my home, and we shall make ourselves comfortable with refreshment while you tell me your tale."

"I wish we could afford to stay." Malok replied. "But, we must be going. My quest to find this Bright Dragoness is most pressing."

"I know it is." Lenairu, plainly stated, and confounded by his host's profound discernment, Malok began to ask how. But, she interrupted before he could say a word. "I have read your thoughts. The gift of Soul-Speaking, Athungar- as it is called in the ancient tongue, is given to all Dragons, and your mind was unguarded and open, plain to my sight."

Shar doubted this greatly, gibing that Malok's thought's had always been spread across his face, to be just as easily read as a book, but the silver Dragoness disproved his skepticism by speaking aloud knowledge that had been withheld from her. "Your name is Shar, the king of your people, and just a moment ago, you were more than a little upset with your friend because he did not introduce you at the first and became ashamed when I noticed his Serpen upbringing. Just now, you have become embarrassed because of my speaking aloud your inward thoughts."

Seeing that Shar no longer doubted her words, and was now staring down at his feet, abashedly attesting the accuracy of her power, with a victorious grin, Lenairu turned back to Malok. "I can teach you how to do this and how to guard your thoughts from others, and much more that is no longer known to even the Masters of the Order. I shall help you find your Dragoness, but first, as my honored guests, you shall come inside and be refreshed." She kindly insisted.

Try as he might, Malok could not help but to admit his weariness, how defeated he felt in this unceasing journey, and how welcome was this help and invitation to rest.

Chapter 22

It took what remained of the morning and the better part of the afternoon for all the Urz and their guests to gather together and take the slow funereal march down the worn, sloping trails to the very bottom of the mountain; all the while, in gentle mist, the rain which earlier had loomed overhead, now came wafting down, wetting every plant and rock and darkening the sky and earth about with a cold, damp fog. It became so gloomy that, to clearly see the path ahead and stay together, the procession had to light torches and walk in tight groups, but even so, this slight precipitation was nothing compared to the deluge that the three traveler's had but days earlier experienced.

Albeit, Calidon for his injuries and earlier afflictions had asked leave from the whole ordeal, desiring needful rest and rejuvenation and would shunt the gentle shower within the comparative comfort of the chief's lodge, making the three sojourners only two. Fast becoming drenched with the rest of the funeral procession, Anur and Feldara could not help but to want for the warm bed and hearth to which their companion had been excused, yet they could not at all begrudge it of poor Calidon, having seen the depths of suffering he had endured.

Despite the miserable conditions, the funerary procession eventually reached the very bottom of the mountain, where the ground became more level, rather than the constant decline, but even lower than the ground they had still to go, into "the belly of the earth", as Gorod had called it.

Feldara could immediately see why it had been named so, for before her eyes, in the slump of a large bowl shaped dale, appeared a great cavernous mouth, with enormous stalactites hanging from the ceiling and with moss and fern covered fallen rock, seeming as jagged teeth, reaching up from the leaf littered forest floor.

Though Feldara had to fight the unpleasant impression of being eaten, the Urz entered into this gigantic maw without any trepidation or fear, only with slow, steady, and somber footfalls and heads held low in reverent mourning. Through this terrible gaping jaw Feldara entered, fully feeling as if she had been swallowed whole by the mountain, for immediately after passing through this toothed gate, the warm darkness of the earth's interior enveloped her, until she could not even see Anur walking but a few feet before her.

Yet, through the deep blackness, the flickering of the torches, with their soft red light, began to bloom, as stars popping into the early evening, so that, little by little, they could see well enough to not clumsily stumble about. Without the slightest slowing of their constant pace, deep into the tunneling recesses of the cave they windingly trekked, though it was not hard going as the descent from the mountain, for the floor was quite smooth, aside from the occasional stray rock or stalagmite, over which Feldara tripped more than she would have liked to admit.

Eventually, as they passed beyond the recollection of their entry or of any light beyond the modest glow of the small braziers, the walls opened up round about them, expanding what was before a cramped tunnel into an enormous circular vault, while the arched ceiling reached for domed extremity so far above them that the feeble light of the torches could not at all illuminate it, and it seemed to Feldara that they truly had come to the very heart of the mountain, the belly of the earth.

It was here that the leader of the procession, the old Znakar, stopped, for as Anur and Feldara slowly became aware, by seeing that the entire wall round about the dome was lined with the peculiar graves of their custom, all Urz who had previously died had here been interred, seemingly from time immemorial. Their sepulchers were not overly intricate or decorated, merely a slot cut into the side of the rock wall and covered over with another precisely carved stone door, making for each Urz a small niche of a sarcophagus, and the only marker upon them was, carved in the stone door, the ornately engraved name of the person whose body therein resided.

The Urz priest said but few words, as the wives and children, fathers and mothers, friends and family loudly lamented the departed loved ones, but it was only of necessity that he spoke not overly long. For, though these Bjarz had died valiantly in battle for a most worthy cause, the mourners could not linger long in the vault of the tombs. As Gorod had earlier explained, the air would not last very long shared among all these people, being already stale and of short supply so deep beneath the earth, and if they tarried, they would all soon sleep with the proud warriors. It was with heavy hearts that those closest to the departed placed them in a pre-cut recess, slowly sealed the stone doors of their tombs, and reluctantly left the sepulchral vault with the rest of the procession.

In the manner of Urz tradition, the mourners, though having been silent the whole trek down the mountain, now loudly let forth their tears in the final departure from their kin, and did not let up until they passed out again from the cave's mouth. Once they had again come back into the light of the living day, out from the deathly dark of the tomb, they slowly began to be more at ease, and Gorod, standing upon a large boulder for to be seen by all, spoke to the people.

"They will rest here forever, but now, we drink to their life." Loudly said he in their language, and the Urz raised up a shout, a cheer honoring the life of their comrades and signaling for the celebration thereof to begin.

The journey back up the mountain was of a much quicker pace, for it was made known to Feldara, now that the funeral service had been completed. Flying, as opposed to somberly treading, would again be an appropriate mode of travel, and needing not another to repeat those words, she instantly gathered Anur up on her back and sped off into the dismal sky and up the mountain's height.

"I despise walking long distances." She let Anur know, as among the lofty peaks, she circled the Urz village below.

"Walking is good and healthy; it keeps one's legs strong and is still the world's most preferred mode of transportation." Anur smugly replied.

"You are only saying that because you cannot fly; if you could soar on the paths of the air, I doubt you would ever walk again, but for necessity." She jocularly flaunted.

"But, I can fly. See me up here on your shoulders with the wind rushing past my face and the ground far beneath my feet." Said he with a sly smile.

She smiled back at him, loving the sight of his face. Though it was grim, cracked by many careworn wrinkles, scarred by recent and long ago battles, and with the inner sorrowing borne of darkest years heavy in his solemn eyes, there was a kindness and warmth of love there, mostly only given toward her.

"Do you really want me to test your theory by throwing you from my shoulders?" She mischievously inquired.

They both laughed, Feldara first, then Anur joining, for they could now tease each other in the honesty and goodwill that they had afore shared, unbroken by contemptuous perceptions, unshaded by pride or guilt. It was the same pure jollity that only good friends can share, completely entrusting their own open heart to the other's grace and kindness; it was friendship, like which they had always wanted to give each other before, but had lately been reluctant in offering, mostly due to their own inner striving. They two, now more than ever before, trusted and realized who the other was: their friend, father and daughter, and they were finally at peace with each other.

They came to earth again upon the village path, just before the doorway of the chief's lodge, and seeing that they were yet a few hours ahead of their hosts' arrival, they decided to check upon Calidon's well-being. They entered the grand house to find the young male lying upon a large cushion, right beside the chief's dais and before the blazing fire, and being overmuch tended by the Urz women who had stayed behind to begin preparations for that evening's bereavement feast. They had apparently fussed over him incessantly, bringing him soup and meats, fluffing his pillow, and otherwise pamperingly supplying his every need.

"I see that you have been faring well." Feldara snorted upon noticing this lavishing of attention.

"I have been well cared for." He contentedly and humbly replied.

"How quickly do you think you could continue our journey?" Anur immediately inquired.

Always thinking on the road ahead, unceasingly remembering their dangerous pursuers, he had already forgotten the purpose of their visit, of asking how Calidon had fared, and had come back to the worry that had been plaguing his every thought from the outset of their journey.

"I should think by tomorrow morning." Calidon offered, but glibly he added. "Then again, I might be so fully stuffed that I cannot move, for these females have been feeding me constantly since I arrived."

"It must be nice getting to stay in out of the rain and not having to walk the length of the entire mountain." Feldara retorted as she helped herself to some of Calidon's extra indulgences, but she, being caught up in the good mood of this morning's conquest, the elation of victory, was only playfully pestering her friend.

"It is good that Calidon has received proper care, for we cannot fully understand the sort of mistreatment he had suffered, to be tortured, to lose control of one's own body and mind. We should not begrudge his duly earned rest." Anur chided, giving Feldara one of his looks, apparently not having sensed the jocund of her comment. Though now that his face was uncovered, his chastening frown seemed far less stern than the one Feldara had before imagined, even affectionate, so that she found it hard to restrain the sudden fit of a giggling snort.

Anur waited until she had excused herself, as if for coughing, before he continued. "That said, we cannot risk staying idle for too long; if you think tomorrow is soon enough for your healing, we shall plan on leaving at first light. We should correct our course by heading directly South toward the plains we had left in the storm. Once there, we shall again turn East and continue on to Doraegonoran, and hopefully, we can avoid any further foes or obstacles."

"Yes, hopefully we shall avoid being captured by the enemy this time." Feldara, with her mouth full of food, interrupted between bites. "No more wandering off to fetch firewood for you." She joked.

Though Anur's pride was slighted by this comment, he regarded it with no more than an inward smile, for he was only glad that his Dragoness was still among the living, free, and happy enough to be irritating everyone so. He could eat a joke or two, especially for his charge, just as he also could serve the dish, but for now, he could not afford anything other than serious planning of their next move. He, more than any of them, had read the signs and seen what kind of enemy they were facing.

"You have a good point hidden somewhere behind that lashing tongue." Responded Anur. "We shall no more be as lax as we have been with our coming and going. We must now lose neither sight nor sound of each other, especially at night, and from now on, we must take turns at watch while the others sleep. For, our enemy is far more cunning and powerful than even I had realized at the first. You may remember, Feldara, how that same storm system, the very one which had tried to drown us into coming here, had formed over the Shadow Lands just as we were leaving our island and followed us our whole journey's length until now. Then, when we came here, to the utmost North, far beyond the common roads of travelers, there was an enemy presence already in this land, seemingly waiting for us to arrive. Only so many separate events must come together before a wise man will call them more than coincidence. We are hunted by a foe far more powerful than Goblins, Trolls, and Ogres; even the terrible Dark Hunters pale in comparison to the one they name 'Master', if even the weather itself is at his command. Worse still, if these forces were placed here not for the sole purpose of subduing the Urz, if they had been sent here, who knows how many months or weeks ahead of us, then we are against one who knows our every move, even seeing into the future."

The food in her mouth lost its savor, and Feldara swallowed the bite of meat she had been chewing, as she contemplated once again the depressing situation in which she had been placed. To run from an enemy was one thing, to run her whole life from an enemy who was great in number and power, who would never give up or go away, who could see where she was going before she went there, was quite another. Her heart sank again into the dark shadows which had followed her all along the way, from the start of her travels, but these were not clouds heavy with precipitation. It was the black fog of despair, that which silently gurgles beneath the surface of everyone's thoughts, waiting only for calamitous incident to strike, for to seep through the cracked floor of careless gaiety and flood the inner heart, swallowing alive all who linger therein.

She faced a two sided choice: to wallow there in the slough of despond and slowly rot in depression and self-pity, or to rise and accept what was and what was to come, hurdling life's difficulties as they came while trusting in the providence of the Eloigal, who sees and knows all things and gives power to the weak, even enough for to overcome their daily trials.

Two choices she had: to despair, or to hope.

Feldara chose hopefulness, for it was far more cheery than any wallowing, shining with the light of optimism, radiating the warm uprightness of strength through perseverance.

"If the master of the Dark Horde can see the future, how come he did not just send his whole army to our island or set great forces of troops against us on our way here?" Feldara contended, refusing to let the enemy earn her fear. "He cannot see the future, at least not very well, or he would have sent more forces here, seeing as we annihilated a whole battalion of them. I say that he was already trying to subjugate the Urz, and when he knew our most probable course of action, he used this installment as a snare for us."

Calidon seemed more to agree with this train of thought, and even Anur paused to reconsider his own worries.

"We should plot a course that he will not expect, something outlandish or out of the way, something that his eyes are not already watching." She suggested, taking another bite of roasted meat.

Anur offered Feldara another of his thin smiles, as his heart inwardly beamed with parental pride, for her astute suggestion cut directly through doubt and dismay to strike an answer within the realm of probability and reality, a solid resolution to a stygian mystery.

"I do think your answer is the more likely." Calidon chimed in, meaning Feldara's proposal. "However, which path we shall now take becomes an issue. Surely all roads between the Aelven Lands and the Order's Realm are being watched or guarded, and we cannot go backward."

"A good point also." Spoke Anur. "We cannot go back; it will lead to being cornered and cut off from any refuge offered by Doraegonoran. To head East from here means we shall fly over the uncharted ranges of the Northern Mountains, and if we do that, we well could miss Doraegonoran and end up in the deserts of the Serpen Kingdom. As you both well know, the Serpen betrayed the civilized races in the last Great War, and I do not trust they shall have changed their ways since."

"Actually, I heard their current sovereign was quite honorable." Calidon offered.

"I still would not trust that people." Anur continued, due to his hermitage, not having heard the same news. "Anyway, it seems the most direct and well watched path is the one which I mentioned, to head due South and then East once we reach the plains. We could, instead, try for the Atsar river—truly an unmistakable landmark. It must be somewhere Southeast of here; we could follow it back North to Doraegonoran."

"There must be a less obvious route than that, for surely, the well-known and highly traversed Atsar will be crawling with the Dark Horde by now." Feldara postulated.

"Maybe the Urz know of some landmark about these mountains which we can use to better navigate our course." Anur suggested. "If only I still had the maps I had brought with me from home, but the Dark Hunters burned all they could of my possessions."

It was useless to inquire of such from the busy Urz maids, for they were cooking frantically, now having heard wind of the rest of the funeral party's nearing. Indeed, there was a sound of song, rough and crude Urz singing, echoing in the air, bellowing up from the vales lower down the mountainside, for the marching Urz had begun their festivities by singing old dirges for mighty warriors now long passed and newer eulogies for the recently departed, as they climbed up ever closer to the mountain's peak.

"They shall not be long now, maybe only another hour or two before the whole assembly reaches the top. We can wait until, what was his name,.. Gorod returns and then ask him if he knows of some ancient pass through the range that shall lead us quietly and safely to our destination." Calidon offered, and they all thought it best to wait for the Urz chief's advice.

It was nearing eventide when all the Urz had finally arrived and joined together again in the great open square at their village's center. The rain had stopped, and the clouds had departed, at least well enough so that the last rosy rays of the sun could tint the gray sky with splashes of blushing pink and sanguine red. As the chief's hall barely had enough room to accommodate all the Bjarz, let alone the rest of the people, they would all gather out here under the open, crimson sky around the long tables set up beforehand, for a commencement ceremony and then depart to their separate feasting locations: here, at the chief's lodge, and throughout the town.

Gorod spoke long, as the people solemnly stood; they did not even as much as sniff of the laden tables, piled high with all manner of food, though they were truly hungry from the morning's battle and the day's long trek up and down the mountain. As their chief extolled the deeds of the dead and the living, they were still as stone, honoring with silence their lost kin, but as soon as the last word was spoken, they all gave a loud cheer and those who would eat here quickly sat down, immediately tearing into the delicious meal.

Once she had made it back to the chief's hall, Feldara found that evening's feasting to be much the same as she had experienced the night before, with similar food, loud chatter, and music, but there were no decorations anywhere to be seen, no happy little paper lanterns to shed their multicolored lights around the village, and there was no dancing.

In all, though the Urz were quite joyously cheerful, there was still an air of respect and reverence about them, for it was in honor of the dead that they now lived fully. Into the late hours of the night and on into the early hours of morning they ate and drank, sang and read poetry, and gave speeches honoring the dead, but soon the pale glint of morning began to lighten the sky, and they stopped, almost suddenly, at the rising of the sun and the breaking of day and retired to their own homes, leaving the cleaning, even the dirty dishes, for later.

Gorod and the Znakar were the only ones who had stayed up to wish their guests farewell, for Anur, Calidon, and even Feldara, though she had protested a little, had gone to bed precisely at the tenth hour, so as to be fresh and fit for their own departure. She had protested even further, seeing Anur don, along with all his other stolen accoutrement- the armor, cloak, boots, and belt, the helm of the slain Dark Hunter captain, but he had silenced her with his own stoic disregard for her disparaging comments. They were now quite ready to leave, with Anur being the most anxious to get going, for he thought that they had already spent far too much time lingering in the mountains, only awaiting the Dark Horde's next attack.

Upon each of their shoulders, Gorod placed his large paw-hands, in turn, blessing their journey with a simple Urz gesture, but when he got to Feldara, he embraced her neck with a great "bear-hug".

"You free my people, fire-bringer Feltra. You free me too. We never forget you." He said, with tears welling in his eyes, though he again turned away and pretended to blow his nose.

But, Feldara could not help letting her own eyes wet, for when least expected, she had found friendship with these people, and especially with Gorod. She would neither forget them, nor their valor or kindness.

"I only wish we could stay a little longer, and really have some fun. I could have taken you flying, if you wanted." She offered, as the Urz chief turned back around.

"No, no, my feet stay on ground." He chuckled.

The Znakar then had something to say in the slow grumbling speech of the Urz, and once he finished, Gorod did translate. "With our people now free from Dark Hunter un-chief, we return to life of peace, but I am thinking dark powers not finish with you. You be hunted, so maybe we send some warriors with you on journey?"

"That might not be a bad idea." Calidon agreed. "We could use a few more good warriors if we run into any further fighting."

"No, for the sake of speed, we shall be flying the whole rest of the way, and I cannot expect either of you young Dragons to carry even one extra person, let alone a weighty Urz warrior." Anur hastily replied. "The only time we shall even touch ground is when we stop to sleep, and then we shall take turns at watch. We cannot afford to be slowed any further."

Gorod then did translate back to the Znakar, who seemed very concerned. He spoke again.

"I have dream, night before last: Darkness covering all lands. I fear war coming to your people. Now you help us and we free, we help you and your people. We go to war, follow you where you go."

"If war is coming, then it shall also come to your people. Should you not rather build up your defenses here in preparation for the coming storm?" Anur questioned.

"No, I think enemy not come back here soon. They hunting Feltra. They not come back until they finish with her, but if we go, more hope for your people, more hope for our people. If we go, maybe we die in battle, but maybe you win. If we stay, and you no win, enemy comes here, and we die in battle. Both ways, many Urz die, but if we go, maybe we help to win." Spoke the Znakar through Gorod.

"When all warriors leave, we send women and children far into mountains to hide, and all Bjarz come to help you fight. If enemy come back here, they find nothing, but we will be seeing them in battle." Gorod added.

"Very well, I see you have already made up your minds about this. I can only hope all goes well for your people, for we owe you all a debt of gratitude for helping us. If ever I live to see the day, I shall gladly repay it." Anur consented, realizing he held no sway with the determined Urz.

"Urz hold no debts, tiny-black-man-friend Anur." Gorod happily replied.

"If that is so, we do, indeed, have one more favor to ask. How shall we best get to the great city, Doraegonoran, from here. It lies far in the East and, maybe, to the South also; the enemy will surely be between us and there." Feldara inquired, remembering Calidon's suggestion from the day before.

The large Urz chief's brow furrowed as he again stroked his protruding lower lip, for he had to think long and deep for an Eastward pass through the mountain, and then how one should recognize its landmarks from the air. It had, indeed, been a very long time since any of his people had traveled very far East, though unbeknownst to them, in their wide ranging hunting trips, they had gone as far West as the Aelven Realm's most Northerly forests.

"There is one pass in mountains go East, but it not go far, not all the way to end of mountains, only to next bend in mountains." He replied after much thought.

"Is there a way we can recognize the pass from up in the air?" Feldara asked, hopeful for some manner of landmark.

"Yes, there is Big Stone." Gorod explained, as if the existence of the "Big Stone" was universally recognized.

"What manner of 'big stone' is it?" Anur inquired, hoping for more detail, as any large boulder could be considered, especially among mountains that included millions of them.

"It, well,.. big rock, cut with hands, but not hands of Urz. It old, older my people remember. You see it if take pass go East from here. From sky, you see it far away when you not close. You no miss it." The Urz chief replied, using more his hands and arms, rather than words, to describe the monolithic stone.

"I suppose that shall have to do. If you say that we will see it, I shall take your word." Anur replied, more than a little puzzled, for from Gorod's feeble description, he could only guess as to the actual size and prominence of the carved rock, though he truly was thankful for any help that was offered.

They then said their last words of thanks and well-faring, and with Gorod's help, the Znakar blessed their journey, even as the two Dragons, with Anur well seated upon Feldara's shoulders, slowly rose up and off into the brilliant golden light of an early morning sky.

"Blessing be upon you all. May Boag's light shine upon your path, making bright even the darkest hour."

Chapter 23

They had finally found it, after nearly a whole day of scrambling tirelessly through the dank and dark shafts and galleries of the abandoned Dworvish mines. Zurthaud and his men had at last found the one tunnel that led from these empty quarries under the mountain ranges, those which stood, upon the northernmost side, fast beside the city of Doraegonoran.

Many years before, at none other than Orthard's behest, had the last Dworvish miners ceased their delving in these forgotten passages, back when they had all been forcefully, and wrongfully, expelled from the Order. It was now, only thanks to a formerly exiled Dworvish Paladin, Himmel, with his brethren, Gimmel, Noff, and Toff, some of the few Dworvs who had unlawfully stayed behind to follow Zurthaud, that they were led surely and safely through the pitch-blackness of the corridors. Many times, by the careful guidance of these brave people, they had narrowly avoided death by falling many fathoms downward into some abyss.

"Dworvs don't really make maps o' their mines, ya'know. Why, we remember 'em like the back o' our wrinkly hands while we're down in 'em, but if'n we've been away for too long, well, we tend a forget some o' the minor details." Himmel explained, seeming apologetic for having not led them so straightaway to the entrance of the Keep.

"I thank you for a job well done, Himmel." Zurthaud heartily commended, while Himmel's Dworvish brothers chuckled over 'miner details' and boasted claims of how they or another Dworv could have found it faster. "I am just glad we all made it here alive, quickly or not. Now, you Dworvs must guard this passage with your lives, for if we become cornered inside the Keep, this very tunnel may likely be our only way of escape. The rest of us will go on from here, and quietly, for stealth is our only ally within these walls. Shed no blood that need not be shed. We do not war with the frightened servants, but with my father only. He shall pay for his crimes, but let the innocent and ignorant go free."

With that, the rest of the Paladins, thirty hardy Men of war and twenty bow wielding Aelvs, proceeded down the remainder of the passageway to the very door of the Keep. It was a round portal in shape and made of heavy oak with iron banding, but they found it shut with only a simple lock on the inside. With a magic spell of heat and destruction, Zurthaud cut straight through the bolt at the crack of the door, where wood met stone, and the party quickly, and as silently as possible, entered therein. Though the heavy door creaked ferociously on its worn rusted hinges, there seemed to be no one about to hear, for it was through a deeply subterranean basement that the mines gained access to the Keep.

It was the back of a dark passageway in an unvisited, and apparently unkempt, part of the fortress, and Zurthaud had himself never been here once before. Lighted by the torches they had brought along, the chilling sight of the iron bars of long unused prison cells promptly informed him where they had arrived; it was the dungeon.

In the long past golden ages of Threa, there had not been any kind of prison within the Order's fortress, but even before the tyranny of Orthard, the Paladins had unwillingly found need for holding cells. It was here, back in the days when the Order had no inner strife to deter them from their true duties, that Paladins had brought their captured criminals, to await sentencing or to serve punishments of time, yet even with this justified usage, the grim, abandoned ward seemed not a kind place to stow even the most deserving of convicts.

As they slowly walked down to the very end of the corridor, Zurthaud hoped that he could avoid sending his father to such a fate, that perhaps, once he managed to get the upper hand by letting the Dragons into the sealed stronghold, his parent would just give up and resign, but just as much as he hoped, he doubted. He knew exactly how stubborn and relentless Orthard could be.

Eventually, they came to a door at the opposite end of the hallway, and seeing that it too had a bolt that was easily cut, they proceeded through the groaning oak portal. This time, their entry was noticed, for to their shock, they had stumbled into one of Orthard's many secret evils.

They had come out from a disused and forgotten dungeon into another prison, newer, very much in use and filled with inmates. As soon as they entered, they began recognizing some of the imprisoned, for these captives were none other than former colleagues, even former Paladins: Dworvs, Aelvs, and Humans, all of whom were thought to have left the Order. These were they who had spoken too loudly against Orthard's oppressive hand, who had fought long in the lower councils for equality and fairness of law, they who were thought to have either willingly disavowed or had been exiled from the Order. Now it was known what had become of them, when families heard not from those they assumed were at the Citadel, and when the Paladins had inquired of their fellows in their respective homelands and found naught of them.

Stealth was, at best, forestalled when, through the red light of braziers mounted on the walls, the prisoners saw who it was that had entered from the closed, unused door at the end of the hall. Some of them cried plaintively for help, frantic for escape when salvation seemed so near, but the most of them silently jumped to attention and came quickly to the doors of their cells. They knew that if Zurthaud's men were here discovered, their long desired freedom would leave with him.

With tears of anger burning in their eyes, Zurthaud's soldiers cut and pried the locks with spells similar to Zurthaud's bolt cutter, but they could not undo the shackles bound to the prisoners' hands. These shackles had been made with magic, with old Dragon-stones that had been stored in the Keep and previously forgotten before being secretly repurposed, and thus they were impervious to any sort of spell and bound just as well the magic of their wearers as their bodies.

"How long have you been down here?" Zurthaud asked of one of them, a man seeming the same age as his father.

He could see that the prisoners had not been treated very well, for they were all gaunt, unshaven with long locks of matted hair, poorly clothed with rags, and stank like a filthy latrine.

"I have been in Orthard's thralldom for almost fifteen years, and some have been down here longer than I. Some who were with us are now no more." Replied the elderly man. "Are you that one boy the Dragons were training, Zurthaud the son of Orthard?"

"I am he."

"I am glad to say that you profited well from their tutelage. You are nothing like that rat's bastard that claims to have sired you." Grimly smiled the old man through his long, gray beard.

"What is your name, and why were you imprisoned?" Zurthaud questioned, already knowing the answer to the latter question, but wanting to know more about this new-found friend.

"I am Lorn. I was a member of the High Council until I spoke too loud and often for kinder, fairer treatment of the other races. I was the very last Paladin to ride upon a Dragon's back, before everyone stopped being a companion to their companion, for Orthard put so many restrictions on flying that you basically had to ask his personal permission to do so. I snubbed him and his ridiculous red-tape my last free day. I got up on my Dragon's shoulders, Sicaron his name was, and we flew seventy circles above the Keep as protest, all without Orthard's approval, of course. When we came back down, no one said a word, not even your father, who was ever so red-faced with fury, but that night I was dragged out of my bed and thrown in here, no court trial, no hearing, not even a sentencing. The last time I heard of anyone from the world outside was when that damned man came to my very cell, telling me that Sicaron had been searching long for me among the Human villages, gloating that my Dragon friend had finally been slain during a scouting mission. I spat on him, and they beat me for it, beat me until, for weeks after I could not stand, but I would do it all again, if it could bring my friend back from death." Spake the man, and as if he had himself not endured these atrocities, but distanced, detached, as if he had only looked upon them from afar, as if it was so long ago he could hardly remember.

Zurthaud did not know how to respond to this poor soul's tale, but any thoughts of simply letting his father go freely upon his way after all this was over vanished from his mind; Orthard must now be brought to judgment, to pay in full for his many crimes."My father shall, indeed, pay back many times what he has dealt so cruelly upon every prisoner here." Zurthaud stated, as his men finished freeing the last of the prisoners.

However, they now had a harder task upon them than merely sneaking through the Keep to let in reinforcements by opening one of the many Dragon-sized doors, for now they had to consider these miserable captives. To get them outside, to freedom, must become their main priority, and even the bringing of such long overdue and deserved punishment to Orthard, must become a secondary objective to protecting from any further harm these pitiable men.

"We must press onward." Zurthaud commanded. "How many prisoners are here with you, Lorn?"

"Almost thirty." He replied.

"Then, let all those who are fit enough for combat be given a blade or bow from our spares. There will not yet be enough to go around, but we shall disarm any guards we confront." Spoke Zurthaud.

"There is also a small garrison and armory at the end of the hall, just on the other side of the door. With this many on our side, we can take it and any weapons and provisions we find there." Lorn suggested.

"Yes, but we must do it quietly. We cannot now afford to sound an alarm, for I doubt many of these former prisoners could survive the day long trek back out through the mines." Bid Zurthaud. "Also, we must attempt to spare the lives of the guards we encounter; I will not have any more blood be shed than necessary."

"I will try to honor your wish. Though, I cannot speak for all of us." Unhappily muttered Lorn, as he motioned to the other freed captives. "What we suffered has not entirely imparted compassion for our keepers."

With that, Zurthaud's men hastened to arrange arms for the few prisoners, less than half, who seemed well enough to fight, and they slowly crept toward the door at the opposite end of the dungeon's corridor. Zurthaud again took the lead, but he did not just cut straightaway through the bolt as he had the other doors. Cautious of the garrison Lorn had mentioned, he used magic which allowed him to see through the door and walls, and luckily he had.

There were about a dozen guardsmen in the large open chamber, with two leaning right against the door leading to the dungeon, two each lounging by the three other doors on opposite corners of the room, and the rest gathered about a table before the hearth near the center of the garrison hall. Ending the spell, Zurthaud gave a nod to three of his comrades, and they stepped forward to the door. They readied themselves, and at the end of a count, one cast a spell to silently open the door, while the other two seized the door guards so hastily that they had not time enough to make a noise before they were quietly dragged into the dungeon's hallway.

Cut off from the light of day in this underground area of the Citadel, the guardsmen had to rely on the light of their dim fire and the scant wall-mounted braziers for to see, and these cast long shadows and left many dark corners in the dismal chamber. Not a one of them had noticed anything amiss, even the absence of their two comrades, who had been nabbed, stripped of their weapons, and altogether sorely frightened. Without making a noise, even the slightest creak of hinges, the door was quickly, quietly closed again, and only thereafter did Zurthaud stare the two terrified guards in the face and begin to address them.

"Do you know who I am?" He whispered to the trembling soldiers.

They could only nod their heads, "yes", for their mouths were still firmly shut with the palms of their assailants' hands, lest they make any noise to alert their comrades.

"Then you know why I have come here. I promise to spare your lives if you help us, for only Orthard can be held fully responsible for the misdeeds of this shattered Order." Zurthaud explained, and he motioned for the guards to be let a little loose. "I want you to call for one of your friends to come over, just one. Tell him that there is a problem with the prisoners, and nothing more. If you betray us, you will surely die."

Reluctantly, the guards agreed, for these were the most cruel and base of Orthard's men. They were rough and vile, and should really have never been allowed to join the Order, but such were the soldiers Orthard had ever more preferred over the kind, brave, and honorable enlistees. Yet, out of fear for their own lives, they did as they were told, and one of their friends came right through the door into Zurthaud's trap.

He was also grabbed up, restrained, and his weapon taken, all without a sound. In the same manner, Zurthaud captured two more of the guardsmen, but their captain eventually became suspicious, ending the possibility of conquering this garrison so easily.

"No, everything is under control. The little tarts just got unruly with us, crying for mercy, or sunlight, or something, that is all. We shall teach them a lesson and come right back up." Replied one of the captured guards, as Zurthaud instructed.

Seeing their use for these men was at an end, Zurthaud had them taken back to the very same cells where they once had jailed others and had them locked within, yet as the crude mercenaries had neither knowledge nor skill in magic, unlike the previous occupants, these new inmates had no need for enchanted shackles. Regular old steel bars held them quite well, and displeased as they were with their situation, they seemed ironically well-matched with their new accommodations.

Now would come the tricky part, of quietly and quickly subduing the rest of the guards without alerting any of the others. For this task, Zurthaud selected some of his Aelven bowmen, as they were lighter of foot and frame and could easily scamper about, even a well lit room, almost too quickly to be noticed. He sent them in six pairs, hugging the walls and ducking below the dim, flickering light of the braziers, two for each guard that remained on the other three doors, about the outer edges of the chamber. The Aelvs had a harder time of subduing their prey, for they were, indeed, lighter of frame than the Humans and generally less strong of arm, but by the time they had grabbed the last of their targets and the rest of the guardsmen had become aware of what was happening, Zurthaud and those with him had come pouring through their doorway and tackled all the remaining jailors.

Those Paladins who were formerly prisoners did then attempt excessive violence toward their loathsome wardens, they who had so cruelly mistreated them, and one of the hapless guardsmen was slain even, before Zurthaud could restrain them.

"Did I not say to keep the shedding of blood to the very minimum, only when most necessary for our own survival?" Infuriated, he asked of them, even as he stood between them and the terrified jailors.

"We only seek justice for the wrongs done to us. Lo, there is the very man who beat me sore, and only for the cause of spitting on a trash heap named Orthard." Spake Lorn, as he pointed his newly acquired sword toward that deserving guard.

Though it was not he who had drawn first blood, Lorn had no intention of staying his comrades' blades, for indeed, they had suffered many wretched years of merciless, inhumane treatment.

"Then let there be justice, but justice only and not revenge. This man beat you sore? Then, give him the lawful retribution, thirty lashes, but take not his life; leave that for the proper courts once we have brought these foul men before them." Zurthaud persuaded.

Lorn put down his sword and picked up a lighter spear, a javelin for throwing, from one of the weapon racks along the walls, but he did not intend to skewer his nemesis. He turned about the sharp steel tip, holding forth the majority of the haft, gripping it close to the spear-head, and had himself a nice, long stick, perfect for a whipping, and whip he did. Thirty lashes across the back did the yelping guard receive, but Lorn spared whacking his head or breaking the bones of his arms or legs.

"Are you now satisfied?" Zurthaud annoyedly asked, for though he had not moved to prevent the jailor's beating, he had neither enjoyed watching it.

"I am." Coldly replied Lorn, even as his fellows began to find their own rods of correction.

"No. That is enough." Zurthaud sternly chastened. "We have wasted enough time and caused enough racket with the one beating. I understand your desires for justice, but to carry on now and squander your opportunity for freedom from this foul place is foolishness, not to mention unfitting for those who call themselves Paladin. We shall be better than our foes."

Thoroughly scolded, the former captives ceased this wasteful and hateful revenge seeking, and they placated their exacting of justice, for the time being, by merely imprisoning all the remaining guardsmen. Once done with that, they could finally equip for themselves some proper clothing and armament, and even feed themselves from the stores within the dungeon's garrison, and at last, the whole company, minus four- who would stay behind with the unfit prisoners and keep them safe in the now secured guardroom, readied to move out again.

Through the narrow, low ceilinged corridors they quickly sneaked, slowing and peering about every turn and intersection, for though this section of the Citadel basement was dark and quiet, being the storehouse where all the various goods and treasury were kept, the dim torchlit halls were often patrolled by guards. One such patrol of six soldiers passed them by, completely unaware of the nigh fifty armed men huddling close to the shadows of the wall, just around the turn of the corner, and they remained oblivious even as the company silently crept on behind them.

Eventually, Zurthaud's men did make it to the exit of the basement levels, coming to a large intersection at the center of the labyrinthine hallways. One great oak door stood before them, heavily barred and studded with steel nails, and this time there would be no easy entry through the magical cutting of lock, bolt, or hinge. For, this great door was laden with inscriptions describing the myriad enchantments warded over it, so many as to seem it was protected from any forced entry, and there was even written at the very bottom of the gate a kindly posed suggestion to turn about and forget ever entering without permission.

____

"I had almost forgotten about this door." Zurthaud muttered to himself.

Though its name had been lost to the years, it was, indeed, a famous door of the Keep, having been fashioned by the hands and magic of Dragons long dead. It was supposed to be ultimately impenetrable, even mighty time and decay could not scathe it, but there were made for it an ever increasing number of keys, as many had unhappily locked themselves without or within, so that now nearly every guard's ring had a key for it, nearly.

Somehow, Zurthaud had managed to steal, seemingly, the only set in the dungeon that did not have a key to unlock this door, and he could tell quite easily which one it was. These keys had all been marked with the icon of a Dragon upon the bow and were shaped rather oddly, for to fit in the unusual Dragon fashioned lock.

For a moment, it seemed as if their undertaking had come to a halt, needing much backtracking, for to find and acquire another key-ring, increasing their chance of being found out or embattled, but Lorn allayed all their fears. He simply strode up to the door and casually knocked upon it.

"Who goes there?" Called the voice of the guards beyond the door.

"It is I." Lorn called back, hoping his voice would not be recognized through the muffling of the thick wood and steel.

"Is that you Vorgen? What do you want?" Inquired the voice.

"Yes, it is." Lorn flatly lied, as a large smirk spread across his face. "I have been locked out, and it is my turn to go off duty."

"How did you get locked out again?" Returned the voice, becoming shrill with annoyance. "Did we not give you your own key-ring just yesterday? What, did you lose it already?"

"I apparently have the only ring in this entire castle that has no key for this damned lock." Lorn replied, adding some truth to his tale.

"What? Did Jerel from the prison trade rings with you? That rat's bastard, he knows you always are getting shut out. Fine, come on in; we shall get you, yet another, new set." Spake the voice again, even more annoyedly.

The door was opened, and not waiting to see what they were up against, Zurthaud's men burst through the entrance. In a split second's decision, they could not afford to plan past the door's opening; they had no choice but to rush it or stay locked out.

Thankfully, though this room was large, the first Dragon-sized room they had encountered, there were few guards within, and these were caught completely unaware. The two who had opened the door were overtaken and immediately cast aside; some sitting at a table before a fireplace near the middle of the room, attempted to rise and draw swords, but they were restrained by the speed of Zurthaud's men.

The last few guards left in the chamber were those who stood close by the other entrances, and they would have attempted to flee except that, thanks to the Aelven bows, they had been pinned, by their shirt sleeves, to the selfsame doors, with gracefully aimed arrows.

There was no convenient cell to lock the guards in this time, so that the company had now to think of a way to bind these men. They found the answer to be the shackles which the former prisoners still wore, and much to their amusement, with the right set of keys, of which there were many in this central guard station, the loathsome cuffs had swapped owners.

Though they shut again the enchanted, Dragon-forged door, so that no more reinforcements could easily come up from the cellars and dungeon below, speed became utmost importance, for with this central room filled with shackled soldiers, Zurthaud's company would surely be found out by relieving guards coming down from the multiple stairs to the floors above. It was now only a matter of time that the whole of the fortress should be on alert, and they raced up one of the circular stairwells with hardly a care for the few small patrols they overtook, trying with all their might, lest they become cut off from all aid, to beat the sounding of the alarm.

They broke through a smaller wooden door, the last barriers between the basement floors and the Keep proper, and out into the beautifully pillared and arched marble sanctum of the grand main hall they crashed, bowling over every doorman in their way. It became a full on fight, as Zurthaud and his men now had to battle their way through the throngs of soldiers that were gathered here in this massive chamber, spacious enough for several Dragons to fly about in without fear of colliding.

While Zurthaud's men attempted to still obey their leader's command, and spare the lives of these pitiful soldiers, their enemy, for the most part, did not share this sympathy. Though many did fall on their faces begging for mercy, most of the frightened men who battled against them could only assume that their very lives were forfeit, for the Paladins had somehow breached the castle's defenses and gained access to the very center of the Keep. They fought wildly, as if for their very lives and did wound many of Zurthaud's men, even killing a few, but the advantage was with the true Paladins.

Magic could be very handy if used properly, and in this particular situation, when the killing blow was to be spared, the casting of non-lethal spells was crucial. Whole battalions were sent flying through the air, head over heels, by a forceful magic blast; others found their weapons quickly rust into dusty vapor right before their eyes. In this manner, the ten to one odds of the dire battle swung in Zurthaud's favor, and his men subdued or, regrettably, slew every last one of the soldiers present within the great hall.

<>< ><>< ><>

"Shut and seal every door leading out of the hall!" Zurthaud yelled, as soon as the fighting had died down. "The majority of the troops will have been stationed in the upper floors and towers; so, close those passages first. I need volunteers for to take the gatehouse with me."

Off to the main gates he ran, not waiting to see if anyone followed, but several, more than should have gone, did chase after Zurthaud, as he tried to get to the main doors before reinforcements could arrive.

They exited out the main hall through its giant double doors, swung wide and open as they had remained for centuries. Not even in this time of siege had anyone attempted to close the ancient and incredibly weighty doors, for they had no modern pulley system with counterweights to help move them. Originally, Dragons had been the porters and guards for these massive, solid steel doors, as they were the only people strong enough to move them, but many hundreds of years of peace and never any direct assault on the Citadel itself had made the gargantuan gate almost useless. Through these and onward through the smaller entrance hall Zurthaud raced, trying with all his might to make it to the end thereof, for within sight now was the only slightly less impressive doors of the main entrance. Already, he could hear the alarm bells clanging, and the shouting and tramping of many men, but he was nearly upon the side access for the gatehouse.

Just as his fingers touched upon the door handle, an arrow whizzed past his face and sank deep into the wooden flesh of the gatehouse door, and from around the corner of the side hall to his left began to pour the strength of the Citadel's garrison. Shouting as they came, the fortress guard ran with all their might and shot bolts aimed for Zurthaud and his companions, for they knew if the gatehouse were taken, the Dragons would enter and easily conquer all who remained therein.

However, the reinforcements were too late, and as the last of Zurthaud's detachment entered the gatehouse, they slammed fast the door thereof, shutting out all the howling soldiers and the sound of their projectiles thudding harmlessly against it.

Immediately, they were set upon by the gatehouse guard, who had apparently been soundly napping right until Zurthaud's men had entered, but after only a short exchange, they were quickly dispatched. Sadly, their surprise attack only cost them their lives, and only one of the soldiers within the gatehouse was left to cower and beg for his life.

"Get up. We did not come here to slaughter feeble minions. It is my father, and him alone, we seek to bring to justice. Your life we give back to you, and you can repay us by helping to open the main gates." Zurthaud promptly commanded of the prostrate guard, for to quickly allay his fears.

Now the tables were turned, even as did the wheels of the pulleys slowly opening the gates, and Zurthaud could hear the sound of Dragons, roaring and carrying on, as they swiftly perceived that the Citadel's entry had been won. Zurthaud had worried that the reinforcements headed to the gatehouse, once learning that they could not overtake Zurthaud would, instead, go after his men in the main hall, but his fears were quickly allayed. They were still shouting profusely just outside the door, but it was not of rage or indignation over being outwitted.

In an attempt to prevent the Dragons from entering, they were now being forced by their idiot captains to form a shield wall at the entryway, just under the arch of the door, but the greatest shouting was not even the giving of orders. It was the cry of dismay and sheer terror that burst forth from the lungs of the despairing defenders, and the clamor of arms was of them dropping their swords and spears, completely disregarding their foolish captains, to flee wildly through the corridors, as though they were madmen.

At last, Zurthaud could hear a familiar sound roaring above the din.

"Get out of my way, you miserable rats, lest I squish you." Threatened the booming voice.

An ironically gentle knock on the gatehouse door a moment later, caused Zurthaud to crack a smile, and he strode over to answer the door.

"Who goes there?" He called, already knowing the answer.

"It is I, and I should think you stupid for not recognizing your own friend's voice. Now open that door and come out before I rip it off its hinges, for I have had neither sight nor smell of you in what seems like ages." Grumpily demanded Theros.

"Alright, alright we are coming out." Zurthaud replied, as the other Paladins with him laughed a little; though, the guard with them seemed likely to lose control of his bladder.

They swung open the door to find their view blocked by the big red Dragon's muzzle, and he must have seemed quite the sight to passersby, sitting with his face to the wall like a cat before a mouse's hole.

"Get out here already, you blasted Human. Let me look you over, and see if you have gotten yourself killed." Bellowed Theros, but when this close to his mouth, it sounded more like thunder than spoken word.

"I would, but you have blocked the door with your fat head. I would name you stupid, but that I am too glad to see you." Zurthaud retorted, beaming with the glad smile of a reunited friend.

With a huff, Theros then did back off enough that they could exit the gatehouse, and the Paladins were able to exit freely. Yet, did the terrified guard remain inside, cringing behind a barrel; Zurthaud decided to let him be, as he was now too occupied with being scoured by the glaring and prodding of his friend's ludicrously protective mood.

"Cease from this nonsense. I am fine." Zurthaud cried out, as he held up his arms to defend himself from all the snuffling and nuzzling.

"Nonsense!" Theros indignantly returned, though he did halt his investigating. "Nonsense is the last time that you and I parted, for then you jumped off into space from my safely soaring wings, plummeting to earth like a stone. I cannot help but to worry over your self-destructive tendencies."

"How goes the battle?" Zurthaud asked, looking around at the hallway.

It would have seemed more warlike of a scene, but that there were only two bodies lying upon the cold stone, face down among the piles of strewn weaponry. Apparently, they were the victims of trampling from the panicked retreat of the frightened soldiers, but at least one was still alive, crawling about in a daze. Further down the hallway, the sound of Dragons roaring and the crashing of steel and stone signified that the struggle was yet to be concluded.

"In our boredom, waiting for you to accomplish your mission, we took five of the seven outer wall garrisons and set free some of our captives outside the city, for the younger ones, poor lads, were crying and begging to be let go to their own home and country. Besides that, we have taken the main gate, if you had not already noticed, and are proceeding directly to the most likely location where the vile Orthard should be." Theros blithely reported.

"What horror!" Serc unintentionally interrupted, as he landed before the main gate to the Keep.

Being a doctor, he meant the two unfortunate warriors who had been run over, and without signifying he had even noticed Theros or Zurthaud, he stooped down to lend his medical aid to them.

Though the near incessant screaming of the first confused and wounded man made it hard for the Dragon healer to concentrate upon his task, he eventually made a fine splint out of two handy spear hafts and had even dosed out a little drug, barely being able to force it down the panic-stricken guard's throat for all the wild struggling. Zurthaud could not help but find a little humor in how the giant Dragon handled his hapless patient, for it seemed to him, with regard to proportions of size, rather like a child playing doctor with their doll.

"That will soon soothe your pain and addled mind." Serc consolingly muttered, consumed by his work, completely unaware of Zurthaud's mirthful observance, yet did he hand off his first patient to other staff, even those from the Keep's own medical ward.

Only after he checked the pulse of the other prone soldier, did he begin to take notice of Theros and the Humans watching him.

"Happy with your work are you?" Said he, noticing Zurthaud's exceptionally wide grin. "This poor fool is dead, and that is nothing to smile about." He angrily chided.

"Are you not in the least glad to see me among the living?" Asked Zurthaud, though he knew the aged Dragon cared for him and was only now so upset because of the loss of life going on all about.

"I knew you would come out alive, even if everyone else within were a dead man. Please, tell me you spared some of them." The doctor asked, allowing a little more levity in his voice, though his face still grimaced with the pain of compassion for all the fallen.

As they who had been assigned to aid the aged Dragon in his tending of the wounded carried away both the dead and live man to their separate resting places, they three walked on into the Keep, fully glad to know that they were each safe and well, happy to again be reunited.

They strode on through the entrance hall, which fortunately was bereft of anyone needing assistance, down its length to the grand doors of the great main hall, and much to their surprise and joy found them to be once again manned by Dragons, one on each side. Not in nigh a thousand years had a Dragon been a sentry and door-person within the Citadel, and it was, indeed, a sight to behold, as the young males puffed out their chests and stood at attention, trying to seem important and dutiful all at once. They pushed wide open the great door, as they, wishing their mundane job to be more useful, had apparently somewhat closed the heavy steel gates, and Zurthaud, Theros, and Serc had all to enter in through the cacophony of screeching, rusty, unused hinges. Yet, the groaning of the great gate's hinges was nothing compared to the clamoring of the cheering Paladins who had gathered within, for the company which Zurthaud had safely led through the raid was now joined by their companion Dragons and other comrades.

The massive hall was filled to bursting with the raucous triumphal mob, hearkening back to days of old when all Paladins here gathered to feast and celebrate their fellowship and the goodness of those peaceful times, and as much as it had been a joy to see Dragons guarding the door, it now brought tears to Zurthaud's eyes, to see such restoration of the spirit of the legendary Order come about in his own time and, in part, by his own efforts.

As they had as yet to bring justice to Orthard and the High Council, the joy was short lived, and the cheering was at last abated by their necessary return to duty.

There would still be pockets of resistance hiding out in the dark corners of the Keep for days longer, especially in the basements where the Dragons could not reach; they all had much work to do yet.

"We should head on up to the High Council chamber; that will be where my father is, unless, of course, he is hiding in his own rooms." Zurthaud suggested, as the crowd began to disperse.

"We should take plenty of reinforcement with us, for there will be many soldiers between here and there." Serc suggested. "First, I have some new knowledge from the Dark One's book that I must bring to your attention." The aged Dragon would have continued, bringing to light some yet unheard secret of the Shadow Lord, but that he was almost cut off in mid sentence by the sight of an old friend. "Lorn, is that you?" He gasped.

The former prisoner's face glowed like Zurthaud had not before seen, as the old man ran with the stride of a child to meet with Serc, for in as many years as he had been a captive, he had not so much as looked upon any of his beloved compatriots.

"I thought you had returned unto your own home among the northern villages, but that was more than fifteen years ago. Where have you been?" Serc, astonished, inquired.

"I have been here the whole time, rotting away like a potato down in the cellar." Lorn replied, his smile only thinly masking the hurt he felt in those words, however lightened, for to spare grief or guilt from his good old friend.

However, Serc could not hide his own sorrow and pity for the man he now embraced, and big wet tears ran down his face.

"I am so sorry. Oh, that I had known. We should have come to this point far sooner." Serc grieved, but he pulled back suddenly, recalling something most important. "Oh, Lorn, Sicaron,... How can I say this? He had passed some time ago. He never stopped searching for you."

"I knew of his passing. The same man who imprisoned me delighted so to tell." Lorn gruffly replied, his former callousness returning.

"Then we must bring him swiftly to justice." Replied the Dragon, with grim determination in his voice and heart.

"Are you sure that you can bear to do such a thing?" Lorn asked of the doctor, who let go his friend and turned toward the way that they should go.

"I will be fine." He returned, dismissing such a hint toward knowledge unknown by those younger than they, as he was already heading toward the giant main stairwell.

Zurthaud had then to hasten to find some volunteers, and as they were refreshed and emboldened by rejoining with their Dragon companions, many of the same men who had accompanied him from the beginning of this mission did offer to go with him yet further. Soon, a good sized company, including: Theros, Galrag, Lorn, Zurthaud, and many others, was tailing along after Serc, to ascend unto the very top floor of the Keep by way of the main stair, for from the ground level floor to the very roof, the great stair ran unhindered and unbroken.

Each floor had access to the quadratic, winding stair by an open well, which was not enclosed, meeting with each floor on both sides of the landing, before continuing on and upward, for, though it was not the only way up within the Citadel, it was centralized in its position within the Keep and was the only single stair that climbed its full height.

They encountered no resistance, either upon the stair or on the landings, until the third floor, where were the main barracks of the Keep, for on either side of the spacious well, blocking the access to this level, a crude barricade was piled: of heavy furniture, empty and full storage barrels, and loose piles of brick, among other things. The soldiers behind it must have hastily constructed the palisade after hearing of the main gate being taken, and they now began to shoot arrows and throw spears at the perceived attackers.

Surely, they thought, having so desperately opposed the true Paladins' takeover, that they should all be slain.

However, mercy was in Zurthaud's heart for them, and Serc did neither wish harm upon these hopeless souls, so that they chose not to engage with them. The only return of barrage they offered was of Theros burning down the shoddy barricade, and then, only after he had warned those behind it that he was going to do so.

After sending messengers down to the main hall, for to assign more Paladins who would take and quell the fighting of the third floor resistance, they proceeded onward and upward. Past the fourth floor, where was no opposition, for here was the medical ward. Despite his lengthy separation from the staff thereof, Serc was still much respected here, and when the doctors and surgeons did peer from their rooms and work and saw him with the triumphant Paladins, they became at ease.

Before they returned to their duties, many even did give a short bow to him, so great was his reputation among the healers, but they, most of all those involved in either the coup or the defense, were too busy for pleasantries. Here came the wounded from both sides.

Up to the fifth floor they went, where were the lower courts, the other lesser halls of meeting, and the public libraries, but there seemed no one hereabout at all, so that the troupe did pass by without instance. Onward to the sixth floor they went, and here they did meet the most heavy resistance. For, on this floor of private residences, libraries, armories, and barracks, the majority of the well trained and battle hardened of Orthard's men had planned for their defense, and these were not just the common hired mercenaries which had for so long made the bulk of the Order's soldiers.

These men gathered here, behind afore well-constructed walls of stone with iron gates, were former Paladins themselves, and were they who had before ridden upon Dragons and learned of magic and been true Paladins in heart and deed. They had either willingly or unwillingly gone along with Orthard's ruthless reign, either out of a sense of hopeless and unhappy loyalty to the Order, whomever led it, no matter how evil, or of a lack of compassion for other races, feeling no urgency to stop Orthard aiming his cruelty toward non-Humans.

In either case, these men were honest in their stance defending the Keep and would fight to the last man, if need be, to protect what they thought was right; they were, indeed, truly misguided, but they tried to avoid conflict still, as genuine Paladins were wont. They called out a warning to the intruders before they had yet reached the floor's landing.

"Halt, or we shall fire upon you." Cried their leader, Argamon, a strong and strong willed man who had despised the rule of Orthard, yet out of his faithfulness to the Order, however misplaced, had done nothing to go against its leader. "Traitors to the Order are not welcome in this castle, and we command you to leave, so that peace may be restored."

"Peace!" Nearly roared Theros, as he lifted his head above the last step. "There has here been no peace since before I was a hatchling."

Immediately, whistling bolts of Black-iron responded to his presence, and Theros had to duck or risk losing an eye, though Argamon did shout an order to ceasefire.

"I am sorry for the trouble that has befallen your people, master Dragon; truly I am. But, that is the price we must pay for sincere loyalty to the Order; an honorable soldier must follow his commander, though his commands or person be wise or foolish." Argamon called out, somewhat apologetically. "I gave up rights to be with my companion, even to speak with her. The day that she died, I was on duty collecting taxes from people too poor to pay them. I curse my own self daily, but I dare not disobey. If you are true Paladins as you claim, you will do likewise."

The argument did seem sound to Zurthaud, and he knew not how to combat this line of thought, though he could tell it was flawed, misconstrued. Certainly, his sire deserved no such honorable man on his side, but here was a good man fighting for an evil one, a tragic conundrum.

"You were Ilara's companion, then?" Serc asked, just trying to talk out the situation, for perhaps, through reason these reasonable men could be persuaded.

"I was." Argamon replied.

"She was constantly asking her lover, Sicaron, to spy upon you, for to see how you were faring." Serc revealed.

Upon hearing the name of his companion spoken aloud, Lorn perked up, for though he had caught on to Serc's intentions of disarming these men peacefully, he had as yet to think of how or why he should be involved. True, he had recognized the voice of Argamon, for as their Dragons had been life-mates, they had also been comrades, quite close.

"I am coming up. Do not fire upon me, for I just wish to speak with my friend." Lorn called out.

He passed by Zurthaud and Theros, who could only look on in remarked silence for this display of courage, and though Serc did seem as if he wished Lorn not to go upward into the range of arrows, he too let the former prisoner go. His freedom, to go where he wished, was not now to be denied, not ever again. Upon reaching the last of the stair, Lorn did raise his hands above the level of the floor showing they were empty, for he had laid his weapons down even before speaking. Surprisingly, no one shot at him, and he ascended the last few steps.

"Lorn, is that you." Argamon spoke, his voice tremulous with disbelief. "I thought you had abandoned the Order years ago."

He opened the gate of their palisade and stepped out to meet his friend whom he had missed for so long. The resentment he had at first felt when he thought Lorn had just up and left, even so soon after his loss of Ilara, had long ago left from him. All that remained was the deep joy of meeting again with someone he had thought gone forever.

"I did no such thing, as I will explain." Lorn said, but his voice now seemed torn with a heart-wrenching memory. "I did see Ilara pass. It was good that you were not there, for that dark hour was not as anyone would wish to remember her."

"Oh, that the times of our youth could come back to us again, when there was naught to do but ride together upon the wings of our friends through the laughing roar of wind." Sighed Argamon, as tears threatened to fill his eyes from reminiscing upon his lost Dragoness. "I wish I could have gone with you on that last ride of yours. I can almost remember the taste of the high air and the rush of wind, yet the feeling of flying seems so distant to me, a faint memory, so long has it been from when my feet last left the ground. I was very much jealous of you, but it was rebellion against a direct order, so that I could never have gone. It was a shame unto your otherwise flawless reputation."

At that, Argamon broke his reverie and restrained himself from further display of such sorrowful emotion, which was thought unfitting a soldier, especially of his rank, captain of the guard, but his joy of reuniting with his long lost comrade, called for more than talking. He could not help but to embrace, even ever so lightly and formally, Lorn, and doing so seemed a shock to both of them, but to each for different reasons.

"You are so thin and frail, my friend. In your exile, did you not fare well?" Surprisedly asked Argamon, who had always known Lorn to be the more fit of them both.

Lorn was so astonished by this uncanny display of affection, so dissonant with the hardened, even saddened, soldier who stood before him, that he almost did not reply. Such show of inner feelings was more akin to the younger Argamon he had known so well, yet he did eventually find words.

"I did not go into exile, nor did I leave this place at all." Lorn explained, and he watched his friend's confused expression turn to horror, as he continued his tale. "That final soaring upon Sicaron's back was the last time I tasted fresh air until earlier this morning, for when I had so disobeyed the orders of Orthard, despising the corruption of the High Council, he had me locked in prison from then until now, those fifteen years. Daily was I mistreated, with scant, poor food, bitter water, and harsh words, often were we prodded and poked for our guard's amusement, sometimes beaten. I have slept on straw and cold stone, wallowed in my own filth, and worst of all, had my own enemy gloat to me about the death of my best friend, of whom I was informed had never stopped looking for me."

For a moment Argamon just stood in shock, with his mouth agape, for he could not believe such evils had transpired in this tower once of righteousness, and under his guard.

"But, it was your punishment, for breaking the laws against Dragon riding. Surely, it was only justice." Argamon feebly tried to claim, his own words choking in his mouth for lack of conviction.

"No." Spake Lorn again. "If fifteen years imprisonment is just punishment for the 'crime' of supernal freedom from gravity and deepest fellowship with my friend, then we have imbalanced scales, and though that is injustice, it is rectifiable by a mere reexamining of the courts and amending through law such issues. However, I was dragged from my bedchamber in the middle of the night and thrown into the dungeon, all without trial by any court, and it was intended that I stay there until I died. No one can say that was a mere flaw in the legal structure. No one can argue in defense that such evil execution of petty revenge by incarceration was justice. You may feel that you are honor-bound to follow the will of the Order, no matter how evil the one who leads it, but there is no honor in defending what is evil. Remember the writings of Rathnyalgr, 'Show me your honor, if possible, followers darkness; demonstrate it to me without any righteousness. Yet, mine will be proved by upright word and deed.'"

Argamon lowered his head in shame, now fully realizing how ill-deserved his loyalties were, now truly convinced that he could no longer follow the vile Orthard and still keep his honor.

"I will surrender my command and this fortress, but it must be conditional." Argamon relented, lowering his gaze and voice while drawing his saber and laying it at Lorn's feet.

The men behind him groaned, for they knew that he had given them up to defeat, but neither did they resist his command. They all had respected Argamon for his sure leadership in this trying time, for it was he who had organized and rallied the defenders and made secure the Keep.

"It is for our own good." Argamon shouted back at them, as though he were a teacher correcting school children. "The Keep is lost, as lost as our cause, for we cannot go on any longer and still keep our dignity while fighting for so evil a man. Besides which, we could not last a week up here with our short supplies and an imminent attack from the Dragons. No, we must surrender, and I would have it sooner rather than later."

"What are your terms?" Lorn politely asked, returning to formality.

"First, you must promise my men no repercussions from this debacle. They must be allowed to keep their standing in the Order, if they so choose to stay, and must not suffer harm in any way, either to their health or reputation. Second, you must prove yours is the right side, the true Paladins as it were; you must give Lord Orthard and the other High Councilors the justice you did not yourselves receive, including fair trial and sentence." Argamon humbly requested.

"It shall be done." Lorn returned, as he took his friend by the arm and shook it, making the agreement an oath between them. "You have my word that it shall be so."

As Argamon strode back into his barricade, Lorn returned unto his party to deliver the good news, but as they were well within hearing of the conversation, they needed only the details that had been spoken in lowered voice, mainly the terms for Argamon and his company's surrender.

Though Theros seemed a little upset that they could not now just incinerate the wicked men who had so despotically ruled over their lives and had, instead, to give them fair trial, he complied as well as any of the others, yet was Zurthaud surprised that Lorn had offered such leniency toward his hated enemy and pressed him for an explanation.

"Before, when we were in the dungeons, you had wanted the blood of all who stood in our way, but now you offer mercy to the man who made mockery of your companion's death. Why the sudden change?" Zurthaud asked of the older man.

"Freedom changes oneself." Lorn offered. "In the dark of my cell, I was a hopeless beggar; then, when we had to fight for our salvation, I was like a cornered animal. Now, when I can come and go as I please and fear not for my life, nor worry if I shall get any bread this day or tomorrow, I can somewhat return to the Paladin who I once was. I can afford to offer others the compassion that I was denied, and I have only you to thank, for turning a starving, feral wretch back into a man again."

As soon as more of the Paladins from downstairs had come up to escort Argamon's men out from the fortified sixth floor, Zurthaud and his company moved onward, up to the last floor of the Keep, and though he had been offered a relief of duty and a personal escort back down to the main hall where the Paladins were already setting out provisions and tending and processing the captured, Argamon did wish to accompany them. He explained that he desired to see this whole fiasco through to the end, and thus he and a few others under his command, they who had also unhappily endured the tyranny of Orthard, also came along.

When they reached the seventh floor, the stair ended, for any access to the exterior towers and the roof battlements were elsewhere on this topmost level. As it went in a large circle about the entire circumference of the Keep's interior, around the innermost High Council chamber, they followed the spacious singular hallway, passing the great private libraries, personal chambers of the generals and High Councilors, and some map rooms and treasure vaults until they came to the very opposite side of the Keep from the stairwell.

On the outer side of the hall was Orthard's opulent personal chambers, but the door was swung wide, and investigation found it to be empty.

On the inner side of the hallway was the smaller entryway branching off toward the great doors to the High Council chamber, and these were shut securely with the very last of Orthard's loyalists guarding them.

Argamon tried reasoning with them, for their armor shook as they stood ground before the Dragons. Yet, did they not move, not until Galrag roared mightily, seeming to shake the very walls, and then they did move quite quickly, but for one poor soul who could neither run nor hold his bladder. The rest of the panic stricken men, having reached the end of the short entry hall, began pounding on the massive oak doors, begging to be let in, but Theros and Galrag pushed past them, surprising the soldiers greatly, for they had thought to be more a snack, rather than a mere annoyance. Once these astonished soldiers were moved out of harm's way, the two Dragons breathed their explosive, fiery breath upon the last obstacle between them and their long anticipated objective.

The ancient door, not being one that was enchanted, was blown apart, explosively incinerated, by the fiery Dragon-breath, and the whole of the company stepped within the grand High Council chamber.

Chapter 24

That whole afternoon, Malok spent entertaining the lady Lenairu with tales from his youth, of how he had grown up among the Serpen, for she was delighted to have her two guests do nothing more than to sit upon lush, Dragon-sized cushions and sip sweet, homemade wine from ancient, seldom used chalices, as they regaled her with their life's' stories. Eventually, they came to the present, this very point where they did meet with the beautiful silver Dragoness, thus ending the narrative, and even though Malok thought this all a waste of precious time, he endured it for the help of this powerful female.

She had already proven her prowess in the accurate reading of their thoughts and had even promised to help them find the Bright Dragoness whom they sought, but the waiting, the slow marching of hours, weighed on Malok's heart. Of all people, he knew how critical was the success of his mission, and if Lenairu could so plainly understand the hidden knowledge of others, he began to wonder how she could be so reserved and untroubled when he felt so restless and anxious.

"Oh my, it is about the dinner hour." The Dragoness suddenly exclaimed, after drinking in both her guests' narrative and more wine. "Shar, will you please stoke the fire hot enough for cooking while Malok and I head out to hunt for our evening meal?" She kindly asked.

The Serpen king nodded in response as the two Dragons left from the cozy little cave, and once outside, they quickly took off into the golden, orange light of an early evening sky.

The ground fled beneath them, as they speedily hunted the nearby forests and fens for any savory prey, and at length, they caught two wild boar and a few waterfowl.

Yet, as they returned unto her abode, and Malok grew more and more distraught with all this seeming wasting of time, Lenairu took notice of his depression and swung in close for to speak with him.

"You think our nice little chat, and our hunting, even our eating of food, all a waste?" She asked, giving him a stern motherly glare, both caring and capable of melting stone all at once.

Malok did not respond, his mood was dark, his thoughts inaudible groaning.

"How can you seek well or receive what is good if you are incapable of waiting well and bear what you see as mundane?" She asked, thus penetrating to the heart of the matter.

"Truly you are wise." Malok replied, acknowledging his elder's astute questioning. "But, my heart is aching, and my strength is gone. How can I endure this great task, much less enjoy life's frivolities, when there is so much at risk?"

"Eating is not frivolity; it is necessity." Lenairu returned, as they again came to ground just outside her cave. "And, it is just as necessary to wielding magic as it is to living, for the conjuring of spells and the gathering of energy cannot be done in a body without sustenance. The quiet staid mind required to hear the thoughts of others, or to see beyond the physical world, cannot be obtained without patience and singularity of focus. These have I been attempting to coax you into all afternoon, and I am pleased to say that you are making progress. Perhaps, after dinner you shall be refreshed enough to partake in the hidden knowledge of Dragons."

Malok was stunned and slightly peeved, for he thought that, had he known the idle hours they had spent conversing was the start of his own tutelage, he would have tried all the more, and all the faster come to the state of mind and body that was required.

"You mean to tell me that this whole time you have been trying to teach me a lesson?" Malok plaintively inquired.

"All life is a lesson, as we Dragons know, for though we engage in structured study, lecture, reading, and writing, we realize, this being how we raise our young, that every moment presents an opportunity to learn and to grow. Nothing is idle waste; everything is fully enjoyed, never rushed or forced, always balanced and peaceful." She explained, her kind smile returning.

"Why did you not tell me this sooner?" Malok asked, not at all understanding why this Dragoness could not grasp the importance of his quest. "If you had but explained to me what it was that I should know, I could have well been ready to receive your teachings by now."

"I know how dire your situation. I understand the urgency of your search, but you miss the point of my lesson entirely if you think you must exert great effort to concentrate fixedly upon refreshing and clearing your body and mind, or if you require me to lead your mind to rest and bring peace to your soul each time the stresses of life press down upon you. You must learn to let yourself rest, to quiet yourself, to see past the obvious snares of anxiety and useless fretting, so that you can overcome these temporary obstacles, and the only path to this is letting go of your troubles." Lenairu stated, forcefully yet still very much kind.

"How can I do that, when it is so pressing, so imperative that I find this one? How can I let go?" He frustratedly cried out.

"That is easy to answer. You must give your concern to someone else, someone you can trust to care for that problem, worry, or doubt just as much, and more even than yourself." She plainly stated, as if the resolution were so simple.

"If I cannot bear the weight of this woe, then how can I dare give it to anyone else? To whom can I give it, to you?" Malok asked, his voice rising with incredulity.

The lady Lenairu shook her head, almost as if in disappointment, though her tone was still of a gentle tutor. "While it is true that others like me can share in your burdens, as I am so doing even now, for by aiding you I bear some of the weight. There is yet another of whom you should already know. One whom all Dragons know in their heart of hearts, for we all are His children."

"Who?" Asked Malok, though the answer itself came to him even as the question left his mouth, for all Dragons know this answer.

"Why, Eloigal, of course." She kindly replied, knowing that Malok too had come to this answer. "He is greater than all, for He made all things. Not only did He make the whole world and all that is therein, He sustains it and cares for it. As strange as it may sound to those whose minds are not awakened to this knowledge, or worse refute the great mystery as impossible, though nothing is more true, Eloigal is love; He seeks personal relationship with you and I, and all his created people, to the astounding point that His heavenly hand will stoop down to our dismal mortal world and lift us and all our burdens up, even to His very heart."

She spoke no more of this, leaving Malok to brood over her words and teaching style, as they strode again within her home.

Shar had a marvelous fire roaring in the designated pit, just inside cave's awning, so that the smoke ran not into the home, but rather curled in puffy gray billows up around the edge of the ceiling and on out into the open air. Upon this they cooked the fowl, for they were meant to be the Serpen's supper, while they Dragons would dine upon the boar. Much to the surprise of Shar, who had thought that "wild" Dragons ate everything raw, Lenairu knew much about cooking and helped him to season the birds quite well with fresh herbs, onion, and even a little salt, which she pulled from a small porcelain box, that which lay, among multitude other functional items and trinkets, upon one of the many shelves fire-carved into the walls.

At last, with the soothing scents of roasted meat and the warm, earthy taste of fresh pork in his own mouth, Malok began to relax a little, for he had taken to heart the words of the wise Dragoness. The massive task he had undertaken could not be accomplished or aided by obsessive worry, bringing stress to his mind and body; anxiety could not solve his problems. He did not forget, nor cease to care for the resolution thereof, but he realized that only through peaceful mind and rested body could he move forward.

He gave his cares up, let the weight fall, like a heavy pack, off from his shoulders, yet he knew that they were not discarded. He let them go to the One Who cares for all things, The Eloigal, for the One Who made the world would sustain it. His children, He would not forsake, and their worries and fears, problems, and whole life, He held tenderly and securely in His omnipotence. If anyone could do something about anything, it would be Him.

After dinner Lenairu became suddenly more serious, for she knew now her pupil was ready to receive her knowledge. She strode out into the dying light of evening unto the very shore of the pristine lake, and she motioned for Malok to follow. Though, Shar thought it best to watch from where he sat upon the front porch of the Dragoness' lair.

"Sit beside me here, at the edge of the still waters. Clear your mind of restless thought, as we wait for the setting of the sun." She instructed.

And, there they two sat for almost an hour, until the darkness of night finally engulfed the world and the small light of the few evening stars grew to a fabulous twinkling dance of myriad luminous bodies. It pained Malok to be so still, for never in his life had he for any moment been so motionless. He had always been one to go and do, never one to stay idle for very long, or even to rest longer than necessary. To stay in this meditative state for so much time, was near impossible for him, and he ended up catching himself daydreaming and fidgeting more than once.

However, time did pass, with Malok remaining as quiet and peaceful as he could manage, and eventually Lenairu broke the overwhelming silence.

"Now, stretch out your magic to the water." She spoke. "Only touch it with your mind for now, command it not. What I am teaching you is the technique of Atsarocu, also known as Peering, which Dragons have used for many generations to see and communicate over great distance; by it we could look upon others and speak with them, and they us, even from across the whole of Threa. Over time, we found this magic to have many other applications than just calling upon far removed loved ones, for by this method one can send their own eyes throughout the world, to gaze upon anyone or anything they so desire, unless, of course, the said focus is guarded against Peering by other magics."

Malok did as he was told, feeling for the water with his mind, and soon he realized now why he had to become so calm to accomplish this. Even as the lake was still and silent, so his mind must be, for every thought that passed through his brain seemed now to cause the surface of the water to shimmer and ripple. Even his surprise at affecting a disturbance of the pool created some small waves.

"Concentrate." Lenairu calmly instructed, and through quieting himself again, Malok was able to return the water to its previous serene condition.

"Good. Now comes the tricky part, for you must visualize in your mind the image of the person whom you seek. Try now to picture the Dragoness of your dreams; bring her forth from your thoughts." She bade him.

This proved far more difficult for Malok, for as he tried to recall exactly how the beautiful Bright Dragoness appeared in his dreaming, the water became ever more disturbed by his mental activity.

"Focus only upon the coarse image of the Dragoness, not every detail about her. Set her in the forefront of your thought and do not worry so much about every little part, else you will lose the whole of her image for the sake of a single facet." Spake the Dragoness.

Though Malok could see before his eyes the water of the lake begin to shine as with the light of the stars, glowing ever white and brighter, he could not afford to focus upon it, for his mind must now be fully fixed upon her whom he had so earnestly sought.

"Good." Lenairu exclaimed. "Now project this vision onto the surface of the water, use it to conjure her form."

Malok tried to grasp what he had been told and so do, and at the same time attempt to keep his thoughts from wandering. Suddenly, the pool's shimmering heightened and that which he envisioned in his mind was before him, a static, lifelike, though lifeless, portrait of the young Dragoness.

"Excellent, but do not stop at this point. Now that you can see her, search for her. Use the water as your eyes, to show her unto you, for all the water of Threa is connected, whether through what floats invisible within the air or through the rivers, lakes, and seas. Through its presence, nearly everywhere, you may Peer anywhere." Lenairu happily directed.

It was all too much to do at once, to still his thoughts, focusing upon the Dragoness, to gaze upon and not become distracted by the enrapturing image before him, and now to command, through his outstretched psyche, inanimate water to obey him. Malok groaned as slowly the lake began to increasingly bubble and slosh about, and the luminous image of the Dragoness faded from before him.

"I cannot do it. It is too much for me." He complained, for it seemed beyond his capability.

"Try it again." Lenairu commanded, quite sternly, for she was not so interested in seeing her dear pupil give up so swiftly. "Walk yourself through the steps, returning to the place where you were. Do it again and again until it seems they come all at once, for much practice makes easier any task. And, do not ever feel ashamed that you cannot accomplish a new undertaking at the first attempt, for hardly ever is something so easily obtained worth anything. Besides, many young Dragons, especially those given more to the elements of fire or the land, go many years without ever being able to connect with the cold non-thought of the water's essence."

Malok did try it again, and again, and again, and just about the time he seemed so worried and frustrated with himself that he could not even cause the lake to sit still, Lenairu stopped him.

"That is enough. You have again become too concerned with the necessity of finding this Dragoness to effectively Peer upon her. You know the technique, but you see only what your troubled mind cannot do and it only troubles you more." She gently rebuked, but Malok's heart only heard the sting of correction.

He became quite cross and violently splashed the water with his outstretched claws, and the groan of disappointment now became a cry of anger and sullen defeat.

Yet, the Lady Lenairu was quicker than Malok could react, and before he could say a word, her hand was upon his. Her other arm went about his shoulder, and she pressed his cheek against her own. She held him there in the closest likeness of a mother's benevolent, nurturing embrace that he had ever felt, and realizing this, he wept aloud.

Not in self-pity, nor even in some sense of foiled overconfidence or expectancy, for Malok had never allowed himself to become so self-infatuated. Rather, he leaned opposite, evaluating his own self as less worthy, unsure, weak, different, ugly, a failure in all that he attempted, and this simple embrace stunned him to the very core, bringing him hope and encouragement and that maternal affection for which he had always longed and never before found.

"Such hurt inside of you, some of it is caused by others, and some is of your own making." Lenairu softly spoke to her foster-son, for so now she surely saw him. "You must let go of every past failure, yes, learning from them, but not ever should you gnaw upon them like a bone. They will rot your spirit from within and, if you let them, keep you from ever again trying anything, but you are better than all that you think. You are more valuable than all these stars in the sky, and they would all be cast down and forgotten only to have you walk among us. Your failure can make you strong, even as your success, and more even, but you must not let them sour your heart, or tarnish your self-worth. Come now, child; try it again."

Malok then did let go, not only of his cares again, but of himself as well, for he could not amend the past, nor could he be perfect in the present or near future. He accepted who he was, failings and successes, scarred and whole, and strove only now for this moment to live and give his all, not being held back by the weight of misery he had piled upon himself. As he let go from the loving embrace of his dear teacher, he did clear his mind again, stretch out to the water of the pool, envision the Dragoness, and seek her through the element's powerful gaze, and, surprisingly enough that he almost again lost control, he immediately succeeded.

There before him was the Bright Dragoness not as the still, lifeless imagination he had impressed upon the lake earlier, but here she was in living motion and color, lying upon the ground next to two formless blurs, which somehow Malok knew to be her companions. Her restful breathing made her golden chest rise and fall regularly, and her loud snoring could easily be seen by the moving of her mouth and nose and even faintly heard, as from a great distance.

"That is her!" Malok exclaimed, as Lenairu looked on, beaming with pride and happiness.

"Do not lose focus. Try now to know, through the Peering eye, whereabout she is." Lenairu excitedly explained.

"She is somewhere to the North and far to the West of here." Shouted Malok, somehow sensing this through the waters' perspective. "I can see the mountains all about her, perhaps, mountain ranges between the Aelven lands and the Order's realm."

Suddenly, his focus having shifted to where the Dragoness was located rather than upon her person, Malok's vision was filled with swirling images of these mountains, and he nearly became lost in a kaleidoscopic sea of these.

"Stop!" Lenairu shouted, even as she put her hand over Malok's eyes.

The lake rolled in huge waves as Malok's Peering was interrupted, but it was thankfully so.

"At this stage of your mastery, you must never lose focus during Atsarocu, for you could look and look whither your mind wandered until your eyes fell out, losing all sanity in the process. To properly end a Peering session, simply close your eyes for a bit, until the water moves again and the images dissipate. Only when you are much more practiced can you use Peering to search about for what you have never before seen or experienced." Lenairu sternly warned.

She then lifted her hand from before Malok's face, letting him see again, for she had promised another technique to show him.

"I shall also now teach you how to read other's thoughts and to guard yourself from both Atsarocu and Athungar, or Soul-Speaking, as these magics are all related in technique. Guarding against Peering is much the same as Peering itself. It does not require you to know that you are being Peered upon, but you must still follow the same steps with the same clarity of thought. You must cast your magic, creating a cloud of non-vision existing about you, reaching out to the water about you as you had done before, but this time cause it to hide you, keeping others from using it to 'see' you. This might have some adverse side effects, such as not being able to see your reflection in water, but you can cast and retract this spell as often as you like once you have mastered it. For guarding your mind from others, among the many spells that you may cast proactively, there are two simple methods to use during the moment when you perceive someone is currently reading your mind: either you may run many useless thoughts through your mind, focusing on nothing of value, or you can focus solely upon one thing, so that nothing else may enter or leave your mind. Either of these methods are most effective, for one cannot read what is not written in a book, so the same with thoughts. One cannot read a thought that is not there, memories that are not currently being recollected cannot be read by another, unless of course they were to Scour your mind, causing you to recollect what they wish to know. It is dark and evil, a forbidden and impossibly difficult magic. To Soul-Speak to another's mind, you must reach out to them as you did with the water, to touch their consciousness as you touched the water's. As the water felt cold and lifeless, people shall feel warm and alive, with each person giving you their own unique sensation of mind's presence. But, be warned, if you invade another's thoughts it may not always be without consequence. Some strong minds, skilled in advanced guarding techniques, may even attempt to ensnare, drive insane, or destroy your own mind in retaliation, yet more commonly, most people cannot always think kind thoughts. Sometimes, what you learn may simply hurt your pride or lessen your joy and opinion of others. You may try reaching out to my mind to read it, if you like. It will be safe for me to do so, but if you were to attempt this on one unskilled in mind defense, say Shar for instance, you might unintentionally, out of distraction, place a thought in their mind that should not be there, or suddenly cutting off the connection, leave them with no thought at all- like a mental hiccup. Do you see how the singularity of focus is so important in all three? It is a very dangerous business, and you should not ever take this, or any other magic, lightly, only utilizing what you have here learned when it is most desperately needed. With magic, always exercise much caution and much more discretion."

Malok was rather dissuaded, but being reassured of Lenairu's control over the situation, he reached out with his mind to her own, as he had done with the pool. Instantly, he was met with the warmth of compassion that flowed through Lenairu's consciousness, and he sensed that he was being allowed free entry. He then "saw", or perhaps "felt", how she was greatly delighted at his success.

Her voice came to him then, seemingly at the back of his mind, just past his ears. Unlike audible sound, it echoed through his thoughts, wispy, ethereal, and non-physical, as if she were speaking inside a cavern. Yet, it was her voice, for sure, speaking her words.

"In this way, when minds are connected, Dragons can communicate soundlessly. Merely think of what you wish to say while you are connected with the person to whom you wish to speak and they shall hear you. But, be careful; idle thoughts can still be translated as images and still be just as dangerous when merely reading another's thoughts." Lenairu Soul-Spoke to him.

"What is the difference in reading one's mind and speaking to another through mind connection?" Malok thought-asked.

"It is the difference between spying upon someone and having a conversation with them." Lenairu thought-replied. *"Usually reading another's mind is considered, at worst, an attack, and at best, just plain rude, but to connect to another's mind to begin a conversation with them is not so frowned upon. Yet, it is still something that only those who know each other well do together often. To have physical conversation first is considered proper etiquette, as I did with you, when you first arrived at my door. Only after I had greeted you did I then reach out with my mind, attempting to converse there. Admittedly, I was a little hasty in commencing unspoken word, but you seemed like a nice young Dragon, and mind-talking is far more efficient than pumping air through lungs and wagging tongues and lips for to speak."*

Then Malok sensed that he was being pushed out from Lenairu's mind, and he ended his connection with her.

"Most excellent." Lenairu spoke audibly to him. "I knew that Peering would be the most difficult for you to grasp, yet as I suspected, like with most Dragons, you took to Soul-Speaking very well. So, in one night you have realized three of the many techniques that have been forgotten among the Dragons of the Order, and even what took many of my children years to learn." Then realizing how late was the hour, she concluded their lesson with an invitation. "I know that you must be yearning to go to your Dragoness, but you will not travel very far or fast without sleep. Would you care to stay for the night?"

It was a welcome suggestion, and Malok, his spirit lifted and relieved by his recent successes over failure, joined her and Shar, gathering about the dying fire, talking merrily until midnight when they were shown to an unused guest room and soft, Dragon-sized beds, whereupon they quickly fell into sound and peaceful rest.

Chapter 25

They had surely found it, as Gorod had said that they would, and easily, for from the air, after only their second day of flying East through the lofty, cloud swathed mountain range, Calidon had spotted it while yet a great way off. Now as evening was quickly being swallowed up by the night and the once day lit bright peaks of the mountains started to become darkened looming shadows, did the three travelers come close enough to marvel at it, the great stone.

The name which the Urz had given to this monolithic obelisk was surely an understatement, for it sat in a green grassy vale between two encircling arms of the Northern mountain range and jutted nearly as high as they into the darkening sky. Of the same rock as the mountains was it cut, a lord of monuments, smooth and well shaped, three sided, with beveled edges, and flat upon its lofty top. Upon its sides, scrawling downward from the rim around the gigantic column's crown unto nearly half its height, strange yet artistic markings had been finely chiseled, as for their meaning, none of them knew.

"Should we land upon the flat top and there make our camp? Surely, no enemy could assail us there." Calidon asked, though with much trepidation.

The whole of the vale, but especially this humongous structure, gave off an aura of reverential fear, and they dared not to even fly any closer toward it.

"Perhaps not. I sense there is some significance to this place, that to which we must pay respect; besides, the valley has no passes into it by foot. No enemy could thus come here, and the last I knew, no flying creature would be any threat to us. Let us, instead, land by yonder stream and camp beside it." Anur replied, pointing to the small brook which flowed down from one mountain's snowy heights and into the depression, then disappearing into unseen subterranean grottoes beneath the high peaks.

When they landed in the nightly shaded glade, they immediately noticed the stillness and the silence of it all, the absence of life and noise, for there were no birds about, either in the sedges by the brook or in the lush carpet of vibrant grasses. Neither were there any insects, not one cricket chirping, thus explaining the absence of flowers and trees in the valley, for there would be no one to pollinate them. Neither were there any deer or any other game creature, not even rabbits; nor were there any fish or even bugs in the stream. They were completely alone, isolated from the whole outside world, within this untouched grove, and they felt it, in their bones and on their skin.

"As we discussed, there will be no fire again tonight, and that only partly because there is no wood hereabout with which to make one." Spake Anur, only a little remorsefully, as he dismounted from Feldara's shoulder and took off the helmet he had confiscated from the Dark Hunter's captain.

He had been forced to promise Feldara that he would not wear it constantly, and he had agreed only to wear it at certain times: in battle, to hide his identity when necessary, and to keep the wind off his face while flying. He now had to take it off again, as he was doing none of those. Though with some apprehension, did he remove the well fitted helm, for his old reclusive habits, had somewhat resurfaced with the acquisition of this new gear.

"As for turns on watch, I will go first tonight, for I took second last night, and then you two must come to agreement on who shall take second and third." Spake Anur, as they three situated themselves for the night.

Once they had decided, and not without a little arguing, that Feldara would take the loathsome second shift and Calidon the third, the two Dragons went quickly to slumbering upon the soft, verdant rug of grasses, while Anur sat upon a boulder that was jutting out over the stream, the height of which would give him some vantage point for viewing most of the vale.

Just as Anur suspected, as the late evening darkened until the blackening sky became aglow with stars and the hours wore on to about midnight, nothing eventful occurred. No one else entered or was within the valley, yet did the babbling drone of the brook's incessant flowing tempt him ever to sleep, until at last his watch had ended and he could afford to do so.

He strode quietly over to the soundly snoring Dragons and gently tapped Feldara upon the arm to awaken her, but to no avail. She was quite the sound sleeper, and he softly spoke her name and increased the force by which he attempted to rouse her, until he was near to rocking her whole body with the force by which he pushed upon her. At last, Feldara groggily awoke.

"What?" She grumbled, only half conscious.

"Awake, you lifeless rock." Anur teased. "It is your turn at watch, and I wish to rest."

Feldara was too grumpy upon being awakened to appreciate any of Anur's humor, and she responded not with words but a low, gurgling growl. Nevertheless, she arose, if only to stare annoyedly at her mentor until he lay down and began to doze off, and at last satisfied that he would hassle her no more, and being resigned to her fate of midnight watchman, Feldara decided to refresh herself with a drink from the stream.

It was a cold draught, to chatter the teeth with the ice of the mountains, but nothing had she tasted that was purer and more enlivening than the snow-melt water of this little brook. Feldara drank long and deep; so that when at last she again raised her head, she was thoroughly surprised at the presence which had crept up behind her.

A warm glow, like the fiery gold of the morning, shone about her and reflected off from the stream's surface in a playful dance, and though it was bright, the light did not strikingly cut through the night, as contrasted with the flame of an actual fire or the burning radiance of the sun, but rather softly illuminated the whole of this side of the vale, so that it again seemed as twilight.

Feldara turned about, completely dumbfounded, thinking Anur had broken his own ruling and somehow had lit a fire; though how he would have done so without the presence of dead or living wood within the valley, Feldara had not come to knowing yet. She was still quite sleepy and, as such, slow of mind, but what she saw behind her, fast awoke her.

A massive Dragon stood right next to her, far taller and longer than even the largest Dragon Feldara had yet seen- Yuronon, the bigger brother-in-law of Rathnyaling. From him, this enormous king of Dragons, the soothing glow emanated, for his golden, yet white hot scales shone with an aureate, luminescent brilliance. Though, Feldara had at first been taken aback by this unexpected intruder, the kindness and warmth of his eyes matched with the peaceful halo that gently reflected off from everything about let her know that this mysterious visitor meant no harm.

"Hello, my child." Spake the Dragon, with a voice that boomed deep like far off thunder yet rung as sweetly in the ear as amber honey on the tongue. "Welcome to the vale that has been prepared for us, for the Counting Stone."

He spoke in words from a far removed language that Feldara had never before heard, that which she thought must be Old Draconic, yet she did understand what he said in the plain speech, that which she herself spoke. For a moment, she was dumbfounded and could not at all respond, and she merely stood basking in the radiance of this Dragon's soothing aura, warming smile, and benevolent eyes. However, eventually Feldara found speech again.

"You are my father?" She asked, for so this Dragon had named himself.

"I am every Dragon's father, for I was the first, the created one, descending from no Dragon, but fashioned directly from the mind and Word of the Almighty, the Eloigal." He gently replied. "You are a very special daughter, as you may know by now, for within you is the power of light and the strength of righteousness, by which the darkness shall be broken and the world be blessed, by which our people and the children of men shall be preserved."

Suddenly, all apprehension left from Feldara, and she felt so relieved and contented, free and able to say anything to him, this complete stranger of a

Dragon, her far-removed grandfather. Though she knew not if it were his genuinely compassionate smile or the sincerity of his gaze, or even the comforting warmth of his emitted radiance, Feldara felt as if she had known this sire all her life and were deeply loved by him.

"Why must I be the one upon whose shoulders the world is laid?" She plaintively questioned, though immediately regretted being so bluntly obstinate.

"It is a valid inquiry, one which all who have shared similar burdens do ask, but it is also one with quite simple an answer." Chuckled the large Dragon, his mild laugh reminding her of the copious summer sunshine. "It is because you can. Perhaps, only you, now in this age, on this world, can accomplish this task set before you, and you do have the strength to bear it, to endure, and even to succeed. Otherwise, it would not have been given to you. Indeed, many, if not all, are called to a task, by their circumstances, predilections, passions, and pursuit thereof, but few, very few are chosen to the great deeds which shape our world, make our history, and grant us a future. Chosen by the Almighty Himself- it is a special labor, difficult, yet, if faithfully borne, the most rewarding life that existence has to offer."

"I do not feel so worthy or capable, for I am only a young Dragoness, neither strong, wise, nor skilled at anything. I cannot, as yet, even breathe fire." Feldara humbly muttered, curling her tail about herself ashamedly.

The huge Dragon placed his massive arm about her and drew Feldara close to his side for a reassuring embrace. His touch was supremely comforting, beyond that of any other Dragon, beyond even the affections of her own foster father, like a blanket in Winter or the balmy ocean breeze about her island home, and he spoke encouragingly to her.

"It is not always the strong, the wise, or the talented who are chosen; though they too may be. Usually, it is those who think they have no gift at all, and only looking back at their great accomplishments do they finally realize that they did bear some unique, priceless idea, quality, or ability that belonged to no one else. You are quite fortunate to have come this way, even if trouble did find you along the path, for I have been given the opportunity to show you exactly what is your gift and how to use it." He consoled.

Much to the dismay of Feldara, who could have stayed in the good Father Dragon's strong arms for much longer, years or so, he then relinquished his embrace, and began to saunter off toward the great stone monolith.

"Come." He gently bade, motioning for her to follow him. "Oh, and the breathing of fire, it shall come with your age. Do not worry about that, for it will be soon enough now." Said he, even more lightheartedly.

They walked over to the very base of the monument, and only when he was close enough to lay his hand upon it and stroke the smooth gray stone, did he again turn to face his pupil and resume speaking.

"This is the Obelisk of the Covenant, the chronicle of Dragons. Upon it, starting with mine and my mate's names at the top, and descending toward the bottom, are all the names of Dragons written, those who were, and who are. Whenever a new Dragon is born into this world, their name is also written down, and eventually all the free space upon the stone shall be filled and the ending of time will come. This is a representation of the holy covenant between Eloigal and our people, for each name that is written is not only my child, and their parents' offspring, but also His own. We are engraved upon His heart the same, for we are His children forever. Thus, we are given His Spirit, to aid us from our birth, for to do His good will. Being His children, we do well to obey, but beware that still we are given freedom of choice: to follow His righteous path, or to pursue our own way, which may oftentimes become wicked." He said, explaining the purpose of the giant column. "Come. See your own name written in the stone." He suggested, as he flapped his massive wings and slowly lifted into the air.

Up they flew circling about the great stone chronicle, for a long while they slowly ascended, as there was many, many generations' worth of free space still available upon the monolith's lower reaches. Much further than halfway did they rise until, at last, they came to some very recent writing.

Even as Feldara gazed upon the stone, another few names were being scrawled into it. New Dragons were even now being born into the world, but strange was the manner of this carving. There was no hammer at work, or chisel, nor any stone mason to be seen, yet the names were engraved without any chipping, seemingly burned or impressed into the rock, the end result appearing as finely etched lettering.

"Ah, here it is." Exclaimed the Father Dragon, pointing to a word scrawled but a few spaces further back in the list. "Not many have been born in recent years, for there is great stress among our people. We feel in our beings the growing danger of shadow and live more cautiously, but we are still enough to survive. You are among only a few hundred Dragons born of the same generation, so far that is. Now, look here upon your own name carved into the stone and the covenant."

Feldara did gaze upon the foreign text that was her name, drinking in every curve and angle of each letter. She reached out and touched it with her hand, feeling along the smooth stone and the exquisitely chiseled writing, and though it had been explained in words to her just a moment earlier, Feldara felt now more than ever before that her life was with purpose and that nothing therein, or for that matter anything anywhere else, happened by chance, mistake, or accident. There was order and design for everything, including her own life, and to think that the Lord of the Universe, who had made everything by thought and word, would stoop down to give such to her and all His creation was simply overwhelming.

Tears came to her eyes, of joy and thankfulness and sorrowful repentance for any previous ungratefulness or poor attitude, and Feldara then vowed within herself to live up to the worth she had been given, the task for which she had been chosen, and the life with which she had been blessed.

"This is my name?" She asked, still confounded by the significance of it all.

"Yes, it is written in ancient Draconic, and an even older, dialectal form of that- the language which I spoke and read and wrote with when I still freely walked among my first children." He stated. "Now that you have seen your ordination, I shall show you your gift and how to wield it. Let us move upward."

With that, he ascended to the very plateaued top of the enormous structure, and Feldara followed, landing close behind him upon the flat surface.

Here, unlike the sheltered glade far beneath them, the wind rolled off the nearby mountains in chill gusts, but Feldara felt not the bite of cold in it. The Father Dragon's warm light banished any such frigid temperatures, even those from the icy rushing gales.

"Is this your name?" Feldara asked of some writing carved into the floor just beneath her feet, as though in his presence she could feel like a child again, given to be fascinated anew by everything.

"That is the name of my mate; my name is written over here." Corrected the giant Dragon, pointing to a spot opposite the plane from where Feldara was standing. "My time is short with you, little one. I so wish we could simply talk and enjoy each other's company, but we must hurry to complete your training." He said, rather remorsefully, dispelling any further juvenile inquiries Feldara had wished to make.

"You know of magic. Have you ever wielded it?" He asked.

"No, I was never taught to do so, for though there were many books that I read on the subject, and Anur does know some magic, He never taught me how to charge or cast spells." Feldara stated, regretful that she had not been given this opportunity.

"I feel your disappointment in your father for not instructing you in the ways of magic, but do not begrudge it of him. As he is not a Dragon, there are just some things that he is incapable of teaching to you, yet he tries his very best to raise you uprightly. He gives his all, his whole life for you, and for that he deserves only your praise and gratitude." Chided the Father Dragon, who then became quite serious.

He strode around to the opposite side of the spacious, level roof of the monument, and before he began his instruction in earnest, in a moment's time, he caused all to fall silent, even the wind. Only once all was quieted did he resume speaking.

"Magic is within all Dragons, for it is a special gift given to us by Eloigal. It is the power to replace reality, for a limit of time or effect, with our own will, or more so, that which 'is' with what 'should be'. It will flow freely from within you, but it is not your own power. It belongs to Him. It comes from Him, and it can only be used by our freedom of choice in ways that, ultimately, He permits. There are classifications of spells based on types of effects they produce and for what they are utilized, but this is all Man's influence with their need and duty of categorizing and naming everything. Magic is not limited by technique, institutionalization, charging of 'energy', or any other physical factor. Its power is restricted solely by the imagination of the caster, by how creatively and efficiently they will something in or out of being, and thus it becomes very important to remove oneself from distraction and give forethought to consequences, seen and unforeseen, before and during the casting of magic, lest one destroy what they intend to save or cause chaos rather than bring order. There are certain exceptions to this, your special power being one of them, and these are called 'gifts'- special powers intertwined with one's own soul that have a unique and unchanging quality. These gifts can be anything: from dream-walking, to instantly understanding any language, from having particular attunement with and power over a natural element, to seeing the future. Indeed, you have a very special gift, for within you is the essence of light and the power over its spiritual implications. You can, quite literally, and quite metaphysically, cast back the darkness, just as the sun does the night. For example, when you fought with my son, Calidon, you must have noticed the darkness engulfing him, strangling his thought and life, and wresting control of his own body and mind. This darkness was found concentrated in an evil device, a Bloodstone, deliberately placed around my child's neck for to subdue and torture him, but you instantly shattered the vile Bloodstone, no matter its seemingly irresistible power, and with nothing more forceful than your tears. It was through your gift, even only acting out subconsciously, that you were able to destroy the corrupted Dragon-stone and free your brother from his enthrallment, but I shall teach you how to summon this gift at will, to freely use it in fighting the shadowy evils." He instructed. "Now, search within yourself, find the place where your magic dwells. It will not be within a physical part of your body, but rather a spiritual location, your soul. It may take some time in meditation, but it is there, so that you will be able to find it"

Feldara did then seek this part of her being, that which she had mostly ignored her whole life, for never before had she been taught of, nor herself sought for, her source of power. It seemed as if many long hours passed by in silence, as Feldara sat reflecting upon her own self, but eventually she thought she had found it. It was like a whisper within, and toward the back of her mind, or a warm feeling in her gut, a tingling in her toes; the source of her magic was all around and within her. She had come to the place where it was.

"Excellent." Approved the Father Dragon, even before Feldara could herself rejoice in her success. "Now, draw from this spring, your power; think of a way that it can affect the world around you. However, this phase of magic wielding is most critical, for if you were to do anything too outlandish or if you had need for a more profound action and did too little, there would be consequences. Regard in your mind how the physical world will react to your subjugation or removal of its laws and plan accordingly. Of course, there is a more advanced technique, whereby you can nullify the impact of your magic beyond a certain range of area or effect, but this is much more difficult, as then you would have not only to know how to create your desired effect, but also how to limit it."

"Magic requires a lot more forethought than I had first assumed." Feldara posed, having a hard time drinking in so quickly all this new knowledge.

"Indeed, it does, and that is why there are spells written down and taught among such groups as the Order. They have the wisdom of others who contemplated the desired effect, its repercussions, and perhaps, the nullifying phase, and they need then only read and learn what the original caster did to succeed and do the same. For your gift, there will be no such help, for no one in this world but you has had this unique ability. There will be no wise elder's spells to memorize and practice; you must create your own. Now, do as I had told you. Dwell as long as you like upon it, for the best and wisest use of magic is always long pondered over, thought through, and well crafted."

Again, for hours it seemed, Feldara sat and contemplated how she could show her power without breaking reality in ways with harsh consequence. At first, she thought of casting a great ball of light into the sky, but she thought it over and decided that enemies might be able to see it from far away. Then, she thought of something much grander, turning the night into daytime, but then again, her enemies would notice it, and everyone on all of Threa would be awakened. Besides, she did not know how to get nighttime to come back again afterward, as sleep was still desirable, and worst of all, if she were to move everything around to morning again, she could not fathom what unexpected effects that would have on their world.

Instead of all of these, and many other ideas with big and little effects and consequences, she chose to do something simple and discreet that would have no other action than simple gentle illumination. She chose to replicate about herself the same gentle, glowing aura that resonated from the Father Dragon, and she wished it to be so, mentally drawing it up from the well of her power, until the air shimmered and grew lighter about her.

Suddenly, she shone brilliantly, a little more brightly and of a different color- white, turquoise green, and golden- than her grandfather, but Feldara had achieved her desired affect and removed it from any consequence other than gently illuminating the immediate area.

"I did it." She giggled with delight, as the Father Dragon beamed with pride, but after only a little while, Feldara had tired of her shininess and worried about being seen like this, either waking Anur and Calidon or attracting unwanted attention. "How do I turn it off?" She asked, becoming a little frantic.

The Father Dragon chuckled again, bemused at seeing his daughter's discomfort with her own achievement, which was in no way harmful or endangering, a perfect first spell, well crafted and cast. "Simply wish to undo what you have done, for as there are no unpleasant consequences to fix, you have nothing more to do in ending your spell."

Feldara did so, and immediately the brilliance of her aura vanished, leaving only the dark of night and the warmer softer glowing of the Father Dragon.

"There are many useful applications for what you just did, and furthermore, there are innumerable other utilizations for your power over light. However, the quality of your gift is not that of a mere lamp, for while it may physically enlighten whatever is about you, it is designed to destroy the spiritual darkness that plagues our world. There is no such black evil in this place for you to experiment upon, but the method for drawing out your power at will is the same. Sometimes, what occurs after your gift is used may very well be autonomous from your own will, affecting the physical and spiritual worlds in ways beyond your knowledge, in which it was intended to function- for example, your power shattering the dark Bloodstone for to free your brother without even your knowledge of its existence." He explained.

At length, a great fog began to roll into the vale from off the snowy mountain peaks even as the Father Dragon's visage became sorrowful and his light dimmed. "I am afraid that all my time given to be with you has been used up." Spake he, with much sadness in his voice.

"No, do not go now!" Feldara shouted, even as before her very eyes his form began to fade. "I have so many questions."

"I wish I could stay and give answer to them all, but my body has long passed from this world, and my soul belongs not here. I shall bring word back to your mother, how beautiful a Dragoness you have become, for she asked of you when I left, and to tell you that she loves you and wishes that she could be here with you. I love you also and will be watching, yet from afar. Farewell." Spake he.

Even as the last words left his mouth, the image of the Father Dragon dissolved into the enveloping gray fog; so that by the time he said 'farewell', it was only an echo disparate from the invisible mouth that spoke it.

Feldara was left sitting alone upon the cold stone of the great monument, and tears fell from her eyes, truly of sorrow borne. With the complete peaceful joy of the Father Dragon's radiance gone, and with the relayed message from her mother still burning within her heart, she felt bereft of any friend or comfort. Eventually, she did dry her eyes and remember her two companions slumbering far below her and her duty to watch over them.

Feldara quickly glided down to where they lay, worrying that, perhaps, something had happened to them while she was away, but she found them both sleeping, snoring even, perfectly fine and safe. She awoke Calidon, for such time had passed that it was well beyond his turn to take watch. He grumbled far less than she had, getting up almost immediately, and quickly assumed his duty.

____

As Calidon strode off a way, needing to relieve himself, Feldara lay down beside Anur and snuggled up close to her mentor, the only father she had ever known before this night, and now that she had seen an image of what a Draconic parent should be, she all the more valued Anur. As he tenderly put his arms about her, she could only see him more and more as that father for which she had always longed and became ever more grateful for his presence and guidance in her life. Before she knew it, gone was the lonesome dread she had felt after the Dragon father had vanished; it had been replaced by the love she received from her foster-parent, which left only the good memories of that night. These then turned, through restful sleep, into peaceful, forgetful dreaming.

Chapter 26

The High Council chambers were a complete wreck, with papers strewn all over the floor, a few pieces of broken furniture, and an ugly, ragged gash cracking the giant central table, that at which the councilmen sat when they performed their duties. Here they still sat, in darkness now, for with the windows and huge circular skylight fastly shuttered for the siege, there was naught to see by but a few wall braziers and candlelight from the table's candelabras. Still the room, black as it was, was lit well enough to see within, if only barely, and the High Councilmen did gaze upon the newcomers in amazement.

Or, perhaps, the look they now offered was one of fear, or the desperate, though unspoken plea of unfortunates in need of rescue. Indeed, here they had been forced to sit for two whole days' worth of besieging, waiting for something to happen, and it troubled Zurthaud so. For, what could hold these men here hostage, glued to their chairs, when the look upon their faces spoke only of flight or terror, and at the least, much discomfort?

Truly, some of them fidgeted uncontrollably or gnawed upon their nails, possibly fearing that, finally, their rule was to be overthrown, for with men in power that is what they fear most, and once lost, their penultimate nightmare realized, anxiety over being held accountable for all their past misdeeds drives them to thoughts and deeds once unthinkable. Though, also truly, not all the men who sat on the High Council were evil or callous or weak minded and suffering from pangs of conscience. Surely, some were only trembling in trepidation of what was about to occur, for they continuously gave nervous glances toward the darkened end of the great table.

"Men of the High Council, henceforth you have been relieved of duty on the charges of wrongful conduct and the approval and abetting thereof." Declared Zurthaud, as he stepped forward to address them. "You are stripped of all title and power and must be escorted to the main hall below where you shall await fair trial and sentencing for your individual and joint crimes against the Order and the Free Peoples."

Zurthaud's strong voice echoed throughout the room, undoubtedly heard by all the High Councilmen, yet not a one of them dared to move, nor even respond to him. They kept on looking back and forth from the shadowed end of the table to Zurthaud, perplexed and eerily restrained from any action other than the nervous clearing of throats, and it began to seem that a darkness beyond that which impaired sight had flooded the room and enslaved these men.

Eventually, one voice broke through the umbrous silence, there was still one man who laughed, mockingly guffawing at Zurthaud's command, until his voice rose in brazen, spiteful gaiety. It was, of course, Orthard.

Zurthaud recognized him by hearing alone, though he was cloaked in the deep shadow hanging over his end of the table, for that despicable man could be known anywhere by his harsh, hateful tone. Though, never before had Zurthaud ever heard him in merriment until now, now when he was the subject of his own father's mirthful scorn. It caused the young man's blood to boil as nothing else ever could, for his own father to ridicule him.

"You should laugh not, Orthard, for today you answer for your many crimes." Coldly spoke Serc, seeing that the others, even the angered Zurthaud, all fell silent, unnerved by this hysterical, psychopathic utterance.

"Be silent, dog." Grumbled Orthard's voice, as he rose from his chair and stalked toward them. "Of what crimes am I so accused, for treating the beasts as they are, rather than pandering to their whimsical fantasies to walk and talk like men? I have done nothing worthy of punishment." He said passing through the light of one of the wall-mounted braziers.

Long enough did he linger there for Zurthaud to see that his eyes were red and bleary, as a man having drunk too much, but nowhere, either in his room or in this chamber, had been found the evidence of overindulgence in any spirit, no smell, no empty bottles, not even of his favorite Aelven wine. The gaze of Orthard then fixated upon his son, and it was wild, as of a ravening animal, and Zurthaud, along with the other Paladins, began to sense there was something amiss about him.

"Here is the one worthy of trial and punishment. My own flesh and blood rises up in mutiny against me to take power not given him, a coup among our own ranks, and you gallant Paladins have done nothing, or worse, aided this sick little boy. I am disgusted." Rasped he, twisting truth, scattering lies like seed, attempting to sow a spirit of doubt and discord among those present.

"You say we are animals. Why then do we not just destroy and devour you all now, or before when it would have been easier?" Theros angrily growled, fully through with any debate to be had with so foul a person, but Serc placed a hand upon his shoulder, quieting the younger Dragon. He would not have Orthard validate his false perspective with any outburst of wrath.

"We may walk upon four feet, but our minds are given to higher thought and more righteous cause than many generations of Humans have in these halls dared to aspire. Even now, I can name only a handful who would rise to meet us in greatness of word and deed, thought and character, for most now seek after vain pleasure, forgetting the duty of Paladins, while we have yet kept true to the Order and its statutes, even to our own detriment." Serc calmly rebutted, keeping Orthard from causing strife and debate through a change of subject.

"And, I will testify that your crimes are not only toward Dragons." Lorn added, stepping forward into the light so that all could clearly see him.

Upon seeing his face, many Councilmen broke their silence by gasping in wonder, for they too had been deceived regarding his fate.

"You! How dare you show your face back here, when you disobeyed my laws and were banished!" Screamed Orthard, frantically attempting to cover his egregious misdeed. "See now how all of my enemies here gather to corrupt and destroy what I,.. what we have built."

But, fear was rife in Orthard's voice, strangling the confidence he had earlier possessed. This was one of the many grave errors he had made, a horrible wrong, and it now fully, unabashedly confronted him. Under such pressure, even Orthard could not weasel out from under. As Lorn again told his tale before the High Council, the vile lord could only squirm in dismay.

"What have you built but walls of hatred, divisions borne of wicked imaginations, to scar and devastate what was once whole and clean?" Serc asked, after Lorn had finished.

"These 'walls' were earned, the hatred was deserved!" Orthard shouted, yet suddenly he became calm once again, producing one of his sinister smiles. "Oh, but, you think you all have won this day, this battle, do you? You think I have been idle these last few days, but you should know why it is we have all gathered here one last time, waiting for my announcement, why it was we were wanting to send your miserable kind to the sulfur mines." Spake he, and he reached toward the center of the table and grabbed some item from the darkness between the candle sticks' faint glow. "Here is what we have built, what I have achieved, the weapon of my own design." He triumphantly shouted holding aloft a long tube of iron with a lever and handle at one end. "I have seen the future, one without 'magic' or Dragons. With this weapon, we shall have no need of your people's powers, not your God, nor your aid in anything. Never again will we cry unto you for help, only to see our hopes be crushed, only to fall into despair."

"So, that is what this was all about, everything that you have done, the restrictions, the discriminatory laws, the degradation, the hatred?" Serc replied, coming to a sudden realization, much to the astonishment of the others, for everyone in the room was now convinced Orthard had gone completely insane. "You still blame me for her death and seek to punish me and everyone else for it?"

There was more between these two than anyone could have ever guessed, except for those who were old enough to remember Orthard in his youth, when he too rode upon a certain white Dragon's back. There was once a time when he too, even in his disbelieving, self-centered heart, was once touched by the love and friendship of one of these noble beings, when he too was proud to call himself a companion of a Dragon, but those days had long gone, torn asunder by the encroaching roots of bitterness and hate.

"Of course, I do, you wretched creature. You were the one who stood idly by, doing nothing to help, as she slowly wasted away." Orthard spat. After decades of secrecy, being caught in the moment, he had unintentionally revealed the source of his heart's loathing for Dragonkind, and now he threw all restraint to the wind, exploding with wrathful gall.

"I did everything I could!" Serc cried out, as old wounds were rent afresh. "I could not save the life of your child along with your wife. Believe me, I would have given my own life for her's, and I did everything in my power to rescue her. Yet, when the time came to decide, she unselfishly chose your son over herself. She begged me not to care for her own sake, though, as a doctor, I did make desperate attempt anyway, and despite all my efforts, your wife died bringing forth your own child into this world. In honoring her last wish, I could do nothing to save her while I delivered your son."

Zurthaud was mortified.

All hatred for his father was forgotten upon hearing these words, and the world began to spin, as for the very first time he heard tell the fate of his mother. Though, of course, he had known she had died when he was still very young, before he could yet remember her, never had he realized that she had died because of him, and from the weight of this revelation, he stumbled back a few paces and grew lightheaded.

His father's attentions were drawn unto him by this sudden display of weakness, and a venomous, growling glare grew upon Orthard's face. "Oh, is that how it went?" Orthard sarcastically sneered, in a calmer yet more malevolent tone. "Then, I suppose you and your people were not to blame after all, and I can only condemn a God who does not even exist, really, such a cheap ploy to pass the bottle to some transient, cosmic phantasm, so that you should not have to bear it."

"It is impossible to cast blame upon Eloigal, for He is above all things of this world. Sorrow, toil, blood, and even death are all so far beneath Him." Serc retaliated, angered by Orthard's blasphemies. "You, in your cynicism and unbelief, view death with a hopeless despair and think of it as the end of everything, the ultimate finality, but it is not. Your wife died because the world is corrupted by mankind; by their own sins, evil and death were brought into the perfection Eloigal had made. It is the mercy of Eloigal that our wicked selves are not left to rot in our corruption of His perfect world, neither are immediately consumed by Holy, judgmental fire, but that His mercy is greater even, poured out upon us daily in every little miracle and blessing of life. His mercy was offered to your wife by the ending of her woes, and furthermore, when she, along with all others who believe and call upon the Holy One, perish from this world, they are instantly with Him, brought to rejoice before Him in the Blessed Realm, where they too live forevermore above sorrow and mortality."

In one of very few times, Orthard could think of nothing to combat this argument, for it was put forth from a heart full of conviction, confident in the truth of reality, unswayed by material knowledge, Human philosophy, or emotional distress. It was truth, unconquerable truth, that though mortals may die and Eloigal, in His infinite wisdom, sees fit to allow such, that there is greater mercy at work. For those who believe, death has no power, and is reduced to a mere gateway to that blessed life beyond, the last river to cross.

However, Orthard still wallowed in his obstinacy; even given so much time to heal and faced with a clear exposition of truth, he resisted. In his cynicism, and the apparent madness which had now taken him, he would not, could not allow himself hope.

He laughed.

The many long years after his beloved had passed away he had spent in hating the God he denied existence, yet an odd thing that, to detest what is not. Everything that reminded him of God, he mocked, fought with, and tried to destroy. Thus his contempt for the Dragons, for they are Eloigal's servants. Even his son, for whom he had at the first made endeavor to show love, if only because he was his father, he now completely loathed.

He now, in whatever insanity had so beguiled him as to fashion weapons of unknown malice and lock dignified men in a single shuttered room for two whole days, laughed, a low, long, yet empty cackle, devoid of any mirth, only brimming with his boiling wrath and spite.

"So, even God escapes the blame." He shouted. "I suppose then it must be my fault, as you shall make this whole mess to be. After all, I was only trying to right a wrong, restore justice, avenge the death of my wife."

In frustration, he then stopped to grandiosely flail the weapon about his head, causing all the councilors to flinch and seek cover. "I suppose you all think that I am to blame, that I am crazed. Well I am not!" He screamed. "There is one last person upon whom I can cast all of my wrath, one last betrayer who can take the punishment for the lot of you traitors, and maybe then we can work something out for your 'downtrodden' people. I speak, of course, about the very one whose birth rang the death knell for my beloved. You, Zurthaud, you killed my wife; you are responsible for the death of your own mother." Said he, bluntly pointing his bony finger directly at Zurthaud.

The weight of this claim nearly brought Zurthaud to his knees, for as he struggled not to just crumple to the floor, he could not deny this revelation. His mother died so that he could live. Her blood must be upon his own hands, for there was no one else to bear the load. He alone was responsible; he alone was to blame.

Before the wise Serc, or any other good person, could repudiate any of this, bring any clarity to this realization, any peace to Zurthaud, any closure to the long grieving Orthard, before anyone at all could react to what had been said and did only stare open mouthed, dumbfounded by what they had heard, Orthard raised the secret weapon in his arms and aimed it, as one would a crossbow, straight at Zurthaud.

"I thought you were dead, and a pity it is that you did not remain so!" Orthard poisonously spat, and he pulled the lever on the ugly device.

A great crack, as of thunder, boomed throughout the room, for the wicked device exploded forth fire and smoke from the end of the long tube nearest its target. In the same instant, a bolt of Black-iron, small for its intended lethality, shaped for swiftness and cutting through the air without wavering, shot forth from the tube, propelled by the hot gas and fiery fumes at speeds nearly faster than the eye could follow. It should have struck Zurthaud, for he was not a stone's throw away from where Orthard stood, and it would have slain the young man right there. That bolt of Black-iron would have cut into his chest, devastatingly crawled through his body, and burst forth again from an even larger exit-wound, but that it had been intercepted.

Serc stood before the quivering Human, whose mind had been so dulled and downcast and whose body had been so sapped of strength that he could not have possibly escaped any other way, for the old Dragon doctor had been nearest Zurthaud. Seeing the evil intent within Orthard's eyes, either through general perception, or perhaps from his past untold years of being joined in companionship with him, Serc had leaped in front of the young Human. Even before the bang had uttered, or the smoke and fire poured forth, longer still before the wicked bolt sped out from the weapon, the ancient doctor had moved to protectively shield Zurthaud.

However, it was not without consequence that Serc had again saved the life of Zurthaud, for though the Human had been spared, and likely a lesser metal would have done naught but bounce off the hard scales of the elder Dragon, Black-iron had been designed by the Dark One to be the bane of Dragons. It supernaturally corrodes the scales, skin, and even bones, so that rich, dark red blood now began to pool upon the floor, spewing forth from the wound which the bolt had deeply carved in his chest.

As Serc gasped and fell to the ground, the ashen Paladins came to from their shock and horror. Immediately, Argamon called an order to fetch any and all the physicians they could gather from the fourth floor below, himself shoving two Paladins out the door. At the enraged behest of Theros and Galrag, many others hastened to apprehend Orthard, and the cruel ex-tyrant did neither attempt to resist nor flee. He only looked on, deep within his own internal misery, a blank expression of bewilderment and regret upon his usually callous visage, and did not turn his eyes from the scene, even as he was being hauled away.

The rest of the High Councilors hung their heads in shame, as though awakening from deep sleep, though surely feverish and filled with nightmares, realizing, at last, how they had let so wicked a man govern them as he who would slay his own son, and who did, indeed, murder a Dragon, and they resisted but a little when they too were borne away.

It took only seconds for all this to be done, and in the aftermath everything became still again, as all who remained in the chamber, only they who were close friends, were already gathered about the great healer.

No eye could now remain dry, for he who had spent his whole life mending wounds, lay bleeding out upon the floor agonizing in terrible pain. Every one of them would have given their life or arm to save their beloved friend, mentor, and doctor, but even as they attempted to stopper the wound with any free cloth they had, there was nothing to be done for him. The bolt had penetrated deep within, unto his very heart, and his life-blood flowed fast away from him, soaking deep red all their best, yet futile efforts.

Serc himself could but lay there, gasping in pain, for no remedy, either of skilful doctor's hand or of learned magics, could remove the tainted metal, nor aid him any way; of such was the dark power of the Black-iron. He knew that his time had come.

"Let us have a little light in here, for it is so dark." The old one calmly whispered, and they nearby opened the shutters and sky-light, which had been closed during the siege.

With the glowing of an early evening sun, the beauty of the room was revealed, with its gray stone walls, luxurious scarlet tapestries, and the awe inspiring tile murals upon the floor and ceiling, that which rivaled even those within the Dragon's temple with their artistry and scope, depicting the forming of the Order and the High Council, and at last, the horrible darkness which had festered here was lifted. The once stale, malodorous air became immediately freshened by the soft breeze, which thanks to the height of the tower, so cheerily and easily, blew within. Satisfied with the extreme change in atmosphere, from dark and gloom to light and its warmth and serenity, in spite of his dying torment, the old Dragon motioned for each of his close friends to draw nigh for to bid them farewell.

Argamon, Lorn, and Galrag he reached out through his suffering to touch each in turn, a last affection, to which the old General tearfully replied.

"Save your strength, my friend; the doctors shall arrive any moment, and then..." But, he could not finish his sentence, for the General knew his hope was misplaced. He then only held tightly the hand of his oldest friend.

Unto Theros, who held his other hand and wept, Serc turned. "Theros, I had no children of my own, but I always thought of you as a son. I leave you with all my worldly goods." He wheezed.

Serc then turned to Zurthaud last of all, not out of contempt, for Serc had loved Zurthaud even as he loved Theros- as a foster-son. It was only that the young Human was to receive the most important advice of all and at the hour of his greatest need.

"Oh, Little One," He tenderly spake, seeing the despair in Zurthaud's heart even more than the tears in his eyes. "It was not your fault- your mother's death. It was not your fault, for you were but an innocent babe." Whispered the old Dragon as he laid his head close to where Zurthaud knelt beside him. "If I had not heeded her wish, to bear you alive from her womb, yes, she would still be with us, but if I had done so cruel a thing as to leave a mother alive but childless, I should have received her eternal scorn, and worst of all, I would never have had the joy of knowing you. She made her choice, and it was the right one. It is never wrong to give yourself up, to sacrifice your own good, so that others should flourish, should live. I want you to no longer bear the idly cast guilt, that wickedness inspired a fallen, broken man to thrust upon you. You deserve it not, and you cannot now afford to remain in it. It is my fault you live and your mother does not, mine alone, and let the blame die with me." The old one sighed deeply and coughed and grimaced, but finally a faint smile broke through his torment to grace his lips, as he continued to speak to Zurthaud. "We are nearly whole once more, and all my life's work has yielded such a bounteous harvest. Though I shall not taste the fruit of my labor, I leave it in the hands of the generation to follow. I leave it in your hands, Zurthaud. Stumble not, certainly not upon past failures, nor upon guilt unearned, and that when you are so close to realizing what I could only dream. Prepare yourselves for the falling night, for now that we have gained a little strength, the enemy shall come, attempting to tear it all away. You must lead them, Zurthaud, as you have until now; Lead them on to victory and the glory beyond."

With these last words, fading in strength with each syllable, and these separated ever more by the challenge of breathing, Serc spent all the rest of his vigor. With one last ragged exhalation, the aged Dragon, beloved and respected by all who had known him, friends and enemies alike, breathed his last. His chest rose no more, and the light of his eyes faded to glassy emptiness.

He died.

Yet, even in his last moment, there was peace there surpassing all understanding of why there should be any in such despairing hour, that in which the heart and healer of the Order did perish.

It almost felt, to those gathered, as if they were standing within the temple atop the Dragon's tower, right in the midst of worship with reverential and serene song reverberating the hall throughout, and yet, here they stood in silence and tears, with neither singing nor any joy among them, while the dead lay in such tranquil repose, his lifeless visage bearing a soft, bittersweet smile.

Zurthaud could not restrain himself. He buried his face, wet with the rain of his eyes, in the cheek of his good friend now departed, and he would not cease his grieving. He had regarded this Dragon, not a Human, above all others, even his own sire, as his truest mentor, for the aged one, now gone from the world, had taken up his tutelage from where Lethira had left, and by his sincere affections and honest teaching in all things a just Paladin should know, especially by example, Serc had taught him what a leader should be.

He was consoled by all his friends there gathered, even Argamon laid hands upon the young man, for they all were touched deeply by his sore mourning. Eventually, as Serc's empty body, bereft of his inward being, spirit and soul- all that made Serc himself- began to ignite with the natural funeral pyre of Dragons, Zurthaud had to leave from holding onto the precious head.

He let go of his friend and guide to stand back, lest he too be consumed by the flames of Draconic death, and Theros came over to him and put his arms around him and held him. And, they all stood there watching the body burn until it was ash and nothing remained but peaceful smoke trails wafting upward, even assuredly as Serc's soul had done beforehand, out through the large opened windows into the darkening heavens beyond.

Chapter 27

As the sun began to rise over the mountain's crest, lighting their reflective snow capped peaks as with fires of bright orange hue, Calidon awoke Anur and Feldara, for though they were all short on rest, they needed to get up, find their breakfast, and get going before much daylight was wasted.

With a crisp refreshing drink from the chill mountain stream, Feldara was fully awakened, ready to meet the day, and yet with that same draught, she was also brought recollection of the night before, of her meeting with the Father Dragon and her valuable lesson. Even though she remembered every detail clearly, Feldara still began to wonder if it had all been just a dream, for she felt rested enough, as if she had also even as much sleep as the others. She decided to try testing her gift again, going through the steps of drawing out this power from within herself, shaping it into a desirable effect, and casting it forth, but there were unfortunate consequences to her actions this time.

Feldara had meant merely to cause a radiation of light from the palm of her hand, but her spell was not very well thought through, or aimed. With light often comes heat, so when she cast forth this beam from her hand and it landed upon Anur's backside, who had been busy rolling up the blanket he had slept upon, it did begin to set his pants to smoking. With a yelp, Anur jumped forward, for the prolonged contact with the blade of light, as Feldara had been too busy marveling at it to notice anything else, had nearly burned him.

"What was that?" He yelled, patting out what was almost a fire upon his buttocks.

At the first, Feldara did not know whether to laugh or apologize, but she quickly made herself do the latter.

"What, did you breathe fire for the first time only to scorch my backside?" He nearly shouted, for finding out that Feldara had nearly set him ablaze had removed his surprise, but not his anger.

"No, it was magic, and I am sorry. I did not mean to burn you." She explained.

"Magic can be dangerous. You should not practice it on other people." Calidon soberly informed, as if he were oblivious to the fact that her attack had been accidental, and his incognizant chiding only caused Feldara to exasperatedly roll her eyes.

"Magic! Since when did you learn magic?" Anur asked, completely taken aback, for he had never even attempted to teach her such things.

The magic of Dragons was more unwieldy than that which Humans used, for while the Humans' magic was drawn from their Dragon and, by them, could be controlled with certain restrictive measures, the Dragon's received their magic directly from Eloigal, their power essentially being limitless. As such, Anur had never felt comfortable with trying to teach his precious charge to draw from this well-spring of boundless power, even though he was quite skilled in the casting of afore created spells. He still felt too insecure about his own knowledge and skill to teach on this extensive and treacherous subject, yet he had certainly meant for her to be trained by the world renowned mages of the Order.

Now he had not the opportunity even to aid or guide her mastery of the treacherously potent ability, for his young Dragoness was already causing havoc with it, having in one night learned some of what had taken him many years' study.

"I was taught how to use my special gift last night by the Father Dragon." Feldara plainly stated, as if it were a well known fact. "And, it was an accident, Calidon. I would not just set Anur's pants ablaze for fun."

Anur could but scratch his bald head, for he had never heard of such a person, either in the lessons of his youth, or from the books and scrolls upon their island. Neither had he seen or heard anything out of the ordinary last night, and Anur, of all people, was so light a sleeper he would certainly have noticed any intruder, perhaps even before whoever was already on watch.

Calidon, however, stared agape with disbelief, "You saw The Father Dragon?" He asked, utterly amazed. "He taught you magic?"

Feldara nodded her head "yes" in answer to his question, even as Anur asked his own. "Who is this Father Dragon?"

"The very first Dragon in existence, the Created One," Calidon informed, "It is said, in our legends, that he did not die a true death, merely that his body did fade away, and he was taken from this world to the Blessed Realm. It is also said that he comes forth from that world, descending in spirit and again taking on flesh, for to aid his children at times when he is needed most. Never did I think these stories were true, at least not to that extent, and still I am uncertain. Yet, I do wish that he had said something to me also." Said he, muttering the last bit under his breath, for at this moment, he was somewhat envious of Feldara's supernatural encounter.

"Are you sure you were not dreaming?" Anur asked of Feldara, for he too doubted that a Dragon from so ancient and mythical a time could still walk among the living.

"I did just now, albeit accidentally, cast a spell upon you, yes? How else would I have come to the knowledge required to magically warm your butt?" Feldara bluntly stated, her sarcasm obvious, for she tired of all this undue attention and useless questioning.

She knew what had transpired, and if they chose not to believe her, it mattered little. The truth was the truth, whether or not they accepted it.

Anur was less concerned with the origin of her knowledge than with how she had used it. "From now on, you must consult with me before you think of casting magic, for it is, indeed, as Calidon has expressed, a most dangerous power and should not be strewn about idly. If you were to let forth an ill-formed spell, the damage could be irreversible, such as setting me on fire and burning me to ash. As I am your companion, I can help to control your magic, especially if we were to form the spell together, and if such a spell were to go awry, I am probably the only one here who would be able to negate it." He stated.

Calidon regretfully agreed, for he knew not enough about magic to negate other's spells.

Feldara was just so absolutely exuberant that she had been referred to, by Anur, as his "Companion", that while daydreaming of them going off as Paladins to fight evil together, she happily, though absentmindedly, agreed to the terms, and once that was settled, they quickly finished with Anur's packing up and headed off into the bright morning sky for to find their breakfast.

Unlike the plains, there were no bison here, but many scattered groups of sheep ran, frolicking among the mountains and rocks. These they did not consider, for though, they were all three hungry, the large herds of fattened, grass-fed deer were nearby, upon the steppes and high forests just below these ranges. As deer was much better eating than goat, to a Dragon at least, they made for the Southwestern course that should take them toward the Southern plains and its tasty game, and better still, ever nearer to their ultimate goal, the bright city of Doraegonoran.

At length, they crested the very last ridge of the final mountain to find themselves high above these same grasslands that they had been making for. So broad an expanse it was that they could not even see the end of it, the great Atsar, upon the horizon's edge, and as such, the forest dotted plain seemed to go on forever, even from the vantage point of this high altitude.

Yet, Calidon's mind was not turned to merely observing the scenery; with a finger he pointed to one such grouping of their desired prey, a massive herd of deer scattered much abroad among the grass and deciduous groves.

At his signal they both dove together, down toward their quarry, choosing their particular victim as they closed in, and in a rush of adrenaline and violence, they each, nearly simultaneously, had swiftly descended from on high and landed forcefully upon the backs of their targets, thus crushing the spine and quickly, neatly, and almost painlessly ending a life and their hunt.

The herd was completely taken by surprise, as these were not overly hunted like the deer about the Rathnyalings' home and the two Dragon's had shot down, swift as arrows, from so high above them, yet, unlike the bison, the deer did seem to realize what had happened and quickly fled afar, as fast as their bounding legs could carry them, to taller grass and dense brush thickets.

They three settled down to enjoy their meal together, with Calidon lighting a fire for Anur to cook his meat upon, and for a great while, as they sat back in the warm glow of the late morning sun and ate their meat, it seemed as though the day would wear on as yesterday had, uneventful, even peaceful, bereft of all the danger and woe they had so feared should be pursuing them. Still, they ate quickly and quietly, for though they were so close to their goal and the safety that it offered, by Anur's calculations, now only two day's journey by Dragon-flight from the great city, he did not wish to be kept out in the wilderness any longer than they had to be, as easy prey for their enemies.

However, afar off in the distance, so far away that when before they had looked to the horizon they had not even noticed it, then but a dismally black stripe across the panorama's outer edge, there loomed another massive storm, brooding dark with clouds and malice. A peal of thunder, an ominous ringing of doom, sounded forth from the South, and they all jumped. They could fully recall, with much dread, the horrors of their last encounter with such twisted, evilly bent storm systems, and they wished not to suffer such woes again.

"Surely, we have neither seen nor heard any enemy, and yet, here again come those vile clouds." Calidon sullenly whined.

"Perhaps, it is not a sign that we have been spotted, but rather a sign that our enemy, not knowing our location, is still searching for us. Perhaps, they again wish to force us to take a path of their own choosing, afore prepared to ensnare us. We should keep moving, stay ahead of the storm and what it drives us toward." Anur suggested.

It sounded as good a plan as any other and was now simply the only course of action to take, for they could not hope to turn invisible or expect their enemy to just pass them by. So, again they took off into the air, but this time they beat their wings furiously, pumping their massive flying arms in hurried rhythm of frantic pace, trying with everything that was within them to outrun the oncoming squall. It was to no avail, for the wind moved against them, even as the looming thunderheads rolled onward, faster than any natural force could push them. Though it was not night, soon the shadows grew thickly about them as the giant wall of storm blotted out the light of the sun, and eventually, despite all their effort, they were once more completely overtaken by an evil tempest.

They groaned within themselves, thinking that again they should suffer the onslaught of torrential downpour, but the wind howled on and the dark clouds swirled overhead, even the thunder did peal all about them, but there was no rain, nor even any lightning. These clouds had not passed over the sea, nor had they picked up any other water; they were merely blackened by the evil intentions imbued into them and could not even give the slightest of benefit to the land underneath. They were dry, empty, without any mercy for the parched ground or any relief for the thirsty grasses, a threat and a portent of malevolence, nothing more, nothing good.

Realizing that they should, at least, not become drenched, they flew on, thinking for a while that the absence of rain was something for to be glad, yet by the time midday had come, they had grown so weary of the depressing darkness about them that they yearned to stop for a moment of rest. They descended down into a stand of pine, some of the last between here and the Shadow Lands, aside from lonely isolated trees dotted throughout the land's predominantly deciduous forests, and they gathered under the groaning boughs for a little reprieve from the howling wind and dismal skies.

"Such evil weather, a dry wind without any rain, and yet the sky darkens as for a fierce storm." Calidon muttered, as he settled underneath a nicely sheltering fir. "No doubt this is the Dark One's doing."

"Yet, no enemy has presented themselves to oppose us." Anur spoke, as he too huddled next to Feldara under another conifer. "If we keep our heads, remain calm and not carelessly fall into this trap, we might yet well escape to Doraegonoran without again being caught or even noticed." He counseled.

"Perhaps, this storm is for another purpose altogether." Added Feldara, rather hopefully, for she had no desire to remain the full fixation of the dark powers.

A smell of burning caught their attention. It was not that scent a of a clean wood fire, merrily billowing smoke as it cooked a meal or warmed a house, but it was a rather dirty, smoky odor, as though trash were burning. Mixed in was the unmistakable stench of scorched flesh, which caused them immediate alarm.

"You two stay here. I shall investigate." Anur commanded, even as he sneaked off into the denser part of the pine wood.

It seemed an eternity as the two Dragons waited upon him to return, for they knew not if even now they had fallen again into the clutches of the Shadow Lord. Suddenly, a snapping of branches startled Calidon to jumping, but it was only Anur as he strode back into the pine strand with much less stealth than with which he had left.

"What was burning?" Calidon boldly asked, as though he had not been so surprised a moment earlier.

"Come and see." Anur instructed, cold of voice, plainly stricken by what he had experienced.

They three then went forth, through the conifer thicket, and all the while they strode among the burgeoning darkness, the reek of burning became ever stronger about them. At last, as they passed the last of the trees and stepped out into the tall sedges, they saw what had caused all the smell. They could not have seen it from the air, as the sky was darkening as unto dusk, and it lay in a hollow just a short way beyond and beneath the hill upon which stood the pine strand.

There below them, about a dirt road spreading from North to South, lay the remains of a small town. It was in ruin from arson of the buildings, but it was no accidental fire. Each home had been set ablaze, and many now were but ash. The crop fields had also been laid waste, and the dead livestock were scattered everywhere, left to rot where they had been butchered or be set upon by the gathering, circling carrion birds. Just outside the town was a large heap, a mass of twisted blackened forms, even now acridly smoldering, and with much horror, Feldara came to the realization that this must be what remained of the people who had lived here.

"This is terrible. Who could do such a thing?" Feldara wept.

"This is the work of the Dark One. He shows no discretion between warrior and farmer, innocent and guilty. Men, women, and children: he slays all who are in his way." Solemnly spoke Anur. "I am going down to search for survivors, make sure the dead are properly cremated, and dispose of the livestock. You two go back into the shadow of the trees and keep watch for me from the top of this hill. There is no telling how many of the Dark Horde are about, but it would take many to so overwhelm and slay these people."

Calidon vomited.

<><><><><>

Several hours passed by as Anur completed his task, for he searched very thoroughly for any sign of life about the desolated village. No one had escaped; none had been spared.

He then had to gather the farm animals together, and much to the dismay of the vultures, he burned their bodies in a separate pile from the unfortunate people. They who had been slain and so uncaringly heaped and cremated, Anur set a thick layer of stones over, so that no scavengers could get at them, but he could not mark the grave with any epitaph, as by now he could find no words of any kind, let alone eloquence.

Finally, as the already dismal sky darkened unto night, he returned to the top of the piney knoll, and just in time, for the sound of marching was fast approaching from the road.

Even as Anur darted into the thick cover of conifer boughs, rejoining his Dragons, a large mob of Trolls and Goblins came stomping around the bend leading around the hill.

The anger among the three companions burned nearly as hot as the funeral pyres below them, as they espied the savage killers of the poor denizens. It was apparent, by how the battalion of Dark Horde was jeering and carrying on, that they had been the ones responsible for this wicked act, and they were even now returning to set up their camp near the ruins of the town.

"We should leave." Anur suggested, and not out of cowardice.

Feldara gave him such a look though, as to melt stone; she would not, could not, let these monsters go unpunished for their barbarous actions.

"We should not engage this small party of warriors, for if even a single one escapes our wrath, the enemy shall become aware of our presence here. We lose our advantage of stealth and risk being caught out in the open again." Anur explained, even though he too longed to avenge the innocents who had been so cruelly slaughtered.

Movement and noise closer to their location startled them to attention again, for two Trolls had climbed the little hill and were coming straight toward them.

"Get the wood for fire, slug. Stand guard on that hill, you maggot. How come we always get the hard work?" Grumbled one Troll to the other, but they had not yet espied the two Dragons and Anur.

Quickly, it became apparent that their hand was now forced, for either these two Trolls would eventually spot them and sound an alarm, or they could slay the Trolls and risk their comrades sending out a search party after them. Anur knew now that they had no choice but to strike first.

Quietly, he sneaked out from the strand of pine and crawled low upon the ground, concealed among the dense grasses, toward the two approaching Trolls. Eventually, they split up, each going to their respective duties, and at this point Anur struck.

The one on watch duty, he slew first, swiftly and nearly all at once grabbing his feet, pulling him down to ground, and slitting his throat. The other Troll was now a good way from Anur and nearly upon the two Dragons, but they were not sitting idly while their mentor did all the work. With a quick swipe of a claw, they pulled the Troll into the thick pine clump with them, even tearing him in half with their ferocity.

Anur crawled back into the pine clump with them to discuss their next move. "We a forced into action now, for we have taken out their firewood gatherer. They shall soon be wanting him, for though they might never have inquired about the guard, it is going to be a cold night." He stated.

"We should attack from the air, spew fire all over them. True, it will scatter the survivors, but we can easily pick them off before they send out any messengers. If that fails, we can just go after the messengers too." Calidon suggested.

It was the young male's turn to receive a blistering glare from Feldara, but he did not immediately remember that she could not yet breathe fire. He could only submissively shrug, as she sighed exasperatedly.

"Regardless of whether or not you can breathe fire, Feldara, I still think attacking from the sky will be our best advantage here, for with your viewpoint, you two will easily spot the runners making to get away. I will attack from the ground, cleaning up after Calidon's passes." Agreed Anur. "Just try not to incinerate me also." He sincerely requested of the Dragon

With that settled, much to Feldara's annoyance, for she wished to be a bigger part of the battle than to just circle above and take out fleeing Goblins, they set out for their positions. Feldara and Calidon headed to the far side of the pine grove, where they would soar off high into the sky, well out of their enemies' sight, and circle back around.

It took only moments before the Dragons were already in position above the camp, and now they only waited for Anur to get near enough the town ruins before Calidon would start his first dive. He approached faster than they expected, but not without their notice, and they began the attack.

Calidon ripped downward, like a falling stone, and just before he hit the earth, he opened his wings and, slowing just enough to break his fall, let forth his fire. In screams of alarm and agony, the enemy responded, but they had few archers. It mattered not, as Calidon had already sped away, and their missed bolts hissed in the empty air.

Anur then came among them, and with his green lighted magic blasts and sword made short work of, first their bowmen, then the rest of the disorganized rabble. In a panic, the battalion broke asunder, and Goblins and Trolls fled in every direction. Even as Calidon descended again to set ablaze the majority of the remaining soldiers who foolishly chose to stick together in a closely clumped group, Feldara realized it was her turn to join the fray. She dove for the nearest enemy, and with a fearsome roar, she ripped it apart, still in flight, gliding but a few feet above the ground. She would kill five to ten of theses monsters in such a way before ascending to gain momentum for another dive, and in this manner she, along with Calidon's help, had soon slain the last of their dispersing foes.

It had not occurred to her how fast and far the Trolls had run, until she looked back after finishing the fight and saw the remnants of Calidon's first attack still blazing brightly quite a way off, but soon she covered that distance and landed beside Anur, who had the nerve to be seated quietly upon a rock, just a short way from the fires that had once been the Dark Horde.

"How nice it was to have you helping us." Feldara cajoled, upon seeing him so reclining.

"What? Surely you did not think that I was going to run down all those Trolls." Anur retorted, as he folded his hands behind his neck.

"No, but you probably would have given them neither chance nor reason to flee. If it was not for Calidon's suggestion, you would have easily slain them, one by one, all night long." Replied Feldara.

Anur did not argue, even as Calidon landed close beside them.

"I do doubt they shall be cold tonight, Anur." The Dragon stated, trying to conceal a self-congratulatory smile for his perceived whit.

"Did it take you this whole time to come up with that poor excuse for humor?" Sneered Feldara, though she and Anur both cracked a smile.

It was not so much that they rejoiced in the suffering and fear of their foe, for surely, no matter how vile the Dark Horde was, it would have been wrong to exalt such things. Mostly, they were caught up in the rush of battle, but also they were joying in the success of their plan, and the righteous avenging of the innocent slain townsfolk, and even the sharing of their company. All these they valued more worthwhile than the lives of the fell monsters, and rightly so.

However, their mirth was abruptly ended, for the clouds suddenly drew back like a scroll being swiftly rolled up, revealing a night well lit by the stars and a little sliver of moon. Upon the blackened skeletal remains of one of the ruined houses, a sole figure slowly crawled, like a lizard, across the ashen beams and burnt panels.

"What is that?" Feldara asked, completely bewildered, for she had never seen such a creature.

It awkwardly scrambled about on all four, Black-iron clawed feet, and it wore nothing but scraps of Black-iron mail and a weird, angular face plate that revealed only its lip-less muzzle and sharp teeth. Upon this mask was carved a large "X" shaped symbol, which in this night, glowed red hot, as if by some inward fire or magic.

"That is a Nokre." Anur spat, a tremor in his voice. "We need to flee, now!"

Even as he made his command the strange creature elevated its head and howled, and its eerie, resonant moaning was unlike anything Feldara had ever heard, not even as the dark wolves had howled. It was altogether otherworldly, as if it were the noise that a long dead corpse should make, though they, indeed, neither rise nor speak.

They took to the air, and looking back to the ground below, Feldara espied the unnatural animal melt into a puddle of black goo and move no more. They took off at a quick pace, but already, as Feldara was still glancing behind them after the fate of the Nokre, winged shadows appeared, barely silhouetted against the faint light of the moon.

They had been found!

Chapter 28

For two whole days, Malok had been racing after and gaining ground on his quarry. Every few hours or so he had been able to find a source of water and Peer upon the Bright Dragoness, and thus adjust his course, as he had pursued her, North and West, over the wide expanse of the Order's Realm. It was a hard flight, for the young Dragon would hardly stop, eventually landing only to eat or rest briefly, or because Shar had begged him to do so. As difficult as the whole journey had been for Malok, flying at breakneck pace for long hours, even harsher it had seemed from Shar's perspective, for the Serpen King had to endure the whipping and roaring of wind and the prolonged periods of silence and boredom, as Malok concentrated only upon soaring ever farther and faster. Even the chaffing of unwanted places, as he rode unsaddled upon his friends hard back, sorely grieved the unhappy Serpen king, until the late afternoon of the second day.

They had only just landed in a grassy field, nearby brook and forest, sedge and wildflower, to eat their meal of freshly hunted deer, and Shar was finally unwinding but a little, when once again Malok, immediately after hastily finishing his food, had insisted they keep moving. At first it was only expressed in attitude, a sighing groan of thinly veiled, complaintive fatigue, but Shar had, indeed, reached the end of his patience and self-control.

"What is that all about?" Malok asked, as he arose, and not too kindly, for he had also grown weary of flight and wind, and the ever declining optimism of his friend.

Shar could restrain himself no longer. "What do you think this is about?" He shouted, throwing his arms into the air and falling back into speaking in the Serpen language. "I am painfully tired of this chase. I am exhausted, wind burnt, vexed of mind, and chaffed of buttocks for all this cursed constant flying. I want a break. I want sleep. I want hot food and a soft bed."

"Then go back to your fine palace, little prince. I have something to do." Malok gruffly retorted. "Even now we are closing in on the Bright Dragoness, and I will not turn aside to petty comfort, especially not because of your whining."

"Curse you and your imaginary friend. All she has brought us is misery. You do not even know that she is real, or do you think that images conjured from the water can be trusted more than the sand?" Shar yelled. "For all you know, she never even existed, much less needed you to drag me, gallivanting, across the wide world to rescue her. You are such a gullible dreamer."

"At least, I have the honor to stand by a friend in need. You would rather I had gone by myself." Malok roared. "Well, I will have the honor of my race, and you can just walk home."

"That is all you have ever wanted." Shar cried out, his eyes welling with tears borne of long repressed feelings of betrayal. "You care no longer for the Serpen, for my people, nor for me. You would discard us like waste just to be with your 'Dragons' and your fake lady-friend."

"That is not true." Malok retaliated, though, upon seeing his friend become tearful, with more restraint, for it was something that he had never seen the uncommonly reserved and blissful Shar do in all his life. "You know that I love our people, and you know that I love you, even when you are being a rock-head."

"Then why, this whole journey through, have you constantly been embarrassed of me and the customs taught you by my people, earnestly seeking to be less and less perceived as Serpen?" Shar interrogated, folding his arms across his chest, for he referenced the words of the lady Lenairu, how she had spoke aloud Malok's thoughts.

"Is that why you have been so cross with me lately?" Malok asked, for he regretfully recalled the instance.

"Yes, it is, and I want to know why it is so, that you can act one way when no Dragon is watching but become a completely different person whenever we enter one's presence." Shar pressed, arms still folded tightly and accompanied by a pronounced frown.

"Because," Began Malok, and he too choked a little on his answer, for it was an issue near his heart also, "Even though everyone in the kingdom knew my name, and you and Ulam treated me as your own family, I have always felt different, awkward, as if I did not ever belong. I felt always as if I were outside looking within, wishing I could be at home with you and our people, but never really being able to do so. I have felt a stranger to my own skin my whole life, for though I was raised a Serpen, I am not one. Even now, when I have found fellowship with my own kind, I feel estranged, as if I am not truly Dragon either. So, I belong nowhere now, neither Serpen nor Dragon, and I chase after a vision like a fool, hoping that, perhaps, when I get to the end of this journey, I shall finally find someone who is like me, who knows what I have felt all these long years. Maybe, just maybe, I shall find somewhere to call home."

They stood staring at each other for the longest while, each trying not to come to an embarrassing full sob in front of the other. At last, Shar opened his mouth, attempting to diffuse the situation with some whit.

"Well compared to your misery, my day seems not so bad at all." The Serpen King muttered indirectly.

Malok could only sigh, for this weight had lain heavy upon him. His whole life had he lived in disquiet and yearning, and now it would seem that he should never find any solace, a place where he could belong.

"You know that my home has always been yours, and I never regarded you as anything less than a brother." Shar spoke, trying to comfort his friend, and he strode over and embraced him. "You will always belong with the Serpen, weird shaped, four-legged, flying, and all else. You will always be a part of me."

"I know this, and I am sorry that I had expressed embarrassment for you as my companion and the Serpen as my people. I just wanted to be accepted by my kind, and yet, they freely gave such blessing, leaving me to seem more a donkey than a Dragon." Malok apologized.

"I forgive you, as I always shall." Spoke Shar very seriously, but then continuing on with a growing mischievous grin. "Besides, I have already gotten what I was really after, for here we have been standing about, talking all this time. I think this has been long enough a break."

Malok was astounded. "You would start such an argument with me just to get a few minutes relaxation?" He growled.

"Well, that was not my intention, but it does seem to have worked out that way." Shar guiltily mumbled, as he looked away, far across the distant rolling plains.

"Alright, get upon my back. We have wasted enough daylight." Malok demanded, though he inwardly laughed at his friend's jocularity.

The Dragon had never intended, with the voicing of his heart's desiring, to hurt his dear friend, and he truly loved his adoptive people. Malok only rued that he had ever been ashamed of his Serpen peculiarities, and he vowed never again to be so foolish. He had come to realize, in great part thanks to the lady Lenairu's wise counsel, that he could truly be both Serpen and Dragon at the same time, for these two separate identities were of what made him unique. There was no reason he could not love both people and express himself in both Serpen and Draconic ways.

"Did you hear what I said, or is that head of yours too rocky for sound to penetrate?" Malok playfully inquired, after Shar had not hearkened unto him and only stood staring off into the distance.

"What is that?" Shar distractedly replied, for he was truly espying something afar off.

Malok then did turn to see by what it was his friend had become so transfixed, and he could barely believe his eyes.

____

In the desolate lands of the Serpen, a storm rises only every once in a long while and comes either from the far Northern Mountains or the Southeastern sea, and still, these seasonal rains were light showers compared to this gale. Here and now, a massive wall of pitch black thunderheads came rolling toward them, rising up in fury from the South.

Never before in all their lives had the desert dwellers seen such a dark, dense, and enormous storm system, and they were simultaneously enchanted and terrified by the sight of it.

"It is a great mass of clouds, so that it must be a storm, but I have never seen one as this." Malok eventually replied. "Here, get upon my shoulders, and we shall go where it is not. For, I do not like the look of such a squall."

Yet, the Dragon soon found as he raced off into the sky, that such an enormous weather system could neither be outrun or flanked. It seemingly spread across the whole of Threa, blotting out the sunlight and bending every tree with its dry, hateful wind, and though Malok was not an unskilled flier, it easily overcame the two travelers.

"It is dark as night out here, but the sun had much further to go before it set." Shar complained, as he fearfully scanned the sky about them.

"I can see well enough to fly on, but it may become unsafe to do so. Let me know if you hear any thunder or see any lightning. I should hate to be flash-roasted." Malok replied over the roaring of the wind about them.

On they flew for many miles, with the monstrous storm having no end in sight, yet from his vantage point high in the air, Malok could see a rather strange occurrence. Upon the ground below, there began to appear a great number of fires being lit in the villages further toward the South, that which were nearest the Atsar river. Indeed, so many little bright burning balls arose that an eerie red glow shone upon the undersides of the dark thunderheads, and it changed the whole sky underneath the black cloud cover from a dark night to a blood red twilight.

Malok could not imagine why so many fires should burn, but that the Humans had become afraid of the dark and were trying to ward it off with excessive light. However, as the young Dragon drew nigh to investigate, he found the actual cause for the reddening of the sky and the lighting of fires to be far more despicable, for under the blanket of storm and its covering darkness, the Dark Horde had begun to move.

Rising up from the South, in much the same manner as had the great squall, the armies of the Shadow Land had marched forth in long lines, with many, many battalions, thousands upon thousands of soldiers, and they had begun spreading across the land, taking to the dirt and cobblestone roads, that which were meant to connect the realm in trade and communication, for to speed their progress. At every split of the road they happened upon, a battalion of mixed soldiers would break from the main group, travel down its length, all the while pillaging and setting ablaze every town and farm they came upon.

It was an organized slaughter, an extermination.

"The Dark Horde has crossed the Great Border Wall and the Atsar!" Malok gasped, and for a moment he hovered there, shocked by this appalling sight and terrifying revelation, not knowing what he should do first.

As many of them had been only farmers relying on the Order for their protection, the Humans below were undoubtedly being massacred in great number, and Malok desired most of all to aid them. However, he knew that the Paladins were somehow unaware of this surprise attack, and needed to be warned if any sizeable and effective resistance was to be mustered. And still, his heart told him that his Bright Dragoness was out here somewhere, perhaps, even now imperiled by the same army of savage monsters.

After only a moment's hesitation, he chose to aid those in immediate and apparent danger, flying straight toward the ever increasing number of bonfires, and he fast came upon the battlefront. The nearest village was just now being overrun by a large mob of Trolls and Goblins who had broken off from the main force. Fortunately for the poor Humans, who were huddled behind a last defense barricade at the center of their town, Malok arrived just in time, and he quickly proceeded to drive off the battalion of monsters with bursts of fiery breath.

"Go! Head North, to the nearest city!" Malok shouted at the petrified villagers, once this regiment of Dark Horde had either been incinerated or scattered and a pathway had been cleared, by which the Humans could escape.

The people fled from their palisade of overturned carts and stacked barrels, grabbing only what necessities were already within reach, and ran for the road going North, as Malok covered their retreat from the encroaching main host. In this manner, these folk outran the slower march of the dark army, and Malok could turn aside to help other towns and farmers in like manner. Still, the single young Dragon could neither stop nor abate the relentless onslaught, and many miles worth of crops and thousands of homes were torched and otherwise destroyed.

Eventually, the Dark Horde became aware of Malok's presence, how he did harass their movements and slow their advancement, and they brought forth ballistae with which to shoot him out of the sky. It became ever more wearisome and risky for the Dragon to swoop down to attack their ranks, for they would fill the air with whistling Black-iron bolts, enough even to make him change course, lest he be hit. Still, the towns were burning all around, and the beleaguered Humans, from all across the wide expanse of prairie, fled North, as far and as fast as they could run.

"Where are the Paladins?" Shar cried out. "Surely, they must have seen or heard by now that their Realm is burning to ash?"

Malok searched the ever darkening sky, yet there was no help to be found, either for to aid him in halting this invasion, or to help with the escaping civilians. The only assistance he had received was that of a local lord, whose few armored knights, mounted upon horse, did ride at the fore of the black tide, stinging the monsters with a barrage of crossbow bolts, and with feinting charges, mow down some of the less tightly grouped formations of enemies.

Malok did descend to speak with their commander, a young, flaxen haired man, even at his tender age lord of this province, but not having the time to land, he hovered just above the ground to converse.

"Is there any way you can send word to the Paladins of this terrible invasion?" Malok asked over the shouting of men and the neighing of horses, the crashing of weapons and the roaring of the enemies' battle cries and horns.

"My Lord Dragon," Spake the young lord, with as much composure as he could muster. "I have already sent my fastest horse to Doraegonoran, but it is, at least, three day's ride from here. The only quicker messenger we should have is you, brave Dragon, and we have earnest need of your presence on this field, lest we become the only fixation of the enemy and be completely annihilated."

"Is there no help for us, then?" Shar called down to him.

However, the young lord could not answer, for having reached the end of the time available to remain stationary, due to the ever forward charge of their opposition, the knights had to fall back yet again, and Malok, finding himself within ballistae range, had to head higher into the atmosphere.

All then seemed hopeless, to the young Dragon, who earlier had been so close to the end of his quest, for he was now extremely weary, having spent so much time and strength in reaching the Bright Dragoness. There was now no allotment for any rest, for in the waging battle, that of most dire need to protect the poor and helpless people, their homes, and livelihoods, he found himself one of the only participants on the side of good. He could not now retire from the fight, yet every muscle in his body ached, every bone groaned. All that he longed for was this night to be over with, and he dreaded the thought of making yet another hazardous strike at the enemy's ranks. So, weary was he of the battle that he began to make mistakes, was nearly shot twice, and on the return to higher, safer altitude, he almost missed the joyful sound.

At the first, it was as a distant horn call, faint and unimportant, but as the trumpeting call drew nigh, Malok recognized it as none other than the roaring battle-cry of many Dragons.

He turned about his gaze to the North to see them coming, the great beating of wings and rending of clouds, the shimmering of myriad colors, all seemingly blood tainted in the red fiery light. It was, indeed, many Dragons, but these bore no companions on their shoulders, and far more terrible to their foe were they than any Paladin.

These were "wild" Dragons.

The knights below gave such a cheer, for now their relief had come, unexpected salvation from upon high. They knew these Dragons, for they were also local lords, not of men, but of fire and the open sky. With flame hotter than any earthly source they breathed destruction down upon the Dark Horde, for they dove in upon them too swiftly for any dart to find a mark. As they passed overhead, with fierce and chaotic magics they dismembered what remained of the host, and in one such strike, they accomplished more than Malok and the knights had done all evening.

But, they were not yet through with their foe. They landed among the monsters, scattering them with claw and tail, tooth, fire, and more magic, and so violent and effective was their attack, that the entire host of Dark Horde began to break ranks, quickly dispersing abroad. Some retreated in ordered regiments, but many of the legion simply ran in terror, screaming and yowling as they fled in every direction.

Malok was completely taken aback by the ferocity and the power of these free Dragons, for more as forces of nature had they fought than as soldiers in combat. He was still opened mouthed, even as he landed among them.

"Hello, young one." Greeted a large brown male, "I am Drowon, and I can speak for my neighbors here. I see that you have long been fighting this filthy rabble; are we very late to the battle?"

"Greetings to you, and well met, Drowon. I am Malok, and I have become so weary of combat that I can neither remember when the Horde came upon us, nor how long I have been set against them." Malok replied, as he touched earth again, grateful for a moment's rest from flying.

"When I first noticed the fires, it was about late afternoon." Shar spoke, able to answer the question, for he had naught to do this whole while but to uselessly cling to Malok's back, as he had neither bow nor pole-arm with which to help fight their enemies.

"Ah, you must be Paladins, seeing that a companion is astride your shoulders." Spake Drowon, giving Shar a slight bow as greeting. "I thank you, Dragon-friend, for your record keeping. It informs that we were not too far behind the assault, for it was about that time we first spied them from our gathering nearby upon the higher plains. Though we had already here mustered, having earlier heard the horn call, I feared that we should be very late, costing the lives of many unfortunate Humans."

"We are not Paladins, truly." Malok replied. "They have yet to make presence here, and I am left to wonder if they are even aware of this invasion. Either their border guards were overwhelmed and got no message out to them, or there is no such watchman to speak of. Yet, you say yesterday there was a horn call?"

"Indeed, we all heard the ancient trumpet, the Dragon-horn, the power of which is to gather our people together for battle. I am surprised to find this assault was not the reason for which it was sounded and the Paladins absent, but there have been many unusual disturbances, rumors, and tales from The City of late." Replied Drowon.

"Yes, there are strange goings on in The City these days, maybe, enough even to keep them from their sworn duties." Concurred another Dragon, causing all the others to discuss what should have happened to cause such silence from the Order.

It was then that the knights rode up to where the Dragons had incinerated and broke the advance of the Dark Horde, distracting them from their debating, and the young lord who led the brave men quickly dismounted and strode up to the "wild" Dragons.

"My lord Dragons." He wept, as he bowed before them upon the scorched ground. "I owe you and your people our lives. Many are saved alive this day because of your actions. How can I ever repay you?"

"You can start by getting up off the ground." Chuckled the great brown Dragon in front. "Truly your thanks are enough, and I am only sorry we did not get here the sooner. Indeed, our work is yet to be done, for though we have broken their ranks, we must ensure that the horde does not regroup further to the South, and does fully leave from this land. Human lord, you must, of course, attend to your people: the defense of your towns, the gathering of the scattered and injured, the burying of the dead, and so on. We shall pursue the foe southward, to the far side of the Atsar. Young Malok, we see that you are most weary, having striven through from beginning to the end of the battle, and we bid you take leave from this field. Go and find rest, for we here shall, most easily, have the day."

"Then, I shall head back to Doraegonoran, for the Paladins must be warned of what has transpired." Malok offered, though he dreaded the thought of flying back all the way he had come.

"Why should we bother?" The young Human lord, scoffed. "They have proven neither to care for the people, nor to honor their oaths, for while they are glad to extort tributes, they make no endeavor to render what service or protection is bought or owed, as exposed by their absence today."

"Nonsense." Drowon exclaimed. "For, there are still Dragons within their ranks, and Dragons are not oath-breakers. There is, no doubt, either some manner of foul trouble keeping them from coming to our aid, or they, along with us, were taken completely unaware by this assault. We must be patient with them, for to continue in service to the people, they have long endured the reign of a despot. After such trials, they would not now forsake their sworn duty. Young Malok, we shall send a messenger from among us to the Paladins. You need not worry about this, for you have well earned a reprieve from such tasks. We must go now, lest the enemy regroup."

With that and another trumpeting roar signaling the ongoing battle to resume, the free Dragons all took off, like a whirlwind, toward the fires further South, shooting out their own streams of bright incendiaries as they fought enemies all along the way.

The young Human lord bade Malok and Shar thanks and farewell, and he then mounted his horse and rode off, along with all his knights, to the lingering, aforementioned, responsibilities of caring for his people. Thus, Malok and Shar were left alone in a field strewn with carnage.

"So much for our break." Shar quipped, as they took off into the sky, for to leave from such a gruesome place as this battlefield.

They resumed their Northwesterly course, as before, assuming that during the hours of fighting, the Bright Dragoness had not changed her path, yet as they flew on but a little way from the field of battle, they could see that the free Dragons had not quite exterminated the Dark Horde's presence from these lands. By their assault, the Goblins and Trolls had, indeed, been swept far and wide across the plains of the Human Realm, but they were still causing destruction in any place to which they had scampered. Their little broken packs of survivors were still attempting to sack and murder, burning down any isolated homes they came across, attempting to slay any lone Humans they found, but these small groups of villains could do little but harass the villages and annoy the towns.

The Humans had, at last, organized and armed themselves with any tool or weapon they could find to help drive off the barbarous invaders, and even now, many other lords less local than Athard, had arrived with their knights and other soldiers. However horrible the damage and loss of life, it was still inspiring to see the ingenious and spirited people all come together for the defense of their homes and the common good; left far behind were their everyday squabbles and disputes, as they united against doom from their vile attackers.

"They shall soon have this rabble routed," Shar contemplated. "Allowing us a chance to rest. In fact, that grove of trees looks like a good spot to spend the night."

It was a large strand of pine, the first they had seen since they crossed over the Northern Mountains, for as they had been traveling most recently, further South, they had only encountered the single conifers growing, almost out of place, among the generally deciduous forests.

"I suppose we have earned it." Replied Malok as he began his descent to the ground.

However, he began to notice the disturbing scene about this pine wood, for just down a short, soft incline from the grove, there was a ruined town, burnt to ash, apparently another victim of the invasion Two dead bodies, both Trolls, were lying in the tall grass where he did land, and many others were strewn about the town and the fields beyond.

"There was a scuffle here too." Malok exclaimed as they investigated about the area heading down into the burnt town's remains.

"Great, we go from one open graveyard to another, such an unpleasant country." Shar muttered as he hopped down from his friend's shoulders. "Such a nice place to lay our heads, right beside some severed ones and their disemboweled bodies. Too bad the townsfolk are not still about, for I would like to get a look at the stalwart people who did in these Trolls so neatly."

"It was not the Humans of this village, but Dragons who did this. See the particular scorch marks on the ground; only Dragon-fire burns the soil that way." Malok explained as he touched the burnt earth.

"Then, who was it that made all these expert sword cuts?" Shar antagonized, for he had noticed those immediately, being himself learned with a blade.

"Perhaps, it was a couple of Paladins, but that would be strange too, since they surely would have joined in the battle further South if they had been out here already fighting." Malok guessed.

"Well, in any case, we cannot sleep here tonight with all these corpses about." Shar spoke, shivering just thinking about such a gruesome situation.

"What, are you afraid of the dead? Shall they rise again to feast on your flesh and gnaw your bones?" Malok teased, but Shar was, indeed, frightened unto such effect.

"Speak not of such things." The Serpen king hissed, as he returned unto his friend so that they might be quickly leaving, but as he did so, he stepped in something gooey and viscous, altogether disgusting. "Ah, what is this, some Goblin's guts?" He shouted, adding a few curses.

Malok could see that it was no such thing, though still most unpleasant, for it was a thick oily liquid, like tar, but more slimy than sticky. It had not originated from any dead body, which Shar was most grateful to learn, but had rather leaked from a larger pool of the same goo which had clung to the rafters of one charred house.

"Perhaps, it is some residue from the fire, as if some substance or foodstuffs the Humans made had been consumed to a point where it is no longer recognizable." Malok posed, but this mystery was just as unsolvable as the one before.

"Whatever it is, I shall want water with which to wash it off. Let us go find some." Shar pouted, not at all enjoying his new footwear.

"I could just breathe fire to cleanse it from you." Malok joked.

"And, char to ash my whole leg with it? I think not, and I am done playing today. Just help get this off my foot and find a sleeping spot without dead bodies. Thank you!" Grumbled Shar as he hopped back upon his fiend's shoulder.

"Just keep that goo off of me." Malok exclaimed, only partially in jest.

"Why? You can just burn it off." Spake Shar, getting in one last jab.

Chapter 29

It was the Dark Hunters again, the fiendish servants of the Dark One, and this time they came flying through the air upon some hellish creature. All black, draped in shadow, these beasts soared effortlessly, gliding through the air like a fish through water. Their wide, toothless maws, upon stunted, neckless heads, gaped wide, while their flat bodies, made mostly of their wings, caught the wind and pushed it past their whip-like tails. They had no arms, no legs, no eyes; they were horrific to behold, unnatural abominations bred for only two purposes, one of which was immediately obvious.

They were very competent fliers, now closing in fast upon the Dragons until they were right above them, flying so near that Feldara was tempted to reach up and bite at them. Their second quality was revealed only when, at the command of their wicked riders, a pair of the creatures folded their wings over each of their targets, pressing down against the two Dragons' wings with their own thick, fleshy folds. Their underbellies were so sticky and hampering of her flying, that Feldara found she could not possibly fight against them and stay in the air at the same time, for with their ensnaring appendages, these things had been designed to subdue Dragons.

Seeing her distress, Anur was already busy with trying to pry loose the nasty animal with one of his swords, but even as he did so, the Dark Hunter that rode upon it dismounted onto Feldara's back and began fighting with him. They two fought with swords upon Feldara's back, even as she fought against the entangling abomination and with gravity's indomitable pull, but it was a losing battle for them all.

Try as she might to stay aloft, Feldara gradually descended lower and lower until she suddenly crashed right into the top of a taller oak tree. Both Anur and the Dark Hunter were flung from off her back, yet still the viscous grasp of the flying monster held fast Feldara's wings. Even when they both slammed into the ground below with enough force to knock her unconscious, it did not let go.

It was only a few moments later that she came to, her head throbbing as though a hammer were pounding from within her skull, like a Dworvish miner trying to chisel their way through rock. As slowly the world permeated through the fading black fog of her previous incapacitation, she found the horrible animal still stuck upon her, having wrapped itself even more tightly against her body, even to the point of restricting her breathing.

She reached back and tore at it with her teeth and the claws of her hands, furious that it had caused her to fall from the sky, and it bled dark and slimy excretions all over her. Still it held onto her as she ripped it to shreds, never once uttering a sound or even wincing in pain. At last, when there lay more disgusting mess of creature on the ground about her than on her own back, was the vise-grip of its wings released and Feldara was free of it- all but the smell, for she was drenched with its foul blood and mucous.

She slowly rose, still faint from her concussive blackout, and checked herself for injury, of which she found none. She next tried to wipe off the creature's filth, but with her rubbing, she found it only to be smearing and not so easily removed. It held onto her every bit as well as had its owner.

"Anur!" She called out, worrying for his well being, for though the squishy body of the winged beast had broken most of her own fall, he had been thrown through the air at great speed and height.

There was no response, none but the musical chorus of nocturnal insects and frogs, for they had landed in a marshy area surrounding a slowly flowing creek. With the night now in its fullness, she began earnestly searching about for him in the dense thickets of cattails, for under the shadow of midnight, she began to fear a Dark Hunter lurked behind every tall bush and willow bough.

Though she thoroughly scanned the area about, Feldara found no trace of her mentor, and she surmised that he must have been flung farther from her than first assumed, as neither he nor any Dark Hunters were nearby.

Roaring and the whooshing burst of Dragon-fire in the sky above her head, reminded her that Calidon still battled his assailants, for having with fiery breath dispensed of the other monster attempting to forcefully ground him, he now retaliated against the remaining Dark Hunters, diving, rolling, and otherwise dodging in the fierce yet graceful dance of aerial combat.

Though it gave her some assurance that she was not yet alone in this conflict, Feldara was still much too woozy from her fall to join so soon with him in skyward battle, and most importantly, she still had yet to find Anur. She began plodding along the bank of the creek, heading in the direction inertia would have propelled him, but Anur she did not find.

She began to hear noises that stuck out against the clamor of nature's usual nighttime symphony, the scuffing of loam and leaf, or the snapping of a twig or two, but so faint and far between and so cloaked by the din of other natural noises were these occurrence that, though she became ever more timorous, she tried to dismiss them as only her imagining. She chose further discretion, opting for more stealthy and reserved approach to her searching. Like a great cat, she slunk off into the tall grasses by the water's edge, silently continuing her hunt for Anur, hoping that he was well, but not now daring to call out for him, lest she draw more unwanted attention.

Eventually, she came to a large bend in the creek where the wide turn had formed a large pool surrounded by an expanse of bank. The bank itself was of the same worn stones which had once also been part of the creek bed, now displaced by time, flood and drought, and the waters ever wandering course. Around this pool, with its extended stony bank, was a clearing where the trees and brush had not come so far as to the water's edge, but had stayed at a distance, for the bed of stones blocking their encroachment. Here the faint silvery light of the moon shone down against the water's surface, diverging in refracted sheen, revealing all within the clearing, including several dark figures emerging from the shadows on the far side.

One of them raised his hand, as if in greeting, certainly indicating that they had spotted her, even though she was doing her absolute best in trying to sneak about. She already knew who they were, even from this distance being unable to fully make out their appearance. It was the Dark Hunters, and they offered no such niceties as greetings. They had only intended to get her attention, call her over to make parlay or mischief of some kind, and reluctantly, growling with frustration and enmity the whole while, she strode over to meet them.

Any other time, she would have just flown away, seeing who they were and that they had apparently lost all but one of their winged mounts, but she could not do so now, as she had also seen their captive, whom they dragged out into the open alongside themselves to be clearly seen by her. Revelation came, too late now that she had been noticed, that she had again fallen into another of their foes' inexplicably well organized, almost clairvoyant, traps, for somehow, they had caught Calidon. Apparently having lost the aerial conflict, he had been knocked unconscious and tightly wrapped up in the folds of the very last of their mounts' wings, and due to his comatose state rendering him incapable of freeing himself or fighting back, he was a second time to be used against her, now as a hostage.

"Come here, Dragoness!" Shouted one of the Dark Hunters, causing Feldara to growl all the louder. "You can see that we have captured your friend. Come quietly, without struggle, and we may even kill him quickly."

As much as Feldara hated to submit to these devils, she could see no other alternative, for to combat them now would be to risk the life of her friend, her family. So she thought of Calidon, if Anur was her father, the kind red male was her dearest brother. Anxiety rose within her soul like bile in the throat, as she strode over to just the very opposite shore of the creek from the Dark Hunters, and she whispered a silent prayer, that everything should turn out alright in the end. At the first, she tried negotiating with the vile men, hoping to buy enough time for figuring some way to avoid their snare or devising a counterattack, and free her companion.

"If I come with you, you must promise to let him live and set him free right away." Feldara haggled, but they were not biting any lures. They knew they had the upper-hand.

"You are a little too bossy for one without anything to bargain," The Dark Hunter mocked, evoking malicious chuckling from his comrades, though he himself did not laugh at all. "I am done playing, for you have proved most trying a quarry. You evaded capture in the Aelven realm, then slew our brothers in the North, and somehow you even managed to hide from the Kragon's eye for a little while. Yes, very clever you are, but we have had enough of you and your tricks."

The Dark Hunter raised a new weapon, not a sword, but a small crooked dagger, rusted and with nasty nicks and splintering all over, for he fully intended to gruesomely murder Calidon with this horrible Black-iron knife. Feldara was speechless, at a loss of thought and word; nothing was coming to mind, no plan, not any spell, or any other course of action. She was paralyzed with fear, for no matter what she did now, one of her most beloved friends in the whole world was going to die, and she would be the cause of it.

No one could offer her any help or advice, for Anur was nowhere in sight, and Calidon was in so futile a position that he may as well have been snoring.

"This one dies slowly, now that you have so tried our patience with your insolence!" Shouted the Dark Hunter, but his blade never fell.

All of a sudden, there was a squeal from somewhere off to Feldara's right; it silenced the Dark Hunter, stayed his hand. He and his men all turned to face whatever had caused such noise, and for at least a moment, the fiends were at a loss, completely dumbfounded. They neither anticipated nor prepared for any such interference, and only after more shouting and screaming had erupted from that side of the clearing did they react at all.

"You four, go find out what that was." Eventually shouted the Dark Hunter after he came to his senses, for he, the one with the crooked dagger, was apparently their new captain.

The dispatched men sneaked off into the cover of the undergrowth's shadow, and nothing more was seen or heard from either those four or any other thing from that direction.

"Now, where were we?" Asked the Dark Hunter captain, as satisfied with his level of response, he returned to his manipulations and gruesomely hopeful execution, but he never got the chance to again threaten Feldara or his other prisoner.

As he again raised his hand to strike her dear brother, the emotion that had been rising within Feldara reached its peak. All the stress and anxiety, the wrath and rage, even the fear and sadness came to a breaking point and boiled over. She screamed out against Calidon's executioner, of defiance and anger and the desire to save her beloved friend, and with that groaning roar, she released all of it. Something popped within her chest, bursting through a sphincter that before had sealed away what was inside her, and an intense heat poured from thence, burning up through her throat.

In that same split-second, an explosion of flame blasted forth from her mouth, instantly consuming the Dark Hunter, completely incinerating him and his two remaining companions, and from there it spread out, blanketing all the far bank in hottest Dragon-fire, covering Calidon in warmth and melting away his fleshy prison. Almost as soon as it had happened, the tongue of fire dissipated, as the gasses needed to create the flame had so quickly spewed from her, as yet untried, second lungs.

Feldara could hardly believe what had happened; she had breathed fire!

Her joy was short-lived, for now that their primary snare had failed, the Dark Hunters were forced to spring the rest of their trap. They came forth from the shadows were they had been waiting, for the whole clearing had, indeed, been surrounded by them, except for the extreme right-hand side whence had come the wailing from before. They were still very many in number, and they now all came charging inward, heading straight for Feldara.

However, she was truly not alone, not in this fight. She would have been easily overwhelmed, completely overpowered by the mob of formidable adversaries, but that the cause of the aforementioned distraction and ruckus from the right side of the glade then revealed itself; it was none other than Anur for whom she had been searching. Like her, he had almost stumbled into the same snare, but that by good fortune and he not being the intended target, it had not yet closed about him. Being on the outside of their encircling tactic, he had been able to surprise the foes on the side nearest him and thus break their ring. He now cut through the ranks of the black robed devils, shouting as if he too had the ferocity of a Dragon, and no one could keep him from joining with his beloved Dragoness.

The small glade erupted with warfare, and the little brook ran crimson with blood and bodies, as Anur and Feldara battled against their fell enemies. She poured forth flame in every direction, in between fiery breaths, swiping with her claws and biting with her teeth, becoming a veritable whirlwind of death-dealing Dragoness; all the while, Anur wielded his favorite short sword and another blade, a long, straight dirk, with unparalleled martial skill.

The tide of the battle would certainly still have turned in favor of the Dark Hunters, for they were many. Their numbers seemed endless, as they came pouring into the clearing from the wooded thickets upon all sides, as they again closed all around their prey.

The Dark Hunters were fell warriors, not at all incompetent. They evaded Feldara's claws and teeth and shielded themselves from her fire-breath with their dark magic, and they were every bit the equals of Anur's swordsmanship. They even began to strategize against the Dragon, summoning long spears into their hands, for to keep further out of the reach of her claws and teeth, and using bows with Black-iron tipped arrows.

Just when it seemed that there would be no hope for victory, no matter how fiercely Anur or Feldara fought, there was another disturbance outside the enemy's ranks, for it was then that other unexpected allies came bursting forth from their own place of hiding. With another flash of explosive fiery breath a strong, yet lean, black Dragon, almost invisible against the night sky, along with his companion, a creature the like of which Feldara had never seen before, also entered the fray.

Her saviors on the other side of the creek fought through the Dark Hunter's ranks until they were also alongside her. So ferociously and skillfully did they struggle, that the night-black colored Dragon seemed even more a destructive, rage driven force than she, and his companion with his extremely slender and agile body-type allowing him to roll and duck away and into strikes like a Human opponent never could, and with his smaller, quicker armament, a neatly curved sickle-sword, was as much a match of the Dark Hunters' blade wielding as Anur.

Together, they four combated the foul hunters for more than an hour, giving much punishment and receiving only a little. The Dragons fared the worse, being larger targets than the others, and they became covered from head to toe with arrow shafts. Thankfully, no eyes were put out, as was intended by the archers, for the Dragons would spin and dodge, always moving, to avoid the dreaded blinding. The barbed tips did only bury themselves shallowly within their thick, scaly hides, making them appear as some giant pincushions and angering them against the sting of the darts. Anur and the lanky companion of the black Dragon did then focus upon these sharpshooters, and they broke through the ranks of encroaching swordsmen to rush upon the bowmen and slay them. Such fierce skillful fighters were they, that in so doing, not one of their foes' blades touched them, yet was many a close shaving avoided. Their opponents were, indeed, terrible, more skilled than nigh any other enemy, but with their archers dead, the Dark Hunters lost any hope of easily disabling the Dragons. With only swordsmen left to fight two fire-breathing death dealers and a couple of superior blade-masters, the black-robed men turned to more arcane tactics; using magic, they now came at the heroes.

Flashes of green, red, and blue light awakened the night sky, as the Dark Hunters displayed their uncanny prowess in the unnatural power with blasts of force and fire, lightning, and other energies. Only Anur was skillful enough to combat them effectively in this way, for truly, he had his training in magic with the Order of Masters. He shielded all the others with strong defensive warding, and even retaliated with caustic projectiles of his own. Feldara, with her limited knowledge, could only attempt to disrupt their spell casting with blinding flashes of light and some few other effects, while the black Dragon and his lanky companion could only look upon the proceedings with an expression mixing fascination with horror.

It was when the Dark Hunters began to combine their physical attacks with these magical ones that the strange comrades again found something to do, for with sword and spell used in collaboration the battle came to its last intense forays, as the Dark Hunters used every last trick and tactic in their arsenal.

Finally, when it seemed that the heroes would tire and be overcome only by the superior numbers of their assailants, the Dark Hunters' were all slain except but for the last two of their number, and this remaining pair, realizing the futility of their situation, fled on foot into the darkness, even as the third to last of their brethren was struck by Anur's sword and fell to the ground.

The stillness and hush of night returned immediately to the corpse choked brook and its floodplain, a stark contrast to the previous clamoring of war. The victors then just stood there for a while, able to accomplish nothing other than panting, resting, calming from their adrenaline rush and blood-lust, recovering from the shock and exertion of battle. No one spoke, no sound was made but for Feldara and her strange rescuer Dragon slowly plucking out the arrows from their scales and dropping their clattering shafts and tips upon the stones and, of course, the steady babbling of the reddened brook, which now seemed a raging torrent compared to the profound quiet, yet after only a short while of this post-storm calm, the strange companion of the black Dragon broke the silence.

"If I have not yet earned my rest, just kill me now, for I am too tired to live any longer." He quipped, and he slumped to the ground, unharmed but quite ready to sleep for a day and a half.

His lightheartedness calmed them all, even causing Feldara a slight smile at his antics. While Anur joined the black Dragon's comrade, sitting upon the ground, Feldara strode over to her Draconic rescuer, and though she knew they had never before met, something about his visage, his bearing seemed almost too familiar, like a distant relative or a long lost friend. Little could she yet know that he felt toward her much the same, only stronger, for he had truly seen and long been in pursuit of her.

"I must thank you for saving our lives. Without your ambush, we would have succumbed to theirs." Feldara gratefully expressed, giving her best attempt at a formal, Draconic, bow.

The black Dragon reciprocated every bit as clumsily as Feldara imagined she had done. "You are most welcome. I could not just stand by, or rather, sleep by, and let these evil men have their way." Said he, as they both sat down and began pulling out the arrows still stuck in their hides. "I am Malok; may I ask your name?" He inquired, though her name meant not as much to him as her appearance, for he had recognized her as soon as he had spotted her, even among the dense tree cover whence earlier he had started the surprise attack.

"I am Feldara." She replied, and having finished with all her stuck arrows, she began helping Malok dislodge the last of his own. "And, very well met, might I add. Who is your friend, and what manner of creature is he?" She asked, for she, only slightly uncomfortably, began to notice and wonder at this Dragon's unrelenting stare, peculiar accent, and strange mannerisms.

"His name is Shar, and we are so close, he is more like a brother to me than friend, although a Serpen. Ours is a long story, and I would not wish to bore you with it now. We have truly come a long way from our home in the Serpen Kingdom, on a mission of utmost importance." Malok explained.

"Oh, really, what mission is that?" Feldara asked, yet truly wishing she could hear of this curious, though charming, young male's whole life story.

"I came here seeking you, Feldara." Malok plainly stated, as if such a thing should be common knowledge.

But, such a purpose was not common at all, and the revelation was entirely shocking to Feldara. She knew that the enemy of all life was hunting her, but now this comely Dragon, a slender youth about her own age, had also been looking to find her. It was more than a little disconcerting, a fact very well reflected by her confounded, open-mouthed expression.

A sudden grumbling from Calidon broke the moment and its tension, for Anur had forsaken introductions to see about the poor Dragon, who only after all the commotion had passed, awoke from his unconsciousness.

"Did we win?" He groggily asked.

Chapter 30

The remainder of that grievous night Zurthaud spent in the worst of depressive slumps, for after Serc had passed away and even the ashes of the dearly departed had immolated to complete disintegration, he had somehow, in the mental and physical numbness of deepest melancholy, stumbled into his father's personal chambers. Even though Zurthaud had not a single fond memory of these rooms, despite their exquisite furnishings and comforts, he found himself sitting on the edge of the bed, wondering why he had been allowed to be born, why he existed. Despair was the slough he sank into, a powerful gloom of depression, as over and again he regretted the beloved Dragon saving him through ultimate self-sacrifice; even his mother's selfless love he rued, that they two should die and he live.

He dwelt upon his own unworthiness to receive such gifts and wished it was rather he who could have died in their place, for the horrible thought fixed itself above all others, that were he never even born, none of the evil that had transpired over all these long, hard years would have ever happened. His father would have had no reason to hate the Dragons or even Eloigal, for his mother would still be alive, even merrily soaring together upon the back of a much less grieved Serc.

Festering in this dreadful conclusion, a profound silence filled his mind and emptiness his heart, as within himself, Zurthaud cursed the day of his own birth. A cold, blank stare was the only expression he could muster, as he brooded long upon nothing and everything, all in the darkest of woe, but as it happened, by poor fortune, his dead glaring had landed upon the open cupboard where was his father's favorite Aelven wine.

As slowly, Zurthaud realized this fact, the idea came to him that he could not overcome his sorrows any other way than by drowning them, and with sudden determination, he arose from where he sat, and snatched up the nearest bottle and a glass. He had never been one to overindulge in anything, neither meat nor spirits, but quickly, and foolishly, he downed a full goblet of the rich, velvety wine. One small glass then became two, then three, and losing sobriety, he thought to thereafter need no more smaller vessel than the whole bottle and put it straight to his lips.

Theros then found him, entering the, thankfully, Dragon-sized apartment which had been built long before Orthard's discriminatory tyranny could have prevented such. "Zurthaud!" He exclaimed somewhere between a gasp and a bellow, surprising and interrupting the Human's intentions, causing him to cough and sputter, as the drink he was about to imbibe had not quite flowed down his throat.

"What do you want?" Brusquely asked the already slightly intoxicated Zurthaud, after recovering from breathing, rather than drinking, wine.

The Dragon became greatly upset seeing his good friend indulge in booze while he too had been sorrowing, for Theros, along with everyone else who had known the elder Dragon, had loved Serc as a father. Now, not only to see Zurthaud's callous, almost selfish, indifference to any other's grief, not to mention his idleness from the massive amount of tasks still to be done for the siege's completion, but to hear the blunt, stolidity in his voice, while yet engaging in foolish pastime, enraged Theros as no word or action of Orthard ever could. For, though he cared not at all what Orthard did or said, Zurthaud's words and deeds did matter to him most of all, and this self-destructive bout accompanied by poorest, blackest attitude, cut right through his scales, unto his heart, even as had the bullet done unto Serc.

"I want you to quit acting the fool, as I see you have now been about since last I laid eyes on you. Put down that vile drink and come over to me." Quite nearly roared the fiery red Dragon, and pointing to emphasize.

It was not so much out of fear that Zurthaud hesitantly obeyed, for he knew Theros would not consider harming him. It was, rather, the Dragon had nearly entirely startled him out of the alcoholic reverie to which he had been so stupidly close to succumbing. Not since that day, sixteen years ago, upon the balcony of his hospital room, had Zurthaud been yelled at by a furious Theros, and until now, he had almost forgotten how it felt to be set upon by a Dragon's wrath. Zurthaud did oblige his angered friend, and quickly, but he did not expect what was next to come.

Theros bent his massive form over the comparatively small Human and wrapped his giant Dragon arms gently about him, holding him close in tender embrace.

"Do you think to be the only one that mourns?" Wept the Dragon, his hot tears falling in large drops upon his friend's shoulders.

Zurthaud wept then also, the numbness of before rushing out of him in a torrent of emotion, through his wet eyes, and he buried his face in the Dragon's enormous chest.

"I should not have been born at all, then none of this: my mother's death, my father's wickedness, Serc's murder- none of it would have ever happened." He cried, letting out into the air the despair he had bottled within this whole time.

Upon hearing this, some of the Dragon's anger returned, and he held Zurthaud out from him to stare the Human in the eye.

"Never say that, nor think that, ever again, for no one is born into the world without purpose, least of all one so noble and accomplished of valiant deeds as you." Theros boldly challenged, and then more kindly, he continued. "It was you who helped me to grieve for my fallen mate when my heart was turned only to hate. It was you who stood alone above all others against the Dark One, seeking to challenge his evil where it dwells. You rallied the true Paladins together from among the foolish and the arrogant. You will go before them still, for now more than ever, we need your strong, youthful, and courageous leadership. We need you. Besides, all those things for which you blame yourself could still have happened whether you were born or not; if not while loving and protecting you, Serc and your mother would certainly have died of something else, as that is the only certainty of life this side of the blessed realm. Perhaps, Orthard would not have fallen to such low depths of evil, but to do so, to resent all that was good in his own life, even his own son, that was his own choice, and the poorest of them."

The Dragon then just continued to hold Zurthaud close to him, until the sobbing and tears had dried from them both.

"I had come to take you to the temple for the memorial service we are holding for the Paladins who fell this day, for Serc; when I had left from there, they were preparing to start, having already finished with the majority of the siege and its duties." Theros explained after a short while had passed.

"How goes the fight? Are we almost done?" Zurthaud asked of him, recovering slowly, yet to be surely over much more time, from shouldering such depressive weight and his slight intoxication.

"We have yet to fully secure the Citadel and complete the takeover, for though the High Council and Orthard have been disposed of, locked away in the same dungeon they had stowed so many innocent men, there are still a few pockets of resistance left, mostly frightened soldiers who know not that they are to be spared upon surrender. These are clustered primarily in the gatehouses and garrisons of the outer city walls and underneath the Keep in the more isolated corners and vaults of the cavernous basement, but even the most well defended and fearfully protected of these are being taken even now, quickly and without much bloodshed, mostly thanks to Lorn and Argamon. Their knowledge of the Keep and high rank, both former and present, have proven invaluably helpful in convincing the foolish to throw down their arms." Theros explained.

"So, what happens then, after all the fighting is over and we have accomplished all for which Serc, and the rest of us, had hoped?" Zurthaud asked, more as an internal pondering than as an actual question, for the fear came upon him that upon completion of this grand task, they, and he especially, would now find themselves without purpose.

"The fight against evil and the powers of darkness is every day, in every choice we make. When this great task is done, another shall arise, and we must meet it." After pausing a moment to think, Theros wisely answered.

____

"Come, let us hasten to the temple before everyone starts wondering what is become of us."

The funeral service was, unexpectedly, the refreshing of soul that Zurthaud had needed, for though all the Paladins who had fallen that day were honored each in turn, no one in recent memory was so exultantly lauded and mourned as was Serc. The worship of the Dragons, praising The Eloigal for their beloved healer's time among them, flowed directly into the dirges and eulogies of individuals, who, one by one, came before the others gathered to speak or sing of their shared life experiences with the grand old Dragon. Reminiscent stories, tales of help and saved lives, remorseful songs of memorial, or ethereal lyric of heavenly bliss- all these poured out, almost unceasingly, from the lips of so many Paladins, all whose lives were touched in some way by the beloved doctor. So many had come together, of all kinds and crafts, all having something to say or sing, recounting and praising his kind deeds and words, his healing work as a physician, his wise leadership, and his whole life, that it was well past midnight before they all had given a testimonial, all but Zurthaud.

Their eyes now turned upon him, for they knew how the elder Dragon had so cared for him, that he had been as much as a son unto Serc. They expected him to speak, even as Theros finished the singing of a simple, yet heartfelt hymn.

Zurthaud loathed himself for the mind-dulling wine he had so foolishly guzzled before, as the service, even as glorious and profound as it had been, had hazily sped along, with clear details blurred by his alcoholic stupefaction, for though he had sobered much by now, he felt not well enough yet to speak with any eloquence.

Still, he arose and took his place at the center of the great sanctuary, upon the speakers' platform. He had no notes, no speech prepared, but he had to speak. He had to say something, not for them, the assembly, the other Paladins, but for himself, for Serc.

"We are at a great loss." He slowly began, truly feeling the blow of those words. "The best of our Order has gone from among us today, and we are left desolate without them, without him. Each of our own hearts has been torn;

we all feel the pain of this loss. No less do I, for I did not have a sire to tell me: that I was worth anything, that I could succeed; to show me how to be a person of honor, how to live in righteousness. No man gave me such kind mentoring, but a Dragon, for it was Serc who taught me that I was worthwhile, showed me by his own example and through his own tutelage. If anyone thinks highly of me, it is because of, so many others, yet the greatest of these- our beloved healer, who invested their lives into my own. Above all others, I call him father, for when I had none, he was there for me."

At this point Zurthaud had to pause, for his own tears welled in his eyes, so that he had to wipe them clear. He had to force himself to continue, through a voice strained with emotion.

"We cannot lose hope now. We cannot stop fighting. We must press onward, to the high goal, ridding our world of the very same evil that has so rent our flesh and souls, that would see the rest of all Threa be wounded, destroyed, even as we. We bleed so that one day our children, our grandchildren, may not suffer the same, that they might have the peace we could not attain. Serc truly believed that day would come. He lived for it, and he died for it. Let us honor his sacrifice, by believing in it, by living for it, and if necessary, even by dying for it."

Even a little more would Zurthaud have spoken, but that he was interrupted. An uninvited guest had crashed through the doors, startling all to turn and face who, or what had so rudely cut into such a reverential service, but it was no one they could have expected, nor chided.

A young, strikingly cobalt colored, Dragon had bolted into the sanctuary of the Dragon's temple.

"Paladins arise!" He shouted, almost roaring in a thick accent, unmistakably that of a 'wild' Dragon. "The Realm is burning!"

<><><><><>

The ash was thick on the ground, black under the blood-red sunrise, so much so that it crunched like snow under Zurthaud's feet, but so constant was the sound that, by now, he paid it little heed.

Though he and the other Paladins had quickly roused from their funereal ceremonies, last night's battle was long over by the time they had arrived. If it was to burn an expansive swath across the South and South-western quarters of the Order's realm, sacking homes and murdering their residents along the way, the Dark Horde had seemingly accomplished what it had set to do. From before the Atsar river, just West of Bythatsar, almost to the nearest reaches of the Aegan mountains to the North, had they scorched and pillaged the land.

Over this bleak desolation, had Zurthaud and his fellow Paladins flown and tramped in darkness, seeing to the dispatching of scattered units of the enemy's troops, and offering aid to the afflicted inhabitants. It was this latter task that had kept him busy the whole night through, for now that the fires had been put out, and the monsters slain, there was still left the overwhelming need of many, many thousands displaced from their homes.

Houses, farms, even whole towns, lay in blackened ruin, while all the survivors shivered in the cold dawn, at last, breaking day upon their lives' longest night, yet as much comfort as was the return of sunlight, it did nothing other than brighten the grave world about them, making visible the past horrors hidden in discretion by the dark. The crunching of the ash did not bother Zurthaud much anymore; it was the bodies, being so many that everywhere he turned they could be seen that upset him.

For the sheer number of them, the people had forgone the usual funeral ceremonies, and under the constant droning prayers of local priests, the families cast their loved ones into piles, already burning from the pyre set ablaze for others, or having already mourned their eyes dry, left them in ordered rows all about to await their cremation. Men, women, and children had all been slaughtered indiscriminately, gruesomely. Past all these Zurthaud strode, as quickly as he could, to their newly established emergency forward base, which lay just outside the North gates of Bythatsar's city.

Unto here were flocking all the refugees of this atrocious calamity, for Bythatsar was a large and secure city. It, along with all the other larger and walled towns, had survived mostly unassailed, and though there were two other cities near this quadrant of the Order's Realm, Grynwood and Plainskeep, to the people, this place alone represented hope and safety, as in ages past, it had never once fallen to the Dark Hordes continuous attacks.

Though they were welcomed into the burgeoning refugee camp, the throngs had made it hard for anyone to move about quickly, and as he had become separated from Theros and his flying transportation by many relief duties, Zurthaud had to push through them to get to the meeting he was to attend. As he passed through the crowds, whisperings of, "Where were they in the dark hours of the night?" and, "Why could they not have come sooner, then my family would still live?" and, "Why did they not help us?" filtered in from every side, past all the shouting, commotion, and conversing going on about him, and these inquiries truly stung, even as the smoldering wisps did his eyes and nose.

He had to bear them, all the night and through this morning, for they spoke truth. And, it was the truthfulness that hurt him most, for he had known a guard on the border wall was needed, just as he should have expected some kind of assault from the Shadow Lands, now that the Oder was divided, at its weakest.

He swallowed this gloom, truthful though it was, in bitterness, naming it another of his own personal failures, and again he wished that another had been in his place at this hour, perhaps, that he had never been born at all.

Yet, he eventually made his way into the center of the camp, where were the tents assigned for the meeting of officers of the Order, leaders of the communities, and noblemen. Here and now, they had agreed to gather, for to make plans and preparation on how to abate this crisis. Even as his boots ceased from the ashen crunching, to the clacking of wooden boards, so placed to keep down the sloughing of mud, he could hear the raised voices, and even more so he wished not to have these burdens of responsibility placed upon him, to be so well-liked, notable, or even needed, that he be called to attend these festivals of argument. His compassion for the suffering masses about him alone compelled him to endure, and to the salute of the door guards, he lifted the flaps and entered, even as the shouting reached a peak.

Zurthaud glanced around the tent, as he entered, to see who were among the many occupants; the seven greater lords of the Human Realm each representing their respective territories of North, North-west, North-east, West, East, South-west, and South-east. The lord of the Southern province would have also been present, but for that he had not been heard from in months, and his lands on the far side of the Atsar were, due to frequent raids, no longer populated. Also here gathered were the mayors of each large city, among which were Bythatsar, Grynwood, Plainskeep, Richmont, Bestford, Muthport, and, of course, Doraegonoran.

These noblemen were all situated around a small wooden table at the center of the tent, along with Lorn; Galrag and Theros were also present, but they could not fit within, so that they sat off to one side of the tent, of which the whole fabric had been rolled up so that they could see within and participate without much more difficulty.

"We have paid tribute to your coffers all our lives, and our fathers', and our father's fathers', but the night grew thick about us and the enemy assailed us. They burned our fields and homes; they slew our children and loved ones. We cried out for help, but you did not come. The 'Paladins' were nowhere to be seen!" Yelled a fair-haired nobleman, the young lord of the South-western province, who still wore most of his battle-charred steel armor. "Less like Paladins, more like dogs you are!" He shouted pointing his finger at a scowling Lorn.

"Watch your tongue, Human, for my teeth care not what noble house from which you descended." Growled Theros, threateningly leaning his head just within the tent.

"Peace, my lord, I have no qualms with the Dragons, for your people did give us aid when the night was blackest and all hope seemed lost. From their mountain homes far to the North, they came to repay the enemy with fire, even as they had so dealt to us." Spake he, gesticulating reassuringly, though not lowering his enraged tone of voice that cracked emphatically with his youth. "I speak only of the fat sow Orthard, and his ilk, his bastard son, and all the cackle of crows that laughingly flock to his folly."

Whether or not Zurthaud had just arrived to hear this latest of insults, Theros would then have heard no more of this talk, but Zurthaud strode over to stand by his friend and held out his hand to stay the Dragon from action, as all around hushed in anticipation of his response.

However, he had no retort for the hurtful, yet mostly truthful, words. He stared down the accuser, eyes bleary and sallow with lack of rest and spent grieving, for he had witnessed all the death and destruction that had been wrought upon these poor souls.

"What is your name, young lord?" Zurthaud calmly asked, for surely, this man was even his younger by several years.

"I am Athard, son of Lothard, lord of the South-western province." Replied the hot-blooded nobleman, defiantly, proudly, raising his chin.

Zurthaud thought about all the ways he could bring this haughty boy down a few pegs from his high perch, but he did none of those. Instead, he gave him a low bow, respectful and apologetic. "Lord Athard, you have every right to speak such words to us; we have failed you and your people. For all this suffering and devastation, which we did naught to prevent or avert, I am truly sorry. " Said he.

For a moment, the young lord stood there clenching his jaw in surprise, and the group about showed no less shock by their continued silence. They had all expected, at least, a little retaliation.

"Your apologies do not put shelter over our heads; they will not feed us today, nor grow enough crops to see us through the winter." Lord Athard insistently argued, at last finding words and faults again.

"That is why we are here gathered," Calmly replied Zurthaud, as he ended his obeisance, "To see about making amends for our lacking protection, to make reparation through supplying the needs of the afflicted, to rebuild all that was destroyed. We only need make plan and preparation, to figure the amount of provisions and shelters we shall need, for to relieve those who are sorely affected. I realize that there can be no excuse for our absence when we swore our service and collected payment for it, but I offer this compensation, in the hope that your trust might be restored when we prove ourselves worthy of it again."

All fell silent again, at least, those not of the Order, for not in many decades had they heard of the Paladins offering such aid to the people.

"Surely, Lord Orthard seeks to turn this calamity into profit, for with this 'assistance' you speak of, we shall be bought, be made his debtors forever." Disbelievingly spoke the young nobleman.

"The vile Orthard no longer holds any position within the Order." Informed Galrag. "He has been deposed, arrested for crimes against the free people, not the least of which were the excessive tributes he levied. We ask for nothing in return; we freely open our storehouses to the poor, as in the days of old."

"Well that is good news, for a long while, I thought we would be paying to put up all of Athard's people." Interrupted Fazil, the mayor of Bythatsar, a rather large, round, grandly mustachioed, old man, long past service in any military fashion; though never was he as accustomed to the blade as commerce, or gormandizing.

Despite sour glaring from the young Athard, the comment did seem to ease some of the tension amongst those gathered, enough that they again felt free to speak plainly.

"If Orthard is no longer Head Consul, who leads the Order now?" Slyly questioned a tall, lean scarecrow of a man, Rothard, lord of the South-eastern province and Athard's older half-brother.

Zurthaud had no answer for this, neither did Theros or Lorn, so that Galrag spoke again.

"Our internal matters shall be handled by our own methods. Indeed, there is no excuse for what happened, but let it be known that we did not forsake our duties for lack of leadership. Truly, we were in mourning for fallen comrades, even as many among your own people do now grieve, and that is the only reason we were taken off-guard." He discreetly answered.

The elder Dragon knew that already rumor of the true Paladins' coup had reached these lords' ears, and they were now only asking about such things to confirm their own suspicions and, perhaps, to craftily pry free any further, yet unheard, bits of knowledge.

Who was to now lead the Order, was a question of great importance to them, whether he were a disreputable or honorable man, for the Lord Consul played such a critical role in their governance. Under the negligent, tyrannical leadership of Orthard the realm of Humans had withered in both power and prosperity, and if another man like him were to rule, they would no doubt be considering some form of revolt of their own. Yet, if a good, sensible man were to step up, there would be no need for such troublesome action.

It was then that, Kellam, the mayor of Doraegonoran chose to speak out. A large, strong man of few words yet much martial and political skill, he was highly respected by the other lords, not only for the importance of his city, but also for his own personal character and deeds.

"I know that in the past, if the Paladins said that they would do something, they did it. With the former Consul Orthard gone, I have much hope they will return to their former trustworthiness." Spake he in favor of the Paladins, for being mayor of the city where long Orthard had ruled, he more than any other nobleman knew how dreadful the situation had become, and how it now again became optimistic.

"In any case, we have already offered our aid, to bicker over that any longer is but a waste of time and of no help to the people you claim to represent." Lorn added, and a little hotly, for he had been at the brunt of Athard's combative accusations until Zurthaud had arrived. "I suggest you start counting your needs, putting them all down in numbers, so that we can accurately know what and how much to start bringing forth from our stores and treasury. Since Athard's lands and people were the most afflicted, I propose we begin with there, with the other lords pitching in to help relieve any immediate needs, and we shall repay you all in due time. All in favor of said course of action, raise your right hand and speak 'yea'."

Every one of them raised a hand; all the lords and officials spoke 'yea'. The motion passed, for it was the only reasonable response.

"Then this meeting is adjourned. As discussed, bring all your expenditure, in writing, back to this same place to be approved, counted, and repaid." Lorn quickly concluded, and he stormed out from the tent, clearly not having enjoyed the uselessness of the arguing and finger-pointing that had taken place.

Zurthaud then turned toward Theros, but he and Galrag were already heading off toward the epicenter of the destruction, for all the Dragons, both 'wild' and Paladin, were still searching afar for survivors among the wreckage of burnt-out structures. One by one, all the others also exited, leaving Zurthaud by himself in the tent, but he too did not linger there very long. There was so much work to be done.

Chapter 31

The morning after the Dark Hunters' attack was more cheerful than Feldara could have hoped, for the sun shone brightly, though not warmly. The night had been chill, and after they had moved a good distance away from the site of where their foes had so thickly been slain, back up out of the waterway's basin and upon one of the many, scattered open glades, they became quite cold, especially after their battle warmed blood started to cool. So much did they shiver that, at last Anur had to risk lighting a fire, or rather, let Feldara light the pile of wood he had gathered. For, now that she had gained the uniquely Draconic ability, she insisted upon herself using it each and every time it was required.

Even in this dismal temperature, she found rest quite easily; perhaps, it was due to the relief from being so pursued by her foes, or maybe the stalwart presence of, not one, but two worthy Dragon males sleeping close beside her. In any case, she had woken fully refreshed and ready to greet the brisk morning air; not so the rest of her party.

Anur was stiff and sore from all the fighting, and made that fact known to all, though unintentionally, by grunting each time he bent or moved excessively, while Malok's companion, Shar, had no restraint in complaining about his lack of sleep, food, and, due to his cold-blooded Serpen body, the overtly bothersome weather. Calidon was also abnormally peeved about something yet unmentioned; though Feldara had her guess that it had something to do about his helpless, and useless, state during last night's battle.

The only person who seemed at all to be even slightly attuned to Feldara's happier mood was Malok, but he did not express it with much talk or laughter, unlike Feldara who was busy recounting her deeds from last night to a less than enthusiastic Calidon. He seemed content with only gazing upon her, as if the sun, moon, and stars paled in beauty compared with her.

Truly, he had not gotten around to explaining the "why" of his mission to seek her out, and though Feldara was curious to find this out, she dared not ask any more about it. Herself, she wished rather not to know, or at least, let Malok explain for himself, but it seemed he had himself forgotten about such details with the passing of the night, that is, until she volunteered to go hunting for their breakfast.

"Let me go with you." Malok insisted, rising from where he sat upon the frost wettened grass.

Calidon offered a grimace, but did not say anything, not even to also volunteer his help. Anur was too sore to be goaded into riding upon Feldara's back, but he made himself busy in other ways, like fetching water to boil, in his helmet, for a crude tea of local herbs, rather than flat-out refuse to go. Shar only huddled under a blanket and made request for something other than deer, for he had become sick of the taste of venison since he had arrived in the Order's Realm- which was very abundant with them.

So, it was that they two took off together into the nipping wind, for to seek their morning meal.

It was only after they caught their last quarry and were taking a moments rest upon the ground, for to skin and bleed their deer- for which they had planned a half-hearted apology to Shar- that Malok broke the quiet of the still morning, for they had hunted mostly in silence.

"You must be wondering why I have been searching for you." He stated, as he finished licking clean his claws from the butchering.

"I must admit, I was most perplexed by that conversation last night; though, we seemed to be distracted from the conclusion." Feldara replied, but then, with a sly grin she added. "Let me guess; is it because I am the 'Light Bringer', the destroyer of darkness, and the bane of shadows."

But, Malok shook his head "No".

"Well that is a relief, because, I have no desire to be such things. At one time, I just wanted to see the world, and now, I just want a safe place to call home. I am tired of being hunted and fighting a war that I want no part in." She admitted, glowering even thinking that the only reason he had come was to find her for the Order to use as a weapon, even against such a horrible foe and for such righteous cause.

"It is no use struggling against your destiny." Malok offered. "One way or another, it will find you, whether or not you are prepared to meet it."

This only provoked more scowling from Feldara, mostly because she knew he was right, speaking with wisdom beyond his years, but noticing her change of visage, Malok continued.

"The real reason I have been seeking for you is much more personal than that." He disclosed, and suddenly becoming more bashful, he began s wiping his claws on the grass rather than speaking.

"Go on, tell me why." Feldara insisted, becoming impatient and irritable after being reminded of her fate.

With a sigh Malok revealed his heart, bared it unwaveringly before her. "I have been dreaming of you my whole life. As you lived and grew, from when I was about ten years of age until now, I have been watching you from afar in my nighttime visions. I saw, in one of these visions, that you were being attacked, and I had come to rescue you from the darkness. Yet, more than that, I feel as if I have known you all this while, as if you were very close, very dear to me, and I have been wanting to meet you in person ever since I fist laid my dreaming eyes upon you." He explained, sheepishly staring at the ground and absentmindedly scratching the back of his head.

For a moment, Feldara did not know what to say, but her characteristically cynical tongue overtook her heart in the race to get words out of her mouth.

"Well I hope to have met your expectations. Do you, indeed, like what you have dreamed about for so long? Or, do you have such honey tongue for all the other Dragonesses you meet." She laughingly mocked. "Have any of them actually fallen for that same tawdry, saccharine love story, or do you make up new ones as you go."

"It is the truth I speak, not a tale, and you are but the second Dragoness I have ever met." He indignantly countered. "Forget I ever said anything." Malok snorted, and taking his two of the four deer they had caught, he bolted off into the air, leaving Feldara to feel quite foolish on the ground below.

Inwardly Feldara cursed herself, for little too late, she realized that he had been honest and open, sincere and not desiring anything more from her than an empathetically listening ear.

With a sigh she hastily grabbed up her two deer, though she had not been so quick as he to have fully dressed them by now, and took off after Malok. It was difficult flying to make pace with him now after he had been so scorned, but when she eventually caught up, she glided in close, for to be heard over the wind.

"Forgive me; I misspoke." She apologized. "Sometimes my wagging tongue gets the better of me and ends in hurting those I care about. Truly, I am sorry for what I said, for making fun of you."

Malok only nodded, for he had been sore wounded that Feldara had ridiculed him for what had so long been his soul's fixation. Still, he did forgive her, as he was not one to hold grudges, and came to the realization that she was, indeed, not some fairy-tale individual who would always understand and accept him, but rather her own person with her own thoughts and character.

"All I meant to convey was how hard it is for me to believe that someone could do such things as know another, and so deeply, just through their dreaming. It does seem rather strange when I repeat it for your own hearing, does it not, that you have been spying upon me my whole life long?" She pressed, sincerely trying to heal the blow she had dealt his heart while explaining her blunt, yet expected, reaction.

"Yes, it is most strange." Malok conceded. "I cannot explain how unsettling it is to see your own body while floating through a dream, and I do understand your shock upon hearing of my watchfulness. Believe me, it was unintentional, mostly, unavoidable, as I have yet to master this strange ability." He explained; then becoming more abashed, he added. "Of course, I did not mean to seem flirtatious or expectant of such reciprocation, which would have been improper having just met you, er, having just met you in person, that is."

"Well, I shall accept your explanation, since you did receive my apology." Feldara replied, fully regretting she had so forcefully quashed his inferred advances from earlier, for she did think Malok a most handsome young Dragon. "But, I hope you now realize that I am not some swooning damsel who needs or wants a chauvinistic male to swoop down and rescue me, nor do I consider your every thought and inner-working. I am a real person, and my own self, with my own thoughts and understanding."

"You have well proven that." Malok replied, mostly to himself, as he mumbled this under his breath and beyond Feldara's hearing.

They then had to cease from this conversation, for having not flown very far to locate their meal, they had returned to their camp and fellows. Soon descending to rejoin them, they divided the spoils from their hunt: a deer for each Dragon and one for both Anur and Shar to share. Calidon was still in a foul mood and would not partake of the deer Malok had caught, but took one of Feldara's for himself, which he immediately regretted for he found himself finishing her rushed, half-done skinning from earlier.

"You barely even pulled out the entrails, so that now the whole carcass stinks." Complained the unhappy male.

"I guess we two shall take your other kill, as we must roast our meat anyway." Anur offered for both himself and Shar, though not enthusiastically. Shar would then have complained also, but that even he thought Calidon had already voiced such so excessive and brilliantly.

While under other circumstances Feldara might have been upset with their objections, she was on this occasion rather satisfied to eat of another's labor, particularly Malok's.

Only a short while later, after they had all eaten their fill, Anur quickly put out the fire with kicks of sod and dirt.

"Let us depart from here, for though we fought well last night and many of our foes were slain, I still do not wish to tarry ever long upon the open plains, especially when our goal is so close at hand." Anur stated, burying the last of the smoldering embers.

"Surely, we have seen the last of those Dark Hunters." Feldara reasoned aloud.

"I would not risk your safety or any other's upon that hope." He replied.

"Yet, we are such a large party now that they should not think us so easy a target." Shar argued, for he was still sore, and bored, from all the flying they had done.

"Do you really not remember the vast army that we fought against last night?" Malok emphatically interjected.

"What army? You fought an army?" Feldara inquired, somehow causing Calidon to grumble.

"You did not hear of this?" Malok perplexedly returned, yet he continued. "The Dark Horde launched a massive invasion of the Order's Realm last night. They scorched a wide swath from the Southwestern border to, nearly, all this far way North.

"That must have been what we stumbled into earlier the other day, for we did come upon a village that had been so attacked, completely burnt to the ground, and its attackers, which we vanquished. But, I had not even considered that it had been anything more than an isolated raid. If that whole assault was just a ploy to draw you out, my point is only further validated." Gravely spoke Anur, then turning toward Feldara.

"Surely, all that was not just for me. It could not be so." Feldara falteringly queried.

The sullen frowns of her fellows conveyed their thoughts plainly, for they did not speak with words but downcast eyes. Even as they came to the truth, Feldara had long before accepted it, yet did she still wish to deny the darkness such power over her life and such dire consequences for those innocents who stood unintentionally between. She longed for the freedom of unimportance, the security of anonymity, and the peace that brought not just to herself but also to those around her. However, she had been given a gift, an ability. To what extent, she knew not, but the darkness feared her, despised and pursued her, so that somehow, she must be capable of causing it much distress, perhaps, even its destruction.

"Then, there is no alternative; we must hasten to Doraegonoran, for your own safety." Malok concluded, inciting more grumbling from Calidon.

Heavyhearted from this grim conversation, none more so than Feldara, they all arose from where they sat, and after Anur had mounted Feldara's shoulders and Shar clambered aboard Malok's, they took off into the sky once more, to complete the final stretch of their lengthy journey, that which had taken Anur and Feldara nearly a month's time.

Were it not for their detours, traveling from Lotheliel to Doraegonoran by Dragon-back would have taken only a few days, yet as so much had happened to them all at once, this whole trip seemed, at least to Feldara, as a lifetime, and their home on the little island far to the South, many leagues distant.

The miles, again, raced below them quickly, yet was there not much beauty in the scenery. The more they traveled South and east, the more ashen and ravaged places they passed over, for truly, the Dark Horde had dealt a terrible blow to the unfortunate Humans who dwelt in these lands.

It brought a great heaviness to Feldara's heart, for to see all this devastation, nearly she came to tears. She swore again within herself that if she had any measure of power, of light or otherwise, that would enable her to aid or assuage the suffering of these people, she would give her all to use it in combating the evil darkness. Yet, she had now not much time to dwell upon this, for the great city, Doraegonoran, was slowly coming into view. As she and the others of her party, aside from Malok and Shar, had as yet to see the grandness of the great walls and towers, they all eagerly looked forward unto the ever waxing form, which had but moments ago only been a darker blot against the backdrop of majestic, high, gray mountains.

Now, as they closed ever more quickly upon the vast Citadel and its surrounding metropolis, all the splendor of the great city came into focus; from its sprawling fiefs and fields of golden wheat, to each of the seven walls, from the huddle of myriad shops, crafters, merchants, and residences among these walls, to the great keep standing on a slight rise, just before the edge of the mountains, at the very far end of it all.

Feldara could not focus on any one of the many details of the marvelous city, for each little street held its own world of people and places. Rather, she had to let her eyes drink in the glorious view as a whole, a panoramic display of civilization's most inspired architectural and organizational achievements. The sight of such magnificence took her breath away, and like the others, stole her thoughts for a good moment. It was Anur who first spoke to break their silent awe.

"That great, lone, domed tower, standing within the Citadel and most near our approach, is the residence of the Order's Dragons, and the Great Temple is atop it, under the dome. Beside it stands the Keep, wherein is the High Council chambers." He explained, pointing his finger to emphasize. "Malok, you have come from here; where should we land to make our presence known and to seek refuge among the Order's ranks?"

"We should head first to the Dragon's quarter." Answered Malok, remembering all the strife of before, the coup and how the High Council and Orthard were to be deposed. "There was much conflict among the Order when lat I left, but there shall be surety of safety within the walls of the Dragon's abode."

This news brought Anur much discomfort, but he kept it hidden with his face under his darkly vizored helm. The anxious energy Feldara felt was not borne of such concerns, for she was bubbling over with excitement to see all the Dragons and the famous sights of the Order's Citadel and the city at large; even Calidon seemed to perk from his foul mood, as he too had been longing this whole journey to see these wonders and be welcomed, hopefully to joining, by the Paladins.

They skirted around the outer wall, so as not to disturb the city residents with much gusting of wind pressure from their wing beats, as they made their approach, and at last they came to hover over one of the many balconies of the Dragon's Great Temple.

They had as yet to notice their landing go unwelcomed, but Malok had not considered this, having experienced such at his last arrival, and the others in their excitement, forgot to ask such questions as, "where had all the Dragons gone?"

Quietly, they touched down, and quickly Anur removed his helm and dismounted, as did Shar also, and they all headed within the vast atrium. Before Malok had a chance to inform them of the custom, though he meant to impress his new friends by knowing something they did not, Anur first, then Feldara and Calidon, even Shar- all laved appropriately at one of the ritual basins and headed on within the great sanctuary, leaving Malok to hurry and do the same to keep up with them, for unbeknown to the young, Serpen-raised Dragon, Anur had been of the Master Order and had taught the rituals and even worshiped with Feldara from when she was old enough to understand such things. Calidon also had been taught the ways of reverence by his parents, for the "wild" Dragons were they who had initiated the practices, for to prepare the mind and cleanse the body for appropriate contact with what and Who was holy. Shar had actually forgotten all he had learned from his last visit, that is, right until the point he noticed Anur and the Dragons washing, and only then remembered that he should do likewise.

Malok did quickly overtake them, for the newcomers were like he had been upon his first visit to these hallowed halls. They all had their faces up, gazing in wonder at the amazingly glorious and intricate murals, all while pacing about in lazy circles, for to observe each single valiant icon and heroic scene. Even Shar and Malok looked up again, smiling, for the marvelously painted ceiling seemed never to fail in catching the eyes and instilling reverence and wonder.

"Hello. Can I help you?" Asked a quiet voice, interrupting their thoughts and admiration.

"Ah, Aelanur," Answered Malok, for he remembered the golden colored Dragon who was priest of this hallowed temple. "See, I have found her."

"Found whom?" Asked the befuddled Dragon priest, for Malok had never divulged his purpose for visiting the Order to him.

Only to Serc, Zurthaud, and Theros had he let be known the reason for his coming to the Paladins, and they had only relayed this to few others: trusted friends like Galrag, and the scouts who would have come to help Malok and Shar in their search had not so many catastrophes occurred lately, seemingly, all at once. Nevertheless, Malok had expected his reaction to be more elated at recovering the last young Dragoness in existence.

"Is that a Troll?" Aelanur asked of Anur, as the priest had suddenly become aware and distracted by him and his most unusual appearance, instead of rejoicing over Feldara's presence.

"No, that is Anur, companion to this Dragoness." Malok returned, deciding to suppress his questions about Feldara's greatly devalued reception. "Do you know where everyone has gone? Especially, where are Zurthaud and Theros and Serc?" Asked he, wishing to quickly change the subject while also beginning to worry the coup had not gone as planned, for indeed, the Citadel and even this temple were devoid of any other people besides they and Aelanur.

"Zurthaud and Theros are both somewhere about Bythatsar helping to relieve all the poor souls affected by that last horrendous assault. That is where I also am now going, for I have offered enough prayer this day to last a week, and my healing knowledge, though quite small compared to Serc's, is much needed." Then becoming very sorrowful, Aelanur divulged what had become of the Order's greatest doctor. "I remember that you had to leave before that day, so it pains me to be the first to tell you of this. He died during the coup, on the last day of the siege. Through his sacrifice and, thankfully, few others, we succeeded in winning the battle, for as he was always wont, Serc gave of his own self for to save another."

Malok did then grieve for the loss of so greatly magnanimous a person, for though he had known the elder Dragon for only a short time, he had come to understand how kind and generous, wise, and caring the great healer had been.

Feldara, seeing his sadness, did then offer him comfort, placing a gentle hand upon his shoulder, and though she knew not Serc nor about the coup, or how the elder had given his life up to save Zurthaud's, she inferred that he had been a very dear person in the lives of all who had known him, even of Malok, and sought to lessen, even a little, the hurt her friend experienced.

"There is no reason for us to stay here." Malok stated, recovering quickly from his mourning, due in part to Feldara's affection to whom he then turned. "We must go to Bythatsar, for to inform Zurthaud of your presence."

"But, we just arrived." Calidon plaintively argued.

"If this Dragoness is so important, I shall deliver the news of her coming to Zurthaud when I arrive in Bythatsar." Aelanur offered. "But, I am a slow flyer, and shall be tending wounded along the way, so that I may not reach him for a day or two at most. May I ask what is so special about our guest? Er,.. not to say that any Dragoness is unimportant, but that she is only one young female, and not a warrior judging by her build. Are you a healer, or a scholar, perhaps?" Innocently inquired the priest, at the end turning to question Feldara directly.

Truly, he meant no harm, no demeaning nature could be found in the mild priest, yet was he socially challenged by his reclusive duties, thus accidentally expressing his curiosity inappropriately forthright. Although upon hearing this, Malok was again taken aback by Aelanur's naivety, so much so that he decided to attribute it to some form of mild dementia or other uncontrollable forgetfulness.

"I am quite unimportant." Feldara smartly replied, becoming annoyed at being so belittled, yet secretly glad that not everyone was so excited as Malok to have found her.

"Well, I shall bring word of your arrival, anyway, for you must have a purpose for coming here, of which I, usually the last person to know any of the goings on around this place, am unaware. I bid you all farewell." Offered the Dragon priest, and after giving a quick bow, he sauntered past them and headed out the temple, beginning a journey that would take him farther from this sacred place than he had been in decades.

"What shall we do know?" Shar irritatedly asked of Malok, folding his arms in annoyance, for he had never been kept waiting in his whole life.

He had also been hoping, since day two of their journey, that they could both go back home as soon as Malok's quest had been completed.

"I guess we should just wait here until we hear word." Malok suggested with a shrug of his shoulders, which, for a Dragon, is accompanied a slight flap of the unopened wings.

"I, for one, would not mind in the slightest a little time for waiting, for resting and recuperating from our hard traveling." Anur declared, and Calidon heartily agreed.

Although Feldara could not think of anything more boring than just sitting around waiting to hear from a person she did not know or care about, she had to admit that the thought of rest and relaxation, especially contrasted with the most recent fear, fighting, and running of her daily life, seemed quite nice.

"Is there any area for bathing around here?" Anur asked, for he had not the time or opportunity to fully clean since leaving the Aelven realm behind.

His simple question only caused the others to realize that they too must be quite dirty, for they also had been too distracted to keep up proper hygiene. Feldara was the most embarrassed of all, as she could not recall the last time she had washed, and she fretted that, perhaps, Malok, or anyone else, had noticed such.

"Yes, Malok, is there any such washroom hereabout?" Shar inquired sarcastically, for he knew full well that though his friend had desired to seem in charge, well prepared, and on top of things, Malok still had not stayed within the Order's Citadel long enough to have become familiar with its layout or facilities, and had no idea where anything was located. Even so, Shar had wished he had been the first one to ask that question, for though he was not abashed by his own stench, he had been deeply craving such comforts.

"Perhaps, we should find another Paladin and ask them." He sheepishly replied, tryingly mightily not to seem unqualified for his most recent heroic status.

"I have seen hardly any other person about the whole place besides the priest, and I have been scanning the walls and windows of the Keep and barracks since before we landed." Spoke Anur, beginning to suspect that Malok was purposely withholding important information from them. "Something has happened to this place; aside from this temple and it's murals, it is nothing like the descriptions I had read. Where are all the Paladins? Where are all the Dragons? Where is the spirit of camaraderie and the happy fellowship of like minds, all in collaboration, seeking, practicing, truth and justice? That priest said there had been a coup; tell us now what has here occurred that could so absolutely steal away the life and joy of this hallowed place."

Malok did not wish to speak about any of the terrible things that had gone on in the Order's Citadel: not Orthard's vile, half-century long tyranny, not the subsequent revolt, and definitely not how Feldara was now one of the last female Dragons in the whole world.

Then it occurred to him that he had, indeed, met with another Dragoness, with Lenairu, so that Feldara was, indeed, truly not the last Dragoness in existence, and perhaps, he too had not himself heard the whole story of why the shining city of the Paladins had become so dark and dim.

"I am not sure I know the answers to these questions myself." Malok disclosed, earning an annoyed, distrusting scowl from Anur. "We shall have to wait for Zurthaud to arrive and answer them himself, for if anyone should know the truth behind all these mysteries, it would be him. For now, let us head over to the Keep and see if there is anyone thereabout who could direct us to a bathhouse or even a creek or pool to wash in and perhaps further accommodations, for I should not like to sleep upon the ground outside when night falls." He suggested.

They all agreed, though some not as cheerily as others, and they exited the temple and glided the short distance over to a large balcony on the Keep's second floor. Upon landing, they found this building to be inhabited, for there was, at least, someone here to greet them, an important looking Human with two guards.

"Hello." Called out the man, even as they touched down upon the gray stone of the Keep. "My watchmen had seen you flying about, to the Dragon's quarters and back to here, so that we knew you were coming. I am Argamon, captain of the Citadel guard, but you I do not recognize. Per Zurthaud's orders, I must ask you to, please, state your names and business here, for our recording, for no one is allowed in or out of the Keep without documentation."

"The last I checked, Dragons were not even allowed in the Keep." Malok replied, confusedly.

"Then you must be returning after the change of command, and I shall inform you what has happened and the new regulations." Argamon explained. "Two days ago the Order underwent a dividing conflict, during which one faction rebelled against certain unlawful rulings by the other..." Began Argamon, but Malok interrupted him.

"I know that part, and obviously the true Paladins led by Zurthaud were victorious. What I do not understand is why our coming and going should be so monitored." Malok inquired.

Recovering with only a little annoyance at his speech's disruption, Argamon continued. "After the coup, the lower parts of the Keep have been made the prison for all the political criminals, the debased rulers who used their position of power to further their own selfish gain and the wickedness and corruption that had so infested the Order. As Zurthaud and his other allies are away, and I am the only Paladin remaining who still holds a formal rank of leadership, until the current crisis with the terrible burning and pillaging of the Southern part of the realm is resolved, access to the Keep and, consequently, its dungeons has been restricted and placed under my careful attendance."

"O, that is fine, we actually have no interest in entering the Keep." Feldara irritatedly interjected; then forcefully pointing to each of them in turn, she continued. "I am Feldara; this is Anur; that is Malok and Shar; and that is Calidon. We just want to find where we can properly refresh from our long travels and where we can lodge for the night without having to impose upon your ordinances. Does that satisfy you?"

"Yes, it does." Argamon replied, albeit more gently than he had afore been addressing them. "There are no Dragon-sized bathhouses available anymore; sadly, they were all converted into other buildings, mostly for Human use. However, I knew of a mountain stream nearby with a waterfall and a deep pool; it was where my companion always went when he desired a washing. Other than that, you could rough it and clean yourselves with your own fire-breath, as I have read the wild Dragons usually do. Regrettably, I am not knowledgeable about the Dragons quarter's current accommodations, for I have not visited in many years. But, again very sadly, there should be plenteous empty apartments within the tower. I would think it perfectly acceptable to, at least temporarily, acquire one or two such for your uses. I wish I could offer you a more hospitable welcome, seeing as you are the last Dragoness, the Bright One, but I have orders assigned to me, important duties to perform. Please, accept my apology; we have fallen far and are yet to return to the glory and charity of the old days, when strangers would be welcomed here as brothers." He informed, and after offering directions to the pool they could use for bathing, he excused himself with a quick bow.

They left from there, each of them low in spirit, for though Shar and Malok had encountered much sorrow at their earlier visit, they had still been greeted comparatively warmly. Without the presence of their afore well-known acquaintances, like Zurthaud or Theros, or even anybody other than Aelanur, who was just leaving, and the dutifully practical, if not austerely blunt and unwelcoming, Argamon, their destination seemed no more cheerful or cordial than the road they had long traveled with haste, toil, and worry.

However, the cool water of the mountain pool, fed by lofty streams dropping a water's fall down into the deep caldera, did help to relieve their weariness and ease their hearts, for descending the gently sloping bank until fully submerged and scouring with a little soap borrowed from a seemingly vacant Dragon's apartment, was, indeed, most rejuvenating.

Chapter 32

Coldness, blackness- these were the horrors that filled the sight and heart of Orthard, but the chilling touch of his cell's stone floor and the darkness of the gloomy dungeon was nothing compared to that icy chill of regret and the numbness following insane ferocity within his own soul. It had been a long time now since he had felt the warmth of kindness or the light of love, for longer still had he been enslaved to the shadow.

At first, it had seemed his own thought, his own will, for he had hated the Dragons, blaming them, blaming Serc for the death of his beloved wife. His attempts to subjugate them, prove their inhumanity were, indeed, his own, but genocide, though he was no stranger to killing, had seemed, even within his own thoughts, quite strangely introduced, as he had always intended to keep the beasts around, as long as they lasted, for the Order's martial superiority. He was not stupid, not wasteful, but even this new depth of wickedness he had dismissed as only the proper conclusion of his loathing.

Then, it happened; the Dark Horde invaded the Order's realm. First only the most Southern fiefs, those nearest the border wall, had perished, and these he thought he could spare. Yet, the dark army attacked Bythatsar, a prominent city, one with great earning potential, and he dismissed the whole event as his son's careless gallivanting, having conspired the whole thing from start to finish, in order to play hero.

The idea had felt foolish, even to Orthard, who knew that Zurthaud was not conniving enough to devise such a scheme, but he spoke it, until eventually, he believed it himself. And, then his son was nearly slain on a scouting mission to the Shadow Land, and the father that still clung to the shards of Orthard's soul had cried out within him in anguish and lust for vengeance. Yet, did he speak against his son, and knew for certain that his own pride, let alone any parental care for his progeny, would never have allowed him to so denounce the truth of what had occurred. Had he been himself, he would have then and there awoken from his stupor and, with selfish, even greedy intent, taken up arms against the darkness, but he did not. Instead, he cursed his son's allies and friends and attempted to write their doom.

Afterward, when he had heard news that his boy yet lived, had he been free to do as he willed, Orthard knew that he would have put aside all differences he had formerly begrudged against his son and made the trip, even begging for a lift from the wretched Dragons, to see him where he lay in the temple, even if only just to see him well and complain that they had not fully cared for his heir, letting him come to such harm, but he did no such thing.

It was at that moment, after all the many others, that he finally realized his mind was not his own anymore, and he attempted to find the culprit and fight off the controlling demon, as his own arrogant self became enraged at the thought that he should be so used by another. But, it was also at that moment that he realized he was far too late, even past pleading with the Dragons to help him with their arcane knowledge and powerful magic.

He could not speak without the darkness speaking through him, nor go anywhere the darkness did not bid him go, nor even lift a finger that was not first thoroughly scrutinized and at last, perhaps, allowed to function.

So it was no surprise to Orthard, that when Zurthaud and Serc had broken through the Keep's defenses and were standing before him, that his words, even drawn from his own memory, were thrown about recklessly, exposing his deepest hurts, playing upon them like a twisted, yet more honest, version of what he had kept suppressed within his own mind for so long, and meaningfully so.

Never would he have ever in all his life, though it went to the grave with him, ever told Zurthaud how he had so felt regarding the boy's involvement in his mother's death. Orthard was yet a father, and though his heart was black as coal, he still had not desired to let that secret, desperate, hateful old grudge come to his lips, had he any control over them, if anything, at least, that his weaknesses be not exposed. All he had ever wanted for his son was the best, the best of everything, and to disclose that one time, sorrow-borne bitterness that had leaped into his heart only the moment after Zurthaud was born, and after holding the helpless little babe in his arms, had faded, repressed, into Orthard's self-imposed exiled thoughts, was the extreme opposite of all his dreaming and scheming.

True, Orthard had been somewhat jealous of Zurthaud's tight knit, familial, following of Paladins, his sway with the young and the brave, but everything that remained of his own self implored the darkness to let but a single tear fall from his eye, so as to lessen, even a little, the blow he had dealt to his boy, to let him know that he truly had not meant the words that spewed uncontrollably, like sewage, from his mouth. He was denied and could not cry, could not call out, could not apologize.

Then he picked up that awful device, the Bullet Projector, as he had so named it back when at the first he still had a little control so as to give names and take delight in overseeing the creation of a weapon that could, perhaps, eventually, replace Humanity's need for magic or Draconic allies, or even God. Had he known what its actual intended purpose had been, never would he have succumbed to his desire for science and Human ingenuity to replace the spiritual and the magical, but he was then only foolishly falling into the snare.

Now, fully caught in its vicious, inescapable net, he could only silently scream as his fingers pulled upon the trigger, his hands holding the weapon before his own son.

But, the bullet never touched the youth's head, and Orthard would have wept tears of gratitude unto Serc and lauded him with praise at his funeral, and his contempt for the Dragons would nearly have vanished, as the elderly Dragon, his dear friend of old, upon whom he could now hold no blame or hatred for anything, stepped before the lad, protecting him, taking the death that had been meant for another.

Finally realizing that, so long ago now, the doctor had tried with as much effort to save his wife as he had now given to save his son, even unto his own self-sacrifice, and that by this act, placing the highest value upon life and protecting the weaker, even unto death, the Dragons were proven to be people, with souls and conscience and high emotion, Orthard could only stare on in total regret for all his life's toil, all his wicked deeds and self-serving hoarding of power and wealth.

His world that he had tried to shape with his own two hands, that he had clung to with such white-knuckled stubbornness, crumbled into dust before him, and just as he was about to pray for forgiveness for such foolish, worthless, wasted living, to a God he had so long denied existence, the darkness took him completely.

No longer could he see; no longer could he feel, not anything but the coldness of his own numb soul. Though time was irrelevant to him in this state, he could still feel that hours were passing; it was the only thing remaining that reminded him of his own existence, the fact that he moved through time.

So it seemed rather suddenly, that a giant, red armored terror without any face in its horned helm began to appear before his eyes, and stranger still to the afore so numbed Orthard, the fiend spoke to him in audible words.

"Ah, my faithful servant, the great Lord Consul of the Order of Paladins, Lord Orthard; you who would have ruled the world of men. My, it seems as though your living conditions have somewhat deteriorated of late." Rumbled the nightmarish apparition, with such a voice, like the opening of a tomb, that his mocking statement carried no humor.

Somehow, Orthard's consciousness broke through the fog for just a moment, and a glimmer of his own free will exposed itself enough that he could finally speak a word of his own thoughts. "Who are you?" He stammered, completely horrified and unable tear his eyes away from the phantom.

"Surely you know me by now." Answered the armored menace, and Orthard had to admit the voice seemed oddly familiar. "I am the one to whom you listened, who now chooses what you hear. I am the one to whom you spoke, who now chooses what you say. I see through your eyes, and tell you what to look upon. I work through your hands, and walk through your feet. I am your master, the Dark Lord, Kragon."

"No, no, no! You are not even real!" Orthard screamed, and his voice echoed emptily from the dungeon walls while someone off in the distance, a guard or fellow prisoner, shouted for him to shut up.

The Dark Lord smotheringly grabbed up Orthard's head in one clawed metal gauntlet and drew his faceless face nigh. "Oh, I am quite real, my dear puppet, though not really here." Said he, as with another Black-iron clawed finger from his other gauntleted hand he blithely tapped upon a singular crystal that hung about Orthard's neck by a Black-iron chain. "If you had paid more respect to the dead, or even the living, we would not be having this pleasant little chat, but life is all about choices. And, now that you have wasted all of yours, I think you should help fulfill mine."

Orthard's hand stretched forth not of his own will, and in his palm a strange black goo flowed out of his skin and began to puddle, so that, eventually, out of the puddle formed a key of cunning design, the bow of which was solidly shaped while the bitting was of an amorphous nature. "You shall have need of this." Again spoke the demonic villain. "The 'Bright One' is here, just dying to meet me, and you shall be the one to introduce us."

"No, I shall not do it! I will serve you no more, foul demon!" Orthard shouted at the very top of his lungs, so that he spat and grew hoarse and red in the face, and though he had tried summoning a last little bit of his former dignity and pride, he could not but feel helpless, as the Dark Lord cackled, a dreadful sound like metal grating against stone, while again someone far off in the background yelled for him to shut up.

"You cannot refuse what is no longer yours to give." Chuckled the Dark Lord, even as he began to fade from Orthard's vision.

"Why me?" Plaintively asked the hapless man, but then the blackness closed in upon him again so that his numbness began to return.

Faintly, Orthard heard a voice echo in his ears, like words spoken in a dream. "Do you not remember?" Sinisterly whispered the Dark Lord. "You chose this."

But, the voice faded away until Orthard was completely alone and could again hear no more, see no more, and feel no more.

<><><><><>

Feldara's first full day in the Order's Citadel seemed a luxury compared to her most recent lodgings.

From her rejuvenating bath of the night before to the comfortable, Dragon-sized bed she had slept upon, and now to the breakfast they were eating, that which Argamon had sent unto them from the Order's provisions, which though a courtesy by any standard, was taken as somewhat of an apology for their earlier standoff- in all these privileges of civilized life, she fully reveled.

Now, as she sat, along with the others, upon the cool, soft grass in the Dragon quarter's open yard, and she munched upon savory, roasted sausage, crispy bacon, and deliciously pan fried potatoes, Feldara began to wonder what other frivolities she could enjoy today. Malok, on the other hand, only became more worried about what he had not seen.

Zurthaud, of course, would be expected to lead the relief effort, and Theros would surely have gone with him. Yet, since Aelanur had left, besides their group, there were no other Dragons about, and he feared that here, more than they had ever been before, even in the wild, they were exposed to the enemy. Still, the walls were unassailed. No shadows covered the sun, nor could any spies be seen lurking about the halls or towers, so that he had to force himself to repress these feelings of dread and looming darkness.

Feldara had begun to notice this gloomy anxiety come over her new friend, and wishing to banish his personal raincloud, she quickly finished her breakfast and made a proposition.

"I think I shall go exploring the city today, perhaps, walk among the streets like I did in Lotheliel. Would anyone care to join me?" She inquired, as they still sat about finishing their own portion of savory breakfast fare.

"I should like nothing more than a little peace and quiet, maybe a book from the temple library, if one of you shall give me a lift before you leave." Anur commented, rising from the grass and brushing biscuit crumbs off his tunic.

"I do not think running about the city would be such a good idea." Malok argued. "It is not as well defended as the Citadel; you could be leaving yourself open to an attack."

"An attack from whom?" Feldara retorted, her tail flicking with frustration at his, seemingly, petty complaint. "We defeated the Dark Hunters, and so soundly this time that they should not be trying their tricks again so soon, if ever again."

Thus silencing Malok's contention, she turned to face Calidon for to see if he was interested, but he chose not to look her in the eye, instead, glancing down and chewing his food, as if he too were uninterested in spending time with her. Feldara could not fathom why the usually cheerful red male had become so sullen and grumpy of late, and so annoyed by his current attitude, she barely gave him any time with which to respond.

"Well, if you two are so fearful that something would happen to me, perhaps, you should come along, for I am going, whether or not anyone accompanies me." She chided, and strode over to Anur for to offer him a ride to the Dragon's temple, leaving the two males to stare after her.

"Oh, what fun you three shall have." Mocked Shar, who had wisely chosen to remain quiet until Feldara had gone. "I think I shall do something, anything else, other than associate with that bossy Dragoness."

"Watch your words, Serpen." Growled Calidon, as suddenly rising from where he sat, he became wroth. "That is my friend of whom you speak."

"Likewise, do not threaten my friend." Malok returned, rather more defensively than he at first intended, and he arose also, to stand between Calidon and Shar.

Calidon did then aggressively tower over the smaller black Dragon, but he did nothing more, only snorting annoyedly before quickly turning about and taking off after Feldara.

Shar made the whistling hiss of a confused Serpen, and spoke to Malok in his native tongue. "What is his problem? I only spoke in jest."

Malok could only shrug, for though he had not known Calidon very long at all, he had thought all Dragons regarded each other more familiarly than to display such hostility toward one of their own.

"Perhaps, he is in a relationship with yon Dragoness?" Shar suggested.

"Now it is my turn to say it. Watch your words." Malok replied, then feeling quite defensive of Feldara, and left wondering why he should care at all.

However, he did motion for his friend to clamber aboard his shoulders, an invitation for him to come along with them.

"No thank you." Shar replied, a sly Serpen grin creeping across his face. "I shall stay here and on the ground, for I think I have had my fill of besotted Dragons today."

Malok did not quite understand what Shar had meant, but neither did he get the chance to question his friend, as the Serpen was already wandering off to do something else, probably more relaxation. Now, he had fast to fly for to make pace with Feldara and Calidon, as they had already let Anur off at the temple's balcony and were winging away toward the city center. By the time he finally caught up with them, they had already landed again, yet this time, instead of the quiet, empty lawn of the Dragon's quarter, they found themselves within a bustling section of an open city square, that which was just beyond the outermost of the Keep's walls.

Everywhere they looked there was a crowd of Humans busy about one thing or another; buying and selling, hauling wares, and running errands- they all seemed but part of one large amorphous, perpetually motive conglomeration, like the incessant waves upon the sea. For a moment, the three Dragons could but stare in amazement upon this sight, as, besides Malok, they had never before seen such a multitude, but eventually Feldara's curiosity caused her to wonder at what each one of these peculiarly occupied people were doing. She began to wander through the crowd observing every activity, examining all the wares in the vendors' stalls and shops, and in turn the mass of Humans started to take notice of her also.

So many times had Dragons flown overhead that the people had become accustomed to the event. Barely any of them even glanced skyward at the approach of the three Dragons, but now that they had landed among the Humans and were walking about the square, the people did begin to stare upon them with the same fascination with which their daily activities were being scrutinized.

Indeed, it had been a long while since the Dragons of the Order had taken time to walk the streets with them, or converse with the common man, longer still since the Dragons had any coin to purchase wares or even traded Dragon's-work for goods or services, as it was called when the two peoples bartered magic, fire, and flying for the myriad crafts of men.

Yet, were these people still aware of the value of having such mighty protectors so nearby, even more so now that they had heard, and smelled, wind of the great burning of the fields and farms to the South-east, and with many merchants offering samples of their wares and the masses making sure to not throng or bump against them, nor point at them, or assail them with questions of insensitive curiosity, they openly displayed their gratitude for this protection with courtesy and respect for the three Dragons.

So it was, as they traveled throughout the square, and then on past the inner gate and through into the rest of the entire city, that they three were met with kind greetings, and Feldara, by the satisfying of her fascinations, acquired many useless trinkets, which she somehow, either by putting them in their arms or hanging them upon their horns or neck spines, caused either Malok or Calidon to hold onto, and some edible dainties, which she herself ate and did not share.

At length, she had such a collection of sampled gifts that she began to be able to trade these in bulk for other more desirable items, like a new sword, of well-made quality, for Anur and a necklace, one that could actually fit around her Dragon-sized neck, made of finely corded leather and a single, large pearl fastened by a curiously wound silver housing.

Malok and Calidon had no such fun, for the drudgery of this endless walking, coupled with the constant stopping for Feldara to gaze upon every other new bauble, seemed to them quite boring and draining, but since they would never give the satisfaction of letting the other see them tire, give up, and go back, they both became ever more weary and unhappy.

At last, they came to a part of the city where the residences began to very much outnumber the shops and the people seemed less friendly, for they neither offered them anything nor did they greet the Dragons as they passed by. The fine houses and merchants, foods, fashions, and boulevards had been left behind some while ago, and the masses were of plain and simple folk.

"What is the matter with this part of the city?" Feldara asked, wondering why the same shine and wonder was not also here, having been replaced by a gloomier spirit of trudging and labor.

"This is where the poor live, the unskilled laborers who work the farms outside the walls and the factories within." Malok replied, having a little experience with the way cities were laid out and with the less fortunate parts of these, for he had been raised among a nation of impoverished people.

"But, why does their lack of money make them go about so sullenly?" She inquired, further expounding her first question.

"They work all the day and take home only enough to feed and shelter their families, and with so little to spare, they see no brighter future than for them to toil on like this until they die." Malok surmised, again from his own experience.

This so bothered Feldara that she began wondering if there was any way she could at all bring even a little light unto this darker place where the people had not enough hope to smile or be at all merry. Looking about she saw all the little children who, after being done with their daily chores and duties, were gathering to play in the quieter side streets and alleys, but they were so ragged and dirty, mostly barefoot. Her tender heart having gone out to them, she walked over to one such group of the street children and greeted them

Surprisingly, they had enough manners to return her gesture, and she was introduced to all of them and talked with them, even about simple and small things. She became their new friend, and they trusted her so much that she was eventually invited to play games with them too. To Malok and Calidon's amazement, who had sat by watching, the whole neighborhood's children began to gather, for it was not every day, that they got to see up close, much less make fun with, a Dragon. For hours it seemed, she chased them and they chased her up and down the street, and so great was the noise of their merry-making that the glum adults began to gather about for to see what was the cause of all the ruckus. Even their stony, downcast hearts could not help but to smile upon all the infectious happiness of the children's game with Feldara, so that in a short while, nearly the whole of this city section had assembled for to watch or play with the joyous mob of children and the Bright Dragoness.

Not until eventide came did the crowd begin to disperse, and even then, the difference in their spirit could be seen and felt. A little jollity, a little love and kindness had gone a great way into lightening this part of the city and its residents. At last, with their suppertime at hand, the children's game had to end, but Feldara had one last idea, one more goodness to give away.

"Calidon, Malok, get over here." She called to the two males, who had refrained from the activity, mostly for all the various objects they were carrying about.

Once they did reach her, which was no small task with all the many trifles they tried to hold in their arms, causing them to clumsily attempt two-legged walking, and all the bangles hanging over their heads and necks, hardly aiding their vision, and in this manner, having to wade through a crowd of children, Feldara started to hand out all the novelties and gadgets she had collected earlier in the day, one to each child, and by some miracle, she had enough to give to every single one assembled.

"Bless you, Dragoness." Thanked one mother who had come to gather up her little ones, and her gratitude was echoed by a chorus of a hundred small voices and even many big ones.

But, Feldara had not done any of this for attention, or even for their gratitude, though she cherished it, offering inn return a polite bow. Out of the kindness of her own heart did she offer any gift, and she only felt abashed that they thanked her at all for a thing so simple as to play and make friends with the children and to hand out her freely acquired presents. Yet, to them her small kindness was much needed; to see the love of another, to hear the laughter of children- these simple treasures, even a little light, were what would help to keep them going through the mundanity, and even the despondency, of a hard life.

But, at length, when it began to become dark and the lamplighters were starting to make their rounds, the many people all dispersed, and Feldara was left with naught but Anur's new sword, her necklace, and her two tired, but relieved at no longer having to carry about her luggage, friends.

"Feldara, you have such a gift, to be able to bring light, even a little brightness, to this place." After a moment of solitude, Malok stated in amazement, for he truly had been captivated with how, almost supernaturally, joy had seemed to flood the once grim neighborhood.

Feldara returned this unexpected compliment with a bashful smile, and she was about to explain that she had not done any of this to receive praise or thanks, only wanting to cheer up the little ones, to bring them a little happiness, when Calidon abruptly spoke over anyone else.

"You are such a honey tongue." Calidon suddenly spat at him. "Can you not cease your boot-licking for even a moment?"

He truly had not meant to voice so bluntly, so callously soon to such an occurrence that he also admired for Feldara's gentleness and benevolence, an opinion that not even he deemed worthy of speaking, but ever since Malok had joined their group the big red male had borne animosity toward him. Somehow, he felt defensive of Feldara, and wanted only to keep Malok from her.

However, it was not Malok who offered any contention; rather, Feldara was very upset with him.

"Calidon!" She nearly roared. "How can you be so offensive? What has gotten into you that you have become so unkind and unpleasant of late?"

He could not answer her properly, and only stood there open mouthed, now thinking his words over and wondering why he had said them. Truly, he could not believe that Malok was so self-serving as to compliment Feldara for her good nature only to put himself in her favor.

"Excuse me." He mumbled, head low with shame, and he turned about and flew off into the looming twilight.

"I apologize for him also." Spoke Feldara unto Malok. "Calidon usually is so gentle and friendly; I have no idea why he has been so mean lately."

Malok also did not respond well, only nodding his head in acceptance of her obligation, for he then remembered what Shar had been hinting at before.

<><><><><>

Zurthaud had been almost too busy even to eat, and just now, he was partaking of his first morsel of food since the night of Serc's funeral. Though the relief effort for the refugees had been very generous and constant, managing and distributing all of the supplies and personnel, so as to make sure all the needy were cared for, had been quite a laborious task, and even though Zurthaud had not been alone in this, with Theros' and Galrag's helping with organizing the Dragons, and Lorn and many of the Human lords overseeing much of the operation, he had still borne most of the decision making. Any question that was asked of him, he had found an answer for it, from where to store and how to ration out the foodstuffs to where and how to lodge each and every one of the villagers from the Southwestern province, and any task that needed an extra hand, he had pitched in, from building temporary shelters to handing out bread and water.

By the end of the two days that had passed, Zurthaud had been worn out both mentally and physically, that the thought of hunger had not come into Zurthaud's mind, nor would it have, so occupied was he by the seemingly more pressing concerns of others.

It was only now that he had been made to sit down and eat something by a random, yet sympathetically concerned, cook who had seen him walk, or rather trudge, past the kitchen facilities, that he had finally stopped long enough to realize how weary and hungry he was.

"Sit you down right here, sir, and I shall soon have out some bread and soup for you." Said the kind chef, nearly shoving Zurthaud to sit at an outer table by the entrance, one of many set in the, again, one of many makeshift dining halls.

Truly, it was more of a hastily staked tent, with no sides, only a roof, and some benches and board tables set in ordered rows down its length, but with the roaring, warming cooking fire nearby, it seemed to Zurthaud as quite a fine place to rest, even if but for a moment. Soon enough, indeed, Zurthaud found himself slurping and sopping rather heartily a most tasty stew and hearty, crusty bread, and it seemed to him then the finest meal he had ever eaten. So famished was he, and now finding hunger again after finally eating, that the cook had to bring out two more bowls of soup and many rolls before Zurthaud felt as if he had partaken of anything at all. Only after finishing his third serving, did he look up about him at all the others that dined herein, for it was the dinner hour.

It seemed, in the warm glow of the dining hall's merrily blazing fire, with all the happy, smiling faces of children, and the careworn, though content visages of the adults, and even some music beginning to start up at the far corner of the hall, that the people were surely healing, that they would eventually recover from all the hurt and the burning and even all the death. The night would soon be over, and the day would come. There was peace here, and hope for the morning. And, at that Zurthaud began to smile also and even allowed his toes to begin tapping to one of his favorite tunes.

"Zurthaud." He heard his name being called, snapping him back to reality from the cherished warmth of the reverie.

He turned about to see the last person he expected.

"Aelanur, welcome. What are you doing all the way out here?" He called, greeting the Dragon priest, and he tried to get up from his chair out of respect, but found that he was rather glued to it by the weight of his fatigue.

Either way, the humble priest would have had none of it, and taking no notice of such, began to elaborate on why he had left the temple.

"I left my sanctuary hoping to be of some aid by either my limited healing skill, or prayer, or anything, and indeed, I have aided many yesterday and today." Spake the Dragon, as he sat down beside Zurthaud, he outside the tent with his head poking in. "Truly, I did not meet as many along the way as I had expected, and to me, the trip from Doraegonoran to Bythatsar seems far, indeed, but once I arrived, I found plenty to care for. My only regret is that I did not come sooner, for arranging the Temple for my absence seems a trifle compared to the needs hereabout."

"Nonsense, your service at the Temple is vital to us, for as you often say, 'Prayer is your most powerful weapon.'" Zurthaud replied. "Besides, we all have our part to do; there have been many, even over many, to help with all there is to do about here."

"I should know; it took me the better part of this day to find you amongst all these people. Though they are well organized, everyone still seemed to point me toward a step behind you all day long. 'He is over there.' They would say, and then going there, I would find that you had already left to help someone else." Aelanur mirthfully explained.

However, Zurthaud's mind had been turned to the care he had for these unfortunate people, they whose woes and wounds which he had been tending. So much pain and destruction had he seen, and now given the opportunity, he could not refrain from asking the Dragon priest something he had great trouble comprehending.

"Aelanur, if the world was made by Eloigal and is even now sustained by His almighty hand, and He is so merciful and good, why then does He permit such suffering? Why do the innocent perish by the sword of the wicked or the scourge of disaster?" Zurthaud questioned, more to Eloigal Himself than to the priest.

"It is a hard question you ask me, a mortal, to explain." Replied the priest, also becoming very sober. "For, the ways of Eloigal are high above us, beyond our comprehending. However, revealed in His word are truths to which we can cling in such dark and hopeless times. He is with us in our suffering, and He bears it even more fully than do we. For, while we can only see our own pain, and sometimes that of others if it is great and visible enough, He sees into each and every heart, feels every lash of sorrow upon His own back, takes every thorn to pierce His own brow. He also works through our pain, for if it is the struggle of trials, we are made stronger, refined as gold, by them. If it is the devastation of calamity, we are made to realize our true dependence is upon Him alone, yet can He rebuild anew our lives, even better than before. You can neither forget that His mighty hand has been drawn many times, both in the past and now, for I have heard many stories as I worked among the afflicted today, and there are many, many tales of the miraculous salvation of the hopeless, the healing of the sick, the defending of the helpless. So many speak, throughout all history, of how Eloigal saved them by some impossible means or another when all they expected was the inevitable end, the sorrow, the harm, the death, that we cannot deny He is present and intimately involved in each and every life and the rescue thereof. And more so; though we, as mortals, in the first abomination of corruption, the primary evil, did shatter the natural order of the world, that which He had designed to be good and without death or any kind of misery, He still bears with us, working all things to our good, even if it be in the very end."

Here Aelanur paused and lifted his gaze upward, but he looked not at the darkening sky, only beyond it. "Ah, that very end, our true home, that perfect place so like, yet better far, by eternity's fathom, than that first world which He made and called 'good', there is no comfort even close to it; that assurance so strong and sweet, that when our bodies, at last, part with the trifles and inconsequential duties that we so childishly hoard in this imperfect and toilsome life, we shall be called up and beyond into the everlasting perfection and solace of the Blessed Realm."

The knowledge that Eloigal saw and suffered with him in his own trials and, at times miraculously, worked all thing toward his good, even to the eternal separation from sorrow in Heaven, did much to relieve Zurthaud, but still he fretted about the poor folk around him. He was not yet fully satisfied with Aelanur's answer.

"Truly my heart is comforted thinking upon our eventual destination, but what about the here and now? The Blessed Realm is a long journey from where we sit, and to reach the heavenly shores you must cross the river of death." Zurthaud prodded, hoping to elucidate a more complete explanation from the priest.

Here the Dragon priest paused, for he had again to think upon his reply to Zurthaud's stiff inquiries, but after only a moment he answered reassuringly.

"Have you not considered that we: you and I, and all others who follow the Eloigal in spirit and in truth, are the arms and legs, hands and feet by which He now ministers unto the world, providing aid to the needy, help to the helpless, rescue to the endangered." Spoke the priest, returning his gaze to Zurthaud. "As I said before, He does still work His miracles as in days of old, but His love is shown to us, like a father to his sons or a tradesman to his apprentices, in that He invites us, chooses us, to participate in and accomplish His work of saving the world and caring for those in want. Speaking on death and traveling thence, indeed, it and useless suffering are horrible things, unnatural in every way, for as in the beginning they were not. Death is an abomination to be fought against and avoided, but its power is gone, torn in two by the Great Sacrifice and by the Law of Grace. Now, we need not fear it, yet neither rush to it, and our enormous task regarding it is to ease one another's passing beyond that final anguish, and on into that sacred peace for which we all strive."

Zurthaud had still much to contemplate, but he relented his questioning. Aelanur's answers had been sound and encouraging, even if they still did not quell the sympathetic hurt Zurthaud felt for the plight of so many wretchedly entreated innocents.

Still, the thought that he was not alone in his compassion, that Eloigal did care for these people, for all of them, had a perfect will that would surely be accomplished, and would watch over and keep them, even supernaturally, did much to alleviate his grief.

"Oh, I do actually have a purpose for seeking you other than for good conversation." Spake the priest, interrupting Zurthaud's thoughts. "I was told to inform you that a certain Dragoness has arrived at the Citadel, one for whom Malok had been searching."

Zurthaud just stared in awe for a moment, for he had thought the search for the Bright One would have taken many months, even years. Never, had he hoped that the last Dragon female, both Human's and Dragon's providential heroine, could be so near, so quickly and easily located, for he had always imagined her quite far away and hidden, isolated in some forgotten and ancient part of Threa.

"I must go to her immediately. Quick, you must help me find Theros, Galrag, and Lorn, for they are my most trustworthy counsel, of whom I shall have great need regarding this Dragoness." Zurthaud exclaimed, as he recovered from his amazement and sprang to his feet.

"I really do not know why we are making such a big fuss over just one person." Aelanur protested, for he had been hoping to rest a bit after his long travels of the day before and his prolonged searching of all this day.

But, Zurthaud had not heard him, for he had run off into the looming night, hastening as fast he could for the last place he had known Theros to be.

Chapter 33

The chill night wind whipped through Zurthaud's hair and cut at his face like cold steel blades, but he cared not. Theros cared neither, for though, thanks to his thick scaly hide, he did not feel the icy sting as did the Human, a person of utmost importance was awaiting their arrival- the Bright Dragoness.

She was the one for whom Malok had long been questing; she was the one for whom the Shadow Lord trembled. Zurthaud too had been longing for this day, in which he could rest easier knowing that one more wise and skilled than he would lead the Order and the free world to victory against the Dark Horde and their terrible master, in which the dying race of Dragons could be saved, for she was not only- as far as Zurthaud knew- the single last Dragoness alive in the world, thus their race's savior, but also the ultimately powerful light bringer, the greatest hero of the whole world, the one and only who, with her luminescent power, could save the world from the gathering darkness.

Many others had come along with them, including Lorn, who rode atop Galrag's shoulders, for ever since Zurthaud's mentioning of her apparent importance, they all had been in anticipation of the "Bright One's" arrival.

In only a few hours' time, they had crossed all the vast distance between Bythatsar and Doraegonoran, and now the great city loomed before them, its tall towers and walls black against the moonlit sky, with only the scattered light of street lamps and unshuttered windows to break it from the umbrous shadow of the mountains behind. Quickly and quietly, they soared across the silent garden of buildings unto the Citadel's Keep, that is, until Theros landed upon one of the top floor balconies.

"Argamon," Zurthaud called out, even as he dismounted from Theros' back and some guards ran out from the under the entryway to greet them. "Where is she?" He asked of them.

But, the common soldiers knew not what he meant, so that they had to fetch the elderly man from his quarters and bed. Donned only in a nightgown, the usually more noble guard captain tried to maintain some composure, but despite his best efforts at making a brisk and elegant stride, still being in the mind of sleep, he teetered slightly toward one direction or another while walking toward them.

"Sir." Said he, giving a salute and standing at attention, for no other polite words could he quickly summon to his tongue at this late moment.

"The Bright Dragoness where is she?" Zurthaud asked again, at first perplexed at the normally keen captain's ignorance of such an important person, but then remembering that Argamon had not been made aware of her status.

"There was a Dragoness, perhaps the one for which you had been searching, along with a few others, who arrived yesterday; they are staying in one of the unused apartments in the Dragons' quarter tower." Argamon replied, letting show only a little annoyance at having been awoken at this hour for such a question.

"Have you been keeping watch over her?" Zurthaud inquired, already mounting Theros' shoulders again.

"No, not particularly obtrusively," Argamon perplexedly replied, for he, though privy to the idea of the Bright Dragoness and the search for her, was not entirely informed regarding her full significance. "For, as you instructed, we have been keeping watch over the Citadel. But, no one, including the Dragon female has gone in or out, or even come near the walls or gates, without my knowledge."

Zurthaud quickly thanked and dismissed the captain of the guard, and he and Theros hurriedly took off toward the Dragons' quarter, leaving Argamon to stand confused and shivering in the cold night wind.

They peered into the entry of every apartment, but did not find any sign of their important visitor, until they came, at last, unto Serc's old dwelling. Here, there was a light flickering dimly out from the main room onto the balcony, and here Zurthaud and Theros landed, with Galrag and Lorn close behind.

As quickly as Zurthaud could hop down from his friend's shoulders, they darted into the main room, and found it occupied by none other than a lone Serpen, resting upon one of the smaller sitting cushions among a pile of scrolls, papers, and books. Zurthaud quickly recognized him as Malok's companion, Shar.

"What are you doing in here?" Theros nearly bellowed, after recovering from the surprise of finding not the one they were expecting.

"Reading." Shar slowly replied, dropping the document he had been examining.

"My friend, did you not learn of Serc's passing? And, here you are going through the belongings of one who is now dead." Zurthaud chided as gently as he could.

"Oh, this is, er, was his abode?" Aghast, Shar stammered, for truly he had not meant to disrespect the noble Dragon's memory by casually rummaging through his belongings. "I am so sorry. Everyone ran off and left me here alone all day, and I was just so bored." He attempted at an apology.

"How did you even get up here, seeing that your Dragon friend is not about?" Theros hotly interrogated.

"I climbed." Shar replied, nervously emphasizing with a complementary motion that caused Theros to snort, as much in humor as derision.

"Never mind that now. Where is the Bright Dragoness, she for whom you and Malok sought?" Zurthaud pressed, ignoring Theros' indignant anger toward Shar's unintentional disrespect.

"Oh, she went out into the city, but that was this morning." Shar explained, as if the fate of the world did not rest with the one person who had gone missing from it.

With Theros close behind, Zurthaud was already heading out from Serc's apartment when he heard a disturbance at the top of the tower. From the atrium of the domed temple, he heard someone cry out the most dreadful words he had heard all day.

"Dark Hunter!"

They two rushed up to the temple's balcony, fearing in their hearts that, somehow, the enemy's most wicked servants had penetrated the Citadel's defenses and either killed or captured their precious heroine. They did not so much as slow themselves to wash in the basins, running past them through the atrium and on into the sanctuary, for without even thinking upon it, they counted this as enough of an emergency that they could enter the holy place without such preparation.

Bursting through the entryway, they found that two of their fellow Paladins had, with drawn swords, cornered the villain between the inner rooms of the priest's quarters and the temple library and any escape from the multiple entrances of the sanctuary, but out of a desire to shed no blood on this sacred ground, they had not yet attacked.

The Dark Hunter himself had offered no aggression, merely standing stone still with his hands raised, as if in surrender, and in one of these he clutched a book. It was not even the Dark Lord's small, black-leather bound tome that he had apparently been attempting to steal, but was rather an ancient hymnal, full of old, Draconic worship songs.

"What business does one like you have in these holy halls?" Snarled Theros, letting flow the rage he had earlier checked.

"I was invited to stay here, in the Dragon's quarter, by the guard captain. Argamon was his name, and I was not told that any building had restricted access other than the Keep." Calmly replied the black-clad figure.

"That traitor!" Theros roared, but Zurthaud had noticed the submissive stance of this usually quite terrible foe, they of whom he had only heard tale but never before actually encountered.

"He invited you, a Dark Hunter, to be our guest?" Zurthaud further questioned, not believing for an instant that Argamon could be so dishonorable or clueless, and wondering what he or this Dark Hunter had to gain from entry to the temple for to steal old songbooks.

"I am no Dark Hunter." Replied Anur. "I am one of two surviving members of the Order of Masters, and companion to a Dragoness, the other member from the same."

Just as Zurthaud was about to inquire further into these claims, Lorn and Galrag arrived, and they had also brought up Shar, who sauntered into the temple at his own pace, hands still slightly wet from washing.

"Shar," Anur called to him "They think I am a Dark Hunter; tell them I am not."

"How can I be sure that you are not, for I am not so certain myself?" The Serpen smugly replied, and no one could tell if he were teasing or serious.

"If you let them kill me, Feldara will tear you to pieces, starting with your smarmy tongue." Anur threatened in a very Anur manner, crossing his arms and lowering his voice just so.

"Oh, it is definitely you." Shar conceded, still murkily between sincerity and jocularity. "My good Paladins lower your swords, for indeed, this is none other than the honorable companion of yon Bright, and violently wrathful, Dragoness, so do I vouch for him." Said he, stepping between Anur and the others, and now clearly mocking the laughable situation.

"You are a horses' ass." Anur vented, relaxing a little as the Paladins lowered their blades, and he would have chucked at the Serpen the hymnal that he had been much enjoying, but that he had too much respect for books and their valuable knowledge.

"Come now; all this is your own fault for wearing that fearsome helm, especially when there is no clear reason for it. You should just take it off until needed." Shar glibly patronized, heartily thumping Anur on the shoulder, which did nothing to alleviate his annoyance with the Serpen.

"If you are the companion, where is your Dragoness?" Zurthaud asked, not in the least bit distracted, even though he had plenty of questions for this strange man.

He had never even heard of the Order of Masters, and then there was the question of why he dressed as did the servants of the Shadow Lord. These were trivialities, though, compared to locating the "Bright One".

"She went out this morning to explore the city." Anur bluntly replied, quite over his, now two, less than hospitable welcomings to the Order of Paladins, but seeing Zurthaud's growing exasperation, he continued. "Fear not, both Malok, whom you know to be trustworthy, and Calidon, the son of Rathnyaling, are with her, for your good Paladin thought her unsafe, even within your own walls. I am also beginning to think the same." He finished with a sting, for he meant his poor treatment, as he figured that the two Dragon males, plus Feldara herself, could handle any small danger that might slip past the city's defenses.

"I know of Rathnyaling; his father was the famed Rathnyalgr, the great hero who first defeated the evil Shadow Lord. In his youth, he was a Paladin, a student of Serc, but for all the oppression, he left the Order and headed to the Aelven Kingdom in the West." Galrag stated, more out of a desire to reminisce than in vouching for Calidon, or even in making conversation.

Yet, Zurthaud had already turned to go. "Then truly, for such esteemed guests, I apologize for our poor greeting, but I have not the time to make amends right now. We must secure the Bright Dragoness within these sacred walls, for we cannot be sure that she is safe until she is here, the only place the Dark One's power cannot touch." Said he, calling back over his shoulder as he exited the sanctuary, but he and Theros did not travel very far.

They had but exited the sanctuary, and were just about to take off into the night, when two figures, shaded by the light of the moon and the deep of night, landed upon the temple balcony before them.

"Who goes there?" Zurthaud asked, for though he could tell they were Dragons, his eyes could not further determine their identity.

One was almost invisible in this hour of dark night, even though the moon was swollen and quite luminously shining upon him. The other was reflective as a running brook in the bright sun of noonday, so that the lunar glow radiated from her like a shimmering halo.

"It is I, Malok." Joyously, called out the umbrous black Dragon. "Zurthaud, Theros, come see who I have found and brought here with me."

They two did race unto the end of the temple's porch where did the other two land softly upon the balcony, and could but shield their eyes from the radiance of the Bright Dragoness. They had to wait until she came under the dome of the temple, for to gaze upon her, yet even then, her beauty was not diminished.

"Hello, I am Feldara." She humbly greeted them, offering a slight bow.

Zurthaud was ecstatic, but it was Theros who was the more emotional. He falteringly stepped forward toward this magnificent Dragoness, and he could barely breathe. He reached her, who was the exact image of the one he had loved most in all the world, lacking only in years, height, and coloring. He barely had to sniff of the air about her, for she seemed to him as a vision, like one of the many he had dreamed, of the happy golden past spent in the loving arms of an exactly alike blue female.

Theros came up quite close to her, tears in his eyes, and he could hardly find words for his mouth. Though neither his lungs or language worked yet, his hand reached forth to tenderly caress Feldara's cheek, and though she wondered greatly at this, in discomfort thinking to withdraw from him, she felt that she should not, that she was quite safe with this unknown, yet very familiar, older male.

To Feldara's mind came the memory of the great Father Dragon and his warmth of love, as Theros gently lifted her face so that he could gaze into her eyes. Struggling through his weeping and emotionally overwhelmed body, he let out all he could muster, a single whispered word.

"Daughter."

And, suddenly everything was well and as it should be, and Feldara buried her face in his strong chest and arms. Sobbing, they fell to the ground in each other's embrace, and they had no need for anything other than their shared, unbreakable, familial love, so that the night had no power, nor did time, nor anything else. For that eternal moment, the world was as complete and whole as Feldara's and Theros' once wounded hearts.

Zurthaud was also overcome with emotion, and though he had the presence of mind to cover his gaping mouth with a hand, tears flowed steadily down his own cheek. Never in all his life had he imagined the possibility that Lethira could have given birth after her brutal combat with Ilara, more so that the child she bore should have lived to adulthood apart from her parents, even more so that she would be the very same Dragoness for whom they had been searching, the Bright One. His questions, his expectations, could wait, thought he, as all the others gathered around, each coming to terms with what was happening in their own way.

Anur had been not far behind Zurthaud when he had rushed out of the temple, for he had surmised the Dragoness for which they were frantically searching was his own Feldara. He had seen the whole interaction, and he had to remove his helm for to wipe the tears streaming from his own eyes. Neither could he have imagined that his precious charge's actual parents were yet alive, and though he felt a small pang of selfish remorse, as now he thought to have been replaced in her heart by another who had not spent the time nor given the care he had for her, his crying was of sincere joy for her, for this joyous and miraculous reunion.

It was a good long while that they all stood or sat there, wet eyed by the overwhelming emotionality, yet lighthearted in the relief and closure of this happy fate, and the night began to grow cold and deep. Eventually, the two Dragons arose from where they had rested both their physical beings and all the weight of many years' worth of sighing and longing and wondering what had become of the other, Theros first, and then lending his arm, helping her up.

"Zurthaud," He joyously exclaimed, suddenly remembering his friend. "See my Daughter. She is alive, and has come back to me."

"I do see." Replied Zurthaud, as he dried his eyes. "Words cannot express how happy I am for you both."

"Who do I have to thank for your care? Who did so unbelievably kind and tremendously great a service unto me, that which I never could repay?" Theros asked of Feldara.

So overtaken by all the flood of thoughts and questions and feelings that she had been experiencing that she could but point her face and look toward her beloved mentor. Feldara then realized, looking upon Anur's weeping visage, again rid of his concealing helm, that life might now become quite strange for her, having two people she could name "father", but having such love for both of them, Anur's already proven, tried, and steadfast, and Theros' now kindled and eagerly awaited in the days ahead, that she knew such inconsequential matters would be smoothed over in time.

As it was, Theros strode boldly over to the much smaller Anur, and after looking him over and in the eye, gave a low, Draconic bow to him.

"I and my family are forever indebted to you for the unspeakable goodness you have shown us. I bow low unto you, and regret that before I had so misjudged you. I name you Dragon-friend, for I have no better words to express my gratitude." Spake Theros with his head upon the ground at Anur's feet.

"Not since my youth has such a pledge been made." Chuckled Galrag, as he stood watching the occasion with Lorn. "Though many a fine Paladin has been worthy of the title, a Human has not been formally named Dragon-friend since before the great darkness of the Kragon."

Anur could hardly bear it, as he was a humble person with no desire for such obeisance. He placed a comforting hand upon the Dragon's brow, and replied. "As for her care, it has been my honor and pleasure, and if I am your friend, you owe me nothing. For, I would hold nothing, especially not this, against a friend."

"Then, grant me one more boon." Requested Theros, as he rose from his humbling gesture. "Were you with 'her' when she died?" Asked he, meaning Lethira.

Anur nodded in reply, but he was quick to answer. "Let me not trouble you with such a sad memory on this happy day. Be with your daughter; be glad in your heart. Afterward, seek me out, and I shall tell you all. I have wept enough today, so that I do not wish to recollect her passing, but suffice it to say, I was with her until the very end, and I did all in my power to ease her passing."

Theros nodded in agreement, even though he yearned to hear what had become of his beloved mate, but he turned again to gaze upon his daughter. At length, he spoke unto them all in as mirthful a voice Zurthaud had ever heard. "Let us bring forth food and drink and make merry, for my child who was lost, now is found, and who I once thought dead, is alive!"

Chapter 34

Neither Theros, nor any of the others, had quite as much stamina as at first intended, so much as to party on through the night, and though they did break out a cask of fine wine and eat of some quickly prepared stores of sausages and cheese, breads and hams, and did talk merrily, Feldara listening to her father speak of his love for her mother, and he listening to the tale of her adventures traveling from her island home to the place where they now sat, by the end of the night's second watch, they had all found a resting place.

Not until very late the next morning did Feldara awake, for snuggled warmly next to her father in his bed, she had the soundest, most peaceful sleep of her life. To her, his very presence radiated security and belonging; it was as if merely his earthy, familiar scent brought a confident serenity and welcome to her soul that only once before had she experienced, in the arms of the Great Father Dragon.

Still, he was fast asleep, and snoring furiously, while she had already risen, so that, reluctantly, Feldara left from her comfortable place nestled at his side, but the morning was so beautiful, with a gorgeously fiery sunrise, that she soon left off her disappointment at his late sleeping. After all, now that she had found him, where would her father go that she could not reach him?

She was about to step out onto the balcony of Theros' apartment from the entryway where she had been watching the glorious morning, when a dark shadow swung down onto the same space she had been intent on occupying. Surprised at first, she quickly realized it was Malok who was landing there, nearly crashing into her.

"Oh, sorry!" He loudly apologized, clearly as surprised as she that he had almost plowed into her.

"You should be." She challengingly returned, more in jest than in anger, for indeed, it was only a near miss, not a collision.

In that moment's time, she allowed herself to look upon him, for she did think the darkly colored male very attractive, his black scales a direct and complimentary opposite of her shining skin. Now, with the hot sun burning in its ascending glory behind his shadowy apparition- almost a satin silhouette against such radiance, he seemed quite handsome, and Feldara found herself remembering and forgetting this being the same way she had felt about Calidon when they first met. However, even more so did she feel this toward Malok; it just seemed more right, as if it were supposed to be how she reacted to him. For, while her heart had quickly waned in amorous intent toward Calidon, as he had found his place in it as a beloved older brother, her romantic inclinations toward Malok only waxed stronger, and Feldara began to suspect the more time she spent with him, the more her fondness of him would continue to grow.

"I was just about to check if you were awake." Malok explained, abashedly backing off a little from his close contact with her.

"I am." Feldara, bluntly replied, having been jolted from her secret thoughts. "Was that all for which you wanted to come here?" She asked, raising a crested brow and hoping that it was not.

"Er, um, no, you see." Stuttering, Malok began to explain, but he took a deep breath mid-sentence, as he wondered how Feldara always managed to get him so flustered. "I was wondering if you would like to go hunting for breakfast with me." He finally managed to get out, though he could not yet look her in the eye.

Feldara could see that he desperately wanted her to go, and she did also want to accompany him. Yet, a thought came to her mind, that she had not seen Calidon all last night after he had excused himself from their presence, and she wondered if something horrible had befallen him again, as he seemed to have the worst of luck.

"I would." She replied, but then it was her turn to look down as she unhappily declined his offer. "But, I have not seen Calidon since yesterday. I have begun to worry and shall have to go looking for him, yet hopefully nothing ill has happened to him."

"Oh, I see." Malok glumly consented, thinking this answer meant something more than it did.

"I would appreciate it very much if you would help me search for him." Feldara offered, hoping to ease her rejection. "Perhaps, after we have found him, we could all get some breakfast together on our return."

Malok did not reply, but with only the slimmest of smiles- almost a grimace- motioned for Feldara to take the lead, and she did, leaping off the balcony ledge, letting gravity speed her momentum a little, then flicking out her golden wings to rise up on lift's resilient and steady push.

On through the late morning, they scanned the ground below and all around for their lost companion, but they found no trace of Calidon within the city. Venturing beyond the safety of the walls for his sake, they two circled high above the farms and fields without, and eventually, as they turned North and westward, they spotted a bright red ball, sitting on a hillock that rose above the country fiefs in the shade of the nearby mountains.

The bright glistening and peculiar shape of this abnormal figure caused them to investigate, for surely it could be nothing other than a Dragon sleeping, tightly curled up for the cold. Indeed, they found it just so, as they descending to the ground again, landed nearby, yet not so close to rouse their slumbering friend.

"Let me wake him." Feldara suggested, knowing that Calidon and Malok were, as yet, not on the best of terms.

Gently shaking his shoulder quickly bestirred him, and groaning with the unpleasantness of waking, Calidon unfurled his body and stretched out in the morning sunlight.

"Good morning, sleepy head; wandering off last night and not returning at daybreak had us worried that you might have gotten captured again." Feldara teased.

Calidon snorted with displeasure at this comment, for he had been greatly embarrassed at having, now two times, been overpowered by the Dark Hunters. Yet, he had gotten away from the others for his own benefit; he had spent the night thinking over how he had been acting, so hostile toward Malok and so gruff and unpleasant with everybody else. He had in the calm of isolation come to terms with his own feelings and had resolved within himself to be kinder and more friendly, even to Malok.

"And, good morning to you, smart mouth." Said he, and rather unintentionally, and borne only of his better mood and resolution for a kinder disposition, he kissed her, quite fully, upon the cheek.

Feldara did not know what to think of this, and she felt embarrassed, for herself but also for him, even as Calidon suddenly realized his overreaching friendliness, while Malok's heart both sank and burned with jealousy. Desperately trying to pretend nothing had just happened, Feldara suddenly backed off and sat down all at once.

"Would you like to go hunting for some breakfast with us?" She invited, as her tail curled defensively about her.

Truly, he had not meant to overstep the bounds of his friendship with Feldara, but seeing Malok's face turn pale, even through his night black scales, gave Calidon more pleasure and confidence than he had felt since leaving his home.

He had no idea how Feldara felt about him, nor did he know what she thought about Malok. As far as he was concerned, he was still running strong in the contest for her heart, and this too he had long pondered upon last night, his love for Feldara, to show it plainly to her by his deeds and words and prove himself worthy of her affections. No longer would he care what Malok said or did to try to woo this beautiful Dragoness; Calidon was determined to win her over. Only, no longer would he despise Malok for his efforts, and he would endeavor to be gentler with him.

However, the young male did not realize that there was no contest; not even a glimmer of hope remained for him to be the person he desired to be for Feldara. No matter what she yet felt, or did not feel, toward Malok, her mind had already been set about his place in her heart. He would never be more than a friend, like a sibling to her, and nothing he did would change that. The only outcome would be a building of tension and a growing strain on their current relationship.

"Of course, I would like to go with you, for I am famished." He exclaimed, though with wide-eyed glance askance, for he was still slightly abashed by his discourteous display of fondness from before and hoping that she had not thought it as weird as had he.

After a bit more yawning and stretching and pretending that they each were not in any sort of conflict with the others, they three took off again into the air, toward the very same mountains that rose as a majestic backdrop for the great city, and began the hunt for their morning meal.

With so many Dragons of the Order in such close proximity, the game of these slopes and valleys, the deer and goats, were very skittish and even more attuned to the approach of aerial predators than were those nearby the Rathnyalgrs, and the three hunters found that, by the time they had gotten close enough to begin their diving descent, their quarry would bolt, dispersing in all directions, and would only regroup into a herd when again well out of range. It had become so frustrating to Feldara that she had nearly given up on eating from these animals, until Calidon came up with an expert strategy.

One of them would head out in a great circle around the location of a larger flock and approach from the opposite direction, causing the flock to scatter toward the other two awaiting Dragons, and this seemed such a sound plan that even Malok went along without the slightest argument.

Winging far out to the right, Calidon enacted his maneuver on a herd of goats they had singled out, being one they had as yet to startle. Malok and Feldara could see him, afar off in the distance, stealthily circling around their prey, and at last, when he had gotten into position, they slowly advanced toward the herd. Suddenly, the goats caught sight or scent of Calidon, as he had stalked quite near to them, and they each had to dive quickly to have even a chance of catching one. But, the pincer movement had done its work, and finding themselves caught between the two groups of hunters, the animals hesitated just long enough for the Dragons to plow in amongst them.

Feldara caught one, which she was quite proud of, while Calidon came away with another, and being very hungry, they sat down immediately to skin and eat their meal. However, Malok had ended up empty handed, for before he had managed to snag a prize, the goats had all dispersed again. Truthfully, in the last moments before their killing strikes, he had noticed Feldara had chosen the same beast he had been eying, and certainly not wanting a collision, much less wanting to catch one and leave her without anything to eat, he had to hastily change to another target, which every hunter knows will most often lead to a miss.

Unfortunately, they had- due to their great hunger- not noticed this before attending to their own kills, and had left Malok to wonder how he was supposed to get his breakfast while they already began to eat. It was only after Feldara had taken her first few bite that she looked up and saw the black Dragon sitting a little way off, trying not to salivate eagerly at their meal or seem dejected by being left out. Indeed, he had made up his mind to poke fun at them for, rudely, going ahead and eating while he waited for them to finish so that they could try this maneuver again and he, at last, feed also.

Feldara felt much pity for him, though, and much shame for having neglected to see that they all had gotten food and could dine together. As soon as she had noticed him- and she alone, for Calidon almost had buried his face in his meat- she arose from where she had sat and took her goat over to him.

"Here, I am sorry; I had not noticed your going without. We can share this one and get another when we are finished." She offered, setting the mutton down between them.

Yet, before Malok had a chance to open his mouth, for he had intended to politely deny her kindness and insist that he could wait to get his own, Calidon had just glanced up to see him with the kill that Feldara had made.

"How dare you take that from her!" Calidon bellowed, mouth still full, as he furiously arose and leaped over to Malok for he thought, or rather from lack of thought surmised, that his rival had taken by force what had belonged to someone weaker than he.

Before Feldara could explain that her offer to share her own food was none of Calidon's business, the larger red Dragon, thinking to be somewhat of a hero for defending Feldara from a greedy bully, had snatched up the carcass and flung Malok to the ground with a forceful push.

"Is it not bad enough that you are too poor a hunter to get your own kill, but now, in weakness, you steal another's?" Calidon roared, and shoved the goat's carcass, now quite dusty from all the scuffling, toward Feldara.

It should have not gone farther than that, Calidon's completely asinine overreaction to a mere misunderstanding, which Feldara or even Malok could have verbally contended, to his ignominy, with their own, truthful explanation of events and scathing reprimand, but Malok was rather done with this maltreatment he had received from the blunt, rude, aggressive, and now assaulting other male. He also rose in fury, and roaring in retaliation, he leaped into the larger Dragon with all his might, and striking him with such force, tackled him to the ground.

The fight was on now, and the two Dragons rolled in the dirt wrestling and beating and biting one another. Even though they had the presence of mind not to use their claws, which would have been an abomination, shedding the blood of another Dragon with the intent of dealing death, they battled fiercely, but Feldara was also quite fed up with all this bickering, hatefulness, and now full-on fighting.

"Stop it!"She screamed, and she unleashed upon them a burst of fire from her lungs.

It did not singe the other two Dragons, but it did get their attention. They immediately ceased from their tussle and pushed away from each other.

"What has come over you two?" Feldara yelled at them both, tears welling in her eyes, for though they suffered some minor bruising from their scuffling, she was inflicted a greater wound by their mutual meanness.

"I was just,…" Calidon began to explain, but Feldara gave him such a glare that he could not possibly finish his sentence, and he could only hang his head low in disgrace.

Malok too could not face her, even though she came to see about him, for Calidon had hurt him sorely in the leg so that he had developed a slight limp.

"What if you have broken his leg, or worse, had killed him?" Feldara asked of Calidon, who could not reply. "And, you." She started to say in challenge of Malok's actions, but she was just so disappointed with the violent manner he had retaliated that she could find no more words.

Even though she knew Malok had been acting in his own defense, he still should not have repaid Calidon's evil with more of the same. They should have both known better, than to behave in such a way, and indeed, their emotional, and hormonal, upheaval was not even a pathetic excuse for their viciousness. Feldara was just so tired of dealing with them both, that she just up and left them there, abandoning her food also, as the taste for anything had gone from her mouth, and she flew as far and fast away from them as she could, leaving the two males to reconsider their shameful conduct.

Chapter 35

It was going to be a good day; Zurthaud determined. For, with the Bright Dragoness found and safe and the crisis of the Great Burning- as it was now being called- behind them, he felt that there was nothing now to overly worry him. He had risen from a restful sleep, a good hour longer than he normally did, and had seen Feldara head out with Malok, so that he did not feel overly worried for her sake. So, now he sat in relative relaxation in the kitchen of the Human quarter's barracks eating a simple breakfast of grain porridge and some bacon, and indeed, so content was he that he hardly noticed the approach of Feldara's companion, Anur. Although, that would have been the case had he even been on guard, for as he learned, Anur was usually as quiet in his treading as a cat.

"Good morning." Zurthaud welcomed, as Anur, with his own porridge and bacon, sat across from him at the long table, for they were the only two people within, other than one lone cook, who had stayed behind to feed the few guards that remained with Argamon in the Keep.

With a grunt, Anur explained why it was not a good morning. "That cook was quite rude; not recognizing that I am your guest, he did not wish to serve me. Instead, he grabbed up a kitchen knife and backed into a corner, and it was only after I started helping myself some of the food he had made that he calmed down enough to even ask who I was."

Zurthaud resisted the urge to laugh, for it was an oddity to him that this person who sat across from him was, obviously, of the same folk as the Dark Hunters, and even more so that it was not in the slightest a consideration of how others would perceive him. Even without his helm, as he was now, Anur would appear to the common man as a Troll, and Zurthaud wished to get to the bottom of this mystery, how a servant of darkness could be the companion of the daughter of light.

"Anur is it? Do you mind if I ask how it is that you came to be part of,.. what did you call them last night- the Order of Masters, and how you came to be Feldara's companion and caretaker?" Zurthaud questioned setting down his bowl and spoon and leaning comfortably upon the table.

Anur, with a somewhat annoyed look, finished his bite of gruel before answering. "It is odd, and somewhat vexing, wording a question in such a way- to ask permission to interrogate me, but to then proceed voicing your inquiries all the same. I have received nothing but poor treatment since I arrived here, so that you must answer my questions before I shall consider yours." He bluntly deflected. "Why is it that here the skies are not filled with Dragons, that there is barely a guard in the Keep, and more so, that there was a sacking and burning of the lands hereabout that was in no way abated by your order, and lastly, why have we been entreated so inhospitably by ones who should be more like us than any other folk, the companions and friends of Dragons, the upholders of truth, justice, and peace?"

Zurthaud was taken aback by this sudden outpouring of enmity, but he refrained from returning any. "We have been going through a very troubling time of late. It started with the man who sired me, Orthard, who became Lord Consul and, due his unwise, greedy, corrupt, cruel, and eventually just plainly evil character, his iron-fisted rule over the Order caused the Paladins and, indeed, all the people of these lands much suffering. The Dragons did fare the worst, for while they were the majority of those who would yet remain in defiance and keep intact their honor and still perform their orderly duties of keeping watch and protecting the people, by combat and tragedy and the evil machinations of Orthard and the Dark Lord, their numbers dwindled severely, until now that only a few hundred remain. As of right now, most of them are still out aiding those refugees made homeless by the Dark Horde's recent attack, and truly we are to blame for not defending the helpless people that night. It was only that we had just finished overthrowing that despot who had so destroyed our Order from within, even striking down our eldest, wisest, and most beloved, member, so that we were in mourning, that we were so ill prepared to defend those whom we swore to protect. I can swear to you now that such a thing will never happen again, for we will post a new watch on the border wall and a new High Council will be elected. Truly, I apologize for our lack of consideration as your hosts, for we did start our relationship in misunderstanding and in mid-crisis."

"Apology accepted." Anur muttered after another mouthful of porridge.

"Now, you said that if I gave an account to you, you would answer me. Please, do, for I am quite perplexed by your appearance and by this Master Order, the like of which I have never heard tale." Zurthaud pressed, as after finishing his breakfast, he reclined.

Anur also finished his bowl of food before giving explanation. "The Order of Masters- you have not heard mention of them? Truly, much do you not know, for we were as the graduates of your Order, the most elite and advanced members of the Order of Paladins coming to serve in our ranks. I was not born among them; they found me, when I was very young, wandering along the far shore from their island, along the coast of the Shadow Lands. I remember little, but I was told that they took me in because I was starving and near death, possibly an outcast of my kind. They trained me in their ways, so that I, probably, know a great deal more about magic, swordsmanship, and Dragons than any Paladin hereabout."

Here Anur paused to drink from his pewter mug, and Zurthaud took the opportunity to ask, yet another question. "Why then have we not heard from the Order of Masters, at least not since before I was born, and our Paladins do not 'graduate' to your Order anymore?"

"We were also destroyed, but utterly, now many years ago; I have lost track how many." Anur explained, his demeanor becoming quite morose. "One night, we were attacked, set upon by the Dark Horde, who came in overwhelming force of number, and when the morning finally dawned, breaking at last that longest, bloodiest night of my life, I was the only one who remained alive."

"It is hard to believe such a tale." Zurthaud pondered aloud, though not out of distrust for Anur's word. "I mean, if our two orders were as close as you say, surely you would have sent word to us of your dire situation, and surely we would have sent aid upon hearing of it."

"By the time the attack came, we had received no new members in many years." Anur returned. "That, I do remember, for the supplies were cut off from the East, the realm of Men and the Paladins. Long had we gone without any aid or trade from Humans or your Order, only the Aelvs provisioned us, and that only upon request. Indeed, we sent out Dragon messengers before that fateful night, but they never returned, not even after the fighting was long over and the weeks after that, which I spent burying our dead and burning the enemy. I long ago assumed they too were captured and slain by the enemy."

Anur here paused again, for the old wounds he had mended and forgotten were being torn open again. He took a long drink from his mug, wishing that it had been filled with mead instead of milk.

"I am sorry to hear of this. Please, forgive me asking this of you; I had no idea of the sorrow which you bore." Zurthaud apologized, regretful that, indeed, he had not ever heard of the Order of Masters or their untimely and doleful ending, and he wished within himself that he could also rectify this shortcoming of the Paladins, yet knowing he could never turn back time to do so.

"There is nothing to be done for yesterday, only for today and tomorrow." Spoke Anur, more in consolation of his own heart. "I still have tale to tell of how Feldara came to be in my life, and that tale is better, for it is only bittersweet with a very happy ending, rather than tragic all through. However, I think it would be best to speak of it first in the presence of your companion, Theros, for it does involve the passing of his mate."

"She was my companion also, before Theros even liked me." Zurthaud mused, again remembering his beloved friend of old, her motherly kindness, how she had practically raised him. He truly missed her, and longed to hear word of her, even if it be only of her passing. Yet, he agreed that Theros should be present when they heard this tale.

Rising, Zurthaud took up his eating utensils and bowl along with Anur's, for he wished to accomplish much more today than conversing with his guest. "Speaking of my Dragon, I should best locate him soon, for we have much to do today. The finalizing of the refugee aid and recalling the Paladins from that task, setting up the new border wall guard, among much other less palatable business must all be done soon, hopefully by evening, and I shall need his aid in all these things."

Seeing that Anur would have nothing better to do, Zurthaud returned unto him from the kitchen, after he dumped the dirty eating implements into the cook's washbasin. "If you would like, I invite you to accompany me, for it is not every day one gets to be in the presence of a Master." Zurthaud offered with a charming, mostly sincere, grin.

Anur was almost tempted to return the expression, and he nodded his head and arose from his seat in acceptance of the offer. He was beginning to like this Zurthaud fellow.

<><><><><>

The morning was moving quite slowly for Theros, for he had woken earlier than usual, for to see his long lost daughter and spend time with her, only to find out that she had already flown off with the young Malok to get breakfast, leaving him alone in the apartment with only the black Dragon's Serpen companion.

Zurthaud and Anur had apparently hitched a ride down with another Dragon, probably Galrag, and would no doubt be eating breakfast in the tiny, Human-sized barracks' kitchen, into which he could not fit even his head. This he considered a great shame, not because the Order had built buildings that were unable to accommodate a Dragon-sized individual, but that he had very much wanted to speak further with the Dark-Hunter-like man about Lethira. Even Zurthaud he would have wanted to spend time with today, but the Serpen companion of Malok, Shar, Theros did not care to be around.

It was not that he disliked Serpen. It was not even that he bore Shar any undue animosity, but this Serpen, once started, would just not shut up.

"I cannot believe he did not as much let me know he was leaving." Complained Shar, which seemed to Theros the only thing that he did.

Even after getting the Serpen some meat, for which Theros had hunted, and for which he had grudgingly returned to his apartment to eat, knowing that Shar would be alone and, though found out to be an excellent climber, possibly stranded in the high and inaccessible Dragon apartment, he still complained. Seemingly, he was upset that Malok had up and left this morning without letting Shar know.

"What friend leaves another friend, a friend who depends on that friend for transportation, alone and yet asleep without even mentioning to another friend, or even writing a note explaining his intentions?" Shar ranted in between mouthfuls of venison.

"What daughter leaves her father in the same way, with whom she had been reunited just last night after sixteen years of separation?" Theros asked, not at all bothered by what Feldara had done, just a little envious of Malok, but only wanting the Serpen to see that others had more to complain about than he and hoping that would silence him.

"See, you know how I feel. We should repay them in some like rudeness, either that or give them both a sound scolding when they return." Shar continued, as Theros realized, the flames of malcontent had only been fanned by his tactic, and still on the Serpen king yammered.

Rubbing his eyes with a hand, as after a long spell of Shar whining in between bites of food, and the increasingly agitated Dragon munching and trying not to listen in relative silence, Theros came to his last resort- threatening violence. "Shar, be silent. I have listened to your incessantly plaintive mouth all morning, and I have grown tired enough of it that, were you to open it again, I would shut it for you, permanently."

The Serpen was about to object to this treatment, but a sound from outside the apartment distracted them both, thus saving him. Theros recognized that it was a voice calling up to them from the ground below, and he arose for to see who it was, though guessing told him it would be Zurthaud and Anur. Indeed, it was they two, for as the Dragon apartments had no access other than wings, they needed Theros to lift them up to his residence. Of course, Theros obliged. He would never leave his friends waiting on the ground, and soon they four were sitting comfortably and, for a welcome change, chatting amiably within Theros' abode.

"We had better leave now, for we have much to do today." Zurthaud suggested, after only a few minutes already getting up to go.

"What did you have in mind?" Theros asked, for he knew of quite a few things he wished to do that would not take him half as far away as the border wall.

"Well, we must finish the care of the refugees today, for most of the homes are either finished or in the final processes of reconstruction. We must also see to the securing of the Aronoran. Both of these tasks shall go together, for we will need our Paladins who are currently busy with the refugees to begin the watches and make any needed repairs. If we accomplish both of those tasks and yet there is daylight, I suppose we should begin preparing our formal complaints against Orthard, for though, above all other of his many crimes, he murdered Serc before a number of witnesses, we must still uphold our system of justice and offer the observance of trial, so as to adequately expostulate his guilt before the judges and the public." Zurthaud explained.

"That is a tall order for one day; I was hoping only to spend time with my daughter and hear of my mate's passing from our friend Anur." Theros wistfully murmured, but a Dragon's murmur is as resonant as a Human's normal speaking voice, so that he was well heard.

"Oh yes, do complain about your circumstances." Shar grumpily mocked, only to receive a wicked glare from the Dragon.

"Since I have already been invited to accompany you and Zurthaud on this day, I could speak of this as we go about your duties." Anur offered.

Theros agreed, but he had something he had wanted to bring with him. "Before we go, we must head down to Serc's old apartment; there is something that I would like to get, something that might help explain what happened to Lethira." He declared, also rising.

After a clumsy sort of mounting- of the like that a Paladin would have been ashamed to observe or take part in, as Shar insisted, even without voice or intention, upon mounting and dismounting first, even if Anur or Zurthaud were directly in the way- the three bipedal people managed to each find a spot between one of Theros' long neck spines. In sitting single-file, it was not so cramped on Theros' back for all three of the smaller folk as Zurthaud would have thought; still, it was too short of a trip for anyone's liking to go on like this- with Shar hastily clambering over everyone, only to have to clamber, again over everyone, off from Theros' back when he landed upon the other balcony, not two stories, and half as many minutes, beneath them. Indeed, Theros, if given inquiry, would have rather suggested chucking the inadvertently uncouth Serpen rider down onto the lower balcony, whether or not the height would cause him to splatter upon the stone, and only carry on his shoulders those with better riding etiquette, yet despite their inward or outward cringing and grumbling at the Dragon-back bumping and scuffling, they eventually all made it into Serc's apartment without too much time wasted.

"What is it that you had needed?" Confused, Zurthaud asked of his Dragon. "Surely, not a medical tome, for reading the names or descriptions of illness or wound that she suffered could not possibly be useful to us."

But, Theros paid him no heed; he was too busy hunting about for something in particular.

"Blast you Shar; these books are all in disarray. Your curiosity of last night has strewn all Serc's records out of order, and I shall now have a hard time of finding what I seek." Theros grumbled, as he thumbed through the once highly organized books and scrolls upon the shelves and in cases lining the back walls of the main room.

After a good minute of this searching, and Shar, arms folded, muttering about how he should not have left home, much less been left bored and alone, without anything to do all the day before, Theros gave up his scanning of Serc's records, for despite the chaotic disorganization, he had thoroughly looked over every shelf.

"I cannot find the black book, the one written by the Shadow Lord." Turning back to face the onlookers, Theros relayed.

It was then that Zurthaud also recounted what Theros was seeking, and thinking quickly, he strode into the back of the apartment into Serc's private chambers. "But, Serc said that he had made a translations of excerpts." He excitedly recalled. "They are on his writing desk, but the black book is not among them." Zurthaud called out, as reaching down onto the low, angled table, he grabbed up and examined the papers, which while conveniently noteworthy sized for a Dragon, were like a large advertisement poster to him.

Abruptly, he realized that these were the last words that Serc had written, and he held them with a little more care, as the others followed him into Serc's study.

"Is it there," Theros asked, even while taking from Zurthaud the pages and looking through them. "That one spell that Serc mentioned just the morning of his passing?"

"What significance does this spell hold?" Anur asked, not aware of what had transpired, where it came from.

"These were taken from a small, black leather bound tome that we recovered from the Ragnor." While Theros read through Serc's notes, Zurthaud explained , but paused briefly as, with eyes widening in amazement, Anur comprehended exactly what he meant. "These are the writings of the Shadow Lord himself, translated by one of our most beloved members into the common tongue from the Old Draconic in which they were scrawled, and this particular enchantment that my friend is referencing involves a manner in which Dragons can be brought under the Dark One's control."

"I see." Anur said, becoming, as did they all, most grave.

"Yes, here it is." Theros triumphantly proclaimed, separating the correct page from the rest. "Will you read it aloud, Zurthaud?" Theros asked, for his thoughts had darkened, lingering upon the method by which his mate had died, and though he wished for some sort of closure, which he thought perhaps this knowledge would partially provide, he could not bear to read the wicked spell himself.

Zurthaud did read the words, which having been converted into the common tongue and moderated in their wickedness by Serc's interpreting had lost all power in their mere uttering. The spell was as thus.

The Curse of Blood-stones:

A chain of Black-iron, in melding of fire, binds to it a shard of purest Darkness.

In these, my Dragon-stones, shall lie my power, my curse, which is Darkness.

When hanging upon the neck, my Darkness shall cover: their eyes, ears, mouth, nose.

As if in deepest slumber, their mind and body shall be numbed,

So that they cannot feel, cannot reach outside the mind,

To think, to perceive, to know that they are caught.

For, in that Darkness, they shall not hear me utter;

In that dream, they shall not feel me move:

Their legs, their hands, their feet; their eyes, their mouth, their throat;

Their lungs, their wings, their claws; their voice, their heart, their mind.

All that they are shall be mine, for the purpose which I desire- to move, to change, to use.

Thus, shall the mighty fall,

And those once free shall be made to serve.

"That is terrible." Shar gasped, eventually breaking the silence that had grown among them since reading the awful spell.

Truly, though the words had been rewritten carefully, so as to diminish the hate and wickedness of the original, there was still much to revile of this horrendous enchantment, for in it was the intent to bind and shackle another being, to enslave them to the will of a dark master.

Anur was the most shocked, for he had seen firsthand the effect of these "Blood-stones".

"Did you happen to see one of these necklaces, wrought of Black-iron with a gem of dark quality, about the neck of my Lethira?" Theros asked, nearly coming to tears thinking that his beloved had been so possessed before her passing.

"No, I did not find anything like that upon her, and she was fully in control of her own mind, unlike those who are under the influence of these Blood-stones. Indeed, I have seen them used before, on a perfectly healthy, kind young male, who never would have dreamed of hurting another Dragon, but he slavered and stumbled like a ravening wild beast and fought against Feldara with ferocity, yet cunning." Anur answered, recalling Calidon's fight with his charge, which he had been able to helplessly observe from afar, even as he had hoped to distract from the fight with the burning of the enemy camp.

"What became of the poor Dragon?" Zurthaud asked, not realizing of whom Anur spoke, hoping that they had ended him kindly.

"Feldara freed him, but she could tell you further how that occurred. At the time, I was too far away, and upon seeing who it was they had so enslaved- too distraught, to more directly intervene, instead attempting to stop the fight with more pressing concerns to the enemy. His name is Calidon, the other Dragon who has accompanied us, as I told you last night, yet he did not return with Feldara and Malok from their visiting of the city. So, for some reason, I suppose he elected to sleep outdoors."

"Wait." Zurthaud interjected. "I remember Galrag speaking of him and his father, but I have never before met this Dragon; I mean, he is not one of our members. Please, tell me again, from where did he come?" Zurthaud asked, quite confusedly, for he had thought all living Dragons were among the Paladins.

"Well, his father is Rathnyaling, son of Rathnyalgr, and he was living with the rest of his family: His parents, Aunt and Uncle, brothers, sisters, and cousins- in the Aelven Kingdom, but chose to come here with us, for to become a Paladin." Anur explained rather casually.

However, Zurthaud could not believe his ears. "Wait. There are other Dragons, other Dragonesses out in the world? Feldara is not the last one?" He asked, completely at a loss.

"You had thought the Dragons only lived among the Order and close to extinction?" Anur countered, as much perplexed as Zurthaud.

All this time, all his life, he had thought, since the Dragons of the Order were so low in number and there were no females among them, that there were no other Dragonesses at all, and that Feldara, being the last one in existence, was the only hope for their kind to remain, to reproduce. No one had told him otherwise, not Serc, not Theros, nor any other Dragon.

He looked to his friend, but Theros could not meet his gaze. He knew, and had known otherwise, and more, that Zurthaud had been deceived, intentionally.

"You knew all this time, and knew that I wholeheartedly believed your people were dying, and you chose not to tell me any different?" Zurthaud plaintively accused his best friend, as he was nearly dizzied by the betrayal as much as he was joyfully relieved for the Dragons.

"It was part of Serc's plan. I did not wish to go along with it, but I did. We all did. Only now that he has passed and what he set out to accomplish has been done, do I feel I can speak freely of what I had once sworn to keep secret." Theros admitted, at last meeting Zurthaud's gaze.

"I can barely believe what I hear, that my most trusted of friends, proven faithful on so many other counts, have so long and so willfully lied to me. Come clean of this deception; what plan do you speak of?" Zurthaud pressed, struggling to keep from seeming as angry as he felt for being so duped, for truly he was glad that the Dragons were not in so dire a predicament as he had always envisioned.

Theros cleared his throat, either in preparation of a lengthy explanation or due to the uneasy tension that had permeated the apartment, before beginning. "After you were born, the discrimination we Dragons and the other races received from the Humans, which had, indeed, existed much earlier, intensified greatly, for as you and I found out together only a few days ago, Orthard made it his personal vendetta. The wrath of my people burned hot against such disdainful treatment and slanderous words, and we met together to discuss how we should react to this injustice. I still remember, though I was a young Dragon, that there were two parties. One was led by Galrag, and he wanted to forcefully overthrow the Humans, even if it meant burning the Citadel to the ground. He was much more hot-blooded back then, a fierce and proud warrior; more than once he has told me how much I remind him of his fiery youthful days. The other group was headed by Serc, and, I now suppose it was for the sake of his past friendship with Orthard and with your mother, he desired not to engage in violence. Instead, he proposed a three step plan, which nearly succeeded without any bloodshed at all, and had Orthard only stayed his final order of sentencing us to death, it would have worked flawlessly. Obviously, his strategy, being the wisest and kindest, was the one that carried the day, and the three parts were thus."

"One: remove from the Order and its jurisdiction all our children, our families, the very old, and any others who did not wish to stay, so that they would be safe and free from any harmful actions that Orthard would take. This phase we enacted so well, over so long a period of time, the Humans and even most of the other races thought we were dying out, and we let them think so. However, they whom we protected had only left for our ancestral homes in the northern Aegan Mountains, the Southeastern forests and those of the Aelven lands, and elsewhere, and we swore an oath neither to speak of this, not to friends or companions, or even to each other, nor allude in any way what actually happened to them."

"Two: is where you come into this plan, for without you it would have never succeeded..."

And, here Theros was interrupted by Zurthaud.

"So, I was, indeed, just an instrument, to be used for the expediting of your plots and plans?" Zurthaud nearly yelled, feeling that his whole life's work had been vainly pursued, that he would have been better off refusing Serc's offer so many years ago.

"That is not true!" Theros forcefully objected. "You have been my friend, not because of some scheme, but because I love you and wanted to be your companion, for even when you were but a little Human child, whose progenitor I loathed with all my being, you had more in common with this foolish, hot-headed Dragon than any other person in the world. And, you are a perfect fit with me. You take my rage and melt it with your compassion; you have always tempered my anger, so that I am not the same stupid, young warrior I once was. You have helped make me the Dragon I am, and I love you for that and much more beside. Of Serc, he loved you as a son, and you must know by now how deeply that he did. And, speak not of Lethira in that way, for she sought you out, seeing how badly you were neglected and abused. She loved you and cared for you before you even knew what a Dragon was, so kind was her heart. Sincerely I speak this, we did not choose you as a tool to fit the position we needed for Serc's plan or because of any influence you had with the Human Paladins, or anything else. We each saw in you the kindhearted, noble, and charismatic man that you were and would become, and we cherished you for it. It was because of your great character that we loved you, and it was because we loved you that, to us, you were the only choice for the great task of uniting the Paladins and leading the Order."

Zurthaud's outrage was considerably diminished on hearing what his closest friend thought of him, of remembering the love his other dear friends had for him. "Why then did you keep this from me, for you knew that I could be trusted?" He inquired, now more in regret of not being included in such an important conspiracy, and for seeming foolish whenever he thought or spoke contrary to the truth, rather than in any anger over being deluded.

"We swore an oath, and Dragons are not oath-breakers. It was, ultimately, too late to inform you, for most all those who had wished to leave had already long gone by the time you became friends with Lethira." Theros penitently explained. "Besides, I thought you would have figured it out for yourself when all those 'wild' Dragons came to help fight off the Dark Horde and rebuild after the Great Burning." He smirked, becoming more lighthearted.

In truth, Zurthaud had neither the time nor brainpower to ponder such things during those few days of ceaseless, sleepless work, but now that he thought upon it, he recalled seeing many Draconic faces he had not recognized. Still, all the "wild" Dragons who had lent their aid were fully grown males, so that anyone who had not seen the battle, with all the "rider-less" Dragons, could have been easily blindsided.

"Well, I am very glad that is now out of the way; I, for one, feel much better." Shar glibly interposed. "But, what was part two and three of the Dragons' master plan?"

With a snort of irritation, fully directed at Shar's incessantly contemptuous tongue, never mind his undue curiosity, Theros continued. "Part Two was to separate the Humans by faction, those who would see reason and follow the old ways in unity and brotherhood, and those who chose to follow Orthard's demeaning idiocy. Zurthaud was instrumental in this, not only because, as I already explained, he was beloved, and certainly became a foothold in the ranks of men- good-natured, trustworthy, and stalwart friend- but also because (and this only by his own natural talent) he was the singular person who could lead all of us together, Humans and Dragons. Step three was much less violent in planning than in reality, for Serc determined that as soon as Orthard's support waned enough, as happens to all who wrongfully rule, we would simply have our Human allies call for a vote and place Zurthaud as head consul. Once elected, Zurthaud would no doubt, even as he is now doing, lead us rightly and treat all peoples fairly."

"I do like that version of what should have happened much better than the coup and the loss of life that accompanied it." Zurthaud thought aloud, again missing the departed Serc and forgiving him keeping secret these few matters.

"I am just glad that the Dragons' situation is not so dire as you had believed." Spoke Anur, rather amusedly. "As she is not one for pomp or fanfare,

I have no doubt Feldara would have despised such importance thrust upon her shoulders."

With a sigh, Zurthaud let go completely the frustration he had let build up in him over hearing of his friends' deception, for truly, he was glad to hear how wrong that he was, to think that the Dragons were helpless to keep themselves from going extinct and that he alone had to fix such an overwhelming problem. Certainly, at the back of his mind, had this anxious fear long gnawed, that these glorious people, including his best friends, would be gone from the world, and now, in great relief, he could finally discard that worry.

"Do you forgive me withholding this from you?" Theros asked, rather sheepishly from the Human.

But, Zurthaud could hold nothing long against his close friend. He uncrossed his arms, and instead opened them in embrace of his friend. "I am mostly just relieved, gladdened to hear that your people are not endangered in so terrible a manner as for years I had anxiously feared, but I am even more gladdened that you can now fully confide in me, that there is no oath sworn secret between us that needs be kept hidden." He explained, then letting go his Dragon. "My, the hour grows later, and we have become so sidetracked from our original purpose of entering Serc's apartment. Theros, I know that we have as yet touched on Lethira's passing, but we have spent much time- and forgive me for being the one to keep us from our duties- but, we must be off if we wish to accomplish all that needs to be done today. If you would fly slowly and just take us as far as Bythatsar, Anur can speak to us of Lethira along the way. We can get another to transport, Anur and I, from there to the wall, for I know that, more so than anything else in the world, especially after such heavy conversation, you wish to be with your daughter today." Zurthaud proposed.

With sincere thanks from Theros for Zurthaud's free forgiveness and their restored relation, and almost more so for his leave of duty, they all left again from Serc's apartment to go about their various tasks, except Shar, for he did neither wish to intrude upon Theros' time with Zurthaud and Anur, and later Feldara, nor did he wish to travel all the way to the border wall, or be left on his own in Bythatsar.

Yet, in the diversion of Theros' apologetic tale and their haste to get on with their tasks, even as Theros winged away into the clearest and brightest of skies, not at all did one of them think to ask why the Shadow Lord's little black book was not to be found in Serc's apartment.

Chapter 36

Feldara was very upset, and so much so, that after she had endured that horrible display of childish squabbling from both Calidon and Malok, she had spent the rest of the morning flying about alone. She had not yet returned to the ground, for she thought that, perhaps, one of the two males might have followed her, and she did not wish to give them any time of day, nor the opportunity to apologize.

At some point during her questioning of why they, especially Calidon, had been so violent, acting so weirdly out of character, she had come to figure that it must be because of her, and she was quite riled at that thought, that she could be treated as some sort of prize, over which to be contested. She had been trying not to let either of them on, that she might be interested in pursuing a closer relationship with them.

Indeed, she thought herself nowhere near ready for such responsibility or even capable of allowing someone so close to her heart as to be her life-mate, even though she had considered the possibility of delving further into friendship with the both of them.

When she had first met him, she truly had though that Calidon could be the one for her, as he was handsomely large and strong, yet she had never felt that way toward him thereafter. Through their time spent with each other, she had grown to regard him as an older brother, and she wished only for that familial closeness with him, that which he was only making harder to maintain with his strangeness, his brash, ungainly, and plainly unwanted, pursuing of her heart.

Toward Malok, she felt differently, completely opposite, a closeness and knowing of his soul that she could not describe, as if she had met him before and had then been good friends. Butterflies floated in her stomach when his low, gentle voice spoke with her so unrestrained and personally, and she sought to know more and more the mystery of this charming black male.

It delighted her to think that she could possibly spend all the rest of her days loving and cherishing him, but she wished that eventuality much further away from now; she wanted life to move more slowly than it was, than it had been.

Indeed, with all her many adventures and all the long traveling, these last few weeks had flown by at a Dragon's racing speed, and she had just wanted to relax and have a little peace and rest. She wanted calm and freedom and the open sky under her wings, yet these two males were ruining that desire, truly a need, and were intent on forcing her to choose one of them and push the other out of her circle of friends.

Feldara decided then, that if these two foolish Dragons were so determined to make her do something that she was very much unwilling to do, she would spend no time with either of them, and she began winging her way back toward the Citadel, to her father, the only male Dragon she ever cared to see again, or at least, at this time.

She reached the city in no time at all, for she had been flying in lengthy, circling paths over the countryside thereabout, and even quicker did she find herself landing upon the balcony of Theros' apartment. Sooner still did she find herself, again, sitting on his bed, the exact place she had started this day, for she had looked about the apartment and not found him to be there.

As she sat, her wrath toward those two boyish Dragons only grew, and she could only detest the way they had acted the more for the way it so affected her. She sat and stewed in her ire, wasting away the hours, until she could barely stand it anymore, and she laid down her head in the big, soft cushion and cried for anger, that she could be so mad at her two friends and so hurt by such foolish behavior.

Eventually, the hotness of her rage diminished, and she found herself only weeping a little, crying herself to sleep, wishing that she could just be herself and not have such problems.

<><><><>

For a good long while, maybe an hour, Malok and Calidon just sat there in the dirt, looking at the dirt, feeling like dirt, for so ashamed were they of the violence and hatred they had shown to another of their own kind, to another Dragon. It was not the way proper Dragons behaved, not even in the heat of passion, and Calidon knew that his father and mother would be most disappointed if ever they heard how he had been acting.

Malok had no such upbringing, but he needed not a good parent to teach him that striking others, or acting in any violence toward another Dragon, was inexcusably opprobrious. He had a gentle heart; truly they both did. Just in the war of love, they had forgotten to show that to each other.

It was Calidon who spoke first, for as the aggressor, he knew it was his duty.

"Malok, please, forgive me. I have been acting a fool and shamefully mistreating you." He sincerely apologized.

"Of course, friend, if only you will forgive me for fighting with you. I should not have done that." Malok graciously responded.

They two arose and gave an amicable embrace, and just like that, they surmounted their fiendish action and hateful thinking toward one another and so moved on to being better, while unbeknownst to them, Feldara was still sitting and fuming.

"Did I hurt your leg badly?" Calidon asked, remembering that before Malok had limped away from their scuffle.

The black Dragon shook his head "no", for he was only sore from the thrashing they had given each other. That was the least of his concerns, for it seemed more and more apparent to him that Shar's jesting from before, about their battling for Feldara's affections, had been astutely truthful.

"I hope that I have neither injured you." Malok replied, though thinking that nothing he did could severely harm the larger male. Then sighing, he relayed what was on his mind. "I can see that you have feelings toward

Feldara, and I have also seen her affection for you. Know that I will not stand in opposition of your love for each other."

So Malok said, though in his heart he groaned, for he had long desired Feldara, at the first to find the Dragoness of his dreams, and then only to grow in closeness of fellowship as the best of friends, and now something more, for his heart longed for evermore of Feldara: her laughter and smile and voice, her approval, her sight and scent, her presence, and all that was Feldara. Yet, he realized that the choice was ultimately Feldara's, and he would be the better Dragon, if she elected to grow only closer to Calidon.

"Do you joke with me?" Calidon asked in befuddlement. "Yes, I do love her and desire her, but I have only seen her affections toward you. I thought myself the one at a disadvantage and having hard to work to make her see my yearning and earnest care for her, and she all this while has fawned over you so."

It took a moment for them to realize that they had so comically envied the other for the care Feldara had shown each of them, but they eventually were able to laugh over their own childish misgivings.

"Listen, we should go to her together and make her choose right now with whom she would rather be, and that will completely settle our grievances." Calidon bluntly, if not humorously, suggested.

"I do not think that idea very wise." Malok disagreed, at a loss for how Calidon could not see that as a horrible solution, how unintuitive he could be at times.

"Why not?" He asked, though the answer did slowly come to him. "Oh, yes, Feldara is very wroth with us right now. For her anger, she would not want to make such a decision, and she would probably tell both of us to go fly into a thunderstorm."

"Right, and such issues cannot be pressed upon someone. She needs to take her time and fully consider what she wants, who she wants. Either way, it is her decision, and we cannot greatly affect it one way or another." Malok confirmed.

"Let us then make a pact. I will no longer press my affections on her, desiring to be seen by her, if you will no longer do the same, and neither will we be played into receiving such to the other's disfavor. Let us not worry about whom she will choose, but let us focus on being better friends to each other." Calidon suggested, sticking forth a hand for to make the truce.

Malok clasped the red Dragon's arm in his own, and agreed, gladly ending this ridiculous and unproductive contest.

"We should go find Feldara, and not to say anything about earning her love, but to tell her that we have made up and shall no longer be unkind toward each other. Hopefully, that will cheer her from the foul mood we gave her." Malok suggested.

"And, let us also bring her the food she would have eaten. Nobody can be happy on an empty stomach." Calidon added.

And, now better friends, and people, than they had before been, they took up her kill from earlier, for to get another would have been wasteful, and took off in the last direction they had seen her go.

<><><><><>

After the long ride and saddening tale of Lethira's passing, anything should have seemed brighter, even the enormous workload that Zurthaud was expecting to greet him at the refugee camp, but even as Theros drew nigh to the city of Bythatsar for a landing, Zurthaud and Anur could easily see that there was not much left to be done for the few remaining refugees.

So quickly and thoroughly had the Paladins and free Dragons assisted in the recovery of the Great Burning's victims, that it had taken only a few days' work to get the vast majority of the farmers and villagers back to their own land and with new or repaired homes and ample stores for the coming winter. Even from far away in their approach, they could see that the once sprawling refugee camp had dwindled to but a few shelters, for the citizens of Bythatsar had taken the rest of the affected people into their own homes rather than let them dwell any longer in the nearly empty camp's tents.

The lord's of the Human Realm, even Athard, were so impressed by the unprecedented level of care and supply that the Paladins and Dragons had offered, that they had made this last day of their concerted aid for this disaster somewhat of an occasion. They had gathered all the people of the town together in the large, open-aired central square and were making speeches, positive and hopeful in nature, looking forward to the good that would come from the Paladins, due to the leadership of Zurthaud and others like him.

When they looked to the sky, and slowly began to recognize that then approached just such the person of whom they spoke, the people let out a cheer and waved at them and the lords began to motion for them to come down and join their celebrating, no doubt wanting some words spoken by the man of the hour.

"Can we just pretend that we do not notice them?" Zurthaud asked, inwardly groaning at the thought of making an impromptu address in front of so large a crowd.

"You are the hero, the leader and face of the Order; such is your duty and curse." Theros replied amid a deep chuckle, for he neither wanted such attention, yet knew that he, despite his enormous size, could slip away unnoticed while Zurthaud spoke.

Anur, of course, wanted no part in this; so that when they landed and the crowd thronged about poor Zurthaud, both he and Theros methodically slipped through the masses, even as Zurthaud was rushed, nearly against his will, to the speakers' dais and the podium. After the lords clapped him heartily upon the shoulders and shook his hand, and after the audience had quieted from their chanting of, "speech, speech," Zurthaud cleared his throat and stood sweating in the seemingly infinite silence of collecting his thoughts.

Eventually, he opened his mouth to plain and simple words.

"This is not a day for occasion, for rejoicing, and not necessarily because of all the innocent lives lost to indiscriminate fire and cruel sword, as the mourning for their passing has been on our lips for many days since, even now; not even because there is still much work to be done, and we have not the time to indulge in such leisure or laxity, as there should always be time for happiness and lightening of heart and spirit. No, the reason we should not mark this day for the honoring of heroes or the exaltation of soldiers' and Paladins' deeds is because this manner of action, this degree of aid and sincerity of compassion, to pour out upon the hurt and the needy, should have been expected, if not expected, then earned by your continual faith and support of an Order that has broken its oaths time and again. This day should be marked, yes, marked with solemnity, by the Paladins, by all of us, as a reminder of how far we had fallen, so as to neglect our duty and so endanger the lives of our people, and we should rejoice only in the knowledge that this stern reminder shall live with us, all through our lives, to chasten the slothful and corrupt spirit that constantly seeks to abide in any leader or person of authority, and so guarantee that never in all our days, and hopefully those of our children and grandchildren, shall such a travesty of disregard for the poor, the common man, and the defenseless, of betrayal and oath-breaking, , willfully or otherwise, ever again be committed."

A long silence followed these dire words, but eventually the people applauded, not in the same spirit of gaiety, but modestly, in understanding of, and agreement with, the message spoken. No more revelry could be expected after such harsh truths were spoken, for though food vendors and entertainers had prepared for further festivities, and now cursed and began closing their stalls and kiosks, the people were no longer in the mood for carousing as if nothing had occurred only a few days past. In gravity, they slowly returned to their homes, for it was still a marked day, a day to remember, but in solemnity- though optimistic, and reverence- yet levity borne of relief.

Again the lords of the land shook hands with Zurthaud, each thanking him for his words, true and simple; although some of them, the fatter and less affected ones, were obviously somewhat upset that their feast day had been abruptly ended. Last of all to come forward and to leave was Athard, he whose lands had been the most charred, his people the most afflicted.

"Truer words could not have been spoken." Said he, quite gravely, though he did heartily clasp Zurthaud's hand in his own. "You are a good man, and wise, and have proven that my earlier ire was unwarranted. I hope your leadership is long over the Paladins, and may your successors strive to be like you."

With that, he left, and Zurthaud stood alone on a dais in the middle of the town square, with only Anur and a few street sweepers remaining to keep him company.

"I could not have done a better job of clearing the crowd and killing the mood had I even taken off my helm." Anur dryly quipped, as Zurthaud hopped down from the stand and approached him.

"I only spoke the truth, and I have no desire to be lauded simply for correcting a mistake." Zurthaud gruffly replied, not realizing that Anur spoke in jest, for it was, indeed, hard to tell. "Has Theros left already?" He asked, for in his speech making he had looked only at the crowd before him, all else dimmed before his eyes, and had not spied the Dragon's escape.

"Yes, for a large red Dragon, he was rather sneaky in taking off, but while your audience was captivated by your very moving speech, he ducked behind a house and leaped into the air without anyone noticing." Answered Anur, a little bemusedly, recalling the Dragon's antics.

"Very well, let us find a ride to the border wall." Zurthaud replied, a slight smirk appearing on him also, as he imagined Theros' determined, and comically inept, attempt at avoiding any attention.

They left from there without much delay, for the streets were mostly empty after all the townsfolk had abandoned their merry-making.

Soon they found themselves in the remnants of the once massive tent city of the refugees, and were greeted by the few Paladin Dragons and companions who remained, as the "wild" Dragons, not wanting to be found out and bound by no organization or oath, had all left much earlier. Galrag and Lorn were among those that remained, and they met with Anur and Zurthaud in the shelter of the last large tent yet upright, once a mess hall and just barely big enough to accommodate a Dragon, to report the finalizations they had made.

"The last of the homes have been rebuilt, and well, so that all the people who were here have a place to go when they leave, and even now, we are dispensing the last of the stores to those who have remained, enough to see them on their journey home and provide for the loss they suffered, that is, to last until the early harvest of next year." Lorn relayed, seeming very much lightened in heart since Zurthaud had last seen him.

Indeed, caring for the needs of others was the best of cures for overcoming the wrongs done to him, especially the providing of such necessities that were denied him. He looked now a very refined, if not martially rigid, older gentleman, rather than the scrounging animal that had been pulled from the lowest of dungeons.

"We have overseen these to the last detail, and after discussing among ourselves, we believe securing the Aronoran should be our next priority." Galrag added.

"Then, we are united in thought, for I had already considered that next most important of our looming tasks." Zurthaud agreed. "Let us take the majority of the Paladins here and go directly to the wall. The others, we will send to regroup back at the Citadel, gathering the scouts and hunting parties, or any stragglers out in the field, on their way, and from then, we can make a watch of half or a third of our number."

"Thereafter, we will need to focus on our reorganization, replacing the old High Council and selecting a new Lord Consul, and then we shall have to see about the trials for the former members." Galrag spoke again, and this he said more gently than his other words.

For, he knew, even though the former Lord Consul was more a beast than a man, that he was still kin to Zurthaud, and that the Human, though now distanced in heart, mind, and physical presence from the miserable ex-despot, still sorrowed over the grievous words uttered and the atrocities committed and had taken very personally that his own father, though now disowned, could have been such a deplorable villain.

With a sigh Zurthaud thought about how he would have to again face that wretched murderer, and he loathed the possibility that he might have to hear his voice, or worse still, his defense for his actions. "We will come to those things soon enough, for now, we have a sieve for our southern border, a fact that the Dark Horde and their master know well. We must secure it, and quickly, before any further attacks."

A few receipts and papers were left to be signed, for the transfer and use of goods, but quickly they finished with that and left from there out into the open center of the tent village. A nearby Paladin was given the order, and he blew upon a trumpet to signal the other members to gather there.

Although, it was almost unnecessary to do so, for with nothing left to do about the camp, they had all been eagerly awaiting Zurthaud's next orders, many even sitting just without their tent of meeting.

Galrag had the largest voice, so it was he who addressed them. "Paladins, gather yourselves and pay attention. I want you twelve to tear down whatever tents remain and return them to their rightful place. The greater portion of who remain shall go with us to the Aronoran; except you four, go and fetch any members afield and return to the Citadel to await further command. See to it." He loudly shouted.

Well trained, they instantly dispersed to the various duties described, and the Humans and Aelvs who had not elected to disassemble the impermanent city all quickly mounted their Dragon companions. Galrag leaned down and stretched forth an arm to accommodate his "riders", as did all the larger Dragons near his size, but Zurthaud did not take the lead spot upon his back.

Galrag and Lorn had gotten closer over the past few days, having many shared memories and experiences, and it was the older man who took the coveted seat among the larger spines just before the Dragon's neck. Anur and Zurthaud mounted first and moved further down his back. Even with this preferred order, the seating took a few seconds, perhaps a half minute, still much less than whenever Shar was involved, and the great elder Dragon soon bore them all up, with ease and haste, into the afternoon sky.

It was not a very lengthy trip to the great wall, for at this point, the Atsar river was at its nearest to the massive construct. Very soon, they could see it afar, its white stones dazzling the eye with their bright reflections, yet even from this distance, they could tell it was worse off than they had expected.

Truly, the tales of their scouts were accurate. The wall had long been in disrepair, yet to see what was before them, what was once so great and pristine a monolithic guardian, yet now a ruin: chipping, crumbling, collapsing in places, was more than they had expected. For miles and miles, the wall stretched from one end of the peninsula which was the Shadow Lands, from the sea at the East coast, to the Crydan bay on the West, and for each of these miles, the wall had one flaw or another.

"Was this stone not under the same enchantment as the stones of the Citadel?" Zurthaud asked of the elder Paladins.

"If memory serves, yes, that is correct." Galrag confirmed over the wind's roaring.

"Why then is there so much damage to the structure? For, I thought that spell protected the stones from natural weathering and even magical attack." Zurthaud questioned, unhappy about the level of disrepair that had been allowed.

"Look at the ground, and it will tell you the story." Galrag explained, pointing down to emphasize. "See the Shadow Lands; see how the soil is dark, ashen black, yet dry, cracked, completely useless and infertile. And now, compare it to the grassy turf on our side of the wall, though it does become more brown and withered as it comes closer to the border. The lands of shadow are cursed: from the soil to the sky, cursed of their master and their people, condemned by their own evil and malice, and it is a slow, yet constant, evil that, like the crashing of the surf against the cliffs of the shore, breaks down, over time, even the strongest of magic wards. Many, many hundreds of years, nigh a thousand, has this wall stood, and all this time has it held at bay the corruption beyond it. Slowly degrading, slowly failing, if it is not repaired soon, it will altogether decay into rubble and ruin."

"Look." Anur suddenly exclaimed. "The enemy needs neither stair nor ladder, for in this spot, the damage is so severe that they can walk over upon the piles of fallen debris, and so cross easily into our lands."

They did see this gaping hole, and even the signs that it had been used recently, for strewn about were various items of camp and guard of the Dark Horde's monsters: burnt out fire-pits and braziers, rough, stained, and dirty half-pitched tents of unknown hide, horrid standards with the skulls of men hung upon their crossbeams.

"Here we shall land and set up our strongest watch. Thereafter, we should send an inspection down the full length of the wall, from ocean to ocean, so to make fast any such gaps until further repairs can be made." Zurthaud suggested, but here he was cut short by an all too familiar sound.

It was as the sound of a bee, a whistling, buzzing noise, yet a bee of the size needed for this sound's loudness was, thankfully, not to be found anywhere. It was the horrendous, unmistakable, dissonance of Black-iron ballistae bolts as they whipped through the air toward their target, and painfully acquainted with this sound, no order need be given before they all started evasive maneuvers.

Nonetheless, someone shouted the alarm. "Ballistae!"

Even as Galrag ducked lower and began diving toward the ground at an odd angle, Zurthaud began scanning about for their assailants, only to realize that there were none on the ground below, for the shots were coming from the wall's own guard towers.

The enemy had already taken the Aronoran; the great wall had fallen.

Chapter 37

Feldara awoke to the sound of someone entering the cozy apartment, and it annoyed her greatly. Although her wrath had much subsided, so that now she was only irritated rather than furious at this disruption of her slumbering, she was still in no mood to be pestered by such disturbances. She even tried to lay her head down again and return to sleeping, but whoever had come into Theros' apartment would just not cease their scuffling and rustling, so that she eventually arose with every intention of dispatching the intruder.

However, her anger had to be cooled, for she could not go and kill Malok's best friend. Indeed, Shar had climbed back up into Theros' apartment from wherever he had earlier been skulking, and now he was up to his old shenanigans of digging through the Dragon's belongings as if he owned every curio or book that he touched.

"What do you think you are doing?" Feldara loudly confronted him, scaring the life out of the Serpen, for he had his back turned unto her quiet approach.

"I was looking for a good book to read, but your father seems to have no taste for literature, only some old, school curriculum and boring medical tomes." Shar replied after recovering from his fright.

"Do you not know that it is rude to rummage through other people's property without asking?" Feldara inquired, only now half-angry with the uncanny Serpen.

In answer to this question, Shar could only scratch the cresting ridges above his eyes in embarrassment, and though he truly had not considered such an act offensive, for being royalty the only property he was used to handling was his own, he now understood it to be socially awkward and unacceptable, at least, when he was caught.

"Well then, what are you doing in here? For, this is your father's house and not your own." Shar returned after a moment of his own abashed stupefaction, though more in curiosity than retaliation.

"I wanted to be alone." Feldara unhappily replied. "And, you are ruining that." She added as a dry jest.

It was then that Shar decided that he might like this Dragoness more than he had earlier thought, for she, like him, also had a humorously barbed and quick tongue. Yet, he could relate deeper than that alone, for through her shield of sarcasm and cynical wit, he saw, as plainly as if he were feeling so himself, that she had suffered great hurt.

"Why did you want to be alone?" Shar cautiously asked; though in sincerity he spoke. "Where are Malok and... that other guy?"

"I have no desire to talk about that or either of them, and I also want you to leave now." Feldara grumpily replied, becoming sullen and defensive.

"What did they do this time?" Shar interrogated, becoming mock-angry also, as if to take Feldara's side on the matter, whatever it was.

Apparently, Feldara really did want to talk about what had happened with somebody, anybody, for she suddenly unloaded upon Shar all her wrath, along with every detail of what had earlier occurred. By the time she had finished relating the tale of her ruined breakfast and their shameful behavior, Shar and she had both to sit down, he for the length of the story, and she for the resurgence of her rage.

"I see." Shar answered, almost wishing he had not inquired further. "Well, I suppose that was quite fiendish of them."

"Indeed, it was." Feldara huffed, her tail writhing with the anger she felt at recollecting such foolishness.

"So, you do care very much about one of them." Shar intuitively surmised. "Otherwise, you would not be so upset by their actions."

Feldara could but stare, speechless, at this profoundly accurate estimation.

"Oh, yes, your face right now solidifies my claim." Shar giggled, but he had quick to dodge a swipe from Feldara's hand.

"I shall rip you in half!" She nearly roared, thinking that the Serpen had only inquired of her to exploit her emotions. However, Shar was already out of reach, and truly she had no desire to pursue him any further or to actually maim him, even were he any slower.

"I meant nothing by it." The Serpen defensively squeaked, revealing his intentions, though not his body, as he cowered behind a low table. "I only wanted to say that, since you care about them so much, you should let go your anger and forgive them, for indeed, their offense was only boyish, an enactment, however improper, of their own passions, their feelings for you. I bet, even now, they two have gotten over their silly, little rivalry and have made up with each other, and here you are, unable to appreciate either of their affections, as you sit and froth in your ire."

Feldara had then to seriously consider this, for, in spite of it sounding from the mouth of a jester, what Shar had said was very sound advice.

"I suppose you are right, but you cannot tell either of them how I feel, especially not Malok." Feldara threatened, though her fury had been diminished toward the surprisingly astute Serpen.

"Oh, so it is Malok you rather prefer?" Shar jibed, earning him more fiery glaring from Feldara.

However, another disturbance at the entrance saved him from further attack, for the sound of Dragon's wings flapping heavily, for to land, and a voice calling Feldara's name flooded in from the apartment's balcony.

"There you are." Theros exclaimed, heaving a sigh of relief, for it was he who had arrived and hastened within his own house. "We had been looking all over for you."

He rushed to embrace his daughter, never having wanted to let go his long lost child to begin with, though knowing it would be impossible, at least most uncomfortable and embarrassing, to go about with his brutishly large frame permanently affixed to her.

"Well, I am sorry that I worried you, but I was only here and safe this whole time. I can still go places by myself, yes?" She reassuringly answered, as her beloved father had yet to release her from his strong arms, yet as he did let her go, Feldara had another question pop into her mind. "Hold fast; who is this 'we' that you speak of?"

"Your friends are of whom I speak, Malok and Calidon, for they saw me returning from Bythatsar and stopped me to ask if I knew your whereabouts. I thought this somewhat alarming, since you had gone off with them for breakfast and I had not seen you since; so, I joined in their search, making the City and the Citadel my first stop. How glad I am to have found you here and safe, for I began to worry that the Darkness had come for you again." Theros explained, as he sat and curled his tail about him for to quiet his nervousness.

They became slightly sullen hearing a reminder of the wretched presence that sought Feldara's life, but the day was not all ruined by the two boyish male's foolishness, nor had Feldara been captured, so that they could not long remain low in spirit. She was not utterly downcast by any of this news, for though causing her father some anxiety was regrettable, the worry she caused Malok and Calidon over her disappearance was a most welcome, unexpected, and harmless vengeance.

"Well, you have found me, unscathed and unassailed, and with such a devoted and strong father to protect me, I doubt either you or I had much to worry about at all." Feldara happily comforted. "We should not be spending our day in here, certainly not fretting over things that could have been, or even what has happened. Instead, let us go out somewhere and have some fun."

Shar was most game for this and heartily agreed, and not only for becoming bored with probing through Dragons' belongings. Since he had been able to help his new Dragoness friend with releasing her hurt feelings from earlier and even with realizing the power she held over this situation with her two suitors, he now wanted very badly to see how much she could manipulate the two love-struck males into fretting over her, or doing her bidding by the threat of her departure.

"Should we not first find Calidon and Malok and let them know you are well?" Theros obliviously inquired. "What happened this morning, anyway?"

"It matters little now; besides, I would not have you sharing my anger over it." Feldara answered, even as she arose to leave from the apartment.

Befuddled, Theros followed, still confused as to what could have gone on among them, but resolved not to let such, supposedly, petty things affect the time he spent with his daughter, he took Shar upon his shoulders and followed Feldara out into a fine, blue, afternoon sky.

<><><><><>

The air was thick with the deadly Black-iron bolts of the Dark Horde's ballistae, and so suddenly and unexpectedly had they released them that the Paladins were hard pressed to dodge or deflect them.

Only one Dragon was slain outright, with a nasty impaling wound, yet in his last breath kept his wings open enough that he would glide, rather than plummet, to the ground below, avoiding taking his companion to death with him by the fall from great height. Others suffered lesser wounds, gashes and cuts, but this and their comrade's death only enraged them.

With roars and a shouts of fury, though they were tired well beyond fighting their best, the Paladins ferociously retaliated. Blasts of fire and magic struck the enemy emplacements upon the wall, slaying many hundreds of the Goblins and Trolls who dared strike at them, but the guard towers, where were the ballistae placed were nigh impregnable from the air.

The malicious bolts kept sizzling out from the windows of these, causing Zurthaud to have no other choice than to give the command to land, for to take back these strongholds.

"Galrag!" He called to the Dragon, as they circled one such tower. "Only your voice can be heard over this din. Give an order for the companions to dismount and take the guard towers, while the Dragons provide support from the air."

Even as he did so, the elder Dragon descended, dodging bolts or catching them with his hands, and smoothly gliding he approached slowly and closely enough that Lorn, Zurthaud, and Anur could all, leaping from his back, disembark upon the roof of their tower even while he kept on soaring. It was then that Zurthaud realized they were in the thick of it, for having hidden most of their number within the guard towers, the Dark Horde's presence on the wall was much greater than he had at first expected.

With fury in their blades they fought, cutting down every Troll or Goblin that had operated the rooftop ballistae, and every one that was guarding these, and even the ones that dared come up through the trapdoor that led further into the tower. All around them, whenever there was room enough for it without hurting his allies, Galrag spat fire and cast magic to destroy whatever foes the three companions missed, and at last they had cleared the roof of the tower. Though he knew more enemies waited within, ready to spring upon whoever opened the door in their ceiling, the Dragon had to prioritize, and he flew off to assist others in more dire need.

"We have to approach from another entrance. This one is too obvious, and probably, also too well defended." Zurthaud suggested, as they took a hard earned breather, for as they had an advantage dispatching their enemies who came up from the door, so too would their foes when they opened it to descend within.

"Where else can we go? Without a Dragon and without this door, we are stranded, useless on this rooftop." Lorn objected, though only trying to brainstorm, as he was genuinely unable to see another option.

"I have an idea." Anur said, and with that, he abruptly vaulted over the crenellations.

Lorn and Zurthaud both rushed to the ramparts, worried that, somehow crazed, Anur had plunged himself to his own doom on the ground far below, but he had not died. He had cleverly landed upon a windowsill only a floor below the roof, and he now motioned for the other two to join him.

"You can go; I am too old for such nonsense. Just do not forget to let me in, when you get the chance; I would hate to be stuck up here all night while my comrades battle." Lorn spoke, shaking his head in disbelief.

"Scared of a little fall?" Zurthaud jokingly asked, as he too climbed over the battlements, although much slower and more cautiously than Anur had.

Once on the sill, which thankfully was not belonging to such a window with a ballistae mounted behind it, as otherwise their ploy might not have worked out so well, they two crawled, one by one, through the narrow window opening and into the tower.

It was dark inside, lit only by candle-light, and they struggled getting their eyes to adjust quickly. Thankfully, no enemy yet came upon them while in this vulnerable state, for this room of the tower was empty, unused for anything other than storage. This they determined by the barrels full of ballistae and crossbow bolts and other stores: moldy cheese and bread on the shelves, swords, spears, and such tucked into various racks and corners.

Quietly, they came to the door of this room, and slowly they opened it a crack. Beyond it was the main staircase, which led in continuous, winding circles from the top to the bottom of the tower, and within that staircase were many Trolls and Goblins, all eagerly awaiting the opening of the trap door in their ceiling, which was just around the next corner and out of Zurthaud's view.

"They were ready for us." Zurthaud whispered to Anur, as they drew back from the door. "How do you want to go about this?"

"Use our element of surprise, of course, to work our way to the roof-door; we get Lorn in on the fight as quickly as possible, so that we have better odds. At the very least, we will have a clear way back to the roof, where, if we end up getting overwhelmed, we can more easily hold off these beasts." Anur astutely replied.

Zurthaud did not like the fact that they would be forced to fight in both directions, up and down the stairs, but there was not any other sensible option. They each charged a spell, and on the count of three burst forth through the door into the stairwell.

Red and green light flashed from their hands, killing many of their foes and blinding the others, and these others they then waded into, swords flailing and yelling like madmen. Taken so completely off guard, the Trolls and Goblins could hardly react with anything other than shock at Zurthaud and Anur's surprise entrance, and they two almost reached the roof-door before their astonished enemy retaliated at all.

It was then a much harder fight than either of them could have expected, as the Trolls were armed with their usual long spears, which in the close quarters of the stairwell were excellent at keeping them out of harm's way while also staving off Anur and Zurthaud's short swords with deadly, accurate jabs, and the Goblins were neither defenseless, as their crossbow bolts zipped past Zurthaud's ears many times, with one such even pinging off of Anur's helm.

Slowly, it worked out that Anur held off the advance of reinforcements from the lower depths of the stairwell while Zurthaud worked his way toward the door in the ceiling, and with great struggle, dodging and weaving, whirling, slashing, and stabbing, they two battled until, clearing the last of their foes between him and the door, Zurthaud shouted to Anur.

"Hold them off a little longer while I open the door."

"Lorn," He called through the thick wood to their comrade above. "Refrain from decapitating me; it is I, Zurthaud."

So warning his friend, Zurthaud undid the heavy wooden crossbar, which the enemy had replaced for to shut them out; setting this aside, he quickly flung open the trap door, so that Lorn could join their fight. The older rider was, indeed, ready for battle, though his sword was not drawn; instead, he held a large glowing orb in both his hands. Zurthaud knew it as some form of magic, but as it was of older origin than his limited studies, did not recognize the spell, and even as he turned to rejoin the fray and help relieve Anur, who all this while had been quite hard pressed to hold up his end, he wondered what the old Paladin had planned.

"You two, step back against the wall." Lorn called down to warn them, even as he set the radiating ball on the top-most step of the stair.

Only when he had seen that Zurthaud, and eventually Anur had done so, did he set the magic ball free, giving a little push to get it slowly rolling down the stair.

As it tardily, almost laughably, bounded down the steps, it grew in size, until, after it had well passed Anur, with bright flashing crackles of energy, it fully filled the height and breadth of the stairwell so that nothing could pass by on either side, above, or below and scraped noisily against the walls. Still slowly tumbling down the stair, it eventually met with the encroaching troops of the enemy, but the magic ball's relentless progress was not at all delayed.

As it proceeded, it nearly instantly disintegrated any flesh it touched, so that in a few seconds it had destroyed the first few ranks of the monsters who would have attempted to challenge them, and once the ranks behind began to notice what manner of doom the magic ball brought to them, they tried to flee, even clambering over one another in their haste to escape the unstoppable magic spell. Eventually, it cleared the steps, one way or another, of all the Goblins and Trolls, and still it continued, rounding the corner and rolling on out of sight.

"I have never seen the like of that spell." Zurthaud muttered in amazement, for he had thought their battle to be much harder won. "What was that thing?"

"The spell is called 'bottled lightning'; it is a classic Draconic form. However, the technique of having it grow while rolling slowly down a stairwell my generation knew as 'the broom', a silly but apt name for a singularly effective device I had thought quite useless until now."

With much regret, Zurthaud wished he had earlier known of such a technique, for it would have been most useful in that horrible battle against the Nokre in the Ragnor, perhaps, even saving the lives of a few of his comrades. Much knowledge had been kept from the younger generations of Paladins, as if the old techniques and strategies were to be despised as obsolete, or maybe, that the elders thought the young Paladins undeserving of their teachings. Both were fallacies, for Zurthaud knew that there was great wisdom in the old ways, and the young needed to hear the wisdom of their elders, or else the accomplishments of their forebears would decline, as their descendants would not have the knowledge necessary to uphold them.

This was, in part, why the Aronoran lay in ruin, why the Order had become so weak. The wise spoke not a word to teach the learner, though many, pleading, bent their ear to listen, and the proud and foolish of the youngsters scoffed at the tried and tested ways of their elders. Yet, what was in the past could not be changed, and Zurthaud only vowed that, if he had any say, there would be much more complete training in the future of the Order. Once again the elders would pass on their stores of wisdom to respectful, hungry young ears, and perhaps, even a Master Order could again be built up from the freedom of such valuable knowledge and the communication thereof.

"That spell was quite handy." Anur added, as he at last reached them, for his fighting had been quite a few steps below them. "You shall have to teach it to me sometime."

"Perhaps, when we are not fighting for our lives, my friend." Lorn replied with a slight, wry grin. "Let us continue, for there shall still be side rooms and halls to clear further down."

The rest of their fight for the tower went on steadily, without incident, as clearing each windowed room of ballistae operators was a simple enough task, for after Lorn's spell had so completely wiped out the enemy from the stairwell, no more came from there below, either in assault or reinforcement. Shortly, they cleared the last room that housed artillery, and with their whole tower cleared, they then headed without by a door that led onto the main body of the wall, the connecting ramparts between each tower.

At such an opportune time, even, for something of a spectacle was occurring, and right before their very eyes, for the captain of the Dark Horde, the fiend that commanded this enemy force, stood fast upon the roof of the next tower over.

His silhouette black against the dying light of a setting sun, clothed in spiky, Black-iron, plate armor, with a horned helm not unlike his master's, and clenching in one hand his dreadfully brutal and massive, Black-iron mace- it was none other than the terrible king of the Ogres, Og "the Killer of Two". A most dire foe, indeed, was the Ogre king, for he had earned his title by slaying a total of two Dragons in previous skirmishes and had as yet to be repaid for such offenses.

With his free hand, he now flung, like javelins, the bolts from the destroyed ballistae around him at the Dragons that flew past him, even as his rallying cries called his remaining troops to repair and utilize the dreadful weapons. Though many Dragons drew nigh and fain would cast their blazing breath upon the rooftop, clearing it of all the foul Horde, the Ogre king's aim was so deadly and true that no one could get close enough to do so, for just as the Dragons came in range to blast the foul villain, so did they also come in range of a well flung bolt, and had quickly to dodge it or be impaled.

So might have the Ogre king won the day, for the young Dragons nearly gave up their assaults toward him. In this way, the terrible Ogre king could have, at least, slowed the Paladins attack to a standstill, were it but for Galrag. The elder Dragon, full of cunning and wisdom from nigh a century of combat experience, was the only one who yet dared assail the tower upon which Og obstinately stood fast.

Though in his despicable, grunting tongue he cursed the aged Dragon, much and loudly, the Ogre king could not even get close to hitting Galrag, for though he was the largest of targets, he flew with a speed and skill learned by his many years' experience and easily dodged the projectiles cast his way.

With his acrobatic antics the wizened Dragon drew his opponent into a fit of rage, yet not purposelessly, as each pass by the tower and dodging of a bolt moved Galrag just a little closer to it. At the last of the passes, Galrag put his back to the sun, and mindless with wrath, the Ogre king drew aim with eyes toward the blazing, blinding light. Like lightning's swift strike, Galrag sped toward the tower, and the sun's dying rays served true and hindered the monster, blinding him, making poor his aim. By mere inches, the last bolt he cast missed Galrag, and seeing the trap into which he had fallen, the Ogre hastened to defend himself from impending Dragon fury.

With a roar, Og attempted to strike down Galrag with a blow from his mace, and though the stroke was swift and strong, far beyond a Human's, able to shatter a Dragon's bones where it fell, even under their scaly armor, the elder Dragon, even while ramming into the Ogre with such force as to unstoppably tackle him, leaned into his opponent's blow and caught the weapon in his own arm before it had gained enough momentum to severely injure or cripple him. Galrag still bled from cuts by the vicious mace's flanges, yet not as much as the Ogre would. With a roar of fury, the Dragon opened wide his massive maw and enveloped the screaming Ogre's head within, down to his neck, helm and all. In the same second, with all his force and fury, Galrag severed the Ogre's head from his shoulders with a single savage bite, and so vicious and mighty was this bite, that the sound of his teeth chomping together could be heard, even by Zurthaud, Anur, and Lorn from down were they stood below the tower.

The Ogre's limp body fell away from Galrag's crushing teeth, even as Galrag arose and spat out the severed head and its putrid taste from out his mouth, and with another roar, this of proudest triumph, he spewed forth his fiery breath upon the tower's top, incinerating all the carcass of the Ogre king and all his henchmen, who unable to comprehend their leader's sudden defeat had stood by helplessly.

Thus was the end of Og, king of the Ogres, "the Killer of Two", and thus was the end of the battle, as the remaining enemy forces lost their will to fight and began to retreat as best they could. Seeing their great leader so slain, down through the guard towers and out onto the desolate, blackened plains of the Shadow Lands they all scattered, though the Dragons made sure that hardly any made it very far into their own land, and then only a handful completely escaped from their fiery pursuit.

However, the Paladin's work was far from over, for they knew that the Dark Horde could well return, and with greater numbers, or that perhaps, there were other placements of enemy troops along the length of the wall. And, Zurthaud called up to Galrag, for to relay as such.

"I see there is still much cunning and fighting spirit in our renowned elder general." Exuberantly cajoled the Human, for he was very much glad that his friend had overcome so terrible a foe and that, with few casualties, they had together won the day against their enemy.

"Do not test me now, boy, for my blood still boils from the heat of battle." Growled the Dragon, as he glared down at them from the heights of the tower. Although a slight grin betrayed his true, lighter mood, for slaying such a wretched animal that had dared to offend the Dragons by taking the lives of, not one, but two of his kin, was a great victory and alleviation to him.

"Well, if you can spare the time, I would ask of you to, most graciously, sound a call for gathering." Zurthaud gibingly instructed. "If it suits you, let us meet on the grassy field, on the Threan side of the wall."

With a booming voice, Galrag sounded the order and himself glided down to the wall, for to pick up Lorn, Zurthaud, and Anur on his way to the ground below. Once there, Zurthaud gave a command for to take a well-earned rest, as he discussed their next moves with his close comrades.

"We cannot waste time with all of us together scouring the whole wall for enemy emplacement, assuming there are anymore, or that there are not positions even more fortified than here, that which we could not so easily overtake." Galrag brought up as his first point. "It was a hard won battle, at least regarding time spent, for though we lost only two of our brothers, it is close unto nightfall."

"Agreed, we must make a strong stand at this point, and only once the breaches are fixed hereabout, move on to other, less secure sections." Lorn added.

"Yet, we cannot sit blindly, supposing there are no other gaps in the wall, and let the Dark Horde easily retaliate against our lands. We must make certain that this is where they came through for to hurt us so deeply by the Great Burning." Zurthaud objected.

"You can send out scouts to search the rest of the wall, and if needed, send a messenger back to the city to gather reinforcements. At the least, we should know from whence the enemy can assail us, and that without committing your entire force to such a costly endeavor." Anur suggested, which earned him praise from Galrag; although the Dragon muttered an admission that he would have advised the same were he given the chance.

"We may as well send out our messenger now, for we shall need a change of guard by midnight, as none of us could stand a full watch after our battling." Zurthaud added, accepting the tactful compromise.

"Yet, we should be lucky to get one by first light." Lorn interjected, evoking a tired sigh from some eavesdropping Paladins.

"Our scouts can go on reconnaissance after we have refreshed ourselves with a bit of food and water; they would need that much rest." Finished Zurthaud, after he shooed away the unintended listeners with a commanding, though not dispassionate, glower.

So it was, after they had supped a little from meager, packed provisions, with the Dragons having to scrounge the nearby countryside for some game, that they all who were neither couriers nor scouts settled into a long and sleepless night entrenched atop the guard towers of the great wall.

Chapter 38

Feldara, Theros, and Shar had a rather fine afternoon together, for they had leisurely enjoyed some of the favorite spots that the older Dragon had known: the little cleft in the rock wall, beside and under the height of the city, where he and Zurthaud had spent many of their free hours; a little grove of trees, not too far from the city walls, among which he had first professed his love for Feldara's mother; his favorite view of the city, whether sunrise or sunset, from atop the mountain nearby its back-side- all these and many others, each with their own story and reminiscences. With joy, he recounted all them, the fond and even the painful memories; with eagerness Feldara drank in all these tales, treasuring each one, even as the beloved person who shared them.

Shar cared only a little less, for Theros could tell a story rather well and, as difficult as this task seemed, even as indomitable as defeating the Dark One himself, managed to entertain the Serpen king.

The end of the day brought the best stop, for Theros had intended to save this place as last. He led them nigh the center of the city, where was another large open court, like that before the outer gates of the Citadel, a place that Feldara had somehow, though given its sprawling immensity, understandably missed during yesterday's exploration of the vast metropolis.

Within was a beautiful public garden, full of all manner of fountains, flowers, and fruit trees, and at the end thereof were two great, stone towers, in height nearly rivaling those of the Keep.

These towers were rounded and enormously wide, and joined to each other at intervals by sturdy bridges; ornate stone carvings of various patterns, and plant and animal likenesses, lined the many decorative corners, gables, and arches.

"This is a beautiful place; what a magnificent building." Feldara exclaimed, as her eyes drank in the fabulous sight.

"It is called, the Adthonler, something like- 'the welcoming house for strangers' in ancient Draconic, and it is one of the oldest buildings in the city, an historic landmark. It is an inn, and remains the largest throughout all this realm, perhaps, the other lands also. It is, or at least, was the last place in the city that served Dragons. In fact, once when I was a child, my father took our family here to dine. I figured that, if they are still able to accommodate us, we could eat our evening meal here." Explained Theros, happy to recount the building's history, along with his fond memories and high hopes for their own experience.

Down the white, cobblestone paths lined with flowers and sweet long-grass of the luscious garden they strolled, leisurely taking in the pleasant scent of each fragrant herb, until they came unto the large double doors, clearly Dragon-sized, of the nearest of the two buildings. An attendant, in fine livery, was already there to greet them.

"Lord and Lady Dragon, we have not had the pleasure of serving your people in many, many years. Please, come in, and I shall make certain that the necessary arrangements are made to suit you." Spoke the eloquent, although surprised, doorman, as he hid his astonishment at having Draconic customers with a graceful bow and opened wide the doors.

They three did then walk into the most opulent structure in all of Doraegonoran, for even the Dragon temple's grand sanctuary had not the gilded splendor of the Adthonler's luxuriously decorated halls. Though the inn lacked the same soul and reverence that abounded in the temple, there was, perhaps, less gold in all the Order's treasury than was painted on every ornamented pillar, corner, and crown-moulding, and every few feet of spare wall was fit with a gold-framed, well-polished glass mirror or window that stretched from the gilt baseboards to the mouldings. Every few feet of wall that had not a mirror or window, and every alcove in between, displayed elegant vases and baskets overflowing with the gorgeous flowers from the garden outside.

Even Shar was left with his mouth agape at such glamorous decoration, and so much were they all overwhelmed by such munificent adornments, that they hardly noticed the two ushers guiding them from the entry hall and into the dining rooms. Not until they were finally seated at their table, which was comfortably Dragon-sized on one end, yet by craftily raised seating, easily accessible to Shar on the other, did they fully recover from such uncommonly beautiful interior design, to notice that they had caused somewhat of a stir among the other patrons, and even with the serving staff.

Not in many years had Dragons dined indoors among Human company; not in decades had the inn received such guests, so that now, long-unused methods and techniques of accommodating their guests were being reviewed and utilized, and all on short notice. In spite of the hushed, though by way of their glances, obviously pointed conversations of the other customers, and in spite of the inexperience of the waiters, there was an air of pride and joy that the Human people once again shared company with and serviced the Dragons; though, Shar was not by any means ignored, he certainly did not receive as much awed attention.

Indeed, even as they had been seated in this largely unused section of the restaurant, where were the giant tables and booths, sized and styled for a Dragon's comfort, the staff had quickly to pull away dust covers and set the utensils and various other accoutrements. Only after pretending that such unseemly nuisances had never been, were the three unusual guests offered choices of what was to be their meal, and what was to accompany that as drink, among these, many old dishes that the poor, unsuspecting Human chefs had not prepared in generations, but as Shar, besides basic foods, knew only of dishes from his homeland, the only one of them who had any experience ordering meals meant especially for Dragons was Theros.

Certainly taking into consideration the untried cooks and servers, he requested something simple- a classic Dragon's meal of raw, skinned, cleaned, and spiced whole venison covered with a thin, but savory, gravy, along with potatoes and herbs boiled in the fat of waterfowl, and all accompanied by a robust, red wine to drink; this, perhaps, being even the same dish he had eaten the last time he had been here, so many years ago.

It was brought out before them in less time than Theros had anticipated, and he made sure to notice such, being the expected polite thing with which to compliment the servers at this point. Although in the same amount of time, Shar had gotten bored enough to attempt self-amusement by flicking and flinging the small flowers, which were laid in arrangements or strewn upon the table, toward Feldara's general direction while either she wasn't looking or was otherwise unable to chasten him for it with growl or glare. The chefs who had so prepared their meal also came out with the food, which was carted in on giant silver platters, for they wished to see their guests reaction, whether they had made well, and to their liking, the ancient dish, and this almost as much as they wished to see a Dragon here, close enough to touch.

It seemed rather odd to Feldara, all this attention and just over her eating food, but after they Dragons each had a deer, and Shar had a venison steak prepared in the same way, for he had no experience with any of the Human style food they offered, and had each taken a bite, they then exclaimed how delicious it was.

It was the polite thing to do, of course, as Theros quietly explained before their meal, but besides being absolutely true, it was also the only way they would be allowed to dine in peace, as once hearing their guests' satisfaction the happy cooks retreated to the kitchen, with much swaggering and self-congratulating, and the waiters heaved a sigh of relief and ran off to attend to other guests.

Really, it was the best food Feldara had eaten since she had been in the Rathnyaling's company, and she devoured it happily. Shar jestingly complained that his steak was undercooked, for it was raw like theirs. But Serpen could tolerate raw meat as well as Dragons, and he swallowed the rest of it in a single big Serpen gulp and after expressed to them that it was exceptionally well flavored. Although he said nothing else about the dish, Theros remembered it tasting much better when he had last been here, but he had to admit, the company and service were just as excellent. In all, with fine wine and food, they had every bit as good a time as he had hoped, and when they had finished, he purposefully paid a great deal overmuch, for to let the good people know how much they had enjoyed the experience and their kind service.

Unceremoniously, they left their pay, along with the good bit extra for the exceptional service and deliciousness of the food, on the table and slipped out the door, with only the host and doorman to wish them a goodnight, for they all had enough fanfare spent upon them. Filled with laughter and sustenance, they strolled again through the florid gardens until it was almost too dark to enjoy the sight.

It was then that Malok and Calidon finally found them.

"Where have you three been? All day we searched for you." Malok sincerely inquired as he touched down before them, with Calidon close behind.

Shar was about to open his mouth to brag of all the good things they had enjoyed without the two males, but that Feldara answered first, and much less jocundly.

"Why should either of you care? Are you not too busy fighting among yourselves?" She hotly shot, giving them both a glare that could melt stone as easy as her own fire-breath.

"Fighting? You two are old enough to know better." Theros scolded, rather more fatherly than he normally would have intended, but the wine, food, and good fellowship he had just enjoyed made him more comfortable, at this moment with anything. "And, over what?"

But, Shar gave him a knowing look, and his slightly slowed consciousness, at last, came to an accurate conclusion. However, he had no need to chasten any further, as Feldara was still quite hot-blooded toward them.

"They think to compete over me, as if I could be some manner of trophy." She condescendingly spat, earning a shrinkingly chastised posture from them both. "I shall have you know, were either of you the last male Dragon on all Threa, I would be no nearer to considering you for my mate. I am too sickened by your objectifying behavior toward me or your barbaric contention toward each other to even think kindly in your general direction. So, if you do not mind, be gone, and may I not see you again."

And, with that, she smartly turned about with her back toward them and sat behind her father so that he stood flabbergasted between.

Theros, though very disappointed on hearing unkind behavior had occurred, was not half so angry as Feldara, so that now he felt a little sorry for the seemingly despondent males, and could not bring himself to chastise them further. Shar, however, could not help but point and twirl his finger at them and give them mockingly snarly glares, yet his efforts at lightening anyone's mood was, at best, ineffective.

Malok was so distraught, so hurt, by Feldara's words that he took off into the sky before he thought anyone could see the tears welling in his eyes, for he truly cared for Feldara, loved her, and desired her love. To hear that she cared not at all for him, even if only as a friend, even if only spoken insincerely in a moment's anger, stung worse than a wound of the flesh, worse than hearing these words from anyone else, worse than anything he had ever felt before.

However, Calidon caught a glimpse of his sorrow, how much more Feldara's words had affected Malok than him. At length, as they stood or sat in silence there in the night's chill, he finally realized that Malok cared much more for her than ever he could, for he felt only the mild shame of being caught in an undignified act, not any rue or rage upon hearing her scorn.

Indeed, he felt now more foolish than ever to have thrust his own superficially amorous feelings between Malok and Feldara's truer, purer love, but also something else he felt. Indignation, he felt its hot burn rise in his chest, that she should so callously entreat Malok, full well knowing that he cared so much more for her than even he did, causing him such distress and sorrow.

"You are mean, Feldara," Calidon suddenly heard himself say. "To say such things to him, as if I ever had a chance with you. There never was a contest, nor could there ever have been, and you have known that this whole time."

She did not turn around, though she heard Calidon clearly; she could not let him see the tears welling in her own eyes. Thankfully, Theros told him that it would be best for him to leave right now, before anything further wounding was said among friends, so that she did neither have to respond nor turn to face him.

So it was that Calidon left from there, almost relieved, that he had come to the understanding of such truth and had spoken it aloud. He no longer had to worry about winning anyone's affections; he could be just himself: sometimes too foolish, sometimes too wise.

By now, Theros could see that Feldara was sobbing, and he sat with her and put his arm around her. He knew of nothing to say, and somehow he felt that he need not say anything. He only wished Lethira were here, for she always was so good at comforting others; surely their daughter would have been no exception.

Shar, on the other hand, never knew when to be quiet.

"Ha! You sure told them. Worry not, my dear Dragoness. There are plenty more fish in the sea, or birds in the sky. You can pick your animal." He giggled, almost astoundingly unsympathetically.

Theros could hardly grasp how the Serpen could be so insensitive, especially in a matter regarding his dearest friend, but then he recalled their dinner.

"Shut up, you fiend. You had a Dragon-sized goblet of wine and are much too drunk to stand, let alone speak with any reason." He more exclaimed than scolded, to which Shar smiled, cast both hands up in the air, and plopped down upon his backside to emphasize.

<><><><><>

It was only slightly after midnight when the retaliation came, when in an instant, the Nokre swarms were upon them. Marching in total silence, without even the noise and mist of breathing, indiscernible in their own dark coloring from the blackness of the barren earth of the Shadow Lands, they had approached nigh the Great Wall undetected, almost until it was too late. If it had not been for the alarm of the diligent Paladins on watch, who heard more than saw the muffled scuffling of a thousand footfalls and their subsequent clambering up the sides of the walls and towers, for certain Zurthaud would not have lived to see the sun rise.

As it was, he was now back to back with Anur and Lorn, fighting for his life in a way he had not yet been forced to, for savagely he battled, with sword and spell, against the unending tides of Nokre claw and fang. Galrag had taken off into the air, as had most of the Dragons, for there was not room enough for them to stand and fight upon the tower roofs. Some had found this out the hard way, having suffered, like a larger bug overwhelmed by ants, the slashing and biting of mounds of the ravenous horde, as they crawled and clambered over and upon them.

The air was their only escape from such death of a thousand cuts, though already two had fallen by too late heeding this necessity, and this only for the sake of their companions, who, despite noblest sacrifice, inevitably shared their same fate.

Even with the Dragons, unassailed by the earthbound foe, providing great cover of furious flaming death and catastrophic blasts of magic, even with their own fearsome swordplay and spells, the Humans and Aelvs left upon the towers would surely be overcome in a matter of minutes, for so hastily were they assaulted hardly any had managed to mount upon their companions.

"Galrag!" Zurthaud, though hoarse from exhaustion, yelled as loudly as he could. "We must retreat. Hover over here nearest Lorn, about the level of the tower, and we shall jump to you!"

With a quick roaring command for the other Dragons to follow suite, Galrag heard and did just so, though with his head level in height to the tower's roof, he could no longer provide as good covering fire. As the Nokre brutally pressed ever more overpoweringly about them, Lorn jumped on first, being the nearest and, at length, with a clear path. Together, Anur and Zurthaud, slowly backed toward the edge, even as with doubled ferocity the Nokre leaped and charged upon them, and hardly could they fight them off, though they fought as madmen and animals for their own survival.

Zurthaud was nearly forced to go next, as when faltering in a sudden misstep, Anur saved his life by quickly pushing him off the tower top. Though, not near enough to land on Galrag's head, the elder Dragon saw what had happened and caught Zurthaud in a massive hand before he fell out of reach.

Now in the thickest of frays, Anur could hardly do naught but swing his sword wildly and let loose what magics he knew without thinking hard upon them; not even a single step backward could he take, lest his enemy fall unrelentingly upon him.

But, he was not alone in his struggle, Lorn continued to cast spell after destructive spell at their foe, and though he had been busy fire-blasting Nokre from crawling up his side of the tower, seeing his ally in close peril, Galrag rose above the level of the roof. As Anur could not have possibly come to him, the Dragon came to Anur, and just as he was about to be undone by the aggregating monsters, he was snatched up out of danger by the other of the Dragon's claws.

Having, at last, escaped the perilous rooftop, they three could breathe a little easier, but as each tower had a similar fight raging atop it, their battle was nowhere near over. Even with the aid of their airborne brethren, some Paladins did not manage to clear the roofs in time, or were simply overtaken by the sheer numbers of the untold masses of Nokre. By the time the last of their number had reached the safety of a companion's back and the sheltering sky, fifteen Humans and Aelvs, and three Dragons had been slain by the Nokre's vicious surprise attack.

"That was too close!" Zurthaud exclaimed, as he having scaled the Dragon's arms, rejoined Lorn and Anur upon more comfortable Dragon-back seating.

"Close? Many good Paladins have fallen this black night!" Lorn objected, though not particularly against Zurthaud , for he knew that no one could have foreseen such swift, devastating retribution from the Dark Lord.

For hours more, the Paladins rained down fire and magic upon the Nokre, even until the Wall began to glow red with the heat of their assault, but their enemy did not retreat.

Even when all the Dragons and their companions were safely out of reach, completely unattainable to the pedestrian and weaponless Nokre, the vile monsters continued to ascend the wall, now only to sit still and quiet as though made of stone, harshly contrasting their previous insatiable savagery. Even as they burned and melted in the Dragon and magic fires, they stood, with even a soft whisper of laughter, crazed and evil in timbre and intent, wafting in the wind and their ashen smoke.

Only when the sun, at seeming greater length than any other night in the Paladins' lives, eventually crested the horizon, and the Aronoran was observably devoid of all life and Nokre, did they cease their counter-attack and retire upon the grass before the Order's side of the wall.

They did not speak, nor at all rejoice in victory, for too wildly had this fight been waged, too many comrades had been lost. The worn and battle weary Paladins only sat despondently in hushed clusters of close friends, as though they had been the ones to suffer defeat.

"We cannot withstand another assault like that." Anur spoke, at last, as he, Lorn, and Zurthaud rested against Galrag's massive side.

"Perhaps, if there was quicker warning of their approach, we could have fared better." Zurthaud offered. "Maybe, we could set up a perimeter guard, further out, upon the dark plains ahead."

"With whom?" Lorn suddenly spat. "The men are all tired; there is not one of us with the strength left to stand watch or patrol all night upon the black earth of the Shadow Land, much less to fight off even one more army such as we have faced. We are overspent. We are too few. There is no hope here for sustained defense, much less victory."

Many ears other than the three around Lorn heard his words, much to Zurthaud's dismay, and all their spirits began to melt, their courage waned. Even Anur, with his visage hidden by a helmet, seemed more downcast than usual.

Then Galrag arose.

"We cannot give up." Spoke he, as nobly and loudly as he could manage. We cannot ever give in to defeat, no matter how tired we are, no matter how weary of battle and death, for if we fall, if we fail, if we turn to our homes and comforts and, like cowards, run from this fight, there will be more lost than this here wall. To what shall we return, if the Dark One wins this war? If we here falter, it shall all be consumed by this vile darkness, and there shall be no more homes, no families, no livelihood. We are the last, and only, line of defense, the lone guardians standing between Ragnor and death and all our loved ones. We cannot give up."

With what little eloquence, and energy, he had now depleted, Galrag sat down again upon the grass, and though everyone was still exhausted from a night spent in battling for their very lives and they all longed for rest and peace, a new fire of determination was kindled in their hearts to resist, even unto their last breath, this cold, cruel darkness that would wish, even as they witnessed with their very eyes and wounds, to take all life from the world.

"I will take first watch on the wall, while the others rest." Zurthaud proclaimed, as he stood, ready to take his post. "Who will take second?"

Anur arose and a few others.

"Forgive me my earlier remarks, for so long I previously dwelled without hope, I forgot what a precious thing it is to lose." Lorn meekly asked aloud of Zurthaud, so that all who had heard him before could now hear him again. "I will take the third watch."

He stood and so did many others.

"Then it is settled." Said Zurthaud. "Here is where we shall make our stand. To live or die does not matter, for if we fall, we shall fall on this ground, rather than see our homes and families ravaged by the darkness."

Galrag waited until the others returned to their recuperation, talking and eating upon the grass about the wall, before he began further military advice to Zurthaud. Lorn and Anur accompanied him up the steps of the wall to where Zurthaud chose to take his watch alone.

The grown man sat upon the battlements, his feet dangling rather childishly over the wall, as he sat and watched the morning sun rise ever higher into the sky over the blackened land before him. The Dragon's intrusion was welcome, even though he knew it to be of more pragmatic and discouraging nature.

"Our situation is dire." Galrag began. "Truly, we are stretched far too thin right now, and those with us, though now in better spirits, are physically incapable of much further defense. However, we are not hopeless. The messenger and the reinforcements he sent for should be arriving soon, allowing those of us who did not volunteer for an extra watch to get some true refreshment, after which we could go ourselves to search out the remainder of the wall for enemy emplacements. While we are handling that, I suggest we send out another message to the mayors of Bythatsar and Doraegonoran to lend us stone and workmen to repair the damaged sections of wall hereabout, and maybe even reinforce it in some ingenious new way against Nokre assault."

"Wise counsel as always." Zurthaud consented. "But, there is so much more to accomplish right now than just the defense of the realm. We still have matters back in Doraegonoran to attend, such as: what to do with all the remaining prisoners of the revolt, including the former Lord Consul, there is Orthard's trial that must be finished, and also I have as yet discovered the importance of the Bright Dragoness, er Feldara. Besides which, a new High Council must be elected, which requires, at least, a quorum of Paladins to attend, plus all the ruthless tyrannies of Orthard that must, in law and writing and recompense, be undone."

"Then here we must part ways." Spoke Lorn. "You must attend those duties of state, and Galrag and I shall oversee the defense and reconstruction of the wall, that is, if you think you can trust me to hold myself together."

Here the old man's eyes fell, for now in right mind, he regarded with shame his earlier words of tired and anxious despair.

"Certainly I can. You have proven yourself time and again; though you might, as the rest of us, stumble or become a little weary on the way and need good friends and counsel to lift you back to your feet, I have complete confidence that you can do this task, even the harder of the two." Zurthaud, as putting a kind hand upon his shoulder, encouraged the worn soldier.

"I doubt ours shall be the more difficult path, for while we deal with obvious darkness, quick to attack and quick to fell, you shall attempt to overcome a more treacherous snake than ever was, and in his most favorite territory, the arguing and twisting of words. I should rather swallow a Nokre whole and kicking than go to court with that vile purveyor of lies." Galrag grumbled, and not untruthfully.

"In any case, my path shall lead back to the City and my Dragoness; I have much desired to see her face, hear her voice, and share her company, this being the longest I have been without Feldara for some time." Said Anur, rather solemnly, but then more lightheartedly added, "Who knows what trouble she's gotten into in my absence."

Chapter 39

Even the glorious gardens of the Adthonler, glowing with the golden radiance of the dawning sunlight and wafting the luscious perfumes of a thousand flowers, could not lift Feldara's spirits. She had sat there, all night long, and now into the early morning, in the very same spot she had sat the evening before, the very same spot where she had so coldly refused the love, admiration, and even the apology of her most beloved of friends.

She longed to take back her words, just like she inhaled the dew moistened air of the morning, but they would not, could not ever return. The culmination of all yesterday's exasperated frustrations with the ones whom she loved- they had been words of malice, hurtful and completely untrue, and she could only hope to somehow smooth them over, as polishing tools to rough stone, or as unthinkable as it was, be forgiven them.

But, she had seen the tears well in Malok's eyes; Feldara knew her venomous speech had cut deeper than she had ever intended. While her father and Shar had slept soundly through the night, Feldara could only anxiously, sleeplessly, wonder if the damage she had wrought in her lover's heart was irreparable.

Indeed, Feldara was in trouble, and like most of the trouble she had gotten into, it was completely her own fault. She had at first tried to argue within herself that the two males had forced her into this position of spiteful rejection by their own unruly, selfish, and vile actions, but Feldara knew that they had not the power over her as to make her jaw flap up and down, push air out her lungs and across her tongue, lips, and teeth, and cause her thoughts, her detestable, vengeful thoughts, to thereby leap out and poison the love and friendship they had shared.

Feldara alone had the control over how she reacted to any situation, and what started within her as righteous indignation had fermented into petty, vindictiveness. In but a few hours, she had let herself forget the reason why she had even been upset with Malok and Calidon, so that instead of rejoicing that they had overcome their disagreements, she had trampled all over their affections.

She felt stupid, and of course, she could not have felt stupid right before she blew forth spite. Only in hindsight could she regret opening her big mouth.

Feldara wished her father would awake and offer her comfort, but he was nowhere near to rising. Last night's big meal and plenteous drink, though not as proportionate a draught as Shar's, had the happily resting Theros, his broad chest rising and falling with slow, rhythmic breathing, or rather snoring, to deeply slumbering to at all be roused.

Even Shar's biting quips would have been preferable to the despairing self-talk that cluttered Feldara's restless mind. She almost could not stand to bear it anymore, so that she had to rise and do something, anything other than listen to the bitter, scathing voice within.

Feldara walked a few paces away, so as not to disturb her sleeping companions, and she leaped into the air. With another stroke of her wings, she was free of the ground beneath, but her own self-loathing was not so easily escaped.

Heavy as her heart was with all these woes, she barely paid any attention as to where she was headed, and certainly turned in one big circle more than once. However, she eventually found her way to the same mountain stream fed pool that they had all washed in the day of their arrival in Doraegonoran, and with a slow descent, more led by the heaviness of her heart than the descent of gravity, Feldara landed upon its pebbled banks.

Hoping that its constant scouring would clean out her fears and despondency along with any dirt on her skin, she sat like a rock in the flow of the little waterfall at the pool's head, letting the rushing torrent swirl over and around her scales, but while her outside was soaked and scrubbed, her inside remained dank and drear.

A voice sounded over the rushing of the water. It was Malok.

"Feldara." He called to her by name.

Though, she desperately wanted just to fall weeping into his arms, she instead acted as if she had not heard him, but he sat upon the bank too, as she had done, seemingly with the same heaviness, idly casting pebbles into the deeper parts of the pool, waiting until she came out of her shower. Finally summoning enough inner fire to not seem like a petty little girl who needed a big strong Dragon to hold her frail, emotionally wracked, carcass, Feldara stepped out from the flowing stream.

"What do you want?" She answered, not too kindly. "You know that I am still cross with you."

"I do. It is all I could expect from you after the way Calidon and I have treated each other." Malok began, as he arose from where he sat and walked toward her. "I have come to apologize for my behavior. I wish I could take back what I did, how I reacted, but I cannot. I can only seek your forgiveness and attempt to be better than I was the day before."

She did not respond to his words, even though she inwardly rejoiced that he spoke them to her, for even if he had said nothing of import at all, she would have delighted at only the sound of his voice. Feldara could neither look him in the eye, as seeing she did not answer him, Malok drew closer.

"If it is Calidon whom you choose to love, then I will, I must, accept that. Please, go and be with him, and be happy, and take my blessings with you both. But, let my actions not rob me of your friendship, for I..." And, here he choked, for the young Dragon's heart raced to think upon this, let alone voice this. "I love you, Feldara, and I cannot bear to think of a world without you."

Feldara let his words sink into her, as plain water never could. Sweeter than the richest Autumn honey they seemed, and by far more desirable to her. Yet, in drinking in this pure nectar of announced passion, she almost did not bring herself to respond again, so that Malok with sorrowful glance downward toward the dark depths of the pool, turned to go, not even knowing to where he should.

"Wait." She spoke, almost letting fly her earlier feelings of desperation through the cracking of her voice. "I must apologize to you also, for my words last night. Indeed, I do have a bad habit of speaking the most horrible things when my blood grows hot, and what I said was cruel, and untrue, and I wish that I had not even opened my foolish mouth."

Malok then turned about to face her, and she strode near unto him.

"But, you are an idiot." She blurted.

"I know." Malok glumly replied, his heart falling thinking that she was to completely reject, and chide, his profession of love for her.

"You are as dumb as a rock if you think I would let Calidon have your place in my heart." She whispered to him, forgetting that she had not wished to reveal all her own emotion toward him, that she desired not to be the maiden in distress, a trophy of love. That was all petty nonsense to her now; openness, sincerity was all she required. "I love you." She murmured again, her face so close to his that their breath was hot on each other's cheek.

Naught else was said in that moment, when time stood still between these two young lovers. Naught else needed saying; only their eyes searched into the other's soul and found out their own intent to be pure, their words spoken before as truthful as ever they had uttered, their desire sure, their love earnest.

He bowed his forehead down to rest against her own, and their muzzles they pressed against each other's. Eventually, his lips found her's, and they kissed long and passionately, the warmth of their love undiminished by the cold sprinkling of falling water from above or the lapping of gentle ripples from the pool below.

At length, they ceased and returned to gazing one into the other's eyes, until Malok looked down and took up her hand in his own.

"I do not know the proper words, as I was not raised in the tradition of Dragons." He spoke, at last. "But, may Eloigal hold me unto them: I pledge unto you my life, all that I am, in love, for forever."

Feldara giggled a little, causing them both to smile, for he knew that she did not so in scorn.

"You do not like my vow? I can learn the proper Draconic ones if you wish." He offered.

"No, your vow is fine." She replied, unable to keep from smiling, for the joy of her soul was springing out from her like sunlight from the breaking storm. "Your words are more than fitting; they are beautiful. Yet, I only can recall Calidon naming you a honey-tongue, and so you are."

And, they did share in each other's levity and laughed together, for so weary had been their hearts, that now lightened, they burst forth in gaiety.

"I accept your vow, and shall pledge unto you also." Spoke she. "May Eloigal bind my heart to my vow: that it is yours forever, and no other's, to love you and only you with all that I am."

The silence that followed bothered them not even a little, for they could have stared into each other's eyes and held each other's hands for all eternity. Yet, was it interrupted at length, as Calidon did land nigh unto them.

In silence, he strode toward them, and though he had not witnessed, nor heard their vows, it seemed, somehow, that he sensed the love that had here been professed. For, when he reached them, he threw his arms around the both of his friends, as they all stood so close together, and he embraced them both.

"I see you two have made right with each other." He finally spoke, as he let go of them.

Feldara could not meet his gaze, for she felt as though she had let Calidon on and had been unfair and unkind with his affections. Yet, before she could speak, Malok took this burden from her and explained what had transpired between them.

"We have just finished making vows to each other, my friend. We are life-mates." He happily relayed to Calidon.

The larger Dragon's face saddened a little, and his eyes fell. Even though, having seen Feldara's love for Malok and Malok's love for Feldara, and having already come to realize and accept that they would be together, he had sincerely desired in his heart for this love to be shared between Feldara and himself, yet Calidon's countenance was only darkened for a moment. With a smile on his face, his soul and eyes rose with honest joy.

"Truly, I say this, as I know that there has been much strife among us, I am happy for you, for you both, and I heartily bestow my blessings upon your union." Spoke he, and then jesting, as his heart had also been lightened from a burden, that of unrequited love, he continued. "I guess I should leave you two alone now, or something, this being your mating day."

Feldara shoved him into the pool, at which they all laughed heartily.

<><><><><>

Up to the fifth floor of the Order's Citadel, where were the lower courts and councils, Zurthaud climbed, and though, due to his lacking of rest from night battle and first watch, the many steps of the central stairwell seemed much more difficult a challenge than they had so many days before during the siege, even when they had been fortified against him, he surmounted them with determination. Though his heart still felt pity toward the monster who had been his sire, he would not falter in his decision. For his crimes, Orthard must be punished.

Death was a penalty served rarely among the Paladins, for though they fought against the forces of darkness and slew them without much hesitation, as was ultimately necessary when at war and with such merciless foes, the lives of the Free peoples, sentient people, were held as sacred, given and sustained by none other than Eloigal. As it was spoken by Order judges long past "To earn death, one must have unjustly taken the life of another", and so, as corporal punishment, it was reserved only for murderers.

Many had Orthard slain, directly and indirectly, but the cases Zurthaud would take against him, that for which he now strode into the lower Court of Justice, were certain to be inescapably condemning.

The Court of Justice was one of three courts that were held in great halls located at the very end of the central hallway upon this level, past the rooms for lower councils and meeting halls, and each had their unique emblem emblazoned upon a tapestry of appropriate color hanging above their respective grand double doors. The lower Court of Justice handled all cases involving crimes and evil-doing, and their emblem was of a golden scale holding a sword in one balance and a shield in the other upon a field of red.

The lower Court of Holdings, with an emblem of a bronze scale holding soil on one balance and grain in the other over a field of green, resolved all issues of monetary and property disputes, and the lower Court of Civility, with its empty silver scale over a blue field, tended to issues of general complaint. Other than the emblems, each court was the same within, a long, well lit hall lined with chairs for audience, at the end of which was the judge's dais and the podium for witnesses and speakers.

"Lord Zurthaud," Greeted the court's chief judge from her seat upon the dais, as Zurthaud entered quickly through the large double doors; she was a wiry, aged woman named Veringa. "I expected you sooner, but I suppose now would be the best time for this, now that the Citadel has been scoured of all resistance to your party and some semblance of normalcy has returned to these halls."

Her manner was brusque, her glare demeaning, for the nobles, judiciaries, councilors, and clerks who occupied these positions and quarters had despised Zurthaud's coup. Their business of politics in danger of disruption or dissolution, they had either to flee the Citadel, having caught wind beforehand, or had to bear being locked within it for the entirety of the siege. Only the bravest of them had remained, or at all returned, and not without their prejudices against one whom they thought a usurper and contentious warmonger.

"Greetings to you, Lady Veringa, but I am no Lord." Zurthaud politely engaged, not at all taken aback by her hostile mannerisms, for he expected even as much from the lawyers. "I have come before you today with a case against the Lord Consul emeritus, Orthard; he is to be charged with murder."

"I see no papers in your hands; where are the documents of charges? Or, do you expect us to also cast aside both law and order to suite your whims." The judge replied, raising a thin and condescending brow.

"Which law is it that we discarded so flippantly as to earn your ire, the law of a madman who would insult, denigrate, expunge from this Order without cause, and finally sentence unto death thousands of people, only because they differed from himself, or even yet more petty, because his wife died in the care of a doctor from said people?" Zurthaud calmly inquired. "I do not presume to teach one so educated in the ways of justice, only to remind you that laws are only as righteous as their source, and unfortunately, the fount of this institution's laws has long been the reeking, stagnant, poisonous slough of corrupt men's whims. Law must be true, built of truth, or it cannot be law, only mere opinion and empty regulation. Only the laws of Eloigal are so pure as to be true, without bias, for He is holy and true, without any flaw or evil. If they are not founded upon, or at all contend with, His word, the proceedings and decisions of these subordinate courts lose their very foundation and principle upon which they stand, and can only be disregarded by those who abide by Eloigal's conflicting higher law and moral truth."

"A pretty speech, but I am no worshiper of any 'god', and your words still do not account for the lives of men, lost while standing in opposition to you. Justify that, if you can, or rather, only be grateful they had no widows to sue for justice. Your religion would then be of little help in my courtroom, where if there is any 'god' it is justice." Lady Veringa coldly returned, unwilling to silently accept Zurthaud's much needed, and pride wounding, lesson.

"On the contrary, my religion is especially charged with the care of widows and orphans, and as I afore stated, you have no premise for 'justice' without an ultimate standard for it. However, further discussion on the matter, how those men chose to oppose us and, in the heat of conflict- war- were slain unintentionally, without desire for their death, and only under greatest necessity for our own self-preservation, only takes us farther from my original reason for coming before you. And, I should hate to waste your precious time any further." Zurthaud sagely contended; then gesturing toward the writing desks upon his left, at which were seated many clerks, he continued. "I humbly request that the court scribes document the Order's charges against Orthard, as is commonly done for many other cases."

"Very well." Judge Veringa huffily conceded, as she motioned for the clerks to make ready. "Proceed with your accusations."

"Foremost would be the murder of Serc, the venerable Dragon doctor, who in defense of my own person, and witnessed by multiple others, was killed by the hand of Orthard, who utilized a previously unknown, experimental weapon of despicable origin. Second shall be the murders of several Paladins, who due to complications from their poor treatment, died in the dungeons, under Orthard's orders. Third shall be Orthard's attempted murdering of all two hundred of the Dragons who serve the Order as Paladins, by sentencing them to work for unknown extension of time within the depths of the sulfur mines. I could continue with other high crimes, but these are all the charges of murder, intended and committed that the Order chooses to bring forth at this time, as we believe these to be sufficient for conviction and punishment."

____

"Well, I suppose if you argue as heatedly for this case as you do for your 'god', it should, at least, be worth this court's time and adjudication, if only for the sake of spirited debate." Spake Veringa, then directing her attentions to the scribes. "The proceedings shall begin an hour before noontide in three days; you are dismissed."

Even though the antagonistic judge had intended to unbalance and anger him, clearly disgruntled with Zurthaud's leadership, she was due respect, and with as prompt and courteous a bow Zurthaud could manage, he briskly strode out of the courtroom. Though she were brusque and bitter, though her personal beliefs differed greatly from his own, Zurthaud honored her position above her person and above his own pride, yet he would not waste a second longer than he must in the presence of a person who, though unwaveringly devoted to justice, that which was true or that which was falsely placed upon man's wavering beliefs and standards, had been so combatively unpleasant.

A booming voice called his name, swapping his grimace for a smile, for it was none other than Theros, who, having been allowed within a keep so long bereft of Dragons, though all the great halls, corridors, and most of the rooms had been built to accommodate their size, seemed slightly out of place within.

"My friend." Greeted the Dragon, throwing one of his giant arms about the Human. "How long we have been apart that I wish never to part again."

"It is good to see you also, though it has only been a day and a half since you left, and you had good excuse. I trust you spent many pleasant hours with your daughter?" Zurthaud replied, trying not to be physically crushed by the Dragon's affections.

"Indeed, we enjoyed a day of sights and a meal at the Adthonler, but I awoke alone in the splendorous gardens before the grand inn this morning, with all my fellows, even my daughter, having run off already without me. Being without company, when I heard you were returning to the Citadel this morning, I hastened my way to meet you." Theros relayed.

"You left the Bright Dragoness, I mean Feldara, alone, and you know not where she is?" Zurthaud asked, suddenly very serious, almost panicking.

"From what I have been told, she has two love-crazed Dragons constantly fighting over her attentions. She should be the safest person in all Threa right now." Chuckled Theros.

"I still do not like that neither you nor I know where she is. You heard the Dark One's speech back in the Ragnor, he is seeking her out, to destroy her. She must be the key to defeating him, his antithesis, for he fears her. That being so, we must know her whereabouts at all times and be ever vigilant to protect her." Expressed Zurthaud, a little more defensively than he wished.

"My daughter is not a weapon, but she is a full grown Dragoness. She is more than capable of defending herself; besides which, if anything were to threaten her, I would rend anything to pieces, even the Dark One." Theros growled, made angry, not by Zurthaud's prodding, but by the thought that anything should attempt to harm Feldara.

Theros then let go his Human friend, and as they began to walk back out the main corridor, he casually changed the subject.

"How goes the defense of the wall, or have you encountered any resistance at all?" The Dragon inquired.

"Oh, there has been resistance, to say the least; unfortunately we lost eighteen of our members last night and three from the night before. I only left them when the reinforcements I had earlier requested arrived about noontide today, and then only in the capable command of Lorn and Galrag. Those two have grown rather fond of each other, and shall be an excellent team of captains, manning the defense and repair of the wall, so that I can breathe easier and need not rejoin them until after certain things have been settled here." Zurthaud explained.

"These 'certain things' must be putting forth the vote for a new High Council and setting the date for your father, er sire's trial." Elaborated Theros, and here they paused a moment as they came upon the main stair. "Up or down?"Asked the Dragon, meaning the direction they should take on the stair.

"We go upward. Yes, those are some of the 'certain things' I must attend, but I have so many more matters that require my decisions, my attention, that I have nearly converted the High Council chamber into a logistics office and law study, for not only do I need to finish the last bit of documentation for the relief we offered to the refugees and the conciliatory payments to their lords, but I must also prepare a formal case against Orthard. Not just a few words and some witnesses, it must be solid and undeniably proving of his guilt, or he will find a way to weasel out of punishment."

"That is quite a workload." Theros exclaimed. "Is there anything I can do to help?"

"Perhaps, if you can think of a way to quickly gather a quorum of Paladins whilst we are stretched so thin, I have not a single person to spare as a messenger." Zurthaud glumly replied, then more humorously, continuing. "Hopefully, they would elect someone else as Lord Consul; then I could leave off these bothersome duties and return to wall defending or something else as equally taxing."

"Nonsense! You would make an excellent Lord Consul; you already are. Nevertheless, it would be an impossible task, of late, gathering all the necessary Paladins in one place, but perhaps, there is a way we can gather their votes without the need for all the quorum members to be present at the same time to cast it, such as by paper ballot, and I think I know of someone or two who may be able to fill the role of messenger, carrying the ballots back and forth. With their aid, we could take that item off from your list of things to do; all we would need to know is the number of members, how many Paladins make a quorum, and who to deliver papers unto." Theros helpfully suggested, as they mounted the last step and arrived on the seventh floor.

"Well, that is the tricky part. Orthard's specified quorum was twelve, the exact number of High Councilors, but in times past it had been the High Council and all the lower councils and at least a quarter of the total members. However, with the necessity that all of Orthard's 'laws' be undone, I believe- and especially for this particular election- that all Paladins should have a say, all members should vote." Zurthaud countered, as they strode down the main hall toward the High Council chambers.

It was Theros' turn to contend, as they entered the stately hall of their destination. "And, what wisdom is there in such nonsense as a vote like that by the total populous? Much more than half of our current members are those who willingly followed Orthard and obliged, or even agreed with, his stupidities of hate and segregation, and should we give them the chance, they would cast their vote for such a one like themselves, maybe even re-electing your despicable sire, and only because they know his name and are upset by our little coup." He then paused a moment, trying to think of a better method, before continuing. "Instead, let a vote be cast for a new lower council first, a Council of Electors, and let these councilors be those who are selected by their respective peoples, such as: the Dworvs elect a Dworvish lower councilor; the Aelvs, an Aelven councilor; Dragons, a Dragon councilor; and Humans, a Human councilor. There will then be equal representation of all parties in one council, and they then can cast votes for members of the High Council. Afterward, the newly formed High Council and all the lower councils can elect one of the already selected High Councilors as the new Lord Consul."

"That is not a bad solution to our dilemma, for the thought had not entered my mind that the men formerly benefiting from Orthard would do such a thing, even as to reinstate such a horrible excuse for humanity, though it were a likely outcome. Such well-intentioned policies, as this my thought, gone awry by the manipulations of the corrupt, are, no doubt, partly why the Order has declined as it has. We should also consider a limit of time for each councilor to serve, so that, if one is poor of decision making or is simply evil, like my... like Orthard, they can only serve for so long before a new councilor is elected to replace them, hopefully correcting any wrongs."

"There, that is the solution!" Theros, happy to have helped resolved such an important policy change, nearly bellowed in excited agreement. "There must be a term limit on all who serve as leaders: councilors, judges, even generals; no more should any one person be able to rule as a tyrant over us their whole life long, upon an unlawful and unrighteous throne of their own making."

They had to cease from their conversing, at the moment, for they had come nigh unto the charred wreckage that had once been the great doors of the High Council chambers and had to pay attention stepping over, and not tripping upon, the mess of ashen wood and melted, twisted metal. Within was just as Zurthaud had earlier described, a total mess of papers, but at least, the skylight's shutters were open so that fresh air and light could enter the grand circular chamber. Yet, this was not a completely desirable effect, as this illuminated and made quite present a large, dark stain upon the stone floor of the room; it was in the exact place where Serc had breathed his last.

"The cleaners and maids have tried everything." Zurthaud mournfully detailed, as entering the room, they both had become silent and glum upon noticing the significant mark. "Yet, nothing will remove that stain. It is almost a fitting reminder, a warning against unchecked corruption, but that a friend had to die to give it unto us."

"I do not wish to speak of it; just have them cover it with a rug, or something." Grumbled Theros, most melancholy, as he felt a stab of pain, almost physical, from recalling the horrible day.

"No, his memory is worth so much more. We will cut out the stones and replace them with a fitting and somber placard." Zurthaud contested, but not unkindly.

"His memory is worth more than even that, though I suppose it would be proper, yet it is his life I wish to recall, not his death." Theros contemplated, at first somberly, and them more brightly. "You know that, among all his other belongings, he bequeathed unto me his doctoral texts, implements, and supplies, and I have not a single idea how to use any of them."

"You could give them to Aelanur; the priest might use them, as he does have some medical knowledge." Zurthaud suggested, while he seated himself in one of the empty High Council chairs.

"I shall give him what would spoil if not soon used up, such as the tonics and poultices, but I think I shall keep the tomes and instruments. Perhaps, I could someday learn how to heal, rather than only harm." The Dragon chuckled as he too sat at the High Council's table, though not in the tiny, Human-sized chairs.

"Did you manage to find any more of his notes from the Dark Lord's black book?" Zurthaud asked, suddenly remembering the Dragon doctor's final and unfinished task.

"I did manage to locate and categorize most of Serc's papers, even after that pest of a Serpen had wrought more disorder than a whirlwind; many useful bits of information had he translated and recorded: the Bloodstones, some blueprints of the Ragnor, and other pertinent plans and schematics. I even found designs that I believe are for that abominable device Orthard used to kill,.." Here Theros stopped, for he did not wish to finish his sentence, nor did he wish to recall it. Yet, did he linger in silence, the painful memory already dredged to the surface of his mind, and only after a good moment did he continue. "Well, if they match the device as much as I could discern, they would prove collaboration with the Dark Lord, which is outright treason against the order, and that he is even more mad than I previously thought him to be."

It was sickening for Zurthaud to hear, though not unexpected, for it was not a far leap for one used of darkness to have conspired with its master.

"I shall have to read those schematics. If you are right, it would be damning, and there would be no chance, however slim, of Orthard escaping justice." Zurthaud mused, but then became sorrowful that such a person was once his father. "Long ago, I did not wish to believe he was capable of such things, that he was just an unkind and unpleasant person, but he truly is evil, perhaps even all along."

"I doubt he set out one day and decided to become the Shadow Lord's henchman; rarely does one do just so." Theros offered, seeing Zurthaud's distress. "It probably happened over time, slowly, day by day, with greed and corruption making way for worse and worse evils."

"It started with losing my mother." Zurthaud recalled, truly depressed to remember such conversation. "He blamed Serc, me, even Eloigal for her death. He let bitterness take root in his life, and it destroyed him."

"I am sorry this has been also your tragedy." Theros compassionately offered, as he put a massive arm about his friend. "I wish you could have had a good father, like mine. He is still a good father; I shall have to take you to meet him someday, when all this quiets down a little."

"Just rub the salt into my wounds." Zurthaud jokingly retorted, but then more seriously. "I should love to meet your family, and I am just stunned that you managed to keep them all hidden, even from me, this whole time, secret visits and all."

But a moment they spent basking in the warmth of friendship and the happy thought of good times to be had, hopefully in the near future, but Zurthaud then remembered his veritable mountain of work. He began scouring through some of the papers that had been strewn upon the table.

"Ah, here is my case against Orthard. I must begin preparing my arguments and counterarguments today; so, I shall have to ask you to bring that weapon blueprint to me as soon as you can. And, we should definitely be checking those schematics for the dark tower; they could be crucial if ever we get to the point where we could invade the vile fortress." Zurthaud requested, as he began to scribble some notes

"Certainly, I shall get them at once." Theros agreed, immediately rising from his seated position.

"Oh, and did you mention that you had found someone to go as messenger, to help gather ballots for our vote?" Zurthaud asked, barely glancing up enough to notice Theros' head nod an affirmative. "I hate to ask you this, especially since we just now got to spend some time together after being apart, but could you, please, take care of that for me? I have not the time or sanity to extend myself to one more task." Yet, this time he did make sure to meet the Dragon's affectionate gaze, somewhat hurt by the prospect of their parting again so soon.

"Of course, you can consider it done." Theros saluted with a smile; though, in his heart he sighed as he purposefully strode out the door and to a near balcony.

With winged stroke he took off into air, off to find his messengers, three young, probably idle, Dragons with whom he was very well acquainted.

Chapter 40

Feldara had not been happier in her whole life; never before had she felt so elated and carefree, not even in her first ever flight across the dark waves surrounding her island home. Nothing prior could compare with this overflowing fount of joy and love she was experiencing within herself and also resonating from her mate. His presence, just the warmth of his body nigh unto her, was comfort, strength, and excitement.

Sitting beside her, sharing his fresh kill with her, upon a grassy hillock, he seemed more beautiful than ever, with his deep black scales absorbing the light of the sun into their abysmal pools of non-color, though his physical attributes were the least of what captured her attentions. His smile was her soul. His laughter was her heart, and every time they locked eyes, her breath was stolen away. Everything about him, all of which she had noticed before, now seemed new and strange, and yet familiar and satisfying.

She had barely even noticed Calidon the whole day, though she and Malok had happily agreed to get some breakfast with him, using their tactic of the day before to again hunt the timid deer of the nearby mountains and steppes. Even as they ate their meal together and chatted in the golden light of a bright and clear morning, Feldara could mostly only nod in reply toward anything that Calidon said, for she was not able to take her eyes off Malok or cease to drink in his every word.

Another visitor interrupted their feasting, yet as it was Theros, it was truly a pleasant disruption.

"Father!" Excitedly greeted Feldara, as the older Dragon landed nearby them, and she quickly arose and ran over to firmly embrace him.

"Good morning, my beloved daughter." Replied Theros, who was surprised, though not disappointed, to be saluted so forcefully. "Why the joyful mood today? Have you made right with your friends?"

"You tell him." Feldara, cheerfully demanded of Malok, who immediately was somewhat less thrilled to break the news to the larger, stronger, and notoriously foul tempered older male.

"We um…" Began Malok, but Feldara in her jubilation could not wait for him to finish.

"We are life-mates now, avowed lovers." She jubilantly shouted.

The look on Theros' face was worthy of painting: a mixture of shock, joy, trepidation, paternal love, and fatherly protectiveness that was somewhere between an elated smile and a confused grimace.

"But, I just found you." Said he so sweetly unto his daughter. "And, now you want to steal her away!" He nearly roared at Malok.

"That would be the way of things, sir." Calidon imprudently chipped in. "A young Dragon finds a young Dragoness, and they go off on their own to…"

The fire in Theros' glare, which could not be met by the young Dragon's gaze, instantly cut off, as though by magic, anything more Calidon was to say. Yet, as he returned his gaze to the eyes of his precious daughter, and then again looked upon her dearest Malok, in whose own eyes was no guile, only sincerity of love for her, Theros' heart began to soften, until he finally broke the present uncomfortable silence.

"Yes, Calidon, I suppose that is the way of things." And, then he held his daughter close to him, and only after a long, warm embrace did he pull her away to ask her the most important question. "Do you truly love him, beyond looks and fine talking, for he has both? Do you love, and will endeavor to love, Malok with all your heart?"

"Yes, I do, with all my heart. However silly I have been about telling you, I was honest when I made my vows to Malok; I am sincere now, and I will be steadfast farther along when life's trials assail us." Feldara replied, a little annoyed that her father asked this of her, as if she were some flippant child incapable of reasoned decisions, yet knowing that he only sought what was best for her, as any good father should.

"I know you are a good Dragon, for you have already proven yourself in saving Zurthaud's life and in seeking out my daughter, saving her from whatever dark premonition you saw." Said Theros, turning a softer look toward Malok. "I trust you with my daughter's life, and I give my blessing unto your union." He then sat down upon the grass next to her. "I only wish I had more time spent with you as you grew up, to hear your laugh and see you play as a little child; I feel as though I were robbed of years' worth of time. Yet, those days were the treasures of another, and he must also hear of this good news."

"Oh, yes!" Feldara exclaimed, suddenly arising. "How could I be so thoughtless? We must tell Anur at once; besides which, I have seen him barely a moment since we arrived here."

"You must also make known to Aelanur, the priest, your union, for to consecrate it before Eloigal. They should both be found at the Citadel, for I had met Zurthaud there before coming to find you. Both he and Anur had returned together." Theros, shouted after her, as Feldara then grabbed up her new husband and winged off into the sky with him, for to deliver the good news unto her foster-father.

Only after they had left, and Theros had mirthfully chuckled over her high-spirited joyfulness, and he and Calidon were left alone upon the bare grassy knoll, did Theros, eying him as with malicious intent, relay unto the younger male his previously held purpose for seeking out the other Dragons. "Come along , young Paladin; you and I have some work to do. I was hoping to garner help from a couple other Dragons, but now that they are, well,.. a couple, it looks as though you and I are the only ones left to play messenger."

<><><><><>

<><><><><>

After being dropped off at the Citadel by one of the messenger Dragons returning from the wall, Anur had parted ways with Zurthaud to search for Feldara, and nearly half a day later, he eventually gave up, yet only because he knew she was safe.

He had managed to track her trail well enough to determine that she had met with Malok and Calidon at the bathing pool before winging off elsewhere, which had been quite difficult to do, considering Dragons mostly fly about which leaves no trace, hardly even scent. Truly, he felt foolish for going that far when he had neither been invited nor given reason to worry for her safety, for if she had wanted his company, surely by now, Feldara would have sought him out.

So it was that he had returned alone, in melancholy, to Doraegonoran, not really in great hurry to get anywhere but rather strolling along, trying to figure out what he should do with his life, now that he was so removed from the center of Feldara's. She had been the sole fixation of all his thoughts, actions, worry, and hope, so that his current status, and what to do next, was somewhat of a mystery to the man. Until recently, he hadn't been apart from his charge for more than a few days, but now he felt distanced from her so much more than just physically. Their relationship had changed, and this frightened Anur, who loathed the insecurity of change, more so in this than in all other things, for he loved Feldara. She was not just some plot of ground he had called home; he had left even that for her. He feared, above all other things, that he would be removed from Feldara's attention, from her love, and from her presence.

Anur had to stop walking for a moment, for to swallow the anxiety building as gall in his throat. He breathed deeply and reminded himself that he should only be happy for Feldara finding her place among her people, with her genuine and very much alive father, and he knew that any other thought must be driven by his own selfishness or insecurity. Still, he could not but feel a pang of sorrow, yes, a little jealousy for being replaced, and yet Theros was blood to her, how could he compete with that bond. He could not and he should not, nor should he feel this way.

Attempting to cast these poisonous thoughts from his mind, Anur was then only left with loneliness, missing his foster-daughter, and depressive sadness that she did not seek him out for companionship and cared not to hear his voice or see his face. He almost wished he could allow himself to begrudge the affection that Theros had received from Feldara, if only to have a target upon which to unleash the frustrations borne of such disregard and subsequent isolation, but that he knew acting out on such despicable thoughts would only make things worse and assuredly drive Feldara further from him.

Having to trek through the bustling city, which with his helmet covering his face had not been a complete disaster of terrified populace running for their lives, Anur had almost reached the front gates of the Citadel wall when the familiar sound of a Dragon descending for a landing overhead disrupted his train of thought. He immediately spun around, hoping that it was Feldara, but was only slightly disappointed to see Calidon carefully landing within the busy city square.

"Anur, it is good to see you again." Happily greeted the young Dragon, as he touched down not a stone's throw away.

Again, Anur's helm had come in handy, as he had been the only person so close to Calidon's landing who had not to shield their eyes from the scattering of dust, blown into a small cloud by winged downdrafts upon the city's mostly clean streets.

"It is good to see you also, my young friend, but I am looking for another Dragon about your age. She has been quite hard to find lately. Have you, possibly, seen Feldara about?" Anur replied.

"Oh, yes, I have." Calidon jubilantly reported. "I had followed her up to that spring in the mountains, where we had bathed the other day, intending to apologize for the argument we had the night before, and well, for a few whole days before, actually."

"You two had gotten into a fight?" Anur asked, upset that he had only just now heard of this, thinking that he could have, perhaps, helped resolve the issue that had sprung up between them.

"Um, yes." Calidon abashedly admitted. "But, everything is alright now. We talked through some, er, disagreements we were having."

"I am glad you two were able to resolve them and forgive each other, as most quarrels between friends truly are petty and not worth the holding of grudges, but where is she now? Where is Feldara? Is anyone with her? Is she safe?" Anur hastily inquired trying to move the conversation forward, as he was not overly concerned with Calidon's embarrassment. Rather, he wished to hear news of his beloved Dragoness, and perhaps, find her whereabouts, maybe, spend some time with her.

"That is what I was about to tell you- the most excellent news. Feldara and Malok are newly sworn life-mates!" Calidon elatedly informed. "I came upon them only just after they had made their vows unto each other; they should have been heading to the temple for Aelanur to make their union officially recognized."

For a moment, Anur could not speak at all, even breathing seemed an awkward and unnatural choice, for the flood of emotions that entered him upon hearing theses words was more than he could stand at once. He was foremost overjoyed to hear this happy news, and then he was worried for her, that her heart and life was now held in the hands of another.

Alongside these, was he also saddened, troublingly so, for he should not be saddened at all upon such a glorious day, at such joyous news, but by twofold cognizance was he tormented: first that he should be giving away his daughter, though his foster-daughter, no less beloved than one of his own flesh, and to such a stranger unto Anur, for he had hardly spent any time getting to know Malok; secondly that he should be pushed even further out from Feldara's familial circle.

Anur was so overwhelmed that he just slumped to the ground, and he moved not, though Calidon earnestly asked, and prodded, about his wellness. Finally, he seemed to hear the young Dragon calling his name, as though he had awoken from sleep and dreaming.

"Anur, are you alright." Concernedly asked the young male, as he tried to gently raise Anur to his feet.

"I am. I am just so,.. happy to hear this news." Anur falteringly replied, as he tried to steady his wobbling legs with Calidon's help. "Please, see if you can find Feldara and tell her how happy I am for her."

"Can you not tell her yourself? I shall take you to her." Calidon merrily chuckled in reply, completely unaware of any emotional distress that he may have stirred up even as the dust of his previous landing.

"No, I... Well, you see how I have taken it; I am a little surprised. I need some time to recover. Please, go on ahead and give her my regards." Anur contended, as he struggled to get to a nearby stone-carved bench.

"Very well." Calidon relented, the look of concern not fading, though Anur's words seemed reassuring. "I shall be sure to deliver your message to her." Then, remembering that he had further work to do. "Oh, yes, messages, I almost forgot!" He exclaimed, as he shot back up into the sky.

Anur still trembled as he stumbled over toward and sat upon a nearby bench, though no longer from flooding of multiple emotions; a single one, the worst and hardest to rid oneself of yet remained- anxiety. With it present, joy soon became absent, and Anur's hopeful desire to share in his charge's joys was dashed to pieces, as he yet again, questioned his place in her life.

A Dragon grandfather would make sense to her children, but he would only be a source of confusion to them. Worse yet, with the oncoming familial responsibilities to her mate, and then to her children, and also to her father, when would Feldara even have time for him? He would be forgotten, and maybe not even because Feldara chose to exclude him, only because she had no time for Anur, none at all.

He was not needed.

He would be useless to her, less than baggage or unwanted company, and Anur could not live with that burden upon himself, much less thrust it upon Feldara. In his anxious depressive state, he could not bear to imagine awkwardly facing his Dragoness in her day of joy, thus souring it, nor even ever again, even so much as he could not wait around the corners of her life, slowly becoming nothing to her. He felt he no longer belonged here with her, even as he felt that he no longer belonged anywhere.

He got up, but not to enter the Order's Citadel, nor did he head toward the Dragon's temple and the matrimonial ceremony that was sure to be within. Anur stumbled past person after person, through the thronging crowds, until he again reached the last gate of the city, where a guard finally stopped his forward momentum.

"Hold a moment sir. May I ask where you are going?" Politely inquired the guard, as he did to nearly everyone, at least those that caught his attention , who entered or exited this gate.

For a moment, Anur just stared at the man, who could not have possibly known what had happened either within or without Anur's mind, but at last he answered him.

"I am going home."

Chapter 41

Time seemed to slow for the two lovers, as Feldara and Malok flew close, side-by-side with each other, and naught else did they notice but the other, not the toiling city beneath, which they had passed with hardly a glance, nor the towering Citadel of the Order. Only when they had arrived at the Dragon's quarter and Malok, being the first to wake from their wakeful dream, indicated to land at the temple, did they notice the world about them enough to gently float down to one of the temple's balconies.

Even when reaching their destination and entering within the porch, under the dome of the temple, did they remain distracted from the rest of reality, enchanted by each other' beauty, laughter, and smile, so that they almost forgot to lave before entering the sanctuary.

Not even Aelanur's eloquent dissertation upon the virtues of matrimony could fully wake them; they were truly enthralled by each other's love. The Dragon priest had a wealth of patience, or was expecting such from two young lovers, most likely from many decades prior experience, for without grumbling or complaint, he repeated nearly every question he asked of them twice or more and quickly officiated their nuptials according to Draconic tradition: having to say certain specific vows, that which were founded in their Holy Scriptures, and having their names and status written together in Old Draconic for the temple's records.

Even when the priest gave his final benediction to them and dismissed them did they hardly notice.

"I said, I bless you both in the name of Eloigal. May your lives be long and happy and your union strong and fruitful." Repeated the priest, finally betraying some slight frustration. "Have either of you heard a word I said?"

"It was a lovely orison. Thank you for performing our matrimonial rites, Aelanur." Feldara quickly obliged, before Malok could, more truthfully, admit to their absentmindedness. "I especially enjoyed the scripture about us being joined together as one flesh."

"That verse has far more meaning than that of the carnal. Of course, I expounded on that already, how that is to be lived in your lives: putting each other before your own selves, loving each other as your own body, serving each other as if serving your own body, and I hope that you were listening then. How many more happily married people there would be in this world, if only they regarded their spouse as their own flesh and bone, treating them just as well as their own selves." Grumbled the priest, but he well knew how the passionate fires of young love burned, hot and to the exclusion of all else. "Well, I suppose you two shall have many years to figure that out on your own. I dismiss you both. Go forth, be fruitful and multiply." He sighed, choosing to not let their infatuation annoy him further.

"What was that, priest Aelanur?" Malok dazedly asked, to which the priest sighed again, shook his head, and took his leave of them, as if they would notice that either.

Eventually, they did cease from their gazing, cooing, and giggling long enough to notice that they had been left to themselves within the temple's vast, yet empty, sanctuary.

"I remember you wishing to find Anur, for to tell him the good news; would you like to do so now?" Malok asked.

"I would." Feldara replied, as she led the way out of the temple.

"I wish Shar were anywhere about so that I could also tell him. Besides ourselves, our companions should be the next to know of our union, and yet they are nowhere to be seen." Joked Malok, yet Feldara thought this not so funny.

"Anur is far more than just a comrade who rides into battle on my back. He is more like unto a father to me, and though I love them both dearly, I know him better than even my blood father. Indeed, it troubles me that I have not seen Anur hereabout. Aside from our vows of love so recently expressed, these past few days that we have been apart have been horrible, and I miss him and begin to worry for him, as though he might have gotten into trouble without me." She half chastened and half sobbed.

"I did not realize he meant so much to you, and I apologize for making light of his absence. Truly, Shar is more like a brother to me than anything else; we did grow up together as such, so that I can somewhat understand how you feel toward Anur." Malok related, as they exited by one of the temple balconies into a sunny afternoon. "However, I do have a very serious question."

Feldara could not guess what he could be inquiring about, so that she had to pause before taking off from the balcony. "What is it?" She asked.

"With you having two fathers, shall I have to ask for Anur's blessing also? Requesting it of Theros was terrible enough, but I should hate to also beg it from Anur. For, while your father is the kind of Dragon who would rend me in pieces outright, Anur is more the subtle kind of person who would reply amiably, even if he despised you, and then, afterward, if he felt you were to cause his Dragoness harm, would slit your throat while you slept." Malok teased, cracking an askance smile.

"O, you do have him figured out. Worry not beloved. I shall keep watch through the night." Feldara retorted, though in such a way that Malok could not tell if it was in jest.

As she did consider this proposition fairly feasible, Feldara leaped from the edge of the balcony and into the air before Malok could further question her outlandish response or whether Anur would actually kill someone in such a way, if he did so detest them, or whether Malok was actually so loathed by Anur, and so in danger.

He followed after her into the clear blue sky, wondering if he should spend a few nights without sleeping, and they proceeded together to scan the Citadel below for any sign of Feldara's beloved mentor. They entered within the great hall of the Keep and looked about for him within, even asking the door guards if they had seen Anur, but they had not had anyone of his description pass them by. Eventually, they headed without again, and thinking he had gone out unto the city, they flew over the vast metropolis searching for him. They passed several times over each section of the city, but there was no sight of Anur. An hour passed by, nigh upon two, before Malok suggested they leave off their hunt.

"Perhaps, he chose to stay at the wall with the other Paladins." Malok offered, as they settled upon the roof of a sturdy tower to rest a while.

"My father mentioned that Anur had come back to the Citadel with Zurthaud; we should have found him there, if not about the City. Malok, I am beginning to worry for him." She expressed, flicking her tail in anxious exasperation.

"I am certain he is fine. From what I have seen, Anur is a very capable warrior; there are not many foes that could stand against him. Besides, we are within the great City of the Order; with all the walls and guards, there cannot possibly be any dark fiends hereabout." Malok spake trying to comfort her, though he could tell his words had little effect.

It pained him to see her so frustrated and worried, so that he wished to do anything to take these hurtful feelings from her. He did then recall one person who might be able to help with both the problem and Feldara's reaction to it.

"Alright, I think I know of a way we can find Anur." Said he arising. "Follow me."

Again they took off into the air, but not to hover above the City. They headed South at a good pace and for many miles, over plains and across the great Atsar river; so far and long they traveled, that it grew well into the afternoon and nigh unto evening before they slowed their pace, signaled by Malok that they neared their destination.

"Why have we come so far out from the City? Would not Anur be there, or close to there, if anywhere?" Feldara skeptically queried.

"Maybe, but I know someone who, I believe, can help you find his exact location, even if it is somewhere hidden or unexpected." Malok simply answered.

It took him but a moment to see where they should land, and down he descended. However, the closer they came to land, nearby a forested hillock with a small lake before it, the more distraught Malok became. He knew this location, or at least thought he had, for he had been here before.

While searching for one whom Feldara loved so much, Malok could not help but remember how the lady Lenairu had helped him find the one he now loved so dearly, and he had thought to bring Feldara unto her, for to learn the technique of Atsarocu, as he had also done, so that she could find Anur and even never truly lose sight of him again.

Yet, the closer they came to this plot of ground, which Malok was absolutely certain of the exact same location as had been the home of the beautiful silver Dragoness, the less familiar the place looked, for much had changed since last he had been here. The lake, which had been clear and transparent, unnaturally so, was now like any other still body of water: covered with green algae nigh unto the middle, rushes overgrowing its banks, and water murky and colored of sediment. The hillock into which her home had been fire-carved, which had before been kept and tidy, was also overrun with thick clumpy grasses, bushes and brambles, small and large trees, so that the path from the door thereof to the lake was eradicated and all other aspects obfuscated.

"What has happened here?" He gasped aloud, as they landed near the shore of the lake, which was now muddy rather than sandy.

They walked up to the hillock, and indeed there was a round hollow into it, into the rock of it even, a sure indication that there was, or rather had been, a Dragon's home here, yet it did not proceed quite far into the hill, barely being more than a perfectly shaped overhang, and all covered with mosses and ferns.

"Lady Lenairu?" Malok called out, and though they both expectantly waited for reply, no one returned any greeting.

"It looks as though no one has lived here for many years. Are you sure this is the right place?" Feldara questioned, just as confused as was Malok.

"I do not understand how this can be." Malok declared, most perplexed. "Shar and I met a wonderful Dragoness here not a few days ago. She taught me a technique of magic that helped me find you, but now what was once a home has been reclaimed by the wilderness and, indeed, seemingly abandoned for a greatly long time."

"I believe you saw what you saw, and experienced such, but perhaps, it was borne of magic rather than reality." Feldara suggested.

"It felt real, very real." Malok wistfully sighed, as he turned to leave.

"This all reminds me of an encounter that I had before." Feldara recalled, but then remembering Calidon's envious reaction to the tale of how she met the Great Father Dragon, she chose to leave off any further elaboration.

Yet, had she spoken of him, they might have considered that a Patriarch must needs have a Matriarch, just as the Sun needs the Moon, and that she who had entertained and instructed Malok could have been even as the Moon to the Sun in whose light Feldara had basked.

After slowly returning in defeat unto the small pond, which was alive with the sounds of the just awakening nocturnal inhabitants- various frogs and insects, Malok plopped down upon the muddy bank, casting a forlorn glare to the water, water so murky that he could barely see his reflection from it. Indeed, the only thing clearly visibly reflected was the sun beginning to set in an early evening sky, and Feldara, for she sat beside her mate trying to comfort him with a gentle stroking of his hand.

An idea came to her then, and Feldara immediately voiced it aloud. "Since this Dragoness taught you the magic technique, and you have used it successfully before, maybe you could now teach it to me." She happily suggested, causing Malok's smile to return.

"I could try; it was very difficult for me to learn, so that I do not know how well I can teach it." He humbly admitted. "You must form an image in your mind of who you want to see, and once you have a good idea of that, you have then to stretch forth your mind unto the water." He instructed.

Feldara did so, and shortly, just as soon as she decided to imagine Anur with or without his helm on, his image began to slowly appear on the surface of the water.

"Alright," Malok began, amazed that she could perform this technique with relative ease, for the water of the pond did neither ripple nor wave, as steadily Anur's image remained upon it. "Now stretch out your will to the water, command it to find Anur for you, as if it were your instrument through which to see him, for all water upon Threa is connected."

A small ripple lapped outward from the pond's center, but surely the image of Anur remained until it morphed into the Peering of him in reality.

So clear and bright was this scene that he could easily be viewed moving about and all the country beside him, and from what Malok could tell, he was upon some road, passing by few travelers, and headed toward the setting of the sun.

"Well, where is he?" Feldara asked, causing another small ripple to lash forth from the pond's center, but still the Peering remained constant and steady.

"Upon some road heading west." Malok replied. "Other than that, I cannot tell."

"Is he safe?" Feldara asked again.

"Yes, he is safe. You can see everything around him so clearly; how can you not tell for yourself?" Malok queried, a little annoyed that Feldara had so capably and easily accomplished what had taken him many hours and attempts, and that she was also asking rather obvious questions, as if to rub her accomplishment in his face.

"I have my eyes closed, stupid." Feldara hotly retorted, causing more ripples.

Indeed, Malok had his own eyes fixed upon the lake once the visions had begun and had not bothered to check if Feldara was also looking upon them, and now that she was dissatisfied with his explanation of the goings on in the Peering, she attempted to see for herself. Just as quickly as her eyes opened, the water sloshed about as though a great stone had been thrown into its depths and the viewing faded from sight.

"Are you pulling my tail?" Feldara crossly demanded, at which Malok stifled a snorting laugh. "There is nothing to be seen on this stupid pond but algae and our reflections."

"Never would I lie about something so important to you; I swear to you. You conjured a perfect Peering, first try, and Anur was plainly visible, in living motion, just as I said." Malok happily assuaged.

"Why was he on some road somewhere? Why has he not come to seek us out?" Feldara worried aloud. "Come, let us go to him." She insisted rising from where she sat on the lake shore.

With a sigh, Malok followed, as they had been searching for Anur all afternoon and he wanted to spend less time on their mating day worrying about him, who Malok knew could handle himself, and more time in each other's affections. Taking off into the brazen evening sky, they left the mysteriously abandoned Dragon home and headed off into the West and the setting of the sun.

For many miles, they searched the ground below, scanning road after road with their excellent eyes, which did naturally become telescopic when needed, yet not even a single person halfway looked as if they could have been a disguised Anur, as he was taller than most Humans and had a unique stride.

They stopped on the crest of a small hill that overlooked the roads nearby, and spread before them, they could see the country all about: the beginnings of the Southern Mountains that would reach and join the Aronoran and stretch beyond, unto the Southern Sea; the farmland about, still scorched from the Great Burning, letting them know that nearby, just beyond the horizon lay the city of Bythatsar; the river itself, the Atsar, flowed as a silver lining upon the farthest Northern edge of their gaze.

Still there was no sight of Anur.

"We should head farther North, so that the Atsar is on our Southern horizon; he is probably on one of the roads up that way." Feldara pondered aloud, halfway directing her words to her husband, who stood dutifully by.

He could see the worry in her eyes, hear it in her voice as a slight tremor, and he wished her not to be troubled so. Malok only wanted to take her cares from her, even if he had to bear them all himself, and he put his arm around her shoulder, drawing her near to his heart.

"I think we have searched long enough today for Anur." He gently suggested, earning a contentious glare from Feldara. "I know that is not what you want to hear, but maybe Anur does not even want to be found right now. Perhaps, he is seeking a little solitude and isolation. He is perfectly capable of fending for himself, and we saw ourselves that he was in no danger, just alone. So, let us stop fretting, find some dinner, and spend the rest of the night enjoying each other's company."

Feldara hated how reasonable that sounded, and wanted very much to swipe Malok's kind smile right off his head for saying what he did. However, she had to admit, at least to herself, how rational his words were, and could not allow herself to maim her new husband, especially not the parts she wanted to kiss.

"You are right." She conceded, plopping on the ground in defeat.

"We can continue our search in the morning." Malok added, plopping down beside her, as in mimicking her mannerism.

It brought the slightest crack of a smile to Feldara's face, him mock pouting with her, and weakness exposed Malok pestered her further, until she produced a full grin. At which point, she arose and pushed him over and leaped into the air again, and laughing, she called for him to follow her.

In the gathering of the stars above the last red shades of the dying sun, they hunted together, and finding deer less skittish this far away from the

Order's Citadel, they soon had caught their meal and ate it together upon the grass of another hill.

Far away from the rest of the world, they were free to talk and laugh and tease and play as they wanted; the serenity of their remote location was only matched by the energy of their own company. On into the darkening of the sky and the rising of the crescent moon, they lived; they began to know each other- through words first, then affections.

Suddenly, they found themselves facing each other in the deep of night, yet illumined in the silvery moon's light upon the grassy knoll, and with a touch, the holding of each other's hand, the warmth of passionate love began to pervade their presence. Malok, who could bear no longer to only look upon his beloved, was the lead, the first to draw in close: touching his chest to her's, tenderly grasping her arms in his hands, and pressing his lips to her own in a kiss like they had not shared as yet: reaching, searching, desiring, yearning. Their long muzzles fully embraced each others' lips; their tongues intertwined. For so long, they let the world turn about them, until as spontaneously as they had started, they again released each other from their Dragon's kiss.

The night and his dark coloring lent not well to seeing, but she needed not so much to see his black form to perceive and savor his strength of body, his greatness, his burning of love, and earnest desire for her. He however, could see quite well her bright and shining body in every curve and detail which he craved, for the moon reflected the light enchantingly off from her luminous skin even more easily than from the heavenly body's own surface.

He knew hardly how, for his eyes had not strayed from her. His own body had not ceased to touch hers, yet had he slowly taken his place with her, and gently grasping her body, he rose above her and reached over her, so that he could, and did, lay his neck alongside hers and whisper gently into her ear.

"I love you." Said he, his warm breath tickling her cheeks.

"And, I love you." Feldara softly replied, as her neck curved so gracefully so that she could continue to keep his dark comforting eyes within her own gaze.

No better friend could she long for. Not Calidon, in all his goodness, strength, and kindness, could she ever compare to this beautiful male, nor even her fathers, or anyone else. Her love for Malok was beyond all other loves, for he was now her life-mate, her soul's completion, above vows, and distance, above physicality, or emotional discord, sickness, health, wealth, want, or even life and death. He was her own self, her other half, and as much as she knew this of him so did he of her. He knew any joining now in the body was nothing compared to their connection already established, their spiritual unity, consecrated solemnly before their Creator and in the deepest part of their being, in their souls.

The beauty of the simple smile which she then did offer, caught his attention, distracted him, if even for a moment's time, for it was the absolutely, most incomprehensibly lovely aspect he could yet fathom about her. He could only return her graceful expression with his own boyish grin, before they were completely lost to each other in the passing of the night.

They two were one.

Chapter 42

Shar had been quite bored, for ever since awakening in the garden of the Adthonler; he had been unable to locate a single one of his friends, neither Malok nor any of his newer ones aside from Theros, who could not be woken despite Shar's best, most annoying attempts. Eventually giving up on either rousing Theros or finding anyone familiar by the time he hungered for breakfast, he had been left to his own whims and mischief, and mischief it had mostly been, as his strolling through the city had been nearly as disruptive as Feldara's own spree, although in his case, the merchants and shopkeepers were generally more likely to gasp in shock and disgust, and in such stupefaction become incapable of offering him any wares, and especially not for free.

About lunchtime, it had become quite apparent to the Serpen that Humans were quite unused to encountering his kind, much less entreating them with courtesy and respect, for having entered an establishment of much lower repute than the Adthonler, a tavern of some sort, he had been left to sit idly at a table, unserviced and unwanted, for almost a half hour. Then, when he attempted to complain about their complete disregard for his existence, much less his appetite or wallet, a couple of strongmen simply tossed him out on the street. Eventually, he did find a more hospitable cafe, whereat he was serviced and only stared upon as though he were the only Serpen the waiting staff had ever seen, and probably so.

Shar could care less what all these Humans thought of him, as he was, after all, a sovereign king of an entire nation. It was, rather, a source of amusement to the Serpen, to see how most of them hardly knew how to engage with him, as if he were not a person or tripping all over themselves and their words. Almost comically, some bumbled and mumbled about, unsure of how to

address him without referring to derogatory slang for his kind, or there were
the obviously rude and unpleasant sort, who went out of their way,
inconveniencing themselves, to do or say stupidly offensive and unpleasant
things unto him. Once or twice throughout the day, he had just burst out
laughing at these pathetically petty displays.

Of course, there were Humans that had treated him with respect and
common courtesy, earning Shar's appreciation and delight, but these
encounters then seemed so uneventful, humorless, and even boring to Shar as
when compared to the atrocious, yet hilarious, acts of the others.

Yet, past all the laughable acts of vulgar disrespect, or even the few acts
of sincere hospitality, he found himself in the rare position, as far as his
experience went, having lived as a very popular royal among his people, that of
being an outcast, which did feel so lonely to Shar, especially with neither sight
nor sound of his friends all the day long.

About eventide, he was strolling along his return trip to the Citadel
through the byways and back alleys that meandered through the various
housing districts, when he noticed a large group of children; Shar did ever so
much admire children for their peculiar innocence, as without the baggage of
society, politics, or history, they were usually the first or only Humans to ever
warm to him. Having desired a few of his own, and having made plans as such
with a special someone for when he returned to his own realm, he decided to
get a closer observation, for studious purposes, as if these children could
provide some insight into how his own might behave someday.

He didn't like what he saw.

One child, smaller than the rest, was being surrounded by a mob of his
elders and tormentingly harassed, and no adult was there to come disperse
them, or settle argument, if dispute there had been.

"Hey, you kids!" Hissed Shar, striding toward them for to stop the
ruckus before it could get out of hand "Leave him alone!"

"Or what?" One of the bigger ones replied before he had truly caught
sight of who had ordered the cessation of their cruel fun-making.

"Or, I shall gobble you up, whole and kicking." Maniacally laughed Shar, as screaming and hollering, the mob of children, having finally seen who had come to get them, all scattered as fast as their feet could run.

The poor victim child, who had been shoved to the ground, could hardly believe that he had been so abandoned to such a fate by his "comrades", for so he probably still thought them, even so abused, and as Shar approached, he cried out.

"Oh, hush, silly little babe." Grumbled Shar, as he helped the boy to his feet. "I am about to eat no one; Human children taste awful. Are you alright? Did your friends kick you while you were down?"

"I guess I am fine." Whimpered the little boy, as he struggled to hold back tears, for he was not yet sure if he was still about to get gobbled, yucky or not.

"Well, tell your playmates not to be so rough with you, or I shall be back to get them." Shar explained, mock seriously, as expressed by the winking of an eye.

Fortunately, the little boy finally understood what Shar was about, and laughing his acknowledgment, he ran off to rejoin his group, if he could find them not cowering under their own beds.

"Now that my good deed for the day is done," Shar thought to himself, as he continued onward to the Citadel. "I am free to get fat and drunk and comfortable."

No surprise to Shar, though polite enough about it, the gate guards did not wish to let him inside without papers, such as Ulam would have carried on summons from Orthard, for these were of the men that Argamon had been leader and not of the Paladins who, at Zurthaud's deathbed, had greeted him and Malok, nor witnessed the Dragon's deeds, neither did know at all that Shar was a companion of a Dragon, of whom Shar still had caught neither sight nor scent. Little did this matter to the Serpen, for after being told, rather discourteously, to slither off somewhere else, he had merely wandered out of their sight and then clambered up and over the outer wall. Indeed, climbing was hardly more difficult than walking for a Serpen, for they could flatten their whole bodies against a surface and dig in their sharp claws for to easily scale most any wall, even one quite smooth and crag-less as the Order's Citadel walls.

Once down again upon the other side of the wall, Shar had no problems with anyone treating him poorly; that being because there was no one within the Citadel, was only slightly disappointing to him. Indeed, after the scouring coup, which had cleaned out all the non-member courtiers, merchants, and diplomats along with all the unsavory, Orthard approved thugs, and with all the Paladins dispersed about the realm to various tasks, the grounds of the Citadel seemed more a ghost town than a usual bustling, thriving castle-town. Yet, there was one person, in Shar's mind the most important individual of the whole Order, who still lingered about these halls, and left from them about as much as the Dragon priest, Aelanur.

Off he went to visit this invaluable person, his favorite resident of the whole castle, the cook, who surely would be within and hard at work, for a cook can hardly forsake his duties any more than a doctor. Truly, this hash slinger had, at the first, been the most hateful Human he had yet encountered, offering many insulting slurs whenever he saw the Serpen, but the pride the man took in his craft prevented him from yet serving an inedible meal to Shar. The fires of hatred would have then been stoked but for the delicious fare served; instead, they dwindled and smothered under the downpour of compliments Shar offered before and after each delectable meal. Over the few days that he had eaten at the Paladin's table, the contemptuous chef had slowly been won over, even to where he had apologized for his previous offenses and then became rather fond of the Serpen who only had praise for his cooking.

Of course, the ever hungry Shar was intentional in his buttering of the coarse Human, for he knew how to keep his meals coming hot and good, how to keep his plate unbroken. Into the mess hall attached to the Human's barracks he sauntered sniffing loudly of the air, though his people would easier smell by flicking out their tongues.

"My, how scrumptiously savory smells this fine kitchen today." Crowed the Serpen, as he sat at his usual place.

Immediately upon hearing his voice, the cook could be heard back in the kitchen bustling about to hurriedly fix a plate for Shar. In half the time it would have taken the Serpen to walk into the serving area and fix his own plate, as did everyone else, the cook came proudly striding out of the kitchen with an enormous tray of a plate piled high with this evening's supper.

"Shar, me Serpen lad, welcome back, sir. I have got the right stuff for you here, yes sir." Flaunted the chef, as he set the huge plate loaded with fine foods before Shar.

"Why, Venrogan, you master chef, you have outdone yourself with this awe-inspiring feast!" Shar exclaimed, gasping exaggeratedly, never-mind being on first-name basis with the cook. "Why I regretted missing dinner here last night, for I was sorely disappointed to learn that even the Adthonler has not come close to the taste of your culinary craft."

"O, now I know yer pulling on me leg." Laughed the chef, so hard that his massive belly joggled horribly.

Indeed, though the chef did make fittingly tasty food, it was an outright lie.

"But, I ken yer saying. Their victuals is much too dainty for a hungry man like yer 'n me, and pricey." Agreed Venrogan, the cook, as he heartily slapped the Serpen upon the back.

"That reminds me, I do have here something for you," Shar slyly offered, after wincing from the cook's painful show of affection. "A small token of my sincerest gratitude for all the supremely delicious meals you have served me."

Reaching down into his knapsack, the very same which he had brought all this long way from home and kept strung across his shoulders all this time, he pulled out a large bottle of the very best local spirits he had found in his searching of the markets earlier in the day. The cook's grin got so big that it ate up his whole face, as full knowing how potent and enjoyable this elixir was, he merrily accepted the bottle, and he gave the Serpen several more slaps on the back, each one more hearty than the last.

"Yer a good lad." He laughingly bellowed, as he pulled the cork from off the bottle using only his teeth, and after fondly smelling of it, poured some into a nearby clean cup. "Share and share alike, me friend." He declared, offering the single cup to Shar, yet laughing all the way, stealing the rest of the bottle back to the kitchen, where he would remain for the rest of the night, as he would soon be incapable of walking to his bed.

The meal, though simple fare, was quite good, excellently prepared and seasoned, and Shar quickly downed the tasty morsels of salted pork, sausages, cheese, breads, potatoes, and various other vegetables. However, the liquor was horrible, so much that Shar couldn't stomach more than a swig, and along with his dirty dishes to the sink, he returned the nearly full cup to the kitchen, for the cook to finish later, who was sitting by the hearth and already talking and laughing to himself,.

With a full belly, yet a sober mind, Shar strolled out from the mess hall, vowing to return only a little later for some dessert, for he desired a walk in the looming dusk, as the glimmering stars were just peeking out of the blackness at the far Eastern horizon while the fiery orange of the sun, in all the glorious ruddy hues, slowly descended below that of the Western.

Across the deepening shade of the common lawn he sauntered, not really going anywhere, eyes looking for nothing in particular, only absorbing the resplendence of the painterly colorful twilight hour.

Far across the lawn, a movement caught his eye, a door of the inner wall, that of the Keep's bailey, was being opened. Slowly and suspiciously, as if the doorman desired to draw no attention, without creak or whine, the wooden door was swung just barely wide enough to be opened a crack, and eventually, slithering out the narrow opening, a sole person exited from therein. Against the shadow of the outer courtyard, like a black cloud on a moonless night, this singular shadow crept; clearly a fiend up to no good, it pressed hard against the wall, blending well with its camouflage of darkness as it slunk about.

"Most peculiar." Shar thought to himself, and determined to see for himself what this sneaky specter was up to, he followed after it.

By way of hugging the wall, the villain avoided detection by anyone other than Shar, for there were a few light patrols upon the top of the outer wall, every few moments flashing their lanterns out and down into the courtyard on one side and the city streets on the other. Waiting in the shadows beyond the reach of the lantern light until these guards had passed, the villain suddenly leaped upon the face of the wall and stuck like a lizard.

"A better climber than I, is this weird one." Shar mused with astonishment, as with apparent ease the phantom scaled the smooth stones straight up to the top of the wall and jumped over the battlements to the other side.

Shar was hard pressed to make pace with the climbing speed of this shadowy foe, especially after such a heavy meal, but about the time it had reached the bottom of the other side and began running off into the streets, Shar had made it to the top of the wall. He took note of its path before he followed suite, descending the wall, yet after the scoundrel turned a corner and fled down a side street, he had to jump down the last few meters and take off sprinting for to keep hot the pursuit.

Through the back alleys of the city, of which Shar was thankful to have visited earlier, so as to be better acquainted with their particular layout, or lack thereof, the mysterious fiend darted at break-neck pace, and though Shar was no quick runner and again hard pressed to keep up with it, he was not so far behind that he would lose his quarry. On and on they raced through the streets, with Shar only far enough behind to remain unnoticed by his target, yet strangely enough, in their course throughout the whole city, which did not necessarily sleep when darkness fell, they passed not a single person in the way. Through all the graduated sectors of the city, they passed, until they came nigh unto the very last gate, the only gate of the outer wall, the main gate of the city, and seemingly disregarding any possibility that it could be apprehended by the gate guards, straight for these gates headed the dark foe.

Though he thought to himself that surely the night watchmen would arrest this blackguard if he intended to pass through the gates, Shar wondered whether or not he should attempt to apprehend this villain before or after it did pass through them, for he had, as of yet, no idea who he was chasing. The thought then occurred to him that perhaps he had been chasing down a friendly messenger, causing Shar to suddenly feel rather foolish for all this running, if it did prove to be needless, and he slowed his steps for to call out to the mysterious runner.

"Ho! Are you friend or foe?" He shouted, an acceptable question to any unknown person at night, but the shade paid no heed to his words, neither slowed pace at all.

"Guards, stop this man!" Shar called out to the gate guards, some of whom stood at attention even at the gigantic hinges of the great gate, within perfect range for interception, and they did move to position themselves, obstructing the road from any traffic, of which, strangely enough, there was none, save for the running man and Shar. However, they did nothing to detain the shadowy villain, and it passed on between them, racing off into the night beyond the dim light of the city's braziers and lamps.

"Why did you not stop him?" Shar gasped exasperatedly, as tired from all the running, he stopped to catch his breath before them.

In but a moment, he saw why, for these were no ordinary night watchmen. Before him, blocking his path rather than their ally's, stood a troop of the black-cloaked Dark Hunters, and above him, upon the ramparts of the gatehouse, stood several more. They kicked the long dead body of an actual gate guard down to the ground before him, for to silently, mockingly, prove their control of this place.

"We will by no means impede the Vessel, and neither shall you." Gratingly spoke one of the black-robed fiends.

Before he had time to question this saying, "the Vessel" they spoke of, another of the Dark Hunters stepped forth from the group and stabbed him in the gut with a nasty, jagged dagger, which at any other time than now, when he had been so winded after chasing that shade, he could have dodged.

Gasping from shock and pain like burning fire, Shar slumped to the ground and could do nothing but clutch at his belly, from which flowed his warm, wet life-blood, while the Dark Hunters, one by one, slipped out through the ajar doors of the gate, leaving him and all their other victims to lie on the cold ground of the deepening black night.

____

The sun shone brightly through the window of Zurthaud's quarters, so clear and brilliant that he could not help but arise at its dawning, and even as soon as his eyes opened, he hastily arose, cleansed himself, and dressed. Today was another big day, the day of his father's trial; it was the ending of a long endured reign of tyranny and the beginning of a new day of freedom.

Down the hallway of the Human's dormitories he ran, even from the same room he had kept his whole life, down the stairs past the kitchens, and out into the common yard between the separate quarters. So stark and still and quiet was the morning and so early he had awoken, early enough to need not race unto the courtrooms, that he thought to take a stroll down the same path he had walked nigh sixteen years ago, over unto the Dragon's quarter, up the stairs to this section of wall's ramparts. Down he stared at the silent, empty courtyard, at the still barren patch of dirt where he had last ever seen his Dragoness companion, Lethira, who had awoken his heart to love and kindness.

"This day is for you." Thought Zurthaud to himself, perhaps even unto the Blessed Realm, where dwelled his long passed Dragoness. "For you, Lethira, and your people, today is your day of victory."

Watching the last fogs of morning fade into the rising warmth of the morning sunlight, he rested only a brief moment there upon the wall, for he had a busy day, and tough battle ahead.

A battle, indeed, thought he to himself, though not a battle of swords and magic, a war of words and wit, for Zurthaud feared that, even yet, if conniving and weaseling enough was the speech-making of Orthard, his sire could yet be loosed to walk freely. The judge who sat over the proceedings, Lady Veringa, was no friend to Zurthaud's cause, hiding complacency and dislike for her own inconveniencing behind a thin excuse of impartiality and equality, and if Orthard presented to her the more convincing argument, even a false one, he could be cleared of many charges, possibly even the murder of Serc. Though steps had been made so that he would never be permitted to rejoin the ranks of the Order, Zurthaud knew he could, and probably would, stir up much trouble without, if he were to be set free.

Down the steps he trod again, down again to the courtyard, and crossing it, unto the Keep. The Human door guards posted here at the Keep's main gate almost called for him to halt before recognizing him at a distance; instead, they saluted his approach. He slowed only a little, for to return their gesture, as he hastened inside.

It was not for need of being prompt that Zurthaud quickened his pace, but that he was just so nervous, he had not much practice with the court proceedings, being secondary in his mind to skills of battle. He was anxious to win this case, and not lose, setting Orthard free, and he hoped not to blunder, as he felt to have done more often than not.

There was but one Dragon guarding the inner door of the Keep's grand hall, one of the same two who had volunteered days before to this duty, and he no longer was so enthusiastic as to keep the great steel doors closed until passerby would need them opened Though the horrendous grate markings upon the floor and ceiling indicated he had tried to maintain such inordinate vigil, at least until his friend had been reassigned to other duties, he now had it swung wide and propped open, as previously it was, and only needed salute Zurthaud, as returning the gesture, the Human passed on through.

Up to the fifth floor Zurthaud strode, bounding up the steps by two and three at a time, and down the long hall unto its end, and into the Court of Justice. He was the first to arrive, but for the clerks who were busy about their duties.

It was they who had to proof-read each side's arguments, for to help make certain they were free of logical fallacy, hearsay, and other such blunders before being presented, and already they had Zurthaud's papers, evidence, witness list, and notes all arranged neatly upon a desk before his seat. Strangely enough, there were no papers, not even a single scrap upon the desk before Orthard's chair, even though Zurthaud had made a personal order that his sire be given full access to paper, ink, pen, and any book or resource he needed for to make his best argument of defense.

"Clerk," Zurthaud called to one of the many who stood by. "Where are the papers for the defender's argument?" He asked, thinking that, perhaps,

Orthard wished to delay his nigh inevitable sentencing through non-compliance of court procedure.

"I am afraid that the defense has, as yet, presented no papers for their arguments. We hoped to receive even a word or two by today, but the lord emeritus Orthard has yet to make coherent request for any kind of legal counsel or even pen and paper. There could, possibly, be a mistrial due to the lack of cooperation from the defense; in which case the date of trial would have to be rescheduled." Informed the clerk.

Zurthaud was beginning to feel unsettled, for it was rather odd that Orthard would turn down a chance to argue on his own behalf, as that seemed to be his favorite pastime aside from collecting taxes and crushing liberty. The arrival of Lady Veringa distracted his dwelling upon this, for upon her appearance, he and all others present in the court had to rise from seating and greet her with a formal bow, an act signifying their respect for her position and judicial rulings. Once she had finally adjusted her flowing robes and sat upon the judge's dais, the regal Lady would have started proceedings but that she too was slightly early, so instead she gazed about the courtroom, and also finding Orthard not yet present she voiced her concerns to Zurthaud.

"Where is the defendant? Was he not adequately notified of his trial?" She brusquely asked of him.

"I am unaware of his exact location currently, as he should right now be en route, with his complimentary guards, but rest assured, the accused was prior informed, upon the date of presented charges, by your own court's clerical staff, as to the date, time, and nature of this trial, and was even granted full access to all necessary resources, as required by law, all of which is recorded in my court documents." Zurthaud replied trying not to sound too curt, for it was much too early to be dealing with the foul attitudes of uppity politicians.

"There is yet a quarter-hour until the exact time of trial, my Lady." Informed one of the nearby clerks.

"I shall be forced to declare a mistrial and reschedule if he does not appear; I do hope that you actually have done as you said." The judge gruffly declared to Zurthaud, apparently feeling it much too early for any sort of courtesy.

Zurthaud just held his tongue, and in uncomfortable silence, they all stared at each other: Zurthaud, Lady Veringa, the court clerks, for a good long while, nearly the full fifteen minutes. Just when Lay Veringa was about to again ask for the time, a loud clanging of metal sounded from above; the clamor of tolling bells descended upon their ears at a volume too loud to be ignored. It was the warning bells of the Citadel. Something had gone terribly wrong.

Suddenly, just as Lady Veringa was about to complain about all the ruckus and inquire as to why the castle's alarm should be sounded, a young Paladin, one of those set to bring Orthard forth from the dungeon burst through the grand doors of the courtroom and shouted the worst of messages.

"The prisoner has escaped! Orthard has escaped!"

Chapter 43

"Good morning, beloved." Murmured a gentle voice into Feldara's ear, and she opened her eyes to find her Life-mate, Malok lying beside her upon the cool, dewy grass of a golden morning.

His arms wrapped tight around her, as had they been all through the night, she could not but move closer unto him, and she desired nothing else. To wake alongside her dearest lover was her heart's fulfillment and her soul's completion. She was full: of peace and joy, happiness beyond all bounds, and she felt that the sun, in all its luminous glory, could not burn as bright and warm as the elation which now she felt.

Through her groggy, half-open-eyed morning vision, she reached with her arm for his head, and shortly finding him, she gently caressed his cheek and pulled his neck down to her for another kiss. His lips were sweeter than honey to her mouth, and not wishing to be anywhere else in the world, she caressed them long with her own.

He almost laughed, for joy of his own, and a bright toothy smile shone through his otherwise darkness of form. She could only meet his grin, the apple of her eye, with a smile of her own. So that in pureness of satisfaction with life and love and all things, they lay together out in the morning sun upon the grassy knoll, spending time only in each other's company.

"I should get some breakfast for us." Malok suggested, at length, attempting to rise, but she held onto him, unwilling to lose the warmth and the presence of his body next to her own.

"Let the world pass us by; only stay here with me." Feldara murmured into his ears, as she reached unto his mouth for another kiss.

He waited until their lips again parted before contending. "You shall be awfully cranky, if we do not eat by noon." Malok jested, and knowing how truthful that was, she only halfheartedly laughed in agreement.

They got up and stretched together, limbering and shaking the remaining dew drops from off their bodies, and just when the world could not be more right and his desire for her was kindled again by the sinuous straining of her body and they had locked eyes with each other and leaned in together for another kiss and more love-making, Malok broke away, his attention ripped from her by an object fast approaching.

"What is it?" Feldara asked, seeing the troubled look on his face, as Malok stared off into the distance behind her.

"I think it is a Human." Malok guessed, perplexed and somewhat unnerved by the awkward way this person strode- quickly, savagely, and straight toward their direction.

Feldara slowly began turning about to see, but she only caught a glimpse of the shadowy man, before, roaring defensively, Malok shoved her aside and swiped an angry clawed hand at the Human who had rapidly crossed the distance between them and leaped toward Feldara. She now spun about to see what manner of fiend assaulted them, and caught sight of the tattered, distorted Human, for so it was: smelly, unkempt, grim, and dark of visage- as it was violently cast by Malok's strike several yards away from them and plopped into the ground like a pile of wet rags.

However, their foe was not defeated, for without cry of agony, or even of rage, its body bleeding from the gashes Malok had rent in it, it quickly arose, and its bones cracked with the unnatural movements as it reformed a somewhat stable posture and charged them again.

"Go away, villain! Leave us be!" Furiously shouted Malok, attempting to reason with the creature if any were to be had.

However, the beast-man heeded not his words and only charged them again. Malok again struck at it with his claws, but the fiend was not cut or thrown this time. With sly movements, it clambered on and over Malok's talons, so that he did not even graze it with them, and then leaped from his hand as though it were a springboard.

It passed over Malok and landed behind him. And heeding him no longer it sped on toward its true target, Feldara, but she was not quite caught off-guard. Mostly out of surprise, somewhat of defensive instinct, Feldara had sucked a good draw of air into her lungs, and now, with a crack like thunder, she released her fiery breath. In violent explosion, her flames poured forth from her mouth, bathing Malok in their warmth and protection while scorching to cinders the grass and ground all about him, but she knew that she had missed the foul creature.

The vile fiend had scurried to the side, avoiding some, though not all, of Feldara's blistering attack; still with flames hungrily licking, charring, its side closest to the blazing Dragon-fire, it again rushed at her. She had not but to move her head to spew forth her flaming breath into its path, but Feldara found the villainous beast too quick for her. In a flash it had ducked too close to her chin, underneath the arc of her fire, and grabbed onto her forefeet.

Panicking at this monster's touch, Feldara screamed a roar, rather than leaning forward her head, again bringing the fiend into range of her destructive breath, or even curling her tongue just so that her fires would wind around and, in superb defensive shield, kindle to flame the air around her body, and she violently struck at the dark beast with her claws.

The vile creature, this Human turned animal, though cut, burned, broken and bleeding from all the ferocious attacks from the Dragons, unshakably clung to her one hand, and no matter what she did to it, though she nigh ripped it to shreds, Feldara could not at all get it to release its grip.

Suddenly, the wretched assailant began to vomit vile black ooze that could never have originated from food, and in such volume that could never have fit within a Human's stomach. On and on, it retched upon the ground before itself, and though Feldara, completely disgusted by this, twisted and struggled wildly, and though Malok tried grabbing hold of it and pulling it away from her, by unnatural force it held fast to her hand and to the ground.

A pool of the tarry, black soup began to form before Feldara, yet the Human did not cease its agonized shuddering and eliminations, not even to breathe. So it was that Orthard, once Lord and High Consul of the Order, died in a puddle of his own filth, and out from the blackness of this liquid began to rise an even more terrible form.

To Feldara and Malok's horror, out from the goop slithered: first the deep red, faceless, and horned helm; then the same red, spiked, and cloaked armor and mail of the dreaded adversary of all life- the Dark Lord.

"Malok! Malok! Help me!" Feldara screamed, well terrified of this daemon's appearance.

Malok set upon the Shadow Lord with a ferocious assault of fire and claws and teeth, but the armored giant hardly budged at all from the slashing and clawing and biting and burning. With but a simple backhanded strike, the Dark Lord sent Malok hurtling through space to land on his backside but a short distance away, yet even as Malok arose from the dirt, even as, roaring in anger and fear for his beloved's safety, and leaping in attack, unconcerned for his own life, toward the most dreadful of foes, the Dark One cast his black cape about Feldara, drowning out all her light and beauty in an unnatural shroud of evil shadow, and in the next moment, withdrawing it from where she should be, revealed her to be gone, whisked away from where she had stood only seconds before.

It was as if time stopped, the world ceased its motion, as Malok looked in appalled confusion upon the bare spot of ground where only part of a second earlier his life-mate had stood, and seeing the expression on the young Dragon's face, that of horror mixed with anger and despair of losing his soul's mate, the terrible crimson armored villain laughed, long and twisted and deep.

"I shall kill you!" With all his breath and rage, Malok hoarsely shouted, as he finally reached the Dark One and unleashed his fury.

However, a wicked, jagged-edged scimitar came from nowhere to appear within the Dark Lord's hands, and with it, he struck the assailing Dragon. Malok could hardly avoid the surprise weapon, and was thrown to the ground again, this time bleeding from a ragged gash hacked down his side, but even so wounded, the young Dragon had avoided a certain death-blow from the cruel weapon.

His vainglorious celebration of triumph, of crushing all happiness, hope, and light, cut short by Malok's assault, the Dark Lord turned his attentions to taunting the injured Malok. "Ah, 'the dreamer', or should I say, 'the thief'; it is most pleasing that my ultimate victory is also vengeance for your offences. You stole my precious things; now I have taken yours."

Malok cared not to hear any words from this horrible foe, especially not this gloating, not over stealing away his beloved, and roaring furiously, he charged the Dark One yet again.

"Calm yourself, child; I shall give you a chance to win her back, of course." Continued the Dark One, as he slowly descended into the puddle from whence he had come. "I am fair, even generously benevolent. Come to my tower, and you may challenge me again for the fate of your Bright Dragoness. And, do bring all your friends, especially Zurthaud. I should hate for you to die alone."

With that, his boasting, complete, the Dark Lord sank into the depths of the black pool, and though only seconds away, Malok could not reach him fast enough to grab hold of him, or otherwise prevent him from disappearing. Even attempting to go after the Shadow Lord by way of descending into the ooze himself proved futile, for though Malok tried his very best to swim down into it, the puddle proved to be less than an inch deep for any other traveler and most foul smelling.

There was nothing he could do now to save Feldara, and the utter despair that Malok felt overwhelmed him. He could do naught but writhe and wail and scream in agony for his wounds, both of the flesh and of the soul.

<><><><><>

Anur felt stupid.

All night long he had cursed himself for travelling so far from his dearest charge, from all the people he loved most in the world, and only for his depressively perceived uselessness. It should not have mattered to himself, certainly not so much as it had, that he would become an outlier in their happy Dragon family; he could still be content as only observing, even from a distance, the joys of those whom he loved best.

Such a life had no glory, no great appeal, but Anur did not care for such attentions anyway. If Feldara could hardly afford him a goodly amount of time, but would once in a while cast his way one of her bright smiles or the musical sound of her voice- it would be enough. Besides, he knew, without a doubt, even considering the formidable Theros, that he was the one most capable of protecting her; he above all others could watch from the shadows, waiting, able to defend her life at a moment's notice.

And, it was this very parental desire to protect his beloved Dragoness that had driven him mad with indecision, until, after pacing in circles for hours, fighting his own self, Anur had finally turned around and headed back down the Eastward road, back to Doraegonoran and his dearest Feldara. All night long, by his keen vision and the light of the moon avoiding stumbling over stones or cracks in the road, he had nearly run all the way until morning.

When the sun did at last crest its golden fire over the sleeping hills about, Anur was nearly a half day's march from the City, yet in the dark of night, had he taken a wrong turn and ended up further East than the nearest highway to the city, that by which he had come. Indeed, he was closer to Bythatsar, which would have now been only a quarter day's walk to the North and West, but it was not so crucial a detour that he retrace his misspent steps. The next junction down this well worn road would have another branch, another road leading North unto Doraegonoran and to his Dragoness.

It was then that he heard it, even as he came into sight of the next fork in the road; from off in the distance, a sound chilled him to his bones, even though, walking through the night and thus warming his blood, not even the cold of the pre-sunrise morning had so iced his veins. It was as a dying animal crying out in its final agonized throes, forlorn and hopeless wailing, but it was unmistakably of the unique quality of a Dragon's voice. His heart now racing, Anur's fears took dreadful shape in his mind, and he forced his feet to do likewise, not away from the desperate cry, but toward it.

Mounting the grassy knolls nearby the road, he could barely make out the form of whoever it was who had so cried out, but as he descended into the small vale and climbed the next little hill, ever nearing the aching, doleful, mourning, as of one who longed for even death as a release from their terrible anguish, Anur finally identified the source.

He could only quicken his pace, nearly stumbling and rolling down the next hill in his haste, as in between ragged, anxiety shredded breaths, his lips silently muttered prayers for this to be something, anything else than his worst fears come true and upon those whom he loved the best in all the world. Yet, his nightmare came to life, as Anur crested the last hill, nearly upon his hands and knees, from exertion as much as overwhelming terror, only to find Malok, his beloved Feldara's life-mate, bleeding out upon the ground, sobbing and howling beyond all sense or control.

The only thing Anur could say, then scream, as loud as his tired lungs would screech was a single word, "No".

No, it could not be, should not be, must not be, yet it was.

Having no need to ask what had happened, Anur only picked up Malok's head and held the sorrow-crazed Dragon in his arms.

Anur wanted to blame himself, his absence, for this, but he knew that would at best be foolish, and at worst, egotistical, to think that by his presence alone the Dark One would have been completely thwarted. He had to force himself to realize that he could not possibly have foreseen what had happened, nor could have hardly prevented it; also, neither would he have wanted to deprive a happy couple of privacy just to be their bodyguard. The enemy had known this, waited for this opportunity, and struck them when they were all divided from each other, even by necessity, when they were the most vulnerable.

It would be easy to fall back into the old habit of self-pity, but it was also pointless. It would be hard to keep going, to break through his own pain and self-loathing, but it was vital that he do so, and everything else that he could. It was necessity for Malok, for his gaping wound to be sealed and his bleeding stopped, and it would not be done by itself. Anur tore off his tunic shirt, and ripping it into strips, he used it for immediate, yet temporary, clotting.

"Anur, he took her. He took her!" Malok wildly raged.

"I know." Anur broodingly replied, as he anxiously tried to think of a way to stitch or bind the gash. "We will get her back." He promised, to both Malok and himself.

The sound of wings beating off in the distant sky could not possibly bring Anur any great measure of peace, yet did it offer that he should be spared the sorrow upon sorrow of losing two of his cherished family in but one morning, that Malok should receive proper care for his seeping gash and not die of blood-loss.

Chapter 44

Two Dragons had to carry him back to the Order's Citadel, and if Anur had not been there, they would have needed a third to hold him still.

Malok, crazed in desperation and blood-loss, had wanted to immediately pursue the Shadow Lord, to set out for the Ragnor right then, gaping wound in his side and everything. He cared not if anyone else went with him; he cared not that he would have died, even along the way, not even in combat for his beloved. All he desired was to have Feldara back beside him again. She was his light, <u>his</u> Bright Dragoness, not just <u>the</u>; she was his soul's completion, his better, prettier, smarter, and funnier half. Without Feldara in his life, Malok did not even care if he lived at all.

But, his good friends reminded him that there was still hope, that the Dark One had given him a whole seven days for which Feldara should still be alive, and that a healed, whole body, with many reinforcements, would be far more successful at a rescue attempt than just Malok, half-dead, alone. So it was that he had let them, and reluctantly at that, drag him into the Keep's fourth floor Medical Hall, into a sick bed, improvisedly Dragon-sized, within one of the many spacious and windowed rooms of the restful healing ward.

"How could this have happened?" Zurthaud asked himself over and over again as, just without Malok's room he paced back and forth within the large and open main corridor of this ward.

In one fell stroke, the Shadow Lord had snatched away all hope for victory: Feldara, the Bright Dragoness, had been taken, probably killed. Malok, her life-mate, had been gravely injured, along with his Serpen companion,

Shar. The man who was once his father, Orthard had escaped justice and died as a thrall of evil.

And, perhaps, this last one hurt Zurthaud even as much as the other losses; deep down, Zurthaud had hoped, like all those with wayward or downright wicked parents, that his sire could possibly be redeemed, that forgoing a death sentence, a life-sentence in the Orders dungeons could have reformed even the proud Orthard into a humbled, penitent Human being who actually had a heart and soul. Maybe, Zurthaud could have even withstood a visit to his cell once in a while, and given much time to heal, could have come, at length, to forgive the man.

Now, he would never know.

A voice like thunder, shouting and roaring with nigh the same volume, interrupted Zurthaud's thoughts and stopped his incessant tramping. Even from further down the main stair of the Keep, Theros could be heard and recognized, and though Zurthaud was glad that he had come so quickly from his mission of delivering ballots, for his presence was needed here where the hurting of his friends and family was greatest, Zurthaud was almost himself frightened by the ferocious cacophony quickly rising, like a whirlwind, up to the same floor.

"Where is he?" Could finally be heard distinctly, as the large red Dragon bounded up the last step and turned the corner into the same hallway that Zurthaud tentatively occupied.

"Here is the room." Replied the unfortunate guide, another male Dragon by the name of Codalts.

One of the company that had gone out with Zurthaud in an attempt to apprehend Orthard before he could cause much damage, Codalts had been Theros' substitute, letting Zurthaud ride upon his shoulders, until, upon finding Malok and Anur, he had been given new orders to quickly fetch Theros. Indeed, being the fastest flyer of that posse, he had completed his mission much sooner than Zurthaud had expected, and when he saw that he was no longer needed, he just as swiftly dismissed himself.

"Zurthaud, what happened?" Theros asked as he quickly approached, and with such broken, anguished expression that the Human nearly wept for it.

"I cannot rightly tell. Somehow, Orthard acquired a key, which he used to free himself, and then, by night, raced all the way from Doraegonoran to the plains just beyond the Atsar. From what Anur has said, and what I have heard from Malok's blabbering, using Orthard, the Dark Lord then came forth and snatched Feldara away." He explained, even as Theros stepped over him to get to the door of Malok's room.

"Is he alright?" Theros asked, most concerned.

"He should be; the wound from the Dark Lord's sword was not charged with any vile magic like that which I endured, so that with poultice and stitching with Black-iron needles and bandages- all wielded by careful physicians' hands- he should soon mend well enough for another fight." Answered Zurthaud.

"That is good; because I am going to kill him!" Theros roared, even as he crashed through the doors into Malok's room.

However, Theros' rage over Malok's failure to protect his only recently reunited, long-lost daughter was crushed by the pitiful sight of the poor, black Dragon lifelessly slumped over the Dragon-sized gurney. Theros could bring no harm or anger against him, and only silently strode across the room, lay down beside the tortured Malok, and like he were his own son, held his wounded form in his arms.

"Lord Zurthaud," Greeted a familiar voice from the hallway.

It was none other than Lorn, who having finished with securing and starting repairs for the Aronoran wall and already having heard of the horrible news, had come as quickly as Galrag's wings would carry them both.

"Lord? I am no Lord." Zurthaud replied, even as the elder man held forth his hand, which he did clasp heartily.

"Did Theros not yet tell you?" Galrag questioned, even as he rounded the corner and, with his massive frame nearly filling the breadth and height of the corridor, sat down behind Lorn. "The lots were all cast and gathered by late last night, and we spent until morning counting them. By unanimous vote, you are the new Lord Consul." Said he, a quite rare slight smile touching his lips.

The news was not entirely shocking to Zurthaud, as he well knew how all the other Paladins already looked to him as a leader, but to hear of the decision, of the faith cast upon him, along with all the heavy weight of responsibility, was nonetheless stunning. Immediately, his instinct was to feel overwhelmed, unworthy, ask for an excuse or a recount, but just as suddenly, he quelled these negative emotions. Zurthaud knew, with the same certainty that he had been chosen by the other Paladins, that he must dutifully perform this role; there was none other who would fill it.

"What about the High Council and the Electors? Were they not selected first?" Zurthaud inquired, hoping that his and Theros' new system had been effectual and well carried out.

"Indeed, they were, but mayhap, with all the votes being cast in such close succession and without much debate or polling, the choice of the people had been slightly skewed and the process too hasty." Relayed Lorn. "Nevertheless, it was a good trial of your voting system. As you instructed, the first votes were taken from the general populace of each race for the Council of Electors, and their Electors are: Aelanur- for the Dragons; Argamon- for the Humans; Efarnuil, Anfanuil's brother- for the Aelvs; and Himmel- for the Dworvs. They then elected to the High Council: Me; Galrag; Theros; Gimmel; Noff; the Aelvs- Thryzanuil and Elyriana; and the Humans- Ruad, Carathad, Bron, Udrik, and you, of course. Afterward, all the lower councils' votes were gathered and combined with the votes of the High Council resulting in your promotion to Lord Consul."

"Why then had my vote not been asked for?" Zurthaud contended, still a little shocked at how quickly this had all been achieved and of suddenly bearing this great weight of responsibility.

"It would have mattered little." Galrag chuckled. "You would have been the only Paladin to cast a vote against you."

"Very well," Spake Zurthaud after a reflective pause. "I accept the honor and will strive to uphold the traditions and principles of the Order, but any further ceremony regarding such things must be forestalled. My first act as Lord Consul is to declare a state of emergency and war against the Shadow Lands and its dark master, and we must immediately begin making preparations-gathering arms and allies and drawing up stratagem for assault. If any of the High Council opposes this decision, let them speak and we shall hold a formal vote; otherwise, I already count your endorsement."

"I am sure that, given the recent attacks and conspiring, no one among the High Council would be foolish enough to yet sue for peaceful resolution, not when the southlands still smolder and an innocent young Dragoness has been snatched away for some wicked purpose." Galrag agreed, confirming due the change of circumstance, a stark contrast from his earlier position.

Zurthaud detected a hint of fatherly protection in his motives, for to rescue Feldara was on the front of the mind for all who knew her, and this elder, once a father himself, knew better than most the anguish of losing a child to the darkness. He would not stand by, watching Theros suffer letting go his precious daughter, even to strengthen their weakened Order.

"We shall rally the troops, and have the Aelv and Dworv members request reinforcement from their respective kingdoms." Lorn offered.

"And, I shall summon the whole host of the Serpen army." Screeched a familiar voice from behind Galrag.

It was Shar, as they saw only after Galrag awkwardly shuffled about in the hallway, rather too cramped for him with all these other people, to make room for the Serpen to pass. Into their midst he trod, a kind nurse offering her assistance to his hobbling, for he was still weak, yet wholly stitched and mending, from his ugly stab wound. It was rather a mean look, uncharacteristically so, that his gaze bore, and not all from the pain in his gut.

He had been laid low, he the king of the Serpen, and in no honorable fashion, and he was most peeved by the whole affair, feeling foolish for not having figured out sooner the events of the escaping runner and the identity of the Dark Hunters posing as gate guards, and angry that he had at all been assaulted, he of royal blood and bearing, and worst of all, had been left on the cold dirty ground for nearly a half hour before the next shift of gate guards discovered him and their comrades' demise and brought him unto the Order for medical attention.

"Even if we were to send word by Dragon messenger, which is truly the quickest method, it would take nearly a month for the Serpen to muster, cross the great wastes, and finally meet with us upon the blackened plains before the Ragnor. We cannot afford such a delay, and for aid that might not ever come." Galrag objected. "There is no guarantee that your king will support us at all, for as his father did the exact opposite in the last war, I can expect no more favorable outcome."

Shar turned his fiery glare upon the Dragon, who was surprised by this, though not as much as Shar's next words. "I am their king. An attack upon me is an attack upon all Serpen; they will come, and not late. I have already summoned them with the Sovereign's Stone." Said he, holding aloft the expertly shaped, ruby like gem, which shone with a light of its own, that which Ulam had packed with his belongings, so long ago now that even he had almost forgotten he had it with him until he lay bleeding in the deep of the night wondering if he would make it alive unto the morning.

"Is that a Dragon Stone?" Zurthaud asked, confused as to what was this magical item, for it appeared as such, magical and of the same kind of spell laden jewels which the Dragons created and used.

"I have no idea of what you speak; these Dragon Stones are foreign to me. My people do not remember how we acquired this sacred relic, for it is so old. Only, upon your mentioning, I do remember there is a legend telling of a Serpen saving a Dragon's life and receiving a magical payment. But, right now, that matters not. What is important is the function of this magical item, why my royal ancestors have held it in our family for all these generations, for when in dire need one touches this sacred rock, my people are made to know, beyond doubt, that he who holds it has need of them and are summoned. I held the Sovereign's Stone in my hand last night, even as I lay dying in the street, and I hold no doubt in my heart that my people will come. And, they shall not be wasting time crossing the wastes on foot, as only an imbecile would think; they shall, of course, be travelling by ship." Shar explained, only slightly less agitated upon delivering such welcome news. "Now, out of my way, commoners. I wish to see my friend." Said he, mostly joking, but much to the nurse's derisive eye rolling, belying just how the Serpen, tired of hiding his identity, had freely exploited his status for any influence or benefit it gained.

And, with a final huffing snout raised in the direction of Galrag, who had not meant to offer any insult in his historical observation, Shar entered into Malok's chamber and had the nurse shut the door behind him.

"I suppose that is good news, even if he shall become insufferable now." Galrag grumbled, only after the Serpen King had exited, giving Zurthaud and Lorn a little of very scarce amusement.

Even as they attempted to resume their discussion, a messenger frantically darted up the stairs into the hallway amongst them; he took only a moment to catch his breath before he gasped out his urgent missive.

"Lord Zurthaud," Said he, surprising Zurthaud that word of his appointment to office had spread so rapidly, zooming even more hastily than this quick courier, so that even lowly envoys now should know to address him as 'lord'. "There is a disturbance outside the gate. Argamon has requested your presence immediately, for a foreign army is fast approaching the city."

"Is it a horde of Serpen warriors?" Zurthaud grinned, half expecting to be relieved that Shar's army had arrived miraculously early.

"No, my lord." Panted the messenger. "They are,... something else."

Shock took Zurthaud, Lorn, and Galrag for but a moment; quickly gathering their wits, they hurried out onto the nearest balcony of the medical ward and, after the two Humans hastily scurried onto Galrag's shoulders, ascended into the midday sky. It did not take them but a moment to soar over the breadth of the city, unto the outermost gate, and soon they were joined with the other city guards and Paladins atop the gatehouse and battlements.

Argamon, who had rallied the few defenders, as he still assumed his captain of the guard duties, strode over to Zurthaud as soon as he saw that Galrag had landed, for to explain the situation.

"Lord Consul," Argamon saluted, causing Zurthaud to wince that such a venerable soldier felt they had to pay him any such dues. "Our scouts spotted this large group of arms-bearing foreigners approaching the city from the West road; if you look through my spying glass here, you should be able to see for yourself why we called for your special attentions."

"Please, Argamon, there is no need for you or anyone else to address me by title; just Zurthaud is fine." Zurthaud humbly offered, as he jumped down from Galrag's shoulders to take up the handy telescope and peer through its magnifying lens.

Once focused on the advancing horde, he was immediately surprised, for Zurthaud had never before seen the like. Marching in organized, though unusual, fashion were a few hundred bears, and very odd bears these were. For, they did walk like men, comfortably on their back legs and wore finely crafted leather and lamellar, or chain mail armor, steel helmets, and long fur capes and carried various weapons in their paw-like hands and on their shoulders.

"Argamon, who are these people?" Zurthaud asked of his guard captain.

"Forgive me, Lord Zurthaud, for I shall continue to call you by your title, as I must set a good precedent for my men." Humbly replied the honest soldier, as he reclaimed his spyglass. "We have no idea; not a one of us, and a few learned mages are among these Paladins, have ever read of such a creature in any of the familiar historical tomes. What we do know is that they have as yet made any aggressive maneuvers to warrant our retaliation, for they have passed by many farms and hamlets without even stopping to speak to the residents, let alone raid or otherwise harass them. As such, we have not engaged in any sort of defensive measures, though they have all this time drawn ever nearer to the city. I sent for you as quickly as possible, for to receive your direct orders on forward procedure with these,.. bear-men."

"Have we yet attempted contact with them?" Zurthaud inquired.

"No, Lord Zurthaud; we were awaiting your orders." Argamon dutifully replied, then aside mentioning further. "I had hoped you knew them, for your uncanny charisma seems to attract all sorts of unusual compatriots."

"I know them not." Zurthaud smirked, slightly bemused by Argamon's thoughts on his friendships. "So, we should send out a parley to curtail their advance, and see about their intentions, hopefully greeting them should they prove friendly." He suggested.

Back onto Galrag's shoulders he and Lorn clambered, and roaring a command for the few other Dragons here gathered to bring their companions and follow, the elder Dragon leaped from the wall, flying straight for the tribe of mysterious visitors. They touched down again a little way before the tramping horde of bear-men, just far enough that, if necessary, Zurthaud, who was joined by Lorn in dismounting, could again easily hop aboard Galrag for an escape.

The troop of bear-people stopped their forward march upon seeing the group of Dragons assembled before them, yet did one of their number, a large, and seemingly regal, brown-furred bear-man, step forward before his group, supposedly to represent the rest.

"Greetings, yet unknown people from the West. You have passed, perhaps unintentionally, into the realm of Men and the Protectorate of the Order of Paladins, and as such, if indeed, you can understand the words which I speak to you, we require you to state your intentions for coming to these lands." Zurthaud sternly, though not unkindly, declared.

The large bear who stood before his people cleared his throat conspicuously and proceeded to address the Paladins in intelligible words, albeit heavily obscured by his thick and breaking accent.

"Hello, tiny-man-people and Fire-bringers. We are Urz; we come from mountains far away North and West. We be looking for Fire-bringer Feltra. We are friends, her and tiny-black-man Anur, and other Fire-bringer friend, Calton. We come to help fight bad-Darkness." Spoke Gorod, chieftain of the Urz.

Just as Zurthaud was about to question the claims of this bear-person, for he knew not who was this Feltra, and Anur's name he had only barely caught, a young red Dragon, none other than Calidon, apparently also known as Calton, swooped down to join with the foreigners. Apparently, after having finished with his delivery of ballots, he had dawdled about or otherwise not been present enough to know about the events of this morning, for he joyfully welcomed those who were estranged to Zurthaud and all the other Paladins but were friends unto him.

"Chief Gorod, it is good to see you again." Exclaimed the Dragon, as he offered the Urz a hearty embrace.

"Oh, it you, no-more-crazy-Fire-bringer friend of Feltra, Calton; good see you again." Gorod waveringly replied, though he did return the Dragon's warm gesture. "Hoping you still no more crazy."

"No, I have been quite well, thank you." Calidon obliviously cheerily returned. "Oh Zurthaud, I am glad you two have met; in the coming battles, we shall have need of these strong, brave Urz warriors, the Bowers." Said he noticing the stupefied group of Paladins opposite him and the Bjarz.

"Word is Bjarz. We Bjarz, not bow-Urz. Now being no more silly; take us to big-house on mountain-made-by-hand-with-many-stones. We go see Feltra and tiny-black-man Anur. We eat, drink together tonight; tomorrow, together we fight bad-Darkness." Gorod returned, a little annoyed that the other Paladins had as yet to heed his earlier stated wishes or greet him more politely.

Now having determined that the Urz were to be friend rather than foe, Zurthaud, Lorn, and Galrag- all three drew nigh for to have conversation more comfortably with Calidon and Gorod, without raised voice or shouting, for what Zurthaud was sorrowfully burdened to say next need not be loudly proclaimed.

"Calidon, we first wished to inform you in private, but you were nowhere to be found earlier. I am afraid that now I must make this known to you and before your friend, Gorod, and cannot help but darken what bright

morning you alone have had. Feldara has been taken by the Dark Lord."
Zurthaud solemnly stated unto them both.

For a moment, they two stood glaring at Zurthaud, but eventually
Calidon had suddenly to sit, or rather plop, upon the ground for shock and
sorrow. Gorod, however, lifted up his voice in a terrible roar, and all his Bjarz
followed suite, drawing their weapons in anger for what had so disturbed their
chieftain. Yet, soon realizing he had lost his composure and caused his warriors
to become hostile, in turn causing the Paladins to assume a less friendly and
defensive posture, Gorod motioned for his company to quiet and to sheath
their weapons.

"We go rescue her, now!" Nearly yelled the Urz to Zurthaud, as he
could barely contain his sorrow and rage upon hearing of Feldara's fate.

"No." Galrag forcefully intervened. "We will rescue her, and soon, but
no small company of soldiers will successfully assault the Ragnor. We are
waiting, for our allies to assemble and for our plans to be drawn, and not a
moment before we are as well prepared as possible shall either we or you set
foot upon the soil of the Shadow Lands. I have personally felt the blow of a
failed attack on that fortress and its Dark Lord; we shall not make the same
mistake again. This time, we shall prevail."

The words sunk into the heart of Gorod, for after a moment of
consideration, he nodded his head in approval. Though he still hurt for the loss
of his friend, he could not deny the elder Dragon's wisdom.

"You and your Bjarz will need refreshing for the battle to come. Be
welcome in our lands, and take the course of action which at the first you did
recommend. Eat and drink a little, rest, and be ready, for we will be setting out,
as a great host, on the morrow." Zurthaud added, seeing how distraught the
Urz chieftain remained.

"Yes, this is good. We will follow your words; rest today, free Feltra
tomorrow." Gorod, after more reflection, unenthusiastically agreed.

"Calidon, since you well know these good people and brave warriors, I
place you in charge of their care; you must see to it that they are given adequate

food and lodging within the Citadel." Spoke Zurthaud as a command to the young Dragon.

Yet, poor Calidon still sat upon the grass, tears welling in his downcast eyes, so that Zurthaud was compelled to attempt to comfort him, for he had sought to give the orders as a distraction from worrying over the fate of his dear friend.

"We were given time to rescue her; it is what the Dark Lord spake, even this morning, unto Malok, when he took Feldara right from before him. If he spoke lies, then I shall personally cut out his tongue, if anything does reside under that helm, but if he spoke truth, then we still have hope that Feldara yet lives and that we may yet save her." Reassured the Human, even as Calidon turned his face away so that his weeping would not be seen.

"How could this have happened? We were within the Order's Realm; the Aronoran has been reclaimed. She should have been safe; she was with Malok. I know he would give his life for her, as well." Calidon blubbered, unwilling to accept the dire circumstances that had become his reality.

"He nearly did, trying to protect her." Galrag gravely added. "The young, black Dragon lies sorely wounded in hospital. You may go to him, but first, you have been given a command by your Lord Consul. As a good Paladin, you must see to your duties, even when struggling through your own storm."

The older Dragon placed a comforting hand on Calidon's shoulder and helped him to stand.

"I too wing this darksome path, though torn to the bone from the loss of a loved one. May it be that there is hope and light at the end, but nevertheless, we must keep fighting." Galrag exhorted, though again wracked with the painful memory of his son's untimely demise.

Attempting to subtly dry his wettened eyes, Calidon stood with new resolve; he would keep going. He would keep fighting, and he would help rescue Feldara, or die in the attempt. With a slight nodding bow, he motioned for Gorod to follow him, for he would show them to good quarters and see about their provision within the Citadel.

"Please, come with me, honored guest, Chief Gorod and his Bowers." Calidon politely entreated, though his grim face still betrayed that he would rather be elsewhere, that he would rather set off then and there, to the Ragnor, even alone, to rescue his friend.

"It Bjarz!" Gorod nearly roared, throwing up his arms in frustration, though he did follow after the red Dragon, for what irked him so was certainly not his friend simply mispronouncing a title, but rather the distressing news of Feldara's capture.

The Paladins respectfully waited until the great procession of Urz had tread on past them and unto the city before Zurthaud issued his orders to them.

"You six," Commanded Zurthaud, addressing the escort that had accompanied him, Lorn, and Galrag. "Fly back to Captain Argamon and inform him of what has transpired, that the Urz have presented themselves as friends and allies and will be welcomed into the City and housed in the Citadel."

"And, what shall we do?" Lorn asked, as he, Galrag, and Zurthaud found themselves alone upon the grassy field before the road.

"We shall continue our discussion, of tactics for our assault, but elsewhere." Zurthaud replied, becoming most serious. "From what I recollect of the Dark Lord's gloating, he has spies or means of seeing most all that transpires, save for in one place."

Galrag made as to look about for unwanted eavesdroppers, as he questioned Zurthaud's answer. "I see no one about, but for the Urz warriors and Calidon, already distant, heading for the City. Who is there about to spy upon us?"

"I know not how it is done, but your recalling your son, Galrath, has brought him also to my mind, him and our fateful mission of that night, now seeming long ago but for the hurt of his loss, for while he was your son, he too was my friend and like a brother to Theros." Zurthaud tried to explain. "Though I would do anything to take back that dreadful night and keep those dear companions alive, and here now with me, the Dark Lord revealed through word and deed that, while our plotting was made in extreme secret, so that neither you, nor Serc, nor anyone else knew of our venture, he had been expecting our arrival that night."

"The Dark Lord does lie, and a great deal, but your words I trust and your experiences seem to coincide with what you believe. However, how can we even go on living, considering for a moment that our enemy knows our every step, our every word? I would rather die than be so exposed to those wicked eyes." Lorn pondered aloud, his anxiety over such horrible knowledge made known through his pacing and wide eyes. "Where is it, this hidden place, wherein we can find some peace, some privacy?"

"I do believe I know, as should you both." Galrag stated, even as he turned his gaze toward the location.

"It is there, and only there that we will discuss, strategize, and make firm any future plans." Zurthaud replied, with a confident smile, for he too knew the place.

With Lorn being the only one yet unsure of their destination, the two Humans mounted upon Galrag's back and they headed off toward their only known safe haven.

Chapter 45

Accommodating the Urz turned out to be quite a more difficult task than Calidon had expected, for with their large size, which was, excluding the enormity of mature Dragons, greater in height and breadth than any other creature to occupy the spaces of the Order, the Human's barracks and other facilities constructed for similar sized peoples, like the Aelvs and Dworvs, were unusable.

Also, were the many spare dormitories of the Dragons' Quarter unattainable, for even if the Urz had no objections to being carried up by Dragon wings to their lodgings, which was most certainly not to be the case for such simple, terrestrial people, Calidon despised the thought of being their singular winged ferry, ever flying to and fro, from ground to tower and back again. Already he was to be at their beck and call, and he had no desire to make his job any more difficult.

So it was that, remembering his time in the great-hall of the Urz chieftains, he thought to lodge them all together in the main hall of the Keep, and after being given their options for potential housing, Gorod thought this the best of Calidon's suggestions, especially compared to sleeping outdoors, as they had done for some time now on their journey, and significantly better than going anywhere by flying. After only a few modifications, such as filling the hall with as many long tables as they thought they would need and gathering a good supply of pads and blankets for the Bjarz to make comfortable their sleep, Calidon and his few helpers set about acquiring some provisions for their guests.

Of course, the Human cook, Venrogan, and whatever staff he had taken on, were set to preparing Human style victuals and rolling in several large barrels of ale, which he immediately said would not be enough for the gathering and proceeded to order more brought up from the cellars, but Calidon also surmised, with the aid of Gorod's suggestion, that some local game be hunted and roasted. Eventually, upon the return of the dispatched Dragons, including their host, Calidon, with plenty of venison and with the extra ale and myriad Human foods, which while quite standard foodstuffs, the Urz thought most exotic and tasty, and a huge fire roaring in the hearth at the end of the hall- the whole company began to feel very welcome, even cheery.

If it were not for the purpose of their stay, and the most beloved, yet missing, company, such a gathering and feasting would have been made a grand occasion, but as it was, that Feldara was still held hostage and war was to be made against the darkness on the morrow, the Bjarz kept low their tone: hushed in conversation, without laughing, without music, so that the somber mood was, especially to Calidon's recollection, seemingly even less celebratory, more serious and weighty, than the feasting made in honor of their fallen brethren after their burial under the mountain.

As they ate and drank their exceptionally splendid midday meal in relative silence, Gorod, who had not left from Calidon's presence, but for when the Dragon needed to fly somewhere, made conversation with his friend.

"What is plan for attack tomorrow?" Asked the Urz, after a huge gulp of ale. "Where is bad-darkness? How many little and big monsters we fight?"

"It is to the South." After swallowing his mouthful of deer, Calidon replied. "There is a place, a fortress, called the Ragnor; that is where we will fight the enemy. There will be many, many wicked little creatures, but that matters little. If I die to free Feldara, it will not matter, only that she is alive and safe." He finished determinedly.

"Ah, yes." Gorod replied knowingly, though it was probably more the liquid courage's fault. "Feltra, she with you?"

"No, she is being held captive." Calidon perplexedly answered. "Have you not been hearing anything?"

"No, no. Feltra with you?" Gorod tried to clarify, but had to result to making a rude gesture with his hand to get his point across.

"No!" Embarrassed, Calidon sharply denied, but then more wistfully added. "No, she is with another Dragon, one whom you have not yet met."

The look of disappointment and disbelief on Gorod's face needed no added words.

"What?" Calidon halfheartedly defended. "She chose him, and not without a stupid, childish fight from me."

"She almost die for saving you; then turn around to someone else?" Gorod mused aloud, and only continued after another drink. "I thought our women crazy."

"It was her choice, and not a crazy one." Calidon replied, coming to her defense rather than his own. "If I love Feldara, and I do, now as only a friend, yet hopefully a very good friend, I must respect her and her choice."

Gorod was silenced for a moment, but as he ever became more addled by the ale, he soon had more to say. "I must see this one Feltra choose over you; he must be very big, strong, Fire-bringer." He chuckled into his tankard.

As peeved as Calidon was with this prying and prodding, he could not help but appreciate the Urz chieftain's high hopes and regard for him, that the one to win Feldara's heart had to be so much more seemly and physically fit than himself, and trying not to comment on how much smaller than he was Malok, he hid his own smirk in his tankard of ale.

Even taking his sip, the half smile that came to him was ripped away by concern for his rival-turned-friend's well being, for all this day, ever since learning of his fate only earlier that morning, he had wished to see about Malok.

"I too wish to see my friend, for so I do think of him now, even as a brother. His wounds, earned in dire attempt to protect dear Feldara, are proof enough of his honor and worthiness of her love and only make me to hurt the more for her loss and his." Spake Calidon, even as he arose from his supper, leaving it yet unfinished in his haste to go unto Malok.

Gorod too did arise and, tottering a best he could after the Dragon, followed him without unto the Keep's bailey yard.

"Why we go out here?" Gorod asked, as he looked up to the heights of the impressive structure of the Keep. "Way to hos-spit-all inside big-house, I think."

"Yes, but it will be quicker to fly up to the Medical Ward's floor, rather than drudge up through four flights of stairs, especially after all that food and drink." Calidon explained, even as he lowered an arm for Gorod to more easily mount his shoulders.

"Oh no. No, no, no. Gorod will no be flying; his feet belong on ground." Stammered the slightly inebriated Urz, all while gesticulating emphatically.

"Come now." Slyly contended Calidon, as he slid his lowered arm closer to the Urz chieftain. "Surely the great chief of the Urz, greatest of the Bjarz is not too scared of a little height and wind?"

For a moment, Gorod contemplated whether he could ever again live with himself after declining so tauntingly proposed a challenge, but even as drink got the best of his sensibilities, his Urz pride overtook his fear.

"I drink just enough for this." He muttered as he clumsily clambered onto the Dragon's back.

Pausing only long enough to make sure the Urz had good enough of a hold that he wouldn't immediately fall off, Calidon leaped into the air to the tune of the most strange noise, for an Urz' scream is somewhere between the squealing of a pig, though that of a massive sized boar, and the whining of a whipped dog, though indeed, quite a large dog. It was almost unwarranted, but for the sudden jolt from the ground, for with but a few flaps of his wings Calidon had already landed upon the main balcony of the fourth floor.

As Gorod slid off the Dragon's back and into a heap upon the floor of the balcony, cursing the skies and kissing the stone, Calidon went within to inquire whereabout was Malok's room, for he had as yet known. A few nurses attending to a rather boisterous patient, whose voice Calidon thought he recognized, happy to be distracted even for a moment from their most intolerable convalescent, directed him, personally leading him to Malok's room and, though at first frightened by his appearance, especially with him as inebriated and so aggravated from the flight as he was, making sure that Gorod was able to follow. Thankfully, for Gorod's poor state, it was only a short trip down the main hall of this ward.

Regretfully no longer being needed, the nurses tardily returned to caring for their most demanding invalid, leaving Calidon to enter upon the dismal scene alone.

In the center of the room, Malok lay, asleep, upon a large mattress, and beside him sat Theros, who with a slight smile acknowledged Calidon's entry. Behind them, in a chair over against the far wall, sat Anur, gaze ever watchful underneath his helm- once again donned, and he arose and greeted the young red Dragon with a kind embrace.

"How is he?" Calidon asked, nervous for what he should hear, be it too bad of news.

"His injuries are rather minor, considering with whom he wrestled; the doctors have skillfully mended anything rent apart within and have stitched up his outside. It may be that Malok shall stand and walk on the morrow, though not much else for some time after." Anur replied, with gratitude in his voice.

"I cannot imagine how he feels, for though his physical wounds are not so grave, he must nearly have died within himself, as would I, to see Feldara torn away and be so helpless to prevent it." Calidon sorrowfully mused, as he came over to stand beside Malok upon his sick bed.

"Yes, he has been most distraught. We all are, but he the most, almost losing the will to live." Anur somberly answered, as he too came to stand beside Calidon.

It was then that Gorod came stumbling into Malok's hospital room, and squeezing between Calidon and Anur, he tottered over to stand leaning upon the Dragon. After staring for a good moment over Malok, and in turn earning glares from Theros and Anur, the former of contentious indignation over the unknown Urz's unwarranted intrusion into a rather private, familial setting, the latter in surprise that Gorod had arrived within the Citadel, for Anur had not previously known of it, Gorod opened his mouth, loosened along with his discernment by the earlier quantities of drink consumed.

"This is Fire-bringer who Feltra with? He so much smaller than you!" Nearly shouted the Urz to Calidon, who flinched at such volume and such proximity.

"What is this thing?" Theros growled. "Get it out of here!"

"I apologize for him, Theros." Anur consoled, trying to calm the irritated Dragon. "This is not just some strange bear-person; he is known to us, and a stalwart friend at that. He is Gorod, Chieftain of the Urz, and is usually quite a bit more kind, wise, and sober than today. Calidon, when did Gorod arrive, and why is he drunk?"

"Tiny-black-man-friend Anur!" Gorod nearly shouted again, and as if he just now saw Anur, though earlier he had pushed him aside for a view of Malok. "It good see you again, but this day is no good. Feltra has being taken by Dark-bad-one; so I drink today-ing and fight tomorrow-ing."

After this, the exceptionally strong mead called up from its hiding place in the cellar started to really catch up to Gorod, so that he forgot that his friends could not understand his native language and continued on speaking only in the Urz tongue. With all the noise then being made, and from before, Malok began to awake, and though Theros fain would have kicked Gorod out, even without the window and off the balcony, for he so despised drunkenness, he paid him no more heed once Malok's eyes opened, solely focusing upon his injured son-in-law.

Slowly, Malok's gaze searched around the room and eventually settled on Calidon, and a new wave of anguish and guilt spread over the poor Dragon.

All his regrets and torments over not being able to protect Feldara now mingled with doubts that he was at all worthy to be her mate, and that, should Calidon have been her lover instead, he certainly would not have succumbed to the Dark One so easily as Malok. Perhaps, Feldara would still be here if the strong red male had been her chosen lover, and so his thoughts boiled within the agonized black Dragon.

But, Calidon was no mind reader. He was not privy to these fears and uncertainty, and greatly surprising Malok, who thought only to be subjected to stern rebuke or disdainful mocking, he spoke kindly to his injured friend.

"I hear it is not as bad as it could have been, and that you are well on the mend, brother." Calidon comforted with a hopeful smile, sincere in his well-wishes. "I hope to see you out of this bed in but a few days."

"He took her, Calidon." Malok whispered, fighting back bitter tears. "He took her right from before me."

"There was nothing more you could have done, and for all that you did, and I do know that you spent yourself trying to protect her, you were laid low, even unto death." Calidon comforted, placing his hand affectionately upon his friend's shoulder. "Now, you must get well, so that we can go to Feldara's rescue together, and I swear unto you, though I die in the attempt, I will aid you. I will bring her back to you, alive and whole, and maybe, we shall survive, shall all grow old together. My children and yours will play in the meadows while we laugh at stories from these days, and all the dark shadows that so thickly shroud, even to drown, the light and hope of this day, shall be gone, dissipated like the morning fog. But, you must rest now and gather your strength, for the fight ahead of us will be the most difficult of our lives until now."

Though Malok was weak from his injury and the following surgery, so that he could not talk loudly nor move much, he did whisper his gratitude to Calidon for his unusually well spoken consolation, and so relieved was he by these kind and hopeful words, he again drifted off to sleep. Theros was equally impressed and moved, and through his watering eyes he clasped the younger Dragon's shoulder in his hand, and they all stood there watching and praying over their common loved one as he rested, until at length, Gorod remembered some of his language skills.

"What you speak, so beautiful." Slurring his words together, he bawled.

<><><><><>

Of soreness and blood loss, Malok had slept fitfully throughout the day and awoke only when those who cared for him had arrived to see about his wellbeing: Zurthaud had stayed with him in the early morning; Theros and Shar had arrived shortly afterward; even Calidon had come by later on in the day, swearing his aid in freeing Feldara; but Anur had surprised him.

Malok had never been sure that the gray skinned, black robed, melancholy enigma had cared for anyone other than Feldara, yet had Anur stayed with him from the time that he had found the young Dragon lying in a pool of his own blood, even until now, long after the others had left for food and rest. Theros had gone and come back, along with Shar who had eventually been forced to return to his own hospital bed for the night, and the Dragon had then made known that he would stay the rest of the night, so that Anur could leave and refresh himself. Still, Anur denied any such opportunity, instead, insisting he remain by Malok's side.

Now that it was nighttime, and the proper time for sleeping, and everyone else had left but for Anur and Theros, who both slumbered for weariness, Malok could but lie awake, for his mind was only upon Feldara. He was so desperately worried for her safety that she was all he could think about. He shuddered to imagine his comparatively lavish treatment to her dark and dismal fate; he strove not to dwell upon thoughts of her being tortured and disfigured for the Dark Lord's amusement. His own health suffered for how troubled he was for her.

At length, he could not take it any longer, and against doctor's orders, and the pain of his wound, he struggled upright and out of bed.

He wobbled across the floor of his room and to the balcony, and through silent, though awkward steps, he managed to sneak past his two good friends and out onto the lofty porch. He would then have stretched out his wings to the dark moonless sky, but that he was so weakened by his injury he could do naught but lie back down upon the cool stone and lament his disability into the chill night air. He then wished for a bowl of water, remembering that he could Peer for his mate, but he had not any now and cursed himself that earlier he had not the presence of mind to take the water which he had been given and do so.

Even the air of this evening was dry, were there a way to collect its water and Peer through that, and he mourned that there was neither sound nor sight of rain or its approaching. He could do nothing, only cry out to Eloigal for aid.

At his lowest, Malok pleaded with The Almighty, that something, anything, good could happen: that the pain he now experienced, of his heart and his body, would be extinguished so that he could be well and fit to go unto Feldara; that the Dark Lord be removed so that he could see her and be with her. Yet, as Malok lay there pouring out his soul's discontent as a drink spilled and wasted upon the floor, no supernatural miracle occurred, no sudden transformation of his horrible circumstances, and he felt somewhat disappointed and estranged, as though contrasted with someone more devout, his prayer went unacknowledged. However, change did come, still and small as it was.

A quietness pervaded the cold night, a tranquility that overrode all else; where was before only anxious distressing for Feldara, now peace flooded Malok's senses. His mind had been cleared of worry; his heart had been lightened. The need for rest overtaking his scattered, clamorous thoughts, Malok's eyes slowly shut for the heaviness of consciousness, and with thanks for even this little blessing, of sweet rest, he fell into a deep slumber.

Seemingly as suddenly as he had drifted off to sleep, he was again awake, as though he had rested well a full night and now came upon morning. Feeling energized, he arose and stretched, but amazingly, upon remembering such, through all his turning and twisting, he felt no wound upon his side. Malok reached with his hand, and surely there was no gash upon him. With joy he started to convey his findings to Anur and Theros, but almost tripped over a large black lump in his way. To his surprise, he passed through the object, rather than stumbling over it.

A sly smile came to Malok's face, the first he had experienced since Feldara had been taken, as he began to realize what was happening. He looked upon the lump that he should have tripped over, which now he floated above, and saw that it was only himself, sleeping restfully upon the stone balcony. He had again come into this strange state, this dream-walking, that so often before he had entered, and as much as he chided himself for forgetting that it should be possible this way to both see and rescue Feldara, he doubly thanked Eloigal for such providence, leading him to again utilize his special gift.

Without wasting any time, for though the night was young, there was none to spare, Malok sped off, winging his way South toward the Ragnor. The journey that would have taken hours, even the better part of the night, seemingly passed in mere minutes, and soon the dark tower appeared before Malok, ever as imposing and dreadful as he imagined it should be. But, the young Dragon spent no thought on the ominous structure other than to scour its outer surface for a way to pass within.

Finding that, unlike other walls and floors, he could not phase through the seamless and windowless Black-iron sheet walls of the Ragnor's exterior- by an unseen magic being blocked from so doing- and discovering the main gate below to also be tightly barred and locked, he sped up to the roof, yet upon reaching the peak of the tower, he found the sole opening thereof also fastened shut.

Pondering how else he could enter within and hoping, yet considering how well closed was the fortress, suspecting that he had been expected to attempt such a dream rescue, he sat upon the vast roof of the structure, until askance faint light caught his attention. As it was so out of place in the Shadow Lands, Malok gave this dim luminary his full attention, and affirming its location, even ventured a further investigation.

Upon the low hills surrounding the vale wherein stood the ominous dark tower were many smaller forts, emplacements of much lower quality, quite pregnable, some blatantly slipshod in their make. Looking down into these lesser battlements, Malok found them to be the living quarters of the Dark Lord's multitudinous hordes of Goblins, Trolls, and Ogres, for here they stood watch, shuffled about in mundane thralldom, and raucously feasted, gambled, and scrapped. The faint light which earlier he had glimpsed from the top of the Ragnor was just one of myriad small fires, which by crafty brazier design were partially concealed from the air and surrounding land, and by which the various minions had little enough light to see about their business.

As he hovered close above the nearest and most impressive of these minor forts, a voice called out, loud enough that Malok thought he was being addressed, and startled, he hastened to hide himself in the shadows of the clouds.

"You there! Yes, you, where do you think you be going with that grog?" Shouted a large Ogre guarding the gatehouse of this battlement.

As obviously, Malok carried no grog, he truly had not been spotted, and put at ease again, the young Dragon sought to ignore any further conversation, until came the interesting reply from the grog bearers.

"It be no grog; it be The Master's wine. He has demanded a larger sum tonight than his usual; we been bouncing barrels into the tower all night." Answered a pair of Trolls, who toiled, rolling a large barrel along the cobblestone lanes within the fort.

"Very good of you not to be pilfering our camp, yet see to it you drink none of that either. I need not warn you what became of the last maggots who gobbled The Master's choice spoils." Laughingly taunted the Ogre, as struggling with their load, the Trolls made rude noises and gestures toward him.

Now Malok knew that if he followed these two Troll peons, they would show him a way inside the Ragnor, and stealthily he whisked down into the fort's courtyard for to see if he could, indeed, pursue them yet remain unseen.

Without so much as stirring the dust and cobwebs of the unkempt garrison, Malok landed just behind the two Trolls, even as they hastened to roll their barrel on through the street, yet did they not proceed without the gates, nor toward the Ragnor. Unto their own fort's keep did they trundle, and Malok felt somewhat annoyed, that these two should have wasted his time by lying so blatantly and only to steal drink. Just as he was about to leave off from following them, the guards of the fort's keep halted them, shouting out their own greeting.

"More wine for the Master? He been taking a sum tonight." Jocularly exclaimed one of the Trolls guarding the keep's shoddy portcullis of an entrance, and unbeknownst, he dispelled Malok's doubts toward the wine bearing Trolls' truthfulness.

"Three ravens crow at midnight." Flatly blurted one of the wine bearers, clearly annoyed by all the stopping and questioning.

"Ah, he well knows the password." Chuckled the other keep guard, but then becoming serious. "See to it they not been followed." He demanded of his comrade.

Before Malok could think to hide or flee, the other Troll guarding the gate took a torch from the brazier and ran out into the fort's courtyard; quickly, he came right unto Malok, so that the light of the torch clearly revealed the Dragon for anyone to see. Malok could do nothing but stand there, stunned that, having had nowhere to hide or flee, he should be found out so easily, and the Troll stared straight at him, unable to have mistaken him for anything other than a Dragon and an intruder. However, the Troll then looked past him, and to the left, and to the right of him, and said nothing until he raced back to the keep's entrance.

"It be all clear, boss." Plainly, even disappointedly, stated the Troll guard.

Malok was even more bewildered now than before, for he was certain that he had been caught. Surely, there was no way the Troll could not have seen him; even as Malok again took in a breath, he could still recall the foul reek coming forth from the Troll guard's mouth- for he had been so close to him. Malok began to wonder if he had become invisible, or if perhaps, he were not truly here, as in a normal dream. The Dark Lord had seen him before, but maybe, that was because the Dark One had such power as to detect his presence, when in fact, Malok was not fully, physically present.

"Good. Master says we must be extra careful no one finds out about the secret tunnel." Blurted the 'boss' Troll, even as he motioned for the wine bearers to pass.

Even as they faded into the gloom of the keep, Malok, having found out about this secret tunnel, was determined to follow the wine bearers, and he decided to put his invisibility to a truer test. He marched forward, even unto the gate guard's faces, and quietly spoke.

"Three ravens crow at midnight." Said the Dragon.

The gate guards did not so much as stir or at all acknowledge him; on they looked, past him, their expressions every bit as bare as the courtyard. With a bemused smirk, Malok squeezed past them into the keep's entryway, and caught up to the slowly rolling wine bearer's barrel. Through the grand hall, past all the drinking and carousing guards, then through a doorway and down a long twisting flight of stairs, Malok followed close after the two Trolls, and all went well until they came to the bottom of the stair and, immediately coming across a fork in the crudely carved tunnel, the Trolls had a dispute as to which way they should go.

"It be to the Right." Insisted the first.

"No, it be Left." Countered the other.

And, Malok was forced to wait upon them as they bickered back and forth, for he certainly knew not which direction to take. Eventually, the second Troll proved himself correct.

"No, it be Left; I swear on me spawner's skin. We took Right last time, as you said, and we walked all the way around to the fort opposite the tower." Spat the correct Troll. "We had to go in from the far side; took us a whole three hours longer than it should."

"O, you be truth telling. Master was wroth, but we blamed it on the poor quartermaster." Recalled the first Troll, and much to Malok's unheard contempt, they continued on rolling down the Left-hand tunnel.

All went straight and smoothly from then, and Malok sped ahead of the slow, lazy wine-bearing lackeys unto the end of the tunnel. Thereat, he passed through the secret gates of the Ragnor, swung wide in anticipation of the wine bearers, and the few guards there stationed, and Malok came within the dark tower.

Though at first, Malok thought he would go horribly astray and should opt to wait for the creeping progress of the two Trolls, for to follow them up certain paths to where the Dark Lord would be serviced his wine, he soon found out that the tower's design was far less complicated than to warrant such fears as becoming lost. As wandering about upon this plain basement floor of the tower, a garrison for the gatekeepers, Malok found that only a single stair exited from it, and looking into this stair, he perceived that it spiraled about the whole circumference of the tower and stretched from top to bottom and was the only access to each and every floor.

With such a convenient layout, Malok wasted no time with searching for a way to ascend the tower, up the full height of the tower, to the very topmost floor, Malok raced, and to the end of the stair he came, so designated by a door, deeply scratched and dented by some horrible occasion, blocking his path. Trying it, Malok found the door unlocked, and he slowly, fearfully, creaked it open.

He knew this room when he saw it, when from the damaged door, he slowly slinked within, for it was where he had been teleported during his last dream-walking episode. It was here he had encountered the sleeping Dark Lord, and from here taken the wicked sword that should have slowly leeched Zurthaud's life from him.

With dread he recalled that night and the terrible encounter with the Dark One, but with joy, his eyes, after scouring the blackness of this dark chamber, landed upon a most glorious sight. Shining as though the moon had peeked within this hellish blackness and came to rest solely upon her, Feldara lay soundly sleeping upon the cool stone floor. He bounded over to her, and made as to grab her in his arms, but then noticed the Black-iron chains.

He had nothing with which to cut them, for his claws could not. His fire, also, would be nigh useless against it. Only good quality steel could cut Black-iron, for it was against mundane metals rather weak. Either that, or Malok could use magic to release her bonds, and that stronger than any spell here placed to fasten them, but he had not yet been taught any such magic and could not fathom how to invent his own spell for it. So here was he stuck, so close, yet still so far from his beloved.

Knowing that, possibly, she could hear him no better than the Trolls without on the battlements, Malok chose to reach out to Feldara with his mind and in that way, at least, communicate with her. "*Feldara.*" He whispered into her consciousness, as he tearfully lay with her upon the floor of her prison.

Even in such hopeless circumstances, he could but smile, as certainly hearing him in her dreaming, she stretched and mumbled and smiled herself amidst her sleeping, and for a moment, Malok forgot everything else as he lay there holding his beautiful beloved. Yet, eventually, he felt his time growing short; he felt the warmth of sun on his face and back and knew it came not from this dark and gloomy place.

"*I am coming for you. I know the way now, and I shall not tarry.*" He softly murmured to her, and he wrapped himself around her.

To a bright flash of glorious light, that of the sun's full dawning, Malok next opened his eyes, and he found himself again upon the balcony of his room in the Order's medical ward.

Chapter 46

With the remembrance of her beloved having called her name, Feldara awoke, or so she had thought, for it was hard to tell. She now experienced the completely foreign and unsettling sensation of having her eyes wide open, yet still seeing nothing, for the darkness about her was without any light whatsoever. The deep consuming blackness, that which disoriented her senses, preventing her from seeing anything at all, was so thick and impenetrable as to have become palpable.

Yet, touch was more honest than sight, and she could feel the coldness of stone or metal against her skin, upon which she sat and her back rested- a smooth floor and some sort of rounded beam, like a pillar for support of a roof. About her, she could feel the sickly chill of metal: coiled as a chain around her waist, locked and shackled to each wrist and ankle, and probably, immutably fastened to either the floor or the pillar-like object.

She was trapped.

Even the brave Feldara was enfeebled by the sinking, despairing realization, and in panicked, though futile effort, she struggled mightily against her bonds. Yet, after prolonged straining, resulting only in cutting her wrists and ankles with the harsh edges of the Black-iron shackles, she found herself firmly, inescapably, restrained, unable to but squirm into a standing position, or slump to the floor, only a couple feet's breadth from the solid, unshakeable pillar. Unfortunately, tiring herself was not the only consequence of her noisy retaliation against her imprisonment; her captor had taken notice of her wakefulness.

Unable to see, Feldara could only hear the heavy treading of the Black-iron boots thudding and scuffing against the slickness of the hard floor, and like a dead, icy winter wind scraping against the sill of a window, the metallic rasping of breathing inside the Black-iron helm- signaling the ever closing approach of her terrible warden.

"Who are you? Where am I?" She roared out into the blackness from whence came the noise of her tormentor's advance, yet only her own echo, as within a large hall or cave, answered her.

She cringed when the tramping of the heavy boots ceased, when the icy breath could not only be heard but now felt upon her cheek; the noxious odor of blood and death filled her nostrils, as just before her must have stood the vile enemy. Even so warned, Feldara's heart still skipped beating when, with a flick of the clawed, gauntleted fingers, the Dark Lord summoned a match's worth of flame into his metal palm, instantly illuminating the nearer part of the enormous hall, the uppermost room of the Ragnor, and the soulless countenance, the dreadful, faceless visage of the red, horned helm.

Had she any less self-control, Feldara should have screamed, that so near and so ominously loomed the horrible villain, the enemy of life and light, the Kragon, but she restrained herself, the parts she could manage, as her heart and breath came with the force and speed of one utterly mortified by the sight before them.

"Good, you are awake. It would be hardly worth all my prior effort to only now kill you as you slumbered; now you can scream in agony as I take your life, and all the hope, from before the eyes of your beloved friends." Spake the Dark Lord, his grating voice like a tomb being opened. "As for your questions, you should know well by now. I am Dragas Kragon, the Dark Lord; the very topmost room of my tower, the Ragnor, is this, your final resting place."

For a moment, any further words, any inquiries or rebuttals, were stuck in Feldara's throat by the dryness and swelling born purely of anxious fear, but she had to know what should further become of her. Her curiosity overrode her terror, and after swallowing the lump that had formed in her throat, she questioned the evil warlord.

"Why? Why me? I am nothing special, not even so much as others have made of me." She interrogated with the burgeoning questions of her soul, for long had she wondered this.

"Indeed, why you," Nearly chuckled the Dark One. "Perhaps, it was the wrong time, the wrong place, for you from the start, and now, I have managed to spin my dark webs of half-truth about, so that everyone, even those closest to you, has come to believe that you are some sort of special savior, some hero, who has any power at all, even to defeat me. Perhaps, it was by my design that an insignificant nobody should be planted in others' minds as this hero, exalted beyond realistic belief, so that when she falls, when she dies, so too shall their hope, and as they all lie dying with her in their hopelessness, my darkness shall, indeed, take full root and snuff out the light."

Here Feldara's heart fell, for though she wished all her life that truly she were a nobody, to be freed from all the expectation, the responsibility of, say, a hero, even more deeply within her soul, she had longed for such to be true, that she could make a difference, that she could do that which was great and high above her own person, that she could be "the hero".

To hear that it all was planned by a nefarious blackguard for his diabolical machinations, that by his design, all her life's worth should have the opposite effect of her desiring, to bring low rather than enlighten, truly shook her to the core of her being and depressed her spirit. Yet, did the Dark Lord continue.

"Perhaps, it is all true, and you are some manner of chosen one, who born with purpose and significance, alone has the power to defeat me."

And, here Feldara took heart once more, for she instantly remembered the shaping of her life. It was not all by the planning of darkness, for it was filled with goodness, which can only come from the Lighter of Lights, from Eloigal. To her memory came all such good that had been given unto her, by which she had been blessed, from her foster father, Anur, to her life-mate Malok, and all so many other people and things; truly, she was not born to suffer or to be meaningless, or even to be used as a tool of darkness. She had purpose; she had a name, written in stone. Her heart turned to the words specifically given to her by the Great Father Dragon; his spoken warmth of truth was certainly no lie. Feldara decided within herself, then and there, that her destiny was what she chose, not the consequence of others' choices or dark designs, and she chose to be the hero, The Bright Dragoness.

"Either way," Continued the Dark Lord. "Your part is accomplished; by their love for you, all your companions shall be drawn here. By Zurthaud's affiliation, all the Paladin's shall too come, and they shall all die. Nothing, no one shall be left to stand before me, and my darkness shall consume the world."

As completing his depressing monologue, the Dark Lord arose to leave his prisoner to lament their doom, but Feldara's fiery spirit had been kindled by his words, not extinguished. She nagged him as he turned about to go.

"Why then do you not just end me now, if my part is finished, indeed? Unshackle me and take me out, if you dare, or can you not? Perhaps, it is because you are too scared?" She mocked, truly wishing that he would unshackle her, if only to stretch and relieve her aching and bruised joints.

The rate at which the foul demon turned about again was so slow as to be painful, and though Feldara was still fearful, she had resigned herself enough to her fate, or her glory, that now what should have terrified her only seemed comical.

"You surely exert great effort into appearing frightful; I suppose you must, since you are too dreadful to have any sort of life or friends." She ridiculed, but was immediately made to regret her wagging tongue.

With but a stride, the Dark Lord was upon her, and grabbing her by the jowls in his one free clawed gauntlet, so that the nails of which dug bloodily into her cheeks, he hoisted her up to what should be his eye level, even as she strained to stand and was pulled against the weight and confinement of the chains.

"Do not taunt me child!" The Dark Lord shouted, voice booming like thunder. "I fear no one, and the only reason you live, is because it pleases me to slaughter you before your loved ones, and not sooner." Then becoming calmer and letting loose Feldara's jaw, so that she fell to the ground, he continued. "I once had a life; I once had friends and family. When I came into my dark power, they all turned on me, every last one, and so, I killed them all, every last one. This is the cost of being born of darkness; this was my curse."

Becoming pensive, the Dark One turned to face away from Feldara again, and she could only wonder that, perhaps, she had managed to reveal some skeletal remainder of a person buried beneath the depths of evil thought and deed.

"I see you do, indeed, think yourself this great hero, this Bright Dragoness," As after a moment of reflection, at last spoke the Dark Lord. "It matters not. Even if you are of the light, with all its power and splendor and life and love, I am of the darkness. I am the one shadow which voids the vast expanse between such stars."

Feldara would have questioned him further, but that the Dark Lord extinguished the little match light he had summoned from his palm, and the world was immediately engulfed in the all consuming blackness from before. No heavy footfalls did she hear, nor ringing of breath, but Feldara felt that the Dark One had left from her presence.

Left unto herself for unknown time thereafter, she tried returning to sleep, wishing that this was all some bad dream, a nightmare, for there was naught else to do. But rest did not come to her, only fitful tossing and turning to the tune of chains clanking and grinding, coarsely rubbing against her scales. Eventually, in her attempt at rest, she thought she caught a glimpse of some luminescence coming from the blackest depths of the room, that which was opposite her. She thought they resembled two large eyes, glowing a deep, dark red, staring her down from across the expanse, yet whenever she tried to focus, gazing upon them, they disappeared, only to reappear once she looked elsewhere.

Eventually, she grew tired of this game, and she called out to whatever it was.

"Who is there?" She shouted, her voice echoing loudly around the spacious chamber.

A soft low noise, almost so that Feldara thought she only imagined it, responded to her, yet its thrumming, growling vibrations resounding to her convinced her it was, certainly, another large creature within the room. Suddenly, the glowing eyes seemed to burn brighter than before, and Feldara grew very drowsy. She thought she heard someone, deeply rumble the word, "Sleep", but she could not possibly have, as she instantly became more at ease and drifted into unconsciousness.

Chapter 47

Hope dared to rise with the sun that morning, for even though the light and inspiration of Feldara had been taken from among them, all her friends and family were united together and determined to rescue her and end the Dark Lord's reign. No one was as lively and full of optimism as Malok, for apparently, he had awoken before the dawn to stroll out upon the balcony, which was where Anur found him sitting.

He had rushed without to check upon the young Dragon's injury, for the doctors had warned against too much movement, that which would tear open his sutures before the flesh healed. Yet, upon checking his side, Anur found hardly a mark upon Malok, only the thread used for stitching and that having fallen to the ground where he had lain; it was as if his terrible wound had vanished overnight. Even as he knew their presence should no longer be needed, Anur did call the physicians to attend their patient, if only to confirm the miracle he witnessed.

After being awakened by all the commotion, especially that of the physicians' scurrying about in their examinations, Theros joined them upon the balcony, and Malok relayed to them all what had transpired last night.

"Then, she is still alive? Has she been harmed?" Anur interrogated, desperately worried for Feldara's safety.

"She was as well as could be expected and has not suffered any further abuse than the wearing of shackles against her skin." Malok explained, even as the perplexed medical staff scratched their heads and, finding him whole, hastened off to another patient's care. "Besides that, the Dark Lord seems not to have touched her at all."

"Plainly, he seeks to use her as bait, luring us all into his ensnaring clutches, and it is not as if we could do anything else. I for one, surely along with you two, cannot forsake her, even if it means my own death." Theros grimly surmised, nearly supplanting the hope that had sprung up for Malok's wholeness with a more bitter melancholy.

"If we know it is a trap, and it can be nothing else, then that already takes away many of his advantages, surprise for one; in our position, our best strategy will be to remove as many of these handicaps as possible." Anur wisely stated, letting in yet a little more light of hope, for they needed as much of that as possible.

"The knowledge I gained from my adventurous reverie last night will prove most useful; I can only hope it turns the tide in our favor." Malok offered, wishing that he had simply been able to cut Feldara loose and carry her away from that wretched tower.

"Save any further explanations of what you encountered for Zurthaud's strategy meeting this morning." Theros warned, even as he glanced around. "For to keep them secret and out of the Dark One's ears, he has said we should not discuss any plans outside of it."

"Can you yet fly?" Anur asked, trying to return the subject of their conversation to the brighter matter of Malok's swift recovery.

"I do believe so." Happily replied the young Dragon, and he arose from where he sat and stretched his wings.

"Then, let us gather your friend, Shar, and head out to the fields for to hunt your breakfast; if the doctors have so discharged you from serious care, you must soon return to activity and exercise for your health to fully recover." Anur suggested, as he too arose.

Unusually, Shar was not difficult to rouse, for his wound, though well bound and healing rapidly thanks to the regenerative qualities of his kind, still hurt him badly and he hardly could sleep soundly for it. Yet, after another quick explanation of Malok's miraculous soundness, and Shar's genuine rejoicing for it, he suddenly felt well enough to join them, and they all headed out through the nearest balconied window and took off into the crisp morning air.

With the aid of an expert hunter of the area, Theros, the scattered herds of skittish deer were much less of a challenge to hunt this morning, for the older Dragon knew many tricks to fool the beasts, such as: coasting low toward the ground, just below the ridgeline of the next hill or mountain for to get as close as possible out of sight and without disturbing the air; flying forward with beating wings in time with the gusts of wind, yet only soaring and hovering in the still air; and using cloud cover to conceal ones' shadow. In no time at all, they settled on the grass to feast upon several exquisite, fattened yearlings of the flock, yet knowing the hour of the strategy meeting was soon approaching, they did hasten their meal. With just enough time to spare, they finished with breakfast, winged back to the Citadel, and touched down upon the Dragon Temple's balcony.

"Why has Zurthaud selected this place, even wonderful as it is, for his meeting? Would not the halls or boardrooms of the Keep, the High Council chambers for one, better suit such an occasion?" Malok asked, as they laved with the water of the basins before entering the sanctuary.

"I believe it had something to do with a saying of the Dark One, and I should know, for I was there the night that Zurthaud first confronted him. The villain can see most anything." Theros started to explain.

"From the standing bowl of smoking water?" Malok guessed, for he too had earlier seen the magical instrument on his first visit to the Ragnor. "I wonder if it is by Atsarocu- that is, Peering."

"I know not this Peering of which you speak, but perhaps so- through the basin he looks and can spy out most anything, save for one place, which he did mention. My guess is that, as Zurthaud must also believe, the Temple is that one place into which the Dark Lord cannot 'peer'." Theros concluded, even as they strode into the sanctuary.

Zurthaud, Galrag, Lorn, Argamon, Calidon, Gorod, and a few other Paladins- all members of the newly elected High Council, and in the case of the Dworvish and Aelven Councilors, representing their respective peoples- were already present, and Malok and his companions found a place among the circle which the delegates were forming, so as all to face each other, around a low round table with a map and some crude models of the Ragnor and other places of importance set upon it. Only after several lords of the Human provinces and cities: Athard, Rothard, and Kellam among them, entered the Temple by the aid of Dragon escorts, could they sit down- the Dragons upon the floor and the others in various chairs thereabout- and commence the meeting.

Yet, it took these Humans a moment to find their places, for as they never had been within the Dragon's Temple, the wondrous architecture and murals, as with all other initial visitors, took away their breath and attention for a brief moment, thus slightly delaying the proceedings.

"Welcome" Zurthaud humbly greeted them all, as after everyone had finally taken their seat, he stepped forward into the circle, before the round table amidst them. "Now that we are all here gathered, we shall commence with planning our strategy of attack against the Ragnor. Many of you, even now, have doubts and fears, for to set against the Dark Tower so boldly has never before been done. Of all the campaigns, of all the long years, centuries, of war, the realms of Men, Dragons, Aelvs, and Dworvs have only responded to the incessant attacks from the Shadow Lands with defensive measures. In times long past, the Aronoran wall was built; in later days, Rathnyalgr the Wise led the defense of the great city in the Battle of Doraegonoran; until now, when we have defended our homes and cities against pillaging, raids, siege, and the Great Burning. No more, now is the time that we take the fight to our enemy, for he has forced our hand."

He gave a moment of silence, for to let his words sink into the air, the impossible task to be spoken into reality. Yet, just as Zurthaud was about to continue one of the Human lords raised his hand.

"The rumor in my province is that the Dark Lord snatched a young Dragoness from my country." Interrupted lord Rothard; in his dry wispy voice, seeming far more antagonistic than his eyes belied. "Is that why you now ask us to die for you? Is the life of one Dragon female worth all the lives of men you will commit to battle?"

The room drew silent again, enough that all their breathing seemed loud in the hushed hall.

"She is my daughter." Spoke Theros, after Zurthaud could not answer, for how could he convey to the unmagical, pragmatic Humans the importance of the Bright Dragoness. "And, I would die for her; I and all who know her."

"I would not, and cannot force this upon anyone, nor will I speak for anyone; I will not decide the fate to befall you. If any among us so choose to leave from this meeting and to abstain from committing themselves, their people, or their resources to this venture and this battle, you may go." Zurthaud gravely conveyed, cutting off any harsher words to be given by Theros, and for a moment of silence held in these halls, Zurthaud thought that the Human lords, in favor of safety, comfort, and wholeness- all sacrificed for one Dragoness, might not lend their aid.

"It is a coward," Nearly shouted lord Athard, as he stepped forward opposite Zurthaud. "Who flees from the day of battle when his friends and allies call for aid, for so the Paladins have again proven themselves, and the noble Dragons had always been. I do not forget that this young, black lord of sky and fire," Said he motioning toward Malok. "He and his companion, a Serpen no less, were the first of all to aid us when thickly the smoke of our enemy's wrath choked the night sky, and never will I forget the hour of our salvation, when from the North and the mountains the Dragons swooped with fury and flame down upon the savage horde. And, may I die long before I forget the aid which the Paladins then gave to us, in recompense for their absence from battle, and that in mourning over a fallen comrade; there is not a single man or family in my entire realm who shall spend the coming winter in either want or homelessness. For all that the Dragons and the Paladins have done for me and my people, it is well earned that I do here pledge myself and all my fighting men unto your service until our foe lies vanquished at our feet."

Moved by the words of this young lord, wise and honorable beyond his years, the mayors of Bythatsar and Doraegonoran both stepped forward and pledged their men and service, and eventually all the Human lords, to varying levels of enthusiasm, even Rothard, promised their aid. Only once everyone had again taken their places, could Zurthaud continue.

"It is good that you have joined with us, for even if you do not value the life of one Dragoness, one person, as do we, well worth the wealth and effort of the whole world to save, you must realize that if we fall in battle, it would only be a matter of time before the Dark Lord turned to eye your own lands and people. If we fail, the desolation that ensues will make the horrors of the Great Burning seem as a merry harvest-tide bonfire. So it is as a necessity that we come together, all of us working and fighting as one, as in days long past, to accomplish what none of us could do alone."

Their decisions finalized, their pledges made, Zurthaud counted all the Human lords as with them, along with the stalwart Dworvs and the steadfast Aelvs, the Bjarz who had ventured forth from their mountain home for just such a purpose and battle, and even the Serpen by the word of their trustworthy King, and he approached the table for to discuss their purpose for meeting- how to assail the unassailable.

"You must all know, the armies of the Dark Lord are comprised of various races of savage monsters: the Ogres, Trolls, and Goblins; also, in his arsenal, are the mindless Nokre. They all have one thing in common; they are all utterly dependent upon their master for orders, for leadership. If all day long we killed monster after monster and beast after beast, it would matter little if he yet survived, but if we slay the Dark Lord, his horde will scatter; so that we must prioritize his death above all others."

"What if the Shadow Lord does not present himself in the open and he merely hides within his tower, even as he does now, so that we cannot assail his person directly?" Asked Thryzanuil, one of the two Aelven High Consuls, as Zurthaud came to a stopping place.

"We have an elite unit that is prepared to enter the tower." Zurthaud muttered in answer, at which, expectedly, Galrag contended, for though he had been with Lorn and Zurthaud as the day before they had plotted their strategy, he still did not particularly care for this course of action.

"Seeing as this is the same manner of plan which caused the death of my son, how can you expect the outcome to differ from your first attempt?" The elder Dragon challenged, though more in wanting for further explanation than contesting for another ploy, as in their talks the day before, they three had concluded that this stratagem, though risky, would serve them best.

"This time is different, because we enter the Ragnor for another purpose than to only assassinate the Dark Lord." Zurthaud calmly defended. "It will be a small squad of volunteers, whose primary goal will be to extricate Feldara from the bonds of the Dark One; if we succeed with finding her and freeing her, we will immediately flee without the Ragnor, drawing him out with us. Once he is without his tower, he becomes a plain target for every spell caster, every swordsman, every single warrior and weapon, and against such an assault he cannot possibly last."

"And, what shall our forces do in the meanwhile, stand about without range of their ballistae?" Dryly stated lord Rothard.

"There are outer fortifications on the hills all about the Ragnor." Malok stated, suddenly stepping forward and pointing to the approximate locations on the table map. "I have seen them. It will be necessary to take at least one of these forts, as they defend the easiest way within the tower- a series of secret tunnels."

"How do you know of this?" Asked one of the more speculative Human lords, only just beating Rothard to the question.

"I have seen them." Malok calmly repeated.

"But, there is yet another simpler means to access the tower. There is an entry on the roof top." Zurthaud offered, not doubting Malok's knowledge, but just as perplexed as everyone else how the young Dragon had come about it.

"The Shadow Lord must have despised your earlier usage of it, for the entrance upon the roof has been sealed shut." Malok replied. "Other than the front gate, the only other way within the dark tower is through these secret tunnels."

"Then, our forces shall take them, and handily. Here we can encamp, set up siege engines and hold defensive positions, until the Dark One is drawn out." Galrag encouragingly strategized. "But, as we have witnessed before, the counterattack of the Dark Horde shall be fiercer than their initial defense."

"Yes, like that night upon the Aronoran, there shall be many Nokre sent out after us." Lorn chimed in, heartened by Galrag's renewed enthusiasm. "After taking the lesser forts, the Paladins must concentrate on keeping the ground between the main tower and the outer battlements well engulfed in flame, or they shall be overrun."

"Bjarz will take all little-towers, smash all monsters inside, and keep other monsters from coming back." Gorod asserted, smacking the table quite soundly to emphasize.

"The aid of Aelven bows would then make extra secure these positions." Added Elyriana, making note to send such a message to the Aelven forces already en route.

"But, crossing this terrain we could not have such artillery in place as would be required to even scratch the dark tower, or its master, especially on such short notice." The Mayor of Bythatsar whined.

"Ya need not worry 'bout that." Grinningly confirmed Gimmel, winking heartily to emphasize. "We Dworvs will be bringing our best toys."

Everyone then began to work together in earnest, adding their own touches and insights to this foundation of a plan, so that all the ideas had to be written down and every group given specific and punctual objectives, and it was also then that Zurthaud turned over such planning to his trusted general and friend, Galrag. For, the elder Dragon was better suited and more experienced than Zurthaud could ever hope to be on the minutia of warfare, neither would the Human be upon the plain of battle.

The people who were closest to Feldara: Malok, Theros, Anur, Calidon, Shar, and Zurthaud were to be the special team to enter the Ragnor; none of them could trust another to take their place. No one else in the whole world could possibly care more for her than these six, and they needed to solely focus upon their special objective.

"How is it that you have come to such knowledge?" Zurthaud asked of Malok, as he left from the din around the table map to join in close conversation with his special company.

With a sly smile, Malok began to divulge all.

<><><><><>

So it was that their planning session continued on unto noontide before everything was finalized and all the other leaders knew of Zurthaud and his company's action and had agreed on how best to take the outer forts and so distract the Dark Lord while those few entered within the dark tower.

"That should be it; we have prepared as well as possible. Let us depart from here, gather our troops and allies, and muster before the Aronoran. We shall then make good our plans against the Ragnor and the Dark One." Galrag spoke in conclusion of their meeting.

In haste, they departed thence, for much needed to be accomplished and in such short time. Messenger Dragons were immediately sent out to the Dworvish and Aelven hosts to inform them of the strategy meeting's outcome, but in order to conceal their tactics, the greater part of what was to be relayed was only in written letters, tightly bound and packaged, with instructions only to open them upon the day of battle.

The Paladins were quickest to muster, for the speed and ease of Dragon flight made sudden the gathering of their number within the Citadel and city and even the stations upon the Aronoran just earlier taken back from the enemy. Every Dragon and every two-legged companion was before the walls of the Aronoran by the early afternoon, and once there, they sent out further messengers and scouts and prepared a camp for the expected host.

In the coming days, as a slow trickle of water, the armies of Men began to steadily rally unto the wall. The lords' knights, heavily armored and upon warhorse; also their foot soldiers, trained men-at-arms; the militia of the greater cities, called out by their respective mayors; and even many volunteers of the common folk, workers, farmers, tradesmen, and merchants- anyone who eagerly desired the downfall of the Dark Lord and an end to his villainy, they all flocked to the banner of the Paladins, gathering together at the camp. Well before eventide of the third day, such a multitude of Human forces had already arrived that the provisions which the Paladins had first set up could not possibly attend them all, and further fires, food, and tents had to be acquired for them.

By the scouting and returning messengers of the Dragons, the progress of the other armies had been tracked.

The Dworvs, whose kingdom was the closest by- being settled in the Dorian Hills to the East and with their great royal halls under the Skye Mountains upon the rocky eastern coast, were already assembled and well into march. Even with their heavy, slowly trudging force of enormous siege engines, pack animals and beasts of war, and of course considering the difficulties of their stature, they had made timely progress, earlier that day having crossed the Atsar, and were set to encamp only a few miles away to the East.

The Aelvs, who were much further distanced, almost as far away as the Serpen, had elected to move their army by water, and with their fleet of ships cutting across the Crydan sea and skirting around the dark peninsula, their queen had already made plans to bypass any meeting with the other armies and instead approach the Ragnor from the South, hopefully gaining some advantage by encircling their enemy.

Yet, by nightfall of that third day, there had been no sighting of the Serpen army, and though none could tell by how he bragged of his fine military, this was much to Shar's disappointment. Only by knowing his friend so well could Malok tell that he was so distraught, but still, did he have faith, along with Shar, that the Serpen would come through, even when the rest of their friends worriedly began to doubt.

Though the darkness loomed about them, clawing at the edges of the camp fires' illuminations, and the steady flow of new arrivals had ceased, and all the great host settled in their position to pass the night, naught but the most battle-hardened soldiers could sleep, for all were on edge, nervously dreading the coming days. All minds there gathered began, at least once, to consider that one of the next sunrises which they saw might be their last, the calm of the night around them only juxtaposing their inner turmoil.

Suddenly, amidst the talking and the few games of cards or dice, someone could stand no longer the quietness which so contradictory stood, starkly opposed to their own angst, yet did they not flee, nor rabidly cry unto the bleak sky, fitted only with the slimmest light of a crescent moon and the dimmest of stars. They sang.

Malok heard it from where he and the other Dragons had stationed themselves upon the wall, partly to keep watch and partly to avoid clamoring among the Humans in their crowded camp. He knew it to be an old song, for the tune was one that, even in the far off Serpen Kingdom, he had heard more than once. And though the words thereof were foreign to him, as the Serpen had fashioned their own, he deeply felt the intent of the lyric.

The Dragons around him joined in as quickly as the second phrase of the verse, for his people, with their sonorous tones, were always fond of song, and soon nearly the whole of the camp had lifted up their voices together, an hundred thousand strong. Though not all sang with bard's fine voice, rough and gruff warrior Humans and Dworvs, and the growling, off key contrabass of the Urz- who knew neither melody nor lyrics yet sang anyway- among them, the sheer volume from the multitude seemingly shook the stones of the great wall and certainly reverberated off from thence.

Only by the time they had finished their chorale did they realize just how thunderous their clamor had been, for in response, the Dworvish camp, miles apart, could be faintly heard belting out a rowdy Dworvish drinking song, which caused the few Dworvish Paladins there among the Human camp to laugh and shout in encouragement and pride.

Only when the tune had faded, for the words were unintelligible at this distance- known only by heart of the few Dworvs among them who had taken to singing along with their kin, did any other tune arise from the throats of the Humans, and in quite the orderly fashion did another start a melody and the others join in. On through the night, the two camps traded their songs back and forth, each like the little fires before them- a small flame of hope and warmth against the impending doom of the darkness about, and only until the second watch did the enthusiasm wane.

It was then that one among the "wild" Dragons introduced his song. It was unknown to the other peoples below, so that they could but listen, yet did nearly all the Dragons join in on the slow dirge-like chant, save Malok. To him, this lyric was just as unfamiliar as it was to the Humans, but he recognized that its words were in old Draconic and the tune was similar to many of the old hymns which the Dragons did sing within their temple. Indeed, it was one such hymn of worship that they sang over the awed gathering below, and though they all understood not a word, the blessing held in the text was powerfully felt by the whole camp and understood upon a much more spiritual level as a prayer for protection in battle.

When the last held note, long and reverent, died away into silence, and the Dragons ceased their singing, no other tunes followed, for not only were their restless spirits comforted and their souls heartened unto the victory that they must win in the coming days, they also could think of no song in the common language fitting to follow after so hauntingly beautiful and yet so soothingly uplifting a melody. Even from the Dworvish camp, much to the bemused disappointment of the present Dworvs, there came no response, and eventually, calmed and quieted, many among the camp began to take what little sleep was left for them.

Anur, who had stayed close beside Malok and Shar, and they close beside Theros and Zurthaud, could only surmise with one wise comment. "As many have said before, there is a power in music."

And this thought clung to Malok as, almost unwillingly, he drifted off to sleep.

Chapter 48

Darkness, visible, nearly palpable darkness, the kind that prevents one from seeing their own hand held directly before their eyes, was Feldara's world now; it was her sight, her touch, her hearing, her meat, and her breathing. Her whole existence was enshrouded, consumed by the complete blackness, void of all light or anything else.

Time meant nothing to her, for by the lack of markers, she could not tell its passing. But for her dreaming, waking and sleeping were the same to her, and the lines between the two were so distorted by the lack of light or food, or anything other than utter darkness that all her wakeful hours began to intermingle with those spent asleep.

With the imposed inactivity and the deprivation of all stimuli, she had forgotten her hunger and her thirst, and very nearly would she have forgotten all else, had but her wrists and ankles been free of the wretched shackles of Black-iron. Though in the first few hours and days of her capture she had struggled vigorously against them and by doing so rubbed raw in a few places- down to the cutting of her flesh even, she now strained against their painful grating and rasping as little as possible, moving at all only if completely necessary.

If it were not for two things, she might have gone mad for all the horrible torment her world had become, succumbing to this imprisoned state as her only life, amnesiac of her past and disregarding any other future.

Yet, periodically, almost to be assumed as daily, she strongly felt the presence of her beloved. Almost as if Malok were right beside her, right there with her in the very room wherein her every passing hour was a struggle to exist, she sensed him, even more tangible than the darkness about. The succor this brought to her weary, starved mind and soul was more than good food could have then brought to her body; it energized her and gave her hope: that he had not forgotten nor abandoned her, that Malok would come to rescue her.

Better still, though Malok's perceived company, when each time manifested to her, was so nourishing, there was within her another presence, another Spirit, and perhaps, it did take the smothering and blackening and silencing of all other things and doings and people in her life to sense this other Force so strongly. Nevertheless, as it had been with her always, so it was with her now, even in this hellish dungeon of nothingness; as light shuttered within a lantern, or fire within an oven- or a Dragon, though unseen, it shone a light of goodness within her life, burned a fire of hope within her heart.

It was even the same One she had felt oftentimes, when calling out in the night, when singing of hymns and worshipping, in prayer, in the joys of life's sweet pleasures, and most profoundly of all, within the Dragon's temple. It was the Spirit of Eloigal who dwelled within her, who now sustained her, gave her hope and strength and existence, even in this dreadful prison. Eloigal had never left her, never once, and now, when all else was taken away, was even more mightily present.

The knowledge that she was not alone, that these two- her beloved mate, and the loving One, the all-seeing One, the Omnipotent One, the nearest One- were with her, even here, even now, was enough to keep her going.

And, with this hidden strength and sustenance, Feldara worked her hardest to not be idle. Though her mind was fogged by the nature of her dark environment, and more so, as if a spell had been cast upon her, she kept thinking, plotting her escape, for she abhorred the position in which she had been placed- that of the helpless maiden in distress, and the position into which those for whom she cared most were inextricably forced- the doomed rescuers bound for a trap. But, if only she could free herself, the whole plot would come crumbling down about the Dark Lord's smug crown, and she and her beloved and their friends would be the victor.

So, she ceased not to ponder ways in which she could free herself and that without attracting any attention to her liberated state, for she could think of many magics with which to incinerate, or otherwise burn free from, the Black-iron bonds. Yet, were all these methods utilizing heat and therefore light, for Feldara knew not how heat of enough strength to undo her shackles should exist without fire, and then how fire should be made that gave off no light. She thought, and this in moments of complete frustration with their clinking and clanging, grating and biting, to magically blast the chains asunder, but she was also certain such a method would be easily heard by her, no doubt, watchful captor.

Eventually, ruling out more obvious methods, such as merely undoing the locks of the bonds, since these would also be too obvious unto her jailor, Feldara settled on magically rusting the Black-iron, and at a slow enough rate so as to not be immediately noticeable to any vigilant eyes. She concentrated her will, formed well the idea of the spell, and released her magic upon the world, and to her delight, she began to feel, as if slowly being filed or under severe, prolonged weathering, the dust of the rusting metal start to gather upon the floor beneath her.

After so long a time as it took her to become tired enough to fall asleep twice, days or hours she knew not, Feldara began checking her work, and surely enough, one of the chains, which carefully she held in her hand so as not to make any noise, came apart, completely disintegrating at the points of greatest stress. She could have shouted for joy, but that she had the presence of mind to refrain from any such noise making.

With but a little more work, she had gotten all four shackles off from her, and was nearly free from the thick chain strung about her waist- the last one still tying her to the floor and the pillar, but then did something extraordinary occur.

Light began pouring into the darkness, a thin sliver at first, seeming so out of place and luminary that the beam assumed an alien quality, and it being the only thing she had actually seen during her long dark time imprisoned, to Feldara's beleaguered mind, at this moment, it seemed nearly the most beautiful thing she had ever seen. However, slowly the beam of light began to broaden, and then the noise hit her, the horrible whining and squealing of metal on metal, so that Feldara began to realize that it was not so strange a phenomenon as at first she had supposed.

As it began to be visible from the ever increasing lightening of the room, the arched spaces between several such pillars as the one to which she was attached were like windows and shuttered by huge metal sheets, and these now being folded back into their places, revealed the lighter, though with the horrible storm clouds still blacker by far than fair weather, open sky without the tower and even the dark outline of the surrounding lands beyond.

Quickly, Feldara worked to conceal her magic, holding the shackles onto herself as convincingly as possible and, with her tail, brushing most of the rusty dust right out the window behind her and off from the tower, and not a moment too soon, for the heavy plodding of Black-iron boots upon the hard floor soon dispersed the former silence.

The Dark Lord came into her field of view, but this time not near her. He stood above her, upon a higher half-level separated from the lower floor by a pair of stairs and some sort of dark hole, seeming as a cave, between them. Without a word, he began to stalk toward her, indolently descending one of the sets of stairs, and at length, striding across the floor toward her.

"This is the day," He finally spoke, with even less cheer than a gallows. "The morning of the contest, the performance."

"So, all this is like a game to you: the fear and anguish, suffering, and death- all the innocents you murder- it is all a sport?" Feldara questioned, mostly to draw his attention away from any signs of her success at freeing herself.

"No, not sport, deadly serious, but a drama nonetheless;" He replied pensively, even while bypassing her, striding to the precipitous edge of the tower floor, for with his faceless helm, to gaze without the expansive window made by the opened shutters. "For now comes the decisive act- when the hero must rescue their beloved from certain demise and Good combat with Evil unto the bitter end, deciding not only their own fate but that of the entire world."

<><><><><>

Almost a week full of tedious marching had passed between the mustering at the Aronoran and this morning, and though the trek had been painfully slow, due to the earth-bound progress of the great combined host of Humans, Dworvs, and Urz, their last night spent out upon the blackened plains of the Shadow Lands, which had been meant as a refreshing reprieve from all the long days of tramping- with the Dragons lazily, yet incessantly, circling overhead- had seemed, to Malok, at least, the longest, hardest part yet of their journey. To be so close, unto his beloved, yet so far, was agony beyond words, eased only a little by his nightly dream visits unto her.

However, long before the sun's rays began battling with the thick, black, yet rainless blotting of evil clouds, which did constantly smother the sky above the Shadow Lands, and a little light would, refracting, escape and disperse enough for the world below to see by, the army was already on the move again; so that, by the time the sun had, indeed, crested the horizon, and the scarce light made it easier for to find footing, they all, at last, came within sight of their dreaded destination- the Ragnor.

The dark tower rose, stark and stranded, up from the dark earth, to tear into the base of the horrible clouds with its mace-like ornamental flanges and drive, by its unnatural and despicable appearance alone, a shudder of fear into each soul whose eyes gazed upon it. Yet, long before that, came the low hills thereabout and the battlements of the smaller forts upon them.

"This is the day." Zurthaud somberly stated, as he stood nearby, along with Theros Calidon, Anur, Lorn, Galrag, and Shar. "Whether we live or die, Feldara must be freed and the Dark Lord destroyed."

Yet, for a moment longer, perhaps somewhat in troubled, primal reluctance of committing to so daunting and dire a task, they lingered in silence upon the rocky little hill, that behind which the host, for to conceal its presence from the minions of the Dark One, had camped in a craggy gulley.

"Galrag," Zurthaud spoke, at last breaking what silence could be had besides the howling of the wind between all the rock and stone about. "Give the order; commence the assault."

With a roar, Galrag signaled their army, and after Lorn quickly mounted his shoulders, along with all the other hundreds of The Order's Paladin teams of Dragons with their Companions, together with the hundreds of their "free" Draconic brethren- nigh a couple thousand strong, each responding with roars of their own, took to the pallid sky. The deafening volume of their war-cry very nearly shook down the walls of the nearest fort, as the gravelly earth trembled with the reverberations of their bellowing, even as against the murky gray canvas of clouds, the air came alive with the myriad colors of the Draconic host.

Quicker than the enemy could sound an alarm, with a fiery blast of breath, they came down upon the first forts in waves until not a single creature remained alive upon the parapets, and fastly following, rallying with battle-cries of their own and many horn and trumpet calls, came the Urz, Human, and Dworvish militaries, for to wipe out any remaining defenders and make secure these forts against counterattack and recapture.

But, the Dragons sped on, breaking into groups, heading towards the other outlying forts. It was then, as they began to disperse, that with shrieking alarms and clamoring bells, the enemies' defenses began to awaken, and like rain, the sky began to fill with Black-iron bolts from the many once shuttered windows, and ballistae, that opened upon the sides of the Ragnor and upon the walls and towers of the various outer emplacements. So thick were the deadly missiles, that there was no hope of dodging among them, and a few Dragons perished at the sudden outburst of retaliatory fire, but the "free" Dragons knew spells with which to protect themselves and their brethren. With knowledge uncommon to the Order, they cast forth energetic shields of light and magic above and before and below them, and by these magic shields disintegrated each bolt that aimed true to strike them.

All seemed to be going well at the start, for quickly the Dragons made full circle about the Ragnor and had scorched each of the outlying battlements with, at least, one fiery pass, and already the Aelven forces could be seen joining the battle on the side directly opposite the initial assault, their stealthy entrance hardly noticed by the enemy but for the twanging of bow strings and the whizzing and striking of arrows, each one fatally accurate to a target.

"Now comes our part." Zurthaud commented, then turning to Malok. "Show us your way into the Ragnor."

From the hillock, they winged their way toward the nearest of the forts, that which was the first to be attacked by the Dragons, and found the Dark Horde's resistance there still quite strong, for the various monsters had many crenellations, towers, and other interior spaces in which to hide, thus very many of them had been missed during the first fiery pass and, now exiting from their hiding places, were ferociously defending the walls from any ground assault of the Humans, Dworvs, and Urz.

The three Dragons dived down upon the defenders, scorching again the battlements with their flaming breath, giving the Dworvs just enough time to set up some of their siege ladders against the wall, up which the Urz and Humans hurried for to quickly engage and to take control of the fort's outer walls and gate.

Even as Malok, Calidon, and Theros touched down upon the cracked and crooked stone of the inner yard of the fort, their forces had finished with the last of the enemy without, leaving only those that remained within the inner buildings- the keep and a few barracks houses, and though the heavy metal doors of the barracks houses were soon to fall to the battering of Dworvish rams and Urz clubs, the keep was seeming much harder to penetrate.

The bare, cubic structure was perforated by many cracks and windows, through which the defending monsters cast their Black-iron darts, and the main gate thereof, at the top of a small flight of stairs, was inaccessible to the larger, wheeled rams of the Dworvs and, with sturdy portcullis, resisted the bashing blows of lighter rams and arms. Though the Dworvs, seeming to have a tool or weapon for every sort of situation, did call for such to be brought up from their ranks for to tear down the portcullis and smash through the gate, the six comrades, Malok especially, wished not to wait any longer than necessary, as precious little time could be spared.

Remembering from his dreaming adventures something that might be useful, Malok began searching about the keep, ducking below the windows, yet beyond the murder holes, for to stay out of sight and range of the enemies' constant rain of projectiles; eventually he found what he had been looking for-a small, unassuming, postern gate, hidden within an artificial crack in the keep's walls. Motioning his fellows to join him, he rapped upon the door as lightly as he could manage, and hoping this ploy would work, he spoke in the highest, squeakiest voice he could muster.

"Let me in!" He squealed, a rather fine imitation of a Troll. "Three ravens crow at midnight!"

Against all sensibility, the door grated open just enough for a foolish Goblin to peek out and, before any within could slam it shut again, though indeed, seeing the ruse for which they had fallen, the Goblin and those with it did try, Malok quickly wrenched the door open and breathed fiery Dragon breath within, clearing a path for Anur, Zurthaud, and Shar to enter the fort- for this door was too cramped for even Malok, the smallest of the three Dragons, to fit within.

In less time than anyone expected, for certainly those three waded through a surprised enemy with all the fervor their mission imbued, even as Malok, Theros and Calidon returned to the front gate of the keep, the doors thereof and the portcullis opened from within, and still fighting with a few remaining Trolls, Zurthaud, Anur, and Shar reunited with their reinforcements.

The flood of Urz, Humans, and Dworvs quickly relieved the three from any further conflict with the tower's defenders, and soon, the whole of the building was conquered and every last one of the monsters within was slain.

"Now we must find our entry point." Malok advised, as they six reunited among the strewn bodies within the main hall of the little keep.

"Everyone, look for stairs leading down." Zurthaud shouted as a command, causing all the nearby soldiers to begin searching along with them.

Eventually, the secret passage was found, for at the very basement of the fortress, in a vile cellar, below what would be assumed a kitchen for all the various stores and decaying animal carcasses, was a great hole, a tunnel, seeming to Malok exactly alike to the one he had entered those nights before.

____

"Get a message to Lorn, Galrag, Chief Gorod, the Human Lords, and the royal leaders of the Aelvs and Dworvs." Zurthaud spake to those nearest soldiers as were there. "We have found our way and are commencing with our part; take and hold your positions until such time as we emerge, or Eloigal save us, until retreat becomes the only remaining option."

And with that, for Malok, Shar, Calidon, and Anur already were speeding on ahead, Zurthaud and Theros followed after, on into the darkness, the void, and what thereafter awaited.

<><><><><>

Though vision was obscured by the thick swirling of clouds about and below the great open windows, Feldara knew now was her best possible chance of escape, for the Dark Lord seemed distracted, even turning his back upon her. It was as if, now that the day of battle had come- though Feldara could neither see nor hear any, her presence meant nothing to the armored fiend; whatever the issue, she wasted not this gilded chance to try for liberation.

With a single quick motion, she threw off her thoroughly rusted shackles and chains and leaped to her feet; in only another instant she had bounded off the edge of the Ragnor and into the thick, gray mass of clouds. She opened her wings and took flight, and miraculously, without any apparent retaliation from the Dark One, she was freely soaring through the wet fog.

Given any other moment, she would have grinned in satisfaction and laughed triumphantly that her plan had been so perfectly enacted and victory had been achieved, but the only thing on her mind was finding Malok and Anur and Theros and Calidon and letting them know that she was safe and leaving this horrible place far away in distance and time. So without any sense of direction, she tore away from the clutches of the Dark Lord and flapped her wings as fast as she could, heading further and further into the enshrouding cloud cover.

Even as Feldara flew for what seemed to her as many miles, the thick clouds obscured her vision; only once she heard a pleasantly familiar sound did the misty pall subside, parting as if a curtain. Suddenly, she found herself leaving the ground of the Shadow Lands by way of a rocky coast, and below her surged a sea's crashing surf- to her the sound, smell, and sight of home.

However, this was not the same cold, dark water of the Crydan Sea; it was blue, clear as a gemstone, and warm to the touch, as she soon found out by landing upon a somewhat calmer stretch of pebbled beach. Here, at last, in a huge sigh of relief, she breathed her first lung-full of fresh, clean, and ocean salted air, that which she had not savored in so long a time now. Finally, with the warm, sweet wind, she tasted freedom.

For a good moment, she satisfied herself with nothing more than letting the waves wash over her aching, slightly swollen hands, feet, wrists, and ankles, caring not that the salinity of the water stung the places her shackles once rubbed raw, but after a minute of refreshing her soul from her previous ordeal with the solitude of the private beach and wresting free herself from the remainder of her squalid fetters, once again lifting her gaze to the horizon, she remembered that her friends and loved ones were coming to her rescue, perhaps, even now beginning their dire attempt, and the words of the Dark Lord, that it was all as a snare for them.

The worry that Malok and Anur, Theros, Calidon, and Shar, unaware of her freedom, would storm within that dreadful dungeon only to find, not her, but defeat and death at the hands of the Dark Lord, stormed within her again. She frantically began to search the world about her, hoping for some landmark that should lead her to them, for to warn them, but to no avail; even the Sun, which would have been enough to determine much of her position and the general direction to travel, was thickly shrouded by the heights and depths of the nimbus towers overcasting the sky. She was completely disoriented, upon the unfamiliar shore of an unfamiliar land.

Her sight abruptly fixed upon some objects far off in the horizon, catching her eye only because they moved parallel to the shore line rather than perpendicular, as did the wind and waves; straining her eyes, the distant black dots waxed in detail until she could determine the sleek bottom of the forms to be brown and gray wooden vessels, above which hung the triangular white sheets of sails. They were ships, and a great many of them, all sailing together, in tight formation and clipping speed; to the South they hurried, following the coast, apparently a navy, probably to join with the battle at the Ragnor- wherever it was.

Feldara took off over the waves, hurriedly flying after the ships, for surely they, with their navigational instruments and charts, would be able to help her find the way unto her beloved ones.

Chapter 49

The tunnels leading under the grounds without the Ragnor seemed all the same to the untrained: dark, damp, disorienting, but Malok, through his many nightly dream visits to Feldara, had learned the exact route. Quietly, the six comrades followed after him; quickly, almost too quickly to be safe, they raced through the black, trusting the Dragons' exceptional night vision to lead them rightly.

After what seemed an eternity of stumbling and crawling through the utter darkness, Malok signaled for them to halt, for a dim, red light began to shine through the shadows at the far end of the tunnel, signaling they had reached the end of the subterranean segment of their journey. Slowly, he stalked forward peeking around the last corner, and only after a long moment of scanning the areas beyond did he draw back into the shadows to join with the others.

"There seems to be no defenders here; only, a heavy Black-iron grate has been dropped, blocking our path." Malok informed.

"Then, we must break through it quietly, so as not to lose our element of surprise." Zurthaud decided, with the others agreeing.

With the Dragons and Shar closely following, he and Anur then sneaked up toward the massive portcullis and began to cast magics upon it. Their first few attempts, to burn or break the darkly imbued metal met with failure, but eventually they found a method by which to dissolve it, as if by acid, and slowly began melting through the crossbars in their way. After only a few minutes, they had made a hole large enough to fit themselves through, and with the Dragons help, eventually a large enough section could be removed so that they all could make their way past the obstacle.

Silently, they snuck within the dark tower, the only sound made being their scuffling steps and breathing, which seemed astonishingly, frighteningly loud in the absence of all other noise, for even the noise of battle without could not be heard in this place so far beneath and within the fortress.

"It troubles me, that our intrusion should be so unchecked." Shar worried aloud, his echoing words tearing apart the palpable silence.

Even though Theros shushed him with a threatening glare, for they all dreaded that then, as if spoken into existence, their presence should be noticed, and the enemy pour out upon them from the surrounding halls, corridors, holes, and cracks. Yet, did he voice their own thoughts, for surely a gate such as this should be guarded at all times by a garrison, and that housed in the barracks, which even now they tramped through.

"Normally, this lower portion of the tower- some kind of barracks complex- was bustling with Trolls and Goblins, even a few Ogres, eating, drinking, and otherwise. I too wonder that now, when attack has come, there are not, at least, a few left to defend this entrance to the Ragnor." Malok divulged, even as they slowly pressed on, cautiously peering around every corner and into every shadow.

"Obviously, as we expected, we are headed into a trap." Anur surmised, his voice yet more grim than usual. "The Dark Lord is giving us free passage, for now, until the snare is sprung."

To the final doorway of the room they warily paced, but the whole way through the garrison they remained unmolested; not a single monster assaulted them, nor was seen any living thing. It was as if the whole of the Ragnor had emptied, and what once was a riotous bastion of cruel warfare had become a husk, a silent, musty tomb.

On and up the seemingly unending spiral of stairs they slowly ascended, half expecting, at every landing of the previous flight- where were doorways leading to interior and exterior halls and rooms for that floor- to be spotted and attacked by defending hordes, but as onward they climbed, the only resistance they met was the steady drudgery of hiking up the over-many stairs.

At long last, they came to a floor that Zurthaud recognized, for looking through the doorway leading to the interior halls, he caught glimpse of the standing basin, still smoking, far off in its distant corner at the very end of the hall. Recalling that fell night, seeming now ages ago, he dared not let his gaze linger, for fear that he should espy the remainder of his friends there lost, and he resolved not to lead his current party to any similar fate. He stopped them there, upon that landing, before that hall, to advise them, to prepare them as best he could for what horror they soon would face.

"Theros and I have come here before." He began, as they all rested a moment from the long hike up the tower's stairs. "We two have faced the Dark Lord and yet lived, and we count ourselves not skilled, but fortunate. He is a terrible foe. Blows that should have slain any other mortal creature merely slowed him; even a blast of magic, cast violently from Theros' hands, which should have destroyed any living thing, knocking him from his feet, only enraged him. My word of caution to all of us is to stay clear of his blade, which will be difficult, as one could not possibly expect a being that size to move as swiftly as he does, and to watch for any sign or movement indicating the casting of a spell, as any arcane thing unleashed from his hands or mouth would be certain doom to the unwary. We must go in quickly, grab Feldara quickly, and leave quickly. If pressed to defend yourselves, or in attack, make it hard, fast, and just as rapidly retreat, or, the Dragons especially, shall be easy targets for a foe that quickly counterattacks after effortlessly shrugging off a powerful strike."

Here he paused, for anxiety caught the better of him. With the memory of that dreadful night and the friends he had lost, into Zurthaud's mind wriggled venomous, paralyzing fear- fear of failure, of him leading these fast friends also unto their doom and thus the whole world unto its end, of darkness, the encroaching, unrelenting, devouring darkness.

But, a certain weight bore down upon him, yet not the weight of responsibility. It was of a different sort, the kind of heft that comes from the affections of another, the touch of another, which alleviates rather than encumbers. For, Theros was beside him and, seeing the pain come into his friend's eyes and the tremor into his voice, he had placed a large comforting hand upon the Human's shoulder. It was this contact that reminded Zurthaud that he was not alone, and that here were his good friends, ready, eager to bear and battle these fears alongside him.

"I fear that I may not see some of you tomorrow, but I pray Eloigal bless us each to witness the light on the other side of this dark day, one way or another. One way or another, we cannot fail. We must rescue Feldara, and we must win, a victory over the darkness, for all who have fallen, for all who live, for all of Threa." Zurthaud finished, looking long into his comrades eyes, even as his own wetted.

They had naught else to say; they were all of one mind- rescue Feldara, defeat the darkness, or die trying. On up the last flight of stairs they ascended, coming to the same Black-iron door at the very termination thereof, for the dents and scratches, the markings of struggle ending a life, still remained upon it. Having no more need for secrecy, already surmising that their arrival had been long expected, they blasted open this door with concussive magics and leaped within the topmost floor of the Ragnor, into the Dark Lord's personal chambers.

The clanging of the metal door's clattering upon the cold stone floor of the room only haunted the grand expanse of the empty hypostyle chamber for but a moment, for as at Zurthaud's and Theros' first visit, the Dark Lord again regaled his guests with music. A haunting melody screamed out from the pipes of the massive instrument, which Zurthaud recognized as the very same one which the Dragons had sung but a few nights ago, yet what was once a soothing prayer, was now twisted with chromatic tones and atonal harmonies into a gruesomely sacrilegious parody of the reverential moment.

They did not waste time listening intently to this obscene grandstanding, but immediately began searching the room for signs of Feldara. Malok eventually happened upon the remnants of her chains, and about the same time as the Dark Lord finished with his ostentatious exhibition. In the quiet after the cacophonous music, a silence only broken by the howling of wind from without the wide open shutters, the malevolent form came to loom over them, standing at the railing of the second level's balcony.

"Where is Feldara?" Malok roared, even as Theros hovered high enough in the air to confirm that she was not held by the Dark Lord upon that upper level.

"Where, indeed, is Feldara?" Gratingly chuckled the horrible armored giant, to them speaking a mystery. "I suppose that now, it matters not. You, the important guests, are all here. Here, at long last, are all the 'heroes' gathered: Zurthaud the failure, Theros the hothead, Malok the thief, Anur the manic, Calidon the simpleton, and Shar the jester."

"Heed not his words." Counseled Zurthaud, feeling the sting of them, yet still wishing to protect the others from such tricks. "He purposefully chooses them to addle you."

"Yet, the truth should not 'addle' so, or do I name any of you falsely?" Again sneered the Dark Lord. "A more pathetic company could not be found in all Threa, and I would know. I have long looked upon your little lives and heard your whispers, your plotting against me. Assuredly, the Temple was hidden from my gaze and all that transpired within, but I needed not to hear and see what already I had manipulated into being. You are here now, because I willed it, because I gave you no other choice, and you will die here, you and all that have come with you, because I have willed it. I am the darkness, I am the void that consumes all else."

Malok did not pause even a moment to listen to the Dark Lord's self-congratulatory monologue, his eyes desperately scoured the room for any place to which Feldara could have been moved. He had just seen her in this very spot through his dream-walking of the previous night, and here her former bonds had been removed. He could not allow into his mind the horror that she had been only previously slain, and besides, no blood was upon the floor anywhere, no stain of ash from her body burning. Surely, the wicked Dark One would have "willed it" to be a spectacle, and that left only two options.

Feldara must either have been moved to somewhere else within the tower, or else she had escaped by herself. Since the latter option seemed least likely to Malok, he could only wrack his brain to recall if they had somewhere along their journey up through the Ragnor, perhaps, heard her voice call out to them or otherwise missed some sign of her presence upon another floor. Yet, was there one last place to check for Feldara within this barren penthouse.

The black void between the two levels of this floor, atwixt the curved sets of stairs that connected them, the cave-like crack, loomed before him menacingly, and unto it, as if called by name, even as the Dark Lord blathered, Malok cautiously strode. With hesitation in each dreaded step, Malok slowly approached the dark chasm, with each step a palpable sensation of panic growing within him. It was as if he instinctively knew therein something horrendous dwelled, and against all such natural inclination and sense, he came nearer unto the unseen resident.

"I would not do that." A cold voice disturbingly called down to him, even as Malok nigh entered into the crevice.

It was the Dark Lord who had spoken, as he looked down from his perch directly at Malok, though not out of concern, only wicked amusement flickered as a snake's tongue in his gravelly tone. "You do not want to wake him."

Suddenly, just as was spoken, Malok felt a presence watching him, not the Dark lord above, but another terrifying phantom, before him. He turned his gaze back into the darkness just in time to catch a glimpse of two soft red lights, as a fire burned down to embers glowing from far away. He began to back away, even before he heard the scratching upon the stone floor, felt the thud of something heavy striking it hard, and he retreated unto Anur and Shar who had joined him near to the dark maw.

"It is too late now." Knowingly scolded the Dark Lord. "Against all odds, perhaps, challenging only me you might have even succeeded, but now you must contend with Dragas."

Out from the abyss slowly emerged the enormous form: first the black crooked horns, wine-red crested brow, and red, malevolently glowing eyes, then the black-toothed muzzle, the powerful frame, the black-clawed hands- the largest Dragon that any of them had yet laid eyes upon. However, his presence was not of an ally, for his eyes relayed no understanding only rage.

His growling visage betrayed no semblance of friendship, only a threat of bloody violence.

Tossing his head back, the dark-red Dragon, Dragas, roared, an unearthly, deafeningly loud, passionless howl of purely animalistic rage, and lowering his seething gaze upon Malok, the gigantic Dragon charged. They had hardly any time, Shar and Anur, to duck to the side and avoid the monstrous beast's rampage as, to the tune of the Dark Lord's mocking laughter, he chased Malok across the room. Only Theros and Calidon dissuaded Dragas from pursuing Malok any further, even though the smaller black Dragon took wing and fled without the tower to escape being mauled, for though it was blocked by a spell of his own, they cast magic toward the huge frame of the beast, thus distracting him, yet also earning his ire and violent attentions.

As the humongous Dragon turned about and took flight, for to pursue the already airborne Theros and Calidon, The Dark Lord leapt down from his perch to land before the nearly stupefied trio that remained grounded.

"We cannot let the Dragons have all the fun." Sinisterly chortled the Dark One, as out from nowhere, he drew a terrible weapon- like a long sword but with a hooked axe blade instead of a pointed tip.

However, Anur was not about to have any fun; seeing that Feldara was no longer here, fearing that the worst had befallen her, he only dwelled upon the business of death. He rushed the armored giant and struck hard at a weak point of his armor, but with speed to match, the Dark Lord parried the blow, causing Anur to quickly withdraw, lest he suffer counterattack. Even, as Anur retreated, Shar was already upon their foe, striking from an awkwardly low angle that only a flexible Serpen could manage.

"We care not for your idea of fun; tell us where you hid our sassy, loudmouthed friend and we shall be on our way." Shar taunted, as after his attack was also parried, he too had to fall back.

"And, I care not for her; I have all the guests I really wanted. Besides, what will it matter when not one of you shall leave this place alive, let alone ever see her again?" Icily replied the Dark Lord.

Yet, before the word had finished spewing from his unseen lips, Zurthaud was at him, casting a spell of fire, like that of Dragon's breath, scorching the demon and a good area about him. Though it seemed to have little effect on the Black-iron clad fiend, the spell did cause him to falter long enough for Anur to follow up with another strike from his short sword. Thus, they pressed their attack, one after the other, leaving no room for the Dark Lord to retaliate, for even as the one finished and faded away, the next struck.

Meanwhile, the air above was as a game of tag, deadliest tag, for the smaller Dragons were hard pressed to keep out of the clutches of the enormous Dragas. As one fled from him, twisting and circling and diving, and weaving in and out of the pillars, within and without the tower, the others would try to attack, and though Theros landed a good blow, drawing blood, on the back of the larger Dragon's neck, they could do little more than divert the humongous beast from further pursuing his current prey before they too became the fixation of his frenetic hounding.

"This is going nowhere." Malok yelled to Theros from across the vast room, as for a moment he could breathe after Calidon became the newest bait. "We have to try something else."

"Agreed, but what and how?" Theros yelled, as after blowing some fire into Dragas face, he had become the nest target.

"You and Calidon are bigger and stronger than I. Let me be the bait and the two of you try together to pin him." Malok conveyed, even as he flew down and scratched the great Dragon's backside.

His claws hardly could pierce the dense scales, but Dragas still felt the blow and, enraged, turned and flew after Malok, giving Theros and Calidon their chance. With a little plotting between those two, as Malok scurried in and out of the tower between the pillars, the giant Dragas, snapping and roaring, closely tailing, they determined the best way to seize their overly large opponent, and as Malok returned within the tower from one of his excursions without, just as Dragas too followed head first, they leapt upon the massive Dragon from their ambush spots- one at each of the pillars on either side of his path. Catching his huge head within the tower, his colossal body without, and using the pillars for extra support, they actually managed to trap the irately howling Dragas between them, and held him there. Malok immediately spun about, and with the others, began to attack the larger Dragon with claws and teeth and magic, and for a moment, it seemed that their fight would soon be won.

However, though Calidon had poked one of his eyes to shutting, and Theros had bloodied his side of the Dragon's head with his biting, and Malok had tried his best to knock out all of Dragas' teeth with a furious slashing of claws, the power of such a titanic Dragon could not be long restrained. With a final roar of indignation and a shake of his huge head, the monstrous Dragas released a blast of magic so forceful, that it tossed each of his assailants through the air and across the room, and only when Malok looked up from his undignified landing in a pile at an opposite corner of the room, did he see how little damage they had actually done.

The eye that Calidon had caused to shut was open, albeit wetted, and the blood dripping from the other side of Dragas face was all from superficial wounds. Malok could barely see any of the scratches he had landed upon the face and muzzle, and only one tooth had fallen out. Even the magic that Theros and Calidon had cast, that which should have been most effective blasts and disruptions, had done absolutely nothing, the insane Dragon being shielded by protective spells, seemingly already in place from before the battle had started.

Yet, Malok had not long to lie head down and tail up against one of the pillars, for with a vicious growl Dragas again came at him.

The Dark Lord, having been up to that point engrossed in defending himself from Anur, Shar, and Zurthaud, appeared distracted by the ensnaring of his Dragon, for at the same moment that Dragas was captured, so did he turn to face his thrall and endeavored to come to his aid. Had not Anur cast a clever spell, certainly the three Dragons would have then been slain by the Dark Lord's interference, but seeing his foe's intent before his footsteps, Anur acted quickly and cast magic like unto a net about the Dark One. Strands of green light shot forth from Anur's palm, scattering upon and about the armored giant, and falling from Anur's hand to land upon the floor, then became taught, fastly tethering the Dark Lord in place.

"How cunning." The Dark One spat, unhappy that his movement should be impeded. "I should have expected such techniques from one of the Master Order, or should I say from one of my own Dark Hunters?"

"I do not belong to you, vile fiend; I am the last of the Order of Masters, whom you slew." Anur retaliated, even as he strained to maintain control of the ensnaring spell.

Shar attempted then to strike the Dark One, but though entangled by the cords of light and unable to move his weapon to defend himself, the Dark Lord shot from his clawed fingertips arcs of black lightning which scorched the poor Serpen and cast him backward across the room. Zurthaud, seeing this, cast a spell about the Dark One like a sphere of orange glass, which stopped the terror's magic from issuing forth, for when next the Dark Lord cast forth lightning from his gauntleted hands, it merely swirled about within the sphere of Zurthaud's casting, rather than scalding its intended target, Anur.

"Try to hold him, yet a little longer." Zurthaud yelled to Anur, as with outstretched palm continuing to cast his own spell, he slowly backpedalled toward where Shar lay, for to see about his injuries.

There Anur stood, alone before the Dark Lord, who though bound physically and magically had yet to be fully subdued and well knew yet more ways with which to attack them, for he continued that which he had started, to assault their minds.

"It was not I alone who murdered, cold, in their sleep, those of the Master Order, or do you not remember?" Sinisterly uttered the Dark Lord. "I can tell that you do not; how could you? You were then but a child; so I will gladly aid your recollection. You see, that wretched island was perfectly defensible against all my plotting, for the Dragons thereon could spot from a great distance any forces I moved against them and, then readied, sink them in the waves surrounding long before any could land upon their shore. However, as usual, the Order of Masters was renowned for their kind deeds, for their compassion, and I at last, found this to be their weakness. For, I casted out of their clan one of my Dark Hunter's little babes; surely they dissented, but after mercilessly slaughtering the opposing parents, the rest of their tribe bowed to my superior stratagem and left the child upon the shore of the sea, starving to death before the eyes of the Masters. They could not help but take in the wretched outcast, the pitiful, malnourished whelp; does this yet sound familiar? Little could they have known that I planted upon said whelp a small token to remember me by, a Bloodstone, of course, and when the time became right, their defenses lax from years of peaceful ocean breezes wafting the palms and utter silence from my dark shores, I awakened my little pawn. Yes, death and blood flowed like water that night, but I was not the only one to shed them."

At first, the words of the Dark Lord came as untruthful to Anur; he rejected them as outright lies. Yet, as the demon continued to speak, long repressed memories suddenly jogged to recollection. Now unlocked from subconscious vault, Anur suddenly saw, plain as day, the very Aelv who had rescued him from slow, tortuous death, who had raised him, like a father; he recalled his name, Thavanael and that of his Dragoness companion, Thergera. He remembered the last night seeing them alive, on watch in the outpost atop the small hill, for a siege had long been ongoing: the Dark Horde crowding the shores, all on alert, their messengers, if returning, hopeless-without promise of aid- mostly not at all.

He remembered getting out of bed, walking out unto them under the light of a reddened moon, putting a spell of sleep upon them, of taking a dagger and plunging it repeatedly into the heart of the Aelv, until the blood splattered all upon his clothes and pooled on the ground, of smothering the unconscious Dragoness with another casting of magic. He remembered the walk back into the compound, when all the Dark Horde had silently stolen in among them, when all was chaos, and only being able to stand in the midst of it all, unmoving.

Then the laughing, the horrible, jubilant laughing amidst all the agonized screams of the dying, the removal of his necklace and the spell, and as Anur returned from reverie, there it was still, horrible, grating, malevolent laughter. Seeing his pain, feeling his anguish, as Anur's magic broke from his lack of concentration and mental distress, the Dark One laughed. Calmly, the evil warlord stepped out from the broken remnants of Anur's bonds of light and the physically penetrable bubble of Zurthaud's magical defense, even as Anur, wailing and trembling uncontrollably, slumped to the ground.

Zurthaud saw it all happen from where he knelt attending Shar, who though unable to continue fighting due to the severe burns, for his sword arm dangled, smoking and limp, was yet alive and in stable enough condition to arise from where he had been thrown. Though the Human had tried to shout encouragement to Anur, to not listen to the Dark One's words, for obviously, even if truthful, they were used in ploy, and those enthralled by the Bloodstones, he knew to be unable to control themselves, his words could not cut through the trauma that consumed the suffering form curled upon the floor. As, still laughing, the Dark Lord stepped over the prone, defeated Anur, to slowly close in upon him, Zurthaud knew himself to be again alone in facing the terrible foe.

The battle was not going well, for after their fortuitous initial assault, the Dark Horde had quickly recovered and unleashed the full wrath of their counterattack. Galrag, along with most of the other Dragons, were forced to the ground by the heavy rain of ballistae bolts, which were the sun present- for their thickness- would have blotted it out like the storm clouds that actually had. He and Lorn had set up sort of a command post upon the keep of the tower which Zurthaud and his company had at the first taken, but with the other forts, they had not so much progress. Only about half of the outlying forts had been taken, and without the heavy air support of a great many Dragons, the other buttresses had managed to completely repel many of the ground attacks from the Humans, Dworvs, and Urz.

Now that their progress had slowed and their advantage of air superiority had been lost, the front gates of the Ragnor had opened and the Nokre had been unleashed. What once started as a trickle of the pests among the counterattacks of the other monsters, which harassed and often defeated their attempts to take one of the other forts, was growing, soon to become an overwhelming flood of the mindless flesh-eaters; indeed, the Nokre swarm was so thick upon the Aelven side that their forces had never linked up with rest of the armies and were completely on the defensive, being hard pressed to avoid the three forts they had taken becoming overrun.

"We shall fly out, regroup, and proceed with hit and run tactics- in and out of range- repeatedly striking until we gain some ground." Galrag insisted, posing the strategy he thought best to press their assault.

"T'would be nay use." Returned the Dworvish King, Dimwi, with support from Athard and Kellam. "The moment the Dragons leave our positions, the Nokre'll overrun us; 'tis only their fiery breath keeping 'em at bay."

"Then we can split them into groups: some to defend, some to attack." Lorn pressed, even as a ballistae bolt shattered upon the magic barrier placed over them by a nearby Paladin Dragon and his companion. "Gentlemen, if we decide upon nothing, this fight will be lost very quickly; we are on the very knife's edge of defeat."

"We have to make a move; we must rescue the Aelvs. They are now nearly overwhelmed." Informed Argamon, his back turned to them, his eye in his spyglass.

Before anyone could say another word, a great roar was heard, almost as loud as a Dragon's, and they all turned to look toward the sound. They could clearly see a commotion at another of the forts upon their front, for apparently, a charge had been issued and the defenders were sallying forth from it.

"It is that fool of a bear, Chief Gorod!" Galrag exclaimed, informing the others, for without their own magnifying instruments or Draconic telescopic vision, they could not have determined such detail from so far away. "He and his troops are all barreling into the thick of it, no doubt seeking to relieve the Aelvs."

"We have to support him," Shouted Argamon, as he put away his spyglass and joined Lorn in climbing aboard Galrag's shoulders. "Otherwise, they shall all be slain."

"But, if we do, we risk ourselves and all our own men!" Shouted Rothard, even as Galrag began taking off the roof.

"We have no choice now; the Urz have decided for us." Galrag hotly replied, and he then roared for to summon the Dragons for a charge.

If it seemed at first to them that the battle was lost, now entering the thickest portion of the Nokre swarm and the Dark Horde under the black rain of the ballistae, before the dark tower, only to join with the brave, though foolhardy Bjarz in what surely was to be their last charge, certainly felt to them as their final hurrah. Yet, not a one of the entire host gave place to fear; even the men who would rather have been cowards and saved their own skins, such as was voiced by Rothard, thus encouraged by seeing those with greater valor, joined with their brethren.

With another shout of battle, though this one of ragged, weary voice and maddened heart hoping not for victory or life thereafter but only to die with fire and honor, the whole of the armies of Men and Dworvs and Dragons rallied and poured forth from their taken strongholds, quickly catching up to the Urz and their fellows, and the fighting was thick and bloody in the valley before the Ragnor.

The magnificent chief Gorod of the Urz was the fiercest warrior in the fight, the first into the brawl; a great sword in one hand and flanged mace in the other, he waded into the mass of enemies wildly beating them hither and thither. A battle cry sounded from his parched lips, now clear to his allies from where they joined in the clash with his people, "Feltra! Feltra!",which he held and repeated as long as his lungs had wind enough to shout, and which his Bjarz took up with him.

He was not the first to fall; long did he battle. Unto the complete utter side of the field he cut his way through the throng of monsters, unto the bottom of the hill upon which sat the first, most beleaguered, position of the Aelvs, who wearily gave a cheer to see his valiant efforts, and having driven an ever narrowing wedge into the enemy ranks, he did not fall even long after they had closed in again behind him, cutting off him and few other Bjarz from the rest of his men. Though the Aelvs, seeing his courage, then took heart and, sounding horn of charge, did rush out to meet him, and though Galrag and a few Dragons were nigh upon his place where he stood ground, fighting until he tread upon a mountain of corpses, for to rescue the fearless chief, eventually the sword and mace could not catch all of the crowding swarm of Nokre and other monsters, and the Urz chief, most noble and awesome of warriors, did begin to sink, gradually, blow by blow, under the sheer weight of bodies piling dead and alive upon him. It was a ballistae bolt, one among many shot without aim or care but toward the enemy, that finally laid him low, for the Black-iron missile caught him squarely in the middle and brought him down, so that the encroaching Nokre did then bury him under their teeth and claws.

Only moments too late, Galrag winged down to help his Bjarz surround the place where unto he had come, and the Aelvs charged down into the valley around them, thus relieving them from the immediate fighting. The Bjarz dug through the piles of flesh to find him, and dragged him out therefrom, while Galrag kept the ballistae bolts at bay with a magic shield and Lorn and Argamon sought how they could possibly attend his wounds.

"Neither more brave nor foolish warrior has ever there been." Lorn remarked in awe, as he gazed upon the mortal injuries and realized that there was little he could do now to help him, though he and Argamon did try.

Though with their limited healing magics and a nearby Aelven medic's skill they tended to his battered broken body, as Gorod lay upon his back gasping and bleeding, he slowly began to fade away. Looking into the sky in his few final moments, he saw what the others had not yet, what had inspired his courage and foolhardiness, and, in spite of his dying pain, a peaceful smile came to his face.

"Feltra." He whispered, a mystery to all those but the fellow Urz within hearing, and thus thinking on his dear friend, for whom he had sacrificed all to rescue, Gorod closed his eyes for the last time.

"He has passed." Argamon said to his nearby Bjarz, who hovered about in shocked and worried silence. "Perhaps, leading us all thereto, but if in battle, one would wish to die as he."

As the closest Bjarz cried out in lamentation and carried Gorod's body from the field, with grim expression Lorn and Argamon returned to Galrag, fully thinking the conflict lost, knowing in their tactician's mindset that they had committed too fully, forsaken their defensible positions, and in the rush of charge, seeking to relieve the Aelvs, then Gorod, they had spread themselves too thinly. They knew full well their lines would soon be crushed, but for that the unexpected happened.

A horn, unlike any of those which were used by their allies or their enemy sounded from behind them, from the former positions of the Aelvs, and a chorus of noise, like the receding of the waves of the sea, both in tone and volume, erupted thereafter. They three turned about just in time to see the formations, row upon row of shields and spears, marching steadily toward them, coming over the rocky hills through the passes and roads between the emptied forts.

The army of the Serpen had arrived, and so great was their host that the ocean-like noise of their hissing battle cry, and the thunderous thwacking of their spears and polearms against the metal boss of their large square shields, in unison raising such a terrible cacophony, catching the ears of the Dark Horde, that it caused the monsters that were not the mindless Nokre to fearfully begin a retreat. The commanding officers of the Serpen gave a shout, and another horn call blasted forth, and the Serpen host, hissing and clamoring with their weapons began a charge of their own.

Those three battle-hardened, aged and experienced Paladins could not help but to grin, as the ranks of Serpen rolled around them to join the fray, for the thought of reinforcements at this late hour had seemed a distant hope, and now seeing hope fulfilled brought only pure elation.

"Maybe, we will win this day, after all." Galrag voiced aloud, as his Human companions again climbed aboard and they too returned to the fight.

Chapter 50

Having swiftly raced over the cracked and broken ground and gravel, just underneath the heavily overcasting gray misting of the nimbus cloak, finding her way by the advise, instruments, and special senses of a seasoned guide and new friend, she had made short the long journey from the coast to the interior of the Shadow Lands. Now within sight of the dread, black tower, Feldara could not even notice the insanity of the fighting going on underneath, not even when certain other of her good friends had sighted her- radiant like a star against the cold gray backdrop- and, thus emboldened, aspired to greatest of deeds; she only could hasten unto it with all her might and quickness, each flap of her wings a matter of life and death, driving her ever nearer to her beloved's rescue.

Ulam could only hang onto the spines of her back for dear life, unable even to afford any breath for speaking, so dire was the situation and so unused to flight was he. He had quickly deduced the identity and appearance of this Bright Dragoness, and with her help as much as his, they had quickly pinpointed the location of their king, to which the Sovereign Stone summoned Serpen were magically drawn, and to the Ragnor, and had expedited the arrival of the Serpen army, which would shortly follow, as close to racing Dragon flight as terrestrially possible.

Without pausing even to look out for what awaited, Feldara broke through the last few obfuscating clouds and burst into the topmost floor of the Ragnor. What greeted her was the most horrible of scenes, nigh unto the mounting fears accompanying her hurried flight.

Anur lay upon the floor in tremulous stupor near the center of the room; Shar, half burned, slumped against a pillar nearby them; Calidon, just then, was flung hard, enough to the breaking and scattering of the stones thereof, against one of the staircases and painfully cried out; Theros wrestled with both hands and feet the jaws of an enormous Dragon- the second largest that Feldara had ever seen- who attempted to bite or devour him, even as Malok attempted to dissuade by wresting the back of their head and gouging their eyes; Zurthaud, hard pressed to do anything else, was atop the second level, ducking and dodging the relentless attacking of the Dark Lord and his terrible blade and magics.

It was all so much chaos that Feldara hardly knew what to do; everyone desperately needed her help and all at once. For a moment, longer than she wanted but less than it seemed, Feldara found herself frozen in place with indecision and conflicts of priority, but quickly she hastened first to Anur, even as Ulam dismounted and saw to his king.

"Are you alright?" She worriedly inquired, steadying the poor man from his tremors.

Tardily, once seeing her face and hearing her voice, he seemed to awaken from whatever horror had seized his mind; gasping for air, he whispered her name.

"We need you, Anur; please, be alright." She begged of him, holding him in her arms.

But, she could not long stay there. The fight was far from over; she was still needed elsewhere. Ulam, who had gathered his master and supported his limp with a shoulder, had made his way over to them and offered to keep watch and assist Anur while she aided the others. Quickly, she made her way over to Calidon, who seemed unable to yet arise, for he lay groaning in the rubble of the stair.

"Feldara!" He excitedly choked, amidst his pain.

"Can you move?" She tearfully asked, as nearing him and seeing the state of the stair, she feared paralysis from his back being broken.

"Give me a minute, and I shall be back in the fight. Seeing you alive and well brings me much strength." He wheezed, as unsuccessfully trying to get up, he could only grit his teeth in anguish.

"The fight is over; we are all leaving, just as soon as I gather everyone." She stammered, hardly able to keep herself together, now having witnessed the agony of both Calidon and Anur and being caught in the adrenaline of battle.

She hated that this was happening, that her friends and family here suffered for her sake, that some hateful demon had used her to bring about such pain and bloodshed, that there was war and death at all in the world, and she wanted quickly for it all to end, or at the very least, to not be because of her.

However, leaving the dark tower would not be as simple as last time. The Dark Lord, having cast more of his lightning toward Zurthaud, had nearly caught the man off guard this time, and though the Human had managed to deflect the sizzling tendrils with magic of his own, the force of the impact had blown him off from the balcony. A tumbling roll saved him from death and breaking anything other than his ankle, but Zurthaud's landing spot was right near where Calidon lay and Feldara stood beside. And, in pursuit of his prey, coming to peer over the banister, the Dark One immediately noticed her reappearance.

"My, my, the Bright Dragoness, returning just in time to watch her precious friends die, how tragic, and stupid; I let you run, gave you full leave, and this is how you repay my generosity, by attempting to save these condemned fools?" Spat the Dark Lord, turning his faceless gaze upon Feldara.

"Why? Why must you be this wicked, loathsome monster?" Feldara screamed in retaliation more than questioning. "Why must you cause all this pain, shed all this blood?"

"I already told you once; shall I repeat myself?" The Kragon thundered, as he slowly menacingly, paced down what was left of the stair. "I am the shadow between the stars; I am the abyss. I cause the light to shine so brightly; without me, it would all be gray. I make necessary 'the hero'; I give them purpose. I am antithesis; I am darkness."

"All you need do is look around at all the broken lives your 'shadow' has touched, to see that your little job has helped no one for the better, to be better. Your logic is not just flawed; it is insanity." Feldara growled, even as seeing the terror draw near she redoubled her concurrent efforts to raise Calidon from where he lay.

"Perhaps." Was the Dark Lord's single word response, as he strode down the stair, ever closing upon them.

However, try as she might, it seemed they would not be able to flee in time, for Calidon was stiff, nigh unable to move at all, perhaps, indeed, paralyzed. Nevertheless, Feldara did not, could not leave from his side, slowly hauling him to his feet, then trying to drag him further away, even as without any urgency, the Dark One gradually neared them a step at a time.

Suddenly, the fiend was upon them and without word or laughter, without any chance for either Zurthaud, who was overcoming what pain he endured in attempt to rise and aid them, or Calidon to do anything, the Dark Lord raised his terrible blade, aimed truly for Feldara, to strike.

Grunting, she waited to feel the tear of flesh, the warmth of flowing blood, and the blazing fire of neurons piercingly declaring her appalling, fresh wound. Feldara wondered, in that microscopic eternity of waiting for injury, if it would be a blow to her death, a decapitation or a severing of an artery, if she were ready to die. She closed her eyes for that split of a second, and internally said farewell to everyone she loved, especially to Malok; she made peace with all of the life she wanted to, but would never live. She committed herself to Eloigal.

Yet, the split of a second passed; the time it would have taken for the blow to fall had passed. She still lived and felt not the pain of wound, nor any pain at all, only the heft of Calidon in her arms. She opened her eyes and looked behind her, to where the Dark Lord would have struck her, knowing not what could have stayed the demon's hand, but immediately wished for any other reality than what had transpired, than who had stopped it.

Anur was before her, arms stretched wide, for to take up as much space as possible; his trembling gone, firmly he stood in defense of his beloved Dragoness, his charge, his daughter. Upon seeing her, he had been reminded of all the good in his life, of all the good he had striven for, next to his Bright Dragoness, the vivid horrors of his past had faded; his guilty hands, which had shed so much blood, though some not of his own will, seemed to him redeemed by her love and presence- she the joy and paramount of his life.

There he stood, though his purple blood trickled down his side from the cut he had borne for her sake, for, seeming himself surprised, the Dark One had left the blade where it had stuck-below Anur's broken collar bone, just above his heart.

Eventually, everyone came to realize what had happened all at once, and as the Dark Lord withdrew his blade and readied to strike again, with magic, Zurthaud blasted the fiend back into the shadows of Dragas' lair. Weeping, Feldara could not help but release Calidon for to catch Anur, who, unable to stand any longer, slumped to his knees.

She buried her face and tears in his bloodied tunic, as they clung to each other.

"I am sorry." Anur wheezed, even as Feldara tore off his helm, to both see his face and help him breathe more easily.

"For what? You have done nothing wrong." She whimpered. "You saved me."

"No, I forgot." He whispered, the strength fading from his voice and body. "I forgot you hated it." Said he regarding his helm, halfway causing her to laugh. "But, I also forgot, even for a moment how good my life has been, because of you, because of you, Feldara. You saved me."

His ragged breaths came ever more slowly, as Feldara wracked her brain for any way to help him, to save him; here he lay dying, in her defense, and yet, she had saved him? As Ulam left from Shar's side and came unto them to try to staunch the bleeding with even his own robes; and somewhere off in the distance Zurthaud, who attempted to rise using his sword as a crutch, yelled for them to ready themselves for the Dark Lord's retaliation; and Calidon, helpless on the ground, full well knowing who had taken the blow, for in his facing position had seen Anur come to their rescue, that blow which he wished his now useless body could have received instead, loudly wept; Feldara could only wonder at Anur's last words and cry over his broken body.

In her pain of loss, she could not fathom how love and joy and life shared save a broken heart; she could not process anything. Her heart hurt so much, that one so beloved to her should die in her arms; she could only cry. Until, somewhere, deep within herself, she remembered something- a tune, a song, not any words, for these escaped this faint, suppressed recollection, but a clear melody and the feelings attached. Like a peculiar scent recalled from childhood days, or the actions ascribed to instinct, or the emotions of a dream, the details of which long forgotten, it came to her suddenly, triggered by what now stimulated her subconscious.

Out of desperation, unable to do anything else but weep over Anur, Feldara began to hum the little tune. Even as the Dark One began to emerge, slowly stalking forth from the shadows toward her; and Zurthaud and Shar came to stand in their last strength between; and Theros and Malok, who had by now seen her and availed to come unto her, still struggled mightily with the terrible Dragas; her humming became vocalization, and what was once a quiet, simple lullaby began to grow in volume and power. What was once mere song, sound waves gently vibrating the air, morphed and changed, becoming ever more miraculous and transcendent of any temporal melody; her voice was filled with magic, her magic- of the light, the bane of darkness.

Suddenly, the cloud cover, the thick gray fog without the Ragnor broke, rolling back as an unloosed scroll, tearing apart as though by wrathful hands, and light, glorious light of a brilliant noonday, burst into the once darkened tower. Everyone had to shield their eyes from the sudden flash of brightness, to shield their gaze from the radiance of sun, but also of Feldara, for she and the air all about her glowed from the radiant magical music emanating from within her. Just as the room filled with light, so too was it flooded with sound, the sweet lyric singing slowly replaced, overcome by an otherworldly harmony of tones until Feldara's comparably more humble timbre was altogether replaced by the heavenly drone.

Though they all rejoiced to hear it, for the overwhelming sensation of joy was borne upon the supernal symphony and mixed within the deluge of illumination, even to they who received it gladly, the overwhelming force of it was nigh unbearable; Zurthaud, Shar, and Ulam, crouching and gritting their teeth through their smiling, all dropped their weapons to stop their ears, a near soundless clatter comparative to what rang like bells around; Theros and Malok, weeping though laughing, ceased from their battling to cover their ears.

However, to he who was of the darkness, who could not ever receive anything wondrous or good, it was absolute annihilation, for the Dark Lord, having no ear to plug, no eye to cover, could but turn his faceless face to the blazing of the light all about and, though nearly completely drowned out, scream in anguish within the engulfing tide of lustrous sonority. Writhing in incomprehensible agony, his armor crumpled as he within melted into a puddle of black liquid, which spread, smoking, upon the floor of the room only long enough for Feldara's radiance to sear it into nothingness, not even ash to blow away in the wind.

Longer still did the music and light last, long after Feldara's mouth had shut and she along with the others had only listened to and watched its resonating pulses and gleaming refractions. Only after the echoes had faded, and the others about began to rise from their cowed state, did she return her full attention unto Anur.

She laid him on his back, as comfortably as she possibly could, for to look into his eyes and touch his face. Within them, she did not see pain, neither disappointment as she had once before imagined, nor annoyance with her childishness, nor dismay of life's good pleasures; she saw only joy for her appearing, peace for his fate, pride and approval for her power and victory, and a soft, thoroughly happy smile.

"Please, do not go. I love you." Feldara pleaded with him, hoping beyond possibility that Anur could.

He could barely mouth the words, his breath and strength gone; she could barely hear him whisper.

"And, I love you, daughter."

The tears and mourning that flooded forth from her at this last breath, for his chest rose no more and the light faded from his eyes, seemed to Feldara even more powerful than the magical brightness and song from before, for she was shaken to her very core by them, by the grievous sorrow from which they stemmed.

But, Malok came swiftly unto her and, holding her tightly, ceased not to kiss her head and cheek, and it seemed, at least, in his arms, that the pain of losing Anur, though not at all diminished, could somehow be endured and the gaping wound of him torn from her life, though still a scar, mended.

<><><><><>

Ever since Gorod's valiant yet fatal charge, the battle turned in favor of the combined forces of Dragons, Humans, Aelvs, Dworvs, Urz, and now Serpen, for with the great number of their well equipped and well trained spearmen joining the fray as reinforcements, the bold maneuver had begun to drive back the encroaching counterattacks of the Dark Horde. Galrag, Lorn and the other generals and leaders began again to hope for victory, yet could they not count the day won nor rejoice, not until the light of the sun broke through the dense cloud cover.

Comparative to the earlier gloom, the sky seemed to have burst into flame, especially the very top of the Ragnor, as the height of the once drear, black tower became aglow with light. The various monsters- the Goblins, Trolls, and Ogres began to wane and cower, and the Nokre, suddenly still and unresponsive, began to shudder then melt as the unusual brightness burned from the heavens down upon them. What was left of the enemy forces then broke and ran, wildly fleeing every which way, and with much cheering and cries of triumph the host of Paladins and free peoples pursued them beyond the hills surrounding the vale before the Ragnor, scattering them into the wilds of the Shadow Lands.

But, Galrag and Lorn, and many others of the Paladins, had not forgotten those who had entered within the dark tower, and seeing the large, wide windows of the topmost floor, they hastened thereunto, for to see about their comrades. And finding them there, still sorrowing over Anur's passing, they gathered around joining with them in their mourning, for many, many such beloved friends had fallen.

So it was, that several hours after, long, long after the fighting had ended, that a solemn gathering of the wounded and the fallen ensued, continuing on until the late evening, when the last of the bodies had been accounted for and assembled, yet without the vale of the Ragnor, for no one wished to see the remains of their loved one lie a moment longer nearby that evil place. A camp was pitched upon the other side of the small surrounding hills, and since none of them could rest well enough to sleep, a solemn vigil was held therein, to fully mourn their fellows.

Throughout the night, as Feldara clung to Malok and Theros, nearby the makeshift field hospital, wherein lay Calidon and Shar, the lamentations of the various peoples could be heard: song and dirge, eulogy and memoriam, and much languishing cries.

Yet, was their grief not without hope, for they knew, even through their tears, weeping over those with whom they had now to part ways, even by such terrible and painful and sudden means, that death was not the finality of their existence. They had assured hope to meet those whom they loved yet again and did not doubt that, even now, the whole of the Blessed Realm was only made more joyously wonderful by those who newly entered, and that the Eloigal, with loving arms wide open, had received them to the greatest of celebrations, that which those who remained behind could only partially imagine the full glory and bliss and peace thereof.

Chapter 51

The warm sand, balmy breeze, scent of surf, and crashing of waves did much to relieve Feldara's poor spirit, for they were the comforts of home. She had cried far too much in the past week: first over Anur, whose death she still mourned; then learning of Gorod's fate and his wild bravery, an act for which she secretly blamed herself; then more so, hearing of Calidon, whose paralytic state persisted well after the night of rest first recommended, that the doctors of the Order could do nothing for his condition; even for Shar, who otherwise unharmed, had need to adapt to his nigh permanent discoloration, for the Dark Lord's lightening, having singed his flesh, had grayed one half of his body's otherwise dark blue scales, like a log unturned on the fire.

She breathed deeply the salt seasoned ocean draft, sighing on remembering all the horrors of last week, the sorrow still stinging her heart, but curling her tail about her sandy feet, she exhaled contentment, gladness to be home.

She had traveled here as part of a strange caravan: the host of Urz upon the ground, with Gorod in the honored head of the train, bearing up their fallen upon their shields, carrying them home to rest with their ancestors underneath their mountain; the Dragons and Companions circling overhead, Theros with Zurthaud and Galrag with Lorn taking turns carrying Calidon, who could by no means yet fly, hoping that his family, with their extensive medical knowledge could aid in returning some of his mobility; and Malok carrying Anur, thoroughly wrapped and embalmed, securely upon his back.

Unfortunately, and much to Malok's dismay, Shar could not accompany them, for as Ulam explained, after using the Sovereign Stone and its peculiar call, his people had need to see their king whole and healthy, lest they worry unduly for his safety, and lest the other aristocratic houses begin to plot for a new successor to the throne. It was with a tearful goodbye that the Serpen king left from his Dragon brother and Feldara, and through many embraces and kisses they promised not to part for so long, but to soon see each other again.

A few days of travel brought them quickly from the Order's realm unto the Urz's mountain, and in spite of the sorrow of their people on learning of their chief's death, they were still well received by the Znakar and stayed as honored guests for the funeral ceremony of their fallen warriors. Though the Urz's feasting and collective mourning was set to last for many days for so great a warrior chief and his Bjarz, with another of the Znakar's blessings, the troupe departed upon the morrow, for they had yet many days to travel.

They then delivered Calidon to his family but a few days after, who welcomed him and his friends with joy, yet even proud as they were to hear tale of his brave deeds, did sorrow over his injury and Anur's passing, and the Rathnyaling extended family comforted each other and their guests for yet a few days more.

Even though this reunion of family and friends was gladsome and a healing balm for the wounded hearts of their guests, Feldara and Malok had yet one more trip to make, and with overmuch love and well-wishing, left from there, saying their goodbyes to Calidon and his family, and also to Galrag and Lorn. Though they offered to yet accompany Feldara, Malok, Theros, and Zurthaud, it was decided that it was more needful they should quickly return unto the Paladins and see to the recovery of their Order rather than attend further their friend's grieving, and so they left for Doraegonoran, while the others went on to the isle of the Master Order.

For it was here that Feldara had wished to inter Anur, although the Urz had invited them- truly a great honor for an outsider- to bury him in their people's funereal vault alongside Gorod. Upon the higher of the two small grassy hills, truly their most favorite spot on the whole island: her for staring off into the wide world beyond, his for together spending many idle sunsets only in each other's company; thinking of no better spot in the whole world, and imagining him wanting nowhere else, she had buried him there.

____

As the day wore on and Theros, Malok, and Zurthaud had busied themselves with some light repairs and clearing of the brush from the aged structures, she had sauntered through the jungle unto the shore. There she now sat, unable yet to linger long at her favorite spot nearby his grave, nor to join with the others among the buildings that were once her house and playground, all for fear of longing to see Anur there, and yet knowing she would not. All the memories, even sweet treasures as they were, would only remind her of the hurt she endured and how she missed him so.

Sitting upon this lonely stretch of white sandy beach, off into the horizon beyond the cresting waves she stared, knowing that in a better place her foster father now resided, truly reveling in that peaceful assurance, yet still feeling the pain of his passing; it was there that Malok found her.

"Theros says, all the nesting houses seem to be in good shape, and Zurthaud found the library. With a little more help, we could restore the rest of the compound, even raise the walls about." He happily relayed as he approached.

Yet, Feldara did not respond with words, only a detached, thoroughly dissonant smile, and Malok, knowing that she still grieved bitterly, and seeing her there, only took her in his arms and held her.

"He would really appreciate it," She replied after a good moment of resting in her mate's soothing embrace. "That you are all fixing up this place."

"This is your home, is it not?" Malok said with a kind grin. "I cannot have my life-mate living in rubble."

"Yes, it was; it still is, just as long as you dwell here with me." After a pause, she returned along with a slight smile.

"If this is what you want, it is what I want also." Malok replied turning more serious.

"I think so." She mused, digging her claws into the sand, really unsure of where else she would rather call home. "I have been giving thought to a lot of things."

"Like what?"

"I want to truly rebuild what was lost here, not just the buildings, maybe restart the Master Order." Feldara answered, pensively, for she knew not what the future held, or even if she was capable of such an undertaking.

"I think that is an excellent idea, a wonderful tribute to him," Malok returned, again holding his beloved close. "Just as long as we do it together."

"Yes, together." Feldara agreed with a bigger, heartfelt grin, and they two sat there for a good moment longer, wafted by the sea breeze, staring at the blue-green expanse before them, enjoying nothing more than to be held by the other.

"Then, first things first," Malok suggested as he arose and helped her do the same. "Let us join Zurthaud and Theros, whose stomach is already grumbling louder than his mouth about this time, and go hunt for some dinner."

And so, they two strode off together, side by side, down the sandy beach, which already began to tint fiery orange by the eventide light of the sun, thus ending one story, and beginning another.

Glossary

Characters

Aelanur- Dragon Paladin who serves as the priest in the temple atop the Dragons' quarters tower

A-Chatsron- The Great Father Dragon, the first, the created one, the progenitor of all the Dragons of Threa

Anur- Last surviving member of the Order of Masters, Feldara's mentor; not quite Human, but most easily mistakable for a Troll

Argamon- Human Paladin and Captain of the Guard for the Order of Paladin's Citadel, once the Companion of the Dragoness Ilara

Aris- Young Dragoness, daughter of Yuronon and Rathnyala

Anfanuil- Aelven Paladin, Companion to the Dragon, Teror, and friend of Zurthaud

Athard- Human, young lord of the South-western province, son of Lothard

Arthaud- Human Paladin, Companion to the Dragon, Silecs, and friend of Zurthaud

Baltor- Human Paladin, Companion to the Dragon, Thol, and friend of Zurthaud

Bron- Human Paladin, elected High Consul

Caelon- Dragon Paladin, Companion to the Human, Losal, and friend of Zurthaud

Calidon- Young Dragon, son of Rathnyaling and Crasra, aspires to be a Paladin, big and strong, and smart, but tends to figuratively bite his own tail quite often

Carathad- Human Paladin, elected High Consul

Chassia- Young Dragoness, daughter of Rathnyaling and Crasra

Codalts- Dragon Paladin, a scout and messenger, swift as the wind

Crasra- Dragoness and the Life-mate of Rathnyaling, mother of Calidon, Sengis, Vol, Chassia, and Sachru

Dimwi- King of the Dworves

Drowon- Dragon of the Aegan Mountains, accepted to speak for his neighbors

Dyreft- Human Paladin, Companion to the Dragon, Galrath, and friend of Zurthaud

Efarnuil- Aelven Paladin, brother of Anfanuil

Elyriana- Aelven Paladin, elected High Consul

Fazil- Human, Mayor of Bythatsar, renowned for his fine moustache, gourmandizing and exceptional rotundity

Feldara- Young Dragoness, daughter of Lethira and Theros and, by mentorship, Anur; the "Bright One" gifted with special power to defeat darkness

Finiriel- Captain of a band of Aelven rangers who kept watch over the Southernmost outpost of their realm

Galrag- Dragon Paladin, Companion to the Aelv Reythanuil, "The General", great leader and tactician known for his stubbornness and gruff nature

Galrath- Dragon Paladin, son of Galrag, Companion to the Human, Dyreft, and friend of Zurthaud

Gimmel- Dworvish Paladin, brother of Himmel, Noff, and Toff

Gorod- Urz, the Chief of the Urz and warlord of the Bjarz, a great and honorable warrior

Himmel- Dworvish Paladin, brother of Gimmel, Noff, and Toff

Ilara- Dragoness, Life-mate of Sicaron and mother of Malok, Companion of the Human Argamon, and really bad at selecting jewelry

Kellam- Human, Mayor of Doraegonoran, well respected for his few, yet pertinent words, martial prowess, and political tact

Kragon, The- The Dark Lord, The Shadow King, The Dark One, darkness incarnate, evil ruler of the Shadow Lands

Lenairu- A mysterious Lady Dragoness renowned for her kind deeds and wisdom, a great help and tutor to Malok

Lethira- Dragoness Paladin, Life-mate of Theros and mother of Feldara, Companion to Zurthaud and like a mother to him

Lorn- Human Paladin, Companion to the Dragon Sicaron and unofficially to Galrag, once a great voice of opposition to Orthard

Losal- Human Paladin, Companion to the Dragon, Caelon, and friend of Zurthaud

Lothard- Human, lord of the Southern province, father of Athard and Rothard, his seat of governance was at Farmersrest, currently missing and presumed dead

Malok- Young Dragon, son of Ilara and Sicaron, raised by the Serpen Vizier Ulam, Companion of the Serpen King, Shar Koman, gifted with a power over dreams and visions

Noff- Dworven Paladin, brother of Himmel, Gimmel, and Toff

Nyalanya- Young Dragoness, daughter of Yuronon and Rathnyala

Og- King of the Ogres, and Killer of Two, slew two Dragons in previous battles without having been immediately incinerated

Orthard- Human, Lord Consul of the Paladins, sire of Zurthaud, a despicable person whose self-indulgence, hatred, and despotism nearly destroyed the Order of Paladins

Rath- Young Dragon, son of Yuronon and Rathnyala

Rathnyala- Dragoness doctor and Life-mate of Yuronon, mother of Aris, Rath, Thinru, Ruderon, and Nyalanya, and daughter of Rathnyalgr, just as capable a doctor as her brother Rathnyaling

Rathnyalgr- Dragon Paladin and great hero of a bygone age, father of Rathnyaling and Rathnyala

Rathnyaling- Dragon doctor and Life-mate of Crasra, son of Rathnyalgr, tutored by Serc to become an equally great and renowned healer

Reythanuil- Aelven Paladin, Companion to the Dragon Galrag, exiled from the Order of Paladins

Rothard- Surly Human lord of the South-eastern province, eldest son of Lothard

Ruad- Human Paladin, elected High Consul

Ruderon- Young Dragon, son of Yuronon and Rathnyala

Sachru- Young Dragoness, daughter of Rathnyaling and Crasra

Sengis- Young Dragon, son of Rathnyaling and Crasra, their most medically inclined child

Serc- Dragon Paladin, great leader and healer, renowned and beloved for his faithfulness and gentleness, like a foster father to Zurthaud

Shar Koman, Ss'al Musst'ra- King of the Serpen, Companion of the Dragon Malok, smart-mouthed and overly fond of pampering, yet fiercely loyal to his friends

Sicaron- Dragon Paladin, Life-mate of Ilara and father of Malok, a legendary scout

Silecs- Dragon Paladin, Companion to the Human, Arthaud, and friend of Zurthaud

Sutton- The Headman for the obscure Human village of Nitenmile

Teror- Dragon Paladin, Companion to the Aelv, Anfanuil, and friend of Zurthaud

Theros- Dragon Paladin, Life-mate of Lethira, father of Feldara, Companion to Zurthaud, known for being hot-headed and quick to action

Thinru- Young Dragoness, daughter of Yuronon and Rathnyala

Thol- Dragon Paladin, Companion to the Human, Baltor, and friend of Zurthaud

Thryzanuil- Aelven Paladin, elected High Consul

Toff- Dworven Paladin, brother of Himmel, Gimmel, and Noff

Udrik- Human Paladin, elected High Consul

Ulam- Serpen Royal Vizier, fiercely loyal to his King and country, practically a father to both Shar and Malok, having raised each of them from infancy after their respective parents passed away

Venrogan- Human Head Chef and Lieutenant Quartermaster of Provisions for the Order of Paladins, untrained in classical Threan cuisine, but a reliable and industrious cook

Vol- Young Dragon, Son of Rathnyaling and Crasra

Yuronon- Dragon and Life-mate of Rathnyala, father of Aris, Rath, Thinru, Ruderon, and Nyalanya

Znakar, The- Urz, the spirit-man or shaman of the Urz, an ancient priestly druid who uses his wisdom to advise and encourage others

Zurthaud- Human Paladin, Companion to Lethira and Theros, sired by Orthard, renowned for his honesty and integrity

Places

Adthonler, The- The third oldest building yet standing in the city of Doraegonoran, while other lesser structures were built before the Adthonler, they eventually vanished- deconstructed on purpose or by time- while the great hotel has remained nearly entirely unaltered from its original construction

Ae River, The- The other great river of Threa, starting far in the North, it slowly winds its way through the Aelven lands down to the Crydan sea

Aegan Mountains, The- Aegan- From the Old Draconic, literal meaning- "These mountains", the Northernmost mountain range of Threa

Aelven Lands, The- The amorphously undefined geography in the West of Threa, consisting of mostly dense forests, which the Aelvs sporadically settled along the Ae River; ruled over by the Queen of the Aelvs and her matriarchy, separated from the Human Realm by a great expanse of unsettled wild lands

Akum, Ss'al- (The Great Wastes) the vast desert of white sand that covers the majority of the Serpen Kingdom

Aronoran, The- From the Old Draconic, literal meaning- "The significant place of stopping", the great wall that separates the Shadow Lands from the lands of the free peoples of Threa, built by the first Paladins with Dworvish cut stone affixed by the magic of Dragons

Atsar, The- From the Old Draconic, literal meaning- "Water"; the longest river of Threa and of great importance to the Human Realm as a major trade route and a natural barrier from the tribes of monsters living to the South

Bassar, Ss'al- The home and sole city of the Serpen Kingdom, once renowned the world over for its lavish markets and exotic goods of all kinds, the Serpen people and their chief city had greatly declined due to their siding with the Dark Horde and losing in the last war, subsequent punishments and embargoes from the Order of Paladins and the other free peoples led to mass poverty among the Serpen and a diminishing of their kingdom

Bestford- A City of the Human Realm known for its many bridges spanning the Atsar River, being the "Best Ford" for many miles about

Bythatsar- The second greatest city of the Human Realm and likely the oldest, being founded by Humans and not Dragons, long standing upon the very banks of the Atsar River, it has served as a major hub of commerce for the entire world of Threa

Citadel, The- The stronghold of the Order of Paladins, sitting just under the Southernmost peaks of the Aegan mountain range and at the end of the city of Doraegonoran, the Citadel was built with the aid and magics of the first Draconic Paladins in much the same manner as the Aronoran wall; it is the second oldest building yet standing in Doraegonoran, as the Dragon's tower, with their living quarters and topped by their domed temple, was constructed first

Counting Stone/Obelisk of the Covenant- (Cainaeg Cronan- Old Draconic) A massive stone in the middle of the Aegan mountains magically inscribed with every Dragon's name, a visual representation of the Eloigal's covenant with the Dragons of Threa; in ancient times, Dragon parents would take their children to the Cainaeg Cronan to see their own names etched upon the monolith and to teach them magic, but about the time of the founding of the Order of Paladins, the custom began to lose favor due to the continual Draconic diaspora making such pilgrimages untenably lengthy; by Feldara's day, it was nearly completely forgotten by all but the most traditional and local of Draconic families

Crydan Sea, The- From the Old Draconic, literal meaning- "This cold", a cold sea that separates like a great bay the West coast of the Shadow Lands from the land of the Aelvs

Doraegonoran- From the Old Draconic, literal meaning- "The significant place that is a city in the mountains", the chief city of the Human Realm, home to the headquarters of the Order of Paladins, founded by Dragons, it is the oldest city in all of Threa

Dunn Mountains, The- A sprawling mountain range upon the East coast of Threa; Long ago the Dragons and Dworves disputed over mountainous territory until an agreement was made giving to the Dragons all the mountains to the North and West of Doraegonoran and to the Dworves all the mountains to the South and East- primarily the Dunn Mountains

Dworvish Kingdom, The- The realm claimed by the Dworves, mostly underneath the Dunn Mountains, but with a few minor/miner settlements above ground

Farmersrest- Once a major city of the Human Realm, it was neglected by the Order of Paladins under Lord Consul Orthard due to alleged laxity in protection taxes; it was shortly after discovered to be abandoned and its entire population, including its lord Lothard, missing

Grynwood- A major city of the Human Realm sitting just Southwest of Doraegonoran in the midst of a large forest, supplied the majority of all lumber and timber to the rest of the world, as the Aelvs were very much against any tree chopping

Human Realm, the- The lands occupied by Humankind, extending from the headwaters of the Atsar River in the North, from the Southern tip of the Aegan Mountain's range all down through the steppe and plains, along the course of the Atsar River and South of it unto the Aronoran wall, unto the foothills of the Dunn Mountains to the East, and ending at the city of Plainskeep in the utter West

Isle of the Master Order- A small island in the Southern half of the Crydan Sea, turned into a training ground, base of operations, and fortress by the Order of Masters

Lotheliel- A major city of the Aelven Lands sitting on both sides of the Ae River about a day's foot travel from the coast of the Crydan Sea, a major hub of culture and trade for the Aelvs, it rivaled and eventually outclassed even their capitol, though the Queen of the Aelvs never even once considered moving her seat of governance there

Muthport- A major city of the Human Realm sitting at the mouth of the Atsar river beyond the outstretching of the Shadow Lands' peninsula, at the very top Northeast coast of the Crydan sea, a major trading port, receiving all merchant ships and cargo from the Aelvs, and most from the Serpen, to be taken upstream the Atsar to the rest of the Human Realm

Nitenmile- An unimportant Human village just about a lazy day's walk Northwest from Bestford

Plainskeep- A major city of the Human Realm, the home city and seat of governance for lord Athard, serving as a fort upon the western frontier of the Human Realm, a single, seldom traveled dirt road connected it to the far distant Aelven Lands

Ragnor, The- From the Old Draconic, literal meaning- "Place of evil darkness", The home of the Dark Lord, a singular tower, impossibly constructed of Black-iron, the tallest structure in the world of Threa, surrounded by a ring of low mountains covered in lesser fortresses; deemed impregnable, no one had ever before dared to assail the evil stronghold since its sudden appearance just before the beginning of the last great war

Richmont- A major city of the Human Realm, the closest Human settlement to the Dworvish Kingdom, it almost solely benefited from their craft and trade and grew quite wealthy by reselling to the rest of the Human Realm the high-value Dworvish goods, chiefly: gold, metalwork, and gemstones

Serpen Kingdom, The- The lands occupied by the Serpen, to the Northeast of the Human Realm, consisting mostly of desert with some pockets of grasslands hidden in the rocky steppes surrounding their coastal mountains

Shadow Lands, The- The home of the Dark Horde, the dry barren earth grew little sustenance under the scowl of low craggy mountains, and the sky was perpetually shrouded with thick black, though rain-less, clouds; it was written that water and grasslands once were there, until the arrival of the Dark Lord and the raising of the Ragnor

Magics and Objects of Intrigue

Athungar- From the Old Draconic- literal meaning, "All souls connected", also called **Soul Speaking**, a spell by which one can communicate directly to another without speaking audibly

Atsarocu- From the Old Draconic- literal meaning, "Water Sight", also called **Peering**, a spell by which the caster uses water to search for and observe another object or person

Black-iron- A vile metal found only in the Shadow Lands, able to cut through Dragons' normally impenetrable scales, otherwise, less favorable than regular iron- being slightly less durable- and much less flexible than steel

Bloodstones- Dragon Gems imbued by the Dark Lord with a horrible curse that allows him to control the one who is bound to them, usually worn on a chain of Black-iron about the victims neck

Dragon Stone/Dragon Gem- Gemstones or pearls imbued by a Dragon with a certain magic spell for a specific utility, usually for use without the caster's direct or constant involvement

Dream-walking- (Eosnor- Old Draconic) A magical gift that allows the bearer to exit from their own sleeping body into a state of existence not actually present in the real world but still able to affect it

Magic- An ability, innate to Dragons, by which the natural laws which govern how the world works are allowed to be shifted, changed, bent, or otherwise broken and replaced with the will of the caster up to a limited time or effect

Spell- A specific technique for utilizing magic designed to produce consistent and expected results and mitigate counter-effects, usually taught by written or verbal instruction

Peoples

Aelvs- The fair folk, given to nature and things that grow, lovers of the arts, lighter and usually slightly smaller than Humans but with keener senses

Dragons- The flying folk, rulers of sky and fire, lords above all who are proud, lovers of freedom and spirit, the largest and strongest of all the races

Dworvs- The sturdy folk, given to rock, metal, and things of the earth, lovers of craft, smaller but much more hardy than Humans

Humans- The special folk, given to whatever their heart desires, capable of both great good and great evil

Serpen- The folk that look as snakes with arms, hands, legs and feet, about the same size and strength as Humans, but slimmer and with lankier appendages, given to sand and soil, lovers of trade and mercantilism

Urz- The folk that look as bears walking upright, much larger than Humans, but smaller than fully grown Dragons, given to the high, cold mountains and forests, lovers of the hunt and of battle

Monsters

Dark Hunters- A mysterious race of monsters, who due to their slight resemblance, some might at first mistake for Trolls, serving as the elite operatives and commanders of the Dark Horde, for their intellect is comparable to that of Humans- though constantly turned toward evil- and their prowess with any weapon and even magic make them formidable adversaries

Goblins- Diminutive monsters, about waist high to a Human, whose faces resemble those of pigs, crafty and cunning, devising and constructing most of the Dark Horde's structures, armor, and weaponry; in battle, preferring to hide behind the other species of the Dark Horde, serving mostly as archers and artillery personnel

Nokre- Mindless monsters, reptilian and ape-like in appearance and stride, about chest height to an average Human, conjured by the evil will of the Dark Lord for the sole purpose of tearing to pieces with their claws and teeth anything that stands before them

Ogres- The largest and strongest of all the monsters of the Dark Horde, the greatest of which could stand just above shoulder height to an adult Dragon, with limited intelligence for most of their species, they serve mostly as heavy hitting brutes, but some exceptional specimens have served as generals and commanders of the horde

Trolls- The reptilian monsters that make up the primary force of the Dark Horde, slightly taller and stronger, though less intelligent than Humans, they most often form tight phalanxes of spear and pike that are tough to break through or scatter

Winged Beasts- The mindless monsters that serve as flying mounts for the Dark Hunters, seemingly especially created by the Dark Lord for the purpose of capturing Dragons

Worgs- Regular wolves of the Shadow Lands mutated into hideous monsters by the Dark Lord's vile magics, their bite is venomous and, when surgically equipped with Black-iron claws and fangs, they pose a danger even to Dragons

Sayings in Old Draconic

The Song of Lethira

Natsra, Ownyi Natsra hosh longu chalts

Adj eo anong <u>tha</u>lon tsar acse <u>tha</u>l ocu Ownyu

Ocu <u>thi</u>rg adj cain adj ha adj loodj adj <u>tho</u>l eocirs

Sedj <u>tha</u>l Ownyi ecs <u>the</u>locs no eo anong tsar alts hare deo Ownyu

Eloigal theld Ownyu ecs Theldar astse Sothelan sharownar ther

Ownyag <u>tho</u>l Ownyu anong Eloigal tsoh Aolar acse <u>the</u>cirs krag

Ar <u>thi</u>s lyre Ownyu intse ha oth <u>tho</u>l astse Sothelan sharcar ther

Sharown anong ha adj lyre Aoror acse ecs krag

Eloigal ocu adj deo Ownyu

The Curse of the Kragon's Sword

Tse djonts <u>th</u>is kror

Aownyou kood

Necs tse krag <u>th</u>is

Reg

Ownyou soon sic <u>th</u>al

Adj res kror

Djoon ownyou hay no

The Curse of Blood-stones

(As Translated by Serc)

A chain of Black-iron, in melding of fire, binds to it a shard of purest Darkness.

In these, my Dragon-stones, shall lie my power, my curse, which is Darkness.

When hanging upon the neck, my Darkness shall cover: their eyes, ears, mouth, nose.

As if in deepest slumber, their mind and body shall be numbed,

So that they cannot feel, cannot reach outside the mind,

To think, to perceive, to know that they are caught.

For, in that Darkness, they shall not hear me utter;

In that dream, they shall not feel me move:

Their legs, their hands, their feet; their eyes, their mouth, their throat;

Their lungs, their wings, their claws; their voice, their heart, their mind.

All that they are shall be mine, for the purpose which I desire- to move, to change, to use.

Thus, shall the mighty fall,

And those once free shall be made to serve.

Eloigal Salthur Ownyis

(a Hymn)

Eloigal salthur Ownyis

Eloigal salthur Ownyis ecs tse Krag

Ownyis no<u>this</u> astse Kralon

<u>Th</u>althur oth krag<u>this</u>

Ha en kral

Sedj Ownyu ownyagral ar <u>this</u>

Lors cas are adj hare sic Threa

Salthur ar <u>this</u> chedj

Creo no eo tso kror

Sedj creo tso <u>th</u>al

About the Author

C. R. Adkins is an amateur writer with no formal training in literature other than an abounding love for great works scribed by a plethora of fine authors. However, he does hold a Bachelor's of Music Composition from Northern Kentucky University, which is surprisingly applicable, as skills and techniques learned in composing music do seem to translate somewhat to literary composition.

He currently resides in the northern Kentucky area where he works in the Healthcare industry; and enjoys the company of his family, the conveniences of the Cincinnati metropolitan area, and the natural beauty of the surrounding farm and woodlands.

If you would like to contact the author, you can e-mail: CRAdkins4444@gmail.com

Thank you for reading this work; I really hope you enjoyed it!